Main illustrations by Flashers, now available at on the internet at www.Flasher.co.uk. (For more details, see page 546).

Secondary illustrations of new video stars Javier Duran and Jan Novak and Andel (in *Puda*), courtesy of Mike Donner and All Worlds Video. Free catalogue: 1-800-537-8024, or fax at 619-298-8567 or look on the internet for a complete gallery of stars: www.allworldsvideo.com.

Worldwide Praise for the Erotica of John Patrick and STARbooks!

"John Patrick is a modern master of the genre!
...This writing is what being brave is all about.
It brings up the kinds of things that are usually kept so private that you think you're the only one who experiences them."
– *Gay Times, London*

"'Barely Legal' is a great potpourri... and the coverboy is gorgeous!"
– *Ian Young, Torso magazine*

"A huge collection of highly erotic, short and steamy one-handed tales. Perfect bedtime reading, though you probably won't get much sleep! Prepare to be shocked! Highly recommended!"
– *Vulcan magazine*

"Tantalizing tales of porn stars, hustlers, and other lost boys...John Patrick set the pace with 'Angel!'"
– *The Weekly News, Miami*

"...Some readers may find some of the scenes too explicit; others will enjoy the sudden, graphic sensations each page brings. Each of these romans á clef is written with sustained intensity. 'Angel' offers a strange, often poetic vision of sexual obsession. I recommend it to you."
– *Nouveau Midwest*

"Self-absorbed, sexually-addicted bombshell Stacy flounced onto the scene in 'Angel' and here he is again, engaged in further, distinctly 'non-literary' adventures...lots of action!"
– *Prinz Eisenherz Book Review, Germany*

"'Angel' is mouthwatering and enticing...."
– *Rouge Magazine, London*

"'Superstars' is a fast read...if you'd like a nice round of fireworks before the Fourth, read this aloud at your next church picnic..."
– *Welcomat, Philadelphia*

"Yes, it's another of those bumper collections of steamy tales from STARbooks. The rate at which John Patrick turns out these compilations you'd be forgiven for thinking it's not exactly quality prose. Wrong. These stories are well-crafted, but not over-written, and have a profound effect in the pants department."
– *Vulcan magazine, London*

"For those who share Mr. Patrick's appreciation for cute young men, 'Legends' is a delightfully readable book...I am a fan of John Patrick's...His writing is clear and straight-forward and should be better known in the gay community."
- *Ian Young, Torso Magazine*

"...'Billy & David' is frank, intelligent, disarming. Few books approach the government's failure to respond to crisis in such a realistic, powerful manner."
- *RG Magazine, Montreal, Canada*

"...Touching and gallant in its concern for the sexually addicted, 'Angel' becomes a wonderfully seductive investigation of the mysterious disparity between lust and passion, obsession and desire."
- *Lambda Book Report*

"Each page of John Patrick's 'Angel' was like a sponge and I was slowly sucked into the works. 'The Kid' had the same effect on me and now 'What Went Wrong?' has blown me away!"
- *P. K. New York*

"John Patrick has one of the best jobs a gay male writer could have. In his fiction, he tells tales of rampant sexuality. His non-fiction involves first person explorations of adult male video stars. Talk about choice assignments!"
- *Southern Exposure*

"The title for 'Boys of Spring' is taken from a poem by Dylan Thomas, so you can count on high caliber imagery throughout."
- *Walter Vatter, Editor, A Different Light Review*

Book of the Month Selections in Europe and the U.K.
And Featured By A Different Light,
Lambda Rising and GR, Australia
And Available at Fine Booksellers Everywhere

*These boys have the stuff
dreams are made of...*

DREAM BOYS

A New Collection
of Erotic Tales
Edited By
JOHN PATRICK

STARbooks Press
Sarasota, FL

Books by John Patrick

Non-Fiction

A Charmed Life: Vince Cobretti
Lowe Down: Tim Lowe
The Best of the Superstars 1990
The Best of the Superstars 1991
The Best of the Superstars 1992
The Best of the Superstars 1993
The Best of the Superstars 1994
The Best of the Superstars 1995
The Best of the Superstars 1996
The Best of the Superstars 1997
The Best of the Superstars 1998
What Went Wrong?
When Boys Are Bad
& Sex Goes Wrong
Legends: The World's Sexiest
Men, Vols. 1 & 2
Legends (Third Edition)
Tarnished Angels (Ed.)

Fiction

Billy & David: A Deadly Minuet
The Bigger They Are...
The Younger They Are...
The Harder They Are...
Angel: The Complete Trilogy
Angel II: Stacy's Story
Angel: The Complete Quintet
A Natural Beauty (Editor)

Fiction
(Continued)

The Kid (with Joe Leslie)
HUGE (Editor)
Strip: He Danced Alone
The Boys of Spring
Big Boys/Little Lies (Editor)
Boy Toy
Seduced (Editor)
Insatiable/Unforgettable (Editor)
Heartthrobs
Runaways/Kid Stuff (Editor)
Dangerous Boys/Rent Boys
(Editor)
Barely Legal (Editor)
Country Boys/City Boys (Editor)
My Three Boys (Editor)
Mad About the Boys (Editor)
Lover Boys (Editor)
In the BOY ZONE (Editor)
Boys of the Night (Editor)
Secret Passions (Editor)
Beautiful Boys (Editor)
Juniors (Editor)
Come Again (Editor)
Smooth 'N' Sassy (Editor)
Intimate Strangers (Editor)
Naughty By Nature (Editor)
Raw Recruits (Editor)
Dreamboys (Editor)

Copyright 1998 by John Patrick, Sarasota, FL. All rights reserved.

Every effort has been made to credit copyrighted material. The author and the publisher regret any omissions and will correct them in future editions. Note: While the words "boy," "girl," "young man," "youngster," "gal," "kid," "student," "guy," "son," "youth," "fella," and other such terms are occasionally used in text, this work is generally about persons who are at least 18 years of age, unless otherwise noted.

First Edition Published in the U.S. in Sept. 1998
Library of Congress Card Catalogue No.   97-065259
ISBN No. 1-877978-93-0

Contents

Introduction:
HEAVENLY SEX
John Patrick
SPRING CHICKEN
John Patrick...25
THE BIG SURPRISE
John Patrick...36
MY PEN PAL
Dan Veen...43
SWEET DREAMS
Peter Z. Pan...55
MOROCCAN DREAMBOY
Frank Brooks...64
ISLAND FRUIT
Thomas C. Humphrey...78
GOLDEN BOY
Thomas C. Humphrey...86
BOUND VIRGIN
Jack Ricardo...98
A RANDY YOUNG
COWPOKE
Jack Ricardo...105
COWPOKE DOWN UNDER
Rick Jackson...112
A DREAM IN DENIM
Peter Eros...126
DREAM SOLDIER
William Cozad...134
GETTING SHAFTED
Leo Cardini...143
MILK BATH
Jason Carpenter...158
MAKING MARK
Tony Anthony...163
MY NEW MASTER
Tony Anthony...176
FARMBOY DREAMS
Rick Jackson...185
THE FARMBOY
& THE STUD
Rick Jackson...192

TRUE BELIEVERS
John Patrick...199
GINGERBREAD
HOUSE
Peter Gilbert...206
OH COME, ALL YE
FAITHFUL
Peter Gilbert...234
GETTING STUFFED
James Hosier...250
BONGIORNO, JOHN
James Hosier...260
ENGLISH LESSONS
Tim Scully...285
STRIP
FOR STARDOM
Tim Scully...301
THE NUDE-SWIMMING
POND
Ian Cappell...318
THE STUFF DREAMS ARE
MADE OF
Bert McKenzie...325
BLUE DUNGAREES
John Patrick...333
VOLUPTUOUS
Antler...339

PLUS
Bonus Books:
DREAM BOY
They all wanted him so
badly, it was sinful.
A Romantic Novella by
Kevin Bantan...341
And
HEAVEN SENT ME
The Collected Sexual
Adventures of The Saint
by John Patrick...427

Editor's Note

Most of the stories appearing in this book take place prior to the years of The Plague; the editor and each of the authors represented herein advocate the practice of safe sex at all times.

And, because these stories trespass the boundaries of fiction and non-fiction, to respect the privacy of those involved, we've changed all of the names and other identifying details.

"You are the subject of so many people's fantasies you don't have to have any of your own. You are the dream. You don't have to have any."
— David Leddick, My Worst Date

. . .

"This man fully lived up to my vision of what a fireman should be. His very broad shoulders were packed into the telltale blue fire department T-shirt, the rest of him into jeans and boots. His short dark hair begged to have someone's hands—preferably mine—run through it. He had the shadow of a beard. He was the most beautiful thing I'd ever seen. I glanced over and saw that (my friend) Grace's eyes had practically rolled back in her head, and she was beginning to drool like one of those pictures of a medieval saint in ecstasy over being pierced by God.

"We stared in awe as our firefighter walked through the aisles, both of us carefully searching for signs that he might be available. Whenever he passed behind a pillar or display, we held our breath waiting for him to reappear. We bobbed and ducked and scurried after him, following silently.

After a minute of watching him, I surmised that there was no one near him who might be a potential significant other, and a quick scan showed that the ring finger of each hand was bare..."
— Michael Thomas Ford, describing his dream man in his book, "Alec Baldwin Doesn't Love Me."

"*Every night in my dreams / I see you, I feel you / That's how I know you go on / Across the distance and spaces between us...*"
–"My Heart Will Go On" (Love Theme from 'Titanic'), lyrics by Will Jennings to the #1 best-selling single, included on the #1 best-selling soundtrack to the #1 money-making movie of all time, thanks in large measure (in our opinion) to the millions of teenage girls who have seen the film four or five times, all because of our favorite dreamboy, Leonardo DiCaprio. Frontiers magazine said this song had "the gayest lyrics ever, and is perfect for remembering all of those ex-lovers...my favorite being 'Jack, I'll never let go!'"

INTRODUCTION: HEAVENLY SEX

John Patrick

In his marvelous memoir *The World, the Flesh and Myself*, Michael Davidson recounts many years of meeting the boys of his dreams throughout the world. For instance, in Bali, in a hamlet called Selatt, surrounded by terraced padi-fields, Davidson stayed in a rest house where, "for a few rupiya one could get a dish of rice, a flagon of *tuak* and a small room; and where, after gently making known to the Mayor one's amorous preference, one's desires were mysteriously fulfilled. Nothing was said; nobody appeared during the evening's supping and drinking; but when one went to bed one would find, wistfully smiling from the gloaming of the room, a tender brown creature who took it for granted he was staying the night. There would be no question of payment: the Balinese weren't interested in money; but if one made a present of a new sarong, there would be abounding and touching gratitude.

"That's how I came to know Ktut...one of the sweetest and most affectionate companions I've had, who stayed with me for all the rest of that blissful month and travelled with me all over the island.

"But then, like all one's loves made fleeting by the compulsion of time, bliss came to an end; I had to go back to the world: I had to leave Ktut, pathetically forlorn, but enriched by several new sarongs and, I hope, some sweetness of memory."

Davidson says that his "highest, most intense pleasure or happiness is of the mind; and comes from seeing, being with, touching, looking into the mind of, a boy who, emotionally, mentally, rather than bodily, is *simpatico*; and from visually absorbing the multiple delights of his nakedness. Any sexual acts that may, and generally do, accompany, follow or precede this mental joy are adjuncts prologue or epilogue to the essential monograph of the mind. It was at Lancing that I first had this experience, which I call love."

Davidson recounts that his boyhood love, Manson, had been given, unjustly, "the label of 'tart'; it was inevitable, with those great languishing eyes beneath their sable lashes, and the lovely Gainsborough face. No doubt the way he dreadfully greased his hair and combed it backwards into a clinging scalp enhanced the tartish look; I longed for it to be rumpled, unoiled, like a satyr's—yet adored the entrancing occiput its flat glossiness revealed. I suppose he was thirteen; I was nearing fifteen. It began in the cloisters; but it was in chapel that the sudden tidal wave of worship hit me and knocked me head-over-heels. I haven't the slightest idea why: I suppose it was some angle at which I caught his face, some light and shade upon it, some tilt of his head—all I know is that my spirit soared with those fluted pillars into the gothic height, and I walked out of chapel feeling as I didn't know human beings could feel.

"...For eighteen months or so he obsessed me: the thought that he was in the same world, the incessant awareness of his propinquity, somewhere, doing something; the image of his face and head and eyes and smile; the craving to touch him, to be with him; and later, after seeing him in the swimming bath, the sight of his nakedness. But I don't think, in all the length of this passion, I spoke to him more than twice."

Years later, in Berlin, Davidson met Werner. "I had, of course, surveyed the city's swimming-baths; and most afternoons was going to those in the Barwaldstrasse, somewhere in the wilderness beyond Hallesches Tor. And there one day, naked beneath the showers, I found the most startlingly beautiful person I'd ever seen: a living, and lively, Beardsley decoration for 'Salome'—he might have been the original Beardsley prototype, except that he was an improvement on the artist's invention. He had all the Beardsley sin, but none of the corruption; all the grace and *uniqueness*, but without the epicene languor. His was the face Beardsley would have drawn, had he not been dying of consumption. Ivory-white skin, parchment-pale, with a fervent scarlet mouth and huge sable eyes, full of black fire; a mass of romping black hair, thick and lively as a bear's, and the figure of a Gemito fisherboy. To Beardsley he added something of the della Robbia choristers in Florence and a great deal of the famous 'Tripod' satyrs in the Naples Museum. It didn't surprise me to find that this face had been chosen from all over Germany to go on the cover of the magazine published by the Socialist Labor Youth—whose blue blouse and red scarf he wore.

"But, I quickly found, it wasn't only his face that was intoxicating; it was a glittering personality and the incomparable friendship that he gave—in his magic company differences of age, culture, language, vanished: he made me his equal and partner. *Was ist mein ist Dein,* he pronounced early on; and that remained his rule for the next few years—what was his was mine: he would share, when I was broke, his last cigarettes; and gave to the last drop his love and loyalty. I had found at last the 'divine friend much desired'; if one of us was faithless it was I—never he.

"Before I knew what was happening, that first day, I'd been swept on to the back of his bicycle and was whirling down the Friedrichstrasse—to a *schwules Lokal,* one of those 'queer' bars whose discreetly blacked-out facades and somberly curtained doorways proclaimed out loud their nature, where we drank cognac. He was not quite 15."

And then, in Tokyo, there was Keibo: "I find it's impossible to write about Keibo because, I suppose, he's too close to me—though it's eleven years ago now, I feel he's in the room with me. Of all the loves I've had, his has lasted longest; of all the boys I've loved, he, more than any, was the 'divine friend, much desired'—the perfect one. He was 15 when I met him in the Hibiya gardens in Tokyo; today, at 26, his affection is as perfect as ever; and mine for him, though changed in structure, is unalterable in strength. (When) I had to leave him behind, his adoring mother, sweet little Mama-San, had said to me: 'Do you want him for your own? I will give him to you.'"

One of Boyd McDonald's contributors to *Raunch* describes his own "heavenly" schooldays: "In my 8th-grade year I added one more boy to my list. Collin was in the 6th grade and we met because we were both in the choir. Outside of choir practice, the only time we really saw each other at first was in the pool. Collin was very handsome and I knew he would probably be a nice catch.

"One day a bunch of us boys were playing tag in the pool. Collin was also playing and I saw this as my chance to grab him—literally. Whenever I was 'it,' I would go after Collin and tag him on his dick right through his skin-tight bikini swim trunks. By the time the game had ended his cock was stiff. After the game had broken up, Collin and I went to a corner of the pool and talked by ourselves. I told him I enjoyed tagging him and he said he enjoyed it too.

"Before too long we were in the pool locker room, in one of the shower stalls. Assured we were alone, Collin and I pulled down our swim suits to our ankles. Both our dicks were hard and ready for action. I was amazed at how big Collin's was. It wasn't as big as mine and he had no hair, but it was big for a 6th grader. I knelt before him and without hesitation took his dick into my mouth. He climaxed without coming, and I was excited as I waited for him to suck me.

"He managed to take all of it in his mouth. When he pulled back so that only the head of my dick was in his mouth, he would put his tongue in my piss-slit and it felt so good. When I climaxed I came in his mouth and I was astonished that he swallowed every drop.

"Collin and I met regularly throughout the year. Mark, Kevin, and Tommy and I also kept our routines. Among the four of them, I was in heaven.

"But the 9th grade and after was disastrous. Eighth grade was my last year at the boarding school. I hated attending a regular Catholic school. The only thing I looked forward to was the PE class because I could watch all the other guys take showers. The ones I mostly watched were the ones who were small and had little or no cock hair. At night I would jack off while fantasizing about these cocks, but I never made any contacts with boys I could have sex with."

"When I moved to Denver I started college," another guy told Boyd McDonald in *Raunch*, "but was also working in one of the hottest gay bars in town. School suffered quickly and I dropped out. The money was good and the sex voluminous. I had a trick every night and would stop at the bookstore several times a week. Denver was blessed with four baths, including the wonderful Ballpark. I frequented it a couple of nights a week.

"One of my first boyfriends was an alcoholic so he didn't go to the bars. We met at a rest area south of Denver. Kurt showed me all the public places to have sex within 50 miles of

Denver. We had a great time hitting the universities, stores, office buildings, parks, and rest areas.

"My friends all spoke of San Francisco as a gay mecca. I found Denver had all the sex anyone could want if one had a little initiative and would just open their eyes. After 2 years I wanted a change and moved to Dallas. For 8 months I lived with an intense man who was into speed and sex. I had gone to the baths one night and met a fellow. He thought I would be a perfect set -p for Mr. T. I went home with my new friend and another hot guy and we played for a while. Mostly tying his friend up and spanking him. Finally he decided to call Mr. T and take us both to him.

"Mr. T was short, balding, bearded, glasses but generated an air of authority. My friend and I became Mr. T's helpers in a several-hour scene of bondage. I don't remember the other kid's name but I do remember that he had a lot of hangups about sex due to his religious beliefs. He was really into getting spanked and beaten and then getting fucked. Several months after this night the young man committed suicide.

"After a while my friend and the kid left and Mr. T and I were left alone. We got high. We had been up all night and it was now dawn. He had beautiful arms that went down to full working-class hands. Mr. T was a carpenter by day. He had a narrow waist that came down from a full chest. His pubic hair was cropped short and his balls were shaved.

"Later after we had been living together for a while I grew to appreciate his ass. It was always willing to take a hard cock if the man was man enough.

"His cock was not large but it was incredibly suckable and I would learn to spend hours with it in my mouth, going from it to his rose-petal asshole. Mr. T was the first man I met whose ass I wanted to eat.

"Anyway, the first few hours we were alone together, I lay there while Mr. T fucked me, and I sold my soul to this man for the next eight months. He became my focus and all my attention sexually was turned onto this man.

"I had never been jealous about my lovers having sex with other people, but with Mr. T this all changed. We started fucking with other people and it drove me crazy to see him with someone else. I can put this personality change down to the speed we were doing.

"Mr. T and I had many scenes. One night he had me and another kid—who happened to be from my home town in California—tied up, gagged, in the toilet of his apartment. We also drank his piss. Another evening we spent at the tubs—myself getting tied up in a room with the door open. This would get a lot of attention. Mr. T would pick a couple of hot men and invite them in to abuse my mouth and ass. When we would finish this scene we would usually end up in the gloryholes sucking dick like mad.

"By the light of dawn we would be lying on the floor under the gloryholes watching the last few get their dicks sucked above us. We'd still be jacking off there on the floor when the morning hard-ons came in to be sucked.

"Another evening he sent me to the local leather bar. Later he showed up and dragged me out, tied me up and blindfolded me. When we got back to his apartment he stripped me and shaved me completely."

Poet Constantine P. Cavafy dreamed of beautiful boys. He was, in fact, obsessed with physical beauty according to A. L. Rowse in *Homosexuals in History*, who says, "for in the moment of ecstasy there is some revelation of the universe: that glimpse of Eros, which Wystan Hugh Auden talks about in his essay on Cavafy. And this, apart from so much else—consolation in loneliness, the sense of the fragility of beauty, in the death of the young like Patrodus, the epigrams in the Greek Anthology, the touching epitaphs on youth upon marble, the remembered lips and limbs and graces. All served for the inspiration of poetry in a fulfilled experience: 'The fulfillment of their deviate delight is over. They rise from the mattress, dress hurriedly without speaking and leave the house separately. As they walk uneasily up the street something about them betrays what kind of bed assuaged desire. But the life of the artist has gained how much! Tomorrow, next day, the years to come, verse will flow that had beginning here.'"

French writer Henri de Montherlant, Rowse says, would sacrifice anything, or anybody, for freedom of spirit. "This made him solitary, a 'loner' (as Americans call it) by nature and conviction: like de Gaulle, he had the utmost contempt for their illusory values. He rigidly suppressed any expression of his own kindness of heart or compassion—that would be vulgar again. He was dedicated to ancient concepts of duty, honor, patriotism. The paradox was that his inner romantic temperament was in conflict; he repressed it. All the same out of the tension came his powerful genius. Living in a time of crack-up and decay of civilization and its values, he was driven even more into his fortress of solitude, narcissism, solipsism—perhaps the most respect-worthy reaction to the contemptible contemporary world.

"But I wish he could have been a happier man. The conflicts of his passionate temperament (so rigidly controlled by sheer style in his work) emerged early at school. In the intervals of receiving a good classical education at a Jesuit school he embarked on 'sentimental affairs' with other boys. We can see from his later work that they were much more than this. They possessed his mind and soul; he always adhered to the view that childhood revealed the human creature at its best (no illusions about adults), and to the Greek ideal that nature's *chef d'oeuvre* was a youth of about seventeen. (The same was true, he said, among the animals.) Then was the human animal at its most lovable, innocent, spontaneous, generous—this was before the contemporary debasement of youth, we may add.

"At sixteen Montherlant was dismissed from his school, the College Saint-Croix. Though he says nothing about it, it left an indelible mark: it was ejection from Paradise. He does say that for the next ten years he had great difficulty in finding himself again, he made the difficulties or his temperament did for him. ...There is no love elsewhere in Montherlant's work; the rest is sex. His experience of sex was bisexual. He was extraordinarily passionate, and for years thought nothing compared with desire and its satisfaction. The affairs with women went into his novels; he said nothing about the other side to his life: he kept it private, but we know where his heart was, and he had comparisons to live with him. Like so many of his temperament, he found an outlet for it in North Africa. The moment he began to win acclaim by his writings, he left Paris, for some seven years, mostly in North Africa."

In Con Anemogiannis's story "Peephole" (in the anthology *Hard* from Black Wattle Press), the narrator states, quite provocatively, that he was both "born and brought up in a male brothel." Thus, he found his dreamboy right at home!

"...Maybe you want to know what it was about our boarding house that made it so sought after," the narrator says, "what it was about that house that brought so many people knocking on that great Victorian mallet, the great iron banger big as a prick that always startled us from our peace—annoying my father and brother, but not me, for whom it was the single high note of a nightingale. I can't say the house's beauty brought these young moths. No one in his right mind could say it was an architectural pearl beyond price.

"Maybe it was all these youths could afford. Then again we didn't have the sole bright torch visible during the protracted eclipse of their rootlessness. The other hostels in the street were cheap as well.

"I think it was word of mouth. Most had heard of us before they came to our fateful street—Edwina Street, full of so many similar crumbling terraces, tumble-down shacks where the deprived and the emigrant could get down and dirty in blissful relief. Maybe they had heard of my mother. Maybe, just maybe, they had heard of me.

"Does it matter? The fact was they came and there was no reason to be upset about such good fortune when so many of my friends now tell me that the most they enjoyed was an unhappy sexless preadolescence.

"I do have to say though that my mother and I after a while did become the subject of rumor, that people began to talk, but Mother didn't care about my reputation or hers as long as she made money and I did well at school. But I'm running ahead of myself. There will be time enough for scandal.

"Let me first tell you about another rumor, the one I enjoyed. The one that said our street had once been visited by no other than Charles Dickens. And that the biggest house on the corner, the one we occupied, was the house that had given him the inspiration for Miss Havisham in *Great Expectations*. I had read that in the local library, both the rumor (in some decayed parochial history newspaper) and the novel.

"I liked that rumor. I liked it very much. If by accident of birth, poverty, fate, or design I was the new Miss (or Master) Havisham, I had certainly rejected the stale and festering cakes, as well as the coy idea of only holding out a shy hand masked by a glove. I was too busy for that with my lodgers, marrying each of them in my mind as we did the deed. Sometimes when these boy boarders caught me staring at them through the peephole (the signal that I was available) I wouldn't enter. To tease them, to show them that I couldn't be had on every occasion, only when I wished, when I was in the mood. Which was often. My occasional coquettish refusal was a show of power, proof that despite my youth, I was the gay piper leading my lodger rats into my private and steamy sewer. But I refused them only when I was being nasty and capricious. Hardly ever.

"Sometimes I would do the opposite. I would be altruistic, I would let them masturbate me, or suck me because I could tell that they where desperately lonely, because I had heard that the factory where they worked fired them. Or because mother told me of a telegram announcing one of their relatives ... back home ... in Greece, where they had been sending money ... (the place of my picture books and nude heroes) ... had ceased to exist.

"I remember blowing one whose father had just died. My blow job, though beguiling and expert, was insufficient to prevent a new wave of despair and self recrimination welling up in him at his inability to attend the funeral.

"Often if we were having a particularly good time I would open the penny catcher at the bottom of the shower (I had keys), reusing the pennies to prolong our shower, an amphibious pleasure our poor boarders could only for a short time afford.

"But that was a special treat, if what we were doing was particularly fun or dazzlingly new.

"Maybe in a way they were my prostitutes and I much like my mother, both client and madam. Governing them, buying them. Five cents a piece, the way in those days other kids bought pyramid-shaped Sunny Boy ice blocks to lick and suck."

Frank DeCaro in his memoir, *A Boy Named Phyliss*, recalls his father's reaction to his first affair with young Frank's first dreamboy: "...For all the gossip and all my not-so-subtle hints, my father's eyes were closed to the obvious. He knew *something was up* between Kenneth and me, asking more than once that summer, 'What sort of spell does that kid have over you?' But he never imagined it was full-blown homosexual love. Still, Frank Senior always seemed jealous of the relationship I'd forged with Kenneth, envious that I told Kenneth things I wouldn't tell anyone else. 'You always go running to him,' my father would say. And, it was true. Kenneth had become the main man in my life; my father was brushed off to the side. That didn't sit well with him. He felt jilted. It was not an uncommon reaction. When fathers find out their sons are gay, they first turn green with nausea (especially if you tell them you think fellatio is man's work) and then green with envy. First they say they never would have known; then they realize their sons have other men in their lives who are more important to them than their dear old dads are. They hate that. Mothers are the opposite. They know their sons are gay from the time they're children and, once they get over the probably-no-grandchildren thing, they're secretly glad. My mother prayed that I wouldn't turn out like her hairdressing partners. But in the long run, she was comforted by the fact that I was gay. Like every well-meaning but overly possessive mother, she knew that my gayness meant she was going to be the number one woman in my life forever. Lovers would come and go, but Marian would always be my Marian. She liked that idea."

Had his mother known, though, she wouldn't have liked the idea that her son was messing around with Van, one of the older boys he knew, even though it was perfectly innocent, "compared with how sordid I wanted it to be. I'd been playing at his house all day long, which was fun because the place was spooky and old. But I was tired of trying on his sisters' injection-molded plastic wigs and playing Green Ghost and consulting the Magic 8 Ball. I was bored with the girls and their pet gerbils and playing hide-and-seek in the basement. So I went looking for Van. When I found him, he was up in his room doing what teenaged boys love to do. He was embarrassed that I caught him choking the chicken, but, at my urging, he continued. I'd never seen anything approaching adulthood—at least, not standing at attention—and I was bewitched. Compared to my prepubescence, his penis was the size of the Bullwinkle balloon in the Macy's Thanksgiving Day Parade, and, best of all, it was attached to a handsome, olive-skinned boy with the blackest hair, above and below. Impressed by this newest part of him, I asked if I could feel it. 'Well, okay,' he said, rather reluctantly. 'But gently.' So I did. It was as soft as velvet, as hard as steel....''

But with Kenneth, Frank indulged himself: "...Soon we were in each other's arms, our hearts racing, first with fear, then with abandon. We kissed, his tongue parting my lips. Kenneth's kisses were nothing like Michele's or Gretchen's. These were man kisses. How strange his teenaged whiskers felt upon my face. So new, yet oddly familiar. We necked for an hour; afraid of what we'd started, we never let our hands stray past each other's chest. Then Eleanor shouted up the stairs that it was getting late. I had to go. In silence, Kenneth drove me home, our hands intertwined on the luggage-brown seats of his father's white Ford Fairmont. 'I'll see you at school tomorrow,' he said, his hand pulling away from mine, as he made the turn into our driveway on Prospect. 'Tomorrow *night*, too?' I asked. 'Yeah,' he said through the open car window. 'After dinner.'"

Frank's second dreamboy was Denis, who was Irish and "looked like so much Fresca. I'd only been staring for twenty or thirty minutes when he woke up suddenly and caught me. 'What are you looking at?' he said. 'Nothing,' I replied. 'Just you.'

"It sounded weird, and it was. I didn't quite understand my fascination with him. It wasn't anything I'd ever felt before. I mean, I wasn't lying there thinking of 101 Ways to Share a Sleeping Bag, but there *was* something going on that I couldn't quite come to grips with. It was big love. It was big lust. Hell, it was just *big*."

How about meeting your own dreamboy? The key to finding Mr. Right is to be *realistic*, according to Orland Outland in his book *The Principles*. "Yes, our culture continuously feeds us pictures of grade AAA beefcake to get us to buy everything from underwear to microwaves, so it's easy to become convinced that you'll never be happy unless you end up with a guy from the International Male catalogue, who also happens to be a brilliant, witty med student putting himself through school modeling...

"Don't let the perfect man of your dreams become the only

man you'll ever marry. Settling for less than you want isn't the point, but accepting that dream men are usually just that is a good start toward getting a real man. Years of experience has taught some of us that not only does the very best sex not come from the very best bodies, but that often the difference in bed between a marble statue and a buff dude is that the dude is warmer (sometimes).

"...Gay men long ago discovered that the secret of happiness was to become the object of your own desire. Love men with giant muscles? Well, most guys with giant muscles want *other guys* with giant muscles, so why not start spending more time at the gym growing some yourself?

Outland suggests making a list of what you're *not* looking for. "By process of elimination, you come up with a list of what you *are* looking for. Go ahead, build your dream man, and caption him 'Just What I Ordered.' Be prepared to accept someone who's got about 75 percent of what you're looking for."

Outland cannot stress enough the need to be honest with yourself: "You may say out loud that 'size doesn't matter' because you don't want anyone to think you're a size queen—but if you are, you're going to have to acknowledge it. Say it loud and say it proud: 'I WANT A BIG ONE!' Now you know what you want. Excellent! It's time to start looking for it. (But) I have terrible news for you. Your knight in shining armor is not about to break into your apartment anytime soon. You are going to have to leave the house. "

SPRING CHICKEN

John Patrick

"Orpheus had rejected all love of women...
He was even the cause whereby the men of Thrace
transferred their love to their own sex,
toward boys in the brief springtime of life,
whose first blossoms they plucked."
— *Ovid*

It was the spring of 1983, and I had come to New York to see the Metropolitan Opera's "Britain Salutes New York Festival."

I became especially enamored of the Royal Ballet's crop of bright young couples whose movements deliberately evoked *Les Biches*, the model for the ballet's mood of indolence and sexual ambivalence. Like birds, the boys were costumed more flamboyantly than the girls, their shoulders bared and festooned with chiffon flounces in confectionery colors. A woman in the audience joked that they appeared to be more interested in each other than their female partners. So what else was new? It was only an eighteen-minute piece but the joy of it was such that I knew I would be recalling it many times in the months and years to come. I resolved I had to meet the studliest of the boys, the studly one who flaunted his hyperextensions, out doing the others with 180-degree penches. During intermission, through Kurt, an old friend, who was working backstage, I sent a message to the dancer of my dreams.

For the rest of the evening I took delight in fantasizing about running my hands over the smooth firmness of his glorious buns. In my fantasy, after I finished rimming him, I would turn him over and wrap my lips around the huge shaft that I knew would be there. I'd pump him mercilessly with my hand and tease the silky head of his cock with my tongue until I felt him expand to the point of explosion. Then he'd dance just for me as he coated my throat with his cum.

The dancer, whose name was Rodolfo Carobino, was perfectly proportioned for classical dancing: a born prince, but brash, with a touch of the earth about him, so it was not surprising that he did actually show up at Joe Allen's eatery that night. I chose the restaurant because it was only a block from the theater so that perhaps he would, at the very least, be curious enough to check me out. I'd hoped he'd be wearing tight-fitting pants, but he was wearing baggy trousers and a loose Armani jacket. Still, he looked as splendid up close as he appeared on stage.

"So you are the man from the Cleveland ballet?" he asked in precise, heavily accented English. "I did not know they had a ballet in Cleveland." He smiled. I smiled back.

Then he added, "Where is Cleveland?"

Now I laughed out loud. I was instantly smitten. And who wouldn't have been? His smile. Oh, lord, his smile. Let him just smile at me like that again, I quivered, after I made him come, and I would die a happy man. A very happy man indeed.

"Order anything you like," I said, my calmness belying my inner turmoil, my desire to carry him off, back to my hotel as quickly as possible. I pushed the menu toward him.

"You order, please. Whatever is best," he said. "I am completely in your hands."

Oh, he was good. My heart fluttered. I was waiting to be warmed, caressed by Rodolfo.

This is absurd, I chided myself. He's much too young for me, but then I've always been such a sucker for the wrong boys. They didn't die on me. They didn't fade away. They just turned into men, men who never quite lived up to my expectations.

Well, I was glad I'd seen Rodolfo off-stage. Sure he was good to look at, even better to listen to. I decided to discard common sense and let my feelings enjoy the ride.

I told him I was a great fan of the ballet and served on the board of the ballet in Cleveland. I could introduce him to the director and others of importance. He said he would think about coming to Cleveland following the New York engagement. He said he was planning on taking a vacation anyway.

"It's lovely in Cleveland in May," I told him. "You could stay with me. I have plenty of room."

His nodding agreement to everything I said heightened my need. I kept thinking of him on-stage. How he would pose so that his girded manhood showed to its best advantage. The image presented itself to me again and again.

Still, when we had finished our supper, as the waiter served coffee and I asked him if he would have a nightcap at my hotel, he demurred.

"*Permiso*, I must rest."

"Of course," I said, suppressing a frown.

That night I lay awake at my hotel, alone, naked beneath my sheets, thinking of Rodolfo in his room entertaining some slut from the streets. Yet he was gay. I was sure of it. When he entered the restaurant, I knew right away that he was gay because we exchanged that needful look that is natural with our kind, and then he looked away, not wishing to commit. Now it was unfair that the best I could do on this night in Manhattan was to bring my trusty dildo to my ass. I could almost hear Rodolfo's voice as I shoved it in me. I slid the dildo back and forth, moving it in slowly as I jacked off. I imagined flicking my tongue over the throbbing erection of my virtuoso lover, then rolling over and separating the cheeks of my ass. He would invade me with darting strokes. Soon I would be trying to establish a motion that mimicked the action of a hot, jerking cock. He would be such a tease. He would withdraw it, then reinsert it, until he was fucking me wildly, coming deep inside me. At the thought of this, I finally managed to build to a furious climax of my own. Still, it was very unsatisfactory, and I cursed myself for even bothering to get worked up. It only accentuated my need to have Rodolfo's rock-hard prick in me.

It was raining when I returned home, a driving spring rain, sure to make the flowers grow, but it only added to my somber mood. I brightened considerably, however, when I retrieved my messages. My friend backstage at the Met, Kurt, had talked with Rodolfo. Kurt had paid back many past favors by giving me a good report to Rodolfo and the boy had agreed to come to Cleveland for "a holiday," as he put it. I immediately arranged for a ticket to be waiting for him at LaGuardia. How amusing, I thought, for him to return to London to tell his fellow dancers he had taken a holiday in Cleveland, of all places! I had told him Cleveland was situated on a very large lake, but I didn't tell him it had been the butt of TV comics as "the mistake on the lake." Still, if I had anything to do with it, he wouldn't be seeing too many of the sights of Cleveland anyhow.

. . .

On the way home from the airport, stretched out in the leather bucket seat of my Mercedes, Rodolfo was appraising me closely. "You are a handsome man," he said finally.
 I chuckled. "Ha! I'm no spring chicken."
 "Ah, but who wants chicken?"
 I glanced at him. He was smiling that smile again. I smiled back. He was as close to chicken as I'd ever allowed myself. Our week apart had made my desire even stronger.
 "You, I think," he went on, "you are like me. We like beef."
 I reached over and squeezed his thigh. "Yes, beef," I said, but I quickly removed my hand. I wasn't sure yet how to play this one.

I carried Rodolfo's suitcase into the guest bedroom. He stood by the window and those dark eyes now roved over me, settling for a moment on the bulge in my pants. I thought he'd penetrate me with his look alone. He shrugged off his Armani jacket. He looked delicious in his vest, crisp white shirt, and, for a change, tight, tight pants. He knew this of course, and touched his own considerable bulge.
 "Toilet?" he asked.
 I walked over to the bathroom door and opened it. "All for you," I said.
 He swept by me and entered the bathroom, but did not shut the door. I stood in the doorway. I watched, transfixed. He unzipped and spread his trousers apart, turned to show me. "No codpiece, you see," he laughed. "All this is real."
 "Beef," I said.
 He nodded and turned away, to begin peeing. I approached him. My nervous, slightly damp hands glided over his shirt, squeezing; my lips touched his shoulders, his hair, his arms. I ran my hands down his arms, coming to rest slightly above his

pubic hair. I looked down at the pissing cock. Done, he shook the cock and then began stroking it. It started to grow.

"You like me?"

"Very much."

It was shining there: a dildo-thick dick, a souffle fresh out of its mold, ten glistening, moist inches shimmering in the mirror lights of the bathroom. The star of the show. Ten inches, taking a bow. For me.

With no further formalities I pulled his pants below his knees with my teeth. With the fabric stretched between his legs, he leaned against the vanity.

"You suck it now," he prodded.

My mouth dove for the flopping, uncut prick. It lay semi-hard in my mouth. I rolled the head of it around on my tongue. I chewed on the foreskin, tongued the shaft, up and down. When I took it full in my mouth, it firmed up and unfurled into the back of my palate. It further invaded my throat, grazing new places in me. My jaw relaxed. His expanding meat pinched into the corners of my cheeks.

His thumbs smoothed both sides of my jaw, allowing me to gulp more of him, pursing my lips so they would lap over the ridges of his throat-probing prick. Just when the sliding slab started to choke me, my chin landed upon his balls. My mouth made accidental, sex-pig sounds, rooting in the trough of his crotch.

"Oh, yes," he groaned.

Dripping down my throat was a slow trickle of his pre-cum, lubing my windpipe. My head was impaled upon his cock. His balls jiggled just beyond my reaching tongue.

My tongue tested the touchy groove lining the helmet of his cockhead. I grazed the bulb of it, tenderizing his cum-slit. Every slurp made his abs ripple like a wave and smack my sweaty brow.

Surprisingly, his asshole welcomed my foraging fingers, allowing my middle finger to skewer him. With my other hand I poked my own ass, getting it ready. That hardened his prick even more. He began shuddering. His thighs flapped against my ears. His crotch receded for a moment, and my lips were splashed with the first gushes of his orgasm.

His ass clamped down on my finger. Sheer suction power

kept me attached. I slurped up his cum-eruption. So much cum. Oceans of cum. And just when I thought it was over, cum splashes all over my face.

"What do you do for an encore?" I asked, hanging on to the cock, softening in my hand.

"You will see. But I am hungry now."

I took him to dinner at the Blue Fox, mafia-owned so the service, by the Italian waiters, is superb. Rodolfo seemed to feel right at home. Over the catch of the day, I confessed I had never been to Italy because of what I had heard about gay life there, that men seem to confine their pleasures to anonymous sex in tearooms, seedy theaters and remote beaches. He was probably used to having sex in the toilet, so what we had done was right up his alley.

Yes, he said, Italians tend to think of homosexuality as an act rather than a condition. "We say MSM, you know, men who have sex with men, not gay."

I understood this because, while perfectly legal, homosexuality in Italy has been, and still is, heavily condemned by the Church. "You cannot speak out," he said. To speak of whatever was in contradiction with the law of God is unthinkable. He said it was getting better, that Milan was fun, and Rome, of course. Lately Florence, Bologna, and even provincial towns like Padua and Bergamo have some gay activity. "But I am better in London." He smiled. "Best of all, in New York."

The thought of him in New York, at the toilets, theaters, and even in Central Park, his cock hanging out, being sucked by man after man after man, aroused me uncontrollably. I told him I wanted to have dessert at home.

My dessert was to be Rodolfo's cock, in the toilet once again, after he pissed. I took his cock in my mouth, cupping it with my lips and bathing its generous length with my saliva, sucking in as hard as I could, licking the underside of the shaft. As if in response to my thought, I felt his manhood begin to stir, stiffening and thickening at the same time.

"*Oh,*" he said, barely audible. I doubled my efforts and was rewarded with more of him.

Fully aroused now, Rodolfo suddenly shifted position, popping his erect penis from my mouth. He had decided to take me to bed. I quickly undressed and sat on the bed. I lubed myself, then, wanting to see, I propped myself up on my elbows. His impressive prick hovered at the entrance to my waiting man-pussy. Panting, he pulled me to him, ready to enter me, I knew. I braced myself in expectation of the thrust, spread myself wide to better let him impale me on his huge pole. Crazed with lust, I waited for him to fill me. But there was nothing. I felt nothing. I looked down. I could feel the head as it entered me, but sensation ended there.

"Oh, oh," he stage whispered. Seconds later, his body jerked three times. Another incredible load, showering me with it. He sighed with an almost animal-like contentment, then he pushed me away, not so much harshly as indifferently. He fell back on the bed, closed his eyes.

I rolled over him to reach the nightstand.

"What?" He stirred. His voice was raspy and hoarse.

I pulled the large, flesh-colored faux penis from the drawer. "I'm going to fuck myself with this while I suck on you. I'll pretend you're in me."

He didn't argue. I got on my knees over him, started in. His cock responded, sort of, as I pushed the dildo into my ass. "So full," I whispered. "So full of your hard prick."

I felt my climax building, flowing up through me, curling my toes and arching my back. "Yes," I cried as the heat flooded my body. "Yes." I could feel the clutching movements of my muscles against the artificial phallus as waves of pleasure engulfed me. "Yes." Then I slowly withdrew the dildo from my body, reveling in the soft relaxation that always followed a good, hard climax.

"That was so good," I said, my heartbeat slowing. "Not as good as having you in there, of course."

"Tomorrow," he said, rolling over.

I feared I had embarrassed him. At that point, I didn't care.

I took a hot shower then climbed back into bed. Rodolfo was already asleep. At least I wouldn't have to sleep alone. But I was sleeping with a surely soulless beauty, who came for me, twice, in what seemed to me to be a private performance. The ultimate irony, the body of disembodiment. No wonder I was sad.

But, to be truthful, I was no better. While he didn't love, I loved too heavily. I deliberated and obsessed, while he simply danced away. No matter what we were doing, I thought of him, his cock. I drove downtown, introduced him to Herman, the director of the Cleveland Ballet, and left him in Herman's office. I went to the agency and tried to get something done. But I couldn't concentrate. I pictured them undressing each other completely, then lying naked on Herman's well-worn casting couch together, their thighs intertwined and their hard bodies pressed together.... No, that wasn't right.

Rodolfo, who I was sure would someday be famous and honored, would play along, but permit nothing more than a blowjob, which certainly would satisfy Herman, who was older than me but in excellent shape. We were rivals, liking the same thing, ballet and boys, so I did not know him well, but I knew he would treat Rodolfo kindly, especially once he glimpsed that cock.

On the way home, I took the boy for cocktails at the Cadillac bar downtown. All eyes were on Rodolfo, as I knew they would be. He ordered red wine.

"To Rodolfo, who will know greatness," I toasted.

He smiled shyly.

I tried to keep from touching him. But if I didn't have that cock in my mouth soon, I was going to explode.

He stared at me and sipped his wine. "You are a handsome man," he said.

"And beefy," I said, rubbing my crotch.

"I have not been good," he said, looking away. "I have let you down."

"Oh, no," I said. "Not at all."

He told me Herman had invited him—us, he quickly corrected, with a smile—to a party later that night. We stopped at my place to change. I hugged him and he moaned as if he were hurt. His cock swelled against me. I pulled away from him. His eyes were open and seemed frightened.

I realized perhaps he was thinking I would ask for what I

didn't get last night. "You're such a beauty," I said, and there in the living room, I opened his pants and fell to my knees. He groaned like he was being beaten. I licked and mouthed and nipped at him as if I were a slave trained from the age of two for this one activity. I did the best I could, gagged a few times, but didn't give up; I wanted him to free himself in my mouth. He rubbed my hair and caressed my shoulders and fell over my back like a cape as he came. Greedily, I took all he had.

I freed him from his clothes, then led him to the bedroom. I wanted him to take me from behind and wanted him to be able to hold out for a good long while. He lay on the bed, on his stomach. "Do we have time?" he asked.

"Oh, yes. Herman's parties don't really begin until midnight."

I kissed his neck, nuzzled around his underarms, again told him he was beautiful. I began rimming him and, after a minute, he started to groan again and breathe deeply. He lifted his ass to me. I knew now what the story was. I stripped and my cock was at last free, jutting out proudly from my belly. He craned his neck to look. "Beefy," he said, smiling.

I smiled back, then scrambled onto the bed and went back to sucking that ass some more; it smelled so funky, so earthy. He was smooth everywhere else, but had abundant hair on his legs and ass. And what an ass—a hard, muscular dancer's ass. It was an ass that felt even better than it looked as I speared it with my tongue. I abandoned his succulent hole for a moment to lick and suck on his low-hanging balls. He wiggled and squealed, and the muscles of his muscular thighs went rigid. And rigid too now was his cock, which I grabbed and pulled back so that I could suck it. I kissed the tip, then took inch after throbbing inch down my throat. I gagged, then released it to return to the puckering hole.

"Oh, oh, oh" he groaned, then he was still. His breath was shallow, ragged, irregular. My cock was dripping pre-cum as I got into position. He reached back to take my cock in his hand. He gripped the shaft, squeezing tight, then he started to stroke it. I thought he was going to try to get me off manually, but no, he just wanted to guide it to the target.

"Please, a rubber?" he begged, almost as an afterthought.

Yes, I knew he had learned much from his experiences in

New York. Things were crazy now; it was best to be safe. I fished a condom from the drawer of the nightstand and rolled it onto my dick. He took it back in his hand and continued to guide it to his crevice. It was as if he were holding a divining rod searching for a long-lost spring.

He moaned as I entered him at last. He was so incredibly tight I had to work to get even half of my beer can of a cock into him. But, before long, he relaxed, and soon I was driving deep into the yielding warmth of his strong body. Suddenly his whole body tensed, and I began ramming forward as hard as I could. He squealed again, then sobbed, "I'm coming!"

I couldn't put it off any longer. My gushing cum filled the rubber, and when the last jolts of the most incredible orgasm I could remember began to fade, I kissed him on the neck. He collapsed under me and closed his eyes. I rolled off him and lay on my back, still panting. This was not what I had planned on, but it was splendid.

He snuggled close and held me with a tenderness that was entirely new. His hand squeezed my softening cock. "Beefy," he whispered. And I began a silent cry, stifled like a moan pressed into a pillow, and then I was crying, tears rolling down my cheeks.

He lifted his head. "Why you cry?"

I thought, *Why? Because you don't love me, you stud. I'm crying from the frustration of having a fuck like that and knowing you don't love me.* Instead I said, "Because you are so beautiful."

"You are a funny man," he said, lowering his head to my chest.

I had gone from being handsome to being funny. I was making progress.

THE BIG SURPRISE

John Patrick

I shouldn't have been surprised that Joe came into my life again. "All the hard stuff rolls around at least twice," my dad used to say. A friend of mine echoed, "A bad penny always turns up." But to me, seeing Joe again meant I was perhaps getting another chance, like reincarnation or a recurring dream. I looked through the fisheye peephole one Saturday afternoon and saw him standing there, all grown up with a little suitcase hanging from his hand.

"Nobody's home," I said. "My dad died."

"So?" he said, without feeling.

He was a cold-hearted boy, that I knew.

My dad had hired Joe to mow the lawn and wash the cars and do whatever else I was unable to do last summer because I was so sick with mononucleosis. Nobody could figure how I caught it, since I'd never kissed anybody. I recovered but then my dad died of a heart attack, right on the 17th green. Some people said it was heartache that he died of, Mom leaving him like that five years ago, all of a sudden, taking off with the piano player at the bar they always used to frequent.

Anyhow, Joe had been a great help to Dad—and to me, because having him working around outside nearly buck naked all summer long was a tonic that I'm sure speeded my recovery.

"Is it money you want or what?"

"No, not really."

I invited Joe in, but I didn't want him getting too comfortable inside. I had been left with some nice furniture, a good hard couch, and a big chair with an ottoman that drew you down into it so far you almost couldn't get up. If he sat there, he'd be awhile.

"What's wrong? Aren't you glad to see me?" Joe asked, dropping his suitcase by the door.

"It's not that, Joe. Can't you see I'm grieving?" It had become my line, that I was doing all this grieving. It kept a lot of sharks away. I knew Joe was no shark, but he still had a kind of predatory look that had unnerved me from the start, kept me from making any moves at all toward him.

Joe walked into the living room as if he owned the place, just as I had feared. Seeing him in retreat I realized he'd been going to the gym, or mowing a helluva lot of lawns. With 44-inch shoulders and a 29-inch waist, I was sure he was getting more than his share of glances. And offers.

"How'd you get so...well, built?" I asked, admiring his new muscles that bulged in his tight black T-shirt.

"Been workin' out."

"Oh?"

"Yeah, I'm gonna pose for pictures."

"Oh?" I said. Before getting too deep into *that* subject, I told him I'd fix us each a Coca-Cola. Joe sat down on the couch.

While I was in the kitchen, he told me he had come looking for work, to earn the price of the ticket. He had been cruised by an agent at the mall. He'd gone with the the agent, who told him he would set him up for a photo layout, but he had to get to California.

I brought in the Cokes and sat down on the couch next to him. I agreed to pay for the ticket, but exactly what Joe was going to do for the money was not specified.

He drank nearly the entire can in one gulp. Some Coke dribbled down his chin, fell to his crotch. He rubbed the spot, deliberately I thought. He looked up, saw me staring.

"Yeah, I've gotta use my assets, man."

"What?" I asked, lifting my eyes away from his abundant crotch in the white jeans.

"My assets. That's why I'm posing. I want to show it off while I have it. You know what I mean."

"Yes. Yes, I do."

"I don't look it, but I've been around."

"I'll bet," I said, my eyes returning to the crotch again. He pushed back into the corner and spread his thighs. "You like it, don't ya?"

Like it? I loved it! I couldn't deny it any longer. It was there, on display. Joe stroked the bulge.

"Well?"

"Yes, yes," I stammered, replacing his hand with my own. "Oh, yes," I said, feeling the hardness. After fantasizing about it for over a year, I finally had it in my grasp, literally. "I want to suck your big cock," I said.

"That's what I figured. All last summer, I saw you looking at me."

"I was sick," I said.

He chuckled. "But now you're well."

"Yes, yes," I said, unbuttoning his 501's. "Oh, it's so big," I gasped as it flopped into view. I flicked my tongue over the enormous cockhead, in and out of his piss hole.

"Hey, I should shower first," he protested. "I'm all sweaty."

"Oh, no, I love your smell. It really turns me on," I told him, pulling his jeans down, then off. Once I had him nude, I buried my face between his thighs. God, he smelled funky! I took his hairy balls into my mouth and gently rolled them around, lapping them with my tongue. His fingers dug into my shoulders as he spread his legs wider to give me more room. I sucked on his nuts, then I licked them, kissed them, slid my tongue beneath them while running my fingers along the crack of his ass. Moaning, he babbled, "That feels so fuckin' good."

I glanced up at his cute face, saw that his eyes were closed in rapture. I wrapped my fingers around the base of his cock. My lips brushed over its knob, opening to permit its entry into my mouth. I felt a strange elation spread over me as I swallowed more and more of it. "Baby, you're doing good!" he murmured, encouraging me. When I felt his pubic hairs tickling my chin, he cried, "Oh, yeah, suck my big dick!"

As I continued to suck him, I released my now stiff cock from the fabric of the swim trunks I always wear at home.

His hands moved down my back to my ass. He slid a finger between my asscheeks.

"Yeah," he whispered. "I wanna fuck that sweet ass of yours."

"Oh, god, it'd hurt." My voice was dubious. I had gone twenty-three years without it, and I had no plans to suddenly change course.

"Only a little maybe," he said, as if boasting. "And just at the beginning."

I ignored his fingers while I worked on his prick. I could feel my dick oozing precum, I could taste his, and my balls were churning. His slow, steady fingering of my butt was driving me insane. Now two of his fingers were buried in my ass. I gasped out in pleasure.

"Oh, god!" I gasped, letting go of his dick. "I'm gonna shoot!" His finger was joined by a third one and now he really skewered me.

It seemed to take forever for me to finish coming, bucking and swiveling and writhing between his thighs, his erection banging against my cheek.

He pulled his fingers out of me, climbed off the sofa, and spread me out for the next phase. "Now it's my turn," he said.

One of his hands was caressing my buttocks, then I felt his finger find its way back between my cheeks. "Relax now," he said, fingering me again. My cock threatened to come alive again. After a few moments, he removed the fingers, straddled my legs, then pressed his dick home. "Lift up just a bit," he told me, and when I did his dick slipped into my crack. I glanced back over my shoulder and saw him poised behind me, his hand guiding his dick along my crack. Soon the excessive width of it was spreading my cheeks. He smiled at me. I froze. His fingers had paved the way but still—

My ass lips tightened reflexively, and "Relax," he coaxed, bending down, his hand caressing my cheeks again. "You're gonna love it."

His enthusiasm was infectious; I surrendered to him.

"You just push down while I'm pushing in," he told me, his voice gentle. I felt the sofa move as he adjusted his weight before I felt his dick begin to move into my yielding hole. He was moving slowly, carefully. But the pain was incredible. "Oh, god!"

"Push down!" he commanded.

My tears wet the pillows as he slid into me. Finally, his balls landed against mine. I became aware of his pubic thatch tickling the sensitive insides of my ass cheeks. "I knew you'd like it."

New sensations were coming now as my ass adjusted to Joe's commanding presence inside it.

"Raise your ass just a bit more," he cajoled.

Instinctively, I raised my ass up some more and felt some of that rigid shaft of flesh pull from out of me. The movement, stroking my prostate, massaging my ass lips, made any thought of pain and stopping disappear. I looked back at him over my shoulder.

"Oh, god," I grunted. His hand trailed over my hip and took my flaccid dick, making a fist around it and kneading the soft flesh, bringing it back to life. As he came back into me, his hand moved back along the shaft to my bush. "Oh, yeah, fuck me!" I groaned, wiggling my ass against his groin as he came to a stop deep inside me, then pulled back.

I began grinding my ass against him every time he banged into me, wanting more of him. "Do it!" I groaned over and over again. "Oh, please, do it!"

Joe kept banging my ass as I shot all over the sofa under me. I couldn't remember ever coming twice in one hour, let alone in one day. But my orgasms were pathetic compared to his, or maybe he hadn't come in some time. Whatever, he couldn't seem to stop, filling me, then filling me again. But he didn't stay in me long; he lifted off and said, business-like, "Now I need that shower."

If anyone needed a shower it was me. I was coated with cum, front and back, but I just lay still, my ass aching, my heart full.

The next morning, I realized I was in love. He wasn't, of course. I stayed cool. I knew that even if there were no pictures in the offing, he would someday want to make a life of its own. Get married, have kids, own a house. I didn't want to get too attached or hold him back in any way.

But I couldn't help myself: I kept thinking about what it would be like to keep him here. I arranged a flight for the next day, telling him all the flights that day were filled.

That gave me another day, but, at the going rate, he'd already more than earned his ticket.

After dinner, he led me to the bedroom. "I don't think I can take it again, so soon after the first time," I said.

"Bullshit," was his reply.

I lay on my back this time and pulled him towards me. I spread my legs wide as the head of his penis came into contact with my anus. My right hand guided the thick prick into the greased opening. Slowly, inch by inch, he shoved the hard cock into me, stopping only to let me savor the feeling of the big thing flexing inside me. He braced himself above me and was in up to the hilt now. It was pure ecstasy, made only more pleasurable by the slow in-and-out movements he now started to make. Gently he pulled back his penis until I feared that it would slip from inside me. The head of his cock was all that was inside, and he held his position for a moment, then slowly entered me again.

My eyes were transfixed on his shaft as it made its way in and out of me. It glistened with the moistness of the grease and precum. His arms were taut as he worked to support his weight as he began to slam into me. My legs wrapped around him and pulled him into me on his forward stroke.

Our movements became more and more frenetic as I urged him on. "Fuck me," I called out to him, my voice cracking. Joe responded with harder, swifter thrusts of his pelvis. "Oh, yes!" I called. "Ram me with your big cock."

I could feel the spasms start from deep inside, as an orgasmic wave began in each of us. I reached down and jerked my cock. With a deep gasp followed by a moan, I came, splattering my chest. He followed an instant later, filling me. "Oh, yeah!" he said.

Slowly he pulled out, went to the bathroom and washed, then returned to bed. He said not a word. I lay there next to him, silent as well.

After a few minutes, I realized it was impossible: I couldn't sleep and got out of bed. He rolled over and noticed I was pulling on my swimsuit.

"What's wrong?" he asked.

"I've got to go out and check the rain gutters. They've announced a storm watch."

I'd recently begun to worry a lot about rain again, as if I were in danger of some kind.

Joe looked at me as I shimmied into my swim suit. "Wake me if you need me," he said, then rolled over and went to sleep.

I stood there for a moment gazing at him. He was so glorious, and I couldn't help but notice how soft his skin was. Like a baby's, more or less. As tough as he was, I couldn't help but fear the sharks in California would devour this young stud from a little town in Florida. But I had the storm to worry about.

I went outside. The wind was up; a storm was definitely brewing. I got a ladder, climbed up and pulled the leaves out of the gutters. I picked up twigs and some rotting fruit, but it was no good. I was consumed with the notion that Joe was in my bed, naked, and soon would be gone. I knew I should be a grown-up about it all, but I was as big a kid as Joe was.

I went back inside, poured a stiff drink. I started working on a manuscript I was editing. Normally, I like mental games. I find it easy to work and I work quickly. In the past, whatever my situation, I had been able to find peace in work, but there was no way now. I went back to the bedroom to gaze at him again, so innocent in sleep. "Wake me if you need me," he'd said. Tomorrow night, I thought, while he was flying away, that's when I would need him. I lifted the covers to enjoy once more the sight of his massive prick. I got into bed and lay still, afloat in the memories of having that great cock inside me. It had been so good, so much better than I'd ever thought possible. I smiled in memory of it, relaxed and happy, no longer grieving.

MY PEN PAL

Dan Veen

"Hold it, sucker!" I command the Latino stud spray-painting obscenities on the subway wall. In a flash I have the subject apprehended—handcuffed.

"Lemme go, asshole! Sonofabitch!" His mouth sprays more obscenities.

"Fucking pig! *Hijo de puta!*"

"That's it, punk. Talk dirty to me," I growl in his frisky little ear. "Filthy words turn me on!"

My cock hardens in our tussle. Kid's got lots of fight in him. I like 'em like that. My cock could fuck a hole right through his cute baggy jeans and drill right up his tight olive chute. Oh, he's a good weekend's worth of fuck!

Examination of the suspect's personal effects reveals him to be one Ernesto Alferez. Nineteen. Hair:Black. Eyes: Green. Hell, even on his driver's license the kid looks cute. I confiscate the rubbers found on the suspect's person—for later use.

With the cuffs on him, I escort him back to my domicile, a crummy railroad flat situated just around the corner.

By the way, I am not a cop, but thanks to my rented uniform, Ernesto is safely trapped in my dingy apartment before he puts two and two together.

"*Hijo de puta!* This ain't no police station, hombre! You ain't no cop!" The poor kid scrambles to stand. "This the way you get your kicks?"

"As a matter of fact...." My jackboot clamps the handcuff chain to the floor, making him bow at my feet. "...this is the way I get my kicks."

My alleged perp is, for all intents and purposes, subdued, on all fours—gazing up at me rather pleadingly. A hint of respect shows now in Ernesto's eyes.

And who wouldn't respect a basket the size of mine? By the time the evening's over, this mother-strutting hood is going to learn to love my cock. He'll adore my cock. Worship it. My boy will zero in on my cock like it's the fucking center of his fucking universe. Ernesto is looking at my crotch now, gulping, getting the idea, the idea that some great ego-smashing humiliation lies in store for him this evening. Soon, the swaggering proud Ernesto won't feel at home until my cock is skewering one of his hot young baby boyholes. Ernesto has been brought to his knees and his destiny.

He's simmering down now. His skintight T-shirt is sweat-damp, damp with the kind of fear that zaps a man's balls. The abject terror that stiffens his dick. His butt vibrates some, anticipating what's going to happen to it.

"I have to pee," Ernesto fidgets.

"Go ahead."

"No, I have to go to the john. You're not going to make me piss in my pants, are you?"

"Not tonight anyway," I say, though he's secretly wishing I'd make him do just that. This search and seizure of Ernesto's identity will be done my way. "Sure you can go to the bathroom."

"Good. Let me up."

"But first—"

I wait.

A long, long time.

An eternity.

As if I might never say another word and never finish the condition and thus never allow Ernesto to piss ever again.

First what? The question forms on his anxious upturned face. First what? Please tell me. Please. What do you want me to do? First what?

Now Ernesto is committed—a player bound in our game of Master-May-I.

"First—you have to take off your pants. Here. In front of me. I want to see you. Strip down."

Trapped between modesty and need, Ernesto looks up at me imploringly, bladder burning. He's not kidding.

But neither am I. He has to piss. He has to piss so fucking bad. Real bad. Yet he doesn't want the humiliation. He can't bear the discomfort of wetting his pants. Like a baby.

He will strip, all right. He will do it. Even with the hands cuffed. Even on all fours, he'll strip for me. He wriggles out of his pants. He flops around on the floor trying to skin those jeans off himself. Putting on a clumsy strip show. And what a show his weenie balls put on! I get to see that change-purse flopping at every angle. Regular jumping beans.

His jeans hopelessly tangle his feet; he's starting to dribble all over himself.

"Down the hall." I nod approvingly. "Get the seat wet and you'll clean it up with your tongue."

Shackled with his jeans, Ernesto hobbles to the bathroom like a drunk kangaroo. His sex organ (if something so small can be called that) is so decidedly underdeveloped that it inspires in me a mixture of disgust and pity. The better to degrade him with. His stiff peanut-dick bobs in the air, his fuzzy-ripe buttcheeks jiggling.

A negligible pee-pee maybe, but a body overcompensated with muscle. Poor kid's spent years in the gym trying to make up in muscle what he lacks in cock. It would be a shame not to toy with diamond-cut sinew like that. That button-size pricklet of his will be just another decorative accent.

Meantime I stretch myself out on the couch. Prop my feet up on the coffee table. And let my cock out for some air. My cock inflates as I pump it with my hand, so big and obvious compared to Ernesto's size AAA battery. My cock's foreskin slides up and down, ripples wetly around the fat crown. The pink seam of its underside stretches as my meat widens and widens and widens. Ernesto's filth-spewing mouth will look real pretty down there choking on my policeman putz. That gutter-tongue will finally practice the obscene things it preaches.

I picture Ernesto's sweet golden-brown buns hugging my meat, those hunching halves straining and stretching to take all of my gut-busting cock as it expands deep inside him. But first, I've got to teach this graffiti-writing teen a lesson for defacing our mass transit system—paid for with our tax dollars.

He's back and has ditched his jeans. They must've gotten a tad wet on his trip to the john. That's okay. He won't need clothes this weekend anyway.

"Get me a beer," I command him.

Hands still cuffed in front of him, Ernesto hops naked to the fridge, nudges open the door. Standing there in the refrigerator light, he tries to get out a can, but he drops it. He crouches down—picks it up between his thighs—hobbles over to me with it, the freezing beer can squeezed between his knees.

He sidles over to me. I make him hold it there for a while before I take it. His little hard dick stands in great contrast to the beer can. The pitiful difference in dimension is as humiliatingly obvious to him as it is to me. His dick sticks up at me like a useless can opener. I pick the can from between his thighs. Ooops—the cold edge of the beer can grazes his dick. He gasps.

For the first time, he's getting a long, hard look at my long hard cock....

His balls rise in reaction. His small scrot-sac retreats with embarrassment.

I sip my beer. I hand Ernesto a felt-tip pen.

He takes it. His face questions.

"Don't act like you don't know what to do with it, punk. I thought it would be the most natural thing in the world for you. Go on, write with it."

"Write? On what?" His eyes follow mine down to his swollen pin-dick. "Oh, no."

"Go on. Do what you do best, hombre. You like writing on things, don't you?"

"Please don't make me—not on my... my...."

"Take your dick in one hand and that marker in the other and write...hmm, what shall we have you write on it...?"

"Please—not there—anyplace but on my—"

"Yes, I know. Write on it: `TINY SLAVE DICK'. That is, if it will fit."

"Por favor, senor! Es muy sensitivo, pinga...."

"I'm sure your abnormally small penis is a sensitive subject, Ernesto. Everybody must have made fun of it in school. Is it hard? Can that little thing cum? Oh well, it doesn't matter any more because you're not going to use it." I jeer at that nub quivering between his legs. "Now you'll have my cock to play with instead of that sad little splinter. But before you can play with your Master's cock, you have to learn how to take dictation. Write on your little bump: `TINY SLAVE DICK'."

Ernesto bridles at this, but my boot-tip jabbing between his legs up into his asshole convinces him of my seriousness. I also wag my cock before his eyes, like a carrot.

Slowly, tentatively, like a miniaturist touching up a masterpiece, Ernesto begins to dab the letters: T...I....

With his first stroke the marker scrapes his sensitive nubhead.

He flinches. He shivers with the realization of what he is doing to himself. The felt tip marker's touch makes him squirm, his balls jiggle. Pre-cum drools from his button of meat. His dick strains under the marker's strokes, making more room for the rest of his task.

Finally my slave has written the word `TINY' on his tiny dick.

"Now—" I say.

And I pause again. A good long suspenseful time. Making him wait. Making him wonder anxiously, Now? What must I do now?

"Now...write what you are on your dick. Write your name. You know how to spell your name, don't you? SLAVE. You can spell `slave', can't you? If not, I'll have to teach you so you'll always remember what you are. Maybe I'll make you write `SLAVE' a hundred times all over your body."

Just below the collar of his pipsqueak cockhead, he begins writing, tenderly applying his pen to form the letters S...L...A...V...E....

It is one thing to have the idea secreted deep within the private folds of his subconscious, but to have it right there, spelled out between his legs, made public, for everyone else to see, to laugh at, stamped upon that most personal of male organs that Ernesto is a SLAVE—he might as well have himself spread out naked in Times Square!

When Ernesto finishes, he is out of breath. His midget meat is harder than ever. There it is, a written admission of his lowly status before me. Slave. A slave to my cock. A slave to my whim. A slave to my desires. It's the first time he has admitted it to himself. But there it is.

Something in Ernesto must like this ordeal, because he continues now, continues almost without a pause, except he does pause.

"Please, sir." And notice how quickly my graffiti slave takes to calling me sir. "Please, sir, can I please write on it COCK instead?"

His plea shows a true feel for words and their shades of meaning.

"Now slave," I say patronizingly. "What you have there isn't big enough to be called a cock, is it?"

Ernesto looks down upon his small bump of a dick. He'd like to have a big cock, a big fat man's cock like his master's cock, but he doesn't. His puny dick is the shame of the high school showers. His minuscule meat-morsel is the reason he fucks his women in the dark. He looks up at me. At my big cock. Comparing, and ashamed.

He sniffles, "No sir. It isn't big enough to be called a cock, sir."

"What is it you have?"

"I have a dick, sir."

"What kind of dick is it?"

"I have," he blushes, "a slave dick, sir."

"What kind of slave dick is it?"

"I have a tiny slave dick, sir." Ernesto blubbers, staring down like a punished child at his diminutive boy-bump. "A tiny slave dick." He repeats, breaking, babbling now: "A tiny slave dick a tiny slave dick a tiny slave dick a tiny slave dick!"

"In fact, that bit sticking up between your legs is hardly big enough to be called a dick. But for now, we'll just let you call that tiny thing a dick. Go ahead." I nudge him under his beanballs with my boot. "Better write it down so you don't forget it."

He finishes writing D-I-C-K. He needs no further nudging from his Master. The four-letter word barely fits at the base.

Ernesto lets go of his drooling marshmallow putz.

It throbs there, zebra-striped with his own writing. The dusky dickskin is now almost blackened with words. A signed confession of his humiliation. Written acknowledgement of my superiority.

After having written it, Ernest is, like so many other boys I've done this to, transformed.

He wants it now. He is eager for me to dictate more words to him now. Now he is happy to submit, submit to writing whatever I tell him.

But I snatch the marker from his hands.

Starting at his broad heaving chest I write upon his flesh:

COCK PIG

In big bold capital letters I write it, practically carving it into him.

Then:

FUCK PUPPY

Then

BALL BOY

Then (tickling him some):

MASTER'S CUM DUMP

Ernesto responds, revels in the words that cleave to his skin. The burning degrading scrawl of ink makes him writhe.

"*Ay, Dios*, I am...I am...I am your cockslave! Yes, I am your fuck puppy, you ball boy! Oh, please, Master, dump your cum in your fuck puppy, please let your cockslave kiss your cock, fuck your fuckpuppy!"

Amazing how attached he gets to words, once the words get attached to him.

Now, as if all his nasty fantasies have finally been exposed with these words-made-flesh, he cries, "Please! Let me kiss your big cock, Master. Please —"

But I'm not near finished with him yet.

"Get on your hands and knees, cum dump. Let me see that hot asshole of yours. Show it to me."

He does what I tell him. His hot, tight buns stick up in the air for me. The small of his back ripples and torques, eager now for his next humiliation. Straining to look over his shoulder to watch whatever I decide to write upon him. Ready to become whatever I say.

Ernesto's smooth beige backside offers me a clean slate, I slowly spell out along his spine: FUCKHOLE, and then I draw an arrow down to his coccyx, to the hole, the very fuckhole, the arrow's point just tipping into the nibbling pink orifice of his ass. On one of his buttcheeks I write, "FUCK MY HOLE HARD!" On his other asscheek I write "DICK ME DEEP!" Fingering apart his hefty bodybuilder's asscheeks, I can smell the nervous sweat trickling down his buttcrack.

"Oh, please, tell me what it says!" he groans out, moving his ass so much I can barely write straight.

"Hold still!" I slap his butt.

I have spelled out his innermost desires. I have tagged,

labelled and branded Ernest with his own deepest fantasies. His darkest desires forced inside out. His body betraying the filthiest thoughts of his hottest nights.

"Please, Master," Ernesto clamors at my thighs now. "Let me, let me —"

I let Ernesto suck on my balls, since he's been begging to have a taste of them.

"Good boy, good boy. That's my little ballsuckin' baby! You like my big hot balls, don't you? Let 'em slide down your throat like oysters, yeah, that's it."

He has never had a man's balls in his mouth before, although he's dreamed about it, wanted a man's balls, for a long, long time. He slurps loudly, gratefully.

While he sucks, I casually write across his forehead: "COCKSUCKER."

And across his ball-filled mouth, like a hieroglyphic mustache, I write: "MASTER'S COCKHOLE."

"Crawl over to the middle of the floor, cockhole. I want to take a look at my handiwork before I fuck it."

Ernesto crawls quickly, pecs, dick, butt, hardened by the suggestion that his hole is going to be fucked by the cock he's just sucked on.

While he's still on all fours I make him turn around for me. First his butt, then his face, then his butt again. Ernesto spreads his cheeks apart for me obediently. A true masterpiece. I call it, "Tiny-Dick Slave Grovelling for His Master's Cock."

I move into position behind him, straddling his upturned dirty little feet, stopping my cock at the entrance to his butthole. I hold absolutely still while he backs up on it. I watch Ernesto guide my cock into his gutter-buns. His asslips nibble at the gooey reservoir-tip of my rubber. When he gets to my cockhead, his hole opens up like a Venus Flytrap snapping up a meal.

Boy, is he ready! My young and pliable fuckboy rams his asshole home around my dick. Once my cockhead hits the inner rim of his hole, his sphincter muscles clasp shut around the head. Tight. The hole takes some time to fully adjust. I give it a nudge; the head of my whang plows through the ring.

Ernesto lets out a sigh. I can feel a satisfied rumbling welling up in his guts, at first like a purring, then like an engine about to go into overdrive.

"Eight more inches to go, fuckhole!" I tap the base of my fat hole-fucker so that he feels it vibrate inside him. "Cockslave!" I take a long look at my giant purple cock ramrodded into his body. "Cumpunk!" Once I get it all the way in, I probably won't see it again till after the weekend. "Pussyboy! Slavehole!"

With a quick jiggle of his balls, Ernesto begins to railroad my cock right into his ass tunnel. Damn! I never thought a butch type like Ernesto could make such a fine pussyhole for my meat. But he's eager now to live up to the names on his body. Nuzzled up into his warm fuckhole, I could dick this boy doggie-style for days!

His little over-excited dick is flipping around like a light switch. It spritzes a trail of pre-cum wherever I push him around the room. We rest for a minute at the edge of the bed, my cock embedded in his guts. He starts rubbing his nubbin against the mattress as I fuck him around the bed. Then I begin to yank him off, as I start fucking Ernesto back the other way, telling him to lick up his trail of pre-cum. All along the way I'm slamming it into him, pounding his ass. The kid's yapping like a lap-dog. By the time we reach our starting point I'm shooting off, packing his fuckslot with a safe full of cum.

Ten minutes later my cock gets huge again. When I slip a new sheath over it, Ernesto realizes he is in for one helluva weekend.

Around midnight, pinning Ernesto face down on the Murphy bed, I start dicking him again. But then I decide, what the heck, I'll wait and finish this fuck off next morning. Of course my new slaveboy is so horny he can't sleep a wink, impaled all night on my prong. Several times I awaken with him trying to bounce himself off on my cock, giving little grunts of frustration, grinding his ass back to my balls. But I just give his dick-tip a good hard pinch between my thumb and forefinger to put him in a more obedient frame of mind. By morning, Ernesto gives up the hottest slice of Latino asshole I ever fucked!

I teach Ernesto to fetch. He crawls for his dildo and his tit-clamps. I instruct him on their many useful applications.

With these in place, I order him to clean up my apartment, which he does naked—clamped, dildoed—with whimpers of discomfort and frustration. As a reward I allow him to blow me for a while, but before he gets his reward of cum I pull out and play keep-away with him, making him chase me around the room for my boner. The greasy fat dildo splitting his ass and the rattling chain on his tits make this difficult for him, but he's game for anything now. With my bazooka cock, I fire off wad after wad into the air and watch him scamper around the living room with his mouth open, chasing and catching my cum-wads in mid-flight.

By late Sunday afternoon, my slavefuckboy is well-trained and well-fucked enough so I can send him around the corner to fetch me a six-pack and a dozen more rubbers. When he returns, he strips quickly and lets me put the six-pack on his backside while I prop my feet up and watch wrestling matches on TV. This is his idea. Now he begs me to use him like a second-hand coffee-table.

It's almost as if the horny little fucker feels the humiliating words written on him. I love taking tough `straight' Ernesto-type guys and messing with their heads till they're pleading for a mouth full of my cock. Occasionally Ernesto rolls over, tummy up, panting for me to scratch his belly, or begging me to please play with his tiny slave dick.

I reach for it, hold his throbbing knob-head between my fingers, twisting the hard, sticky pucker as if I were adjusting the volume of his groans.

But do I give him relief?

No.

Next morning, just for effect, I stand little Ernesto up and spray-paint his balls blue and his dick green—neon green. His dick stays hard the whole time. Looks kind of like a Christmas tree bulb. By the time I finish his body-painting, Ernesto looks like a subway wall. He whimpers about what his girlfriend is going to say.

"Your girlfriend isn't going to see that dick anymore." No way he'll go to any girlfriend with all those humiliating slogans written all over him. Ernesto's stud days are over. "Not that she's gonna miss your shrivelled up little chili pepper. How can you be a macho stud, when you know you're my cock-slave? Why—" I grin at him, reading him like a book, "it's written all over you."

Then I decide it's time. I put my slimy, condom-covered cock back up against the punk's fuck-chute. This time his hungry hole is so familiar with the drill that it starts snapping at my hole like a starving trout. The sight of those little muscle-bound buns fucking back, hunching hard on my cockpipe, swallowing my fat piece up his fist-tight bung, almost brings me right off, so I pin him down against the hall floor, make him lie motionless, almost creaming off from the sensations of my hog rooting around in his tight ass.

Then it's time to throw him my bone. Still keeping him belly-down against the grimy linoleum, I spread his legs with my knees and start pumping. He's going nuts, can't get enough, trying to tell me just that, but I can't make out the words. Maybe that's because I've got hold of his hair in one hand, and I'm mopping the floor with his squawking face. His tongue is out and licking. If I rode him around like this for a while this dump would really sparkle.

Finally I decide I'm gonna come. I shove my cock all the way up his hole, hard, skidding him a few feet under me like a fuck-sled. Now he's screaming from the friction burns and the ride my prick is giving his prostate. Buried to the hilt, I'm shooting off, bloating the scum-bag lining his well-used fuckhole, slinging his fuckboy load out under him in a slick trail across the floor.

Finally we both lie panting in the middle of the hallway, a stinking pile of sweat and cum.

Before I let him go, I give Ernesto this week's homework assignment:

"Here's an ink pen. During the next week I want you to write on your body five hundred times "I will take care of my Master's cock whenever and however he pleases." Five hundred times. Got that? No more, no less. Write it wherever you have space on your body, but I want it written on you when you come back next weekend. And I want my pen back, too. Present it to me Friday night exactly the way I'm giving this to you now." He grunts as he feels me tuck the pen deep within his warm asshole; it is now a penholder when it isn't holding my felt-tip penis. "Or I'll have to put something else up there to remind you where you're supposed to be keeping your writing instruments."

This one took such good care of my cock, I'll want him back next week, begging for more mouth meat. Dressed, his hard pin-dick is barely noticeable through his jeans, but I know when I order him to undress next week, it'll still be hard like that, having stood stiff at attention all week—untouched by his anxious hands.

Now you might think he'd never come back after the way I've treated him. But then you've never been fucked by my cock before. You see, my cock leaves a mark on people. My cock carves a special niche of pleasure into every hole it fucks, a spot that can only be filled again by having my cock fuck it, fuck it hard, and fuck it regularly.

Wanna try it?

Go ahead. Strip. That's it. Crawl over to that pen. Now, slave, write exactly what your Master tells you....

SWEET DREAMS

Peter Z. Pan

"Sweet dreams till sunbeams find you,
Sweet dreams that leave all worries behind you.
But in your dreams whatever they be,
Dream a little dream of me."
  — *Mama Cass*

Dawn in the Miami Marina. Blissful silence, not a soul in sight. On the deck of the Caravaggio Amor, the waking sun's soothing rays bathed my naked body. This was a daily ritual for me. I stroked my fat cock thinking of *him*—as I did every morning. Only today was different. Today, I would breathe the same air as he. I erupted with a fury, my hot cum spurting on my face, chest, and stomach. *Today* was the day!

I knew who the kid was the minute I laid eyes on him: the bushy blond hair, the deep blue eyes, the cleft chin. It had to be him. Nathan Landis, the resident smart-ass kid on *OceanTrek*, the only TV show I could actually sit through without falling asleep. Nathan was really the biggest reason I watched the show every Sunday night. There was just something about this fifteen-year-old kid that made my fat cock come to life. Now here he was, standing in my boat.

OceanTrek was shooting on location on a small island between Miami and Bermuda. My boat was chartered by the producers to take the actors to and from the set. Nathan had a late call that day, much to my delight, so he was my *only* passenger that fateful trip.

"He needs to be on set five minutes ago!" whined the effeminate production assistant who escorted Nathan to the boat. "You take good care of our little star."

I told him to "fuck off" under my breath as we shoved off.

There we were, just Nathan Landis and me on a picturesque South Florida day. But things were not exactly the way I had fantasized: I stood *alone* at the wheel and Nathan sat quietly in the back of the boat, looking out at the open sea. Not exactly a wet dream come true.

"Beautiful day, ain't it?" I blurted out, desperately trying to make small talk.

"It's too hot," Nathan shyly murmured, quite the contrast from the outgoing kid I was used to seeing on TV.

"It's summer in Miami, son," I said removing my T-shirt. "Why don't you take your shirt off?"

He looked at me as if I had asked him to take out his cock or something. "No, I can't," he stated adamantly.

"Why not?" I asked. "It's just you and me."

"I never take my shirt off in front of strangers," he said. "You see, I'm real skinny. I don't have the nice body you have." The last sentence slipped out, making him blush.

"I can fix that," I assured him. "Come here."

The kid did what he was told: he reluctantly stood next to me. I tried to make eye contact, but as much as he tried, he could not take his gaze off my big, brawny body. He seemed fixated to my hairy chest, licking it with his hungry eyes.

"Hi, my name's Jack O'Brien," I said as I vigorously shook his hand.

"Nathan, Nathan Landis," he uttered, his voice quivering.

"Well, nice to meet you, Nate," I said.

"Nathan."

"Whatever. But since we're no longer strangers, you can take your shirt off."

This brought a smile to the kid's face for the first time. "Okay, I guess," he said with a sheepish grin. Nathan lifted his T-shirt, revealing a beautiful callow torso, untouched by manhood. He had a lanky swimmer's build and small, pink nipples that just begged to be nibbled on.

I was about to wipe the drool from my chin when it happened. The boat's compass suddenly started going haywire as dark clouds appeared from nowhere. I had never before seen rain clouds assemble so rapidly.

Shit, we're in the Bermuda triangle! I thought. *We're right smack in the friggin' Bermuda triangle! This can't be happening!*

Gusts of wind and rain hit us as huge waves began to toss the boat.

"Jack... Jack, what's happening?!" screamed the kid. He held on to me, frightened out of his wits.

I couldn't answer; I was too busy trying to make sense of the situation myself, and trying to get control of the boat. The last thought that went through my head before passing out was that of the Skipper and Gilligan spinning, spinning out of control.

We awoke on a sprawling white beach. Apparently we had somehow been washed ashore. Nathan and I just looked at each other at a loss for words, not really knowing if we were dead or alive or just having some horrid nightmare. There was not a cloud in the sky now. It was as if the storm had never occurred.

"Are you all right, son?" I inquired with genuine concern.

The kid nodded and then asked: "Are we alive, Jack?"

"Yeah, son. By some miracle of God, it looks like we're alive," I replied, caressing the kid's long, blond hair.

After several hours of exploring, Nathan and I discovered we were on a deserted island. It was a beautiful tropical island too, with plenty of fruits on the trees and drinking water in the ponds. We soon came upon a large, crystal clear lagoon with stunning waterfalls all around. The water was a lovely shade of blue I had never before seen. It was breathtaking, to say the least.

"Wow, it's beautiful," sighed the kid.

"Yeah, it is, ain't it," I said. "Last one in's a rotten egg." I playfully bellowed as I quickly undressed.

"But I don't have swimming trunks!" whimpered the kid.

"Forget it, boy. C'mon. Let's skinny-dip." With that, I pulled down my pants and exposed my ten-inch dick to the kid.

It was obvious he had never seen another man's cock before. He was absolutely transfixed by it; you could tell he yearned to touch it, but did not dare. I was now completely naked. The kid's eyes were glued to my virile, teddy bear body. I then let out a hearty laugh when I noticed his gaze still focused on my manmeat.

"Sorta makes you think of a salami, don't it, son?"

The kid nodded in awe as I undressed him. First his T-shirt. His supple chest and arms were lean but well-defined, and he was smooth as a baby's bottom, except for the trace of a few hairs under his arms. I knelt and pulled down the kid's pants and underpants. An amused smile took over my face at the sight of the kid's peter. It was so damn cute! The puberty fairy had apparently gotten stuck in traffic on the way to his house:

but a few strands of blond hair surrounded his peter. It lay dormant upon his ripe, plump balls.

I rose as the kid stepped out of his pants. We looked at each other, smiled, then ran buck naked into the lagoon—now our lagoon.

After hours of frolicking in the water, I sent Nathan picking fruit while I fished with a spear I had made out of a bamboo stick with my trusty pocketknife. Nathan's Boy Scout training came in handy too; he effortlessly started a fire to fry the fish. Of course, my Bic lighter didn't hurt. With our stomachs full, we dealt with the next problem at hand: finding shelter before dusk.

To complicate matters, an ominous looking storm was approaching. The heavy winds came first, followed by deafening thunder, blinding lightning, and ice cold rain. We were two paper dolls caught in a furious tempest. A frightened Nathan began to cry as panic began to set in.

"Look!" Nathan screamed, pointing to a small cave several meters away.

I grabbed him by the hand and made a run for it just as a bolt of lightning struck the very spot we had been standing on, barely missing us. We had lucked out. We found a cozy little cave for me and my cub to hibernate in.

"I'm freezing," Nathan complained, literally shaking. The temperature seemed to have dropped fifty degrees.

"We have to get out of these wet clothes, son," I said while undressing.

Nathan hesitated for a split second, then realized he had no other logical choice. He too got naked. I collected some twigs and branches that were strewn in the cave, quickly starting a bonfire by the entrance.

"I'm still cold," he complained.

"We have to share our body heat," I said, sprawling on the ground by the fire. "Come here, son.

Nathan lay next to me, still shaking. Only I didn't know if he was shaking from the cold or from what he knew was about to happen.

"Relax, son, it's okay," I said, trying to comfort him. "We have to share our body heat."

His small body went limp, surrendering to mine as I took

him into my strong, manly arms. He felt so fucking good in my arms, like he belonged there. Before I could worry about his reaction to my fat hard-on prodding his tummy, I felt *his* fledgling boner poking mine. He was as turned on as I was!

We gazed into each other's eyes, our faces just inches apart, our ardent breaths igniting each other.

"Do you feel any warmer, son?" I whispered.

"Oh yes!" he sighed. "I'm warm all over."

With that the kid began to quiver. I was about to ask him if he was okay when I felt the warmth of his seed gushing onto my stomach. After catching his breath, he looked as if he was about to say something and then thought better of it. Instead his cheeks turned beet red as tears flooded his baby blues.

"What's wrong, son?"

"I'm so embarrassed," he confessed, weeping.

My only thought at that moment was to comfort him somehow. Without thinking, I held his head firmly in my hands and kissed him, kissed him hard. The kid didn't even try to pull away. Instead, he greeted my ravenous tongue with his own, tasting everything my eager mouth had to offer. We were both in heat and there was no turning back now. Our makeshift lair was ablaze with passion.

I rolled on top of him and continued to feast upon his delicate face: his ripe lips, his waxy ears, his tangy neck. But I was insatiable! I wanted, I needed, *more*. I licked my way down his lithe, young body to his armpits. They were warm and musky. After lapping at his pits for a while, I proceeded to his tiny pink nipples. I nibbled on them hard, coming damn close to drawing blood. But the kid didn't seem to mind, he was lost in ecstasy.

I giddily kissed my way down his chest to his tummy, which was still wet and sticky from his premature ejaculation. The taste of cum filled my hungry mouth as I ate it up like a wild animal feeding to survive. But this wasn't enough for me, I still needed more. I rubbed my face hard into his stomach until his white honey went up my nostrils, in my eyes, in my hair. I was drunk on it. My face was a milky white, just dripping with his cum.

After licking his tummy dry, I continued my descent to his prick. Much to my surprise it was quite erect again. *Not yet*, I thought. I decided to save it for the main course. So I started with a hearty appetizer instead: his plump, juicy balls. They were like butter, melting in my sultry mouth. I sucked the left one first, then the right one, then both at the same time. That's when I felt droplets trickling down my nose and lips. Licking my lips, I quickly realized the kid was oozing pre-cum. I couldn't stand it anymore. It was time for the entree.

The kid quivered as I took his peter in my mouth. My jaded taste buds came alive with this choice cut of veal. It was absolutely succulent.

I didn't want the kid to shoot another load yet, so I reluctantly left his throbbing pecker alone. Placing one hand under each supple cheek, I lifted his butt off the ground. I could now see his vestal, pink hole glistening with boy-juice. The aroma was intoxicating, sweet yet tangy like a junior high locker room after gym class. I nudged it with my nose, then opened my mouth just in time to catch a droplet of his juice with my swift tongue. It was fucking delicious! His boy-pussy tasted as good as it smelled. I took a deep breath and dove in, eating him out in earnest.

That's when the guttural sounds caught my attention: groaning, moaning, grunting. Yes, they were emanating from the kid, but they were also coming from me. I was eating him out sloppily and loudly, like a pig at a trough. And I was loving every minute of it. I could tell the kid was about to bust his nuts once more, and this time I wanted to gobble down every last drop of his jism, so I had him sit on my chest with one leg on each side of my head.

"Grab me by the hair, Nate," I directed him. "Grab me by the hair and fuck my mouth like a wet twat, son!" The kid took direction well. He rammed his peter down my throat and fucked my face like a twenty-dollar hustler on Biscayne Boulevard. Within seconds I was swallowing globs of his spunk. I rolled on top of him then and kissed him hard, sharing his cum in our mouths.

My cock felt like it was about to explode. I needed relief—fast! I threw his legs over my shoulders, spit into his pink hole, then spit on my fat shaft. I shoved just the head into his tight virgin pussy, hesitating for a moment. This was going to hurt like a motherfucker. I remembered my first time, when Father

McIntire butt-fucked me in the confessional at the tender age of eleven. Hell, I took it and I survived. And Nathan would survive too. He had to. It was a rite of manhood!

"Brace yourself, son," I warned him tenderly. Then I savagely rammed it into him with a savage fury.

I heard a loud "pop" as a streak of his cherry red blood sprayed my face. I licked my lips, tasting his cherry as I fucked him, fucked him on his back with his legs in the air like the little girl that he was. He looked up at me with tears in his eyes, but I didn't care. I continued to ride him deep, ride him hard, ride him rough. Then I threw him on all fours and mounted him from behind like two dogs in heat. I humped him doggy-style, finally collapsing on top of him while continuing to pound his little ass.

I roared, shooting my load deep inside him. That's when I looked up and saw them for the first time. That's why the kid looked so frightened. There were dozens of huge, black natives standing around us, whacking their horse-dicks. One of the them, the biggest one, hit me across the face and I passed out!

I awoke to find myself tied to a totem pole of sorts in a clearing deep in the woods. Meters in front of me, the natives were gathered over my Nathan, who was tied spreadeagle to a bed made out of stone. A huge black snake squiggled on the kid's naked body. It did this almost sensuously, like it was making love to him. The natives stood over Nathan, chanting and whanking their huge cocks, obviously participating in some carnal ritual. Nathan was also rock hard and he actually seemed to be enjoying this bizarre rite. He was obviously drugged. Or was he?

I screamed at the top of my lungs for them to stop and untie us. This just seemed to anger them. A wrinkled elder blurted out an order and two young, muscular bucks ran to me. They brutally lifted my feet, spread my legs wide, and stuck the snake up my ass—head first. The pain was unbearable as the serpent squirmed its way up my tight asshole.

All I could do was look on as the other savages relieved themselves on Nathan, bathing him with their piss. They then untied his legs and took turns butt-fucking him. One after another, after another, they dropped their loads inside him, then went to dance around a campfire.

Finally, it was the turn of the two bucks who were holding me. They dropped me and ran to Nathan, fighting to see who would go first. One of them pulled out a knife and slashed the other one's throat. He then took his prize, fucking Nathan for several minutes until toppling on top of him. He then joined the others around the fire.

I looked back and could barely see the snake anymore for it had slithered its slimy self halfway up my ass. I was a curious sight indeed. It appeared as if I had a tail like some grotesque Centaur, the half-man/half-horse creatures from Greek Mythology. I tugged on the rope furiously until I was able to untie my hands from the pole. I then grabbed the snake and began to pull on it until I felt its fangs biting down on my prostate. It was clear to me: if I tried to pull it out, it would poison me. Aye, there was the rub.

But I would have to deal with the snake later. Freeing the kid was far more important. I ran to Nathan and began to untie him.

"It's okay, son," I said. "Don't worry, I'll get us out of this." Nathan looked me in the face now. Only it wasn't Nathan anymore. He had the cold-blooded eyes of a reptile, and when he opened his mouth, his serpent-like tongue lashed out at me, grabbing me by the neck and choking me....

"Mr. O'Brien!" It was Nathan's voice. "Excuse me, Mr. O'Brien. You okay, man?"

My eyes snapped open as sunlight flooded them. I was on the deck of my boat in the Miami Marina. I lay flat on my back, my legs in the air, with a twelve-inch dildo up my ass.

Shit! I had fallen asleep. And standing over me with a quizzical look on his young face was Nathan Landis.

"You are Mr. O'Brien aren't you?" he asked. "You're supposed to take me to the set."

"Yeah, I'm Jack O'Brien," I said, blushing. "And I'm very embarrassed."

"Don't be," he said kneeling next to me. "I start every morning the same way. Only my dildo is not as big as yours!"

I was utterly speechless. I just lay there transfixed.

"Take your time," Nathan added. "I don't have to be on set

for hours. Maybe you can show me some of the more exotic sights. If you know what I mean?"

I gazed up and smiled blissfully at my dreamboy. I guess dreams come true after all.

MOROCCAN DREAMBOY

Frank Brooks

The boy on the corner waiting for the traffic light to change so resembled another boy I'd known that I almost called out, "Selim," but I caught myself in time, realizing that Selim, whom I'd last seen nearly a decade ago, had to be twice this boy's age by now and probably wore a beard. In fact, when I'd last seen Selim, whom I'd met on a raw autumn evening very much like this one and who had come to live with me for two years as my houseboy, I'd noticed that his downy cheeks would, before long, be in need of shaving.

The boy on the corner shifted from foot to foot, restless with youthful energy, smiling and attentive, his alert eyes darting and, for the briefest moment, meeting mine. He was taller than Selim had been, about five-five compared to Selim's five-two or so, and slender as a willow. I studied him in profile, noting the downy skin of his neck, the rosiness of his ears, his straight nose and softly protruding, kissable lips. How I wished!

For months I'd been living a monk's life in the country, hardly getting into the city at all and having no visitors as I worked to finish an overdue book manuscript, and the sight of the boy, so bright-eyed and alive in the chill autumn twilight, reawakened my senses and got my blood flowing as it hadn't in months. The light changed and the boy was off, trotting ahead of the crowd of pedestrians. He was moving so fast that I almost let him go, but a quick glance he threw over his shoulder, which, in my aroused state I imagined was for my benefit, got me jogging after him. He hadn't glanced right at me, it was true, but I could dream, couldn't I? Besides, his willowy young form was begging to be looked at longer.

I caught up with him at the next corner, where I studied him again from the side as we waited for the light. I was trying not to be obvious. You never knew when some puritanical busybody, noticing my "perverted" interest, might start screaming or pull out a gun. The boy, although smiling as if aware of my longing gaze and amused by it—dream on, I told myself—failed to look over at me. If I couldn't have him, at least, after memorizing his face, I could sketch him from memory when I got home. The light changed and the chase resumed.

For the next four blocks I trotted behind him at a distance, appreciating his deer-like grace. Then, suddenly, he turned left and was gone. I had an after-image of his glancing back once before vanishing, but that could have been my imagination. At the spot where I thought he'd vanished, I found myself looking through the large front window of the Atlas Restaurant, whose neon sign advertised MEDITERRANEAN CUISINE. Unable to spot him through the plate glass, I went inside.

The candle-lit interior was redolent of herbs and spices and exotic music played in the background. Feeling conspicuous standing there, I took a table in back that was partially hidden by a potted palm, from which I could take a more leisurely look around. What I was doing here, and what I would do if I spotted the angelic teenager, I didn't know. I'd probably just look at him some more. I was being silly, I knew, but the boy had become an instant obsession. I'd been locked away by myself for too long, I realized.

The waiters were all youthful males, each of them cute and sexy, but none of them quite as young or enticing as my boy. One of them, smiling, started toward me with a menu, but another waiter intercepted him, took the menu away, and a few seconds later was standing beside my table. It was the boy himself.

"How are you this evening?" he asked, smiling as if we shared a secret. He spoke with just the hint of an accent, which I found charming and sexy. His waiter's outfit—tight black jeans, white silk shirt half unbuttoned—revealed more of his smooth chest and belly than it hid. As he leaned close to give me the menu, his shirt opened more and I glimpsed his brown nipples and smelled cloves. "Would you like something to drink? I recommend the hot mint tea."

"Perfect," I said, letting my eyes wander over him without discretion. His jeans fit him like skin and bulged at the crotch. I wondered if his basket could possibly contain an over-sized cock like Selim's eight-plus inches.

He smiled as if amused by my wandering eyes. "I'll be back in a minute, sir." As he walked away, his grapefruit-sized buttocks dimpling under his jeans, he glanced back. Talk about seductive! There could be no mistaking that look!

My chestnut-haired little beauty, I thought. He could have passed for an American boy except for that trace of an accent and the way he carried himself, gracefully and with a seductive little swagger that suggested that, despite his youth, he was wise to the ways of the world and the desires of men. I wondered what nationality he was. I also wondered where the restroom was, in case I lost control and had to make a quick trip there to relieve my pent-up need.

"I had them put in extra sugar for you," he said, placing a tall glass of steaming mint tea in front of me.

"Thank you," I said, "You're sweet."

He giggled. "The sugar is sweet, sir. Would you like to order now?"

"The tea will be fine."

"Very good. If there is anything else I can do for you—"

"What's your name?" In my excitement, I was feeling bold.

"Rafi."

"Rafi," I said. "Is that Spanish?"

"No," he said with a laugh. "We are Moroccan here. Berber. You have heard of the Berber?"

"Yes, I think so," I said, although I wasn't sure at that point what I knew and what I didn't, distracted as I was by the realization that the boy had unbuttoned more of his shirt while in the kitchen and now I could see his navel. Not only that, but down the right leg of his jeans there was a cylindrical swelling. I burned my tongue on the tea.

"Careful," he warned. "The tea is very hot. If you need me again sir, for any reason, just clap your hands." He wiggled away, again with a glance back over his shoulder.

I began to fear that I really *was* dreaming. The music, the scents, the mint tea, the boy—all so exotic—they couldn't be real! My hard-on seemed real enough, though, and when I burned my tongue on the tea again the pain was real enough. Not only was the tea scalding, but it was too sweet to swallow. I clapped my hands.

Rafi appeared instantly, like a genie out of a bottle. There was no mistaking a hardon down one leg of his jeans.

"When do you get off work?"

"Late," the boy said. "Very late. It's Friday night, you know. Very busy." He didn't ask why I wanted to know, but was smiling as if it was evident.

I felt myself flushing, as much with the excitement of being so bold as with anticipation at what could happen. "I thought you might like to see a movie or something after you get off work."

"A movie or something. What is 'or something'?"

"We could maybe go for a ride. You could maybe come out to my place. I live out in the country. I've got a fireplace. We could build a fire. Very cozy."

His eyes lit up. "I like fires. We don't have a fireplace at our house. Don't go away, I'll be right back."

Don't go away! Was he kidding!

A minute later he was back, a serious-looking man with a large mustache and wearing an apron standing beside him. This was his Uncle Hashim, he said, who owned the restaurant. The uncle did not shake my hand, but shook his head as if not pleased at all.

"Very difficult," he said in a thick accent. "Friday evening. Very busy. To give up even one boy would be very difficult. Impossible! Very costly! Out of the question. I would need compensation."

"How much, Uncle?" the boy asked.

The man looked grim. "One hundred dollars. Not a penny less."

Rafi looked at me as I sat there with my mouth open.

"One hundred," the uncle said, arms crossed. "Not a penny less. To give up a boy on a Friday evening: Out of the question. One hundred dollars."

Rafi looked at me expectantly. "Pay him," he said, sounding a bit impatient. "Pay him and we can go."

"One hundred dollars," repeated the uncle.

Luckily, I'd just made one of my infrequent trips to the bank.

. . .

He bounced on his toes beside me as we walked up the street, chattering away, but I was too dazed to respond except mechanically. Things were happening too fast for me. I was out of practice. Had I picked up the boy or had he picked up me? Was he real or an image in a dream? Had months of boy-less seclusion finally brought on hallucinations?

I'd parked on the top level of the parking ramp, out of habit rather than necessity. There had been plenty of vacant spaces on lower levels. Years ago, when picking up boys had been a daily habit, I'd discovered that a van on the top deck of a parking ramp made a secluded cubbyhole for quick sex. God knows how many boys I'd sucked off in my van on this ramp and others.

"Cool van," Rafi said.

"Thanks," I said, starting the engine. Boys were always impressed by my van.

I was fighting the urge to drag him into the rear compartment, where I still kept curtains on the windows and, on the floor, a mattress stained with the stray spurts of countless teenagers. I feared, though, that if I got him off immediately he might cancel his trip to the country with me. Some boys were like that, good for one blowjob, and then it was bye bye.

"May I take off my shoes?" he asked.

"I'd be delighted if you would," I said. "Make yourself at home."

With his shoes and socks off, he folded his legs on the seat under him, sitting tailor-fashion. "I have been in America for five years," he said, "but I still don't like to wear shoes. As a boy I went barefoot all the time." He wiggled his bare toes as if bringing them to life again after their shod imprisonment.

"You're still a boy," I reminded him, trying my best not to stare at his sexy bare feet and run off the road. I'm a connoisseur of young feet. He had large, long toes, made for sucking. If the size of his toes were any indication, the size of what jutted from his groin had to be impressive.

"How far are we going?" Rafi asked.

"We'll be there in less than an hour." To distract myself from his bare feet and my urge to rape him, I asked him about the restaurant.

His uncle owned it, he said. His brothers and cousins worked there as cooks, waiters, dishwashers, and so on. They had all worked there since arriving in the U.S. Despite his uncle's constant complaints, business was very good and getting better. I asked him about school.

He enjoyed school, he said, especially science, art, and physical education. I envisioned him naked in the locker room after phys ed class, his cock hard with the excitement of being naked.

He laughed often as he chattered and he kept glancing at me cutely. Once we were out of town I had to grit my teeth to keep from pulling over to have him on the spot. I expected him to slide over and unzip my jeans, the way Selim had often done as we rode together, and to lick and suck me as I drove, or to tease my hardon with his toes. But Rafi stayed put, coyly driving me crazy without laying a finger on me.

Rafi wasn't Selim, I had to remind myself. True, both boys had Mediterranean blood, but they were from countries thousands of miles apart, Rafi from the western end of the Mediterranean, Selim from the eastern. It wasn't fair to stereotype all Mediterranean boys as sexpots. In fact, it wasn't even fair to take for granted that Rafi wanted or would go for sex with me.

What a terrible thought! Maybe all the boy wanted was to see my fireplace. Maybe, despite all that had happened so far, I'd misread the situation. Perhaps, in my lust, I was seeing and hearing things in a distorted way. If I thought about it, the boy and the situation were too good to be true. Things had worked out too easily.

"Tell me something," I said. "Before we met in the restaurant, were you aware of me following you down the street?"

"Of course," Rafi said.

. . .

To have a flesh-and-blood boy in the house again was a revelation. Suddenly, I felt decades younger. Really, what had come over me in recent years, and especially in the last few months! Gradually over the years I'd become a recluse and had grown lazy. Making the long drive into the city and cruising the streets in search of fresh young cock had become too much work. And now it had gotten to the point that I hadn't had a real boy in over two months.

"Cool place," Rafi said, inspecting every book, painting, sculpture, lamp, and whatnot in the place. Selim had been like that, missing nothing and interested in everything. Selim had also kept the house a lot neater than I did.

The farmhouse warmed up fast once I'd built a fire and Rafi soon took off his shirt. The boy means business, I told myself. What a lean, velvet-smooth torso he showed off! When I put on a CD of Moroccan flute music, he smiled broadly and began to play an imaginary flute. I brought out a wooden flute for him, and, as he pretended to play it, he began to undulate and sway, dancing, his bare toes caressing the rug as his fingers caressed the phallic-shaped instrument he held.

I sat on the floor near the fire, watching him dance as I'd so often watched Selim. He was taller and more graceful than Selim had been, and more sure of himself, gazing at me as he danced as if to gauge my reactions to his lissome gyrations. As he wiggled his loins and pointed his toes, I began to squeeze and rub my cock through my jeans. Grinning, he nodded his head "yes" and danced closer, gyrating his hips, the meshed segments of his golden abdomen rippling. I rubbed my cock fiercely, starting to feel delirious.

"Yes!" I muttered.

"You like Moroccan boys," he said, as if stating a fact rather than asking a question.

"Yes," I said again, although the truth was that Rafi was the first Moroccan boy I'd ever met.

He smiled and shoved his naked right foot toward me, toes pointed. I cradled it in my hands and kissed it, rippling my tongue over the toes. He had larger feet than Selim, but they were just as smooth and soft, the toes brown and sexy. I slithered my tongue between them and kissed the instep all over.

"Mmmmmm!" he sighed, raising his arms toward the ceiling, flute held high in one hand, body still undulating to the sinuous rhythms of the music. His smooth armpits were misted with sweat, as were his bronzed, satin-smooth flanks. He pulled his foot free and continued dancing. I undid my jeans and pulled out my eight-plus inches of hard cock.

"It's a big snake!" he said, giggling at the sight of my cock.

Then, still moving to the music, he unzipped his jeans and wiggled out of them. His cock was bone-hard and sticking straight out. As he straightened up and resumed dancing, it pointed up at a forty-five-degree angle, wagging from side to side, a third of his moist cockhead peeking out of its foreskin sheath.

"Beautiful," I said, and he smiled.

"It's not as big as yours."

"It's big enough." I estimated seven inches. Although dwarfed by Selim's unreal eight-and-three-quarter inches, it was larger than the average dick on a five-foot, five-inch teenager, and on loins as slender as Rafi's, it appeared larger than it was.

He tickled his pubic silk as if to draw attention to it. Two whisks of a razor would eliminate it. He took his cock between thumb and fingers, peeling the foreskin completely off the fat, moist, plum-like glans, and the musky aroma of his sexually aroused young male body dilated my nostrils. I stroked my cock, sliding the foreskin, tempted to beat off watching him. Sometimes it was fun to jerk off while simply looking at a naked boy, to show him how much he turned you on.

He let go of his cock and made it flex and wiggle by contracting the muscles of his loins. It was enough to drive me crazy and he knew it, laughing as I moaned. Hands on his hips, he flexed his cock to the rhythm of the music. It was as if he had a finger up his ass rhythmically massaging his prostate. He shoved his right foot forward and tickled my cockhead with his big toe, smearing the lubricant that was oozing out.

"You like Moroccan boys," he repeated.

I fell forward onto my face, lying like a slave at his feet and kissing them. I licked the toes, the insteps, the ankles, and continued up his legs, kissing, nuzzling, and licking. The taste and feel of his velvety skin got me crazy. When I got to his balls, my head swam. I hadn't smelled or tasted young nuts in months. Incredible! It was like tasting boy for the first time. I held his cock at the base and licked it like a candy cane, keeping the foreskin pulled down tight so I could lick the mild, sweet, musky-tasting moisture off the sizzling head. He sighed, his cock flexing, spitting a few drops of boyish nectar onto my tongue. I would have gone down on him, but he pulled back.

"Undress," he said. "It's better with nothing on."

I stood before him naked, both of us looking each other up and down. He leaned into my arms, embracing me as I embraced him, sighing as our mouths joined and we began to kiss. His tongue slipped into my mouth. I go nuts over boys who like to kiss. "Baby!" I muttered, stroking his head, his back, his ass. He squirmed against me, purring, sending little spurts of salivary nectar into my mouth, which I drank greedily. His tongue fluttered all around mine and I sucked on it, squatting slightly, so we could grind our hard-ons together as we kissed. The boy looked flushed and delirious, his body literally trembling. Suddenly he was jerking in my arms and shooting spunk against my stomach.

"Oh yes!" he panted. "Oh yes!"

I held him until he'd pumped it all out, then slid down to kneel in front of him, holding him by the hips to keep him from collapsing. As he sighed, I licked the spicy boy-spunk off his belly, cock, and balls. His cock was still rigid.

"Do you like my milk?" He smiled mischievously down at me.

"Yummy! Give me more!"

"I've got lots more."

I held down his foreskin so I could lick his knob completely clean, then milked his piss-tube and licked off the last few gobs that oozed out.

"Ohhhhhh, suck it!" he moaned.

I swallowed his seven inches to the balls, my tongue churning at the sensitive underside of it.

"Suck, suck, oh yes!" He humped to the rhythm of my sucking, fucking my face as if he'd last got off last week instead of a minute ago. The Moroccan flute music seemed to stimulate him as much as my mouth did, and he wiggled to its rhythms. His balls were plump and silky-smooth, and collided with my chin. "Oh man, oh yes!"

It took me all of two minutes to bring him off again. His fingers dug into my scalp and with a boyish yelp he shot a torrent of cum down my throat. It astounded me how hard and alive his cock was and how powerful his spurts. I've sucked off more young cock than I'll ever remember, but I've never grown used to the force of a youthful orgasm. Each time a new boy nearly blows me away, I marvel anew.

"Feels gooood!" he purred, hugging my head, his pulsing cock buried to the hilt in my mouth.

. . .

A mountain of embers glowed in the fireplace, putting out enough heat to make us both run sweat. We were stretched out together on the rug in front of the hearth, Rafi flat on his back as I licked the sweat off him. After licking him from toes to forehead, I settled down on top of him and sucked his nose. Between our slick bellies, our hard cocks throbbed and slid. Rafi, like Selim, seemed to be a boy who never lost his hardon.

Rafi's long-fingered hands slid over my back, flanks, and buttocks, his nails scratching lightly as his fingertips caressed. "You have hard muscles," he said. "I like hard muscles."

"How about a hard cock?"

"I like a hard cock, too."

"Do you suck?"

"Of course!"

I moved up and straddled him at the neck, sitting lightly on his chest, shoving my rigid, eight-plus inches into his smiling face. He lifted his head forward to lick my balls. I rubbed my cock on his smooth cheeks. His cute face had a sex-dazed, lust-flushed expression. His mouth opened, tongue extended, and I eased my cock into it, continuing to stuff it until my balls were mashed against his chin. When he failed to gag on the deep penetration, I wondered how many cocks he'd sucked in his life, as he certainly seemed experienced. As I worked my cock in and out, his raisin eyes gazed straight up into mine.

"You sure love cock," I said, and he grinned even with a mouthful.

I reached down, playing with his thick, chestnut hair, my fingertips massaging his scalp as I fucked his face slowly. He wiggled his nimble tongue under my foreskin and tortured the most sensitive parts of my cock, and I gasped, working my throbbing meat in circles in his mouth. As Rafi sucked, his right arm jerked, skinning his seven inches of Moroccan boy-meat. He was such a horny devil that before I could get off his eyes rolled back yet again in orgasmic ecstasy and his body made rapid little jerks as the jism spurted from his cock, pelting his heaving belly and my ass like gobs of milky spit. His third orgasm within a half hour was as powerful as his first.

I eased my cock out of his mouth and slid back and down to lap the cum off his stomach and to suck the last oozings from his cock. After months on the wagon, I was hungry for all the young cum I could get.

"How many times do you come a day?" I asked.

He shrugged. "Many. As many times as I feel like it, which is many."

"You don't keep count?"

He laughed. "Why? That would be silly."

"You're lucky to be so young." I flipped him onto his belly. What an ass! I spread his grapefruit-sized cheeks and his brownish-pink anus winked from between them. He squirmed against the rug. "Have you ever been fucked?"

"Of course," he said.

"Many times?"

"Yes. Very many."

"You don't keep count."

"Of course not."

I excused myself and left the room for a minute to get the Vaseline. When I got back I found Rafi slowly humping the rug, his buttocks contracting beautifully. I could have jerked off watching him.

"Who has fucked you?" I asked, kneeling behind him and kissing his delectable young ass.

"Everybody," he said. "My brothers, my cousins, my uncle, everybody. Many men." He sounded proud of it.

"You must like it."

"Oh yes!"

Crouched between the boy's spread legs, holding his tight, elastic asscheeks apart, I licked the length of his moist crack and kissed and sucked his perineum. I nibbled his balls, then licked back up to his asshole to kiss it and tease it with my tongue. Rafi humped faster, moaning. I slipped my tongue up his ass, making him pant and squirm. As I licked him out, his asshole squeezed my tongue. My cock felt as big around as my arm, pulsing with each squeeze of the boy's asshole, aching to get inside him.

Rafi watched over his shoulder as I greased my cock. I worked some Vaseline into his anus and slipped my middle finger inside him.

"Yeah!" he moaned, turning his ass up as I finger-fucked him. "Fuck me."

I got up over him and slipped my cockhead between his asscheeks. He rotated his loins as my cockhead kissed his anus and he kept wiggling his ass as I leaned into him. His asshole relaxed in moments and half my cock disappeared inside him. He raised his ass as if trying to impale himself deeper and I settled down on him, sliding my cock to the hilt inside him. Despite my ease of entry, he was deliciously tight, his asshole pulsing inside, and so hot!

I kissed him on the nape of the neck. "Are you all right?"

"Feels great!" he said.

I started to churn my eight-plus inches inside him, scouring his ass with my muscular belly. As I screwed him, I kissed and licked and chewed on his ears, his cheeks, his shoulders, and the back of his neck. I wanted to devour him. He squirmed under me and I worked my cock in and out, first with short strokes, then with longer ones, until I was nearly pulling out with each stroke, then ramming back in to the hilt. The harder I fucked him, the more he seemed to love it, humping the rug under him as fast as I humped him.

"Fuck me! Fuck me!"

I shoved my hands under his chest to pinch his nipples, which drove him crazy and made his asshole contract. As the sensations surged through my sliding cock, I fucked faster and harder, my belly smacking his butt. His asshole tightened with each penetration, sending me to the brink of orgasm with each stroke. I gnawed at his neck and pulled on his nipples. His skin flashed with goosebumps.

"Ohhhhhh!" he moaned once more, arching up.

"Yes, baby, yes!"

My pleasure reached a climax and I saw stars. Letting go completely, I rammed his asshole and exploded into him as, under me, he pumped his fourth load of the hour against the rug. I slid a hand down his belly and caught his last spurts in my palm. I was in heaven.

...

Rafi woke me at ten the next morning with the urgent message that he had to get to work by noon or his uncle would throw a fit and would surely beat him.

"What time did we get to sleep?" I asked. "For good, I mean." We'd dozed off a few times during the night, only to wake again for more love-making, until at last we'd both collapsed into a more permanent unconsciousness.

"It was getting light out," Rafi said. He was lying next to me on my bed—the bed Selim and I had shared for two years—his hand sliding his foreskin up and down.

"Horny again?"

"Of course," he said, grinning. He reached over and grabbed my piss hardon, then leaned over me and pulled it into his mouth. I wove my fingers into his soft hair as his head bobbed in my hands. He jerked off as he blew me.

I lay there enjoying his talented lips and tongue, reminiscing about Selim, who had so often treated me to a blowjob first thing in the morning. Often I had waked to the feel of him sucking me.

"Rafi," I sighed, "suck it!"

In no time, Rafi's toes began to point and clutch in a way that signaled that he was close, and the sight of them excited me to the brink myself. His hand made squish, squish, squish noises around his lubricating cock. I watched his toes flex, his pisshole gape, and a white stream of jism shot from his cock, pelting my thighs and the mattress beyond them. It was too much! My own toes clutched and I let out a grunt as my spunk shot into the boy's hard-sucking mouth. He swallowed it all.

We took a quick bath, with Rafi sitting in front of me in the tub so I could soap up his back. Looking down over his shoulder, I saw his cock sticking up out of the water. The sight of it excited me again and I soaped my swelling cock, then lifted him by the waist and sat him down on my erection, impaling him from behind. He moaned, then laughed as he bounced up and down and jerked off. Boy-spunk hit the tub faucets and plopped into the bath water. I reached around front to catch some of it, then licked it off my hand as I went off up his ass. We were so soapy-slick that he slipped off my cock while I was still spurting.

On our hurried drive into town, I made a proposal: that Rafi come to live with me as my houseboy. I told him about Selim and our arrangement. He was more interested in Selim's monstrous cock than in anything else, and said he wanted to meet Selim. As for being my houseboy: he assured me that his uncle would never allow it due to Rafi's duties at the restaurant. Although, maybe, if I were a millionaire and could pay his uncle large sums of money to compensate for his absence, his uncle might consider it.

"How much?" I asked.

"A hundred dollars a day," he said. "Not a penny less. I know my uncle."

He seemed so sure of this that I wondered if other men had approached the uncle with similar proposals concerning his ravishing nephew. A hundred dollars a month I might be able to afford, but a hundred dollars a day! No way.

As we pulled up in front of the restaurant, the stern-faced uncle himself was standing out front, watching over two boys not much older than Rafi as they swept the sidewalk. I asked Rafi who they were.

"That one is my brother and that one is my cousin," he said, pointing. "Do you like them?"

"I can't deny that I do," I said.

"I will tell them," Rafi said, opening the door.

Without acknowledging my wave, Uncle Hashim shoved a broom into Rafi's hand and disappeared inside the restaurant. Rafi smiled and waved goodbye. His brother and cousin looked up from their sweeping to watch me drive away. I was hoping they thought I had a cool van.

ISLAND FRUIT

Thomas C. Humphrey

Embraced by a soft corona of street light, the kid stepped out of a darkened cubbyhole produce store and fumbled to lock the door as I came up the sidewalk on my way to the parking garage after a hectic day and more of the night than I like to spend at the office. Until my eyes locked onto him, I was looking forward to nothing but a tall drink, a leisurely hot shower, and a restful sleep.

As he tugged at the door, apparently having trouble engaging the lock, my feet slowed. I did not want to hurry by and miss compiling a complete portfolio of the youngster before me. Like the rapid click-click-click of a camera's shutter, my mind preserved image after image: Hispanic, late teens or very early twenties, medium height and build, dark eyes, short black, tightly curled hair, flawless cinnamon complexion, gold earring, wisps of an emergent mustache, taut black tee shirt accentuating a muscled, V-shaped torso, delectable up-thrust buttocks defying baggy trousers.

He turned and met my gaze and stood with a hand on one hip until I drew even with him, transfixed by his unwavering stare.

"Like what you see, man?" he said, his not-quite-baritone voice edged with challenge.

My alarm system sounded Code Red, and a sudden outflow of adrenalin prickled the hair on the nape of my neck. Two of my acquaintances recently had been assaulted and robbed in separate incidents when they were foolhardy enough to proposition kids exactly like this one. Now, I had been caught —staring hungrily at a Puerto Rican kid whose rigidly formulated macho code of honor might very well demand retaliation, maybe even explosively violent physical retaliation.

Hurriedly, I weighed my options. Walk past with a casual remark and hope he wasn't in the mood for altercation. Turn back to the blare of jukebox music from a bar halfway down the street signaling a safe haven. Say nothing to him, but be prepared to swat him with my attache case and run like hell for the parking garage.

I rejected all the options. "Yeah, I'm always intrigued by beautiful scenery," I said, surprising myself. I stopped beside him, and my eyes slowly panned downward, focusing in on his unrevealing crotch. I strained to appear casual, but the adrenalin was still pumping, and I was poised for flight.

"You want to peel my Chiquita banana, huh?" He cupped his crotch briefly and smiled thinly with a slight sneer, his ivory teeth gleaming like the keys of a Steinway grand.

"Maybe, as long as it doesn't cost too much," I said, my heart in my throat. Staid office manager type that I am, I had never dared be so bold with a strange kid before.

"You always get a bargain at Island Fruit and Vegetables, man," he said, "even after-hours specials." His tone was half-serious, half-mocking.

"Then let's go in and haggle over a price," I suggested, dropping my defensive posture.

"At your service, sir." He half-bowed in mock deference and turned to unlock the door.

Normally, I'm turned off by the idea of the exchange of money for quick, impersonal sex with a stranger and have been severely critical of friends who chase kids like this one. But an almost palpable aura of sensuality surrounded him and fired my lust until my whole body quivered with desire. My deep-seated boredom with routine, coupled with the pulse-quickening excitement of having him on his turf—on his terms—overrode any hesitancy or caution. I was ready to follow him anywhere.

"All we got is a bathroom out back," he said, locking the door behind us. "People can see in from the street out here."

"Bathroom's fine," I said, trailing after him along a display table of tomatoes, cucumbers, and cabbages. "But about the price...?"

I quoted a figure much lower than I was willing to go, suspecting he might like to dicker.

"That's fine, man. Like I said, after-hours special." He pushed open the door of a tiny restroom with toilet and sink and a pungent smell of pine oil disinfectant.

I came in behind him and left the door open. Light seeped in from the street and washed the tiny cubicle with a warm, candlelight glow. We both stood awkwardly silent, not quite knowing how to begin. Then he chuckled deep in his throat.

"Shit, I ain't had nothing in over a week," he said. "I'm so horny I woulda almost let you have it for nothing tonight."

"You'll probably blow your load right away, then, and I won't get my money's worth," I groused.

"Don't worry, man. My nuts are swinging so heavy I think I got four or five loads stored," he said. "You'll get your money's worth, for sure." He moved against me. "Sit on the toilet and let's get going."

I sat down and he moved between my legs, both hands on his hips, his eyes glued to the wall above me like a piss-shy kid among adults at a line of urinals. I slowly ran my palm up his inner thigh, and his leg quivered faintly under my touch. As I bunched the baggy trousers at his crotch, he flinched involuntarily and sucked in his breath. He was already fully hard before I touched him.

I kneaded the ample bulge in his groin, and his legs started trembling so much he reached both hands to my shoulders for support. I unzipped him and tugged his trousers down to his knees. Chiquita banana was an apt description of the stupendous organ confronting me, its scimitar curve defying gravity as it lifted toward his navel. But it was a Chiquita with a large purple plum grafted on its end, the protective covering already partially peeled back to expose about half of the dimpled lobe.

"Nice," I said, grasping the base of the thick shaft with one hand and skinning its uncut foreskin back to free the broad magenta crown completely with the other. "Real nice." I hefted his nectarine balls in my palm while slowly cowling and baring the rim of his cockhead.

"Quit teasing and start sucking, man," he grunted. "I need to get off bad." He thrust his pelvis forward and jabbed his big banana toward my mouth.

I let him in, but continued to tease by going down only just beyond the rim of his cockhead, where I nibbled lightly with my teeth while I swirled my tongue around the glans in broad circular patterns. His breath whistled through his teeth as he sucked in a quick mouthful of air. I withdrew my mouth and pulled his foreskin back up until it covered the tip of my tongue, which probed around his piss slit. His hands on my shoulders trembled and his breath whistled on every quick intake. Again he thrust forward, shoving his cock back into my mouth. I reached around and grabbed an ass cheek in each hand and slowly pulled him into me until his broad cockhead spread my throat and his wiry pubic hair brushed against my lips. I held still and rhythmically contracted my throat muscles around his thick shaft.

"Yeah! Suck that cock, man, eat my *pinga*! Swallow it all, faggot!" he moaned. He rocked back and forth, fighting against my grip on his ass, and tried to move his cock in and out of my throat.

I turned his ass loose and allowed him to fuck my mouth at will. I grabbed his heavy ballsac and milked it down until his balls threatened to tear through the bottom and just held it there, keeping the pressure on. My other hand strayed up his ridged abdomen and I ran a finger around inside his navel. Then I moved on up his hairless chest and rolled one of his nipples between thumb and forefinger, squeezing down hard.

He started thrusting his pelvis in a broad circular motion, shoving the flared head of his cock past my tonsils time after time and then withdrawing almost completely before driving back in to maximum depth. My eyes tearing, I just sat there tugging at his balls and nipple and let him fuck my face.

He was trembling all over in violent quakes, sucking in quick bursts of air and groaning fitfully. He wove his fingers through my hair and tugged my head forward, trying to shove even more of that luscious island banana down my throat. As his assault became more and more frenzied, he began barking out, "Yeah, faggot! Eat that cock!" Just before he reached his peak, his babble was intermingling Spanish and English, "*Si, maricon, si! Chupame la pinga*! Eat my dick! *Mamame la pinga*! Suck it, you goddam queer!"

Before long, his babble was reduced to a regular series of primitive grunts, and his pile-driver assault slammed his pubic bone into my lips with bruising force. His thrusts changed to short, spasmodic hunches, the huge head of his curved cock gliding along the roof of my mouth. His grunts and groans became almost a steady howl. His cockhead swelled against my cheeks, and his cum spilled into my mouth in burst after burst as the thick tube beneath his shaft throbbed and pulsed against my lower lip. His ejaculation seemed interminable. I swallowed what I could, but some oozed back out of the corners of my mouth and dribbled down my chin.

"Oh, yeah!" he sighed when he finally extracted his fingers from my hair and stepped back until his cock was out of my mouth. "That was damn good! Just what I needed tonight."

I gently fondled his balls and leaned in to squeeze the last tiny glob of semen from the head of his cock and lap it up with my tongue. "How long before you'll be ready again?" I asked, suspecting that he would want to hurry away, now that his urgent concupiscence was satiated.

"I'm always ready, man," he boasted, "but I need a smoke first." He fumbled in the deep pockets of his baggy pants and extracted a package of Marlboros and a lighter, making no move to pull up his trousers.

He lit a cigarette and extended the pack to me. I shook my head, and he rested his buttocks on the rim of the sink and blew exaggerated swirls of smoke toward the ceiling while I sat on the toilet and watched to see if he lost his erection. He didn't.

"What's your name?" I asked.

"Fernando. What's yours?"

"Kirk. How old are you?"

"Legal. Are you?"

"You're quite a kidder, huh? I could be your father."

"That would be something new. I don't even know where my old man is."

"You work here at Island Fruit every day?"

"Yeah, we own it. There's my mother and me and my kid brother and two sisters. It ain't much, but it's a living. Only thing I don't like is getting up at three o'clock every morning to go to market. Cuts down on my night life."

He took another long drag on his cigarette, blew smoke toward the ceiling, and doused the butt under the sink faucet. He stood up, and his long curved dick came into reach. I leaned over and took him in my mouth and massaged his beautiful, rounded ass cheeks with both hands.

He stood before me for a few seconds and then growled out roughly, "I wanna butt-fuck you now."

"Oh, I dunno," I said. Looking at that huge, curved, thick

tool in my face, I wasn't quite sure I wanted to surrender my ass to it.

"Come on, man. I'm gonna fuck you," he said. He caught me under the armpits and tugged me off the toilet seat onto my feet. "I need to get inside your ass, man," he said.

His domineering insistence and the urgent need in his voice and face fired me into a near frenzy, and my cock swelled and strained against my trousers. I needed him inside me as much as he needed to be there.

"All right, go for it," I said as I unfastened my belt. "I think I'll like you fucking me. But what I'd like even more is to fuck that gorgeous ass of yours."

"No way, man, I don't do none of that," he said gruffly. "Bend over the sink."

I dropped my pants to my ankles, and my stiff cock jumped straight out. I leaned over, grabbed both sides of the sink, and thrust my ass back. He moved behind me and spat on the crown of his cock several times, slicking up the shaft between spits. After he had it good and wet, he bent over and dribbled spit down the crack of my ass. He pried my cheeks apart with fingers and thumb of one hand and guided the flared head with the other. When he was centered, he pressed forward until his big purple plum conquered the resistant ring and entered me. He grabbed me by the hips and lunged forward, burying himself completely in one movement.

The pronounced curve of his shaft had opened me up as wide again as his natural thickness would demand, a thickness more than adequate in itself. I shrank away from the abrupt intrusion.

"Go slow, man! That's a big Chiquita you've got there," I protested.

"You got a good hot ass. I'm gonna stretch your tight hole for the next hour," he grunted.

He began moving around inside me, without the desperate urgency with which he had fucked my mouth. He twisted and squirmed and pulled back until only the glans remained inside and then slowly eased back in full length, obviously enjoying his experiments in maximum stimulation. I grabbed my own rampant cock and slid my hand up and down the shaft. I started to back into him and then retreat in sync with both our movements, at the same time contracting my ass rhythmically, clamping my sphincter tight around the base of his shaft each time he penetrated me fully.

"Oh, yeah! Yeah!" he groaned. "You're a damned good fuck!" He stopped his movements and slipped his tee shirt over his head. "Take your shirt off," he said.

His big cock still buried in me, I raised up, unbuttoned my shirt and dropped it on the toilet, and then leaned back over the sink. He bent over me until his chest rested heavily on my back and grabbed the sink just in front of my hands. Then he resumed his slow, rhythmical movements inside me. As he fucked me, he rubbed his chest all around against my back.

"Yeah," he whispered, "I needed to feel some skin tonight!" He thrust and gyrated his pelvis for a while and then pulled out.

"Get your pants and shoes off," he said, leaning to pry off his sneakers and tug his pants over his feet.

When we both were completely naked, he sat on the toilet seat. "Sit down on my dick. I want you to ride it," he said.

I straddled him, back to his chest, and eased down on him. He caught my hips in his hands and shoved me all the way to the base of his shaft and moved me up and down on his big cock. When he turned my hips loose and started to caress my chest and squeeze my pecs, I kept bobbing my ass up and down in the rhythm he had established, stroking my cock at the same time.

"Get on your hands and knees," he said, shoving me off his cock.

He screwed me doggy style for several minutes, panting and dripping sweat on my back. He turned me over, threw my legs across his shoulders, and plunged back into me. As he fucked away, I lifted my ass to meet him and let my hands play up and down his back, exploring the ripple of muscles with every movement. Completely surrendering myself to him, I closed my eyes and voyeuristically imagined this virile stud dominating some woman as he was dominating me. I grabbed both luscious ass cheeks and squeezed tight. The powerful flex of muscle on every thrust sent shock waves of desire through me.

He did not quite manage his boastful hour, but he came close, the longest, most intense fuck session I had ever experienced. When we both were about tired out, he grabbed my shoulders from underneath, bent me practically double, and began driving deep into my ass time after time, emitting loud, primal grunts on each hard stroke. Then he pulled out until I began to close around the tip of his cock and drove back in full length with one final, brutal lunge and went rigid as he swelled and erupted in quick spasms—four, five, six in succession—until I felt his come seep around the base of his cock and stream down my thighs.

After we cleaned ourselves off and got dressed, I reached for my wallet and offered him a couple of bills.

"No, man, I don't hustle," he said. His voice had a completely different, softer tone.

"But we had a deal," I insisted.

He laughed, confident and relaxed. "You looked so much like a hungry, scared animal coming toward me outside that I decided to mess with your prejudices a little. You know, hot-tempered, fag-hating Puerto Rican kid, switchblade or gun in my pocket, ready to kill you for the smallest insult, or mug you and steal your wallet."

"That exactly pegs me," I confessed.

"Yeah, but when I saw you were more hungry than scared, and when you mentioned money, I figured maybe you got off on playing with tough street hustlers, so I decided to be what you wanted."

"You sure convinced me," I said, "but does this mean that you're—?"

"Sure, man, but don't tell any of my friends," he said. "But working late and getting up before daylight and playing macho games in between doesn't leave much time for nights like this."

"I hope you can squeeze in another one with me soon."

"Me, too. I like older guys," he said. "And by the way, when I'm not acting like a tough street kid, I do just about everything in bed."

"Then I'll have to get you in bed soon," I said. "I'd like to sample that twin cantaloupe ass as well as peel that big banana. Hell, I might become a regular customer."

Fernando grinned broadly. "Remember, there's always an after-hours special. You won't find a better bargain than this island fruit."

GOLDEN BOY

Thomas C. Humphrey

Engrossed in getting my dad settled into his wheelchair, I straightened up, and a burst of luminescence arrested my attention. I had never seen such hair! It was neither yellow, nor orange, nor bronze; it was a deep, rich spun gold. I stood transfixed by its tremulous glitter in the late-morning sun.

Dad's impatient cough pulled my attention away from the boy and his hair; turning my back on him, I slowly rolled the wheelchair down the ramp into Culver Park, Mother trailing a step behind, and on to the shaded area where the Colquitts were gathering for a first-ever family reunion. The image of golden hair retreated to some recess of my budding writer's unconscious, perhaps to be dredged up mysteriously and fitted into a story sometime in the future.

As I got Dad situated close to the near end of the long line of white-clothed rental tables required to accommodate the Colquitt clan, I again spied the boy positioning chairs among a throng of relatives beyond the far end of the tables; obviously, he was a part of our gathering, although he resembled no Colquitt I had ever seen. For as far back as photographs and faded daguerreotypes provided a record, the Colquitt genes had dominated physical appearance. For generation after generation, the men were dark-haired, tall, gaunt, long-nosed, and stern-faced, with deep trenches around the mouth giving them a hound-dog sadness, even in times of merriment. The women were thick-browed, plain-faced, long-jawed, and horsy. Glancing around, I readily saw these characteristics in my nieces and nephews and younger cousins, except for the boy with the magnificent hair. Of course, he possibly was not a true Colquitt at all, but a stepson or adopted child.

As I moved among various aunts and uncles, pausing for obligatory brief visits, I kept glancing at him and hoping that he was another genetic accident, as I had always considered myself to be. I also was like no other Colquitt I had ever seen, in that I was of medium height, with a rather compact build, a somewhat rounded, lightly freckled face, and deep auburn hair.

Always bookish and artistically oriented, I had known from a very early age that my familial singularity did not end with the physical.

Although possessed of keen intelligence, the Colquitts were very nearly completely practical-minded, yet, in my opinion, cursed by what I considered to be a hired-hand mentality. Throughout their known history, they had been farmers who tilled someone else's land, skilled tradesmen who were someone else's foremen, small merchants who managed someone else's businesses. Even those individuals who had become a part of family lore were struck from this mold. From earliest childhood, I had heard of my great-grandfather's older brother, Amos, who added twenty-five dollars to the family coffers by taking the place of a wealthy landowner's son in the Confederate army. Desirous of seeing the world, he made it seventy miles north to Atlanta, where he was killed in battle at eighteen, proxy for a man who experienced ripe old age. Then there was my grandfather's oldest brother, Aaron, who lost both legs in a sawmill accident while trying to protect the equipment of a logging company that floated huge oak timbers down the Oconee from central Georgia to the coast. The company promptly forgot about him, and he eked out a meager existence afterward, constructing rough-hewn porch rockers and re-caning chair bottoms. Although some of the later generations had become property owners and accumulated modest estates, none of them had ever had the daring to be their own bosses, and none of them had ever shown a spark of artistic creativity.

I had always felt out of place among family, partly because of my artistic leanings, partly because of age. One thing the Colquitts were was prolific. My father was the youngest of eleven children; I was the youngest of seven. Nearing seventy, my father had a sister well into her nineties, and nieces and nephews older than he. At twenty-three, I was eight years younger than my nearest brother, and I had first cousins who were married with teenage children of their own before I was born. Even while visiting with immediate family, I always gravitated toward my nephews, preferring to romp and play with them rather than be uncomfortable with virtual physical and intellectual strangers.

As soon as I completed my rounds among ancient relatives,

enduring the tedium of small talk and repeating answers to the same questions regarding my progress in graduate school, I moved to the edge of a flat, grassy clearing where my younger relatives stood in small clusters apart from the adults and noisily engaged themselves in renewing acquaintances or making new ones.

I had hardly stopped under a towering pine before the boy with the golden hair disengaged himself from a group and moved toward me. As he came nearer, my pulse quickened. Concentrating on his face and physique, not just his hair, I knew that I was in proximity to the most handsome—no, the most beautiful—boy I had ever seen.

His layered gold hair, barely tipping his ears and slightly curling over his collar, with tousled ringlets shielding his forehead, was merely the most singular of his attributes. He was hardly medium height, and his early-adolescent body, not yet filled out, nevertheless was lithe and well-toned. He moved with leonine grace, befitting his magnificent mane, with none of the usual big-footed clumsiness of adolescence. His lightly tanned skin was marble-smooth and completely flawless; he was at the ideal Platonic state of youthful beauty, when not even the hint of a future beard marred his face. As he neared me, smiling through deep red, sensuous lips, his teeth gleamed like ivory carved from a perfect pattern. Up close, his eyes demanded more attention than his hair. They were the deepest blue imaginable, and in the light, they swam in shining pools. His lashes were long and prominent, as if lightly mascara'd in gilt. The total effect was of faceted lapis mounted in gold.

"You're Carey, right?" he addressed me.

"That's right," I answered, taken aback, not only that he knew my name, but that he had sought me out. "And who are you?"

"I'm Jason Bowden." His voice had a scratchy, not yet quite settled, near-baritone timbre.

"How do you fit into the Colquitt clan?" I asked, thinking what an appropriate name, in that he already had captured the golden fleece.

"My mother was Frances Eliot."

"Then your grandfather is Lane Eliot?" I did a hurried mental calculation; Lane was my first cousin, almost as old as my father. "That makes us - what? - first cousins twice removed?"

He flashed a beautiful, disarming smile. "Or third or fourth cousins, something like that. I can never remember all that junk." He laughed softly, a happy, confident laugh.

"Neither can I, cousin." I joined his laughter.

"I read your story. It was fresh," he said seriously.

"Which one?"

"'That Shining Afternoon.'"

The story, my second published one, had recently appeared in a small literary quarterly on the recommendation of an undergraduate professor who had gotten a favorable commentary on it from none other than Harry Crews, at whose feet I had sat in awe a few times. I had read enough Faulkner and Flannery O'Conner—and Crews—to be only faintly derivative. It was published with a headnote saying that I showed "promise of following in the great Southern tradition of William Faulkner." I do have a pretty good eye for local color and an ear attuned to Georgia dialect, but underneath, the story is a rather banal young boy-girl love story, a subject I know nothing about firsthand and little secondhand, it not being a primary focus of my interest.

"It was fresh, huh?"

"Yeah, I like the careful way you describe things, and I could hear the people talking, like I was there."

"I'm pleased. That's exactly what I was trying to do with it. You're a very sharp reader."

"Yeah. I want to be a writer, too."

Just as I was beginning to cope with the visual impact of him, his mind now piqued my interest anew. He was another genetic oddity. I wondered to what deep level of our souls we might be kindred spirits. I had never before dared hope that any relative might share my nature, never having detected the slightest hint of it. Now, in the presence of this beautiful adolescent, two generations removed, I began to wonder.

"Are you writing now?" I asked.

"Yeah. I make myself do a little every day—mostly poems and descriptions of things I see, a few little stories."

"That's great," I said, excited by the belief that this was a serious undertaking for him. "I wish you had some of it with you; I'd like to see it."

He shuffled slightly and looked down momentarily; then his eyes met mine confidently as he revealed his intent in seeking me out. "I wish you would tell me what you think of it. I could send some of it to you, if it wouldn't interfere with your studying."

"I'll make time for it," I promised. "Be sure to get my address before we leave."

We were interrupted by two plain-faced pubescent girls, obviously Colquitts, who moved beside Jason.

"Come on, Jason. Y'all can talk some other time; let's go do something," the less attractive, horsy one said, tugging at his elbow, her voice flat and unexpressive, diphthongs floating like corks through the turbid sea of her drawl.

"This is Tracey—and Karen," Jason introduced them. "They're our third or fifth or some kind of cousins."

"Hi," the girls said in unison and then tittered, uncomfortable in the company of even a young adult.

We were joined by Kevin, one of my nephews, who was carrying a football.

"Come on, Carey, let's play some ball," he said.

"Great idea," I said, hoping Jason agreed.

"Can we play?" Tracey asked.

"Yeah, if you don't mind getting tackled," Jason said.

"Aw, y'all're just going to play touch," Tracey said.

"Then, if you don't mind getting touched," Kevin said.

Both girls tittered again. "Oh, we like that," Tracey gushed.

Jason lifted his eyebrows and rolled his eyes at me in mock exasperation as we headed for the playing area.

It was a hot Labor Day in central Georgia, and, before long, most of the boys had their shirts off. Jason and I wound up on the same team. Tracey purposely chose the opposite team, apparently thinking she would get touched more by Jason that way; she tried to get in front of him or chase him down on every play. I was content just to be near him in our brief huddles and to watch the play of muscles with every move he made.

He was even more attractive with his shirt off. The same even, light tan spread over his entire body, as far down as I could see beneath his modish loose-fit shorts, which rode far down on his hips. The only contrasts to his tan were his well-defined little dark nipples and shadows formed by the ripple of muscles across his back and stomach. He did not have one blemish, one freckle, one mole, one scar visible anywhere. A light patina of perspiration soon glimmered on his skin and produced heightened definition like that of an oiled semi-nude model under strong light. Tiny beads on his upper lip formed a temporary opaque mustache. In the huddle, I noticed only a small tuft of fine gold in his armpits; the visible portion of his body was completely hairless otherwise, except for a nearly transparent tangle on his lower legs.

I had played football in high school, as every small town Georgia boy who is any kind of man is expected to do; by the end of my senior year, I was second team wide receiver and had spent most of my career on the bench. In the Colquitt pick-up game, I was designated quarterback, probably in deference to my age. Though I tried to be equitable to all my team, Jason dominated my attention. He possessed the unconscious grace of a born athlete and the youthful exuberance of a fierce competitor. Something sparked between us immediately, and he reacted to me almost as if no one else were present.

Once, when I apologized for over-throwing a pass to him, he clapped me on the shoulder, flashed me a winsome smile, and said, "That's okay; we're artists, not athletes." Another time, after making a diving catch for a score, rolling on one shoulder and onto his feet in one fluid motion, he ran back to me, triumphantly holding the ball over his head, and leaped on me, arms around my neck, legs around my waist, nearly upending me. "Pretty good throw, cousin," he said.

When the call to eat came, I was reluctant to quit playing. All we athletes lined up together at the long buffet table, sweaty and grass-stained. My mother wrinkled her nose.

"Whew, you stink," she said. "Go sit somewhere way off."

"Think you can stand me long enough to give me a pen and paper?" I asked. I wanted to make sure that Jason had my address.

One thing the Colquitts believe in is eating well. The long table was a cornucopia of Southern meats, vegetables, casserole dishes, and desserts. By the time we made it to the end of the line, most of the young people carried two heaping plates, and we had not begun to sample everything.

"Well, he finally got to meet you," Jason's mother said when we stopped to give her my address for safekeeping. "The only way I could get him to come today was to assure him you would be here."

"We writers have to stick together, you know," I said.

"Scribbling and moping around is about all he does at home," she said, tousling his hair affectionately.

"Aw, Mom, you make me sound like some kind of weirdo," he protested. He turned to me with a shy, private, conspiratorial smile. "Come to think of it, I guess I am."

We joined the other football players under a huge live oak and balanced plates on our laps. Tracey shifted positions to sit beside Jason, her friend Karen trailing after her. Jason tried to discuss poetic form with me, debating the virtues of rhyming and free verse, while at the same time giving adolescent answers to Tracey's adolescent questions; it was quite a juggling act he performed. When we were practically stuffed, he stood up and turned to me.

"I'm going for dessert. Can I bring you some?"

"If you can find some of Aunt Esther's lemon meringue pie; otherwise, any lemon pie not out of a box."

Tracey started to get up and then sat back down. "Will you bring me a piece of cake?" she asked. I could almost see her weighing the advantages of demurely having him serve her against the lost opportunity to walk with him.

"What kind?"

"Chocolate."

"Sure," he said indifferently.

"What are you involved in at school?" I asked her after Jason left, struggling to make conversation.

"I'm a flag girl in the band, and I hope I'm gonna cheerlead for junior varsity basketball," she said.

"It's good to do things like that," I said.

Once she discovered that I did not bite, she launched into a description of how pretty the band uniforms were and then told me how cute her boyfriend, who played football, was. Once she started, all I had to do was nod my head.

Jason handed me a huge slice of lemon meringue pie. "Aunt

Esther said you always did have good sense when it came to food," he said, laughing. He poked the piece of cake at Tracey without comment and sat to dig into his own pie. "Um, I see why you asked for hers," he said, licking his lips.

Tracey broke off a piece of cake and stuck it in his face with her fingers. "Try this; it's good," she insisted.

He accepted the offering and then made a face. "Lemon and chocolate don't go together."

"Wash it down with Kool-Aid," she suggested. She reached to swipe at his mouth. "Here, you left a piece on your lips." She let her hand rest on his shoulder and then trail slowly down his arm.

I watched her with amusement, coupled with an indistinct tangle of emotions—envy?—jealousy?—resentment?—built around the contrast between her open display and my suppressed but growing attraction toward Jason.

Jason again mentioned being able to hear characters in my story talk. I decided to show off a little.

"All you have to do is listen close," I said. "You take Tracey; I'll bet she lives in southwest Georgia, somewhere around Albany."

"Aw, you know my folks," she said.

"No, you just sound like people from around there."

"Well, you're right; I live about twenty miles from Albany." She pronounced it "awl-BENNY," like a true native.

"And, Karen, you live somewhere around Macon, right?"

"How'd you know?" Karen said. "I do; I live in Perry, just south of Macon. That's purely amazing!"

"What about me?" Jason asked.

"You're a puzzle," I admitted. "You're southern, but you don't even sound like Georgia. If I had to guess, I'd say Tennessee or North Carolina, one of the border states."

"Atlanta," he said. "Actually, Avondale Estates."

"Oh, well, Atlanta's not really Georgia," I said.

"Also, I've taken a class to learn standard speech; I want to try to do some acting soon."

"How old are you?" I asked, impressed by his disciplined pursuit of his goals.

"Fourteen. I just started ninth grade."

"Do you play football?" Tracey asked.

"No," he laughed. "I'm trying out for soccer, but I'm not very good."

"Come on, Tracey, I have to go to the little girls' room," Karen said, tugging her to her feet.

"Looks like you have a new girlfriend," I risked after they left.

"Yeah," he said, wrinkling his nose in disgust. "Girls can be real pests sometimes."

"But really nice at others," I said. I suspected that he had a lot of practice brushing off the attentions of those who were strongly attracted to him.

"I don't know about that. Maybe." He switched to a more worthy topic.

As we lazed under the tree allowing our huge meal to settle, I attempted to maintain stimulating conversation while trying to sort through my confused feelings. Jason was little more than a child, despite his obvious intellect, and I was having to admit that my feelings toward him were no longer completely pure. He had captivated me with his appearance, he had intrigued me with his interest in writing, he had flattered me with his attention, he had piqued my curiosity with his cavalier attitude toward the girls, he had fired a little flame of hope with his overall demeanor. But he was little more than a child. I simultaneously felt guilty for my less-than-pure interest in him and began to form a dream of my nurturing his writing and our relationship until he entered college, perhaps where I would be teaching by then. He would be eighteen; I would be only twenty-seven. Anything was possible....

Boredom finally overcame after-dinner languor and someone suggested going swimming. I had trunks in the car, but I felt that I should bow out of the teenagers' company, although I was reluctant to leave Jason. Apparently, he felt the same way toward me. When the others responded enthusiastically, he turned to me.

"Do you want to go?"

"I don't know. Are you going?"

"If you go."

"Okay, let's go," I suddenly decided for us both.

In the pool dressing room, I glanced with curiosity as he slipped off his shorts, but all I saw was the shine of his untanned, rounded buttocks as he pulled on his swimsuit, a white bikini of the type worn by competitive swimmers. Once wet under the shower, it left little to the imagination. A prominent bulge indicated that he certainly was much more than a child physically.

I had to restrain myself from staring. As I forced my eyes away, I experienced the enervating visceral stir, the accelerated pulse, the dry-throat, copper-penny taste of lust. Immediately, I was overcome by guilt and confusion. Never before had I been attracted to anyone so young. Even when I was his age, I was enamored with the senior captain of the football team. I had discovered my sexuality about the time the world discovered AIDS and had led a very careful, mostly abstemious life. As an undergraduate at the University of Florida, I had a rather casual on-again-off-again affair with an older graduate teaching assistant. At Chapel Hill, I was no more seriously involved with an older doctoral candidate. But Jason was only fourteen, and I wanted him. I recoiled from my pederastic desire, but I could not tear myself away from him.

In the pool, the other kids wanted to play sharks and minnows. Tracey tugged at Jason, silently begging him to give her some attention. Half-despising myself, I entered into open competition for him. Having discovered that he liked to dive and was good at it, I kept challenging him, "Do a pike, do a half-gainer, do a swan," kept him on the deep end of the pool away from the others and their childish games, kept him to myself and my growing lust and self-castigation.

Every time he stood poised on the board, then soared into the air, performed his acrobatics, and slid smoothly into the water, feet pointed gracefully, my groin tightened. Every time he emerged and shook rainbowed droplets from his hair, now the rich hue of Florentine gold, I became more enamored with him. When he playfully grappled with me and hugged me to him, his thigh pressed tight against my crotch for longer than I believed accidental, I began to hope that he consciously shared my feelings.

I had read *Death in Venice*, and I was appalled at how, in the space of a few brief hours, I had become, like Aschenbach, captivated by and obsessed with my own Tadzio. Yet there was a distinct difference, major and dreadful, between their story and ours. Unlike Aschenbach, I was fully conscious of my attraction and its underlying motivation. I was so caught up with lust that I already was beginning to calculate a seduction, no matter how loudly my conscience protested against it. And Jason was no prepubescent Tadzio. Obviously physically on the threshold of manhood, he projected a worldly awareness of his staggering attractiveness and undoubtedly possessed a knowledge and understanding of my attraction to him. If seduction occurred, I convinced myself, he had communicated enough, by demeanor and innuendo, to make him a willing co-conspirator. Although my conscience resisted putting my thoughts into action, my mind raced ahead, searching for a practical means to accomplish my intent.

I sat on the side of the pool, consumed by desire, watching Jason's every move with longing, as Tracey enticed him into joining a game at the shallow end. Jealousy gnawed at me, although I was confident of his indifference toward this shallow, plain-faced child who so obviously wanted him that she was making a spectacle of herself.

"Why, Carey Colquitt! Hello!" a voice snapped me into reality.

I focused, hesitated, and then recognized Christie Mullins, a high school classmate, whom I had not seen for several years.

We ran through news of all the old friends and acquaintances we could recall, while her two children, one hardly a toddler, tugged impatiently at her knees.

"Well, I have to get these wild Indians in the kiddies' pool. Bye," she said, after we had about exhausted conversational possibilities.

After she left, I returned to my preoccupation with Jason. I had failed to focus on him for the several minutes I had talked with Christie. All at once, my heart sank; I could not see him. My eyes frantically scanned the pool area like radar attempting to pick up the blip of his distinctive mane. He was not there. I anxiously hurried through the men's dressing room, which smelled of sweaty sneakers and disinfectant, where a few nude preadolescents danced around and popped at one another with damp towels. He was not there. With mounting urgency, I surveyed the throng at the snack bar, where overweight girls devoured chocolate bars and acne-scarred boys gobbled handfuls of buttered popcorn. Jason was not there!

Filled with a completely inexplicable sense of panic, I left the pool area and headed for the family picnic site. Then I caught a split-second glimpse of golden hair as Jason rounded the small storage building at the ball diamond twenty yards west of the pool enclosure. Not knowing how I would explain my pursuit of him, I was compelled to seek him out, driven by a quest as obsessive as that which carried the Argonauts toward destiny in Greek myth.

Silently, I eased around the corner of the building. Jason had not emerged onto the playing field. With familiarity dating back to my Little League baseball years, I knew that the west side of the structure contained a tiny room where bases, the machine for chalking foul lines, and tarpaulins to protect the field during brief rain showers were stored. Jason was not outside the building; the storage room door was slightly ajar. I tiptoed up and peered through the crack into the darkened room, excitedly imagining what he might be up to.

Against the far wall in the half-light which struggled through the grimy single-paned window, I first saw his hair glowing. As my eyes adjusted, I discerned that he was not alone. He and the plain-faced Tracey stood melded together. Jason shifted slightly, and I saw that Tracey's bra was gone, and he kneaded one of her nubile breasts; his swim trunks were around his thighs, and Tracey grasped his erect penis in her hand.

Jason forcefully pulled her tight against him, and their mouths battled in a ravenous kiss. As if they were engaged in an old-fashioned dance, he gracefully bent her backward and dipped her toward the floor. Like the tail of a fiery comet, his golden hair traced an arc through the fading light until they sank into complete darkness. As I turned to flee, the little girl emitted a woman's loud moan of submission and conquest when Jason entered her.

BOUND VIRGIN

Jack Ricardo

I needed extra bucks so I got an evening job as a temp at Macy's during the Christmas season. In the Toy Department, no less. A crazy time, what with rude mothers and wild kids.
On my first night on the job, another temp said, "Beautiful, ain't she?" He was looking at a stunning woman.
I said, "Yeah." Then added, "For a female."
I stay in the closet for no man. The guy gave me a puzzled glare and said nothing. What I didn't know until I took my break two hours later was that Mico, another temp, a cute little bugger who looked like he was just handed his high school diploma, had overheard me. He was either Chinese, Japanese, Vietnamese—or some other nese. Like most Anglos, I really can't tell the difference. Mico and I were sitting in the near-empty cafeteria upstairs. He asked, haltingly, shyly, quietly, "What you said. . . is it what I think? Is it true? Are you . . . homo . . . are you . . . gay?"
"Yep," I said, amused by his naivete.
He didn't say a word, just sipped his soda and eyed me strangely. Longingly? At last, he asked, "How did you know you were gay?"
I smiled and said, "I knew."
"I mean, how, when, where, who...?" he stuttered and stopped. I let him off the hook. "You think you might be gay, Mico?"
"No, of course not, well, yeah, maybe, but I don't know. No. No. I never did anything, not ever. I was just wondering."
Okay, cherries usually aren't my style, but Mico was looking for a helping hand, that was obvious, by his questions, his uncertainty, his interest. He was yearning for a stiff dick to swing on and didn't even know it. At 24, I was no teacher, but I did have a stiff dick. Well, not at the moment. But I could, for Mico. He was small, on the thin side, with shiny, straight, black hair, a quiet smile, and a cute little butt. After the store closed, I walked home, as usual. Mico walked with me. We both lived in Chelsea. He with his family, me in an absurdly expensive

little studio apartment. We got to my street and I asked, "Wanna come up for a drink?"

"Well..."

"A Coke?"

He hesitated for a half second, "Sure, but..." He never finished his "but." He let it hang in the air like a cry for help from a man seeking...well, seeking dick but ashamed to admit it. He sat on the futon, a couch I make into a bed every night, his shoulders hunched, hands clasped between his knees, eyes lifting to mine timidly. I sat across from him, legs spread wide. I dropped a hand to my crotch. "You want it, don't you, Mico? Bad. Real bad!"

"No," he blared, pressing both hands into his lap to prevent his true feelings from being seen. "No. I can't, it's wrong. Everybody tells me it's wrong. Very, very wrong and I'll go to hell. No, I don't want it." Even he didn't believe his words. He stared at my hand circling my swelling dick through the barrier of my pants.

"Take off your clothes," I said, softly but strongly.

"But I...."

"You won't be alone anymore, Mico," I assured him. "I'll take mine off too." I tore off my shirt. "See."

His eyes were riveted to my every move as I unlaced my boots, kicked them off and stood up. I looped my shirt over the chair and dropped my pants. An unashamed hard on was arrogantly outlined inside the pouch of my briefs. He was goggle-eyed, mouth agape, his little chest heaving like the little engine that could. I was waiting, chest hairy and bare, hands on hips, dick throbbing against white cotton. "Come on, Mico," I coaxed, my words as insinuating and as mesmerizing as a single soothing violin in a peaceful concert hall.

"I...I...I...I have a...a...a hard-on...." His face reddened, his hand was clawing at the front of his pants.

"It's not alone," I assured him, shifting my hips, sweeping fingers over the outline in my shorts. "And neither are you, Mico," I added gently.

He toed off his sneakers. He unbuttoned his shirt and let it drop from his back. His eyes were pleading yet fired when he stood up and unbuckled his belt. He eased open his zipper and willed himself to his feet. Bright white briefs broke into view when his pants fell to his ankles. Bright white briefs packed with a bulging dick that was already leaking ooze at the head and smearing the cotton. My dick leaped, my mouth watered.

Mico stepped out of his pants. "You're making me do this," he whispered. "I...I...I...don't...don't...You're making me...."

"Yeah, I am," I agreed. Sure, ahuh. The kid wanted it so bad he was damn near quaking. His chest was bare of hair, smooth, and sent warming thrills to my nuts. I cupped them with one hand and probed a finger into my fleshy sacs. I spied his hard dick waving back through his restricted shorts, urging me on.

"So, it's wrong, huh?" I said, my voice growing in strength. Not a threat, just a warning. "Then you're gonna have to be punished for standing in front of another man in your underwear and with that hard cock sticking out like you're fucking proud of that fucking tool. Get your ass over here." He didn't make a move. Fear overflowed his eyes like a rush of water over a broken dam. Fear and hope. "Now," I commanded, and sat.

He walked to me as if captivated, his eyes alive with expectation, with childish fright, with desire. I locked my fingers around his wrist and pulled him down until he was lying in my lap, his ass two firm, cotton-coated soccer balls, his hard dick sticking it to mine. We both pulsed. "Wrong, huh?" I counseled and slammed his ass with the palm of my hand. The sound was muted by the cotton of his shorts. But that didn't make it any less powerful or any less provoking. Mico grunted, his dick bounded into mine. I said, "If it's wrong, than you're been a bad fuckin' boy, Mico." I flung my hand down again, again, and cracked it over both cheeks. They quivered, Mico shivered. His hands were hanging down, grasping the legs of the chair. He moaned. There was much more pleasure than pain gasping from his throat.

"You gonna be a good boy, now, Mico?" I swatted him again. Again. "You gonna be good?" I said, louder, almost a shout. And swatted him again. He didn't reply, only cried, not tears but pleas for more. Again I whacked him. Again.

"Okay," I said quietly, a controlled caution. "That the way you wanna play?" I tore down his shorts until his ass was exposed. His dick was still entangled in his pouch and mine, but his naked ass was an exceptional piece of fine art. A hint of fuzz was centered in the crack. I whacked him again, then again. The swats echoed in the small room. His cheeks glowed a delicate pink. I shoved my hands between his legs and latched onto a set of nuts that were bubbling stones, boiling with more cum than the kid probably ever imaged he had inside them. I yanked his balls.

Mico yelped. "I'll be good. I'll be good." I was sure he would be. Damn good.

"Stand on your fucking feet like a man and stop your fucking whining," I ordered, and released his nuts.

Mico immediately pushed himself from my lap. His bare ass was exposed to view. A gorgeous view. His stiff dick was still cramped in the pouch of his shorts. I stood up, pulled my shorts down, and kicked them off. My dick sprang up recklessly, too long denied. It slapped against my cockhairs then fell again, and immediately sprang up and stood tall, eying Mico through its drooling slit. Mico eyed back.

"Drop 'em," I said. He stumbled out of his shorts and stood up, damn near at attention. His cock was aiming at my chest. It was smaller than mine, but not by much, and its uncut head had a piece of slime swirling downward through the folds of the skin. The hairs that topped his cock were shiny, curly and sparse. His nuts were damn near clutched to the root of his shaft. I sensed this kid was nearly ready to pop.

I fisted my shaft and slapped my dickhead against his, delivering sparks to my nuts in an urgency that was as gratifying as it was exciting. His dick was jumping around like a self-motored pole, up, down, up. The dickhead was swollen, glowing like a light bulb in the dark night, and leaking with enough slime to coat a willing throat. "Beautiful," I mooned. "Turn around," I said gently.

Mico relaxed and thanked me with his eyes before he turned. Two tiny, dazzling globes were pink with the glow of youth, and a sharp hand. I soothed both palms over each and went down to my knees. "You are so beautiful, Mico," I said, leaning over and kissing his ass, swiping my tongue down his crack. Mico purred like a kitten in a clutter of contented cats. I began gliding my tongue over each cheek, tasting his heat, his tender perspiration, his need. I could feel his body relaxing, enjoying, reveling in a desire too long under lock.

While Mico was engrossed in discovered sensations, my tongue drifted over his ass like a moist summer wind. I reached up and circled my fingers around his hands until they were behind him. He stretched his neck in unleashed bliss. My mouth moaned over his cheeks, his fingers twined through my hair. I reached to the floor, grabbed my cuffs, and had them around his wrists before he knew what had hit him. Mico's body stiffened. I stood up. He turned around, eyes wide and terrified.

"Don't be scared, kid. It's all right. Don't be afraid. Trust me. It's all right," I soothed, my voice gentle, enticing. "It's gonna be all right. It's not wrong. It's right. We're right." My tone instantly changed, grew harder, stronger. "And if you believe it's wrong, look at it this way, kid. You're not going to willingly suck my cock; I'm gonna *force you* to blow me. How do you like that?" He didn't reply. I didn't expect him to. But it's what he wanted to hear. I could sense the hidden fear disappear. But I brought it back when I told him, "Down on your knees, faggot." A drill sergeant ordering his recruit to obey.

Mico seemed as surprised by my outburst as he was pleased. "Take those handcuffs off me, please, Jack, please. I'll do anything you say. Please. I'll do anything you want. Please." He pulled at his bonds. His biceps bulged from the exertion.

"I know you will," I said. His dick hadn't died. If anything, it was delighted as it danced in front of him. I wrapped my fist round the handle. It burned to my touch. It pulsed like a powerful rod hit by a crack of thunder. I squeezed. It shot back.

"Ohhhhh," Mico swooned. His exertions ceased. He became jelly in my hands. Rather, in my fist. I reached under with my other hand and cupped his balls. The flames flashed from his nuts to mine. "Oh, yeah, please, please," Mico moaned, quietly, but as passionately as a lover in a vital embrace.

"I said on your knees, cocksucker," I decreed. "Now," I emphasized.

Mico knelt on the carpet. I held my dick in front of his face, a taunting flag before a calf not yet a bull. But that calf was ready. His mouth was open, his eyes were glazed and begging, and his dick was stiff and throbbing.

"You ever suck a dick before, Mico?" I asked, a tease, as I

fisted my cock and inched it closer to his face. He muttered unintelligibly. "Speak up, prick," I yelled.

Mico started. "No. No, sir," he said, strong, sure. "I never did, never ever...." He again tensed, his shoulders ramrod straight, his muscles knotted, his mouth rigidly clamped closed.

"You wanna suck this hot rod?" I taunted, slapping my dickhead over his cheek then pulling it back. "You want this piece of meat?" I slapped his other cheek. "You want it, kid, you want it?" I kept slapping him with my cock. "And if you know what's good for you, you better tell the fucking truth, Mico, because you're gonna love it, Mico. And this fucking rod is good. Damn good."

Mico was kneeling there on the floor with eyes uplifted, tearing, imploring, loving every second of this torture.

I shouted, "Well, do you want this fucking dick or not? Do you? Yes or no? Answer me."

"Yes, Sir!" he shouted back.

Before the one word was freed from his constrained background, I swiped my leaking dickhead over his lips. Mico seemed to melt within himself. He flicked his tongue out until it smacked over the hardened head. A caress from a loving mate. "Ohhhh."

It was my turn to swoon. I was more turned on than I'd been in quite a long, long while. This bound virgin on his knees in front of me, licking his tongue carefully over my dickhead, was charging me, flaming my nuts, sending exquisite tingles to my brain.

I released my fist and let my dick stand alone while Mico cautiously began folding his tongue round the rim, pausing at the slit to taste the ooze seeping out, gulping, sighing, engrossed in sucking his first cock. He swallowed the entire dickhead between his lips. The sight itself was worth a pound of gold: the dick probing from my crotch and this tender young man at my feet, adoring me, my cock, his mouth filled with dickhead, my dickhead, his hands cuffed behind his back, his dick shaking and as proud as a newborn man. I shivered and swept my fingers through his dark hair. Mico groaned into my dickhead. I eased a bit of heated steel shaft into his mouth. Mico sputtered but didn't spit the cock out. I held firmly to his hair and slowly, carefully, began screwing my firm and fluttering dick in and out of the warmth and hunger of his mouth.

Mico didn't complain. He allowed me to fuck his face. It was then I realized he was a born cocksucker, breathing through his nose and taking my stiff dick down his throat as easily as a baby cow sucks down a nipple. It wasn't long before my entire shaft was buried, my balls scratching his chin. Mico suddenly began to moan frantically. But not because of the shaft jammed down his gullet. He was coming. His cherry dick, without being touched, was blasting off of its own accord into a sphere, a universe Mico craved. I gripped his head, shot my hips forward, clamped my crotch to his face, kept my dick crammed in his mouth, and let loose. My knees were mush and shaking, my dick was leaping and quivering and shooting, my mind was in the stars, as Mico took it all, like the fucking man he had just become.

After I uncuffed him, we sat on the futon, nursing Cokes and glowing. He thanked me for releasing him. Not from bondage of the handcuffs, from the restricted life he had been living and lying. Mico couldn't stay overnight. His parents would be worried. He promised to sleep with me the next time. He *pleaded* to sleep with me the next time.

And, of course, there was a next time.

And a next. And a next.

Then he moved in. We became lovers. My first, his first.

THE RANDY YOUNG COWPOKE

Jack Ricardo

I was driving down the main drag of Gallup, New Mexico in the pouring rain. Neon-lit motels lined one side of the street, a railroad track the other. I pulled into a lot where my headlights beamed over two dilapidated signs. "Rooms—$16.95" and "Public Shower."

A dented pickup was blocking the entrance. I pulled behind it, hopped out of my truck, and dashed to the office. A guy pulled open the door. Water was dripping from his straw cowboy hat, his jeans were soaked, his shirt was sticking to his chest. He was about to make a run for it, but when he saw me he did an about-face. "You gettin' a room?" he asked.

"If they got one."

The cowboy glanced at the clerk behind the cage, glanced at me, then said, "Only eighteen bucks for two. Nine bucks each if we share a room." His boots were scuffed to the point where even polish wouldn't help. And his jeans were worn and holey, his shirt was faded, his hat soiled. He didn't look much different than me, dirt poor. When I hesitated, he said, "Help me out, huh, buddy. I been on the road three days. I ain't had a shower in four, and ain't slept in a real bed that long. I can't afford a room to myself. Whatcha say?"

He was cute when he was pleading. "Sounds okay ta me," I said.

The clerk wasn't happy when we checked in together. He gave us two towels and one key. We dove through the rain for our pickups and drove round back. The cowboy's name was Dwight. He looked to be a bit younger than my 20 years. His hair was wet blond, he was thin, he was masculine. We ran for the room, where we found only one full bed and not much else. No TV, something of a closet, a dresser without drawers, and a sink. No toilet. "Shit, worst than a tornado out there," Dwight said, peeling off his shirt and planting it on a hook. "And I seen plenty of them in Texas. I'm heading up to Idaho for a job at my cousin's ranch. Where you heading?" The same blond hair on his head was plastered on his chest, twinkling with both rain and sweat. I gulped and said, "East to Arizona to stay with my sister a while." I draped my soaked shirt over the arm of the chair. My chest hair almost matched his, in abundance if not in color. Mine was as black as the ace of spades but as wet as his. "Shit, I'm beat," Dwight yawned. "Gonna take a shower and hit the sack."

"I won't argue with that," I agreed.

I watched the cowboy fall back on the bed and pull his boots and socks off. He caressed his toes, stretched his arms, shivered, groaned wearily, then stood and pulled his jeans off. A thin, cut cock and a full set of hairy nuts bottomed a thick brush of more appealing blond hair. I was down to my briefs. My packed nuts began to tingle and awaken my own slab of cut meat.

Dwight wrapped the remnants of a towel around his waist and said, "Shit, wish I could afford underwear. That's why I'm going to Idaho. Ain't no work in Texas."

I tossed my shorts on the chair and tucked my threadbare towel in. It almost hid a growing hard-on. We walked the corridor until we found a door that read, "Shower." The dank room smelled of sweat and mildew and had two nozzles in one plastic pen. We dropped our towels on the bench and turned on the showers. Only one worked. "Shit," Dwight muttered, then stood under the shower, lifting his head and letting the water drain over his body. He turned around. A steady stream rolled down his back, through the crack of his ass, over the mound of his curved cheeks, and down his legs. When he moved aside, I stepped under. We both soaped up and I didn't hide my admiration. Dwight lathered his arms, his chest, his legs, his feet, and his crotch, stopping to pull on a foamy dick, flapping his balls with suds, spreading his legs wide and reaching under to scrub his ass, and washed his hair. I realized I was standing stock still and stroking a slippery hand over a cock at half mast when Dwight stopped and stared at me staring at him. He stepped under the shower to rinse off. Dwight was drying his feet, one foot on the bench, his balls hanging low under the mounds of a trim, rounded ass where more of that delicious blond hair was snaking a trail from the small of his back. My pulse increased. Neither of us spoke when we walked back to the room.

Dwight dropped his towel on the floor. The rain was splattering against the windows, the nighttime traffic flashed headlights through the room. I slung my towel over the back of the chair and lay next to the cowboy. He had his arms over his head; mine were at my side. "I seen you looking at me in the shower," he said quietly, then craned his neck to me.

"Oh?"

"Yeah."

"Well, there's so much to see."

"You queer?"

"I like beautiful things."

"Sounds like my cousin. He's a couple of years older than me and that's what he called my prick, beautiful. He thought it was so beautiful he sucked it." He chuckled. "Yup, he sucked me off." He dropped one hand to his crotch and began to fondle his dick. "He thought it was beautiful. Just like you do."

My hand was already on my own dick, stretching and awakening its power. "You didn't suck him?" I asked.

"Hell, no," he said, then laughed, a quick, embarrassed and playful laugh, remembering. "Well, maybe I did a little, just a little. After he did me. But he didn't come in my mouth. I came in his though. And he swallowed it. Didn't mind it neither, from what he told me." I saw his cock start to grow as he reached under to pull at his balls. I leaned on one elbow to face him, stroking my cock, squeezing the shaft until the head blew up and spit out a drop that shined like a pearl.

"You like it when he sucked ya?" I asked.

He shrugged and said, "Got my rocks off." His cock was now fully erect. It was a beautiful sight. "What do you think?" he asked.

"Yeah, it's a beauty all right."

Our bodies were so close, I could feel the heat. Dwight peered down at my hand, my cock, and muttered, "Shit, that's one goddamed dickhead you got there, friend." He rounded his fingers around his cock until the pressure expanded his own dickhead, pointed as an arrow and glowing like a bulb. A dickhead that screws down a throat as neatly as a bolt fits a matching nut. Shiny dribble flowed from the tip and streaked down the side.

"That the only guy you made it with?" I asked, capping the rim of my dickhead with all five fingers and yanking gently.

"Yeah," Dwight said, stroking a fist down the length of his rod and swinging it like a baseball bat. I reached over and slid the palm of my hand over the hair on his chest. Hairs that flashed in the harsh light like live wires. A sigh started in my gut and blew through my lips. My nuts sparked, my dick throbbed. "Until now," Dwight added, smiling coyly.

I plucked the hairs around his nipples then slid my hand over his stomach, flat as a board and furry as a bear, before spidering down to clutch at his moist blond cockhairs, spiking a fiery thrill to rage through my nuts. Dwight was aiming his magnificent rod to the ceiling. My fingers crawled around and under to brush his balls. The silken hairs, the loose flesh, the hard nuts, sent a swift and heated message to my brain. When I moved to the bottom of the bed, Dwight spread his legs wide enough where I could kneel between them. He dropped his hand from his cock. It slapped against his cockhairs, then did a small, joyful leap. So did my mind. My mouth was open, my tongue was lapping out like a slobbering hound.

I bowed down and ran my tongue lightly over his balls and up the entire length of his cock, lapping out a thick, spiraling vein that ended at a slimy dickhead, which I licked clean. The salty sensation spurred me on. I smothered the pointy head between my lips, moaned gratefully into its peehole, and pushed my mouth down the full length of the rod until my nose nudged the root. Dwight grumbled noisily and gratefully.

I lifted my face to continue my trek, the salty remnants of his ooze coating my tongue as I scraped it through the sodden yellow nest, over the grating hairs of his taut stomach, pausing to probe and tickle his belly button with the tip.

Dwight purred and clutched the sheets with his fingers. I used both hands on either side of Dwight's shoulders to prop myself up. The head of my rod dug into his balls when I covered his pec with my mouth and gnawed, on both muscle and hair, then moved on to treat the other, grinding my dickhead into the bags of his nuts, my own nuts swinging in the warm, damp air. Dwight had closed his eyes. His hips began swaying to the side, back, forth, in an unhurried rhythm. His prick was brushing mine, his dickhead was kissing mine, our four balls were molded into one luscious blob that demanded some quick attention.

I sat back in a rush, the heels of my feet spreading the cheeks of my bare ass. I could feel a tepid breath of air fill my asshole as I smashed my face into Dwight's balls, clutching his hips and snuggling my nose into the manly scent of this randy young cowpoke. The hairs on his balls prickled my face. I inhaled and nibbled them with unabashed delight.

Dwight shifted his ass in small bursts of enthusiasm and brought his arms down to snake his strong fingers through my hair. I slavered over his nuts with much spit and a mouthful of affection. Dwight groaned and, in one impassioned movement, flung his legs around my neck. I wrapped my arms over his thighs and filled my mouth with nuts, chewing them, slurping them down my gullet, caressing those babies with a swift flick of my tongue, the flabby flesh of his balls leaking from my lips.

Dwight kept smashing my head lower and lower and lifting his legs higher and higher, until his balls plopped from my mouth. My lips were slick with spit and sweat and it was so easy to pave a tongue-path from his balls, down the crack of his ass, to a tiny puckered hole that seemed to be forcing out breaths in eager anticipation of the pure sensation it craved. I licked circles around the hairy and taunting wrinkles before I speared my tongue deep inside his asshole.

Dwight gave out with a loud "Whoooo," gripped my head and shoved it up his ass. The warm, wet, velvety touch of his insides compelled pre-ooze to slide from the dickhead clamped between my legs while I devoured one hairy cowboy's asshole. I could have gloried in his hole all through the night but Dwight's legs weakened and fell from my shoulders.

I sat up, my chest heaving, quivering, spit drooling from my lips. I kept one hand clutched tightly around Dwight's nuts while the other stroked my rod, as strong as a log and damn near busting with need. I flopped to the side of the bed and grappled for my shirt, pulling out one rubber and a smashed tube of KY, and was again kneeling between Dwight's legs before he opened his eyes. "What the fuck are you doin'?" he muttered, his voice a labored mixture of fear and hunger and restrained desire.

"I think I'll dick ya," I said, ripping open the packet, circling the rubber down the shaft of my rod until my dickhead shown through clear and tight and zealous through the thin cloudy film.

"I...I...I...." Dwight stammered, his lips fluttering, his eyes glowing, hair stringing over the sweat of his brow.

I stopped his words when I grabbed his legs and slung them over my shoulders, gripped the sweetly rounded cheeks of his ass, spread him wide and rammed my face smack between his cheeks, gnawing his pucker and snaking my tongue in and out of his asshole until Dwight was again mooning like a baby calf and panting like a mountain lion.

I came up for air and squeezed a glob of grease directly on his hole. Dwight's eyes were wild; his chest was rising and falling like the ocean waves in a torrid storm. I wiped a greasy finger around his hole until the tip slid inside.

Dwight groaned and pushed down. The rest of my finger eased into his ass as easily and as lovingly as a sow's tit slides down a piglet's throat. The muscles of his ass squeezed against my finger. They were a living animal, a lascivious animal, an animal in dire need and desperate. I lubed my rod, plucked my finger from his ass, and inched forward until the eye of my dickhead was peeking at his door. It didn't bother to knock. It plowed right in. This cowboy was born to be ridden, and ridden hard.

Dwight yelped like a stuck pig when my dickhead plopped inside; sweat was draining over the thicket of hair on his chest. The potent strength of his muscles contracted around my dickhead as tight as a fist and as sensuous as a ravenous mouth. He reached up with both hands and grabbed my neck, the movement causing the shaft of my cock to glide farther up his ass. He groaned: loud and angry and passionate—and, I thought, happy as hell.

He pulled my face onto his; our mouths opened and swallowed each other; my cock dug deep. Dwight was lost in feeling, in feeling my mouth swallow his tongue, in feeling my hard, pulsing dick up his ass. His balls were smashed into the black hair of my crotch, his dick was palpitating between us on his blond pubic hairs.

I pulled my cock out until I felt the rim of my dickhead reach the rim of his hole, then slid back in like oil down a pipeline.

I lifted my face from his. Dwight was staring in my eyes before he snapped his head back and howled in a tone that rang through the room like a thunderstorm and beckoned for more.

I shot my hips back, then again plowed deep. Sweat dribbled from the hairs on my chest to the hairs on Dwight's.

I spread his thighs wider, held onto his calves and fucked. I screwed the boy's virgin ass with a need that was beyond calling back, rammed my rod deep inside his bowels until Dwight began gasping, groaning, barreling his ass back onto my prick, deep enough to feed his overwhelming need.

We began a joined and recklessly feral rhythm that rocked the bed, that tore into the ceiling of the room, that sent needling slivers of pleasure pricking through my balls, my dick, my brain, and I slammed my rod into Dwight until my cockhairs were scratching his ass rashly, until my nuts became solid stones, until I felt Dwight's asshole tighten and strangle my rod as he shot his load over his stomach, as my own cock throbbed and leaped while spitting its load into the depths of Dwight.

We both squeaked off-key, like spent mice, as I collapsed alongside Dwight, resting my head on his thigh, his barren balls but an inch from my face. "I ain't never..." Dwight panted, "...been dicked in the ass. I ain't...." His breath gave out. I didn't have the strength to reply. I passed out.

The rain was still spattering against the windows when I awoke; the traffic lights still roared by. I peeled the rubber from my soft dick and threw it on the floor. Dwight was lying spread eagle on his stomach, snoring, the cheeks of his ass glowing as white as snow, the bags of his nuts resting beautifully between. I leaned down and kissed his ass, sighed deeply, and slept till morning light. Dwight wasn't talking.

It was only after we were getting dressed and ready to hit the road that he finally spoke. He said, awkwardly, shuffling his feet, his hands stuffed in the rear pockets of his Wrangler jeans, his straw cowboy hat covering his face as he stared down at the worn carpet, "Shit, man, I feel I should thank you, but I ain't sure why." He lifted his head slowly and looked at me shyly from behind the bent brim of his hat.

I tugged my feet into my boots, tucked my shirt into my

jeans, brushed my hands through my hair, and picked up the shorts I had worn the day before. I tossed them to him and smiled. "To help start your new life in Idaho," I said. "Good luck."

Dwight grinned and shoved my briefs in his back pocket. "You, too. Oh, and thanks."

A COWPOKE DOWN UNDER

QM3 Rick Jackson, USN

I lay there wishing the creature would hurry the fuck up. My ankles didn't hurt, but the fishing line had started biting into my wrists as I twisted about to get comfortable. More to the point, I felt more goofy than sexy all staked out on the bed. My position did bring to mind an image I hadn't thought of in years even though it had teased ceaselessly at my nasty adolescent little mind the whole time I was growing to studhood. The clip ran relentlessly through my teenage fantasies as I shanked my crank. I'd seen it in some bad western movie where the Indians had staked a lone cowpoke out to die of exposure in the cruel Arizona sun. I remember nothing about the movie except the Technicolor image of the guy—his blond shock of hair cast carelessly down over a heroic brow, a boyish dimple or two, and a lantern jaw.

I'd always started my workout sessions with his face and then slid down across his powerful tanned pecs as they broiled under a sexy dapple of glistening sweat in that harsh, heathen heat. His belly was flat and hard, but for reasons past understanding, the idiot Indians had neglected to pry my hero from his trou. If I'd been the Indian chief, I always told myself, things would have been done right. The camera would travel across his gorgeous torso, down along his hard flanks, and end showing his toes wriggling, bootless, in the harsh glare of relentless doom.

As I lay there staked out in the bedroom of the small apartment in suburban Perth, I returned for the first time in years to that central fantasy of my youth—and remembered what the B-movie had left out: how I would happen across the poor cowpoke. I'd save his ass from the ants or scorpions or whatever, and he would show me how grateful a good western buddy could be. After I lost my cherry to a girl in high school, I decided I'd just been going through a phase and stopped dreaming of reaming out sun-fried cowstud. Pussy was more immediate than the lost glories of the Old West and, besides, by then I knew what was socially acceptable and what wasn't.

In the years since, I'd often compared my body with those around me. You don't spend four years on a 'gator in the US Navy without seeing hard, naked manhood in its prime; but I was always able to banish the occasional quirky idea about my shipmates as a relic of that unfulfilled phase of my youth.

Lying there, staked out and helpless that day in Perth, I knew one thing for sure: the tart I'd picked up was taking for fucking ever to come out of the crapper. Maybe because it had taken me so long to get to women, I'd never been as interested in sex as most of the guys on my ship. Still, after five months floating around the Indian Ocean with nothing but the usual strained faggot jokes and my hand to keep me company, I needed relief bad enough to try Claire.

A pack of us had gone to a bar our first day in Fremantle. The babes were all over us, fighting to buy us drinks and get us home to bed. I can't think why. God knows the place was crawling with men that would set Hollywood on its ass. I guess maybe we were just exotic or something. I'd held out for something a little fresher, a little more stimulating, but finally, when just she and I were left, I decided it didn't really matter what I blew my load into. I let Claire drag me home. My plan was to pop a nut and run, but she wanted to play cowboy and pioneer wife. At first, I couldn't be bothered with her bondage crap; but it was soon clear I'd tap a gusher a lot faster if I played along. Sweetie had no sooner gotten me staked out, than she had to pee. They always do, for some reason, and never think of it until they start. It's either that or needing a drink of water.

I lay there, my mind drifting back again to the sweaty cowpoke meat hidden inside those dusty pants, and came back to reality to find my dick harder than a rustler's heart. After what must have been five minutes, I yelled at my date to get her ass into gear. At the time, of course, I had no way of knowing the crapper had two doors or that she was long gone.

I nearly shit when the dude ambled out of the john. First a quick thrill surged through me: he was fucking gorgeous. Then my wrists and boner reminded me of my position and made me hope the guy wasn't the husband wronged—though I couldn't imagine what else he could be. Something about the leer on his face didn't seem to fit, but I was past noticing subtleties. I started to babble an explanation of sorts when I noticed his dick. Then I really got confused.

He'd shambled about half way between the door and me and just stood there watching, feet apart, hands by his sides, dick belly-up and beautiful. I felt my own meat pounding against my gut like a Morse key in a lightning storm. Like a fool, I stopped babbling only to ask him where Claire had gone. His grin grew as he pried his dick down away from his flat, hairless belly and let it slap back up with a meaty thwack. I needn't worry about her. She was gone. We were alone. I asked him what the fuck he was up to—and silently felt sure of the answer, deeper within me than I'd known I could feel anything. Something about his stance and manner and, especially, the hungry look on his face as he took inventory of what I had told me the whole story. I never did learn the details—who Claire was, what their relationship was, and or where she fit in. Just then, I was too busy learning the shape of his studly body Down Under to bother about trivialities and later—well, never mind later for now.

I showed him my pissed-off defender-of-freedom persona, explaining what I was going to do to the bastard if he didn't get me up off the bed on the double. The more I ranted and threatened, the wider his grin got, the more his eyes sparkled, and the quicker his dick did a tom-tom imitation against his tanned belly.

When he finally spoke up again in his foxy Aussie accent, he ignored my tirade as irrelevant to our present circumstances and sounded almost as though he were making idle conversation on a bus: "What's your name, Yank?" I tried not to think about his swollen dick—or about my own. I'd never been harder. Despite my cocky talk, I was afraid of what was going to happen; yet every part of my body except my brain yearned for whatever he had in store. Here, at last, I was out of control. Whatever delicious perversion he had in mind was his karma's problem. I was off the hook. At last, those adolescent fantasies seemed close to reality. My dick was so swollen it seemed ready to split down the middle like a frank left forgotten to simmer to bits in a picnic pot.

I growled my name and repeated what I was going to do to him when I got loose, but the gorgeous bastard only grinned harder and told me his name was Alec. He didn't look much like an Alec; he looked more like a fucking Apollo. Looming over me, he was about six-one, 200 pounds of pure surfer-stud muscle. His hair obviously started out a dark blond, but was bleached golden above the neck.

Like my dream cowpoke, he had a shock of hair hanging low across his forehead, setting off thick blond brows that seemed almost to merge above his classic nose. He, too, had dimples and a strong jaw filled with sparkling teeth; but he had more hard muscle than my cowpoke had ever seen. A thick neck led down from his cute little ears to spread into shoulders wide enough to throw an ox. The bastard obviously lifted weights as much as he surfed; his massive chest and bulging arms set off a belly that would have almost disappeared from sight except for the meaty signal pulsing in front. Before long, I was to see his world-class butt, hard and firm, hanging off his hips like some futuristic anti-gravity fuck-machine. I'd see his strong legs and feel the hard muscle of his back. Just then, though, my universe was filled with the biggest, hardest, meanest-looking dick I'd ever seen.

I don't know whether Aussies are uncut more often than Americans, but Alec made me hope so. Oz is supposed to be an enchanted land, after all. At first I couldn't see much of his dick except the bottom, but that was enough. Impossibly hard as he was, a great ruffle of soft, wrinkled skin peeked out from between his dick and belly, making my mouth water as though I were one of the faggot cocksuckers squids always joke about underway. His huge balls hung low and heavy between his legs, swaying slightly as he stood silently before me—waiting, looking, savoring the moment. When he spoke again, almost drooling with every syllable, my last doubts about what lay in store for me vanished: "She said you were the best bit of meat about, she did."

The more I growled about his slut of a bitch and about how he was a faggot, cocksucking, ass-wipe, the harder we both got. He didn't say dick as he eased his way the last few feet to the bed and looked down at me twisting about. I writhed and thrashed, struggling with the physical bonds that held me, yet snapping free the last vestiges of my priggish inhibitions as I inwardly yielded absolutely to the demands of the moment.

His right hand reached out slowly, as though relishing a slight delay to intensify his ultimate pleasure. Deep brown eyes that seemed at odds with his bright, golden hair glowed with a primal hunger. When his fingertips ultimately made contact with my thigh, he might as well have been hooked straight to a nuclear reactor. A spark of lust and excitement and deliciously forbidden pleasure jolted up through my leg to disorient me. Flat on my back, I felt myself swept away by a maelstrom of fears and joys past my understanding. One part of my brain heard a low, bestial groan of exquisite pleasure escape my lips and I knew for certain that I was lost.

His hand on my thigh slid slowly upwards, sending shivers and gooseflesh before it. He stopped inches from my balls and started back down again, murmuring something to himself about softness. His left hand reached out next to glide across the very top of the rust-colored thatch that grows thick on my chest. I've always found it wiry and harsh, but Alec's palm was obviously fascinated by the texture. His own hairless, brazen chest was dappled with sweat and stippled by gooseflesh of his own. Those spaniel-brown eyes slipped shut as his hands continued to take the measure of my body as though every hair and bulge were a religious relic to be venerated.

The smile was gone from his face now; he was beyond boyish smiles. Short, shallow grunts jolted a jerky melody from the very depths of his soul. As his palms eased across my flesh, as his fingers pried away my past prejudices and inhibitions, as my flesh surrendered to him, I stopped resisting the inevitable and lay still beneath his touch. I gave myself up to an enjoyment that far surpassed any spit-palmed adolescent fantasy. His touch glided across my flesh, slowly, reverently, deliciously. His grunts of appreciation grew louder, teaching me to meet his touch with my body, pressing my muscle against his hands, giving him my body as I had yielded up my soul to the wicked, wonderful world he represented.

My own groans of pleasure soon rivaled Alec's and seemed to seduce him from his trance. Those brown eyes opened again and he said something about my knowing what I wanted after all. Like an idiot, I strained at the bonds that held me down; but now I was struggling to reach his massive dick. Escape was the last thing on my mind. I had become a slut.

Right then, I was willing to give Alec anything he wanted, but he wasn't about to accept any gifts. Unless he could take it, he didn't want it. I twisted and torqued my way toward his hands and he pulled backward to take stock of the possibilities. I wasn't sure what to expect. I'd heard about faggots being done up the butt, but he'd have to untie my ass from the bed first. If I was thinking at all, I probably expected his monster dick shoved down my throat. When he really got going, I discovered how sick a bastard young Alec really was.

He started off on my right tit—with his tongue. Alec slid his face over my chest. His breath came in short, hot spurts that chilled the sweat oozing out of my pores. My chest hair rippled like Iowa corn as his panting grew more frantic. When his wet tongue tip slashed down through the forest of rust-colored hair to snipe down at my nubbin of passion-pumped flesh. I'd never thought of my tits as sexy, but Alec's bumpy tongue slid across raw nerves I'd never known I had until I was sure I would come from pure shock.

Somehow I stood up to the tit-torture, even after his tongue slid back between his lips and they went into action. His nose snuffled through my chest pelt while his lips, as slick with his spit and as they were experienced in what young American seamen need, locked around my nipples like a vampire dervish in a blood bank, twisted and tugging, determined to suck up every possible particle of pleasure. His furrowed lips tightened hard with every up-stroke along my blood-gorged stocks and then released their grip to glide down on a hot layer of spit as his bumpy tongue darted deep down my shaft to torment me.

At first, only his nose and lips and tongue touched me, but I was able to smear my chest against his face, begging for more like the slut he had made me. My overpowering urge to grab his blond locks and shove him hard against my chest kept me jerking at the nylon line despite common sense. The bastard had me where he wanted me and was in no hurry at all.

His tongue and lips alternated between teasing my tits and rougher play. Now and again, he'd let a dangerous edge of tooth glide down my stock; but just the raspy, cat-like torment of his tongue was enough to set my every nerve alight. Alec kept using my right tit and then my left until they were both numb with delight. Then the sick slut slipped his face into my armpit and began lapping up the sweaty musk that lived there. Now his tongue slid across my flesh in great canine swaths of wet love that taught me yet another lesson about how a man's body can be used. Too soon for either of us, he'd lapped me clean and moved up across my shoulder to my neck and, ultimately, across to my left ear lobe.

His face pinned my head to the pillow while he went to work. Lips and tongue alternated again, sucking, pulling, scraping, urging my flesh into him as though he were a hyper-attractive man-magnet. The feral snorts of breath that escaped his nose roared into my ear just ahead of his tongue, drilling deeper into my head than any human should have been able to reach. Like a starving ant-eater, he flicked his tongue deep and curled it upwards as he sucked at my lobe with one lip and I cried out every filthy thing I knew. I was past knowing what I wanted. His tongue-fucking was so perfect, so brutal, that I knew I would go mad if he didn't stop; yet, once I'd felt what he could do, I knew I'd never be able to get enough. Almost as though I were watching from outside, I felt my body shiver and thrash, my hips convulsing upwards as they fucked the air and wished it were him. The louder I screamed, the faster his tongue snaked in and out of my ear and the more self-satisfied his porcine grunts of pleasure grew.

Whether to take my mind off my ear or maybe just to be a dick, he slid his fingers down to my left tit and started twisting—hard.

The delicious brutality of the moment transformed what should have been agony into something even worse. I'd been close to a breakdown before; now I slipped over the edge. Sensation blurred into surreal sensation; I was helpless to do anything but clench my eyes shut and wait for the universe to steady itself. I heard myself screaming again but as though at a great distance. One convulsion followed another, each fiercer, more sadistic and pure than the last. Then my brain just fucking shut down.

I remember drifting back to consciousness and thinking how wet I felt. My ear and neck were cold and clammy now; Alec had moved south. I lifted my head and saw him lapping a gigantic and very messy load of my best work from my chest and belly. I'd apparently lost it entirely and blown a huge cargo of Yank seaman semen up into the dense thicket of fur that covers my torso. Alec wasn't letting it go to waste. His lips had surrounded the nacreous globs of goo and was busy sucking them out of my hair. Then he went back, using his tongue to round up any strays that had escaped from the herd.

Turned on as I was, I couldn't do much at that point but breathe. I'll never know how long Alec had been up my ear, but it took me five or six minutes before I could gulp down enough air to live. By then, my captor had finished harvesting my sperm-farm and was ready to get serious—but he wanted an audience. When he saw I would live, he went after the last thick threads of jism left—dangling from my cum-slit and down across my dickhead onto my belly. He started low near my navel and slurped upward. His terrible tongue-tip tore into my jism-hole, drilling out the last of my load before his lips slid slowly upward to encircle my throbbing meat.

His lips had seemed possessed as they sucked my tits, and once he proved what a cocksucker he was, I was ready to nominate him for a Noble Prize for his oral talents. He used the same basic method: letting his lips sneak up on my nerve endings on a layer of hot spit and then ripping into my weakened defenses with his bumpy tongue. Now, though, his suction went into overdrive as well—all while he was working his face steadily downward along my nine thick inches. My dick was so stiff and lying so tightly against my belly that he had trouble bending me high enough to handle—but by now he'd moved between my wide-spread legs and was taking his time. I'd just shot the finest load of my young life, but every throb of my naval weapon brought me closer to doing it all over again. Through the fuzzy cloud of pleasure that obscured reality from fantasy, I remember his snuffling slurps and the shit I was talking. I'm sure I sounded like the worst-written fuckflick of creation, but the torment his face was giving my dick was too serious a rush for me to consider coming up with anything creative.

He worked my swollen dickhead deep down into his throat and locked me in place, scraping the tender pink tissues of his craw across my head, pulsing his suction like an organic milking machine stuck on overdrive. I saw his head bob up and down along my shank and felt his lips at work but my head stayed locked tight and deep inside this throat until I knew I was about to shoot off again. For the first time ever, I felt my load being sucked up from my nuts and knew I was going to hump Alec's perverted, cocksucking, faggot face-hole until it bled.

I was wrong. He did fine until my balls tightened against his chin. Then, just as I was ready to have one seriously fine time, he eased his face off my dick and knelt between my legs, grinning down at me, hoping I'd beg for his service. I did, too—but the bastard wasn't about to swallow my load again—yet.

He watched me squirm for a few minutes and then sank back down to my crotch. Now that my weapon was loaded and ready to fire, he concentrated on my spooge-magazine, sucking first one nut and then the other into his mouth for some rough ball-handling action. They were already slightly sore, first from long, underway weeks of relative inaction, then from the strain of spewing my personal-best load of spunk. His lips locked around my nut-sack and his suction started up, pulling blood down into my nuts and making them swell and throb and ache with the unbearable weight of their next load. I started moaning again and kept it up as he switched back and forth between balls for the next twenty minutes or so.

Now and again, he'd stop and lap the outside of my cum-factory as though he were some cur dog going at his own `nads on a dusty country road. He took time out to slurp along my thighs but the absolute limit in kink came when he used his nose to lift my nuts aside so he could snake his tongue back underneath me. The farther back he got towards my butthole, the better we both felt. I'd have given a nut to give the ass-lick what he wanted, but my legs were tied too tightly for me to arch my hips up enough off the mattress to manage.

When he'd sucked my second load of the day back down where it had started, Alec moved back up to my dick and swallowed me again. He was an old friend and my dick knew what to do. I slid straight down past his tongue and let his throat lock around the head of my joint like a family dog slipping into a collar. This time around, though, he had less chance of escaping my spray. My hips were loose enough to fuck his face, slashing upwards, driving my dick home where we both knew it belonged. His head met my meat on the upstroke and tried to hang on on the down, but now instinct took control of my dick—and his face.

I reamed and twisted and slammed dick deep down his throat until I felt my load being sucked up again. This time it happened faster and with a violence and frenzied ecstasy bred of Alec's need as much as my own. Once again, though, he jerked his head up off my joint; but now he was too late. My plume of spooge shot out, spraying my belly and chest with more thick threads of pearly cum than I'd ever seen. Alec knew when he was beaten.

He wasn't going to slurp up his load, but his lips puckered tight and pressed my dickhead down into my belly fur as I shot spasm after glorious spasm up onto myself. As soon as I was pinned and knew it, his tongue flicked out through his lips, fluttering along the super-sensitive V beneath my dickhead, at once forcing me even harder against my belly and raking a whole other set of nerve-endings that were already exploding. His lips and tongue worked harder, feathering frenzy against the bottom of my dick as one jolt of jism after another spewed out the top. Pressed hard against my belly, my dick pumped the last half dozen blasts of spooge into a pearly pond that formed right at the end of my dick.

If anything, the second load took me longer to lose and was more fun. At least, I suppose it was; since I remember dick about most of the first gusher, I can't be sure. When, at long last, I humped out my last few threads of jism, I was ready to lie back content while Alec licked me clean again. He had other plans.

The moment he saw I was dry, he hopped to his feet, straddled my waist and started to shit on my crotch—at least that's what I thought he was doing. Instead, he slipped his asscrack along the underside of my dick, just grazing the surface and keeping it from going limp. Within seconds, he was gliding along my meat, dipping low enough to drag his ass through the pool of jism that lay just north of my dick. Then on the back stroke, he dragged his butthole harder along my dork—scratching his ass like a dog scooting across a new white shag carpet. Each trip got his butt slicker than the last and made my bone the more ready to see what he had in store.

Now, of course, I'd know what to expect; but when he reached down with his hand to pry my joint away from my belly and eased his asshole around it, I figured my life was just about perfect. In the fear and discovery and mind-numbing ecstasy that had come before, I'd forgotten about my cowpoke fantasy; but the moment Alec slipped his tight shithole past my trigger-ridge and I felt the thrill of reality after so many years of fist-fucking fantasy, that Technicolor cowpoke popped into my head one last time. Looking up at Alec wobbling back and forth as he worked himself down my shank, I knew I'd never have to conjure cowpoke again. From now on this bizarre afternoon would be the yardstick against which all my future fantasies and realities would be measured.

As his shithole stretched its way along, I also knew I'd never bother with the Claires of the world again, either. Some assholes might not like the idea of guys doing guys, but now that I'd felt what a hard young body like Alec's had to offer, there was no fucking way in hell I'd put up with the nasty slackness of slatterns. In fact, watching one expression after another slide across Alec's face as my pole disappeared up his hole, I was even ready to see what his impossible dick felt like stretching my guts apart. It was at least ten inches long—and probably more. His head was swollen enough now that I could see his slit oozing a steady flow of pre-cum. Soon the crater formed by his foreskin overflowed dicklube and a thin trickle rippled down his joint to drip onto his balls and then onto my belly. Almost at the same time, Alec's asshole seated itself around the broad base of my dick, grinding this way and that across my Brillo-like pubes, and his soulful brown eyes rolled back in his head. I made up my mind to find out what it felt like to have a man up your ass.

I lay silent for a moment or two but some ancient instinct set my hips back to work. My ass arched upward, driving my dick even deeper into Alec's butt. His eyes eased open for a moment so he could look at my Navy-issue body one last time before he slipped into a world of his own. His lips parted slightly and the moment was past. He was on autopilot now, stroking up and down my joint, scratching the itch that lay buried deep within him like a bear against an even thicker log. My dick drilled upwards as his ass matched my rhythm, twisting slightly to screw himself along the throbbing blue vein that guided me up into his guts. Every movement stretched my shaft tighter, pulling the twin lobes of my head tighter and bringing me closer to launching an impossible third load up into the secret depths of his guts where it belonged.

Suddenly I felt something hard bounce off my dick as I slipped into him; Alec shivered in a spasm of shattering sensuality so severe that for a moment I was jealous. I didn't know about prostates at the time, but I knew what made him feel good and was determined to deliver. My ramrod changed its angle of entry just enough to slam hard into his explosive buttnut on nearly every stroke—sending one ripple after another of gooseflesh across his body and ripping one animal moan after another from the very depths of his being. Alec was still grinding his ass along my crotch, but now that I knew what to aim at, I went to work pounding his prostate for all it was worth.
My dick loved the firm, slick texture up his ass, but Alec went ape-shit. His head flew back and he opened his mouth for a soundless scream fierce enough to deafen mankind. His gasping breaths stopped dead and, while I slammed harder and faster with every butt-lashing, gut-wrenching stroke, my captor proved he had more than pre-cum down his dick. I'd never seen another man shoot off before. Alec was an impressive place to begin. At first he seemed to be having a seizure, but as his lungs clawed at the suborn air for breath, his massive manmeat exploded, shooting globs of iridescent white shrapnel up onto his body and out onto mine. Some of the larger globs splattered against his hard, hairless flesh and began the slow, easy drip down. Many arced through the air to land on me or on the bed beside me. Once his gusher had come in, Alec reached down to get a grip on himself and pumped his well dry, sending his Australian cream up like an explosion in a fireworks factory.

My rod was ready to keep reaming his butt, but once his body seized up, that tight Australian bunghole clamped down tight enough to break my joint off at the nub. The sight of his jism arcing through the sky, the strangle-hold he had on my meat, the noise he was making, the fierce friction of tender flesh against hard bone, and, especially, the perverse thrill of having my dick up a man's tight ass while he shoot off, all conspired to send me over the edge again as well.

I couldn't see my watch, but this had to be my third cum-crop inside as many hours. Alec had taken his time; neither of us seemed in any hurry other than the one built into a man's nature. Now, at least, I was putting what I had where it would do some good—up his ass to lube it out. My first jolt did just that. I couldn't feel my spooge splash off the inside of his guts, but his butthole magically started slip-sliding along my shank so I picked up my speed and really let the Australian asshole have it.

Alec must have crested first, because when I opened my eyes, he was all doe-eyed and grinning. He was also seriously dripping jism, but at least none of it was mine this time. I knew where mine was. He fucked with my dick for a few more strokes and then leaned forward, smearing his chest and belly against mine. The remains of my second load and his fresh first melded together in milky satisfaction as he eased off my joint so we could get in some quality belly-fucking time. Over the next eight or ten hours, we kept each other from getting bored. By the time I finally fell asleep with Alec lying atop me, I'd learned a lifetime's worth about lust and love—and where a man fits in.

Probably the major disappointment in my life was that I never felt Alec's gorgeous uncut dick up my ass. At one point he did tease me with it, sitting on my belly so I could suck on his `skin and the very tip end of his crank. Why he wouldn't let me treat him the way he deserved, I'll never know. I'm sure he had good reasons—in any case I was bound to do as he wished. I only know that when I awoke the next morning, he was gone with nothing but dried jism on my belly and a lifetime's worth of memories to prove he'd ever been there. I found a knife by my hand and cut myself free. Every muscle I had was cramped and stiff, but at least now I knew how to uncramp the muscle that matters most.

While I took a long, hot shower, I decided to wait until Alec came back, but he never did. I should have wondered why Claire brought me through a door that led directly from the street to the back bedroom. I discovered why easily enough: the rest of the apartment was vacant. Whether it was a model apartment or one Alec just kept rented so he could screw Yank sailors or what I never figured out. I obviously wasn't meant to. Alec had shown me what I wanted out of life and how to get it; if he wanted to be a tad kinky with bondage or shy about the rest of his life, I guess that was all right with me. I left the apartment on his terms—knowing nothing about him other than that he and the single, glorious night we spent together, slavish master and devoted bondsman, would remain with me bright and alive until my final hour.

A DREAM IN DENIM

Peter Eros

He stood at the room's entrance, one hip jutting out, secure in his coolness, serenely unaware of the contrast between his jeans and tee and the restaurant's muted elegance. His eyes, a perfect match with the faded denim of his jacket, swept the room. With his cartoonishly chiseled good looks, this was no punk, however grunge the style. The eyes spilled it. They viewed their surroundings with sophisticated amusement.

I felt a little in awe as I waited for him to strut his studly testosterone across the restaurant to my corner table. He picked up on it and the eyes crinkled in unbridled laughter, his smile cocked with enough sexual firepower to wipe out a busload of high-school wrestlers.

Pagan Spector was only twenty-eight but already a legend, a recording star and a movie and television actor of consummate skill. From his start as a teenage rebel with his own pop group, and then starring in a soap fifteen years ago, he had grown to one of the giants of the entertainment industry, with his own record label, and extremely lucrative profit-sharing deals on all his movies and television projects. I read all I could in the files on him—how his early life on the road proved grinding for him, gigging six nights a week and being crammed together in a tour bus for months at a time, taking its toll on the four band members. The songs didn't seem to fit with what he had become. They resonated with a Nashville-in-exile twang, the south of the border ennui of a lonesome loser.

Here was I, Blain Pantera, a tall, slim, wishfully depraved young man, with olive skin drawn tightly over my bones, dark brown eyes and a mop of black wavy hair; just eighteen and still in college; entertainment reporter for a student newspaper, delighted and surprised that Mr. Spector had agreed to an interview with such an insignificant writer and publication. Surprised too at my own forwardness. Feckless, would-be bodybuilder that I was, I'd seen Pagan at the West Hollywood gym and hesitantly introduced myself, gasped out how much I admired his work, and requested an interview. He'd immediately fetched his appointment book from his gym bag and set-up this mid-day brunch meeting at the Polo Room, which he insisted, with a capped-tooth smile, would be his treat.

When I informed the editor of my coup, the twenty-something acerbic bitch, with typical cynicism opined:

"Pagan's so at ease with his boyish charm, he's forgotten that maybe it's time, at twenty-eight, to grow up. But don't let the charm fool ya'. Go after him, and ask the hard questions, Okay!" Go after him I would, but maybe not in the way the catty bitch meant. I was, after all, both depraved and innocent.

Pagan had been one of my pin-ups for years, but only recently had I discovered why. I had just come out, to myself. I guess I'd grown up around too many straight guys. I'm an only child, raised by my divorced mother, so I'd had no brother to experiment with, and I didn't know any gay guys, or at least, I didn't think I did. Anyway, I'd only masturbated so far, and been willingly groped and sucked off at a movie and in a urinal.

I didn't know too much about what else was possible, but I'd bought a couple of porn books and a video at a sex shop and had a pretty good idea what I'd like to try, as soon as I could find a guy, hopefully attractive, willing to be enticed into my bed. I'd measured my cock too, and found I was a respectable seven and a half inches erect, though I wasn't sure whether you measured on top or below.

Pagan sat and cocked his head with that blithe charisma and winked what I hoped was a seductive come-on. His strong, shapely hand clutched mine and held it for several heart beats. His body warmth was electric. He made my balls tingle just by looking at me. My dick was extending down my leg already, pumped and hormonally engaged. He exuded a narcotic seductiveness. I was as tremulous and expectant as a school girl going to the prom. Sexual tension smoldered in my body like a low-grade fever. Just like a dog rolling on something dead, wanting the smell in their fur—that was the instinctive way I wanted him.

An obsequious waiter bobbed in attendance and Pagan ordered Eggs Benedict for two, and asked the guy to shift his place-setting so that we shared a corner instead of sitting opposite each other. Then, with his knee rubbing mine, he asked, in that distinctive voice, as suave as it is warm, "You know, you're really cute, Blain. Are you a perfect interrogator, an ideal bloodhound, come to ferret out answers? I just hope you're not going to be too hard on me."

His hand snaked into my groin under the table. My cock stiffened even more and my urethra pulsed in confusion as his fingers lightly perused my bulge.

"Hey, Blain, I hope your growing pains aren't too intense. I'm real good at easing that kind of tension ya' know. I'll be happy to demonstrate after breakfast, I'm a world-class masseuse." He winked conspiratorially, adding, "That is what this is all about, isn't it?

"I had kinda hoped," I admitted.

"I'm really glad. I haven't had sex in almost six weeks. Working on a movie really sucks sometimes. What's the longest time you've ever had to go without?"

I grinned ruefully and shrugged as I slipped my hand into his crotch. His cock was a rod against his thigh, twice the temperature of the rest of his body, bulging invitingly against the tight denim, and I was moistening and stretching in rhythm with his hand.

"I'm pretty much a virgin, I guess. I've been mostly self-help up to now," I admitted in almost a whisper, afraid somebody else might hear.

"Holy shit! Are you for real, kid? I didn't know they made virgins any more. God! I just love your wide dark eyes. You're as puppyish as a cocker spaniel, and I hope just as cuddly."

The brunch is a blur in my memory, and the ride in his Mercedes convertible to the Malibu house. The bedroom overlooked the sea. A gentle breeze fluttered the curtains that spring afternoon. The sound of the waves came in through the open window and with it the muffled noise of the surfers and sightseers. The sunlight bathed us in a rosy glow.

He clasped me in a tight embrace and his mouth was against mine in a tender kiss that grew warmer, more desperate, wide open, tongue hard and probing. I tilted my head back offering my throat. My breathing quickened as Pagan licked and nibbled. He slid his hands down my back, untucked my shirt, and eased one hand up my back and the other into the waistband of my jeans. I took tiny bites of his shoulder and he gasped at my ear and then his tongue slid inside, and every nerve in my body stood up and shivered. We writhed against each other.

My hands found his bare waist and stroked up under the tee to his urgently hard nipples. His hand unsnapped and unzipped my jeans and wriggled into my briefs. I lifted his tee and stroked and kissed the dark knobs. He tugged his tee over his head then ripped open the snaps on my shirt and pulled me against him. I pressed my crotch against his and he ground back against me—magnetized.

He pulled away and tossed off his shoes and dragged off his jeans, while I did the same. We were nude and shameless, gazing with joy upon each other's nakedness. Health glowed in the rich coloring of Pagan's classically molded face and body, and lurked in the luxuriant, honey-colored curly locks, clustered in glossy waves on his perfectly shaped head. Small tufts of hair encircled the edges of his large dark nipples, the only hair on his smooth, muscular chest. Happiness shone in the large, dreamy eyes and smiled on the voluptuous lips, while an indescribable expression of fire and force pervaded the whole. He had natural ease and elegance. I was pop-eyed with awe at Pagan's low-slung lemon sized balls and eight inches of throbbing, vein-laced hardness, thrust out invitingly.

"I want to satisfy your hunger Blain. I hope you can satisfy mine. I've searched for love, and settled for sex, up to now, but my itch is unscratched."

He knelt at my feet and slipped his mouth over my sleek cylinder of maleness, pink with the glow of youthful exuberance, framed by a tuft of dark pubic hair and left whole from birth. I was looking down at Pagan's curls bobbing against my hard abdomen. He ran his fingertips up and down along the length of my sleek shaft. I couldn't resist the insinuating skill of his fingers and the incredible suction applied to the exposed head. For someone who'd been on a long hiatus he was sure making up for lost time. But I wasn't used to this. My whole body tensed up suddenly and my hands slammed Pagan's head deep into my crotch.

With a guttural groan, my abdomen contracted tightly and I lost control. I shot globs of thick, scalding cum down Pagan's throat. His head bobbed furiously as his lips and mouth pumped my cock to suck every last drop of my syrupy juice, the flowing explosion dribbling past his lips and onto his chin; and yet he kept me hard and alert. He wouldn't let my cock deflate, sucking and lapping me with his tongue, as he held my orgasm in his mouth for a few moments, like a morsel he was not ready to swallow, turning it back and forth in his throat until he was ready to gulp it down.

He stood with a puckish smirk on his face as I apologized.

"Pagan, I'm sorry, I didn't mean to come in your mouth."

"Don't sweat it, Blain. You're delicious kid, and I don't know of any diseased virgins!"

He wrestled me onto my back on the enormous wolf-skin covered bed. A fingertip traced over the furry, puckered opening of my hole. It contracted with fear. The sphincter resisted at first. He knelt and hoisted my legs over his shoulders, just like I'd seen in a video. His face pressed between my thighs and his agile tongue pressed into my pucker, kissing, licking, sucking it lightly, probing delicately at the tiny ridges of flesh. His hands kneaded my firm buttocks and caressed my thighs. His tongue impaled and penetrated, opening me to sensations I'd read about but never imagined. My entire body turned to jelly. The tension in my ass and groin relaxed and his tongue prodded me deeply.

"Oh, god, yes," I moaned, "I don't fucking believe this, I'm in heaven."

As he slurped and tongued, he grabbed hold of my cock, which was red and swollen again, straining with the sting of impending release. He greased his fingers and inserted two, then three, sliding them in and out and feeling for my prostate. Then with swift single-mindedness he unfurled a pre-lubricated condom and encased his glory. Pagan pressed the fat, spongy head of his cock into me. I was awakened, with one swift priapic thrust, to the joys of anal sex. It hurt for an instant, a sharp, stabbing ache. I gasped. I shifted my hips and tried to adjust to it. I pushed onto it and groaned and winced at the raw, burning jab of pain.

"Blain," Pagan whispered, "please don't."

"But I want it," I moaned. "I want you. I want to feel you in me."

"Slowly," Pagan said. "We have to take it very slowly. Take

some deep, deep breaths and try to relax."

He kissed me as he lifted himself up slightly and a free hand gently massaged my groin, my hips and my lower abdomen. The biting tightness of my sphincter relaxed its grip on his glans. He eased his shaft into me with deliberate care, stopping completely each time I flinched. He continued to kiss me and I greedily sucked at the luscious taste of his lips, tasted who I was, as he slowly made his entry, until he was finally in. All the way in.

He started rocking back and forth, pulling out and shoving in, all the while smiling down at me with those twinkling blue eyes. I wrapped my legs around his back and rocked with his rhythm. My dick was riding up his belly with each thrust. And then I felt him stiffen and he was soon shuddering, filling the condom, writhing and bucking with each spurt of cum, crying, "Oh, yeah, yeah! Oh, fuck, baby, you're so tight! Oh, man, I love it!"

I spasmed uncontrollably and shot my load between us, jetting over both our bellies and chests. I had never shot a load with such intensity before. Nor had my cock remained rigid after cumming. But I was still hard. Pagan collapsed onto me and hugged me to him, gluing us together with cum and sweat. His mouth covered mine and we devoured each other, gasping each other's breath.

At last Pagan slid from me and discarded his condom onto a small dish on the nightstand. He licked down my body, sucking up my cum, until he reached my cock and deep-throated me once more. He swung his body round so that his crotch brushed my face and I sucked his glans into my mouth. He slid his cock smoothly in and out of my mouth. I choked, yearning to take all of him with each slide. He flicked his pinkie in my asshole. Then he rolled to one side and grasped my cock.

"We don't want to waste this, kid. Wow, what a boner!"

He straddled me and lowered himself. My sticky cock head bumped against his pucker and slid easily into his ass. He was pressed tight against my narrow hips and my whole cock was inside him. As he began to ride me I watched his taut belly muscles flex as my prick slid in and out of his gripping channel. The heat of our bodies, the rhythmic slapping of my balls against his ass, and the mere idea that I was fucking my ideal man, all combined to bring me to the edge again. I willed myself to wait for him, but it was like trying to prevent a volcanic eruption. I jerked and thrashed under him, pumping into his body, and let fly with another spout of hot jism.

Pagan's eyes closed and his mouth emitted a long drawn gasp as his prick flexed and jetted across me. He collapsed on top of me and we kissed and fondled each other for several minutes. I think we slept a while in each other's arms.

When I woke he was caressing my face and I embraced his slumber-warm flesh. He turned and slid up the bed as he rolled a fierce-looking rippled condom down the length of his beautiful hard dick, and sank his tongue into my mouth, his hands roaming my entire body. Each touch stung me, fired me, and I thrashed wildly. Our kisses tasted of briny cum. His cock prodded teasingly against my pouting wetness. His penis slid into me with the blunt curiosity of a child's finger. Pagan was still tentative and over-cautious at first, but it was so good to be desired. He glided in and out a few times but it wasn't going to work; he was getting a cramp in the back of his thigh.

"Let me lie down, kid, and you sit on it. That should be easier for you. You do want it again don't you?"

"Oh god, ye-e-e-e-s!"

He positioned me so that I was astride and facing him. Holding the latexed prick in one hand I guided it inside myself. My ring wouldn't yield at first, but I soon relaxed and squeezed about half in. It felt so good I shuddered with ecstasy. I clutched the base of his cock, felt beneath me and parted my asscheeks, and pushed down carefully. Then I stopped and gasped, "It doesn't hurt."

Pagan laughed and winked at me as I eased up and down, slowly at first, getting used to the prick invading me at this angle. I leaned forward, nibbled on his earlobe and he began to fuck up into me. The expanding fullness stretching my asshole wide was better than anything I had ever imagined. Pagan didn't move for a moment or two, just flexed his cock, stretching my man-ring wider. I responded by contracting my butthole as tight as I could. Pagan sighed, "Oh, yes, baby, oooh that's great."

His hands clutched my hips and he thrust up into me, fucking me deeper with every mighty thrust, as my head rocked back and forth and I gulped air so I wouldn't pass out as I rode and he fucked me deeper and deeper with each unrelenting thrust. My butt was slamming down with such force, I know his balls must have hurt. But he didn't complain, he just pounded my butt relentlessly in long, fast, hard thrusts, pounding the breath out of me. Then he slammed in even harder, and froze. His volcanic heat filled my guts. I gasped and took it with delight, overwhelmingly grateful to Pagan for breaking me in so gently. His third ejaculation triggered my palpitating cock to erupt, as his prick spurted at least four more jets into my cum-hungry butthole.

I was aching with pleasure between satin sheets. We both sunk into that sweet reverie, halfway between slumber and waking, between desire and satiety, which anyone who has experienced it knows is one of the pleasanter conditions imaginable.

After a long, cuddlesome interlude, I plunged my tongue into his navel. With the tip of my tongue I drew circles winding outward until I reached the base of his cock. Pagan was semi-erect by now. I started toward the head, cupping the thickening length of him with my teeth. Then I took the glans into my mouth and bit down sharp behind the collar.

"Ouch," he yelled.

In no time he had my legs over my shoulders and his new hard shaft inside me, pumping like a maniac. Then he withdrew, lifted my left leg and carefully entered me again. He was deep, deep into my bottom. Our moans became louder, and his arms tightened around me as my anus shuddered and contracted, milking his cock. We rocked, breathing into each other until we came to crescendo.

Pagan told me he loved me and invited me to move in. I didn't delay. Ever since he's been continuing my sexual education, insisting that I need a fully rounded sex life to be really happy. He bought me a number of dildos in a range of sizes. I haven't managed the Kris Lord dildo yet. I've had my nipples pierced, and he's been teaching me about cock rings and stimulants, like poppers. But most generous of all, he's enlisted help. So far we've had three-ways with the pool guy, the maintenance man, and the window-cleaner.

Best of all is our personal trainer. Josh is a blond ex-Marine with pecs and abs to die for, powerfully muscled legs, a ten inch, wrist-thick cock, and a loner stud air of mystery. He joined us today for the first time. My ass is still glowing from the plowing he gave it. I'm smiling as I finger it.

He came home with us after gym and led the way to the bedroom, pulling off his tee, then slowly unbuttoning his cutoffs before sitting back on the bed, looking at us both with a sly smile. Even half-erect, his cock is impressive: thick, meaty, with a large mushroom head. Sunlight danced over his veined slightly twitching dick meat and the fleshy balls beneath it.

I glanced at Pagan, but his eyes were fixed with a hungry gleam on Josh's naked body. We stripped rapidly and threw ourselves into Josh's embrace, each manipulating one of the huge, upstanding nipples. My cock was at full attention. Pagan was already beating off. I squeezed Josh's cock gently; a little precum pearl oozed out the slit and I knelt and lapped it up.

"Mmm! My favorite flavor."

Josh grinned and pulled us both onto the bed and kissed me, his hands exploring my torso, pinching my nipples, playing with my ass. Pagan lay on his back and put his feet on my shoulders while I manipulated my cock into his ass, and Josh embraced me from behind. Once he was sure I was fully in, he lubed my crack and slowly impaled me. I gasped and grimaced, and Josh paused a bit before he continued working his dick in. It didn't take long before he was plowing my ass hard, driving his dick-meat home with ball-slamming force, while Pagan grasped his legs around us both, pulling Josh onto me. Pagan planted his mouth over mine and tongued me for all he was worth, at the same time twisting my nipples hard. I bucked between them like a bronco in heat. I came up for air and slid my precum-slicked hand up and down Pagan's crank. I felt his balls tighten up in my hand and knew he was about to shoot.

A couple more strokes and he was over the edge, yelling loud enough to bring the roof down, and a mighty load of jism shot out of his dick head, splattering against my chin and chest. Josh roared soon afterward as he squirted his load into the condom up my ass, his arms wrapped tight enough around me to damn near squeeze the air out of me, as I shot my load deep in Pagan's gripping colon. We slid apart and Josh and Pagan licked the jism off my face and body.

I couldn't be happier. I can have one of the best fuckers in the world whenever I want. We savor the happiness given to those who set out to enjoy each other without reservations. It feels so natural to be with Pagan, drifting into sleep with his calm and so beautiful body lying beside me.

My writing's pretty much confined to this diary now. Pagan's in the bathroom, and I'm lying here lubing my asshole in readiness and feeling and caressing the muscles I've built up under his tutelage, especially my anus and prick. I guess my sphincter must be one of the best exercised in the world, and believe me, it's a real pleasure.

DREAM SOLDIER

William Cozad

I'd had the hots for the young soldier ever since I first saw him in his camouflage uniform and highly polished black combat boots.

He lived in my apartment building and parked his old but always-shiny white Ford behind my classic '65 Mustang in the same garage stall. I figured he must be married or otherwise he'd be living on the base.

He was tall and slim, around 25, with dirty blond hair fringing his camouflage cap. But it was his eyes that got me, blue-green, "bedroom eyes."

"I'm Larry Collins," he introduced himself. "Just got transferred up north."

I'd already noted COLLINS stenciled in heavy black letters on his uniform. I told him my name and shook his hand. I went upstairs to my apartment on cloud nine, as if I'd just met the boy of my dreams. It was crazy, I knew, but I was in real heat. Usually I chowed down and showered after work before I got down to any serious meat beating. But my cock was stiff and drooling and demanding immediate attention.

Lying down on the couch, I popped out my boner and stroked it slowly, fantasizing about the blond soldier. He was sweaty after a day of field maneuvers at the base. He peeled off his sexy loose camouflage uniform so that the only things he was wearing were his dog tags and Jockeys. I knocked on the door to his apartment. He invited me in. He knew the score—that I lusted after him. After slurping up his sweat, I sucked his dick. He blew a big load. And so did I, all over my belly, while I fantasized about Collins and jacked off. In reality I thought he was probably humping his wife. Wishing it was me he was slamming his hard dick into, I squeezed the last drops of come out of my spent prick.

So began my obsession with Collins. Seemed like we got off work at the same time every day, because I saw him in the garage. We exchanged greetings and small talk, and often as not I got a boner and went right to my digs and whipped off a load.

I was crazy to be so wigged out over a number that I didn't stand a prayer with, although I fully believed, as Truman Capote said, that you could have any man that you devoted the time and attention to get. Private Collins was the new star of my jack-off fantasies. How I fantasized about the soldier and his private parts!

One day I ran into him in the garage. He approached me with a big smile. For a brief moment I thought that he knew how much he turned me on, that he wanted me to give him head right there in the garage.

"Well, I'm going to do it," he said, grinning.

"Do what?" I asked, reaching for parcels in the back seat.

"I'm gettin' hitched this weekend," he said.

"Oh?" Hell, I thought he was already married, although he didn't wear a ring. Maybe he was shacked up with the girl. "Well, congratulations," I managed weakly.

Now he was totally off-limits—the one that got away. Yet I knew married men, after the honeymoon, play around.

"Uh, a few of my buddies are throwing me a bachelor party Friday night. Since you're about the only civilian I know, I'd like you to come."

"Hey, that's nice. Thanks."

I couldn't get out of the garage fast enough. I went upstairs and started to sulk. My dreamboat soldier stud was getting married. My dick stayed soft. That's what straight guys did: married girls. I'd never get him now. Damn it, you're wrong, Truman Capote. Some straight men can be had but not all.

When Friday night rolled around, I noticed the soldier was already home.

I went up to my place. I wanted to be alone with Collins, not with his buddies around. It was bad enough I was losing him to a girl. I could whack off so I wouldn't be so horny for him and embarrass him in front of his buddies. I got cold feet. Maybe I'd just call him and tell him I couldn't make it, had to work late or some bullshit excuse. But I had to see him.

Standing at the door to 206, I heard stereo music and loud talk coming from inside. Sucking in my breath, I rang the doorbell. Private Collins answered, still wearing his camouflage uniform. His blue-green eyes sparkled. "Just gettin' started,

Bill. Come in." Seated on the floor—there were no chairs in the unfurnished apartment, just a sleeping bag and blanket on the floor and lots of electronic gear—were three young soldiers. Larry introduced his soldier buddies in their camouflage uniforms. There was Guy, a slim Asian; Rick, a cute brunet and Cliff, who was swarthy and hairy. They all looked hot to me. I'd do any of them. But they didn't hold a candle to Larry, the guest of honor.

Larry brought me a cold bottle of Bud. I gave him the gift I brought, a half-gallon plastic bottle of Old Crow whiskey. He thanked me profusely. "Since my friend is so generous," he said, "let's break out the booze." Larry poured us all stiff shots of booze in plastic cups. We drank boilermakers, whiskey chased with beer, and nibbled on snacks with dip.

On the small television monitor in the corner was a hetero porn video, mostly tits and ass, not hard-core sucking and fucking. Maybe it was the Playboy Channel. The soldiers were chattering about the Army, shoptalk, and about Larry's upcoming marriage to Cathy. "Should have kept that thing in your pants, dude," Rick said to the prospective groom.

"It ain't no shotgun wedding."

"True love," Guy cooed.

Cliff just grinned. The banter was lively. I was getting high and felt good, enjoying myself more than I had expected.

Midnight came, and the party wound down. The other soldiers all had duty the next day, so they split. "The place is a mess. Looks like a cyclone struck it. Cathy and her folks will be here in the morning."

"Don't worry, buddy boy. Just suck on that beer, and I'll tidy up." I swung into action, emptying the ashtrays and picking up the empty beer bottles, plastic cups, and snack stuff.

"You'd make somebody a good wife," Larry laughed.

"Too bad you're taken," I teased.

"I like you, Bill. You're a cool guy."

"You just don't know me very well."

"But I'd like to."

I wondered what that meant. Larry said a lot of things that could stand greater scrutiny. I took a slug of whiskey out of the nearly empty plastic jug. He was probably drunk and didn't know what he was saying.

"Nice buddies you got."

"They're OK. But they don't understand me. I think you might." He took another nip of whiskey.

"What the hell's that supposed to mean?"

"Maybe I shouldn't get married."

"All guys feel that way—trapped."

Like I knew what the hell I was talking about.

"No, you don't understand. Got a lot of pressure from my folks to get married; they want grandkids. Lots of pressure from Cathy; she wants a ring on her finger."

"You'll be happy. Somebody to fight with."

"Know something? I think I might be bi—or queer, for that matter."

I shook my head. I didn't think I heard him right. I'd been hitting the booze pretty hard to keep up with the soldier boys. "That's ridiculous. You're one of the most macho-lookin' studs I've ever laid eyes on."

"Sure." He paused, meditating. Then, "Tell me something, buddy. Did you ever make it with another guy?"

"Every chance I get! Ain't no big deal."

Looking into Larry's bedroom eyes that now burned blue with desire, I was shocked when he unbuttoned the fly of his pants and reeled out his cock. It was huge, fat, uncut, and drooling.

I laughed. "Now, that's a big deal!"

"Like it, don't you? I thought so. Suck it for me, pal."

"Oh, Larry, you're drunk. You're getting married this weekend. Besides, I wouldn't want to do anything to ruin our friendship."

"C'mon, do it. You said you did guys. And I want you to. God, I need a good blowjob."

How could I refuse? On my knees on the green shag rug, I crawled over to him. I had become his slave.

"Yeah, lick my dick, buddy."

Sticking out my tongue, I lapped up the salty drool oozing out of his pee hole. I darted my tongue inside.

"Put it in your mouth. Suck it."

I tongued the ridge below the crown. It was real sensitive, and he moaned.

Larry was a take-charge guy. He ordered me to lie back and

he positioned me on my back and straddled my chest. He fed me his big dick, slowly at first, then roughly mouth-fucking me. I loved the feeling of his uncut dick tickling my tonsils, then battering them. I clutched his buns, dug my fingers in.

"Oh, yeah, that's it."

His balls slapped against my chin while he buried his boner down my throat. "Get ready. Take it. Eat my fucking cum!"

As we whitewashed my tonsils, and flooded my mouth, I savored its delicious salty taste.

When he'd squeezed out the last of it, he lifted himself up. He shocked me by ripping open the metal buttons of my fly, freeing my boner. I don't wear underwear to better show off the outline of my cock, and I liked the feel of denim against my cock meat. He kept stroking me, and I was hoping for a mercy hand job, which would have been considerate of him. I was completely caught off-guard when the soldier pulled my cock from its prison and wiped the pre-cum from the head of it. I raised up on my elbows to watch as the soldier examined my cock. "You got a nice one, buddy," he said.

"Thanks," I said.

Slowly he lowered his head. He licked the head, continued stroking. Soon his teeth grazed my cock head and scraped my shaft.

He was curious, no doubt about it now, and just the thought of him down there, trying, aroused me. He liked what he was doing, if his cock was any indication: It pulsed, stiff and proud.

He let go of my cock and lifted my legs. He fingered my butt. "I wanna fuck you, buddy."

"Hold it right there, soldier."

"You're queer. All queers take it up the ass."

"Not me. I'm macho." Of course I was lying through my teeth, but I wanted the soldier to work for it—yes, beg me a little. Of course I'd relent, but I wanted him to work for it.

"C'mon, I know when a bitch wants to get stuck."

"Not me."

"I know you like me. I know you'll let me."

Yes, I let him have his way with me. All the while I was working on a little scheme of my own. I like a man who knows what he wants and takes it when he knows he has your consent, silent or otherwise. He peeled down my jeans and rolled me over onto my belly using my cock as a convenient handle.

Looking over my shoulder, I got really turned-on by watching the soldier bury his finger in my butt. I asked him where the lube was. He got it, went back down. Soon the time had come, and Larry mounted me. I'd taken many dicks before but nothing lately and certainly nothing as big as Larry's. Its stiffness made it seem even bigger. He nudged his flared, drooling prick head into my hole, tearing it apart.

"Easy, stud. It's so fuckin' big."

But once he was in, all systems were go for me. I backed up on his dick, forcing him to slide right in all the way. Larry started off slow, reaming my asshole and stroking it deep. When he hit his stride, I was moaning and groaning, filled with cock. My asshole was burning.

"Oh, do it!" I screamed.

Larry showed his mettle. His cock was even harder, if that was possible. His big balls slapped my asscheeks. Then he lunged his meat in to the hilt and exploded, flooding my ass guts with wad after wad of scalding soldier jism. I clamped my butt muscles around his cock and siphoned every drop of juice out of his balls. I wanted it all and got it. It was a gut-wrenching orgasm for him that left my asshole all torn up and the young soldier panting and spent. His cock softened and plopped out of my butthole. I knew that I had been fucked by a real man when he was finished. I didn't care if he liked it or not—kissed him right on the lips that had been around my cock. I gave him a real sloppy kiss as a token of appreciation for the roughest fuck I could remember.

I hobbled back to my apartment and soaked my sore butt before I could fall asleep, visions of the horny soldier dancing in my head.

Larry went ahead with the wedding. I saw the ring on his finger. I thought I'd lost him forever. But something in his eyes told me differently, though I thought that was just wishful thinking on my part. I didn't see much of Larry after his wedding. I guess he was busy being a newlywed and doing what blissful couples do. I was jealous and envied his wife, but he was taken.

Then one night a few weeks later, I was awakened by a

knock on my door. Looking through the peephole, I recognized Larry.

"Can I come in?" he begged. "I gotta talk to you."

"Sure." I tried to wipe the sleep out of my eyes and shake the cobwebs out of my head.

I told him to come in and I poured us brandies.

"I made a mistake, a big mistake. Cathy left me."

"Oh, she'll be back. I'm sure it was just a lovers' quarrel."

After he calmed down a bit, out came the confession. "I knew after you and I did it that I wasn't ready to get married. I tried to deny it. It isn't fair to Cathy. Now she's left."

"She'll be back. You can work it out. Lots of guys have. And I'm always here to help."

"I need a little help right now," he said, leaning back into the cushions of the couch. I saw he was in need, his boner stretching the fabric of his jeans.

In moments, I had him out of his jeans and in my bed. As he climbed over me and slid his cock in my mouth, I knew my dream soldier was a dream no more.

― *This tale has been especially adapted for this collection from material originally appearing in Freshmen magazine.*

GETTING SHAFTED

Leo Cardini

It was late in the afternoon when I dropped into the Ninth Circle, a raunchy gay bar in the middle of the West Village, to buy some grass. The next thing you know I'm sitting out on the back patio sharing a joint with this cute kid with blond-brown hair, steel blue eyes and a mischievous smile. A real dreamboat. He says to call him Little Ricky, since everyone else does, on account of he's not so tall. Shirtless and disco-trim with a nearly-hairless chest, he's stuffed his tight ass and big basket into seriously worn Levi's with tears across the seat announcing to all the world he's not wearing any underwear. Though I can't fail to recognize the similarities in our appearances, I'm still flattered when one of the waiters says we could pass for brothers.

Well, we get stoned out of our minds and next thing you know Little Ricky's got me telling him what I'm into. And then he's surprised when I say I've never been to the Mineshaft.

Sure, I've heard about the Mineshaft and all the wild sex that goes on inside. Well, he sure arouses my interest (and my dick) as he describes the slings for fistfucking, the tubs for water sports, the walls riddled with glory holes, and the dark rooms packed with men fucking and sucking to their heart's content. But then I really get turned on when he says you can even have sex right at any one of its three bars; like say, bend over the counter with your pants down around your ankles (if you're wearing pants, since clothing's optional) and let some guy stick his dick up your ass and fuck you right then and there.

Yeah, that's my kind of place, all right. So when Little Ricky tells me he works there and I should drop by sometime, I say I just might do that. Though I wouldn't mind getting it on with him, he looks to be in his early twenties, like me, and what really turns me on are men with a little more muscle and maturity, guys who take charge and call the shots. And Little Ricky said I'd find lots of studs like that at the Shaft.

So I get directions before Little Ricky runs off, and now here I am standing in front of the place. It's at the corner of

Washington and Little West Twelfth, right in the middle of the meatpacking district, barely a fifteen minute walk from the Ninth Circle. Two stories high and painted black, the only indication of what might be inside is a handwritten "Members Only" in red and an arrow aimed at its unassuming entrance.

The streets are practically deserted, the place feels like a fucking ghost town, and it's beginning to get dark. I want to enter, but I hesitate. After all, once I open that door and step inside, who knows what I'm in for.

If I smoke another joint first, I figure it'll put me in the mood, so I pull one out, taking the opportunity to transfer my few valuables from my pockets to one sock, and light up. Well, more than put me in the mood, by the second toke I'm intensely aware of the stab of my hard, sensitive nipples against the tight white tee shirt I'm wearing. Another toke and I can't get my mind off the way this same tee shirt stops short a couple of inches above my navel, far above the low-slung waistband of my snug-fitting 501 cutoffs. Another toke and I tune into the feel of my cock and balls rebelling against the threadbare denim in my crotch, forcing the material in back to crawl up into my asscrack.

And then I begin to feel that sweet itch in my hole, reminding me of my insatiable need for men to stick their dicks up my ass. So while I inhale once more, I slip my free hand down the back of my pants. Tight as they are, somehow there's always room for rear entry. And so, middle finger in the vanguard, I descend the familiar groove of my asscrack until, with an out-thrust of my butt, I reach my hole. Though at present it's hardly moist, my finger slides in easily.

Jesus that feels good! Real good. So fucking good, in fact, I almost forget where I am and go to slide in another finger...

...when suddenly someone steps around the corner!

I pull my hand out of my pants, but I'm a split second too late.

"Got a problem back there?" he asks with friendly familiarity.

"No! I just...uh...."

My words dry up when I take a look at him, judging him to be in his mid to late thirties. He's tall and he-man handsome with fairer skin, bluer eyes and blonder hair than I could ever hope to have. Ditto for his broad-chested, muscle-packed body. All in all, he looks like a statue of some Greek hero come to life all decked out in modern-day Village wear: a skimpy tank top with shoe-lace shoulder straps, tight jeans that hug his armor-like thighs and strain against his huge piece of meat, and black cycle boots.

Somehow I manage to hold out the half-smoked joint and ask, "Want some?"

"Sure, man. Thanks," he says, taking it from me and bringing it to his lips, in the process mobilizing a stunning array of muscles I practically groan with the desire to touch.

"Name's Kurt," he says over a lungful of grass as he offers me his hand.

"Fred," I say, thrilling to the take-charge force of his grip.

Well, the joint goes back and forth between us. And as we silently proceed to get stoned, the grass collaborates with the sight of him to make me more aware than ever of the denim in my asscrack inching its way towards my hole, and of the swelling in my crotch as the thin fabric teases the hell out of the sensitive underside of my dickhead.

When the joint's done, Kurt nods towards the Mineshaft and beckons me to enter with him.

"Yeah...uh...well, you see...."

"First time, huh?"

"How'd you know that?"

"I'd remember someone like you," he says checking me out up and down, setting my cock all a-squirm. "But if you've never been here before, you're not a member, and if you're not a member, how're you gonna get inside without a sponsor?

"I need someone to sponsor me?" Little Ricky never told me about this!

"Don't worry," he says reassuringly placing a hand on my shoulder and giving it a squeeze. "C'mon. I'll see what I can do to get you in."

And with that, he escorts me over to the entrance and opens the door. Inside there's a dimly lit stairway with concrete steps and a rickety banister leading up to a second-floor landing I can hardly make out. All and all, it looks more like the interior of an abandoned warehouse than a world-famous sex-club.

Kurt motions me to enter, and apprehensively I take the lead and ascend the stairs. In spite of my anxiety, I become acutely aware of the constant repositioning of my dick with every step I take, and of that persistent ass-itch, as if Kurt's warm gaze, level with my butt as he follows me up, can penetrate denim, a skill he uses to probe around the puckered exterior of my hole.

As my eyes adjust to the lack of light, I reach the landing. On the left, the stairs reverse direction, leading up to the roof, I discover later. And to the right, just inside a dark doorway, my lowered eyes first fall on black, square-toed cowboy boots. Ascending, they take in tight jeans encasing the firm flesh of a Titan of a man with a long, thick dick and enormous set of nuts pressed against his right inner thigh. When my eyes dare to make their way beyond his wide black leather belt, I'm confronted with powerful arms crossed over a well-defined, pec-prominent chest with an appetizing spread of black hair his black leather vest does blessedly little to conceal. When I dare to look up further, I see a ruggedly masculine face with a day's growth of beard, and a broad forehead shaded by the brim of a black Stetson.

He looks me up and down with an assessing frown that makes me think maybe I'm in for more than I bargained for. Escape flashes across my mind, along with the realization that this is the kind of man from which escape's impossible if that's the way he wants it.

"Hi, Cam," Kurt says.

"Hey, Kurt" comes the response in a deep baritone as he breaks out into a smile that makes me realize just how irresistibly handsome he is.

They shakes hands and then Kurt says "This here's Fred. It's his first time."

"It is, huh? Well," he says extending his hand to me, "any friend of Kurt's is sure welcome to...."

Kurt jumps in with, "I told him he needs someone to sponsor him if he wants to get inside."

"You did, huh?" says Cam, once again crossing his arms over his chest and sizing me up. I'm so tense I nearly jump out of my skin when I feel Kurt's hand on my butt slipping into my asscrack.

"But, you see," Kurt continues, "he came here all by

himself. So he's got no one to sponsor him"

"Hmmm. That could be a problem now, couldn't it."

I dare to look beyond Cam for a second. Inside I vaguely make out a shadowed, saloon-like setting and I recall what Little Ricky said about buttfucking right at the bar. Jesus, I just gotta get inside!

"Could you sponsor me?" I dare to ask Kurt, thrusting my butt to close up the gap between his hand and my hole.

"Me? I'm not a member."

"You're not?"

Cam laughs at this and then says, "Hell, Kurt's staff—one of the hottest bartenders we got!"

"Well, can't staff sponsor someone?"

"Well, I suppose they could. But—" Cam continues, grabbing me by the top front of my cutoffs and pulling me so close into him my crotch presses up against his and I have to tilt my head back to see him, "how do we know you're the kind of guy we want inside our little clubhouse?"

"Yeah, how do we know that?" Kurt seconds, closing in from behind until I'm sandwiched in-between the two of them, thrilled with apprehension, and wanting to get into the Mineshaft so badly it's like my life depended upon it.

"Let's put it this way," I hear myself say. "I'd do anything to get inside the Mineshaft. Anything!"

"Anything covers a lot of territory," Cam says, looking down at me.

"Especially around here." Kurt says in my ear with his hot breath.

"I said anything, and I mean anything!" I say, not so sure I really mean it.

"Gotta hand it to him, the kid's got balls, eh Kurt?"

"Yeah. Not to mention a nice hot ass. You know what I think, Cam?"

"What's that?"

"I've got a few minutes before I go on duty. Maybe I could, uh...."

"Try him out?"

"Sure. Why not?"

"Well, I don't know if he's ready for you. You're a pretty demanding master."

145

"All I wanna do is shoot my load."

"Well, it's okay with me," Cam says.

Neither one thinks to ask me how I feel about this. I'm about to protest—more for the sake of appearance than anything else, though—then Kurt shoves me up against the wall opposite the lower stairway.

"Now take off that shirt," he commands, stepping back.

I pull it off, and then go to stuff it in my back pocket when I think "what the fuck," and instead roll it into a ball and toss it down the stairs. Then, with shoulders back and chest forward I look up at Kurt, awaiting his next command.

His eyes scan my chest with obvious approval, and then he grips my nipples between his thumbs and forefingers, squeezing hard and giving them a tug.

I inhale sharply, but avoid protesting.

"Next thing I want you to do is turn around, pull down your pants and bend over."

"But supposin' someone should come in downstairs?"

"Supposin' they should?" he dares me, giving my nipples another squeeze until they ache with pleasure. "Now do you want me to sponsor you or not?"

Wasting no time, I turn around, undo my cutoffs and bend over as I slide them down, holding myself in place with my hands on my ankles.

"Umm. You're right. That is a nice ass," Cam states, seating himself on a barstool just inside the doorway, crossing his arms over his chest again.

"And nice hole. Looks kinda tight, though. You wouldn't be a virgin, now would you?"

"Actually I am."

Like I'm fooling anyone! Actually, I hoped they'd decide to check this out with some hands-on investigative work, but—shit!—I hear the damn downstairs door fly open and someone dashing up the stairs.

I go to straighten up but Kurt pushes me down again, so I grip my ankles all the tighter, terribly aware of my exposed butt. I look out between my legs, beyond the hang of my half-hard cock, and who should I see stepping onto the landing but Little Ricky!

"Hey, guys," he says to Kurt and Cam. "Sorry I'm late."

And then "Hiya, Fred. Thought I recognized your T-shit down there."

"You know him?" asks Kurt.

"Yeah, we've met."

"He says he's a virgin. That true?"

"Speaking from personal experience I couldn't say, but...."

He drops down onto one knee to examine my hole close up. As I feel him fingering me, my hole repeatedly clenches and unclenches, proud of its power to monopolize the interests of these three men.

"Yeah, he's a virgin like I'm a virgin," is Little Ricky's assessment. Then, with his index finger squirming around inside me, he leans over around my left to say, "Hey, for a kid who's never been here before you're sure awfully popular with the staff."

"Well, Kurt's gonna sponsor me inside if I—"

"Sponsor you inside? You don't need—"

Kurt grabs onto Little Ricky's ear, pulling him away.

"Ouch! That hurts!"

"When you open that big mouth of yours make sure you put it to some good use."

"What'd you have in mind?" he asks, suddenly so preoccupied with Kurt's crotch barely inches from his face his finger slips out of my hole.

"You wish. Now make yourself useful and get me some Crisco from the can on the bar."

"Okay. But just a minute."

Prying my asscheeks apart, he's about to bury his face in my crack, when Kurt pulls him out.

"Aw, c'mon, Kurt!"

"Let him," says Cam from his barstool. "Fred's gonna need all the loosening up he can get."

"Yeah, guess you're right," Kurt says, shoving Little Ricky's face into my butt. "You heard Cam. Stick that tongue all the way in."

"Ummm," he manages to comment as he snakes his tongue up inside my hole, driving me crazy with an oozy pleasure that radiates outward from my hole, taking possession of me.

"That's it," Kurt coaches. "Get him nice and wet inside so's he can manage all my dick up his ass."

"Is that what's gonna be inside?" I ask, trying not to sound too eager.

"Depends on how good a fuck you are," he says reaching into his fly and carefully maneuvering his dick out into the open. When he releases it, it flops down heavily in front of my face, overwhelming me with the sudden onslaught of its beauty —pale, smooth-skinned and neatly-cut—and its size: beer-bottle thick at the base, hanging down between his legs with so little taper it dwarfs his cockhead.

"Jesus," I say when it responds to my open-mouthed stare with a lazy stretch, "I'll never be able to take all of that!"

"Oh, I'm sure you will—that is, if you really want to get inside. Just be thankful it's me who's gonna fuck you and not Cam."

The thought of what Cam has packed away in his pants combines with the sight of Kurt's enormous dick and the feel of Little Ricky's versatile tongue in a heady mix that washes over me, carrying me far away from the world I left behind just minutes ago one flight down beyond that door.

Then Cam interrupts with, "Ricky, the Crisco! Now!"

"Okay, okay!" he frets, rising and disappearing into the Mineshaft.

I'm still bent over and I don't know whether or not I should get up. And truth to tell, now that my hole's empty again I'm aware of the difficulty of holding this position.

"Don't you think you'll feel more comfortable without those cutoffs?" Kurt asks, tugging on his meaty dick.

I waste no time pulling off my cutoffs and straightening up, on impulse throwing them down the stairs to keep my tee shirt company, the two of them possibly trampled underfoot before the night's out, but also possibly picked up, examined, sniffed, maybe even rubbed against some stud's crotch, or carried inside to wear!

As I stand there looking down at them, naked except for my sweat socks and construction boots, I soon become aware of my stiff eight-incher. Really! Well, more or less. The show-off that it is, and in spite of its heft and thickness, it buoyantly twitches upwards as if my mushroom-shaped dick-head's trying to kiss my navel, in the process exposing my large, cock-clinging nuts.

Kurt rests his butt against the yard or so of banister parallel to the landing between the two flights of steps, his cock still hanging out. He eyes me up and down with obvious approval.

"Just relax. Ricky'll be back in no time."

Well, I don't know about you, but it's kinda difficult for me to feel relaxed when I'm standing butt-naked with a hard-on in an active stairway waiting to take some stud's dick up my ass. But I manage an at-ease position with my hands clasped behind my back and my feet planted well apart.

"Big dick for someone his size, eh Cam?"

My dick twitches in proud response.

"Sure is. Reminds me of Little Ricky's."

Another cock-twitch and, looking down, I see a drool of pre-cum oozing out my piss slit.

"Umm, I see what you mean. Betcha they'd make one hot threesome, huh?"

But all Cam does is slouch forward on his stool with his back pressed against the wall, his arms crossed over his chest, and his legs spread wide apart as he continues to contemplate my restless dick.

Little Ricky comes back with a big gob of Crisco in a white paper cup. When he sees me standing there, my dick gives another twitch to acknowledge his presence, and with an awed "Jeez!" he falls onto his knees, wraps his lips around my cock and deepthroats the entire thing with surprising ease, burying his nose in my pubic bush.

"Hey!" Kurt says, stepping over to us to pull Little Ricky out of my crotch. He refuses to forfeit my dick and fights Kurt off as best he can. When Kurt finally pulls him away, Little Ricky's wide-eyed and out of control with a crazed look on his face. He struggles to mount my dick again until Kurt subdues him with a backhander against his left cheek.

"Now grease me up," Kurt commands him. "And no more of your funny stuff, or you can forget about getting any of this...."

He gives his dick a shake in front of Little Ricky's face.

"...when you come prowling around my bar tonight."

Something tells me if I ever get inside, I'll be spending a lot of time around Kurt's bar.

"Okay, okay" Little Ricky mutters with resignation, soon engrossed in the task of applying Crisco to Kurt's dick.

While Little Ricky reverently slicks it up, I fall onto my own knees to watch. But then my attention's drawn away from Kurt's crotch by the play of his powerful muscles as he lifts his tank top up over his head, hitching it behind his neck.

When I look down again, Little Ricky's greased him into a good nine inches of smoothly up-curving meat, pale as alabaster with light blue veins just below the surface of his cockshaft. It's thicker than ever at the base, and from the way Little Ricky handles it I can tell it's a rigidly rockhard dick with little give to it, the kind of cock that demands satisfaction on its own terms.

All I can do is stare, mesmerized by its size and beauty as it gleams in the dim light, sticking up beyond the topmost button of his 501's.

"Ready?" he asks me when Little Ricky's done.

Open-mouth and speechless, all I can do is nod yes.

"Then pull down my pants," he commands, pushing Little Ricky out of my way.

"You're gonna fuck me right here?"

"Where'd you think I was gonna fuck you?"

I'd assumed once he was good and ready to shove his dick up my ass he'd bring me someplace a little more private. But I don't complain. Instead, I reach around his towering dick to undo the waistbutton of his 501's and pull them down. You should just see the perfection of his lower abs as they come into view, traversed by the thin line of blond hair descending from his tight, innie of a navel into his pubic bush.

And then, below, there's his two large nuts. He'd shaved his balls—something I'd never seen before. As he steps out of his cutoffs, I'm so captivated by the beauty of his huge, hairless nuts that I can't restrain myself from leaning forward and licking them, somehow managing, as tight as they are in his nutsac, to scoop them into my mouth. He lets out with an appreciative groan and slides one hand around the back of my head to hold me there, encouraging me to give his balls a thorough tonguing. When he releases me, I liberate his nuts so my tongue can explore behind them. But I don't get very far since Little Ricky's managed himself onto his knees behind Kurt with his tongue up Kurt's hole, so I content myself licking the nearly hairless cleft between his muscular legs.

"Ohhh!" Kurt groans non-stop, basking in our attentions.

Then, once he's had his fill, he pushes our heads away.

"Now bend over," he orders, indicating the stretch of railing parallel to the landing.

As I get into position, resting my forearms on the railing, I notice I can see all the way down the stairs to the front door, meaning anyone entering can see me also. But whatever my apprehensions might be about this, I'm distracted from them by the feel of Little Ricky greasing up my hole, using one, two and finally three very inquisitive fingers.

By now my dick's twitching out of control. I let out a whimper of loss when Little Ricky withdraws his fingers and moves away, and then a gasp of anticipation when I feel Kurt's hands on my hips as he steps up behind me and presses his cockhead against my hole.

My hole becomes the center of my universe. On the periphery I see Cam, still seated on his barstool, watching with his legs spread apart, and Little Ricky, momentarily busy wiping off his fingers with a blue bandanna he's pulled out of his back pocket, and then, down below, that door that might open at any time, admitting God-know-who to witness me in the act of getting fucked. But at the core of all this is the sensation of Kurt's fat cockhead pressing against my hole with gradually increasing pressure as his hands tighten their grip on me.

Then his dickhead slips inside with a sudden forward thrust. He lets it rest there. After a pause, he slides in a little more and I go "Ooooooo-w!" as my ass tries to clench shut around the obstruction of his cock.

"Lift a foot up onto the banister. It'll be easier that way," Kurt advises me, pulling out a little.

I do, gripping on the railing to steady myself as I feel my stretched hole relax, once more welcoming Kurt inside me. My dick's still relentlessly stiff and my tender nuts cling tight to the underside base of my cock.

Kurt slowly slides the rest of his dick up my ass. I even manage to help by bending my floor-rooted leg to slide down the final few inches of his cock, flinging me into an ecstasy where I become oblivious to anything but the feel of his massive dick filling my greedy hole. My breathing grows labored, my mouth falls open and I can feel that blissed-out look come over my face I'm told I always get when there's a cock inside me.

"You okay?" he asks, his hot breath tickling my ear.

"Yeah," I hear myself whisper back.

Then he begins to fuck me, slowly sliding his dick in and out my hole, rallying the force of his entire, muscle-packed body in service of his orgasm.

He soon establishes a steady rhythm. One second he's thrust his dick so far up my ass I can feel the bristle of his pubic hairs against my butt, and the next he pauses with just his cockhead inside me as he prepares to reverse direction again.

"Aww...such a nice hot hole," he enthuses as his cockthrusts grow more forceful, sending jolt after jolt of pleasure throughout my body, my desperately rockhard dick jabbing the air.

"Maybe I'll leash you to my bar tonight. Would you like that?"

Somehow I manage to nod yes and grunt out my consent.

"That way, when me and my friends get to feeling horny, we'll have you on hand to take our loads."

The thought of it floods my consciousness as cock-thrust after cock-thrust plunge me into an all-consuming craving, not just for Kurt's dick, but for as many dicks as Kurt has friends who might get to feeling horny. My eyes happen to fall on Cam. There he is looking back with a contemplative interest that makes my resolve that some night—assuming I get into the Mineshaft—one of those dicks that makes it way up my ass is gonna be his.

I go to grab my own dick, only to find I really need both my hands on the railing to maintain my balance against the force of Kurt's buttfucking. But Little Ricky comes to the rescue. He's torn off his clothes, sporting a big, stiff dick that could double as my own, and somehow he manages to squeeze in below me on his haunches facing Kurt, throwing his head back to lick my nuts.

"Oh!" I yell out in pleased surprise when he abandons my balls to slide his lips down my cockshaft. And just as my scream echoes in the stairway, the downstairs door opens and this policeman steps in!

But Cam's still watching me, Little Ricky's still sucking on my dick, and of course Kurt's still screwing the hell out of me, so although I know in some rational corner of my mind that I ought to be alarmed there's a cop downstairs, I just don't care.

I still don't care when I see him mount the steps, and I care even less when I make out how tall, lean and square-jawed he is, with blazing black eyes that sparkle with life. In fact, all I can think about is if I have to go to jail because this cop witnesses the best butt-fuck I've ever had, well, that's okay with me.

"Well, I guess I don't need to ask how's it goin' since I can see that for myself!" the cop says with a wide, engaging smile.

"Hey, Slater," responds Cam, his eyes never leaving me.

"Hiya, man!" Kurt manages to utter as he continues pumping away at my ass.

And "Mmmph," from Little Ricky, whose mouth never leave my cock.

Well, this friendly cop just leans back against the stairway wall, one foot on the landing and the other on the step below it, and watches. And while he watches he unzips his pants, pulls out his half-hard dick, and strokes himself into an erection. He's got a huge, rough-hewn log of a dick that's got to be a good nine-and-then-some inches. One look and I pray it'll find its way up my ass before the night's out.

So Kurt continues to ram his dick up my ass, each jolt shoving my cockhead down Little Ricky's throat, all the while this cowboy and this cop looking on, one just sitting and watching with rapt attention and the other stroking a stiff, inflexible rod that begins to ooze so much pre-cum it streams down the underside of his dick and over the back of his hand.

The atmosphere grows thick and humid with sweaty sexuality. I'm so overwhelmed by everything that's happening it's like I lose touch with gravity, and so I anchor my being by fixing my gaze on Slater's drooling cockhead, while Kurt fucks away at my ass for what seems like a sweet eternity.

Time loses meaning, so I don't know how many minutes have passed when Kurt tightens his grip on me with a drawn-out "Ahhh!" that culminates in him shooting what feels like buckets of hot, steamy cum up my ass.

"Ohh! Ohh! Ohhhh!" I yell, my eyes glued to Slater's dickhead as my cock explodes with its own outpour of jism.

"Mmph!" again and again from Little Ricky as he swallows spurt after spurt of my cum, which is then followed by "Ummm! Ummm! Ummph!" as he thrashes about below me, shooting his own load. When he calms down some, I look between my legs and around the side of his head to see his cum dripping off Kurt's nuts and down his thighs.

But then Slater commands my attention again with "Oh, yeah! Yeah! Yeaaahhh!" and I look up again just in time to witness the first jet of Slater's cum shooting across the stairway, landing warm and sticky between my eyes. After a quick, reflexive blink, I watch him jack off the rest of his load until he's left with a drippy dick and a splattering of his cum on my face and across the steps.

Though I'm sweaty and exhausted, I feel a sense of emptiness several seconds later when Kurt slides his softening dick out of my hole and everyone proceeds to pull themselves together, Little Ricky offering me a jockstrap to wear with "It's okay. It's one of mine."

"So, you gonna sponsor him?" Cam finally asks Kurt.

"Sure. Why not?" he says, giving me a playful slap on the ass as he passes behind me to enter the Mineshaft. Just inside the entrance, he turns, beckoning me to follow with, "C'mon," before stepping inside.

I follow, and discover before the evening's over the advantages of possessing an insatiably cock-hungry hole—especially when Kurt's your sponsor, insisting you hang out at his bar all night long to take it up the ass every time one of his hot, humpy friends gets to feeling horny.

. . .

The next night when I went back, Slater, who's actually a bartender at the Mineshaft, it turns out, agreed to sponsor me in if I proved I really could take all his dick up my ass. It took a little effort, but I managed. Then there was last night when Scarface Jesse—yet another Mineshaft bartender—sponsored me in before he went on-duty, though I first had to prove to him I was as good a fuck as was being rumored about.

So here I am again tonight, finishing another joint and just about to open that door and head up those seventeen steps to paradise, praying there'll be someone to sponsor me inside.

But isn't that Cam I see standing at the top of the stairs, looking down at me and rubbing his crotch?

No, I don't think I'll have to worry about getting inside tonight!

MILK BATH

Jason Carpenter

"Oh, yeah," I sighed, weaving my fingers through his dark, curly hair, holding his head firm as I arched my back and slow-fucked his pretty mouth. "Eat my meat, sugar. Drain me. Empty my balls." He cupped my nuts in his hand and milked my load out into his hot, gulping throat. I came until I cried.

Then I woke up with a load of cum soaking through my underwear and the remnants of a boner receding into my groin. Shit. Then I remembered that it was June, high school graduation was two weeks behind me, and I didn't register for college for over two months. Two glorious months of freedom! Life was good!

Mom and Dad were off to work so, when I crawled out of bed just before noon, I had the house to myself. I intended to use my time well. I dropped my stained shorts in the dirty clothes hamper and headed for the backyard with a blanket and a bottle of sunscreen, my cock swinging between my thighs.

Making myself comfortable beside the pool, I swore I was going to get a tan this summer, despite being a pale-skinned redhead.

It was hot. Perspiration pooled in my navel, ran between my hairy thighs and my balls, coursing down the crack of my ass. I stroked my dick and watched it thump until it was ten inches of hardened muscle.

I had no fear of being seen, due to the six-foot-high wooden privacy fence that surrounded the backyard.

My poker stuck almost straight up, pointing at the billowy cumulus clouds overhead. Squirting a dab of the sunscreen into my right palm, I began to stroke my cut meat . . . slowly . . . slowly . . . paying special attention to the dark purple crown.

The boy who had been giving me blowjobs all through school had moved away before graduation, and I was so horny my cods hurt. "Man, I'm gonna cum like a shook-up soda pop!" I said aloud, feeling hot jizz gathering within me.

A sound—a rustle of dried leaves—came out of nowhere, making my cock wither instantly. I froze, listening, then heard it again. This time I also saw a shadowy movement between the slats in the fence on the south side of the yard.

The house on that side had been vacant for months. But someone was over there now, watching me through the fence.

"Who's there?" I called out, flipping a corner of the blanket over my bare pelvis.

A short silence, then, "Uh, I'm looking at this house. It's for sale, you know?" A male voice answered. "Sorry I disturbed you."

I couldn't be certain he had seen me. "Okay, no harm done," I said.

He cleared his throat. "I wouldn't say that. I scared you out of a major boner just as you were about to come."

My heart raced. "You were watching me!"

A pair of hands appeared on the squared-off tops of the fence sections, followed by the stranger's head as he lifted himself up. Oh, gorgeous! I thought, my dream stud come true! He had raven-black hair, slicked back from his forehead, icy blue eyes and a square jaw with a cleft in the chin.

"Yeah, I was watching. Sorry. Would you like me to finish the job for you?" He asked to my astonishment.

I gulped so loudly he probably heard me. "Come on over."

He swung himself easily over the fence. His cut-off shorts and a T-shirt cropped at a level with his dark, rigid nipples showed off a great body—lean but muscular. I guessed him to be in his early twenties. My eyes were automatically drawn to the heavy basket of manna in his shorts.

He came to my blanket and dropped to his knees beside me. "Hi, I'm Greg," he said, nonchalantly whipping the blanket off of me, exposing my meat and balls.

"Hi, there. I'm Jack," I said, holding out my hand.

Instead of shaking my hand, however, he shook my semi-limp shaft, then circled it with his hand and tugged a few times. Almost immediately my cock bulged to a state of readiness. I thought I had fallen asleep in the sun and was having another splendid wet dream. I hoped I wouldn't wake up too soon.

Greg strummed the sensitive underbelly of my cock with feathery finger touches and rubbed my swollen dickhead roughly with his thumb. When I started to squirm and moan he fisted me, ever more rapidly, until I felt the burning jizz erupt up from my nuts, careen through my stiffened sword, then spew in a fountain of creamy gobs over Greg's hand. He milked me dry, as I grunted and strained my hips upward.

Without saying a word, Greg lifted my right leg, resting my ankle on his satiny shoulder. He took my still-hot cum, smeared it over my testicles, and painted my pink pucker with the slippery stuff. I felt his finger prod my asshole and slip past my ass-ring. He finger-fucked me hard, adding fingers until he had three squeezed together, ramming up my chocolate chamber.

I watched, glassy-eyed as he unsnapped and unzipped his shorts and wriggled out of them. His uncut tool arched up toward his belly from the heavy black mat of his pubic hair. It looked like some native totem pole sprouting up from the forest underbrush—sacred and mysterious—an object I could easily worship. He positioned himself between my legs.

"Oh. Let's go inside," I said, "I have rubbers –"

He shot me a sexy smile and held up a condom. "Like American Express Card, Jack—I don't leave home without 'em."

Greg slipped the condom over his throbbing member and withdrew his fingers from my anus. He held them to his nose and smelled my fragrance before guiding his thick man-barb between my buttcheeks, rotating it until he speared through my dark ring. He plunged forward, filling my ass with his hard cock, embedding it deep into my sweet-meat. I entwined my fingers in his ebony hair and pulled his mouth to mine. He Frenched me, his tongue snaking between my teeth in exact rhythm with his pounding fuckmeat reaming out my boyish butthole. I dug my fingers into his hard, bubble-like ass and pulled him closer until he filled my guts, became one with my bowels.

"Oh, yeah!" he squealed, pouring his snowy froth into my deepest recesses, his balls slapping my asscheeks in an ancient tattoo of lust.

I nipped his earlobe and licked his neck until he finished flooding my guts.

He pulled out of me and tossed the rubber aside.

I leaped up and jumped, cannon-ball style, into the sparkling blue water of the swimming pool. My back-splash doused Greg. He jumped in beside me, grabbing at my dick playfully beneath the refreshing water.

We played grab-ass and cooled off for half-an-hour.

I kissed his chest and held his sac in my hand as we floated upright, our toes barely touching the concrete pool bottom. "I'm sure glad you came along," I told him.

"I'm glad I got to you before you wasted your load."

"Are you seriously thinking about buying the house next door?" I asked, hope filling my soul.

"If I wasn't before, I sure am now. Shit, man, you're such a tender young fucker I wouldn't be able to get you off of my mind."

His kisses were hungry, passionate.

My dong became filled with blood, standing out from my pelvis, pressing against Greg's flaccid hose. He ducked beneath the water's surface and took my hot nuts between his lips for several seconds before surfacing. "Hang on," he said, hoisting himself from the pool. He picked up his shorts and shook them.

Another condom fell to the grass.

Greg picked it up and slipped back into the pool beside me. His head disappeared below the water again. He rolled the rubber over my dick, all the way to my tingling cock hairs, then engulfed my boy-meat with his generous mouth. He bobbed his head, taking me into his throat, suckling me expertly. When he could no longer hold his breath he surfaced.

"Get up on the edge of the pool and let your legs dangle over," he instructed. "So I don't drown!"

I did as he suggested, balancing my ass on the rim of the pool, bracing myself with locked elbows behind me, palms on the deck.

Greg sucked my purple-headed hammer, alternately licking and biting gently until I was ready to pop. I threw my head back and closed my eyes against the glare of the sun. "Eat it, Greg—swallow me whole!"

I leaned my weight forward so I could use one hand at the back of his neck to drag him closer, straining to stuff my whole sex-stick into his velvety gullet. Humping and thrusting I fucked his pretty face with all my being.

My balls contracted into hard stones as the flash of seed sped from them to squirt in copious gobbets into Greg's hungry maw.

He sucked me off until the crown of my cock was an enflamed, tender knob of sensitive flesh.

We crawled weakly back to the blanket and lay in each other's arms, regaining our strength. I had never felt this way about a guy—wanting only to fuck him and be fucked by him, over and over again, as many times as humanly possible.

We each filled our hands with the other's sex equipment and let the sun bake us.

I snuggled against Greg's biceps. "You live alone?" I asked him, afraid that he might be living with someone—that I might be only a one-time fuck for him.

"Unh, uh," he grunted, breaking my heart. "My wife," he added.

I sat up, feeling a frown crease my forehead. "Your wife?"

"Yeah. Strange, huh?"

My lower lip began to tremble. "I... I thought maybe you and I—"

"Hey!" He said, hearing the tears in my voice. "It's not like that. My wife comes from a well-to-do society family. They would shit if they knew she was a lesbian—cut off her money."

"Oh, I see."

"We knew each other in high school," he went on, "and got along well. She came up with the idea that we could marry each other for the convenience of it then fuck whomever we pleased. She gives me a very generous allowance for playing the loving husband at social functions," he said, lifting his eyebrows.

A weight was removed from my heart and my cock.

"Then we can see each other?" I pouted.

"Count on it, Red."

"Not nearly as red as I'm going to be if we don't get out of the sun," I said, feeling my flesh tingle uncomfortably.

We policed the area, picking up the blanket and the limp rubbers that looked like dead jellyfish in the grass, and went inside.

The air-conditioning made goose bumps on my sun-baked body when I walked into the house. I cringed when Greg touched my shoulder.

"You need to put something on that sunburn," he said,

frowning. "Milk is supposed to be good, I've heard. Get some and let's go to the bathroom—I'll put it on you."

Cold milk in hand, I led Greg to the hall bath. "Sit in the tub so it won't be so messy," he suggested.

I obeyed. Sitting there with my knees drawn up to my chest, I felt like a child as Greg poured the milk on a washcloth and patted it gently against my flesh. I shivered. "Are you sure this works?"

"Uh, it works for me," he said in a strange tone.

I looked up at him. He sat on the edge of the tub, still naked, and his dick was a dark, wrinkle-topped flag, hard and beautifully arched.

I took that solid staff in my hand and rubbed it against my shoulder where a thin layer of milk smudged my flesh. Turning slightly, I guided Greg's throbbing meat between my chest and inner arm. He started a slow back and forth stroke, fucking my armpit.

"I've never done this before," he said, thrusting harder as I clenched my arm closer against my side, capturing his fuck-rod in a fleshy vise.

My free hand groped his nuts, rolling them together, tugging at his tight sac. "Oh, oh, ahhh," he gasped, and I felt his steaming cum coat my side, stream over my ribs.

He finished my "milk" bath using his own sweet cum to take the burn out of my skin.

Two weeks later, Greg, and his wife, Stephanie, closed on the house next door and moved in shortly thereafter.

Anyone know how to put a revolving door in a fence?

MAKING MARK

Tony Anthony

"I feel like it now," Dave said. "Where can we go?"

"What about the old shack in your backyard?" I said.

When Dave and I wanted a bit of action in private we usually rode out into the woods, back to the good places we had known since boyhood; but my mountain bike had recently been stolen so I couldn't go far. Dave lived with his mother and brother in an old house on a big plot. Back in the yard there was an old shack, which they used these days to store household junk.

'What if Mark comes back and sees us?'

"It's getting dark. If we leave the light off he won't go there," I said. "Why should he?"

"I don't know," Dave said.

"You worry too much," I said. "It'll be all right."

I brushed my hand across my fly to catch his attention. I have a good length and there's usually a bulge to please the discerning eye. I could usually rely on it to turn Dave on hard.

I wanted to fuck him and I knew that if I did all the right things he would let me mount him. If I got the approach wrong —well, he could be difficult and try to fuck me.

He looked at my bulge and I could see the thoughts in his mind. "Oh, yeah, let's do it," he said.

The old shack was dark inside and smelled of still air. Evening light was coming in through a window so we could see well enough. We dragged a big old armchair closer to the window. I put my arms around Dave's broad shoulders and kissed him while I ran my hands down his back and onto his butt. Not being really that good-looking myself, male beauty is something I have an eye for; and believe me, Dave was good to see. He pumped a lot of iron and had the muscles to show for it. I had always been tall for my age, and slim, and couldn't keep up with him.

"Take my shirt off," he said now.

I lifted it off his shoulders. "Gimme those muscles," I said, kissing his pecs and running my hands over his bulging biceps.

Dave was cute all right, but he was nothing compared to his kid brother. Mark was small and neat, nose turned up like a youngster's, lips like a cupid's bow. Trouble was, Mark knew how very attractive he was.

Dave was the nice guy, steady and good; Mark was a nasty little shit, dabbling in crime, behaving in ways that totally contradicted his angelic looks. At school he got a girl pregnant and denied all knowledge of it. He treated Dave and most other people with open contempt.

Dave doted on Mark. I had always wanted a brother and I could understand why he loved him. Dave said the little guy hated being small, and we guessed Mark was trying to compensate for feeling small by being something in crime.

A bulge was showing in Dave's pants now, so I bent and kissed it. It always turns him on and I heard him gasp.

He's got a good, thick rod and I could see it moving, swelling and angling up his groin. He tried to unzip his fly and I pushed his hand away.

"Open it," he said. "Get it out."

"When I'm ready," I said.

"You bastard," he said.

"That's me," I said. I pressed my lips to the bulge and felt it hard as a rock against my lips. With one hand on his butt I massaged the big dick with my other hand and kissed the hair showing above his belt. He's got a knock-out body, did I tell you?

"You're torturing me," he said.

"You've noticed," I said. Suddenly I wanted him very urgently and I stood and hugged him, kissing him deep, mouth to mouth.

"Take my pants off," he said.

"Later." I put both hands on his butt and felt the big muscles tense and hard. He's got a classic male butt and I love it.

"Come on," he said. "Fuck you."

"No," I said. "It's fuck you. Trust me."

He got his pants open at the waist and I knew he could beat me for strength any time so I zipped his fly open and peeled his pants off. His rod flipped out and stood like a soldier. It always blows my mind to see it stand, so good and strong and male.

Dave tried to get my jeans off but I sat in the old chair and pulled him down onto my lap. My dick is a good length and it got all twisted and bent between his butt and my jeans. I struggled and eventually got it into a position where no bones in it were being broken, though I couldn't be sure by the feel of it.

His dick was sticking up just right for my hand. I played with it, rolling the head between my fingertips and feeling the length of the hard shaft.

Sitting there with the evening light coming through the window, my buddy so close to me, it was truly great.

"Finger me," he said, parting his legs. It looked like I was going to get what I wanted. He maneuvered himself and I got my hand to the hairy cleft in his butt.

"We're lucky to have this," he said. "You know?"

"Yes," I said. "We're very lucky to have each other."

"Show me your lucky dick," he said.

I got my clothes off and Dave went down on me. He likes my length—says it's as good as having muscles. While he was bending I put my hand on his bare butt and felt how good it was. I got a fingertip on his spot and rubbed it the way he likes. "I want to fuck you, Dave," I said.

"Mmm-mmm," he said, his mouth full with my dick.

"Now," I said. "I want you now."

"Uh, hmm," he mumbled.

Was he saying no? I pressed with my fingertip and felt it begin to slide in.

"Now, Dave," I said. "I've got to do it now."

"Mmmmmm."

I put my hands on his head and lifted him off my dick. He wrapped his arms around me and kissed my nipples. I ran my hand over the swelling curves of his butt—they were beautiful enough to die for. "Come on, Babe," I said. "Let's do it."

He bent over the chair, presenting his bare butt to me. His balls were hanging in a way so tempting I had to cup my hands around for a while, feeling the firm stones slipping easily around inside. His hairy cleft was promising me something I wanted really urgently and I lubed his hole gently. When I lubed my length the sensation nearly made me come. His hole resisted my dick for a time before opening and letting my length slide in. I rested it in there, letting him feel my groin against his butt. He arched his back lifting his shoulders up in a way that also raised his butt—ready for fucking.

I reckoned he was mine now. A charge zipped through my dick.

"Christ," I said. "You're good to me, Dave."

"Yes, I am," he said.

"I love you, man."

"I know you do," he said.

"Christ, I love you," I said.

"Are you going to fuck me?" he asked. "Or make a speech?"

"You've got no soul," I said.

"I've got a hole," he said. "Remember it?"

I eased back until the head of my dick was against his sphincter muscle. I could feel the ring gripping. Then I pushed the whole, gloriously long thing sliding back into him.

"That's right," he said. He was trying to sound real cool but his voice shook a bit. "You haven't forgotten."

I began fucking him in a steady rhythm.

"That's so good," he gasped. "That's ... really ... good."

"Tell me about it," I said.

The pleasure in my dick wiped out any more words. Every fraction of slide was generating electric currents that were gripping me in rising tensions. Going in was fantastic. Drawing back was electric. It made me push forward again. And that made me pull back to get more. Then I had to go in again. And that made me ....

I reached under Dave and felt his dick. It was like a column of solid rock. Through his dick I could feel some of the sex gripping his body. Suddenly I wanted his dick in my mouth. I pulled out of him and went down on his dick. In my mouth it was pure ecstasy. Then I wanted to be up his butt again so I left his dick and quickly mounted him, pushing his hips down with my hands so I could spread my legs and really begin fucking him fast.

Dave was going, "Uh, uh, uh."

Each time the full length of my dick went into him it made him grunt. Hearing him made me start grunting too. Both of us were breathing like Olympic wrestlers. I pulled him back against myself so I had the satisfaction of feeling my groin thump against his butt with every thrust. My back was straightening, lifting my head and shoulders. I was standing tall, pushing down on Dave's hips, lifting myself to slam harder against him.

I was ramming fast, making his gasps come quicker.

I could feel the tension in myself increasing. Watching Dave moving below me I knew he was loading up with come. His back started bowing. Reaching under him with both hands I gripped his dick and held him hard while I was humping him. My orgasm was close and I was fighting it off.

Dave was making little whimpering cries and that set me off doing the same.

"No, no, no," he gasped.

"Uh, uh, uh," I was going.

"No—no. Please," he said. "Please!"

I couldn't speak.

"No. Oh, no," he whimpered. "I can't. I just can't take it. Oh, no. Please."

It was really turning me on! He always did this sort of thing. It was the increasing tension of his approaching orgasm that sort of scared him. I knew he was all right. I was fucking him harder. My back was straightening again, lifting my head and shoulders. My hands pushed down on the back of Dave's pelvis, lifting myself. Then my spine was arching backwards. I was looking upwards, my mouth open, air rushing through.

"Ah," I sighed. "Aaaaaahhhhh."

He began bucking under me, lifting his shoulders and thrusting with his pelvis. He straightened up. I gripped his erection. It felt enormous in my hand. I felt spunk squirting out of his dick. His anus was opening and closing quickly.

My own dick was locked in rigid tension and my body began jerking in violent spasms. Something like white heat was spurting out of my dick in quick shots. I had my arms wrapped around Dave and we staggered like wrestlers. I lifted him off his feet before my legs suddenly collapsed and he was supporting himself on the back of the chair again. I leaned on his back while the last of my spunk discharged into his colon.

For a while I didn't know where I was. My mind was reeling,

my nerves scorching in the afterburn of the orgasm. Waves of ecstasy whipped through me and only slowly diminished. My eyes opened in the darkening room.

We stayed like that while the tension slowly eased out of us.

"That was some fuck, Dave," I murmured.

"Fantastic," he said.

I drew my dick slowly out of him.

"Look at that," he said, pointing.

His spunk was liberally smeared over his dick and pubic hair where my hands had spread it.

I collapsed into the chair and Dave sat on my lap again. We seemed to have been on a long trip since he was there earlier. We kissed and relaxed. It felt really good to just be there together.

The door opened and the light was switched on.

For a while it was like a still photograph. In the doorway stood Mark with a mountain bike. He blinked at us. We blinked at him.

"What are you cunts doing?" Mark said.

Both Dave and I were naked and had semi-hards on. It must have been pretty obvious what we were doing.

"We're sunbathing," I said. "What does it look like?"

"Fuckin' faggots," he said. "I always knew it."

"You're a genius, Mark," I said. "Sheer brilliance simply radiates from your nasty little mind."

"Don't get tough with me, you creep," he said.

"Why not?" I asked. "Will you get someone to beat me up for you?"

"Believe it," he said, but he seemed to be losing confidence. Something was worrying him. He looked down at the bike he was holding, uncertain whether to come in or leave. He looked at me and then seemed to make up his mind. He pushed the bike in and leaned it against half a dozen others we could now see in the storage area.

One of the bikes was mine! I recognized colored tape I had put around some of the cables.

"You've been ripping off bikes," I said.

"Fuck off," he said. "Anyway, you two are breaking the law. I'll tell the cops."

"We're over age and doing it in private," I said. "You're the one the cops want."

He started foulmouthing me. It was sad to see such a pretty face involved in arrogant, blustering threats. When he started on Dave and threatened to tell their mother I got really angry.

"Shut up, you nasty little bastard," I said. I picked up a baseball bat and made to hit him. I was amazed when he folded immediately, but I'm a lot bigger than him and I guess I must have looked really mad. He sort of cowered away from me, turning aside and bending down. His perfect little butt was showing tight in his jeans and it turned me on real bad. Suddenly I wanted to fuck him. It was a colossal surge and I could feel my dick hardening fast.

Dave would be devastated if his mother knew he was gay, and I thought I could see a way of shutting up his little brother.

"I'll do a deal with you, Mark," I said. "I won't tell the cops about the bikes, if you get it on with us now."

"What do you mean?" he said.

"Come on," I said. "I've always thought you were gay under that tough act. What do you choose? Cops or cocks?"

Dave put his arms around his little brother and kissed his face. Mark hesitated. Dave kissed him again and ran his hands down over Mark's butt. Mark blinked behind his long eyelashes. Dave laid his hand on Mark's crotch and gently squeezed.

He let us strip his clothes off, and his body was as beautiful as his face. Everything was in perfect proportion with his height. He looked like a boy ten years younger except for his dick—it was a man-sized weapon, no doubt about it. He seemed to be unable to stop staring at Dave's naked muscles, and his dick started pumping itself up.

"I'm only doing this because you guys made me," Mark said.

Dave and I smiled.

"You dick's giving you away," Dave said. "You're loving every second of it."

"No," Mark said.

Dave went down on his brother and the little guy's eyes widened. His pelvis started jerking and for a while it looked as though he was ready to come straightaway. His butt was tense and the curves were unbelievably beautiful. I caressed them and knelt behind him and kissed each gorgeous globe. He was clearly on the verge of coming so Dave and I stood back from him until the tension eased.

Mark clearly liked his brother's muscles but he saw my dick, which was then standing really big and long. He reached to touch my dick and then bent and put his mouth over it. For a guy who behaved like a straight he was learning really fast. In no time he was sucking real good.

Dave got his hands on the beautiful butt and stroked the groove. Then he reached under to hold Mark's dick.

The little guy stood up and we saw the full size of his weapon. Maybe his small body made it look extra big but it seemed really enormous. Dave and I both went to hold it and we were sort of pushing each other's hands away to get at it; so we stood side by side and held our own dicks and slid our hands along them, and Mark did the same for himself.

He was like a guy in a trance and I was expecting him to bring himself through into an orgasm, but he put one hand behind his back and began rubbing his butt.

He was so attractive I suddenly wanted to fuck him and I would have fought Dave off if he had tried to get in ahead of me. I lubed my length and tried to get a finger into that perfect little butt. I was so excited my hands were shaking. His hole was very tight. I made him bend forward and tried again. My finger went in but he stood up clinging to his brother, his face against Dave's chest.

"Bend down," I said. "It opens the hole."

He bent forward and put his arms around Dave's waist.

Dave guided his brother to suck his cock and I worked at the soft spot. My dick was absolutely rigid with desire for that neat little butt. I got one finger in and pressed for two. Mark gasped and moved his butt.

"I'll stop him if you want me to," Dave said to his brother.

Thanks, I thought. That's just what I need, Dave.

"No, No," Mark said. "I want it. Let him do it."

Dave and I glanced at each other. I worked two fingers into him and spread them. My dick was practically roaring to get into him and I had to force myself to not get the head on his soft spot and simply force it in.

"Suck me, Mark," Dave said. And when his brother had his

mouth on the dick he reached under him and touched the monster. "Just let it happen," Dave went on. "Relax and let him fuck you. It's great."

I put my dick in the cleft and tried a push. It didn't go in but I rubbed it against his hole to let him feel.

I got two fingers in again and spread them wide as I pulled them out. After a couple more tries I got three fingers into him. I couldn't wait any longer.

"I'm going to fuck you, Mark," I said. "This it it."

"Are you all right, Mark?" his brother asked.

A muffled mumble came from the region of Dave's dick. It was probably a yes. Either way I wasn't waiting any longer. I set the head of my dick against the little hole and pushed. Nothing happened. I pushed again. Nothing. My need to fuck him was driving me crazy. He was too beautiful. He was bending down for me, inviting me to fuck him. He wanted it. I wanted it. I needed it very urgently. I craved it. I had to have it.

I gripped his hips and pulled him hard back onto my dick. The head slipped away and I put it back in place and pushed hard again.

I suppose I should have gone back to using my fingers and stretching him gradually but by now I was seeing things in a red haze. You little bastard, I thought. Fucking well let me in or I'll smash you into a pulp. I balled my right hand in a fist and punched him twice in the ribs. He grunted and twisted sideways, his mouth still on his brother's dick.

And my dick was in! He must have opened up completely. My dick, the whole length, just vanished into him.

He was so beautiful, and I had tried so hard for so long, the sudden entry nearly made go into orgasm. I was exultant. The prettiest guy I had ever seen was bending before me, my dick was all the way into him, and the nicest guy I had ever known was holding him for me.

I started fucking slow and steady, glorying in the sensation of my long shaft tunnelling his colon. I pulled his hips back against me and pushed extra hard, reaching with the head of my dick as far as it would go. It felt really good to be so deep into him.

I leaned back, arching my spine, letting my dick rest inside him. I think Dave must have envied me.

"Go on," he said. "Fuck him."

There was a light in Dave's eye—a look I hadn't seen before. I realized that Dave had probably yearned to do this ever since childhood and his growing realization of a strong sexual love for males. It must have been really tough growing up with a beautiful brother who you couldn't touch.

I looked into Dave's eyes, and pulled my dick out of his brother's butt.

"Come on," I said. "You do it."

Dave looked at me.

"I'll hold him," I said.

Dave moved around to stand behind his brother. For a long while he just looked at the bent back and the bare butt. Then he grasped the shaft of his dick and placed its head in the cleft.

Mark looked back at Dave. Neither of the brothers spoke a word, but you could sense that behind the look was a long past with a lot in it. I half expected Mark to make some sort of trouble but he just bent forward and braced his shoulder against my bare thigh.

Still looking at his brother's back Dave simply pushed his dick in. The little guy's hole must have opened for him.

I knew this was brother business and I was partly excluded. They were not against me but, compared to them, I was an outsider.

Dave looked at me and I nodded. Slowly and almost reverently he began pumping his dick in his brother's butt. It was beautiful to see—something special between two guys who were extra close. For a while the differences between them were unimportant.

Dave's thrusts picked up speed as the passion began gripping him. He stared at Mark's back and began really fucking him.

Mark was making little gasping sounds and, for a while, I thought he might even be crying. He was facing the floor and I could not see his eyes. I wished his head were a bit higher. I wanted my dick to be in something and his cupid's bow lips seemed a great idea.

My dick was as stiff as a stick and I put my fingers to work on it. With my other hand I cradled and squeezed my balls.

Dave was getting more excited as he pumped his shaft into

the rounded butt. I had never watched him fucking before this. He was a fine sight, muscles working, hands gripping the hips in front of him. At each withdrawal I could see some of the shaft of his dick before it disappeared again into the gap.

Below me Mark was gasping or whimpering and I began to feel a sort of frenzy taking over in me. My hips gave an involuntary thrust as the base of my dick suddenly loaded with semen.

I began speeding my hand along the shaft of my dick. Dave must have noticed it because he speeded up too. He bent forward and was really working hard on his brother.

I wished it were my dick up that sweet little butt. I promised myself an opportunity in the future and, in the meantime, I was glad to see my pal Dave having a great fuck. He was in another world, moving faster and faster. He was breathing through his mouth and his eyes were closing as the thrills zinged through his nervous system.

Watching his excitement increasing got me moving faster. Suddenly my back straightened and I was standing tall, my dick sticking out like a long pole from my groin, the head turning purple with passion.

Dave reached for my dick but had to put his hand back on Mark to keep his balance. My orgasm was close and it looked like Dave was not too far off his.

I wanted to help Dave somehow, help him through his orgasm, hold him or do something to make it good for him; but I was fighting to control myself.

I gasped out a big breath and began sucking in air. The tension in my dick was like an agony. I wanted to hold on until the other guys were coming. It seemed right somehow.

I knew that when I came my spunk was going to shoot over Mark's back and onto Dave's chest. I could see that and it seemed good.

Dave was oblivious to the world, I guessed. His mind would be totally overwhelmed by the sensations burning his dick and the awareness of sexually possessing his brother. It must have been truly wonderful after all those years of wanting. I saw him looking at my dick, staring as my hand flashed along it making it curve upwards, skin over the head gleaming, tight with the pressure building inside.

My gut muscles suddenly tensed, making me bend forward. I straightened up again pushing my dick out as far as it could possibly go. It was reaching for orgasm now and I could not hold it back much longer.

Dave was working like a madman, slamming his hips against his brother's butt.

"Hah, uh, uh, uh, " I was going.

"Oh, yeah," Dave gasped.

Below us Mark was suddenly shaking and twitching.

I guessed he was coming, squirting his semen on the floor. I could hold mine no longer and suddenly it shot out a long rope of white along Mark's back and onto Dave's chest. It shot again in another line on the bent back and a loop on Dave.

His eyes closed and his face screwed itself into an open-mouthed, silent roar of passion and pain. He was coming like a steam engine, ramming his rod in and out in blurring speed. The base of my dick loaded up again and shot another, shorter jet of spunk, another, and another. Mark stood up and I saw his dick, as massive as ever, dripping a long line of white to the floor. His eyes were wide open, staring unfocussed in wonder. It was probably the greatest sexual experience he had ever undergone. He looked at my dick and put his mouth to it, taking the last of the spunk. He stood up again.

Dave's arms went around his brother and held him tight, kissing the back of his head and neck.

My legs were shaky and I sat down in the chair. Mark surprised me by sitting on my lap. Dave sat on the arm of the chair and held onto his brother. We stayed like that while the passion drained from our minds, and our heartbeats returned to normal.

"Jesus Christ," Mark whispered.

Nobody else spoke.

'Why doesn't somebody say something?' Mark asked.

"You were fantastic," Dave said.

"The whole thing was fantastic," I said. "Let's not spoil it with a lot of crap."

"I only thought," Mark said, "that maybe you guys were not happy with how I did."

It was sad really. Here was a little guy who always thought people looked down on him. You know what I mean. He thought being small meant people despised you.

I put my hand on his shoulder. "Believe your brother, Mark. You were perfect."

"You mean that?"

"I want you to come in with Dave and me," I said. "The only thing that would please me more would be for you to give up all that crime shit. You're too good to waste your life on that crap."

"That's right," Dave said. "Give it up, Mark. Please. Be one of the boys with us. We love you."

There was a long silence.

"I don't know," Mark said, getting to his feet and putting his clothes on. "I'll think about it. I just want you guys to respect me."

It must have been hard for him to say that, admitting his need.

"We love you and want you, Mark," I said. "And we'll respect you while you're honest."

At the door he paused and looked back at us in the chair.

"Thanks, you guys," he said. "I'll think about it. See ya' around." He left and closed the door.

I looked to see how Dave was taking it, and he was looking at me.

"I think he'll do it," Dave said.

It was hard for me. I could see how much more he loved the little guy; but I guessed there would perhaps be a place for me and, anyway, I wanted Dave to be happy.

"I think he'll do it too," I said. "I hope he does. He sure loved it."

MY NEW MASTER

Tony Anthony

The blacksmith had knocked me down a few times so I was dusty as well as bruised and a little bloody. When I got to the river and my usual swimming hole I decided to make a good job of washing myself so I took off all my ragged working clothes, and sat down in the water. With luck the blacksmith would leave me alone for a while.

I had snared two rabbits and had them cooking before a fire on the grassy river bank. They might console me for my pains before I returned to the village.

The day was sunny and warm but the water felt cold on my bare skin. I bathed my aching face and felt the bruises. My knees and elbows were grazed and I was so absorbed in carefully washing the dirt out I did not hear the horses' approach. When I looked up there was a knight on the bank looking down at me from his horse.

Living all my life in our little village I had heard about knights but never seen one. I stared at him in silence.

"Well, lad," he said. "Do you not speak?"

He was much younger than I imagined a knight to be; but he was heavily armed and had the self-confidence of a man of rights. He was handsome, with fair hair and grey eyes. His horse was huge, a real warhorse, and his armour and goods were on a pack-horse behind him.

"Stand up," he ordered.

I did not wish to stand up. The cold water had made my cock stiffen and I did not know whether to hold my hands in front of it or be a man and let it be seen.

"Get up when I order you," the knight said.

He could kill me if he wished and nobody would dare to complain, nor would they want to.

I stood up and let my cock be seen. "I meant no disrespect, sire,"

"Who are you?"

"I am in thrall to the blacksmith, sire. My village is back in the forest."

"How came you by the cuts and bruises? Been fighting, have you?"

"My master beats me, sire."

"You're a strong boy. Do you hit him back?"

I felt I was more than a boy, but did not want to argue with him.

"He would throw me out, sire, if I hit him. I would have no work and would starve in winter."

"You would starve indeed," a voice came from the edge of the forest. My master appeared, his hairy face scowling. "Get you back to the forge or I'll thrash you soundly."

The knight rode his horse splashing across the river. "Wait now, Smith. I would have the boy stay."

My master glared at him. "He's in thrall to me. I say where he goes."

It was a stupid and insolent thing to say and the knight sat suddenly taller in his saddle. He rode his horse to where the smith stood. With one smooth movement of his arm he drew his sword and lashed at the man; who fell immediately to the ground. My heart lurched and I stared, expecting to see gushing blood.

"That's with the flat of my blade," the knight said. "Try me again and you might feel the point of it. Now get you gone, you ill-mannered lout."

My master shambled away, pausing at the forest's edge to glare back at me.

"I'll join you," the knight said to me, smiling. "What's the water like? As cold as a woman's heart, no doubt."

I stared at him, the only man I had ever seen best my arrogant master. The knight had saved me from another beating, and now he calmly stripped himself naked and walked into the river to sit down and look at me.

"Best close your mouth," he said. "Or a fly may enter. Come here."

I moved closer to him.

Sitting in the water his head was near my cock and he gazed at it. "There's something I like about you, lad."

I was astonished. He seemed to like my cock and be totally unafraid to say so. There were men in the village who sometimes looked at my handsome face in a certain way, but few would dare do more than that, fearing the gossips.

"Sit here," the knight said. "Next to me." With his hand he scooped water and bathed a bruise under my eye. Then he turned his attention to my grazed knee and in no time I felt his fingers close around my cock. "Do you dislike my doing this?"

"No, sire."

"I thought so," he said. "I could read your eyes when I first saw you. You have a comely face and a good body. Have men told you so?"

I shook my head.

He smiled and put a hand behind my neck and kissed me on the lips. "Those rabbits on the fire: they're yours?"

"Yes, sire."

"Will you share them with me?"

I blinked. "Of course, sire. I would be glad to."

"Good. Let's eat," he said.

When he emerged from the water, his gleaming body white and lean, his cock was standing, arching out long and thin. He seemed not in the slightest way embarrassed but sat with me on the sunlit grass and let me tear off pieces of rabbit for him. When he asked I told him I had snared them.

"Well, lad," he said. "I can fight with sword and dagger, dance at court, and indeed address the king himself correctly. But I cannot snare and cook rabbits. I envy your talents and skills."

I smiled at his kindness, and enjoyed our nakedness together and the sharing of my poor offerings. He looked often at my bare body, and seemed to like it.

"Can you ride a horse?" he asked.

"I can sire, and handle them for shoeing."

When we had finished the rabbits we drank from the river and he took me by the hand and led me into the forest. Pausing beneath an oak he put his arms around me and kissed me on the mouth. "You're a handsome lad. I swear I've never seen a more comely boy."

I could scarcely believe what was happening. I had often wished to be loved by a man, but it had been a hopeless yearning. Who would love a ragged serf, in thrall to a pig of a village blacksmith?

The young knight pulled me to him and I felt his cock hard

against my bare skin. It was all so much what I wanted I felt my mind reeling. When he fell to his knees before me and took my cock into his mouth I could only stare at his fair head and revel in the amazing sensations in my groin. He sucked greedily at me and kissed the shaft and head of it so passionately I was soon about to shoot the white. I did not know what to do. If it went from my cock into his mouth he might be furiously angry, take it as an insult and kill me. If I took my cock out of his mouth without his permission that too might anger him.

I placed my hands on his head and stroked his beautiful hair. "Sire. It is about to come and I do not know what to do."

He took his mouth from my cock and looked up at me. Then he stood next to me and put his hand on my cock and rubbed it gently. "Let it come, lad. Let it flow full."

With great relief I relaxed and watched as the white spat copiously from my cock, again and again, dropping heavily on the summer grass. My body was jerking and twitching and he held me firmly until all was spent. Then he put his arms around my shoulders and held me tightly to his chest.

Having had such sweet relief with him I wondered what I should do in return. Would it be offensive to do what he had done? What would he do if a slave such as I presumed to kiss his noble cock? And what if I did nothing?

The long shaft of his cock stood out proudly, its red head beginning to emerge from the white skin. I yearned to be closer to it, touching it. Carefully I bent and put my lips to the hair that grew so abundantly on his groin, ready to find myself being beaten for insolence. He gently grasped my head and placed the end of his beautiful cock against my lips. I opened my mouth and let the head enter. It was the finest bliss I had ever felt. It was such a marvel I wanted to look into his eyes to see whether it was all real.

I stood and looked up into his grey eyes. They seemed solemn and kindly.

"What, lad?" he asked.

"I cannot believe all this, sire," I said. "It is like a dream."

He smiled and pushed me gently down and I took his wonderful cock again into my mouth. While I sucked his long shaft my hands went behind him and held his soft backside. It was smooth and delightful. I caressed it over and over again. When I felt it suddenly tensing hard in quick jerks he took my head in his hands and raised me.

His cock was standing hard now, arching back on itself like a bow, the red head all out of the skin and straining upward. I wanted to grasp it and work it as he had done mine but he put his own hand to it. I was disappointed at not being allowed to touch it but he held me with one arm around my shoulders while I stood next to him watching his wonderful, magic sword preparing itself. His strong fingers were digging into my bare shoulder and his legs trembling as though they were about to collapse.

He paused for a moment as though waiting for something. I saw the muscles in his belly standing out like ropes. Then suddenly his hips jerked forward and his cock delivered a long stream of white. For a while it was a continuous stream, not spurting the way mine had. I heard him gasp like a man struck suddenly with pain and when I looked at his face his mouth was twisted and his eyes tight closed. His whole body trembled.

In a while it was over. His cock was still stiff but more at peace. His eyes opened and he smiled again.

"Let us sit by the river a while," he said. "You are a good lad. I knew you would be when I saw you. I thank you."

I felt embarrassed. "I'm sorry. I thank you sire. It was a great pleasure, truly."

"Enough of words for a while," he said. "Let us lie in the sun."

We lay for a while, in silence except for the summer birdsong in the trees. The peace was like nothing I had felt before. It seemed too good to be true that this wonderful man had come my way, had come to the aid of a worthless orphan and given him such pleasure.

The young knight lay on his side with his back to me and I gazed at the smooth, white swells of his backside. I wondered if I would ever see such a beautiful sight again. In a while he rolled over and looked at my cock. His fingers toyed with my balls and then the big member.

"Have you ever fucked a man?" he asked.

I was astonished. "No sire."

He looked into my eyes and smiled, saying, "Would you like to?"

"I, well, er...yes, sire, I think I would."

"Good. In my saddle bag there is a slab of grease. Bring it here." He greased my cock and I stared in wonder as he knelt and greased his arse, pushing his fingers in and then wiping them on the grass.

"Right," he said, looking at me. "Come on and fuck me."

Again I could scarcely believe what was happening. Yet there he was on his knees before me, and lowering his shoulders while his bent arse bared its curves to the sky and to me. What I needed to do was clear. I knelt behind him and presented the end of my cock to the gap. When I pushed it was as I feared—my cock would not enter him.

"Push harder," he said. "Come on. Get up and push down hard."

I did as he said.

"Hold my hips," he said. "Pull yourself into me."

I did so and felt the point of my cock parting the hole.

When my cock slid suddenly into his arse I thought I would die with pleasure; but I did not and soon I was fucking steadily.

"That's right," he gasped. "That is good."

He seemed to be in pain and I was not surprised. My cock is not small and I had always imagined it was too big to enter a man's arse. "Am I hurting you, sire?"

"Yes, you oaf. Your cock is huge."

I stopped fucking him.

"Go on," he said. "Get on with it. Fuck me."

And get on with it I did. Fucking him on the green grass by the river, looking around at the familiar trees and the blue sky above, and seeing myself wondering at what they were witnessing. I had never imagined such thrilling ecstasy as was then racing through my body.

"By the gods you're big," the knight said.

"What shall I do, when it comes?" I asked.

"Let it come of course," he said. "Let it come within. Is it close?"

"It will come soon, sire," I said. "If you are ready."

"Yes, yes," he said. "Fuck me hard. Now."

"Yes sire," I said. The plunging of my cock was faster now.

I felt as though I was running downhill. Going faster and faster. Unable to stop.

He raised his head and arched his back, lifting his arse to my groin. I looked at my cock thrusting into the cleft in his white arse. The smoothness and speed of its movement was wonderful to see.

My body was being gripped by a burning excitement spreading from my cock to my groin and on into my belly and on again over all and entering every part of me. I lifted my face to the sky and knew my eyes were nearly closed. My breath was hissing through my clenched teeth. I seemed to be losing my mind. Faster and faster my cock was plunging into him; I had no control over it. It was fucking him whether I wished to or not, but I did wish. I wished it to go on and on, but the pain of my fucking was spreading right through my body. I wanted to stop it—wanted to hold it back from burning me, but it would not stop. And now it was becoming more. And more. And more.

"Oh, god," I sobbed as though I had to weep.

"Yes," said the knight, bowed before me. "Do it now. Do it hard. Harder, harder."

"No," I whimpered. Then it was all coming. Heat was issuing through my cock, running into him, burning me, hurting me. I closed my eyes and tried to control the pain, but there was no stopping it, and it poured from me. I could feel it around my cock deep inside him, my cock slipping in it, sliding and thrusting while my mind whirled as though I were drunk and falling, whirling and falling. And slowly ceasing to whirl and fall. Stopping.

In a while it was over. I blinked my eyes and saw the knight's beautiful white back before me. He was still. Resting like me. I seemed to remember hearing him calling out in passion as I had.

I sank back on my heels, my cock pulling out of him. I yearned to touch his beautiful cock and balls so, greatly daring, I held them in my hand. His cock was still very hard and urgent. I circled my fingers around it and rubbed its length. I heard him gasp and sigh and then his cock was throbbing and pulsing in my hand and his white was running through my fingers and I was spreading it along the long shaft of his beautiful cock and he was happy that I was doing it. We were close then, closer than I had ever felt to anyone. For a while it was as though we were brothers.

My wonderful knight lay on his back, an arm across his eyes, saying nothing. I wondered whether I had done some wrong. I hoped more than anything I had ever hoped before, that I had done nothing wrong. I looked at my strong cock, slackening now and a trail of white coming from its lips.

"Sire," I said. "Was it well with you?"

"Indeed it was, country boy," he said. "It was well." We bathed in the river and then I gathered some berries and we sat on the grass and ate.

"We seem to like each other," the knight said.

"Thank you sire," I said.

"Would you be my squire?" he asked.

I was struck dumb.

As a knight's squire I would travel with him. I would see towns and cities. I might even see the sea that people spoke of. I would be with a man I loved. I would work for him, serving him.

"Well?" he asked.

"I would die to be your squire," I said. "But I know nothing of how to do it."

"That's no matter," he said. "I would tell you what to do. But I am a poor knight. I have no money, or very little. I could not pay you."

"I care nothing for money, sire," I said.

"Good. That's settled then. Have you anything in the village to bring with you?"

"A few clothes sire. My longbow and a knife I made for myself."

I got up behind him on his magnificent horse and, with the pack-horse trailing, we rode into the village. People stared, amazed at the familiar wretched slave riding behind a knight. At the smith's house I slid off the horse and fetched my few belongings.

"Where d'you think you're going?" the smith growled.

"He's coming with me," the knight said. "He is my squire."

"He's my property," the smith said. "I have fed him since he was a boy. If you want him you must pay."

My heart sank at the thought of everything crashing down for me.

"I'll pay," the knight said. He drew his sword and put the point to the smith's throat. The man glared at him and stood his ground.

"I'll give you your life for him," the knight said. "Is it a bargain? Or you can die now. What do you say?"

"This is not lawful," the smith said bravely.

"Do you want to go to the assize court for beating the boy? I tell you now that I would speak against you."

"I have fed him since he was a boy."

"You have abused him since he was a boy. Enough of your arguments now. Be silent or I'll cut your dirty throat."

The knight lifted me up behind him, and from my high perch I watched the village pass as we set our faces to the trail. I thought nothing of the life I was leaving behind, and everything of what lay ahead.

Before nightfall we stopped beside the trail. I unsaddled the horses. In the evening light I shot rabbits with my bow and cooked them before an open fire. That night I slept with my new master under his cloak. He held me in his strong arms. My life was changed. My happiness was bliss.

FARMBOY DREAMS

Rick Jackson

I suppose someday I might run across a farmboy that doesn't stiffen my dick, but I haven't seen any sign of him so far. I've pondered the problem of farmboys a lot over the years and have more or less come to the conclusion that what does the trick is the way they all seem to have the hard, sculpted bodies of young gods and the guileless faces of cherubs. I suppose many years of hefting bales of hay about would have to build up a lad's shoulders and pecs. What really sets farmboys off from their big-city brethren, though, is that they look upon every encounter as an adventure. Maybe living in a midwestern farming town with a population straining at 100 doesn't give them the chance to be as naughty as they need as often as they want. Maybe they crave contact with passing strangers who can teach them new tricks. Whatever the reason, I've never once seen a farmboy I didn't want to do—or who didn't want to be done. Jared is a perfect case in point.

Driving through Iowa late last week, I felt my dick twitch like a dividing rod pointing straight ahead, alerting me to the presence of tight, juicy farmboy butt with a serious craving for bone. Sure enough, just about the time my knob was about to burst, a farming village too small to be called microscopic blipped onto the horizon. It had about five houses, a post office and feed store, and a filling station where a young blond Apollo was pumping his truck full of gas.

He shone out like a Stygian beacon, radiantly tanned and sublimely shirtless in the late-summer sun, a long blond shock of hair dangling low over one brow, his tongue sticking out of the side of his mouth, as though to focus the world's attention on the full, sensual lower lip that practically begged permission to wrap around my bone. From a block away, I could see the firm, full ass that filled out his faded jeans—and wondered as I pulled in for a fill-up of my own just how long it had been since he put that ass to its proper use.

I felt his eyes sweep across my MGB, noticing at once its rakish low-slung style and, more to the point, that it wasn't covered over with a thick layer of country dust the way every other car in the county seemed to be. Then his long-lashed eyes found mine and widened with knowledge and hope and incipient satisfaction. I gassed up in a big-city hurry and sauntered meaningfully towards the men's room. I never made it.

Jared headed me off for the first time that afternoon as I passed a dozen feet from him. He stammered and twitched like a virgin in chain gang, but managed finally to blurt out that the crapper wasn't a good place—but that he had one that would do us both just fine, if I didn't mind following him for a couple of miles. Jared so glowed and throbbed with simple sincerity and farm-country goodness that I'd have followed his tight little country ass all the way to a Christian Coalition rally if necessary.

It was just as well I had filled my tank before we started down our road to love. The kid seemed to lead me on forever, turning down one rutted dusty country cart-track after another until we pulled up next to an ancient barn that was all but weathered to bits. Maybe the trip had just seemed like taking forever because my dick was so cramped up and oozing pre-cum into my jeans with every bump of the road and thump of my racing pulse. Once we were there, though, I realized young Jared had been thinking. Not only would fucking in his old man's barn be a delicious forbidden pleasure for him, but a nice down-home rush for me. Besides, the nearest other human had to be a dozen miles away—far enough off that they probably wouldn't hear him scream or groan or beg for more when I got around to giving his ass what it needed.

The barn was dark and cool after the sun-drenched fields, but we were both naked and at each other so fast that we barely noticed. All Jared had to lose were his jeans and sneakers, so he had enough of a head start to jump me before I had finished shucking my jeans. His face flew towards my dick, but I wouldn't let him have it and gave him some low-slung nuts to suck instead. By the time he'd licked a long day's load of driving-sweat off my balls and I'd lapped my way around his crotch, we were both ready for some real down-home romance.

I eased my lips against his, unsure how fast I could go without spooking him. He shivered deep for a moment like a skittish colt looking for his mama and then wrapped his arms around my back and shoulders, pulling my sweaty body hard against his and urging my tongue far enough down his throat to rupture a tonsil. We rolled about on our wide bed of hay bales as the salacious summer smells of farm and farmboy made me forget the prickling I was getting from the hay. Jared made me forget everything but the powerful yearning of his body grinding against mine, the touch of his nails clawing at my back, the taste of his tongue flicking and slurping against my own, and the low, autonomic moans of a young man in serious love.

Minutes or hours later, I pried my lips from his and eased across his neck to tongue-fuck his ear so hard his brain threatened to rupture. By the time his arms and legs were flailing about and his mouth was agape with groans, intermittently spewing out language that would make his own mama disown his ass, I knew the time had come to put it to the use Nature intended. I didn't have any lube, but when I stuck my tongue into his mouth, Jared seemed instinctively to know what was good for him. I pulled it out wetter and slicker and sweeter than Jack Horner's and reached low to shove it right up his butt.

My first couple of farmboys taught me that a man built like me has to be careful or he can do some serious damage. I always like to take a few extra minutes and pry the hole open before I slam my way inside. Jared was lucky I'm such a considerate, `90s kind of fucker. His asshole was so eager and so sublimely tight and my thick nine inches of big-city meat are so hard to take that I'd probably have crippled the kid if I had just flipped his ass over and fucked it.

As it was, young Jared couldn't decide whether he wanted to bear down tighter, slamming his butt down my thumb until it threatened to gobble my whole hand—or whether he should listen to his reflexes and rocket off my thumb to save himself a world of pain. When my fingers reached down from the crack of his ass and pulled his hairless balls up towards the thumb I'd buried up his butt, my hunky young hayseed abandoned forever any thought of self-preservation and hunkered down for a long, hard farmboy fuck.

I used my free hand to jack his uncut dick, sliding his ample 'skin gently up and down across his throbbing head until it was awash in hot dickhoney. I smeared some across his bare chest and let him slurp some more of the savory goo from my fingers in between all those yelps and moans of ecstasy. The way his butt was clutching at my thumb promised me his ass would need all the lube it could get. After I slipped my paw back down to his shank for another few strokes of the sort of love farmboys know best, I stayed put and built up a load of Nature's best lube.

While I was thumb-fucking his hole and clawing at his nuts and balls, I kept busy on all fronts: my lips and tongue lapping the savory taste of boy-sweat from his soft skin, my body pinning his squirming legs to the hay, my lungs filling ever fuller and faster with the sublime scent of pounding pastoral sex in action. I must have drifted off for a moment the way a man does when he's having hot country fun, because suddenly I felt Jared bucking madly against my fist as his face split wide with the howls of the very damned of hell. His butt cinched impossibly tighter around my thumb and wriggled us both happy. Jared spewed sperm up into his face and onto his chest until he was awash in thick white threads of farmboy love. His hips seemed to buck forever, using my paw to pump every drop he had up from the balls I had so firmly in hand. That load dripped and ran and splattered his hard young body until I felt foolish for having worried about a lack of lube—and for spending too much time enjoying the show when there was work to be done.

His seizures were already starting to wind down by the time I broke free of reverie—too late to catch the most violent contractions of his ass, but still in time for one fine fucking farmboy time. In one fluid, instinctive movement, I unthumbed his butt, rubbered up, scooped a bucket-load of creamy jism off his chest and belly, slathered it down my shank, and slammed my dick up his ass—all before the gorgeous little bastard even noticed I'd stopped jacking his joint and was just holding on tight so he couldn't escape.

Fortunately for Jared, escape was the last thing on his nasty little mind. The minute my dick ripped upwards through his shithole and dislodged nine innocent inches of innards, his straining balls somehow found another pint or two of jism to splash up across his already very sloppy belly and chest. As his balls clenched tight to spray his sperm, his ass and guts locked down even tighter around my shank, trapping me deep up his country butt.

Seconds after the broad base of my bone had stretched his shithole towards catastrophe and my stiff, rust-colored pubes had ground into what was left, Jared's lust-struck brain finally realized what his body had done. His mouth gaped wide but couldn't decided whether to scream out in agony or to suck in air to keep him going. He split the difference and let slip a soft, soulful gurgle that spoke both of the most sublime satisfaction and the most terrible of torments.

Like bedrock reacting to a nuclear explosion, his solid muscle rippled and knotted in waves that swept upwards from his ass until his hard, tanned body was cobbled over with clenched and constricted muscles that mirrored both the agony of his tortured ass and the building ecstasy of his farmboy soul.

While I used my left hand to hold his hips down where they belonged, I pumped fiercely away at his dick with my right— and kept at it until I had reamed his ass raw and he was drained drier than a mummy's gizzard. I lifted my jack-hand back up to his mouth and made him lick his jism from my fingers in between screams and gasps and agonized groans. I kept him busy cleaning me up, partly because I've never liked seeing a good load go to waste and partly because the hot flicking of his tongue across my slick fingers was just too fine to rush. I wasn't even above slathering another handful of his country cream up off his chest and belly to keep the good times going.

Before long, though, I was riding his ass hard enough to buck him off—and that was the absolute last thing either of us wanted. To be on the safe side, I moved both hands to his shoulders to hold him down for the fuck of his life. He slipped and slid against my body on a layer of sweat and jism, but I didn't mind. His stiff tits gouged into my forearms, but that was nothing compared to the abuse his ass was getting.

We were both kneeling on our bed of bales by then and, somewhere along the line, I bent him over a bale stacked next to us. I switched my brain into neutral and my bone into high gear. Every nerve in my body seemed to lase bright with bone-bred bliss, yet my memories of the next many minutes are a blur of indistinct impressions and mind-numbing raptures.

I have no idea at all how long I pounded my stiff dick up through that country tight tail, but I remember being swept away by the mingled smells of farm and boy—the scents of hay and sweat and dust and ass all whipped together by the nasty nine inches of big-city meat that bound us together. The sounds of farmboy groans and my own grunts of accomplishment mingled with the slap of wet hips against tight, sweaty ass. Jared's hands grasped at the back of my neck and tore at my ass, desperate to get more dick than he could manage. Mostly, though, I remember the way his slick guts clenched around my back-stabbing shaft, pointing me towards his prostate, urging me deeper with every relentless stroke, and begging me to stay there as I tore my way upwards against the tide to gather leverage for my next inevitable thrust.

I fucked Jared's youthful body so long and hard that reality itself seemed to fold around my dick to be ripped to helpless tatters. The harder I reamed his tail, the less I knew and the more I wanted until the black mists of man's most ancient and most brutal need wrapped about me and shut out the world, leaving only the two of us pounding away. I surged on, humping Jared's young farmboy butt, slamming his head into the hay, and making him howl until neither of us could bear another inch of reaming rapture.

Eventually, the tight torment of his ass and the scents of hay-bred farmboy and the texture of his muscled body skidding, sweat-slicked and jism-coated, across my flesh, all conspired to short-circuit my plan to fuck him forever. The sweltering summer temperatures and the friction of our bodies and the flames of animal lust joined forces to melt my guts. They suddenly gushed loose, squirting up through the throbbing core of my being to spurt out into the depths of Jared's very soul. My rubber may have cheated his thirsty ass of some creamy satisfaction, but Jared drank deep of the ultimate farmboy pleasure—being bred hard and long by a passing stranger.

He kept on quaffing until my balls ached with effort and both our knees were rubbed raw from the straw. When I was finally drained dry, I collapsed onto what was left of Jared and lay throbbing silently away inside his ass while I caught my breath.

I nibbled his ear and gave it some tongue, but mostly I just soaked up the joys of farm life and put off, as long as I could, climbing back into my clothes and my car and the world beyond Jared's rickety old barn.

I managed to delay the inevitable for several more hours—and would have done better if I hadn't run out of rubbers and if Jared hadn't worried in his callow, Midwestern way about being back where he belonged for the evening chores. By that time, the sun's rays glinting through the chinks in the barn walls had aged from the searing gold of day to the deep Trojan bronze that glows so rich and warm across Iowa evenings. I took some of that glow with me as I left and drove off.

My last sight of Jared—the way I remember him best—was a long, greedy look into my rear-view mirror. I left him, still standing, naked and satisfied, in the wide doorway of the old barn. He was covered in dried sweat and jism with the odd bit of hay clinging relentlessly to his flanks the way I would have done in a more perfect universe.

Still, I can't complain. I will likely never see Jared again, but the memory of that perfect, golden Iowa summer day will remain with me, bright and untarnished, until my final hour. Besides, Iowa is full of farmboys with needs as deep and butts as tight as his. I can't possibly satisfy them all—but I can try.

THE FARMBOY & THE STUD

Rick Jackson

After I'd been on my RFD route across central Iowa for a couple years, the local postmaster asked whether I wouldn't like to transfer into Parkersburg for what he called "the big-city action." He smiled at the idea of Parkersburg being Gotham City as he made the offer, but I expect he really did think sitting on a stool behind a counter would be better than driving a hundred fifty miles a day to deliver my John Deere catalogues and church newsletters. The poor bastard obviously had no clue that the country was where the action really was.

Young Chad is a perfect case in point. I handle a lot of mail a day, but, as a long-time subscriber to adult magazines, I know those plain brown envelopes when I see them—especially if they are addressed to youthful farmboys named Chadwick Jones. I'd more or less watched Chad grow from a barefoot country boy in the Huck Finn tradition into a powerfully built blond icon of all that is great in Middle America.

When his first *Stud* arrived back in April, I nearly walked it up to the house and gave it to him personally—the magazine, I mean—so that it wouldn't fall into the wrong hands. If he was so grateful, not to mention enchanted by a 25-year-old stud in uniform, that he'd haul his ass back to the family barn so I could give him the kind of service many men on my route have come to depend on, so much the better. After some reflection, though, I decided it might be better to wait. I didn't want to spook the kid, after all.

By the time July rolled around and it was nearly time for Chad to go away to college, I knew I would have to take steps to keep the kid from missing out. It took me some time to track him down the day his next issue came, but his reaction to the familiar brown envelope and my knowing grin was well worth the trouble. First he blushed; then he stammered. Then he looked me up and down from a new perspective—especially when he saw my male flag rising along my left thigh. He gave a furtive glance around to make sure no one else was near and then suggested I meet him the next afternoon at the farm's windmill several miles down the road.

An old dirt road ran to the windmill, but no one ever used it unless the pump jammed and the corn fields started to dry out. Chad was there waiting for me, all nervous and beautiful, naked but for his worn 501s and sneakers and a shimmering mantle of such sublime sexuality that Leonardo would have painted him as a Calvin Klein model lighted with a nimbus.

His farmboy grin confessed his lack of experience, but the ratty army blanket he had handy promised he was ready to learn. He mutely led me to a small clearing behind the windmill, where he spread the blanket onto the ground and waited for me to show him what to do. The kid was so beautiful that for a long, slow minute, I did nothing at all but stand and stare and savor the open goodness of his youth.

The harsh Iowa summer heat sent sweat coursing down beneath my shirt, but now and again a cooling breeze would waft over from the tall stalks of corn and tease me with the hinted possibility of relief.

The only sounds for miles were the occasional rusty squeak of the windmill and the pounding of the blood in my ears.

I took my time stripping off my shirt and slacks but finished getting naked in a hurry so that I could watch Chad some more. Standing naked and uncertain against the lush backdrop of green, he looked the very picture of fertility incarnate, Dionysus and Ganymede melded together by some caring god to be my plaything for a long Iowa summer afternoon.

His thick blond hair hung farmboy long, covering part of his cute little ears and the nape of his strong neck. His body, though, was smooth and bare, but for the golden curls at his pubes and pits and the ripple of a man's muscles that surged below. Life on the farm had taught his skin how to wear a deep bronzed tan without losing the soft suppleness of youth. His dime-sized tits crowned pecs that were at once firm and hard, yet not the overdeveloped caricatures so many youngsters vainly crave. Most of all, of course, my eyes were focused down past his firm, flat belly and narrow hips at the gorgeous uncut dick already standing tall and begging for my lips. His tiny nuts were clinched tight and nervous against his body, but that fine farmboy dick was proud and confident enough of its destiny to be called cocky.

I stepped onto the blanket and pulled Chad's body against mine, gently at first and then with a roughness that echoed the savage depths of his need. My hands slipped across his broad back and down to cup the fine, Iowa-bred ass that flared full and ready, magically suspended behind his hips as though daring me to do my worst. At my first touch, those glutes knotted tight with the thrill of possession and flexed and twisted in spasms of instinctive pleasure as I kneaded his ass hard, masterfully pulling his surging loins against my own as our lips met and slowly sealed our union.

His greedy hands were everywhere, coursing upwards from my ass to slide along my flanks and hang from the back of my shoulders, desperate to grind my body against his. Our lips learned our common language and our bodies crushed hard and naked together, sliding on a slick layer of equal parts sweat and raw male passion. The searing sun and plaintive squeak of the windmill faded away, and my senses were overwhelmed by Chad's desperate touch, the heaving power of his loins, and the sweet, savory tastes of youth and man upon his lips.

We somehow ended up on the blanket, a surging, sweaty mass of arms and legs all bucking and pounding at once as our lips and dicks lashed out in a frenzied lust that seemed to belong in those fertile fields but would have been totally foreign to the bland, provincial precincts of Parkersburg.

I remember playing for a time with Chad's gorgeous uncut treasure, slipping his `skin up and down, watching the crystal-clear love-lube ease from his purple slit and flow relentlessly down his throbbing shank. The hard ridge of his corona caressed my fingers as his foreskin slid up and down and up again to prove yet again that a country dick is Nature's most marvelous toy. Chad had long since started echoing shameless moans of raw, wanton rapture across the corn fields. They were so natural and unaffected by the priggish restraints of civilization that I remember thinking it was too bad no one would hear them and share our pleasure. As I absent-mindedly rolled rubbers down our dicks, I smiled again at the idea that giving up my RFD route could ever make me happy.

I pulled Chad's firm young body onto mine and let him fuck my face as hard and deep and long as he wanted while he kept busy returning the favor, sucking my latexed lizard and licking my sweaty nuts until both our jaws were cramping from the strain. He kept his hands wrapped tight around my thighs as though to keep them from escaping underground and out of his reach. My hands slid ceaselessly along his torso and lean legs until, when I felt his balls rising to press firmly against my nose, I put my palms back onto his butt to polish his full, fine Iowa glutes.

Once more they writhed in response to my every touch. As he sucked my dick ever harder, Chad let my fingers grope low into his sweaty, hairless asscrack and wriggled in renewed rapture as my fingers coasted across the tender pink focus of his pleasure. My fingers grew bolder and pressed their advantage home, grinding harder across his shithole as Chad's dick-stifled moans found a chirping soprano register that mimicked in perfect counterpoint the rusty squeak of the windmill.

Soon the action up his ass was too much for him to handle with a faceful of postal dick, and he had to move back low between my legs to finish busting my balls, hollering away like a Missouri hog farmer the whole time. When the tip of my first fuckfinger prised his quivering shithole far enough open to work inside, Chad's body seemed somehow to lift off mine and hover in space for a moment as his ass tried to eat my hand for supper.

I worked a second finger deep, twisting his hole wide and worrying my way across his slick prostate to give him a sense of what had gotten into him—and what was next in line. The sheepish, nervous way Chad had started off made me think he lacked experience, but the determination of his shithole locking around my fingers and showing them a fine country welcome were proof positive that the kid was a natural buttfuck. Something about growing up on the farm often puts men in harmony with nature, but I had never felt anything like the waves of rippling shitchute that invited my fingers in to stay. I got the sense I could fingerfuck his tight farmboy ass all the way until harvest home if I wanted—and that only one thing would make him happier.

Since he wasn't using that one thing, anyway, I figured it was time to put it to work. When I rolled Chad's body off mine and wriggled around to spread his legs, he gave me that nervous grin again. Looking up to me with those big, brown eyes of his, he used words for the first time that afternoon: "I want you to do me hard and keep at it until you bust your nut up my ass. I don't know if I can take all of your big dick, but I want you to make me, hear. Don't stop no matter how loud I holler. Don't stop for nothing. You keep after my ass until you just can't use it no more."

I'm always inclined to go easy on guys that are green as the corn they grow and was feeling especially protective of young Chad. Whether this was his first time or not was none of my business, but I figured that it might be. If so, I ought to give him something he would remember always. If he wanted it rough and hard and long, I could deliver it that way, too.

I checked the rubber to be safe and then nuzzled my thick dick against his shithole. His pucker was hungry for meat and nipped at my knob, begging me to hurry and drive him home to glory. Suddenly in no hurry, I took a second and looked down into Chad's open, eager face and tried to remember how nervous about life I had been at his age. I had been a farmboy, too, eager to experience everything at once, desperately convinced that my life would never amount to anything unless I could get away to the big city and do every wicked, depraved thing I'd seen down at Moody's motion picture theater all those Saturday afternoons I was growing up. I'd gone away and learned where the good life really was and come home to live it.

Chad probably would, too—when he was finished learning. We both knew his first lesson was about to begin and, afterwards, he'd never be the same. I reached low to give his forehead a little kiss and then smiled at him: "You holler all you want. There's nobody to hear but us and the corn. I don't know about you, but I like a loud young fuck who knows what he needs."

My thick, blood-gorged dick slammed through Chad's farmboy ass years too late and ages before he was ready. His whole body folded up around mine in agonized knots that would have broken a rabid storm trooper's heart, but I was worlds past humanity. Every ounce of consciousness I possessed focused on fucking that tight young country ass with all the bestial brutality three million years of genus Homo could muster. I can't explain why I needed to be mean or why Chad needed to have his butt broken hard; all I know is that we both got what had to be.

Chad found voice after the first shock of entry and screamed louder than anything mortal could, but my dick knew no pity. I had no sooner reamed aside nine inches of his guts than I arched my ass towards the sky and dragged seven or eight of my thick butt-busting inches up again. Chad's shitchute collapsed in the vacuum left in my wake, desperately clawing at my bone to stay even as it knew its moment of relief was a short as another searing, gut-wrenching stroke of agony was inevitable. The louder Chad screamed and the more he twisted around on the end of my lizard, the more he fueled the fires of my lacertilian frenzy and the harder I fucked his farmboy ass into the ground.

I'd like to give you a stroke-by-stroke account of what happened over the next ten or twenty minutes—I'd like to know what happened myself. I know for damned sure that I had a good time—and, after I had fucked every nerve ending in his body out of commission, so did Chad. About the time his shrieks became moans of "Jesusssssss!" his pain-clenched fists opened into fingers that raked and clawed at my back and butt until I wondered which of us was fucking whom.

What do I remember other than the soft afterglow of a good time? Well, I remember our bodies sliding together on great splashing seas of sweat. I remember the smell of rich Iowa dirt and ass and man-musk as my dick unstoppered Chad's shithole a hundred times a minute. I remember the way his body shivered when I leaned low and snorted air into his ear. I remember towards the end when even Chad's prayers were beyond him and he met my every reaming fuckthrust with a gasp and a twitch and the sure knowledge that another was about to slam his way. Mostly, I remember the way our bodies surged and pounded and bucked together in perfect harmony —up and down like perfect fucking machines, built to fuck on forever with no wear or tear on any vital moving parts.

Sad to say, though, men aren't machines. After both our bodies had learned new limits, mine finally rebelled. I tried at first to stem the tide, but I had no more luck than old Canute. I shot enough cum up Chad's farmboy butt to give it a separate postal code. I held on as tight as I could and kept him from jetting off my joint like some absurd cartoon character, but the look I saw in his eyes when I was finally drained dry and he was pumped full proved that he wasn't going anywhere—not until I had done him again.

I was late getting back to check in that day—and have had scheduling trouble several times a week since. The postmaster sympathizes with what I have to put up with riding the RFD route, and keeps congratulating me for being so noble and selfless and dedicated to the cause. I've been dedicated to a cause the last month, but it isn't the one he thinks.

Fortunately for the postal service, Chad leaves for college tomorrow so my route should be easier until Christmas vacation —if I don't run across some other young farmboy who needs some *specialized* rural free delivery.

TRUE BELIEVERS

John Patrick

Nate was big and black, and he came to work at my ma's motel after my pa died. I was just a teenager then, confused by most things sexual, but I knew what I wanted: Nate. He had a big smile and a gold tooth in front, and showed a bulge in his paint-splattered overalls that tantalized me. Over the first summer he worked for Ma, he taught my pal William and me how to smoke, and, eventually, bribed us with Kool menthol cigarettes to suck his dick. He did not actually teach us how to smoke, but one day at the market when he caught us stealing Uncle William's King Edward Deluxe Cigarillos with Plastic Filter Tips, he figured he could regulate our tobacco consumption and our behavior by becoming our supplier. It kept us from stealing and he made sure we did not inhale. That was about the best he could hope for. The cock sucking started when he caught me sucking off William one day when we thought he was busy painting one of the rooms.

William was leaning back on his elbows on the floor of one of the vacant rooms, partially nude, and I was on my knees doing as good a job of blowing him as I could considering how big his dick was, responding to his moans and groans. I guess we had been making quite a bit of noise, quiet as we had tried to be.

I had closed the door but I had been so excited about having William's cock in my mouth again I had forgotten to lock the door. Nate burst right into the room, and when he saw us, he smiled and said, "I done thought so," which I suppose meant he'd known all along and was just waiting his chance. Anyhow, he told me not to stop and he stood over us, rubbing his bulge. William had gone limp so I was playing with him a bit, trying to get him hard again, but my eyes were on Nate's crotch.

My voice was shaking and my hands were shaking too as I said, "C'mon, Nate, lemme see it."

"Y'all sure?"

"Oh, yeah, Nate. Please."

The cock was so huge that Nate had a hard time freeing it

from his overalls. When he finally did, after much slow fumbling with his great hands, his cock was pointed up, right up, at me at a forty-five-degree angle. He was unclipped, and his foreskin was much darker than the rest of his teak skin. The shaft was like many things: a baseball bat, a fencepost, an arm, a leg, but it was also strong, powerful. I knew from then on I would be comparing all those things (fenceposts and baseball bats and arms and legs) to Nate's cock, and not the other way around. The base of Nate's massive cock was buried in a forest of curly stiff hairs. His balls, what I could see of them, were the size of baseballs. My eyes returned to the cock; it was bobbing up and down.

I was speechless, but William, always the instigator, was urging me on. "Go on," he said, "see if it's real." William's cock was still quite a memorable one, long and tapering, uncut, as was Nate's, but it bent in a curious way, kind of down and to the left, and the head was bulbous, what I called a sucking head. I loved William's cock, but now I had another one that needed—demanded—my immediate attention.

"It real all right, and it ain't even really hard yet." Obviously, Nate was happy with his cock. A thick droplet of creamy pre-cum dotted the end, and, as I looked from it to Nate's slightly smiling face, William said, "See if you can get it really hard, Johnnie."

I let go of William's prick, which, before this, had been the biggest one I'd ever laid eyes on, and shuffled over on my knees to Nate. Shyly at first, I touched it, stroked it. Sure enough, it started to grow to an impossible length and thickness, and William gasped. I looked over at him. He was blushing. I'm sure he had his own fantasy going on because he often mentioned that he thought Nate was fucking my ma, and every white girl within fifty miles. I knew it aroused him to think about Nate fucking all those women with this huge member.

I was shocked and fascinated at the same time. It was all so new and exciting that I didn't know what I should be doing. I looked up at Nate again, but he had closed his eyes and he seemed to have gone elsewhere. I continued stroking Nate's cock and eventually it was fully hard. Now, seeing how huge Nate really was, William was getting turned on. He began wildly jerking his prick.

"Oh, man, yah gotta suck it," William demanded.

I was still dubious. "Kiss it maybe," I said. "I'll never get it all in my mouth."

"Yeah, kiss it," Nate said, running his hand through my hair.

Wrapping both hands around it, I kissed the shaft, then gave it a lick. Nate smelled strange, much different from William. It was a rich odor that was not entirely unpleasant. The cock stench was as exhilarating as it was foul. I kissed and cleaned the foreskin with wide swaths of my tongue: licking all around the base of the head, tasting the sweat, the manliness of the cock, and then, finally (with a groan from Nate), I put my full lips on the tip and gently swallowed the cum that coated it.

I opened my mouth wider and wider till my teeth were oh-so-gently tapping against the ridge of the hidden cockhead. Then, slowly, I started to push myself onto Nate's cock and pull his foreskin back. In my wide-open mouth, Nate's cock was like a stone covered in silk. Nate growled and his muscle-bound body vibrated.

"Oh, yeah," he moaned.

Encourged now, I really got down to work. Both my mouth and hands were working on him, drawing the sperm from him. Then it was too late. The cum began gushing into my hungry mouth. Just then, William came as well, sending jets of cum to the floor. I gulped and swallowed, consuming every last bit of it, letting it flow down my throat and into my belly. Above me, Nate was covered with a sheen of of sweat and groaned and moaned and cried with the stunning power of his orgasm.

Standing up and wiping my mouth, chin, and face with a large red handkerchief, I smiled at Nate. "Sometime I want you to fuck me," I said.

"Johnnie!" William chortled. "Nate'd kill you, man!"

I tugged at Nate's still half-hard penis. "What a way to die."

"You ain't come yet," Nate said. "I could fuck you now."

Nate inhaled deeply when I dropped my pants and got on the bed on my knees. I looked behind me to see the stud stroking his cock to a righteous state of incredible readiness, considering he had just had an orgasm.

And with that, he spat into his hand and started to lube up

my asshole. Then he carefully positioned himself over me and asked, "Ready?"

"Do it, Nate," William cried, standing beside the bed, stroking his cock to hardness again.

The laborer's cock was like an iron shaft gliding in and out of my most tender and excited opening. I cried out with pleasure as Nate fucked me in the ass, slowly at first, then ever longer strokes, gripping his tool tightly, eyes shut in concentration. After a few minutes, Nate's skillful use of his cock had me close to coming and I begged William to get on the bed and fuck my mouth with his lovely cock while Nate fucked me.

Already sweat was again pouring off Nate, and his dark eyes were fluttering with anticipation of a second orgasm. I had no idea how many young white boys Nate had fucked in his time, but it was obvious he got off on this kind of worship. William's cock slipped between my lips just as Nate exploded with a spasming jerk unlike any I had ever felt. As Nate plunged into my depths, seeking my very heart, my legs seemed to give out, and I came. William's cock slipped from my mouth as I fell to the mattress.

Staggering to his feet, Nate hitched up his battered overalls. Now, after we'd come, it was real quiet. All you could hear was the cars roaring past on the highway.

Suddenly, William broke the silence, screaming "Oh, oh," as he too came for a second time.

Nate's voice was like chocolate. "Next time, I want you both. On your knees, before me."

Just the thought of it got me so turned on, I could hardly speak. "Yeah," I answered obediently. William nodded, but said nothing.

Quickly, Nate was gone.

But when "next time" rolled around, William was nowhere to be found. It was just Nate and me. Nate was painting one of the rooms and Ma told me to watch the office while she went to town. It was nearly noon and everyone had checked out, so the only interruption could have been a new guest, which was doubtful considering how early it was. I hung out the "back in a minute" sign and rushed to the room where Nate was working.

I was breathless with excitement, almost coming in my pants, but managed to tell him we had at least a half an hour.

"Shut the door," he ordered.

After bolting the door, I turned and saw he had already removed his prick from his jeans. He stared right at me, like I was a target, thing to attack. I stood, spellbound, watching him stroke his enormous cock. It appeared even bigger than I had remembered.

He loved his cock, that was clear; the way he massaged it, taking it from the base and working it up in his hand right to the big tip. To make things a bit rough, he'd slam it right back down onto his nuts, making the whole thing seem magnified. Then he would grab both balls into a big sac and point his dick the opposite way. This turned him on, and me, too.

His smile gleamed down at me and he jerked a little faster. "Yeah, get right down 'fore I blast, boy."

I have no idea how long I stayed on my knees before him, kissing it, licking it, sucking it, but I lost track of time altogether. I was rudely brought back to reality when Nate cried, "Oh, boy, your mama just drove in."

"Shit."

Nate stuffed the monster back in his pants and went back to rolling on the paint. I opened the door just in time. Ma was happy to see I was "helping Nate" and said I could stay. This got Nate laughing, and he led me into the little bathroom of the unit, where he sat me down on the toilet and then opened his pants again. The cock was still semi-hard, or maybe it was always semi-hard.

Now, as I peeled back the foreskin, clear cum dripped from the piss slit. Barely touching the semi-hard cock with my lips, I lowered my mouth over it until the foreskin was touching the back of my throat. Saliva ran from my mouth and down the shaft of the pole, into the wiry, sweat-grimy pubic hairs.

As his swollen cock bucked, I hacked, spit, gasped for air. He pulled it out of my mouth and came. I felt the hot gush of his cum against my chest, coating me as jet after jet shot out.

I had managed to fish my own cock out of my shorts and I jacked off staring at the exploding prick before me. All I could hear was our ragged breathing as we pumped our dicks dry.

We cleaned up and went back to work, saying nothing more

about it.

A couple of days later, Nate took me and William fishing on the lake behind the motel.

Giving head was easier for me than smoking. Nate laughed at me when I smoked, but he was relatively silent when I gave him a blowjob.

"Lil' Johnnie," Nate said, "breathe out befo' you breathe in, and you won't be coughin' like a little fool. I know you think you got to do everything like yo' ol' buddy Nathan, but the only reason I breathe in when I smoke sometimes is because ya'll are enough to drive anybody crazy. I don't know whether to smoke or breathe, so I just do both at the same time. Yo' mama got the same problem I do, and I think ya'll is the cause. You boys is just too much. Now breathe out, boy." Then he turned his venom on William, who was reaching for another cigarette. "No, William, you can't have another Kool because I saw you tho' that last one in the creek."

"Give 'im somethin' to suck on, Nate," I said, and Nate was always happy to hear that. He had his shirt off and I admired his chest. I kneaded his tits, both hard knots of dark flesh, lightly covered with hair. I stroked his sweat-matted chest, then his hairy, hard belly. Nate's eyes got big and his lips got stiff over his teeth, and his head started going from side to side.

William followed my hand with his eyes as I unbuttoned Nate's jeans and let loose the monster. William leaned over as the cock began swelling.

As we began stroking the big dick, he held our heads and said, "I don't know if ya'll do me that way cuz you crazy and full of the devil, or because I'm a black man and you think you can get away with it. But I loves ya'll."

"We love you, too, Nate," I said, raising up, letting William suck on the head of Nate's prick for awhile.

"Gonna sit you right down on it, William. You'll like this." Nate lifted William over his cock and we watched it go in. William let out a scream.

"Fuck him like you fuck your woman. Fuck his sweet ass!" I shouted, as William shoved his foreskinned prick into my face, slapping me again and again with it. I grabbed for it, put it in my mouth and let him fuck my mouth while he bounced up and down on Nate's prick, till they both came. When they met at the peak of their respective orgasms, they rocked and rolled so much I thought they would tip over the rowboat.

"Oh, oh yeah,"

I lingered between William's shaky legs, enjoying his cock, which I hadn't sucked in a while. I figured William had been scarce because he was afraid of Nate, but whatever his fears, he was okay with it now. More than okay with it, really. Behind him, Nate smiled, slowly removing the long prick from the tight tunnel of William's sweet, brave asshole. William grunted and I leaned in carefully and pressed my lips against his, tenderly, with feeling. William's mouth returned all of my affection and more.

When Nate was killed in an accident while he was driving the old church bus a year or so later, we were all very sad. He had the biggest cock I've ever known, and he was sweet about sharing it with us. He was one of the most gentle people we had ever met, and when he wasn't singing, he was laughing and joking, keeping the rhythm going. He sang in a high soprano. He would sing soul like James Brown or Aretha Franklin, but the room rocked when he sang gospel. And that day he showed us his prick made us into True Believers. And every time we held it in our hands, sucked it, or took it up our asses, we said, "Praise the Lord!"

THE GINGERBREAD HOUSE

Peter Gilbert

"We'll get as far as we can today and then lie low for a few days," said Hans.

"You don't think they'll come after us?" said Greg.

"Not a chance."

The car was new. Both boys were young, good-looking. Both were heavily and powerfully built. But there the similarity ended. In fact, most people found it difficult to believe that they were twins. Hans's hair was short and fair. Greg's dark curls and complexion had turned many a head in the last few years.

"I wonder what they'll be having for dinner at Christmas," said Hans.

"They'll have to go down to the store and buy something, won't they?" said Greg. They both laughed.

. . .

Some three years previously, the two boys had been on the run. Their parents had been buried only a few weeks previously. For a short time they stayed with an aunt whom they had never seen before but the strain of bringing up teenage twins had proved too much for her. A home, she said, was the only answer. She made a few telephone calls and then told them to pack their bags. They were just fifteen. For three days they hitched lifts in trucks and cars in a desperate attempt to get away from people, people who might read about them in the papers and get them sent back. They reached a small mining town and thought of sleeping in one of the many deserted buildings there but there were people there too. Not many but enough to be a threat. Exhausted, they took the old saddleback trail up the hill. They discovered later that they had walked sixteen miles before the lights of 'The Gingerbread House' came into view.

The house's strange architecture struck them even then as they stood trying to pluck up courage to knock on the door. The roof was set at a strange shallow angle with wide overhanging eaves. A long and ornately carved balcony run across the front of the building. Hans pulled the antiquated bell handle. What sounded like Swiss cow bells echoed inside.

The door opened.

"Yes?"

He was a very little man. Hans seemed to tower over him. He had a lined, tanned face and strangely expressionless grey eyes. He invited them in and seemed to know, instinctively, that they were all in. He sat them down and went into the kitchen, returning with two plates heaped with a stew of some kind. No meal had ever tasted so good as that first stew. Neither of them had eaten anything except scraps from garbage cans for three days. After they had eaten, they told him their story, sobbing out the details. He promised not to tell anybody and had put them to bed, and that was how it had all started.

His name was James Montgomery. He told them to call him James. They were welcome, he said, to stay as long as they liked. Things could be arranged with their aunt. He was certain of that.

All their worries and tension vanished. James was easy to talk to. Interesting, too. He told them about the house; how it had been built by a German baker who had settled there in the days of the gold rush, baking bread in the old bake house and taking it down into the town every morning on the backs of his three mules.

"How long have you lived here?" asked Hans.

"Oh, that's not important. I never talk about myself. Now then, I've just got the one spare bedroom, next to mine at the front of the house. I'll go and make the beds. You need a bath really but there isn't any hot water. I'll get the boiler going in the morning."

They both slept well and were awakened by the sound of chopping wood. They dressed and went outside.

The boiler was outside the house, a strange contraption fashioned out of what looked like an old oil drum mounted over a brick hearth. All that day, whilst they explored the house and the surrounding area, James tended the fire, throwing in logs and whistling happily to himself.

Seven o'clock came round. The boiler was hissing. "Best have dinner after your bath," said James. "This way."

The bathroom had been built onto the house as a sort of annex. They both knew where it was but he insisted on showing them. He turned on the faucets and tested the water temperature on the back of his hand.

"It would be best if you were to go in the tub together," he said. That made sense. The boiler wasn't that big. For a few seconds they waited for him to leave them but he didn't. He sat on the closed lavatory seat smiling at them.

"Get those dirty clothes off," he said. "I'll wash them straightaway."

Embarrassed, they undressed. He got up and collected the discarded shirts, jeans, socks and underwear, put them in a pile near the door and sat down again.

Hans, the taller, got in first. Greg climbed in. It wasn't easy but they managed to arrange their legs so that they sat facing each other with Greg's right leg between Hans's longer limbs.

"Nothing like a good bath," observed James from his strange vantage point. They both needed one. The water rapidly turned grey as they exchanged the soap, the sponge and the long-handled back brush. James said nothing but neither of them could forget his presence. Every square inch of them had been washed and scrubbed. Still he sat there. The water began to cool.

"What are those hooks for?" asked Greg, looking up at the wooden ceiling. Two enormous, pointed hooks were fixed into it above the bath tub.

"The old baker, the German I told you about, used to kill pigs in here," said James. "Hang them by their back legs on the hooks and slit their throats. The blood would run away into the bath. They were very practical in those days."

Both Hans and Greg shuddered.

"I should think you're both done by now," said James. "Stand up."

Shamefaced, and with some difficulty, they clambered into an upright position.

"Could you pass over the towels please?" Hans asked. He cursed himself for not noticing the distance between the bath tub and the towel rail earlier.

"In a minute. I want to look at you first." He got up.

"Please could I have a towel?"

"What big boys you are. Do a lot of exercise, do you?"
"A fair bit. Please could we have towels?"
"Not yet. Turn round."

To face the wall was a little less embarrassing but only slightly so. There was a long silence. They both knew they were being stared at.

Hans started as he felt the man's hands on his shoulders. They slid down his arms and onto his thighs. Then they moved up again until they were on his butt. His asscheeks were pried apart. He felt James's breath on his back. James pushed one hip and pulled the other. Hans turned round. James smiled. A professional, artificial smile. The sort of smile the doctor at home used when he said "Just drop your pants for me, son."

He brushed his fingers over Hans's chest and abdomen, then fingered the boy's pubic hair and... The suspicions that had been building in Hans's imagination were confirmed. James took it between his finger and thumb and gently retracted the foreskin. The touch was surprisingly gentle, as if a butterfly had landed on Hans's cock. He let go of it, felt under Hans's balls and then, without a word, turned to Greg.

Hans said nothing but he was furious with himself. It was to escape this sort of guy that they had run away. Both had heard stories about the staff in boys' homes. It had been his suggestion to run away. They had jumped from the frying pan straight into the fire and it was his fault!

He watched as Greg was subjected to the identical treatment. James said nothing at all. Then, suddenly, it was all over. He passed over the long awaited towels, picked up the discarded clothes and left the room. There was no time to ask him what they should wear to go downstairs.

They took a long time to dry themselves. There was a lot to talk about. There was no doubt that James was queer. Hans was all for getting away as fast as possible.

"A bit difficult without any clothes," said Greg. "Anyway, where would we go?"

It was a quandary. "He seems a nice enough guy otherwise," said Greg who had always been the most practical of the two. "If he likes feeling cocks, what the hell?"

"Providing he doesn't try anything else!" said Hans who had heard rather more of the habits of queers than his brother. They wrapped the towels round their waists and went downstairs.

They had dinner, and watched television whilst James washed their clothes. They watched from the window as he hung them out onto the line to dry. He came in again and joined them but sat, to Hans's relief and surprise, some way away from them. He hardly glanced at them throughout the evening.

The clock in the hall struck eleven. "Time you boys went to bed," said James. "Do you want anything to eat first?"

Neither of them did. The evening meal had been enormous and they had devoured two packets of cookies whilst watching television.

"I don't suppose your clothes will be dry by the morning," said James. "We'll go out and get some more as soon as we can. I think we'll make your bath nights Monday and Friday. How does that suit you?"

"Sure," said Hans, convinced that by the time Friday came round they would both be miles away. But it wasn't as easy as that. It was pretty certain that they would be picked up sooner or later. Was life in a boys' home going to be any better? Probably not. By the time the morning came, they still hadn't made a decision. By the evening of that day, they had. "We stay," said Greg and Hans agreed.

James had taken them out to buy new clothes. A hundred and fifty miles to the nearest big town. They came back with more clothes than they had ever possessed before, a selection of CDs and a stereo player, an exercise machine, stacks of magazines and an expensive wristwatch each.

. . .

A year went by. There was no school for miles so the mornings were dedicated to lessons. James was a surprisingly good teacher and seemed to know a lot. After that, they were generally left to their own devices. They never found out what James did in the afternoons or what he did for a living. He was certainly rich. Their every whim was gratified. The old bake house in the garden was soon full of expensive sports equipment and games that they had tried and then tired of. James' encouraged them to eat as much and as often as they wanted. There were only two drawbacks to life at 'The Gingerbread House' and they were Friday and Monday evenings. 'Drawbacks' was the right word. Every bath session was the same. They stood, side by side, facing the wall whilst he felt their shoulders and arms and their backs before moving down to their butts.

"Ah, yes. Coming on nicely," he would say, rubbing his hands over the smooth, still wet skin. "A nice bottom. Nice and meaty. Let's have a look at the rest of you...."

Every session ended the same way with James gently sliding wet skin back to expose the gleaming, purple heads of two adolescent cocks. He never did anything more. "You're nearly ready," he would say. Ready for what? That was what worried them.

Their birthdays came. James gave them a new motor bike each. Hans was convinced that James would try something that night or soon afterwards but he didn't. Life just went on in the same way, lessons in the morning, lunch, and then they were generally free to do what they wanted, unless they had misbehaved.

"It's the bake-house for you," James would say. "That butt of yours needs some tenderizing."

The interior of the bake-house was, for the most part, filthy. The growing pile of cast-off games and sports equipment was covered with cobwebs. Only one part was kept clean. Running along one side of the wall, just under the window, was a long, very smooth, wooden bench on which the long-dead baker had mixed his dough. A deep, bowl-shaped depression had been carved in the middle to hold the flour.

There was no doubt in their minds that James enjoyed those punishment sessions. He would spend a long time in there, whistling happily to himself as he scrubbed the bench and the long handled dough paddle with its perforated blade. Then, when everything was ready, he would come back into house to fetch the miscreant—or miscreants. More often than not, as is inevitable with twin brothers, he had found fault with both of them.

He sat, perched on the bench, as they undressed, talking about the most trivial things. They might as well have been cutting firewood for the boiler.

"Your buddy was in the store yesterday afternoon, Greg. What's his name?" Never 'I saw' or 'I met'. James never talked about himself.

"Kenny."

"Ah yes. He seems a nice guy. Invite him round some time. The lawn needs cutting again if you guys have time. Ready? Good. We'll do it in alphabetical order."

And Greg would climb up onto the bench. James secured his wrists to the bench legs. That was a safety measure to protect the hands he explained, if the boy in question tried to protect his butt from the paddle he'd end up with a broken wrist for sure. When that was done, his mood changed. They both hated what followed more than the punishment itself. Being beaten sure hurt but embarrassment was worse than pain.

"Isn't that a sight for sore eyes?" James would say, looking down upon Greg's prostrate body. "That's how I like to see a boy. Just look at those shoulders! His arms are strong too. Lot of muscle there. Feel his legs, Hans. Come on. Feel them. Smooth as silk eh? Go up a bit farther.... That's right. That's what I call a perfect butt...."

And despite Hans's desperate attempts to distance himself from the procedings, the inevitable happened all too often. Slowly and inexorably, his cock rose. James pretended not to notice but it was obvious that he had. Smiling to himself, he'd prolong his examination, encouraging Hans to feel here and there on his twin's body.

"A lovely butt. Firm, not floppy. Just feel it. Go on. Knead it a bit. That's right. It'll be even nicer when it's been tenderized."

It wasn't just Hans who was affected. Greg's hard breathing was a pretty good indication that something was stirring in the depths of the old dough bowl. James continued to stroke the boy's thighs and buttocks, commenting all the time until Greg, breathing even more heavily, began to make the same low moaning noise that he sometimes made in the middle of the night. In the privacy of their bedroom it usually prompted Hans to reach down under the bedclothes and set about relieving his own built-up tensions. In the bake house, all he could do was stand there, blushing furiously while his cock strained upward expectantly.

"Hand me the paddle, Hans."

Holding your twin's struggling ankles and watching white skin turn dark red and then purple was a horrifying experience, especially if you knew you were to be the next. Hans often cursed his Austrian-born mother for not giving him an initial nearer the beginning of the alphabet.

Then it would be his turn. The knots were untied. Painfully, Greg climbed down and Hans took his place. The same routine but this time it was Greg ruefully rubbing his own butt whilst James's kneaded Hans's.

"A nice, meaty ass. Soon to be good 'n' ready, I shouldn't wonder. Needs tenderizing though. Put your hand on it Greg. Feels good eh?"

The awful thing was that it really did feel good. Fright of the impending punishment gave way to a warm, good feeling as four hands massaged his butt. He'd feel his cock beginning to dribble into the dough bowl.

"Can't get over the difference in the two of you," James would say. "His legs are longer and his butt's so tight. He's coming on fine. You both are."

Then came the moment that Hans couldn't resist, however much he tried. James' long finger pushing in between his asscheeks, moving around until it felt the boy's most sensitive spot. He could never help exhaling loudly. James's incessant commentary seemed to be coming from another world.

"Just look at him squirming, Greg. Gee! He's tight. Just feel that. Like marble eh? He sure needs tenderizing. Hand me the paddle."

Thwack! The first blow was always the worst. It felt as if the paddle blade had been in the fire. Thwack! Thwack! Thwack! By that time you had to call out. You couldn't help it. Thwack! Thwack! Thwack! His yells echoed back from the brick walls. Then they stopped. There was a moment of silence. James untied his wrists, put the paddle back in the corner and, as they dressed, chatted away as if nothing had happened. More often than not, he'd have to wipe a sticky mess out of the dough bowl but never said anything about it.

On the following bath night he never expressed satisfaction or remorse as he surveyed their bruised butts. He never said "Sorry" when one of them winced at his touch. The perforations in the paddle blade left white spots in the rectangular purple bruises. In the privacy of their bedroom they would count the spots and compare scores. Once, just to try to get James talking about it, Hans told him at breakfast. "That walloping left eleven white spots on Greg's butt. There are fourteen on mine!"

"Oh, yes? What are you guys planning to do this afternoon?"

They talked about him a lot when they were alone. The strange ways of James Montgomery became their prime topic of conversation.

"There's no doubt that he's after our asses," said Greg one night.

"He's sure taking his time over it then."

"Making his choice. Deciding who to screw first," said Greg, "and guess who that's going to be."

"You, of course. Alphabetical order. That's how he always does things. You'll have to tell me what it feels like."

"Balls! It's you he's got his eye on. Look what happened when you bent the tip of the carving knife trying to open that can of paint."

"Yeah. That was kinda weird, I admit."

"Weird? It was surreal, man."

The carving set, in its plush case was one of James's prize possessions. Hans had tried to lever off the lid of a paint can with the knife. It was a stupid thing to do and no amount of hammering would straighten it again. It was the only time they had seen James really furious but Hans hadn't been beaten. He'd been shouted at and called a good many names.

"You going to beat him for it, James?" asked Greg.

James put his arm round Hans and began to massage his butt through his jeans. "No. Not this time. Mmmm. Lovely soft buns. Definitely the nicest of the two of you. Hans will be ready first."

"Hans will be ready first. That's what he said and he was feeling your ass at the time. It's obvious," said Greg.

"Just let him fucking try!" said Hans. Years before, a boy had given him a graphic account of an evening spent with one of the staff in a boys' home.

"It's just like a red hot poker going in your ass. Fuckin'

agonizing, man!"

"He will," said Greg, "and then you can tell me what it was like!"

"Fuck off! Goodnight."

They changed their minds just after their seventeenth birthday. It was Friday night. As usual, they stood in the bath tub facing the wall and counting the tiles whilst their guardian made his usual inspection. Both were so excited at the car he had given them that they hadn't slept much for the past two nights. Hans hadn't wanted to have his usual jerk-off under the covers whilst Greg was awake.

To his horror, the moment James's fingers made contact with his ass, his cock began to rise. He tried hard to think of other things: the car; the journeys they'd make. Where would they stay? Would James allow them to stay out all night? Hans's imagination worked overtime. They could drive down the length of the west coast, stopping on the way of course and then possibly right across the states to the east coast. Florida would be a good place to stay. They could spend a few weeks there; possibly get some sort of jobs....

It didn't work. Seemingly nothing to do with his brain, his cock continued its inexorable movement upwards. He glanced down at Greg. His brother's cock was barely visible.

At first, James seemed to pay it no attention and concentrated on Hans's shoulders, chest and abdomen. Finally, his fingers closed on the stiff and throbbing cock. "Hmmm. I said you'd be ready first," he said. He pushed the foreskin back as he always did and then forward again. That made it worse. Unsmiling, James pushed his hand between Hans's legs and felt his balls. Then, quite suddenly, without any warning, he dropped to his knees, put his hands round Hans's butt and took his cock into his mouth. Hans was so surprised that he nearly toppled over in the water.

Greg must have wondered what was happening, and turned round to see. "Well, I guess you don't need me," he said. He went to step out of the tub. James slid his mouth off Hans's steely hard cock, leaving it nodding and glistening. He looked at Greg as if the boy had suddenly gone off his head.

"No, stay!" he commanded. "How can I compare you both if you're not here." Greg stepped back into water. Again, James popped it into his mouth, holding it like an expensive cigar and then pulling at Hans's butt until as much of it as possible was in his mouth. Hans felt the back of the man's throat against his cock head. It felt good. He was aware of James sucking on it and of James's tongue flapping against the shaft. He began to breathe heavily and his heart thumped in his chest. It wouldn't take long. It never did. There was a dull ache in his scrotum. He felt himself sweating. Any moment now.... It was such a good feeling that he tried to fend it off but couldn't.

"Oh! Ah! Aaah!" One after another the jets squirted into James's mouth. He felt the man swallow. For a few seconds the room went hazy and Hans thought he might faint. He didn't. James stood up. A little pearly trail of fluid was running down one of the folds on either side of his chin. He wiped it away with the back of his hand.

"Nice!" he said. "Very nice. And now for Greg."

But he didn't go to Greg. He went to the wash basin, filled a tooth glass with water and very deliberately washed out his mouth, spitting into the basin like a wine taster and running the faucet for a few seconds.

Then it was Greg's turn. "Not quite so keen as your brother but I guess we can soon put that right," said James. In fact, Hans's performance had roused Greg a good deal. Hans looked on whilst the man slid his hands up and down the insides of Greg's damp thighs, played with his balls and finally with his cock. Within minutes it was standing up, rigid and jerking in time with his pulse.

Hans watched; he couldn't help it, as Greg's cock vanished inch by inch until James's lips were buried in his brother's dense hair.

Greg grunted at first but the grunts soon turned to short sighing noises such as he often made when he was apparently asleep. Hans wasn't aware of the moment when his brother came. One moment James was on his knees. The next he was standing up, wiping his lips. A long, viscous thread dropped from Greg's cock onto the side of the bath.

"Delicious!" said James. "You both are but I think, on balance, that Greg is slightly sweeter. Don't be too long getting dressed, will you?"

"Wrong again, dear brother," said Hans that night. "It's

cock he wants, not ass."

"I apologize," said Greg. "If that's all he wants I don't mind at all. With two motor bikes and a car, I think we've got the best of the bargain."

Hans had to agree but he had, as he said then, misgivings. They both agreed that James was a weirdo; well intentioned and kind hearted certainly but a weirdo nonetheless.

After that it happened on every bath night. A year passed. They had gotten so used to it that their cocks started to rise in the warm water the moment James came into the room. Sometimes he started with Greg. Sometimes it was Hans but there was always the strange ritual of the mouth wash before the second cock slid into James's mouth and always the expert verdict at the end as if they had prepared it specially for him.

"You've become much sweeter in the last few weeks, Hans."

"Nice, Greg. I like the salty taste."

"Hmm. Quite a tang to it this time, Hans. Well done!"

A long motor tour was ruled right out. It would entail missing a bath night. James wouldn't hear of it. Hans suggested that they might go away at Christmas. That too was turned down and James sprang a surprise. A friend of his was coming at the beginning of December and would stay until the New Year. More than that he would not say save that it was a "sort of business visit."

They would have liked to know more. In particular whether the friend shared James's tastes and was likely to require the services of one of them but that was a question which could not be asked. All they managed to find out was that the friend's name was Rod.

"Life's going to be a bit boring until he comes," said Greg, hoping that James would open up and say either, "Yes, and it will be even more boring when Rod is here because we shall be talking business all day," or even "Just wait till Rod gets here. You won't be bored then!" But he didn't.

"What you could do," he said, "would be to refurbish the bake house. Sling out all that junk. You're both eighteen now so we shan't need the paddle any more. That would keep you busy. I don't mind paying you to do it. It'll be a dirty job."

They would have been happy enough to do it without the financial incentive though that made it slightly more pleasant.

They dragged out all the old kit, cleaned it up and took it down into the town and handed it to the delighted warden of a boy's home. They scrubbed the floor, polished the windows and painted the walls. The weeks went by. The bake house looked spotless. The walls gleamed and the windows sparkled. The old steelyard scale used in the old days to weigh flour bags had been cleaned of a hundred years of rust and hung, perfectly balanced, from the rafters. They even polished the old, black oven doors.

"Perfect!" said James. "What about the oven itself? Is that clean?"

"No, it's still full of crud. There's even a pair of old shoes in there," said Hans, who had taken one look and closed the door again."

"Oh I think we should clean it," said James. "It would be a pity to have gotten so far. We ought to make sure it still works."

They protested but he was adamant. It had to be cleaned. For three days they shovelled ash and refuse out of it and got thoroughly filthy in the process. The boiler was going all day long to provide them with baths at the end of the day. It was fortunate that the cleaning took place in the middle of the week. James made no attempt to disturb them as they lay soaking off the dirt. "He probably wants us as randy as hell for when Rod arrives," said Greg gloomily.

"I don't know whether to look forward to the coming or the day the guy leaves," Hans replied.

The oven was finally cleared. "Are you sure it's clean?" asked James.

"As clean as it can be," said Hans. "To get it any cleaner you'd have to get right inside it."

It was a stupid thing to say. "Why not?" said James.

"What about our clothes? You'd never get that muck out of them."

"You don't need clothes. Do it stripped off. Why, I guess that oven would take the two of you."

They didn't think so. On the following morning he went down to the bake-house with them. "I'm sure you'd both fit in there with room to spare," he said. They undressed and, naked, they crawled in.

"See? I told you so. It's big enough for both of you. Move up a bit, Greg."

"Don't shut the door, will you?" said Greg anxiously.

"Don't worry. I won't. You both fit in there perfectly."

"Not much room to move around," said Hans.

"You won't need it," said James. "At the moment I suggest one does the cleaning and the other carries the dirt away. Then change over."

That night happened to be a Friday. They got into the tub as black as miners. It took three changes of water to get them clean. James came up for the ritual inspection. He sat, as usual, on the toilet seat. "Well done, lads," he said.

"If you had closed that door, you could have roasted us," said Hans.

"So I could," said James. "I'd have had to get you ready first though. That takes time."

"Aha! But you'd have to catch us first!" said Greg with a laugh.

"I'm sure I could think up a little trick to do that," said James. "A bath night for example. That would be the ideal time. You'd be nice and clean."

There was something about the way he said it that Hans didn't like. He was used to James's single mindedness but there seemed to be a strange edge in the man's voice. Greg was obviously unaware of it. Ignoring the nudge that Hans gave him under the water, he continued the conversation.

"And how would you do it, James?"

"Oh I don't know. That would be a butcher's job. I guess he'd string you up on the hooks and cut your throats. I'm only a cook."

"Tell us how you'd cook us then." Again, Hans nudged his brother.

"Mmm. Let me think. Roasted certainly but slightly differently. Hans in butter I think. Yes, a lot of butter."

Hans's heart thumped. Only a week previously James had taken delivery of no less than twenty pounds of butter!

"And what about me? How would you do me?"

"Well, you're slightly fatter than Hans. Butter as well of course but I wouldn't need so much. A few herbs too. A spot of garlic maybe."

Hans shuddered. James had planted his herb garden soon after they arrived and had tended it and his garlic patch lovingly ever since.

"It would take a long time," said James, apparently unaware of Hans's unease, "As much as thirty hours and I'd have to baste you every now and then to make sure you come out of the oven crisp and brown all over..."

Hans could bear no more. "I'm ready," he said. Shivering, he stood up and faced the wall.

"Oh! Me too I guess," said Greg and he, too, stood up.

The problem was that Hans was not ready. Hans was far from ready. His cock was like an acorn, barely visible in the thick hair that surrounded it.

Greg, on the other hand, seemed not only unaffected but positively excited. His cock stood out from him and seemed anxious to touch the tiles.

Hans shuddered as James touched his butt. The man's fingernails felt like the prongs of the carving fork. He turned round willingly enough but nothing James could do would arouse his dormant cock.

James tutted impatiently. "It's what you and Greg were talking about," Hans explained, anxious that the giver of cars should not be too disappointed so near Christmas.

"Silly boy. Greg and I often have little jokes like that, don't we, Greg? Boys taste much better alive, believe me. Let's have a look at you, Greg. Oh yes! Quite different. That's how I like a cock to feel."

He was soon on his knees slobbering over Greg. Hans looked down at his bobbing head and wondered....

Try as he might, Hans couldn't put the conversation out of his head. He wanted to ask James about the butter and the herb garden but fear like that seemed so childish. Greg was convinced that it was all a joke. James often made jokes like that, he said. There were the references to "tenderizing" for example. Why, several times James had said that he was good enough to eat. He obviously didn't mean it. Not in the literal sense anyway.

Slowly, Hans's fears evaporated, until Rod's arrival on December 16th. It was a bitterly cold day. Rod was obviously a man of some wealth. Apart from his suitcase, he brought two black leather bags with him, which were deposited immediately in James's study. Hans's suspicions mounted by the hour from the moment the man arrived.

"So these are Hansel and Gretel," he said the minute he was in the house.

"Hans and Greg" said James.

"Pretty well the same. It's amazing when you think about it. 'The Gingerbread House' and all that. Your father wasn't a woodcutter by any chance, Hans?"

"No, he worked in a meat packing plant," said Hans—and the words made him tremble.

"And as for the evil old witch. Well, you're getting old James. As for the witch bit... I guess it's not just their thumbs you've been feeling, eh?"

James had the grace to blush slightly.

"One man's meat and all that," said Rod. "Now, we've got a lot of plans to make. Shall we go into your study?"

"I'll bet he's gay," said Greg that night when they were in bed.

"Didn't look like it," Hans murmured. He was trying to fight off sleep so that he could think carefully.

"Bet you!" said Greg. "Tonight or tomorrow. Funny to think of my cock in his mouth."

Hansel and Gretel. Hans dimly remembered the story. The two woodcutter's children whose parents deserted them in the forest. They found a house made of gingerbread inhabited by a witch who kept them in cages, feeling their thumbs to see which one had fattened up sufficiently to be cooked......

"That's how I like a cock to feel."

"A nice fleshy ass. Needs tenderizing though."

"Butter and garlic."

❧   . . .

There was nothing for it, Hans thought the following morning. He would have to find out one way or another. Greg had been up for a long time and was polishing the car. James and Rod were in the study. He could hear their voices. There was one way he could find out. God help him if James discovered him listening at the door. James was funny about his privacy. He padded to the study door and bent so that his ear was near the keyhole.

"When will you be ready?" That was James.

"About a week before Christmas. I'd like to get it over as soon as possible."

"Me too," said James.

"I don't blame you. Death can be remarkably sudden. Very much alive and kicking one minute and croaking the next. I've seen a good few in my time."

"I just hope it's quick and painless," said James.

"It usually is."

That was it! Conclusive proof. Hans dashed out into the garden. "You look like you've seen a ghost," said Greg. "What's up? You were talking in your sleep too."

Haltingly, still trembling from the shock, Hans told him everything. Greg didn't believe it at first. "It's true, I tell you. It's true!" Hans shouted.

"Keep your voice down. They're coming out," Greg replied.

Ignoring the boys, the two men walked down to the bake house and went inside. They left the door open. Every word they said echoed round the bare walls and drifted back to the boys.

"It's fine," said Rod. "Does the fire actually work? Sometimes the flues get clogged."

"I haven't tested it," James admitted.

"I should get the boys to do that. These old bakery ovens take days and days to get to any appreciable heat. Hey! That's interesting. I haven't seen a scale like that for years. Is it accurate?"

"No idea," said James. "The boys cleaned it up."

"Easy way of finding out," said Rod. "Call them in."

James beckoned to them.

"How heavy are you, Hans?" asked Rod.

"A hundred and forty two pounds exactly," said James. "That's without his clothes."

"I might have known you'd know that," said Rod, laughing.

He made Hans stand on an old box and grasp one end of the steelyard. He slid the counterweight along the other, longer arm. Hans felt himself being lifted. At first he was able to keep his toes on the box but as Rod slid the weight along, he left the box altogether.

"A hundred and fifty one pounds in his clothes," said Rod.

"And all muscle!" said James. "There isn't an ounce of fat on him. It would be much more interesting to do it without any clothes."

"In this weather? Let's do it some other time when the fire's going. Let's have a look at this bathroom. You guys coming or do you want to stay here?"

"No. We'll come with you," said Greg.

"I'd like to install a proper boiler," said James. "This thing might be historical but it's not sufficient and we need a lot of hot water."

Rod wrote something on a pad he was carrying.

"What's this?" he asked, looking up at the ceiling. "Pig hooks unless I'm much mistaken."

"Right," said James.

"Still in good condition by the look of it. Amazing. Hans, can you grab hold of one?"

Still trembling slightly, Hans took off his sneakers, clambered on to the edge of the tub, grasped the hook and let himself swing.

"Just look at that!" said Rod. "A hundred and fifty one pounds! Try the other one, Hans." Hans did so. "Firm as a rock," said Rod. "That's a good ceiling."

The rest of the survey was conducted without Greg and Hans. They went into their room.

"Are you absolutely sure?" asked Greg.

"Absolutely. Christ! You heard. The oven's going to be heated. And they're going to need a lot of hot water. You know what that's for, don't you?"

"A bath?"

"Not the sort of bath you're thinking about. Dad told me. They put pigs in hot water so the hair's easy to scrape off. We have to get away—and fast!"

"How?"

"Easy. We'll take the car."

"People don't give cars to the folks they're planning on murdering," said Greg. "It doesn't make any sense."

"A trick," said Hans. "People like him are full of them."

The kid from the boys' home had told him about the sweets

and the cookies that had tempted him from the dormitory into the warden's apartment.

"A week before Christmas," Rod had said. The days went by and even Hans had to admit that, for a couple of murderers, Rod and James were cool customers. It was slightly reassuring to learn that Rod was married and had two sons and when the first bath night of his visit came around he was more interested in the boiler than in what was happening in the bathroom. He'd spent the day inspecting it and it was slighlty disconcerting to see his shadow cross the window as Greg, followed by Hans, spurted into James' mouth, trying that time to smother their usual gasps.

"See?" said Greg that night as they lay in bed. "It's all in your imagination."

'There are some married guys who get it off with other guys. I read it somewhere," he said. "Anyway, having a wife doesn't stop him from being a murderer."

Greg dismissed the idea entirely. "He's neither," he said. "You must have got it wrong."

"Let's wait and see."

But the days passed normally enough. James and Rod spent most of it shut in the study. Time and time again Hans walked past the door and wondered if he should listen in again. Then, shuddering, he thought better of it. It had been scary enough last time. There was no need to wonder what they could be talking about. Killing two teens needed a lot of planning. They'd be working out how to dispose of the bodies and what to say to the few callers who asked about them. "Oh they've gone on a long motor tour," or 'They've gone to college." That part should be easy enough.

Friday came round. Rod volunteered to fire up the boiler and spent most of the day chopping logs; far more than were usually required.

'Time for your bath," said James at seven o'clock. Rod, apparently disinterested, sat reading some papers that had arrived that day.

It was more difficult than usual to get the bath water temperature right. The faucet spat steam and boiling water. So much cold water had to be added that, by the time they had climbed, in the water was almost flowing over the sides and was still rather too hot for comfort. They washed and scrubbed as they usually did. There was no sign of James.

"Probably inviting Rod to come and join in," said Hans.

"Balls! Rod's okay. So's James really. It's just that he's got a kink about cocks."

"I wonder about you sometimes," said Hans. He did. He sensed, somehow, that Greg never minded what James did to him. Then there were those weird conversations the two of them apparently enjoyed.

"Here he comes," said Greg, cocking an ear towards the door. It opened. To Hans's relief it was only James.

"Sorry I took so long," he said. "I was getting dinner ready and Rod wanted to talk about something. My word! What a lot of water you've used!"

"We had to," Greg explained. "The hot water was boiling!"

"I should have warned you. Rod wanted to see if it was dangerous."

"And is it?"

"Yes. He's going to have a new one put in. Now then, up you get. Be careful not to splash too much."

As they had done over a hundred times before, they managed to disentangle their legs and climb to their feet. They stood facing the familiar tiles.

"Red as a couple of lobsters," said James. To Hans's relief, he started on Greg. Hans watched his twin's face as James's hands moved down from Greg's shoulders to his butt.

"Especially down here," said James, fondling Greg's buttocks lovingly. "A boiled butt if ever I saw one. Good enough to eat."

Hans shuddered. He turned his head to look at Greg's face. Sure enough, his twin was smiling.

"Look nice on a plate, would it?" said Greg, laughingly addressing the tiles.

"It looks even nicer on a whole boy!" James was kneading Greg's butt as if it were dough.

"Stuffed of course," said Greg. "You could use that stuff you made last Thanksgiving."

James turned his attention to Hans but continued to talk to Greg.

"The apple and chestnut? Yes, I suppose I could."

"Not sure I fancy having the wooden spoon in my ass," said Greg.

"Silly boy. You wouldn't know anything about it. You'd have been hanging in here for at least two days. Then I'd need another day to get you ready; take off all this lovely hair...."

His hand slid up and down Hans's legs as he spoke. What had Hans overheard? "About a week before Christmas. I'd like to get it over as quickly as possible." Terrifyingly, it all came together.

He glanced down. Amazingly, Greg's cock stood out proudly.

"Anyway," James continued, moving up to Hans' butt again. "Some boys like things in there. It's a nice feeling. So I've heard anyway...."

"Not us!" snapped Hans.

"No. It's probably an acquired taste," said James, "which brings us back to reality. Turn round."

They very rarely knew what James was actually thinking. He had one of those deadpan faces that gave nothing away. It was impossible to tell from his expression if he enjoyed slamming a paddle on a soft, white butt. A cock in his mouth, it had to be admitted, would make an appreciative smile impossible but when it was over and he'd washed out his mouth it was still impossible to tell what he was thinking.

But that evening was different. As they turned to face him, his face lit up and he actually laughed.

"I've never seen your balls hanging so low!" he chortled. "It must have been the hot water."

"Feels like they've been boiled," said Greg as James stroked his belly with a finger.

"Well that's another delicacy we hadn't thought of, isn't it? Boiled balls. What an inventive boy you are to be sure. But I know something that tastes even nicer."

There was no need for either of them to ask what he had in mind. It was already in his mouth. The all too familiar slurping noise filled the bathroom, synchronizing occasionally with Greg's stentorian breathing.

Hans looked down. The old problem. If Greg had kept his mouth shut he might have been able to manage something. As it was, his cock hung, tiny and flaccid, from his bush. He knew from experince that James was not a man to give up. Dinner might be delayed for hours until he had managed to shoot something, however little.

He tried to think of girls. There were not many in the town and not one of them could be called attractive. Kenny, Greg and he had often moaned about it when they'd been together. Anyway, it was difficult to conjure up the image of a beautiful girl when you were standing in a bath tub listening to your twin brother having his cock sucked dry.

"Lot of guys here go in for cornholing," Kenny had said. "Guy's got to get his rocks off somehow," and Hans had said then what he had said a few minutes earlier: "Not us!"

"Don't knock something you ain't tried," Kenny had said. "Let me know if you change your minds."

In reality, Hans and Greg had paid for their drinks and left. What if they hadn't? Kenny was a good-looking guy; only nineteen and he had remarkably smooth cheeks. The other miners called him 'baby face'.

He knew where Kenny lived. It was a tiny cabin on the other side of the valley. He'd never been inside the place but could imagine what it was like.

"Sorry about the mess. Haven't had time to clean up in ages."

And then, when they sat together on what was bound to be a pretty threadbare old sofa. "Which one of you guys is going to be the first?"

How to explain that Greg always came first? No... Greg was an intrusion. Forget Greg. He'd have to stay at home. Hans, alone with Kenny. That was much better.

"Just can't wait to get my pecker in your tight little asshole," Kenny would say. Would he? No, that would be Hans's line.

"Just can't wait to get my cock in that great ass of yours, Kenny," and Kenny would smile.

"I sure have waited an awful long time," he would say. "Guess I'd better get these things off before you come in your jeans, eh? Sure looks like you've got a lot to give."

How did one actually do it? Hans didn't know. Would Kenny kneel down in front of him? He didn't like that idea. Kenny would lie face down on the sofa with his legs apart. Great big, satin smooth buns. Pushing them apart... seeing his asshole, winking up at him. Getting into position straddled across

Kenny's powerful frame. Pushing downwards....

"Oh! Oh! Aaa-aaah!" That was Greg. The dream vanished but it had done the trick. Hans's cock stood out proudly from his belly.

"Nice one Greg. You did well."

James went across to the basin and filled his glass. His face was reflected in the mirror door of the medicine cabinet. Expressionless, grey, fishy eyes stared at his cock whilst their owner swilled water round his mouth. He put down the glass.

"Now for you, Hans. You're being a good boy tonight. It must be the effects of that hot water. Come a bit closer. Put your legs apart a bit more. That's it. That's fine."

He felt James's hands sliding up the inside of his thighs. "A lovely pair of balls," said James, cupping them in the palm of his hand. "Long immersion in hot water seems to work wonders on both of you. We must try it more often. Loose balls make a nice, sperm-rich juice."

Hans shuddered. He couldn't help it. The man didn't seem to be able to say anything without introducing some reference to food or drink.

"We mustn't let you get cold," said James, misinterpreting the boy's fear. "In either sense of the word, eh?" His lips closed on Hans' cock head.

Back to Kenny. Hans didn't want to but it was the only way.

The inside of Kenny's ass felt warm and wet. There was a hint of something bristly in Kenny's pubes. That was odd in view of Kenny's smooth skin elsewhere. It was a great feeling though. He wondered how Kenny would feel. Did it hurt to have a cock in your ass? The guy from the boys' home said it did. Maybe Kenny would call out. That'd be fun, hearing a great hunk like Kenny calling out....

Something in Kenny's ass came to life and started moving. That felt even better. He couldn't help moaning out loud.

"Big brother's in a randy mood tonight." That was Greg's voice and Greg's hand came to rest on his butt. What was Greg doing there? Greg was supposed to be at home. Ah! He'd come to see what was happening. He'd opened the cabin door silently and was watching, dying for his turn. Screwing Kenny? No. Kenny was going to screw Greg. That was why Kenny had that gigantic wooden spoon out ready. Greg had never been screwed before. Kenny was going to use the spoon handle to open his ass a bit and, if Greg didn't respond, why Kenny (and maybe Hans too) could use the bowl of the spoon on his buns. Make them red. Make Greg cry out for a cock....

"Oh! Oh! Aaah!" Shot after shot squirted out of him. He opened his eyes. James stood up and went to the basin again.

"Very good. Very good indeed," he said. He sighed. "You've given me so much pleasure," he said. "That's the last time. Thank you both." There was a strange catch in his voice as he spoke. "Thank you," he said again and left the room.

"If that doesn't convince you, nothing will," said Hans.

"He means with the old boiler," said Greg who was by no means sure he was right. "You heard what he said. He's having a new heater installed."

"What do you guys have planned for tomorrow?" asked Rod at dinner that night.

"Nothing much, why?" asked Hans.

"Why don't you get the bakehouse fire going? There's plenty of wood left over."

"What for?" asked Greg.

"Well, it'd be interesting to see if it still works."

. . .

Strange images floated into Hans's mind that night. He wasn't asleep—or was he? He could still hear Greg breathing and a heart was beating. His or Greg's?

A long, long time ago.... He was bouncing up and down on a man's knee. The man was wearing overalls. He could see the brightly colored badge moving up and down.

"My little twin! Good enough to eat! Yum, yum, yum!" and he giggled as the man's lips touched his bare skin....

The metallic clang of an oven door closing. "Now just you boys watch that. If it's burned when I come back, I'll sure roast your butts for you....

James's voice, seeming to come from far away. "See, it's big enough for both of you." "A nice fleshy ass."

"A nice fleshy ass." Now he was standing up in the bathtub and facing the wall. The voice was James's but those were not

James's fingers kneading him.

"So I see," said Rod. "Ready?"

An arm went round Hans' neck. He struggled and shouted. He could hear Greg, next to him, screaming. Water splashed everywhere. He lost his footing and fell into the lukewarm suds. He kicked out. A powerful hand grabbed his ankle. Then the other one. He flailed around with his arms. There was nothing he could do. There seemed not be one Rod but hundreds of Rods and hundreds of Jameses. Just like when the mirror on the door of the medicine cabinet reflected the image in the mirror on the wall opposite. Then he was lying in the water, choking as it filled his nostrils.

Whistling happily, James tied his ankles together. He still struggled as the bath water receded below him as James and Rod pulled on the rope.

He was hanging head-down over the tub. Rod, strangely not upside-down as he should have been, was sharpening a knife. The carving knife. The same knife that Hans had sharpened for the last three Christmases and Thanksgivings. Hans knew every detail of that knife from the chipped antler handle to the maker's name on the blade and the bent tip.

Greg hung next to him. They both revolved slowly as they hung there. The tiled wall by the bath; the door; the toilet—and then the awful look of fear in Greg's eyes as their faces almost touched.

He felt James's hands on his thighs. He stopped revolving.

"How will you cook them?" asked Rod, still sharpening the knife.

"In butter. Roasted. I thought I'd serve their cocks separately as a starter and boil their balls."

Rod put down the sharpening steel and stood up.

"I hope it'll be quick and painless," said James.

"It usually is. Which one first?"

"Alphabetical order," said James. "Greg first." Rod stepped forward and grabbed Greg's hair. Greg screamed. The knife flashed. Greg made a strange, croaking noise and squirmed violently. Hans felt his brother's chest against his own, felt Greg's arms go round him, clinging to him.

"And now Hans!" he screamed.

. . .

"...It's okay. It's okay. It was a nightmare." Greg had gotten into bed with him and was holding him tight.

"Jeez! And what a nightmare!" said Hans after a few minutes. "This is ridiculous. I'm going out on the balcony to get some fresh air."

"In this weather?"

"I won't be long."

"I'll come with you."

They put on bathrobes, opened the door as quietly as possible and stepped out of the room. The forest lay still beneath them. In the distance a few lights glimmered.

Voices were coming from James's room.

"They're still awake," Greg whispered. Hans nodded and, pointing towards his ear, he edged along until he was by James's window. Greg followed.

"I guess you'll miss their company," Rod was saying.

"I'm sure I will. But it's the best thing to do."

"I presume you've had your little bit of fun with them."

"Well, yes. That worries me."

"Why worry? Dead men can't stand in court."

"Okay. I've heard enough!" Greg whispered. Together, they padded back to their room and, instead of trying to sleep, silently packed bags and whispered final plans.

At nine the following morning, a plume of blue wood smoke ascended from the bake-house chimney. Hans and Greg were flinging logs into the furnace.

"Hey! That's some fire!" said Rod warming his hands by the open oven door. "I should keep it going, lads. It would be a shame to let it go out and these old ovens take a hell of a long time to heat up. There should be a flue somewhere." He looked up at the wall. "Aha! Yes. Here it is. If the ring is pulled out, the fire won't burn so quickly and the oven will heat up better. You can regulate these things exactly with the flue. High heat, simmering heat, whatever you need and whatever it is will be done to perfection."

"We'll pull it out now then," said Hans. "We're going into town. Shan't be long." They pulled the ring, using the handle of the dreaded paddle. The two men went back into the house.

"Right!" said Hans. "Got everything?"
"Luggage in the car. Money in my pocket," Greg replied.
"Let's go then."

. . .

They had been driving for four days, stopping overnight at cheap motels. 'The Gingerbread House' was miles away. They stopped for lunch at a cheap and not very clean roadhouse. A few men were playing pool in the corner. A juke box blared out the latest hits. Slowly, they became aware of the proprietor staring at them. He was leaning over the counter frowning.

"What's gotten into him?" asked Greg.

"Perhaps he thinks we can't afford to pay."

The man's wife came out of the kitchen with their food, plonked it onto the table without a word and went to join her husband.

"They're looking at something under the counter," said Greg who was facing that way.

"A rat or a cockroach maybe?" Hans suggested.

Suddenly, the man came over to them. "Are you guys Hans and Greg Rawlings by any chance?" he asked.

Two hearts in two chests missed a beat. Again, the dreadful vision of being hung upside down returned to Hans. He felt sick. He wanted to run but knew that his legs would collapse under him the moment he stood up.

"Maybe you haven't seen this," said the man. He thrust a newspaper under their noses.

SO WHERE ARE THE HEIRS?

The headline was huge. Underneath was their photograph. The same photograph that James had taken on their eighteenth birthday. Hans had to read the article three times and then read bits of it aloud to Greg:

Mr. James Montgomery, the multi-millionaire president of the Montgomery Corporation, had died of a heart attack. His entire fortune had been left to the two Rawlings brothers whom he had adopted some years previously but they had unaccountably vanished two days before he died. Mr. Rod Chambers, the dead man's attorney had offered a reward of a thousand dollars to anyone who could give information as to their whereabouts.

Mr. Montgomery, Hans read, had lived the life of a recluse for some fifteen years after an office boy at the corporation's headquarters, had made an unsubstantiated charge of indecent behavior against him. "He'd been seriously ill for some years," Rod was reported as saying. "He was tired and he wanted to go. He intended to make over his estates to the boys on Christmas Day and then to enter a hospice. Unfortunately, he couldn't do either."

"Yes. That's us," said Hans, looking up. "Thanks a lot."

"I won't kid you that a thousand dollars isn't a lot of money to us," said the man, "but if you don't want to have anything to do with it, just say so. We'll keep quiet."

Hans smiled. "I should get on the phone straight away," he said. "That lawyer's phone number is here. When you speak to him, could you give him a message from us?"

"Sure. What is it?"

"Tell him to keep the fire going. We're coming back," promised Hans.

OH COME, ALL YE FAITHFUL

Peter Gilbert

"She might be a bit late. She often is," Simon said.

"Oh, I hope she's not too late," Glenn said. "I'm getting a hard on just thinking about it."

"Me too."

The funny thing about Simon was that, when he first joined the school, most people hadn't wanted to know him. He had been fifteen then. His dad had been appointed minister of All Saints. Neither Glenn nor any of the others wanted much to do with a potential Bible basher. He was good looking; he was intelligent and good at sports. As the months went by, people began to change their opinions.

Simon's missionary zeal was very different from that of his father. What Simon didn't know about sex wasn't worth knowing. Some boys doubted some of his stories but Simon knew all the right medical words for things, carried a large stock of contraceptives and, more significantly, had a noticeable light moustache sprouting on his upper lip. After only a year at the school he had quite a following. If you wanted to be reassured that your cock was developing properly or needed the answer to some question you couldn't really ask your dad, Simon Stoker was the man to see.

"I don't believe you," Glenn had said. They were in the changing room after football.

"It's true, I tell you. You can meet her if you want. She'd like you. She'd like that for sure." He pointed to Glenn's swaying cock.

Simon knew a girl; a really beautiful girl with the most enormous tits. If you let her toss you off, you could play with them. Sometimes, if she was in the right mood, she'd let you go further... much further. Her name was Susan. He wouldn't tell Glenn her family name or where she lived but he showed Glenn a photograph of her lying on a beach somewhere.

"I swear it's true," Simon said. "I'll swear on the Bible if you want me to."

That was enough for Glenn. It had to be true. Ministers' sons didn't say things like that if they didn't mean it.

They stood huddled in the church porch. The rain was falling in torrents, streaming off the corners of the roof and splashing into deep puddles.

"Come on! Where the hell are you?" Simon asked, kneading himself through the pocket of his jeans.

"Where are we going to do it?" asked Glenn.

"There's a room up in the tower. It's used to store old hymn books. I've got the key."

"What about your dad? He might come in the church."

"Not today. He's away doing a wedding. God, I hope she comes soon. My cock's so hard! What time is it?"

"Half past three. She should have been here half an hour ago."

"I know. Maybe she can't come. Let's go up in the tower. We'll be able to see her coming from up there."

They went into the church. Simon led the way through a tiny, pointed door in a side aisle and they climbed the seemingly never ending spiral staircase.

"Here we are," said Simon, unlocking a door. Cold air and rain gusted in. The two boys stepped out onto the castellated square roof.

"You can see every street from here," said Simon. It was true. Down below them, tiny cars sped along model lanes past houses that looked like something off a Monopoly board.

"How will she come?" asked Glenn.

"On her bike."

"There's nobody on a bike for miles."

"I was just thinking the same. This fucking weather! Why did it have to rain today of all days? I've got to get my rocks off somehow."

It was a new expression to Glenn, and he made a mental note to use it since it sounded so very grown up.

"Yeah. Me too," he said.

They went into the tower again. Simon shut the door against the wind and they climbed down the stairs. Half of the way down, Simon opened another door.

"This is the room," he said. "It's ideal, see."

Exactly as he had said, piles of dusty hymn books were stacked against the walls. In a corner was a mouldering heap of hassocks.

"I put these on the floor if I want to have a fuck," said Simon.

That was another good phrase. "It would have been nice to have a fuck this afternoon," said Glenn.

"Yeah. What we could do...."

"What?"

"We could have a bit of a muck around ourselves. I mean.... we both need to get our rocks off, don't we? You don't want to go home with a hard-on."

"How do you mean?"

"Do you do it to yourself?"

"Course I do," said Glenn, trying not to blush.

"What technique do you use?"

"Well, the usual one, you know?"

"With your fingers or with your hand?"

"Depends how I feel."

"Show me."

"What about you?"

"Sure. I don't mind what I do," Simon said, and he began to undress. He seemed totally unembarrassed. Glenn could only do likewise.

"I thought you said you had a hard-on," said Simon.

"It was earlier. Climbing all those stairs probably."

Glenn couldn't help staring at Simon's. It stood out from a really dense patch of thick, dark hair and was enormous.

"I'll put some of these down," said Simon. He grabbed an armful of old kneelers. The room filled with dust. He laid them on the floor and added some more.

"There," he said. "Lie down and I'll get it hard for you."

He was remarkably good at it. In no time at all, Glenn's was as hard as his own. He lay down next to Glenn. "You do me and I'll do you," he said.

The feel of Simon's warm, hard flesh did something odd to Glenn. It was unbelievably exciting, much more exciting than stealing things from shops or firing an air gun at passersby. He tried to synchronize his movements with his heart beat.

"Go slower!" Simon gasped.

Meanwhile, Simon's fingers were going everywhere; under his balls, round his cock, twining in his hair, back to his cock, working the foreskin up and down; up and down, up and down.

Keeping time, for Simon obviously knew what he was doing, Glenn did the same. He watched Simon's chest rising and falling.

Suddenly Simon took his hand off Glenn's cock. "Watch out! I'm coming!" he said. Like liquid icing, it streamed out of Simon's cock all over Glenn's fingers and kept on flowing.

"That was good," said Simon. "You're pretty good at it."

"As good as Susan?"

"At wanking I'd say you're better than she is."

"What else does she do?"

"Oh everything. She likes sucking it. Anyone ever done that to you?"

"No."

"It's a good feeling. Fucking feels better though. Do you want me to suck you?"

"If you like."

It was a pity, thought Glenn, that he was already so far gone. Simon's lips were no sooner round his cock than he had to push him away. He wasn't quite quick enough. Some of it landed on Simon's cheek. Glenn lay back, panting. He suddenly felt rather scared. They were in a church. The door downstairs was open. Anyone could come in. He stood up and started to get dressed.

"We could do it more often if you like," said Simon.

"I don't know." He really didn't. It felt nice but.... "If Susan comes, I wouldn't mind that," he said.

"It's just as much fun with each other. Anyway, with girls there's always the chance she'll get pregnant. I make a lot of spunk. So do you. That was a load."

"Girls only get pregnant if you fuck them," said Glenn. "You can't fuck another guy."

"Yes you can. You fuck them in their ass."

"Ugh! Have you done it?"

"Sure. It's great!"

"I'd better get home. My folks will be wondering where I've got to," said Glenn, casting a wary eye at Simon's cock. Even limp it looked like a potential painful experience.

. . .

"Heard anything from Susan?" Glenn asked some days later.

"Christ almighty! Don't you start on me!"

"I wasn't. It was a simple question."

"Sorry. It's just that I'm in the shit right up to my neck."

"How?" Glenn was alarmed. Had the minister found out about last Saturday afternoon? They hadn't bothered to tidy up afterwards.

"She's got a fallopian infection and she's menstruating. She'll be off line for ages."

Glenn had only a very vague idea of what a fallopian infection must be.

"Sounds nasty," he said.

"It is. It would have been worse if she'd turned up on Saturday. I guess we should think ourselves lucky. You ever seen a cock that's been near a fallopian infection?"

Reluctant to say that Simon's was the only one which he had seen at close quarters, Glenn said that he couldn't remember.

"You'd know if you had. It causes blisters and you can't stop them from bleeding. Anyway, the silly cow has dropped me right in it."

"How? Have you got it?"

"No. But the Saturday after next is our big day and she won't be there."

"Whose big day?"

"Forget I said anything."

"No. Come on, tell me."

"I can't mention names. It's in the club rules."

"What club?"

"Oh, I suppose I could tell you that much. Wait for me outside school. I'll tell you then."

Curious, Glenn positioned himself outside the school gates that afternoon.

"We call it the Freedom Club," said Simon.

"Why? What goes on?"

"Well, Susan wanks us off one by one. Then we have a rest and she choses one to have a fuck with. We all stand round them and wank on them. It's really great. Not this month though. I guess I'll have to tell everybody it's off. It's the one

Saturday when my dad will be away till late at night too. Bloody nuisance."

"Why can't you do it without her? Nobody would be able to have a fuck but at least they'd get their rocks off."

"Who'd do the wanking?"

"Take it in turns."

Simon stroked his chin thoughtfully. "I don't know if the others would like it. None of them would want the job. We like getting our rocks off and shooting the spunk around."

"Seems to me that it's your only choice," said Glenn. The memory of Simon's cock and that exquisite patch of black hair was getting him quite excited. "I'll do it if nobody else wants to," he added.

"Would you?"

"Sure. If nobody else wants the job. I've tossed you off. A few more won't make any difference. How many are there?"

"Four beside me," said Simon. "I'd better show you exactly what to do I guess."

"You told me already."

"We'd better make sure it's right. Are you free on Saturday afternoon?"

. . .

It could be a bit of fun, Glenn thought as he climbed down the stairs. He wiped his hands on a clump of grass in the churchyard and cycled home. He stopped on the way and sat on a roadside bench to read his notes again. He smiled as he looked at the paper. HYMNS FOR SPECIAL OCCASIONS. It should read HIMS FOR SPECIAL OCCASIONS he thought. 'Richard Atkinson (17)' he had written. Richard of all people. It was unbelievable. Richard was the Captain of the football team! Peter Maybanks and Michael Cole were both sixteen. David Roberts was only fifteen.

"Still a kid!" said Glenn contemptuously.

"You won't say that when you see him shoot," Simon replied.

Glenn looked at the paper again. He had written various signs by each name but had been so worked up at the time that he couldn't remember what most of them meant. He crumpled up the paper and threw it into a hedge.

The following Saturday seemed to take longer than usual to come round. Simon caught up with him in the school corridor on Thursday and said that all the members had agreed, regrettably of course. It wouldn't be the same. He'd been in touch with one or two more girls but they were all busy on Saturdays.

. . .

"Richard Atkinson usually comes first," said Simon. They were standing in the church tower.

"I'm not surprised. He's the eldest," said Glenn.

"No. I don't mean that. I mean 'arrives'. He's actually quite slow at the other. Ah! There he is. I'll call you down when we're ready,"

"Okay. Thank Christ it isn't raining."

From his high vantage point, Glenn watched them arrive. Richard drew up on his motor bike, parked it by the churchyard gate. He nipped behind a tombstone to have a pee and went into the church. Peter Maybanks and Michael Cole arrived together on their bikes. Glenn knew them reasonably well. They were stupid, he thought. Stories about them had been circulating for months. They called for each other on the way to school. They always sat together and went home together. If they had dropped a few hints about Susan the gossips would have been quashed. They were both good looking; indeed, Peter's blond hair and bright red Cupid's bow lips had fired the flames of rumor.

He didn't know David Roberts. The boy was half-way through the churchyard before Glenn realized that the tall figure who had loitered outside for some time was actually making for the church. It was difficult to tell from that height, how tall the boy was. Pretty tall certainly. He seemed to tower above the tallest of the monuments.

Glenn sat on the plinth of the flagstaff and waited impatiently. It would be interesting, he thought, to hear what they were saying. Of course they'd be moaning about the fact that Susan had let them down. They'd probably be a bit worried about that infection, whatever it was called. Seventeen-year-old Richard had almost certainly gone the whole way with her.

That was slightly worrying. Could you get a rash on your hands from holding a cock that had been exposed to an infection? He wished he'd asked Simon. The thought of holding it was exciting. It would probably be alright if he washed his hands thoroughly when he got home—and anyway, Richard himself had to hold it several times each day to pee and probably at night for other purposes and, as far as Glenn knew, there was no sign of anything on his hands. It was worth taking the risk....

"Ready!" Simon's voice echoed up the stairs.

Glenn put his hands in his pockets in an attempt to rearrange the bulge that had appeared in the front of his jeans and started to climb down the stairs. He opened the door. The memory of that moment stayed with him for years afterwards. The musty smell, the pile of hassocks, the stacks of hymn books against the wall, the naked bulb and the five naked boys. Richard sat in a corner with his legs outspread. His cock, thick and rubbery-looking, lay on his thigh. Simon, next to him, was perched on a heap of hassocks. His was already stiff, reaching up almost to his navel. Peter and Michael sat next to each other against the wall. Peter's pubic hair was a funny golden color and looked a bit like brass turnings. Michael, on the other hand, was dark. David Roberts sat alone in a corner. His immensely long legs converged in a dense mass of dark hair from which sprouted what looked, at first sight, to be a purple-headed toadstool that gleamed under the light.

"Welcome to the club," said Richard.

"Wish we'd known," said Michael.

"I told you," said Simon.

"We thought it was another of your yarns."

Glenn looked round the room. Five of them! Five cocks, pretty big ones at that, and ten balls all hard at work in their warm sacs making sperms. He wondered who to start with. Richard probably. His cock wasn't completely hard yet. It would be pretty enormous when it was!

"We're going to need a lot of paper to wipe up," he said, staring at it. Both Simon and he came pretty copiously. There were two more boys of their age and Richard was a year older. For some reason, the remark seemed to amuse them.

"Here," said David. He took one of the hymn books and

ripped out a chunk of pages.

Simon stood up, took the key from the lintel above the door and locked it. He tossed the key over to Richard who tucked it under the hassocks on which he was sitting.

"Get your clothes off," said Richard.

"Me?"

"You're the only one wearing anything."

"There's no need."

"Yes there is. We changed the rules," said Simon.

"Sod that. You said...."

"We're allowed to change the rules," said Michael. "Come on. Let's have a look at it."

"And a feel of it," Peter added. "Let's see if Simon was right."

"Can I have the key? I'm off," said Glenn.

"You won't leave here until we do," Richard replied. Glenn dashed for the door and, using all his might wrenched at the handle. It didn't move. He hammered on the rough oak surface and hurt his hand on one of the studs on the surface.

"Don't let him make too much noise," said Simon. "It echoes down the stairs."

Suddenly they were all pressing against him. The smell of their perspiration was almost overpowering. Their strength certainly was. He didn't have a chance. Hands grasped bits of clothing. His shirt was pulled out of his jeans. He struggled for a few seconds. One of his shirt buttons flew across the room.

"Oh, okay," he said. "Let me. Something will get torn."

"That's better," said Richard. Glenn looked down. Richard's cock was stiff and pointing towards him threateningly.

He started to undress. Trainers, socks, shirt, jeans and then, finally, his drawers.

"Looks like you told the truth for once in your life," said David Roberts.

"Told you so," said Simon. "Wait till you see him come."

"Who's first?" said David.

"Me of course," Simon replied. "I got him."

"All the more reason for someone else to go first," said Richard. "Stand back."

Glenn wondered whether to make a dash to the unoccupied pile of hassocks and retrieve the key. It wouldn't do any good, he thought bitterly. Even if he managed to escape them—which was unlikely since he could hardly go home in the nude. He'd have to put up with it. He could have his revenge at school. People would be interested to know that Richard and Simon were queers as well as Peter and Michael. There'd be quite a few broken noses and black eyes when the word got round.

He felt Richard's hand on his behind and shuddered.

"Nice ass," said Richard. "He'll fuck well."

Glenn shivered again. They surely weren't planning to do that to him?

"Yeah. Not today though," said Simon. That was a relief. Glenn relaxed slightly.

Peter, Michael and David Roberts kicked hassocks into the centre of the room. Dust flew everywhere.

"Lie down," Richard commanded. Glenn did so. He stared up at the light bulb as Richard's hand explored his cock and his balls.

"He's coming up," somebody said. It was true. Glenn couldn't control it. The worst thing possible was happening to him. His cock was beginning to rise for a queer! It was Simon's fault of course. If it hadn't been for those two occasions with Simon it couldn't happen. He struggled a bit but hands held his arms and legs. He was powerless and it would be all round the school within hours.

"Time starts now," said Simon's voice. Glenn felt something damp touch his cock. He raised his head. Richard was licking it! He felt the older boy's teeth on his flesh and winced. Richard's lips moved down the shaft dragging the skin back as they did so. His cock head rubbed against something hard. Then Richard started sucking. His cheeks moved inwards, touching Glenn's flesh in rhythmic movements. If you closed your eyes, he discovered, it wasn't so bad.

"Time is up," said Simon. Cold air wafted round Glenn's rampant cock.

"He's good," said Richard. "Very tasty."

Nothing happened. The hands still grasped Glenn's limbs. He opened his eyes. David Roberts held his wrists. Simon was at his ankles. Both were pretty strong. There was no point in fighting. Anyway, it seemed to have finished.

He lay limp and stared at the light bulb. He wondered what

the actual temperature of the glowing filament was. Pretty hot certainly. What had the physics teacher said....

"Your turn, Mike," said Simon.

Glenn turned his head. The image of the light bulb had burned into his retina. He was aware of someone coming over to him and kneeling by his side. It was Michael. Once again he felt a hand on his cock. Once again, lips—softer lips this time—slid down over him. He didn't struggle this time. The best thing, he thought, was to shoot and get it over. Then they'd let him go home. He'd have time to plan his revenge. Seeing Michael's putty-like face smashed into a pulp would be fun. Peter too. Convenient that they always went round together....

"Don't make him come." That was Peter's voice. Peter the pretty boy. Ha! He wouldn't be so pretty when Glenn's buddies had finished with him.

Michael played with his balls as he sucked. If only it were a girl doing that.... Glenn closed his eyes again.

"Time is up," said Simon again. Glenn opened his eyes and just as quickly, shut them again. A long, sickening stream of saliva connected Michael's mouth with his cock.

Again there was a long wait. They let go of his limbs. All thoughts of fight had left him. He felt strangely tired and breathless.

"You can help Pete get ready," said Simon.

"With pleasure," said Michael, wiping his mouth on the back of his hand. "Where's the stuff?"

"Oh, sorry. In my jeans pocket. In the corner."

Glenn watched as Michael went over to the pile of clothes. "Got it," he said.

"Now you, Dave." said Simon. "Be careful now."

David Roberts took his place on his knees at Glenn's side. He really was big for his age, thought Glenn. David's cock brushed against his thigh. Amazing for a fifteen-year-old. Again, he felt lips encompass his shaft. If you forgot who was doing it, Glenn thought, it was quite a nice feeling. He wondered if it would be possible to do it to oneself. Almost certainly not but it was a nice feeling. David made swallowing movements. That felt really good. His body suddenly arched upwards. He hadn't meant to do it. It was a reflex, like jerking your leg when someone hit your knee. A strange, warm feeling spread through his body. You couldn't really blame people for being queer, he thought. They couldn't help it and everybody needed to get his rocks off somehow. None of these guys was actually bad. Richard was okay. He was a brilliant footballer. And you couldn't blame Simon really. Having a dad who was a minister must be like living in prison. As for Peter and Michael... well they were okay. They were peaceful enough characters. As for David Roberts... Glenn didn't know him but he could certainly suck cock and his own was a pretty good specimen.

He raised his head and looked along his body. It was enormous. The tip jerked up and down over Glenn's thigh. He wondered what it would be like to suck it. You'd need a pretty big mouth. That was a point. What about Peter? He hadn't had a go yet. That tiny little pursed mouth of his would have to stretch a bit to take Glenn... even more to accommodate David Roberts or Richard. He wondered if either of them had ever tried.

"My turn," said Simon. David's mouth slid away and he stood up.

"Be careful," said Peter' voice.

"Don't worry. I will. I know when he's hot."

For a few moments, nobody in the room spoke. Strange wet noises came from somewhere behind Glenn's head and he heard Peter moan slightly. What the hell were they doing? He tried to put his head right back to see but the two hassocks under his head prevented him from doing so. They were probably kissing, he thought. That was disgusting! The rumors had been correct. Once he'd actually defended them by pointing out that they were never seen holding hands or anything like that. Now, here they were in a church of all places, kissing each other! Ugh!

"Is that enough?" asked Michael.

"A bit more," he heard Peter answer. "Go in a bit more."

Michael obviously had his tongue right in Peter' mouth. All that slimy saliva....

He was aware of Simon at his side. Simon grinned at him. "Last but not least eh, Glenn?" he said.

"What..about..Peter?" Glenn gasped as Simon's mouth encompassed him. Certainly not least, he thought. Simon's was bigger than his. It felt good too. Those afternoons when the two of them had been alone had been good. There was something nice about Simon's cock. It felt hard and yet it was oddly squeezable. And Simon was certainly an expert when it came to sucking. He wasn't a kisser either. You wouldn't get Simon to do that, thank God. Not like Peter and Michael....

And then a thought struck him. If they really did have their tongues in each others' throat, they wouldn't be able to talk. Perhaps they weren't kissing after all. That was a relief. So what were they doing? It was, he thought, none of his business anyway. His business was to come as soon as possible and if Simon was to be the last, Simon could have the lot: right in his mouth. There would be no warnings this time. He arched up again. Simon put his hands on Glenn's hips and pushed him down so that the rough material of the kneelers again made contact with Glenn's buttocks.

In school they had learned that sperms are made of protein and the body uses protein to make new cells. So Simon would have Glenn's sperms in his guts, digest them and use them to make new cells. So there would be something of Glenn in Simon's body. A nice thought...looking at Simon on the sports field or in the pool and thinking, 'There's some of me in that body.' Simon had a good body too...tall and slender...that long, thick cock and those big balls...all that hair...long legs too....

And Simon stopped.

"Keep going!" Glenn gasped. "I'm nearly...."

But Simon just smiled. "Nice, eh?" he asked.

"Yeah." Glenn sat up and reached down to grip it. His balls were aching. He was seconds away from coming. Simon pushed his hands away.

"Ready?" said Peter's voice.

"Just about," Simon replied.

Glenn heard footfalls by his head and then Peter came into view, towering over him. So there was to be another after all, thought Glenn. That was just as well.

But Peter didn't kneel at his side. He put one foot over Glenn's legs and stood looking down at him like a colossus. Well, not really a colossus. Peter's cock was nothing to shout about. It was standing up, certainly but it wasn't nearly so big as Simon's or David Roberts' or Richard's. His balls were quite big though.

Glenn felt Peter's feet moving up along the outer surface of his legs. Peter smiled again and then crouched down. Glenn's cock rubbed against his skin. It was satin-smooth. Peter reached down, held it with his fingers and moved it around. It touched something hard. Glenn raised his head and, at the same time, his cock head touched something soft and greasy.

Oh no! Surely not.... He swore and sat up, meaning to push Peter away. The pressure on his cock head increased and became painful. His behind was pushed down hard against the rough stitching of a hassock. He groaned. Something gave way. He only had to look at Peter's face to see what it was. His eyes screwed up. His tiny mouth grimaced and something warm and tight slid over the head of Glenn's cock.

Slowly, more and more of it went in. It was like being eaten by a snake. Peter opened his eyes and grinned as his balls touched Glenn's pubes and his soft thighs made contact with the hardness of Glenn's groin.

"Ride 'im, cowboy!" said Richard. Several of the others clapped. They came and stood round in a circle. Lit by the solitary bulb in the centre their faces looked evil and leering.

Glenn shut his eyes. He saw himself fucking another guy! It was horrible. He tried to conjure up the vision of a girl but it just didn't work. The air was full of male perspiration. Now he understood—it would have to be Peter after all. Okay, then. He'd hurt him. Hurt him so badly that Peter would cry out for mercy and try to wriggle off the skewer that pierced him. Peter wouldn't walk down the corridor with that sexy little bum wriggle of his for some time. Glenn clenched the cheeks of his ass. A bit more forced its way in. He did it again. Quite a lot more went in that time. Peter winced and something rubbed against Glenn's cock. The base of it felt like a rubber band was round it. He pushed up as hard as he possibly could. That hurt. He could see it had. Doing it to cause pain was actually a nice sensation. He had a momentary vision of Peter tied to a table screaming as Glenn did something to him. What? Cutting off his balls maybe? They were certainly big enough. He could feel them jiggling against his flesh. No, just sticking something in his tight, round little ass was sufficient. Jabbing it in, really hard, shoving against the tissues and feeling them part to make way for him.

"About now," said Simon.

Glenn's eyes snapped open. They had moved in closer. Hands were working on cocks. Not their own hands. He could see that David Roberts' enormous tool was in Michael's hand and Simon had hold of Richard.

Glenn gave another upward show. Then another, then another. Peter's hand gripped his thighs. His cock seemed to have gone down a bit but then, with a thing as small as that, it was difficult to tell. One more upward thrust and then another....

"It's...."

That was all he managed to say. He opened his eyes wide. Peter grinned as jet after jet squirted into him. Glenn had certainly never produced as much. He lay back gasping. Something wet landed on his face. Another spot touched his belly. He raised his head, just in time to catch Peter's next load on his chin. He went to wipe it away and then even more cascaded down from the rampant cocks of the onlookers. Simon first, then Richard, closely followed by Michael and David Roberts. Jets of pearl white fluid splashed down on to the two of them and glistened against the whiteness of their skins. Some went into Peter's blond hair. He just sat there grinning.

"Dirty sods!" Glenn gasped and lay back, absolutely exhausted.

"From where I was standing that looked good," said Simon.

"Sitting on it was even better," said Peter.

Michael handed them the wad of hymnal pages. Obligingly, Peter leaned forward and wiped Glenn's chest.

"You can get off now. You're quite a weight," said Glenn.

The rubber ring feeling moved upwards as he gently lifted his ass. Glenn looked down at his cock. The veins stood out blue against the gleaming white skin. He tried to sit up but toppled back again. It was an extraordinary sensation. He lay there trying to get his breath back and compose his thoughts. The others all stood round him, wiping their cocks on old pages from the hymn book. Cocks, he thought, were interesting things. So, for that matter were asses. There was Richard's great hairy one. Michael's plump ass gleamed under the lamp. Then there was David Roberts. He had a soft, smooth backside. Or Simon....

... Jutting buttocks and faint traces of hair where they merged into his legs.

... Five asses. Each one different. Each one would feel different and it had been a nice feeling.

Michael giggled.

"What's up?" he asked and managed to sit up straight, mostly in order to get a good view of his next target. It wouldn't be fair to fuck Peter and not Michael. It really did look good; so soft and fleshy.

"Have a look at this," said Michael, handing him a soggy piece of paper.

"Oh come, all ye faithful," Glenn read.

"Next time," he said and winked.

Michael winked back. "Lord, be in my head—and Glenn be in my ass," he said.

GETTING STUFFED

James Hosier

I'm still laughing. Karl has just left. I think he feels a bit better for having told somebody about it. His new collection was interesting. As for the way it started, I haven't laughed so much since my dad stepped in the garden pond.

Karl is my age, and he's German. Not originally German like Mike Braun, but real German. German passport, speaks the language, eats sauerkraut: the whole lot. His dad is something big in a German firm over here.

He has just gotten back from a vacation in the so-called "old country," his first visit there for five years. He was there for six weeks and boy, did he learn a lot!

It started off with lederhosen. I didn't know what they were until Karl showed me. Lederhosen, if you haven't seen a pair, are short pants; very short pants, made of leather. They have a cuff that comes about the middle of your thigh and they're held up by suspenders that go over the shoulders. There's a decorated panel between the suspenders, which goes on your chest.

I first knew about Karl's trip when he showed me these weird pants. I'd gone round to see him about something. Karl doesn't often get angry but he was on that day. His grandfather, back in Germany had gotten Karl's measurements from his mother and had these things made for his beloved grandson.

"If he thinks I'm going to wear these, he can think again!" said Karl. He locked the bedroom door and put them on to show me. He looked like a crocus bulb that had rooted. We both agreed that they might suit Pinocchio, but that no American (or temporarily resident) teenager would wish to be seen dead in them.

"You could wear them at fancy dress parties," I suggested.

"Get stuffed!" he growled.

Karl probably knew about my extremely profitable sideline. By the time I was seventeen I'd been "stuffed" a good many times. I was always on the look out for a new cock or ass for my contacts. The sight of his long, white legs and neat little leather-clad butt made my brain ring like a cash register but I knew Karl was a non-starter. I'd tried hard enough with him but my subtle and not-so-subtle hints had fallen on stony ground. As far as Karl was concerned a cock had two legs and an ass had four. He seemed to have no interest in sex of any sort. He didn't date and he didn't go to dances. We just assumed that it was to do with him being a German. Karl tackled everything in an earnest, hard working manner—except sex. It just didn't figure in his life.

They got to Munich safely enough with the lederhosen at the bottom of Karl's suitcase. They stayed with his grandfather. Now it happened that the famous Oktoberfest was on, it being September. No, don't pick up the pen to write me. The fest starts in September.

Grandfather Huber indicated that nothing would give him greater pleasure than to take his long-missed grandson to the Oktoberfest. Karl had nothing against the idea. He'd heard a lot about it. He was looking forward to going until his grandfather told him he was expected to wear the dreaded lederhosen. There was a family row—a row of huge proportions apparently with Karl slamming doors and threatening to go home. I'd never seen Karl like that but he assures me it's true. The family won. A very sulky Karl got transported to the Oktoberfest in grandfather's BMW. Every time the car turned a corner, Karl's butt squeaked on the leather upholstery.

Shock number one was that most of the Germans there were wearing lederhosen. (I wish I'd been there. My eyes would have been popping out of my head!) Shock number two was the fact that the beer wasn't served in glasses but in huge liter tankards. Once he'd gotten over those, he had a good evening. His grandfather introduced him to a lot of his ancient friends. They drank and ate. They sang ancient German drinking songs. Altogether a good evening if you're a German and you speak the language.

The following evening, the family were all going to see someone whom Karl's dad had known years before. Karl wanted to go to the Oktoberfest again. I can't say I blame him. Coming from a state like ours, where seventeen-year-olds have to ask someone older to buy drink for them and then drink it secretly in somebody's cellar, it must have seemed like being in paradise to be able to drink openly, especially from liter mugs!

Another family row followed but not so serious as the first. Karl's mom said he wasn't old enough to get round the city on his own. Grandfather came to the rescue. He would deliver Karl to the Oktoberfest and Karl could get a taxi back to the house. That suited Karl. He didn't really go much on the idea of wearing his lederhosen in the subway.

He went into a different brewer's tent that time, not wishing to be recognized by grandfather's buddies and have to spend the evening with them. It was fairly early. He sat by himself at an empty table and ordered a beer.

"*Ist hier frei?*" He could tell straight away that, although the guy spoke German, he was a foreigner. He wore a check shirt and jeans; a reasonably good-looking guy, maybe twenty-seven to thirty. Karl said that the table was free. The man sat down next to him.

"Where are you from?" he asked in English.

The man beamed. "The United States," he said, speaking slowly and distinctly. "North Dakota, but I live in Munich. Your English is excellent."

Karl laughed. So did the man when Karl told him where he lived.

"Looks like my lucky day," said the man.

"How so?"

"I've been here for five years but I still find it hard work to talk in German all the time."

"Did you really think I was German?" Karl asked.

"Bavarian actually. Those lederhosen aren't the sort that tourists buy. Those are the real thing."

Suddenly, Karl felt immensely proud. He was a real Bavarian and he looked like one! He told the man about his family.

"I guessed as much," he said, and Karl felt even more proud.

"What do you do here?" he asked.

"I guess you could say I'm an antique dealer. I go for the old traditional Bavarian stuff, buy it, restore it and then sell it overseas. There's a terrific market there. You'd be amazed how many people collect it."

"Such as?"

"Oh, old farmhouse furniture, paintings, lederhosen...."

"You mean people actually collect these things?" Karl was amazed.

"Sure."

"Old, second-hand pants?"

"Fifth and sixth-hand are even more valuable. A handmade, nineteenth century pair of lederhosen will fetch thousands if they're in good condition."

"I'll put these in store when I get home," said Karl. He told the man about them. "I never thought I'd ever wear them," he said.

"They're good ones," said the man. "Don't store them yet. They need to be worn in. They look a bit too new at the moment. Do you mind if I...."

He didn't finish the sentence but put down his mug and, pushing his fingers between the shorts and Karl's leg, rubbed his thumb over the shiny leather surface.

"Very good quality," he said, "and you've got the perfect figure for them."

An alarm sounded in Karl's brain. He said that he thought of me at that moment. Me! I'd never gotten near him, let alone got my hands in his pants. The guy took his hand away. They continued drinking and Karl thought he must have been mistaken after all. The guy said his name was Peter and he had an apartment near the city center.

"What you really need," said Peter, when they were into the second liter of the evening, "is an antique schild, or what you would call a shield."

"What is it exactly?"

"Well, it's the tab that goes between the suspenders on the front. That one of yours, with respect, isn't that good. I've got some back at the apartment. Maybe we could meet again and I could show you."

"If they're antiques, they'd be out of my reach," said Karl. "I know what you mean, though. My grandfather has one embroidered with silver wire."

"That's right. Yours would look a hundred per cent better with one of those. It would look as if you'd worn lederhosen all your life and had transferred the shield to the new ones."

Karl looked round the tent. It was filling up fast. Lots of men were wearing lederhosen but he could only see one silver shield on the chest of an old man whose pallor and spindly legs made it pretty certain that his lederhosen would soon be on the second hand market.

Whether it was the effect of the beer or the excited atmosphere of the tent, Karl didn't know, but he was suddenly desperately keen to have a silver shield. His grandfather would be proud of him and, although he could hardly walk round our town in lederhosen, he could show people the shield. Maybe even start a collection of them—something to remember Germany by. The band was playing traditional music. He was surrounded by people in traditional costume, drinking beer in traditional mugs. Even the beer had been brewed to a traditional recipe. America had traditions, traditions to be proud of, but he wasn't an American. He was a German, a Bavarian, and he had never before given it a thought.

"What we could do," said Peter, looking at his watch, "is go back to my place and I could show you some. It isn't far and I've got the car."

"Yeah, why not?" said Karl. The empty places at the table had been taken by a group of tourists. One look at the women's pale blue hair styles and the men's immaculate suits was enough. These people, he thought, were not part of the great Bavarian tradition. Peter was a foreigner too but he was different....

Just how different, Karl was to find out later. The apartment was an eye opener. Karl knew nothing about antiques but it was obvious, even to him, that every piece of furniture was traditional and worth a lot of money. Only the kitchen was modern but even there, ancient, dented, copper jelly moulds and cast iron pans hung on the whitewashed walls.

"A beer?" Peter asked.

"Why not?" said Karl.

"Might as well have it in the proper vessel, eh?" said Peter. "I hate modern glasses." He poured the beer into a tall, highly decorated mug with a hinged lid. At first Karl found it difficult to drink from it. The lid kept bashing his face but the beer tasted great. Much better, he thought, than the beer at home.

Home? No, not home. Home was Bavaria. He felt warm and

comfortable. Bavaria was his real home now.

"Let me show you some shields," said Peter. He went to the heavy, carved wooden sideboard and brought out a shallow wooden tray. It was crammed full of shields.

Karl fingered them, feeling the decoration as a blind man would but astounded at the workmanship. Each one of them, he thought, would have taken hundreds of hours to embroider. The people who did it were long dead. It was up to him to show off their skill. Maybe it was all some kind of destiny. The lederhosen, the trip to Bavaria, meeting Peter, admiring the shield... everything fitted together.

Peter sat next to him. "Which one do you like best?" he asked.

"Gee. They're all beautiful. This one I think. I like the peacock. What are the stones?"

"Artificial," said Peter. "It's not as valuable as it looks. The embroidery is silver wire but what looks like gold isn't, and those emeralds first saw life as a green medicine bottle."

"How old is it?" Karl asked.

"Early this century. Just before the first war."

"So the guy who wore it might have been killed in the war?"

"Probably."

Karl had to have it. The original owner had been proud to wear it. It was an insult to his memory to keep it stored in a box in a Munich apartment, however traditionally furnished.

"More than I could afford, I'll bet," he said ruefully. "I'd give my right arm to have something like that."

"Would you give something smaller?"

"Such as?"

Peter placed a hand on his bare thigh. "You like it, don't you?" he said. Karl wasn't quite sure what he meant.

"Yeah. It's beautiful," he replied.

"It's yours if you do me a favor in return."

"Sure. Hey! What do you think you're doing?"

Karl knew very well what Peter was doing. The fly on a pair of lederhosen isn't a fly. It's a triangular flap, secured at the top by two buttons. Peter had reached over and undone one of the buttons.

"Leave off!" said Karl. He giggled. This must be some sort

of joke, he thought. He put his beer mug down on the table. As he did so the second button was undone. Maybe it wasn't a joke. When he felt Peter's fingers fumbling with his undershorts he knew it wasn't.

"Shit, man!" he said. Back in the States he'd have hammered the guy but the States were a long way away. This was Bavaria. The room started spinning. He felt Peter's hands on his flesh and felt it responding to the man's touch. That was the one thing he didn't want to happen. He picked up the shield. Peter spoke.

"You like it, don't you?"

There was no doubt at all in Karl's mind what was meant that time. He didn't answer. He shifted slightly and the lederhosen squeaked on the sofa.

"Better get them right off," said Peter. "Don't want to make a mess on them."

That was sensible enough. Still clutching the schild Karl let the man undress him. He wondered about the original owner of the schild. How old had he been? Eighteen maybe? Maybe even younger. Had this happened to him too? Maybe. He had a sudden conviction that it had. He was following a tradition. A tradition started by a teenaged Bavarian who was about to be called up.

It wouldn't have happened in the same apartment. The building was too modern. Not on that couch either, but the sideboard that could have been there. The picture on the wall too. That looked old. It was a tiny little portrait; smaller than a picture postcard. A man; a young man despite his long whiskers beaming down with approval, not frowning like King Ludwig.

The boy had met the man at the Oktoberfest. The year? Nineteen twelve. The man? He was an American.

"There! That's better. May as well get your tee shirt off too, eh?"

It wouldn't have been a tee shirt in those days. More likely a shirt with a separate collar and a tie. The man in the picture (probably looking a little less brown and cracked in those days) had seen and heard it all before. He looked genial and unshockable.

He let Peter lay him on the couch. The man knelt by his side.

"Haven't you got long legs?" he said.

"Have I?"

"Mmm. I like long legs. I like big cocks too. Like yours...."

Karl gasped. Nobody else had ever touched his, let alone lick it. It wasn't such a bad feeling. For an instant he wondered if his predecessor had liked it. He glanced at the painting and decided that he must have done or the man wouldn't be smiling so broadly.

He felt Peter's hand under his balls. His legs stiffened and he gasped again. Then Peter put his mouth right over his cock head and sucked it in. He felt it sliding over the man's teeth and Peter's tongue moving against it. That felt really good. He closed his eyes and tried to think of the boy in 1912 but the present intruded. In America what he was doing would be wrong. He knew that. Why was it that, in Bavaria, it felt so right? In the States he wouldn't have given a guy like Peter a second glance. Karl opened his eyes for a moment and looked down at Peter's bobbing head. His fair hair was flopping about slightly. He was a good-looking guy. It felt great to have a good-looking guy as a buddy, especially an expert on traditions. You couldn't go wrong with a guy like Peter. There was nothing wrong with what he was doing. He thought of the young man in 1912 again. It was all traditional. He let himself go.

He was aware of his frenzied groans and wriggles. He felt it building up inside him until the pressure was painful. Then, with a great upwards heave, he came. He hadn't touched it since he'd been in Bavaria, fearing that the duvet on the bed might get stained. Spurt after spurt shot into Peter's greedily sucking mouth. He lay there passive and exhausted whilst the man licked round his loins and in his pubic bush.

"By Christ! That was good!" said Peter. He stood up and grinned down at Karl. "I was certainly lucky to find you," he said. Karl looked at the portrait on the wall. The man was still smiling.

Peter showed him the bathroom. He cleaned up, returned to the lounge and dressed.

"Who's that?" he asked, pointing to the portrait.

"Fancy you noticing that. Shows you have taste. That's the most valuable thing in the apartment. It's by a famous Bavarian artist who worked here in Munich. Strangely enough, I bought it in the States. The man is an American. Walter J. Stone was his name. He lived here in Munich. It has a weird history. Have you got time?"

"Sure."

"It was taken by an American soldier from the body of a dead Bavarian soldier in the trenches during the first world war. Why the hell a Bavarian soldier should be carrying a portrait of an American, God alone knows."

Karl bent down to examine the picture more closely. "They were buddies," he said. He didn't know why he was so sure but he was.

He felt Peter's hand on his butt. "I wonder," said the man.

"I'm sure," said Karl. "They met, became close buddies and then the war came. They never met again."

"You're quite a romantic aren't you?" Peter whispered, "but who's to say you're not right. Shall we become close buddies?"

"I thought we had."

"We could be even closer. Come here. Let's take that old shield off and put the new one in its place."

He clicked it into place and then took Karl in his arms, hugging him tight.

"Really close friends, eh?" Peter whispered. A hand moved up and down the middle seam at the back of the lederhosen. There was no mistaking that gesture. He looked at the picture. Walter J. Stone was still smiling. He'd given his Bavarian boy-friend the shield.

Then, a couple of years later, the war had broken out. The boy had asked for the picture before he was packed off to fight Walter's own people. They had never seen each other again. It was all so bloody tragic. Now it was up to him, Karl Huber, to heal the wounds and carry on their tradition.

"I'm only here for six weeks," he said.

"I reckon we can do an awful lot in six weeks," said Peter "and you'll be back, won't you?"

"You bet your bottom dollar I will," said Karl.

. . .

"They're real nice," I said, fingering the embroidery. Karl

had brought back eight shields. The one I was looking at was a picture of a butterfly.

"I never really had a hobby before," said Karl.

"It's funny," I said, "and you thought you'd be bored out there."

He laughed. "I was," he said, "several times! That butterfly is real gold and the stones are sapphires! I guess you could say that I've had traditional values stuffed into me."

BUON GIORNO, JOHN PORNO!

James Hosier

I never wanted to go because foreign vacations are not my scene. A business acquaintance of my dad's was to blame. You know already, I think, that Dad's firm, Kookalux, makes kitchens and fitted closets. This guy, Kenneth K. Valdinger, is into Culture (note the capital 'C'). He raved about Rossini. Dad bought a couple of Rossini CDs. Then it was Art. Not LP sleeves. Oh, no! Leonardo da Vinci, someone called Titian—that crowd. He had the idea of turning out closet doors with Old Master pictures engraved in the wood. Can you imagine it? I said at the time it was a crazy idea.

"Look in the Last Supper closet and check we have enough spaghetti, James."

But Dad was sufficiently impressed to start talking to the firm that made the engraving machines. Mr. Valdinger said Dad ought to go to Italy and see the pictures for himself. There was no country quite like Italy, he said. The weather was perfect, the people were friendly, the food was out of this world and, of course there was the Art. It would be a good idea to take the family there, he said. It would do young James good to experience the Old Masters.

Young James was happy enough experiencing young masters. I had three regular clients, none of them older than thirty-five. Three weeks in Italy would mean a considerable loss of income. Unfortunately, it wasn't an argument I could use to my folks. I had to fall back on Janet. Not a valid excuse. Three weeks apart would be good for both of us. End of subject. Start packing.

Andy, Greg and Michael were all very understanding and each said he would be waiting anxiously for me to come back.

"You'll get a lovely, very sexy tan," Michael said, stroking my butt.

"Not there I won't."

"You may. Suntanned buns turn me on."

I said something about not getting much of a chance to get a suntan anywhere. The conversation was not pursued. We were both too busy.

Our destination was Florence. Well... not actually in Florence. Dad resents hotel prices. We were in a small village just outside the city. Discos? You have to be joking! A cinema? I don't think they'd heard of them. It was a morgue.

The inevitable row happened on the second night we were there. I'd been to the art gallery with them. Acute boredom! They decided to go again. I said "No way!" Dad shouted. Mom moaned. It's odd when you think about it. I mean, parents are supposed to love their children. I'm not so naive as to think that Andy, Greg or Michael actually love me. If one of them suggested going to an art gallery, especially for the second time, I know that if I said "No," that would be that. They respect my opinions.

I said I'd go into the city and meet them later. Finally, they agreed and that's how I came to be sitting in the garden of the Ristorante Republica drinking a beer and trying to get my legs suntanned. It was a hot day so I'd worn my shorts.

I never really noticed Nico until he stood up and his shadow fell over me. I was just aware of this youngish guy sitting at a table under a tree sipping coffee and reading a book.

"Buon giorno."

"What?"

"You are American?"

"Yeah."

"It means 'Good day'. You are alone?"

"Yeah."

"Can I join you?"

"Sure."

He brought his book and his coffee over and sat down. He didn't say anything. He just sat and read and sipped coffee.

"What's the book?" I asked.

"Fifteenth century paintings."

"You interested in that sort of thing?" I asked, which was a stupid question. The guy wouldn't have been reading about them if he wasn't.

"I'm an art historian," he said.

I said something about how he ought to meet my folks.

"I'd rather meet you," he said. "Tell me about yourself."

I did. "And you?" I asked.

He was twenty nine, and—would you believe—a professor! He'd written three books already.

"Can't say I'm interested in art," I said. That sounded a bit rude. I'd given him ten minutes on the swimming team, the motor bike and my folks and he'd sat looking interested even though, thinking about it, I guess I'd bored the pants off him.

"I guess it's really a question of not knowing anything about it," I added.

"It's fun," he said. "See the cathedral dome over there?"

"Yeah."

"It's octagonal and yet it's a dome. Forty-one meters across. A hundred-and-six meters tall, and built without any reinforcement. And that was designed by a man called Brunelleschi in the 15th century. Ask a modern architect to do it and he couldn't, not without a lot of reinforcement."

"And that's art?" I said, shading my eyes from the sun.

"That is perfect art. He overcame all the prejudices of the time and created something unique and beautiful. The experts of the time would have told him it was impossible but he did it."

"What was his name again?"

"Brunelleschi. We could go to see it if you want but don't feel you have to."

"Why not?" I said. "I've got nothing else to do."

The cathedral is called Santa Maria del something-or-other. Nico was amazing. I think there was some sort of argument with the guys on the door about my shorts but they let us in, almost bowing. Men unlocked doors for us and called "Nico Professore." We went right up into the dome and he showed me how it was built. You could even see the initials of the guys who did it. Initials of people who'd been dead for five hundred years!

"David!" said Nico. We were climbing down the staircase at the timer. It was very steep and winding and I was in front.

"No, James," I said. I didn't turn round. You need all your concentration to manage a 15th century staircase.

"You remind me of David," he said. "It's your legs."

Click! Amazing! Here was another! I'd left three behind in the States, flown several thousand miles, sat in a garden with a beer, and before it was half finished I'd found another one—or he'd found me. Well, I thought, why not? It would keep me occupied for three weeks and I'd earn a bit of extra money.

We got to the foot of the stairs. There was another session of bows as we said "Goodbye" to the guy in charge and stepped out into the open air.

I looked at my watch. There was no way I could go back to his place then. I was due to be collected from the Republica in about thirty minutes.

"What are you doing tomorrow?" he asked. I said I had nothing planned.

"I could collect you from the Republica and introduce you to David," he said. "Would you like that?"

"Yeah. Sure." We shook hands and went our separate ways. I managed to find my way back to the Republica and ordered another beer. Meeting other guys' partners is not my favourite occupation. The atmosphere is either icy because I'm there or it's like swimming in treacle with endearments being thrown around like there may be no tomorrow. I had a suspicion that Nico's household would fall into the latter category. "David made this cake yesterday. David is so clever. Tell James about that wonderful stew you made, darling." Ugh!

I sipped my beer in disappointed silence. I had nearly finished when the folks showed up.

"I hope that's the first, James. This Italian beer is stronger than the stuff at home and you're not used to it." Ha! I said it was. They sat with me. Dad ordered a beer for himself and a martini for Mom. Nothing, you notice, for me.

"We're late because we just had to see the cathedral!" said Mom. "What an experience! It's amazing...."

I let her go on for a few minutes before I spoke. "Built in the 15th century by Brunelleschi. The dome is actually octagonal. They said at the time it couldn't be done," I said.

Have you ever been in a house where there is a baby just beginning to talk? The baby gurgles something vaguely recognizable as mommy or daddy and the parents stare at each other open-mouthed. Mom and Dad were just like that. Mom even put down her drink.

"Where did you learn that?" asked Dad.

"I went there this morning. Asked a few questions. It was interesting."

Naturally enough, when I announced next day that I wanted to go into town again, I got immediate agreement. They were planning a day in the country but it was no trouble to drop me at the Republica.

"Sure you don't want to go straight to a museum or art gallery?" Dad asked.

"I haven't decided which one to see yet. There's such a lot."

"The Uffizi is marvellous, but don't let me pressure you."

I thanked him for the tip, which I guess made him feel good. In the garden of the Republica I sat with my beer and thought of what he'd say to Mr. Valdinger when he got home. "That lad of mine! Amazing! He really took to this Art thing." Actually, I thought, a visit to the Uffizi, whatever it was, would probably be more enjoyable than meeting David.

Nico arrived. "Buon giorno!" he said.

Maybe it was the beer. Maybe I'm just no good at languages. I tried to say it but it came out as 'John Porno'. He laughed himself silly. "That's your name from now on," he said. "John Porno!" I wasn't that amused but I laughed. He ordered a coffee.

"You're not wearing your shorts today."

"I thought maybe David wouldn't approve."

He laughed. "I'm sure David would approve highly," he said. "Michelangelo certainly would."

I didn't understand the joke but laughed all the same. We finished our drinks. He paid for both and we set off.

"I don't know what to show you first," he said. I guessed he meant his room or David's room or possibly something that David had made. We went through a maze of streets and finally ended up in a sort of town square. The first thing that caught my eye was a massive statue of a young guy—stark naked. It was surrounded by camera-clicking tourists.

"Meet David," said Nico.

"The statue?"

"Sure. David, by Michelangelo. It's actually a copy, but few people know that. The original is in a gallery not far from here. See what I mean about the legs?"

I didn't. "Mine are nowhere near as powerful as that!" I said. Who was the model?"

"Nobody knows. A close friend of Michelangelo for sure. He

was gay."

Aha! We were back on track!

"I beat him in another department," I whispered. "He sure didn't have much of a cock!" Nico laughed. I was expecting him to say, "Let's go back to my place and you can show me." He didn't.

"Beautiful isn't it?" said Nico. I had to agree. "I'll bet Michelangelo did a lot more than just carve the statue," I said.

"How do you mean?"

"It stands to reason. The model was Michelangelo's boy friend," I said. "That's why his cock is so shrivelled up. They'd been having it off before he did that bit."

Nico laughed. "An interesting theory," he said. "You'll have to tell me more."

I'd have been glad to but there wasn't much of an opportunity. He told me that Michelangelo had used a cracked block of marble. He took me to another museum to see another "David"—this time by Donatello. Michelangelo liked his models to be hunky. Donatello, on the other hand, was into much younger, rather feminine boys.

I should have been listening as Nico explained things. In fact I was trying to figure out a way of letting him know that I wouldn't object, if you know what I mean.

"... so that was almost certainly the main inspiration for Michelangelo," he said. We'd left the museum by that time.

"But the main one was the boy," I said. "I can see it all. Michelangelo strolling along by the river, just like us, and sees this hunky young man swimming. 'Hey! Care to come back to my place? I'd like to make a statue of you.'"

"And you think he would?'" said Nico.

"Sure he would. Anybody would. He'd take it as a compliment."

"Would you?"

"Sure I would."

"Then shall we?"

"Shall we what?"

"Go to my apartment?"

"Sure. I thought you'd never ask!"

He'd parked his car, a tiny little thing, near the Republica. I wondered why at first but once in it, I understood. If you want to stay alive, don't drive in Florence in the rush hour.

"Michelangelo didn't have a car," I said. "They'd have walked back to his apartment."

"Uh huh," said Nico. He was concentrating hard on his driving. You have to in that place.

"I wonder what David was thinking," I said.

"I wonder."

"I guess he knew about Michelangelo. He knew what was going to happen. He was looking forward to it."

Nico said nothing for a few minutes. We left the city traffic behind and we were buzzing along a highway.

"He wouldn't have looked forward to it that much at first," he said. "Maybe after the first few times he'd have gotten used to it. It makes the muscles ache."

I actually began to like Nico from that moment. Ninety-nine percent of gay guys don't warn you. Most of them tell you that you're going to love it and you stagger out of their apartment feeling like you've been on a rotisserie.

"I've never had a boy," he said, "but I've always wanted to," and I liked the guy even more. I'd not met a guy who admitted that before. Sure, you can tell from the first few minutes if he knows what he's doing. You can usually get a good idea of how many times he's done it. Leaving out Greg—he's a doctor so his expertise might come from book-learning—there's Michael, the teacher. It isn't book-learning or instinct that tells Michael when I'm getting near to the boiling point and he slides in just when I'm itching for it. As for Andy, well, Andy deals with a cock like it was a candy bar.

Michael once said that a boy was like a delicate violin and had to be played carefully. With Nico, the violin was going to have to show the musician how it should be played.

His apartment was some way out of town, on the eleventh floor of a block. It was a nice looking place with landscaped lawns all round the building. The elevator was clean too. Not a cigarette butt to be seen and no graffiti either. He opened the door.

"Welcome, John Porno," he said. "Would you like a drink first?"

I said that would be a nice idea. He seemed to have just about everything. I settled for a beer. He poured himself a short drink of some sort. Nerves, I thought. The poor guy needed to be put at ease.

"Nice beer," I said. "I wonder if Michelangelo gave David a beer."

"Possibly. Not too much though. The lad would have to keep running off to the privy."

"Yeah. That would have put him off his stroke. Maybe I should finish my beer later."

"As you wish." He drained his glass. "You're certain?"

"Quite certain." I'd been taking several good looks at him over the rim of my glass. Nico was a good looking guy. I don't go for just anyone. He was tall. He had a nice smile. He was only twenty-nine and, from the look of the apartment, he was quite well to do. Most important, he was such a nice guy, the sort of guy I could relate to. He knew a lot about art and I knew nothing but he didn't treat me like some ignorant kid. Nico and I could be real buddies.

"I don't really know where to start with you," he said.

"Start where you like. It's all real and genuine American. Shall I get undressed?"

"Well, if you're sure...."

Strip tease acts are not my line. Trainers, socks, and watch came off. Then I pulled my shirt up and over my head.

"Magnifico! Magnificent!" he exclaimed. "What a chest!" He stood up and, very gingerly, put out a hand to touch my pecs. I think he thought I might hit him. I stood still. "Utterly magnificent!" he said. "Such development!" He stroked my nipples and then my back. "And your skin!" he said. "It's flawless and so smooth!"

Needless to say, all this touching had started to do things to my cock, not helped by my own thoughts as to what he would want to do. Andy, Michael and Greg were all older than he was. A twenty-nine year old, I thought, might take some holding when he got going.

I managed to undo my belt whilst he was examining the top half. My jeans and then my boxers slid to the floor. I almost fell over trying to step out of them.

"Oh!" he exclaimed.

"It often goes like that," I said, looking down at the familiar stiff, purple-headed shaft poking out from my midriff.

"It's beautiful!" he said. He put a hand on my ass and stroked my buns. "So is this," he added.

"Better than David's?" I asked.

"John Porno is much better!" he said. "John Porno is the most beautiful boy I've ever seen."

You get used to this line of talk. They don't mean it of course. The compliments are meant to act as a sort of key to unlock your ass to let them in. Mine was beginning to itch in anticipation.

He stroked my thighs. He touched my cock and stroked under my balls and all the time the flow of praise continued. My thighs felt like alabaster. (I'm not quite sure what alabaster is but I'm sure it's nice.) My butt was perfectly rounded. My cock was a revelation. My belly was wonderfully firm and so smooth. He had to make a real move soon. I was all too aware that if he kept on much longer I'd shoot all over the place. He was good though. His hands were very soft and he seemed to have the art of finding all the right places.

"I see what you mean about Michelangelo's David," he said, fondling my cock again. "This is as hard as marble."

"And you're pretty good with marble," I said.

"I've never used it."

"You're doing okay," I said.

"It's so perfectly in proportion!" he exclaimed. My cock head lay across his hand and he stared at it as if he'd never seen one before. Possibly he hadn't, apart from his own that is. I was anxious to see what it looked like. There are limits as to what my asshole can take.

He put his hand under my balls. That felt good. "And these!" he said. "Utterly perfect! I must take some photographs. You wouldn't object?"

Normally, when people want to take photographs, I don't let them, not wishing to end up as the center-spread of some magazine. I did a bit of quick thinking. It was unlikely, I thought, that an Italian magazine would circulate in our town so I let him go ahead.

He fetched his camera from an adjoining room and made me stand just like Michelangelo's David. Film after film went through the camera. I don't think there is a square inch (or a round inch) of me that wasn't snapped from every possible angle.

Finally, he put the camera down and started to feel all over me again. He started with my face; then my shoulders and arms. His hands moved downwards to my hips and then inwards.

"If only Michelangelo was still alive," he said. "A body like yours deserves a genius."

"He wasn't much of a genius when it came to sex," I said. "He should have done the statue first. Art before ass should have been his motto."

Nico laughed. "My John Porno knows about these things," he said.

"I know that cocks have a tendency to shrivel up afterwards," I said. I wasn't going to admit anything more. Every gay guy likes to think he's the first and only one.

He put his finger against my pubes. He said something about difficulty but I wasn't really listening. I was thinking about Michelangelo and David.

"You have a beautiful behind. It's almost a perfect hemisphere."

That was Nico talking to me. In my imagination it was Michelangelo talking to David:

"Has anybody done this to you before?"

"No, maestro." David sounded a bit nervous as I had been on the first occasion.

"Tell me about yourself."

"I am the only son of poor parents. I came to Florence today to sell some eggs at the market and thought I would have a swim in the river. That's when you saw me."

"Perfect. I like big, strong country boys. I'd like to carve a statue of you. Would you like that?"

"As you wish, Maestro. I am yours to command."

That was a good line. I thought it through again....

"I am yours to command."

"Good. First I must taste your essence." No, I didn't much like that. *"First I must tame you. Lie down on this couch. Mmm.... It is so big and hard. You want it, don't you?"*

"I am yours to command, Maestro."

"Good!" Michelangelo undressing. David turning over.

"Such a beautiful behind. A perfect hemisphere! So tight!

Never been screwed in your life?"

"No, Maestro. As I said... oh! Ow! Aaagh!"

David had been a powerful young man. Old Michelangelo would have had trouble holding him down as he drove into him but I was quite sure he'd succeeded, and pretty certain that David enjoyed it.... David squirming and gasping. Michelangelo thrusting into him enjoying the feel of David's huge glutes against his skin....

Then it happened. There was no time to give Nico a warning and nothing I could do to stop it. Nico was standing behind me with his hands on my butt. Spunk shot in all directions. Some of it went on the wall; some on the floor. It cascaded everywhere.

"Jeez, Nico. I'm sorry!" I gasped.

He laughed. "Think nothing of it," he said. "I'll get a cloth. It was my fault. I should have known."

Red-faced with embarrassment, I helped him clean up. He didn't seem to mind at all. I did. I'd blown my chances, and his, for at least another hour. Michael and Greg back home would have been short-tempered and frustrated.

"There," he said when the last drop had been wiped away. "How about some lunch?"

"Sure."

We went back to the Republica. He bought me a real good lunch, which was more than I deserved. I tried hard not to think about sex so that I'd be on form when we got back to the apartment. Knowing what alcohol does to me, I drank Coke.

"I feel better now," I said. "Shall we go back to your place?"

"I really ought to get straight to work. How long did you say you would be here?"

"Three weeks."

"Good. If I can perhaps meet you in the Republica two weeks from today...."

"Earlier if you like. I've got nothing else to do." I was shattered!

"No. Make it two weeks from today at the same time. I want to be ready for you."

Disappointing, but there was nothing I could do. It was all my fault. I guessed he'd go and look for another boy. He'd probably show the boy the stains on the wall and they'd laugh about the Americano who came too quickly.

He drove me back to the inn where we were staying. I spent the next two weeks with my admiring parents. I told them about Donatello and Michelangelo. I even took them to see David.

"You'd think he'd have something to cover himself up," said my mother, glaring at him over her glasses. "They don't seem to have had any modesty in those days."

"Michelangelo was gay. I guess that's something to do with it," I said.

"And Italian too," said Mom. That was the end of Michelangelo as far as she was concerned. Their interest in Art seemed to diminish from that moment too. They made occasional forays into Florence to look at some museum or art gallery but we spent more and more time doing more enjoyable things like swimming in the local lakes and having picnics.

It was a boring time. Just once something happened that interested and amused me. We were sitting on the shores of a lake eating our picnic lunch. From behind some bushes came giggling and laughter and young voices speaking Italian.

"Local lads," said my father.

"Laughing at us!" said my mother, indignantly.

"They'd better not be! Go see what they're doing, James."

I got up and peered through the foliage. There were six of them, all as naked as the day they were born. Four little boys sat round whilst two elder boys, I guessed them to be about fifteen, lay side by side jerking each other off! Their technique left much to be desired but they both had substantial cocks. I stared, fascinated, watching their balls jiggling up and down. Their eyes were closed. They were about to boil over when one of the younger kids spotted me. He shouted something. They opened their eyes. I expected them to get up and run. They didn't. One of them grinned. He said something and beckoned me. If it hadn't been for my folks I would have accepted. As it was, it was me who did the running.

"What were they up to, James?" asked Mom.

"Nothing much. They're not laughing at us."

"Perhaps they'd like something to eat. There's plenty left over. I'll go ask them," she said.

"No. Don't do that."

"Why not? A lot of kids in these countries don't get enough to eat."

"They're... er... they're sunbathing. In the nude."

"Well! Really! How disgusting! These people don't seem to have any morals!"

"Ken Valdinger should have warned us what they're like," said Dad.

"Certainly he should. And he actually recommended that we should bring James with us. It's like... it's like being in Sodom and Gomorrah!" said my mother.

It was more like being in the Garden of Eden as far as the boys were concerned, I thought.

Seeing those boys gave me an idea. I'd been wondering how to get Nico back. I was determined to let him have anything he wanted. He was such a nice guy. I could suggest a picnic and a swim. If we both stripped off to sunbathe I was pretty confident that I could get him worked up so that we came together.

Waiting was agonizing. It was also counter-productive in terms of profit. I was not earning anything and spending money at a frightening rate. Not that Dad moaned. While I maintained my interest in Art he was happy enough to shell out. Naturally enough I really did visit the museums and art galleries I said I had visited and always came back with ticket stubs and a few picture postcards for him to show Mr. Valdinger, but I never stayed long. I spent the rest of his money on beers in the Republica.

It was there that things started to look up. I'd been to have a look at David again and bought four postcards of him. One for Michael, one for Greg, one for Andy and the other one for Dad to show Mr. Valdinger. I sat in the garden, ordered a beer and wrote the postcards. "Just to let you know what you're missing. I sure miss you." That sort of thing.

I was racking my brains trying to remember Andy's postal code when two guys walked in. One was really aged. Sixty-five, seventy maybe. His face was a mass of wrinkles and cracks. The other was much younger, not much older than I was. He didn't look too bad. In fact he looked pretty good. I guessed him to be twenty-two or twenty-three. They sat at a table under a tree immediately opposite. The waiter went over to them..

"Two beers - er... *duo biera*," said the older man in a really strong British accent. 'Beers' sounded like 'bee-ahs'. Andy's postal code came to me in a flash. I wrote it on the postcard and looked at what I had written. It was true. I really did miss him—and the others. My cock twitched in my shorts. I put the postcard in my pocket and attempted to re-align it so that it didn't show. I was about to get up and go when the old guy spoke again.

"There's something about Italian boys. I've never been able to put my finger on it," he said.

"But you've had your fingers on several of them?" said his young companion.

"On innumerable occasions I am glad to say," said the old man. "When I was a young man the war hadn't been over very long. You could pick up a boy for the price of a packet of cigarettes."

I pricked up my ears and decided not to leave after all. My glass was empty. The waiter came over and raised an eyebrow questioningly. I nodded and he picked it up.

"Now that one over there," said the old man. "He'd be an absolutely delightful fuck. Just look at those long legs...."

"Shhh! He probably speaks some English," the young man said.

"Schoolboy English. If you speak quickly they can't understand you."

I looked round. An obviously married couple sat at one table doting over their toddler, who sat gurgling in a baby-stroller with a comforter in it's mouth. Two businessmen with open briefcases were at another table. There was nobody else. They had to be talking about me!

"He is rather nice I admit," said the younger one, so rapidly that the words ran together.

"Delightful. And I'll wager he's got quite a cock on him."

"Do that trick you played in Tokyo," said the young man.

"Why not?" The old man heaved himself out of his chair, picked up a walking stick and came over towards me.

"*Buon giorno*," he said.

"*Buon giorno*." Thank God it came out right that time. I tried to say it in the sing-song way like Nico said it.

"Do ... you... speak... English?" he asked.

This, I thought, could be a bit of a laugh. "A leetle only," I said.

"You are alone?...er... solo?"

"Si, si," I said. I'd heard the waiters in the hotel say that often enough.

"You... come... sit with us. I buy you beer," he said.

"*Multi graz*i," I said; a phrase I'd learned as a result of my Dad's over-tipping. So got up and followed him. The younger man drew out a chair for me and I sat down.

"Your name?" said the old man.

"Er... Nico. Nico Besozzi," I replied, making an enormous effort to get the double 'z' sound just like the real Nico said it.

"Me Mister Lewis. He... my... nephew. Oh Christ! How do you get that across? He bambino my sister. Name Simon."

"Si—mon," I repeated.

"That's it," said Simon. We shook hands. He had a good grip. His uncle felt like a dead fish.

"You - how old?" I stammered, turning to Simon.

"Twenty." He held up both hands twice. "You?"

"Oh... er... take a year or two off? Why not? I held up both hands and then showed him just one hand and a finger.

"Big lad for sixteen," said Mr. Lewis. "but I've often found that with Italians. They get fat when they're about twelve and then suddenly shoot up and you can take *that* any way you want."

"He could shoot for me any time," said Simon, speaking like a machine gun again. "Just look at that lump in his shorts. Long fingers too."

"Not to mention a delightfully tight little bottom," said Mr. Lewis. "One of the advantages of their diet, you know, is that all that olive oil lubricates their passages so well. You wouldn't have all that trouble you had with Mitsu in Tokyo."

The waiter came over with my beer. In a new, gold-rimmed glass I noticed—and served on a tray. Mr. Lewis made a gesture as if he was writing on his hand with his finger and pointed to himself. The waiter bowed low and left.

"He's really pretty," said Simon.

"Not bad. Not bad at all. Now, if I were a few years younger I'd make him squirm. They knew all about it when my cock was in them, I can tell you."

I had to grip my glass tightly to repress a shudder.

"I wonder if he would?" said Simon.

"I don't see why not if the financial reward was sufficient. Fortunately that is no problem." I relaxed my grip on the glass and stared at a pigeon that was picking up crumbs between the tables.

"I'll buy him for you if you want him," Mr. Lewis continued.

"But you've spent so much on me already. I'd feel guilty."

"You've no reason to. You've had a Sri Lankan boy, a Japanese boy and an Indian boy. Why not add an Italian?"

"I was going to wait till we got to France."

"A bird in the hand is better than a bird in a bush. Speaking of which I should think he's got a nice bush. You've noticed his legs?"

Simon hadn't just noticed my legs. He had started what I call 'movie maneuvers'. His foot had been next to mine for some minutes. Slowly, by degrees, his leg had moved nearer and nearer. He shifted his chair and our knees were pressing together. He wouldn't have got so far back home. I only did it in a movie theater once. I ended up with spunk stains on my jeans and a crumpled ten-dollar bill in my pocket. My cock is worth considerably more than ten dollars.

"He doesn't look as if he needs money," said Simon. "His clothes are good quality. That tee shirt looks American."

I kept staring at the pigeon but my ears worked overtime. I felt a bit like the invisible man.

Mr. Lewis took out his wallet and passed over a thick wad of lire bills. I guess you know Italian currency. They don't seem to go in for low denominations.

"How much should I give him?" Simon asked.

"Use it all if he's good," said Mr. Lewis. "You won't break the bank."

"What about you?"

"Oh, don't worry about me. I'll have a little stroll and then wait for you here. You can tell me all about it."

That was a relief.

They drew me into the conversation to ask if I knew the Regina Hotel. I'd been past it several times. A guy in a gold embroidered coat and top hat stood outside to open taxi doors and swing the revolving doors for the guests, all of whom seemed to arrive weighed down by expensive looking boxes and carrier bags.

I said I did and went back to watching the pigeons. Simon's fingers moved slowly up my thigh towards my shorts. It was time to show that I wasn't averse to what he had in mind. I pressed my leg firmly against his.

"I think he's getting the message," Simon whispered excitedly.

"All boys want it, deep down," said Mr. Lewis. That was a laugh. I could have introduced him to several hundred of my fellow students back home who don't. Maybe, I thought, Italians are different. I'd certainly never come across an open air wanking circle back home.

Mr. Lewis slid his fingertips up and down the sides of his glass. "You like?" he asked.

"Eh? Oh! Beer. Yes, I like."

"Not beer. This," he said. He put his fingers right round the glass and moved them up and down. He had to hold the glass steady with his left hand to stop it falling over. I felt a bit uncomfortable. It was a pretty obvious gesture. I hoped the businessmen or the married couple were not looking.

"Oh, I see," I said. "Yes, I like. I do it with my friends," I said, remembering the boys in the bushes.

"There you are. What did I tell you?" said Mr. Lewis.

"Would you... er... would you like me to do it?" Simon asked.

"Solo?" I tried to look puzzled.

"No. With you. I give you money. You want money?"

"Oh si. I save to buy for me a motor-bike."

"Then you come with me to Regina Hotel?"

I drank the last few drops of beer and looked down at his crotch. Boy was he keen! Looking at his cock filling out under his pants was like watching a 3D photograph in a developing tank. He had a nice one. It wasn't too long or too thick. I was pretty confident that I could handle it.

We took a taxi to the Regina. I'd never been in a place like it. It was a bit like stepping back in time. The entrance hall was wood-panelled and the place gleamed with polished brass.

Simon collected his key and we went up in the elevator. That, at least, was modern. I was relieved to see only one suitcase in his room. The thought that he might have it off with Mr. Lewis would have put me off my stroke. There was one huge double bed covered with a floral quilt and a sofa upholstered in the same material.

He sat on the bed. "Come," he said and patted the bed. I sat next to him.

"I wish to God I spoke your language," he said. "It would make things so much easier."

A phrase came to my mind. I'd first seen it on Donizetti's statue of David and asked Nico what it was. It meant 'Please do not touch the exhibits, but it sounded so nice when he said it that I'd repeated it several times. It was on every show case and every statue in every museum I'd visited so I had lots of opportunities to learn and practice it since then.

"Please do not touch the exhibits," I said, trying desperately hard not to laugh. His hand was burrowing into my shorts trying to find the top of the zip-fastener. He found it and drew it down.

"I love you Nico," he said. Why, oh why, do they all say that? It's balls. All they love is cock or ass and in this case he couldn't even communicate with me—or thought he couldn't. But it didn't deter him from planting a kiss on my left cheek. Well, Italian men kiss each other so I gave him one. That delighted him.

I had to stand up to let my shorts drop round my ankles. He fondled my cock through my under-shorts. "It's beautiful. Magnifico!" he said.

It might not be 'magnifico' but it was certainly magnifying, if you know what I mean. He had a good technique. It was time his totally inexperienced and innocent Italian partner took a hand in the proceedings.

"You, signor. You take off the ... er...clothes also?" I said.

"Do you want me to, Nico? Would you like that?" He sounded like a man who's just won a million dollars.

"Please do not touch the exhibits. I ... er... I think better. I not like to be only person no clothes. Please do not touch the exhibits." I said and another phrase floated into my mind so I added it. "Please do not throw cigarette butts into the urinals."

277

"I don't smoke I'm afraid," he said. I made a note not to use that phrase again. He might not smoke but he sure was steaming. I never saw a guy undress so rapidly in my life. He threw clothes in all directions. He wasn't bad. Broad shoulders; flat belly and strong hairy legs. He also had some hair on his chest and, as for his middle—it was like a forest and if old Michaelangelo had seen his cock he wouldn't have given David a second glance.

It wasn't, as I had guessed, huge. It was just right somehow. A question of proportions I guess. Unfortunately, man has always had a tendency to interfere with nature. Simon's cock would have looked so much better if they'd let it alone when he was a baby. Still, it was a nice one and it stood out eagerly.

"And now you," he said. I pulled my tee shirt over my head and he slid my underpants down. He was undoing the laces on my trainers when I remembered that my socks had name tags in them. They were the ones I wore to school and, for some reason, odd socks often went astray in the changing room.

"I... do that..." I said and sat down again. I got them off and rolled them up.

"That's better," said Simon. Gently, he pushed me back so that I was lying on the bed. He lay next to me and took my cock in his fingers. "Beautiful! Absolutely beautiful!" he whispered. I reached over and took his. It was steel hard.

Now what? I very nearly said it. I was getting a bit worried. I knew I could maintain the "Italian boy" bit for a certain time but my "boiling point" caused some anxiety. I was never aware of it at the time but, according to Greg, Andy and Michael I was prone to gasp things like "Christ! Oh yeah! Fuck my ass!" —hardly the everyday language of an Italian teenager. I just had to keep my mouth shut.

Simon didn't. When he wasn't telling me how beautiful I was, he was sucking on my cock so hard that I felt his cheeks pressing against it. Trying hard to slow things up, I tried to remember other bits of Italian but couldn't. His cock was warm and sticky. His hands slid down my back to caress my ass, kneading it just like the old lady in our hotel kitchen prepared the dough for her pizzas.

He slid his lips up and off my rampant cock.

"I want to fuck you, Nico," he said.

I reckon if he'd continued the blow job for even a few seconds longer he would have blown my Italian act too. I was panting like a steam engine but just managed to get myself back under control.

"I no understand," I said.

"You will. Turn over." He put both hands on my shoulders and twisted. 'Nico' got the message and turned over.

"Beautiful!" he said, yet again. "Such long legs!" He ran his hands up and down my thighs. "Hairy too," he said, "and such a powerful bottom. Open your legs a bit."

I didn't understand of course. He had to do it for me.

Of all my regular clients, Michael is the only one who's into licking out my ass. Greg, possibly because he's a doctor, treats the weekly fuck as a surgical operation even to the extent of putting on a plastic glove before he oils me up. Andy gets turned on by slobbering over my feet—which does nothing for me at all but a tongue working down there turns James Hosier into a sex hungry animal in seconds. The moment Simon's hands parted my ass cheeks and I felt his breath wafting onto my balls, I knew I had a problem. I just had, somehow, to keep my cool.

There was another worry too. The pattern on the bedspread was less than an inch from my eyes. A bunch of grapes with a leaf filled my field of vision. Even I could tell that it was expensive material and I, who hadn't had a wank for days, was going to explode all over it. If only "Nico" could speak English he'd be able to say, "How about putting a towel down?" as James said to Michael.

Worrying, of course, makes a person tense up. "Relax, relax," he whispered. "I'm not going to hurt you." I decided that cleaning bills were his worry, not mine and he went back to work. He was good too. He lapped up and down between my balls and my ass; then he stopped and I felt his tongue curling. Desperately trying to remember that I was a sixteen year old Italian who had never had more than a thermometer in there, I tensed up but not for long. It pushed against me, a creature with a will of its own and desperate to get inside me.

I had to keep my cool. But how? Counting something. That was the answer. The wine bottles on the shelf in the bar of our hotel. A green one on the left, then two brown ones, then the long one with the funny neck. Then came two fat ones in baskets and another dark one.

"Valpolicella!" I gasped. Mum had asked the man what it was.

His tongue went in. An odd feeling. Why does a tongue feel like a coin when it's in your ass? I must ask Greg some day. Maybe it'll give him the hint.

He took it out again. That old familiar wet, cool feeling reminded me of Michael. I didn't stir but was relieved to hear a condom packet being torn open. Out of the corner of my eye I saw him open a drawer in the little bedside cabinet. "Thank Christ for that!" I thought. He wasn't going to try out his uncle's olive oil theory.

I tried not to wince too much as a cold, greasy finger took over from a warm, moist tongue. It went in easily enough. More easily than I had intended.

Then his hands were on my shoulders. Michael wipes his first and Greg takes off the glove. Simon was obviously too far gone to worry about smearing me with whatever it was.

It touched my ass. He took the greasy hand away for a moment, to fumble with it and find the right spot. I didn't help. I was concentrating on the wine bottles again.

I know I shouted out when he went in. I had to. I guess not having been screwed for so long had tightened me up. His hands gripped me hard and I felt his breath on the back of my head while, deep inside me, his cock pushed relentlessly into me, the nicest feeling in the world. It's painful but it's a good sort of pain. The sort of pain you experience when you know you're going to win a swimming race. Every muscle aches but you know it's in a good cause and people are going to pat you on the back and say how brilliant you are.

Which is exactly what he did say. I'm not sure when he came. I know that I was feverishly counting wine bottles, visualizing the next one in the line with every thrust. I know that I shot my load on the second Chianti bottle and he was still going when I'd started all over again.

"Brilliant!" he panted as his cock, shrivelling fast, slid out of me.

I went into the shower first, feeling horribly guilty about the dinner plate-sized stain on the bed-cover. I pointed to it and shook my head sorrowfully.

"Don't give it a second thought," he said. "That's the best souvenir I've had on this trip." I looked appropriately blank.

We joined Mr. Lewis in the garden of the Republica. He'd obviously been out because he was reading an English paper that he hadn't had before.

"Good?" he asked.

"Superb!" said Simon. "He might not speak much English but he certainly knows how to fuck."

"I thought so," said Mr. Lewis. "I'm never wrong when it comes to boys. You were the first, too."

"I wonder," said Simon.

"I can always tell. Look at the way he's shifting in his chair."

The real reason was a very much fatter wallet and four very creased postcards. I stared at him blankly.

"Simon number one?" Mr. Lewis asked.

"Signor?"

"Simon, *nummero uno*?" He made a loop with the thumb and finger and his left hand and slid his right index finger into it.

"*Si signor*. Simon *nummero uno*."

"Told you. Tight was he?" The waiter came up. He ordered beers for us.

"Just right. I wish I spoke his language though. What does *valpolicella* mean?" Simon asked.

"Name of a place. There's a wine of that name, too. Why do you ask?"

"He said it once or twice. Just as I was boring into his asshole and again when I shot."

"Well, at least it wasn't 'no'. Going to have him again, are you?"

"If it's all right with you?"

"Have him every day if you want. It'll be good for you."

It was good for me too. I felt guilty asking Dad for money for artistic excursions with several thousand Lire secreted in my room. I spent every afternoon at the Regina Hotel. I remember every tiny detail of that bed-spread. The stains multiplied but Simon didn't seem to care and I certainly didn't.

The only problem with Simon was that every afternoon was

the same and, of course, we couldn't talk to each other. Money went into my wallet and his cock went into my ass every afternoon but I began to miss the real Nico more and more.

The day came round at last. It was a gloriously hot day. The people at the inn packed a cold box for me. A cold chicken, salad, a couple of bottles of beer and a bottle of wine for Nico and Coke for me. I put one or two other necessities in as well, purchased with considerable difficulty in a drug store in Florence. If you are into suffering embarrassing experiences, try to buy pre-lubricated condoms in Italy. I managed, after being offered finger bandages of various types to get my message across and left the store to a disapproving chorus of "Americano! Tut tut!"

Nico turned up on time.

"*Buon giorno*, John Porno," he said.

"John Porno, Nico. I thought we could go for a picnic," I said. "I've got the stuff here."

"I'd prefer to go to the apartment," he said. "I've got something to show you."

"But it's an ideal day for spending in the open air. Couldn't you show me later?"

"Not really, no."

I was disappointed but I cheered up once in the car. He seemed pretty keen.

"I hope you'll approve," he said.

I said that I didn't mind anything. "Anything," I repeated. He laughed. A good sign.

"I think a person should do anything for a buddy," I added. "Like you and me for instance. If you asked me to do something, it's only right that I should do it. I'm a guest in your country. Maybe things are different here than they are in the States. It's my job to conform."

"I wish all Americans were like you," he said.

"For instance," I continued. "The other day there were some boys by the lake wanking each other."

"What?"

"Masturbating. They were completely naked. Now that wouldn't happen back in the States but this is Italy. If some buddy of mine wanted sex in the open air, I'd be happy to oblige."

"But an American tourist may see you."

"He'd think I was Italian."

"Not with a superb body like yours."

I was beginning to congratulate myself. I'd got the message across. We arrived at the apartment. He opened the door. I nearly fell over with shock.

In the center of the room was another James Hosier, a life-sized, grey, unclothed statue but there was no doubt as to who it was, and no doubt about the state I'd been in. My cock pointed outwards and upwards. He'd even got the veins right.

"Jeez! Did you have to do it like that? What's wrong with the Michelangelo system?" I asked.

"Breaking with tradition. I am overcoming the prejudices of the time and creating, I hope, something new and beautiful. Just like Brunelleschi."

"It sure is beautiful," I said, walking round it. "Beautifully done I mean. I didn't know you were a sculptor."

"It's a hobby. I paint as well. This is just clay. I shall cast it in bronze."

I looked up at "my" face. The mouth was half open, as if I'd been surprised by something.

"It was the moment when you came," said Nico. "I caught a glimpse of your face in the mirror. Wait here. There's something else."

He went into the next room and came back with a picture, a portrait of me! It was just my head and naked shoulders. I was smiling.

"An interesting expression," said Nino. "I noticed it when you first got here. It was as if you were plotting something; something secret. What was it? Can you remember?"

"No," I lied. I felt like a bank robber who's been caught on video. There was a portrait of me wondering whether he wanted my cock or my ass and a statue of me at the very moment when I'd blown my chances.

"If you could get undressed again," he said. For a moment I thought I might have been right after all. I wasn't. All he wanted to do was to get the final touches right. I stood for hours whilst he nicked out little bits of clay here and there and smoothed the surface back again.

"Do you think you can get it erect again?" he said, without even looking at me. Believe it or not, I had a lot of difficulty getting it to respond. Thinking about Janet didn't work. Finally I had to imagine being with the boys by the lake. That worked.

I dressed again and we ate our picnic sitting on the floor at the feet of the statue, and after that he drove me back to the inn.

My folks went overboard about the picture. "What were you wearing James?" asked Mom. "I hope you weren't like that disgusting statue!"

"Definitely not," I replied, recalling David's tiny little cock.

"He's written on the back," said my dad. "To James, American perfection personified. Nico Besozzi. That's real nice."

The picture is hanging on the wall in our sitting room. Dad had a light installed to illuminate it. Now that Nico is so famous, everybody admires it. Mr. Valdinger wanted to buy it.

The cause of Nico's fame is not mentioned much in our family. I am glad of that. It means that when it comes to the States, they won't go to see it. The statue "John Porno" by Nico Besozzi caused an uproar. The press and the media were full of it: "Besozzi has captured the moment of a boy's first sexual experience." That amused me. "The sculptor refuses to name his Italian model," it continued. I was relieved.

The Church condemned it, of course, but the gay press liked it. Some papers were not enthusiastic. "There are few things less attractive than a teenage boy. To have portrayed one at such an intensely private moment is an example of sheer bad taste," thundered our local newspaper. I knew three guys and at least one girl who would disagree. "John Porno" is in Germany at the moment and due in the States some time next year. Go see it. The dimensions are all accurate—I should know!

ENGLISH LESSONS

Tim Scully

"Seen this?" Danny asked.

"No."

The Advertiser must be one of the most boring newspapers ever produced. Danny has bought it ever since he joined the Rangers. I was obviously going to be treated to another reading of his outstanding success on the previous Saturday afternoon. Certainly the Rangers' prospects seemed to have improved since he started playing for them but I wished he would let me read about it for myself.

"German teenager," he read. "Wishes accommodation in your area for six weeks in the summer for improving English. Any reasonable amount paid. Schweiger. And then there's the address."

"So?" I said.

"So why not us? 'Any reasonable amount paid' sounds good. We could do with the extra money."

"We're not that hard up," I replied. Danny had taken over the housekeeping accounts since we moved in and had managed them very well.

"Every little helps. And just imagine. A nice German boy –"

"Yeah, with thick glasses and a wooden leg," I said. "We couldn't even contemplate it. Where the hell would he sleep?"

"In my room. It's never used."

"Out of the question. As soon as he found out we sleep together, he'd be off home like a shot."

"Of course he wouldn't. We'd tell him that we moved in together to give him a room of his own. Simple."

When Danny and I moved into the flat we made a pretence of sleeping in separate rooms for the benefit of my friend Dhasan who lived on the third floor. The pretence had become unnecessary. I was losing contact with Dhasan. I had something much better to do on weekends than fuck Dhasan or suck his young friend Neil Webb. I still saw them of course but neither of them visited. I'd told them that Danny was straight and, although they made eyes at him in the lift, they kept clear.

Danny is nothing if not persistent. He worked on me when I was most vulnerable.

"I wonder what a good German boy would taste like," he said that night, licking the remnants of my spunk away from the corners of his mouth.

"Rotten cabbage probably," I replied.

"I'll bet a good German boy would be a lovely fuck," he said on the following night.

"Meaning that I'm not?" I asked dreamily. His cock was still deep inside me.

"Certainly not but it would be good for you to have a change. I wouldn't mind either."

And so we composed the letter. For eighty pounds a week, two young men who shared a flat strictly on grounds of convenience would be pleased to accommodate the Schweiger person. I got the translation people at work to do a German version and sent both off.

To our surprise, a letter arrived the following week. It was easy to see why Michael Schweiger was keen to improve his English but we managed to make out that our terms were acceptable and that his parents thought it would be better for him to live with two young people. "The other peoples what reply to my ad all are old and I like to be under young peoples,'" he wrote, to our great amusement. I hope the girl in the translation department didn't notice our disappointment when she explained that it was a direct translation from German.

July the thirtieth, and we were both in the arrivals hall at London airport watching the passengers from the Lufthansa flight come through the controls. I had one or two near heart attacks.

"I'll bet that's him," I said as a bearded youth came through with a rucksack almost as big as he was. Fortunately it wasn't.

"How about this one?" said Danny as an extremely good-looking youth wearing an immaculate suit appeared.

"One can but hope," I said. Again I was wrong.

We'd almost given up hope when he appeared. I was sure it was him by the way he put his suitcase down on the floor and scanned the waiting crowd. I waved. So did Danny. "Bloody hell!" he said, with good reason. Michael Schweiger was a stunner. He was tall, I'd say about five-foot-ten. He wasn't so much thin as lean if you know what I mean. Even in jeans and a jacket you could see that. An athlete's figure. He had close cropped hair and there was something about his face which was attractive, even though he was frowning when we first saw him.

"Could still be wrong," said Danny but then Michael noticed us and smiled. My heart missed a beat. That smile would have melted steel.

"Excuse me. You are Danny and Tim?" he asked.

We shook hands. He had a remarkably firm grip. I took his suitcase and Danny led the way out of the terminal to the car park. Michael didn't say much on the journey. He was too busy looking out of the window and flinching at the concept of a nation that drove on the left-hand side of the road.

"Is this your first visit to England, Michael?" Danny asked.

"Oh yes. For many years I want to come but my parents they say I must be eighteen. Until now I stay the holidays with my uncle."

"Your folks were probably afraid you'd fall into wicked hands," I said.

"Excuse me?"

"Oh, nothing."

That afternoon we showed him the sights of the town; namely our appalling dirty concrete shopping mall, which looks like it was made by a giant playing with his Lego set. Danny stocked up on hamburgers, pizzas and German sausage. In the evening we took him out to the George for a meal and a drink. He didn't think much of English beer but knocked back two pints. It was a nice evening so we sat out in the garden. The swans were out on the river. The anglers were telling each other stories.

"Is this better than staying with your uncle, Michael?" I asked.

"Oh. I am very fond of my uncle. It is my parents who say I cannot go to him."

"How will you go about improving your English, Michael?" Danny asked.

"Excuse me?"

"How will you make your English better?" I added.

"Oh this is very easy. On Monday I shall get for me a job and with the colleagues in the working place I will talk English."

We tried to explain that it wasn't as easy as that. There were about three million Brits all looking for work at that time. Michael seemed undaunted. An angler hooked something and he went over to watch it being landed.

"You could see Mr. Parsons about him," said Danny, staring at Michael's back.

"In what way?"

"To get him a job."

There were times, as I told him, when Danny talked utter rubbish. Getting an eighteen year old unknown foreign national into a firm making top secret missiles was the daftest notion I'd ever heard. True I was in Mr. Parsons' good books but I was sure it would never work.

"What about all that grass by the old perimeter track? That needs cutting. It would look much better from the road. And he wouldn't need to go near anywhere sensitive...."

Michael returned. "That man has catched five trouts," he said. "Also many small that he to the water returned." It was pretty obvious that more than a bit of grass-cutting was needed to improve his English.

We explained that he would be sleeping in Danny's room and that, during his visit, Danny would be in my room. He accepted this without query. I expected raised eyebrows or some sort of polite argument on the lines of "I can sleep on the couch in the lounge."

On the following day, a Sunday, we took him to London. Surprisingly, all he wanted to see was the Tower of London and Madame Tussaud's Wax Museum. The latter, which we visited first, bores me. I was taken round there so many times as a kid. Danny took Michael into the chamber of horrors. I waited for them in the restaurant. They were in there for ages. We toured the Tower, or rather he did. I bought him a guide book in German and he went off on his own. Danny and I were both feeling a bit tired. We'd been awake a long time the previous night talking about him.

"Do you suppose he wanks?" Danny had asked.

"Bound to. They all do."

"Mmmm."

I had got up at about seven. I always do. I make a pot of tea for us both and get back into bed. I nipped into the bathroom and had just come out when Michael appeared—totally naked. I averted my eyes but not too late to get a glimpse of a beautifully slim waist and a very nice cock set in a thicket of bronze colored hair.

"Oh. Are you with the bath ready?" he asked.

"Yes sure. Go in."

"I stand always early up." he said, making no attempt to move or to cover himself up.

"Oh do you? In English it's 'get up'. I always get up early." I said, addressing his navel.

"Thank you. When the people correct my English I learn fast to speak it good."

I would have liked to stay and correct that sentence too but if I'd have spent any longer looking at his cock my interest might have become apparent. He went into the bathroom. From the kitchen I heard the toilet flush and the bath water running in.

"If he did, there is no evidence of it this morning," I said when Danny had woken up and I was in bed beside him again.

"Did what?"

"Wank."

"How do you know?"

"Just had a conversation with him. He went into the bathroom without a stitch on."

"Good God! Is he still in there?"

"Yes."

"The tea can wait," said Danny, clambering out of bed. "I have an urgent need to use the bathroom. I'll wait outside until he comes out."

I lay in bed listening intently and trying to visualize what Michael was doing. I heard the bath water gurgling away. Drying himself, I thought. More water noises. Good lad, he was cleaning the bath. I took a sip of tea and then the bathroom door opened.

"Oh! I am sorry. I think you are still sleeping," said Michael.

"Just got up to have a pee," Danny explained.

"Excuse me? Oh. Yes. I understand. You should come in. I

do not mind. In Germany we shame us not for the nudity."

"So I see," said Danny.

"I ... er... like to get up early."

"Me too," said Danny. "Get up as soon as the opportunity presents itself. That's my motto."

"Me also. But I must not keep you talking. You wish to use the toilet quickly."

. . .

Danny threw some crumbs to one of the famous Tower of London ravens. "He really is a little beauty!" he said.

"Not so little either," I replied. "I'll bet yours made his eyes pop out of his head too."

"Not sure he even looked, to be honest. I was too busy checking him out. I like them when they taper like that. 'This way to my feet' if you know what I mean. I'd love to see it when it's saying 'This way to Danny's mouth'. Did you see his ass?"

"No, I missed that."

"You certainly did. You'd go into raptures. Do see Mr. Parsons tomorrow. In this weather Michael would be working in shorts. Just imagine looking out of the office window and seeing that."

To my surprise, Mr. Parsons agreed. He made lots of conditions of course. Michael couldn't go anywhere near this building or that building. He had to stay well clear of the scanning antennae but there was a motor mower and the old man who used to do odd jobs had retired. The security people issued a temporary pass with most departments blanked out and Michael started work the following day. He was good too. He got the mower started without help and waved to Danny and me as we watched him steer it through the undergrowth.

Danny was right about the weather. On the next day, jeans and sweatshirt had been superseded by shorts. Just shorts. Not a lot of work was done in our office that day.

Even better, the pre-ablution chats outside the bathroom continued. Michael was totally uninhibited. He'd stand there with his legs slightly apart and talk about the weather or work or what Mrs. Robinson in the personnel office had told him.

Danny and I stared at him like starving kids looking in a confectioner's window.

By the time a week had gone by I was able to sketch his cock, his balls and his bottom from memory. The office shredder worked overtime.

On Saturday, both Danny and I got up late. I couldn't have gone out to the bathroom even I'd wanted to—you don't when you've got a magnificent cock like Danny's pumping into you.

By the time we were up and dressed, Michael was already up, dressed and watching the morning show on the television.

"What shall we do today?" he asked.

"Not a lot actually, Michael. Shopping this morning. Danny's playing football this afternoon."

"Oh good."

"Why? Would you like to come and see the game?" Danny asked.

"Not really. I make the shopping with you and then I write to my Uncle Otto."

So we saw Danny off and wished him all the best, and then did the shopping. We had lunch and Michael settled down to write his letter. For want of anything better to do, I settled down with a book. Suddenly he spoke.

"A friend of me in Germany lives also in a block like this. He does the sunbathing on the roof. Can you do that?"

"I've never thought about it," I said. "There is a key to the roof. In case the place catches fire and we all have to be rescued by helicopter."

He folded his letter and put it in an envelope. "Can we look?" he asked.

"Why not?" I took the key and we went out to the lift. I'd never been as far as the top floor before. We found the door marked ROOF ONLY. I opened it and we stepped out. A huge air conditioning plant buzzed in one corner. Another small building was marked MAINTENANCE STAFF ONLY and from the intermittent machinery noises coming from it, I guessed it to house the lift mechanism. Apart from that, and an array of aerials, it was one vast empty space. I wasn't too happy about the tiny wall round the edges and didn't go near it. Michael did and leaned over to look down at the street below.

"This is a good place," he said, and began to peel off his clothes.

"You need something to lie on," I said. He was undoing his jeans. They slid down. If I stayed much longer there was a severe danger of something embarrassing happening. "Hang on. I'll go and get a towel. A couple of towels," I said.

"No. I go. I am younger," he said.

"Not like that you won't," I replied. "You'd frighten the old ladies." His boxers gaped open in the front to reveal a tantalizing glimpse of white skin and dark hair. In truth it wasn't so much the old ladies I was concerned about. On Saturday afternoons both Dhasan and Neil were in the block and if one of them was to encounter him in the lift, he'd be invited in for cucumber sandwiches, cakes and I don't know what else.

Michael laughed. "They were expensive but still they show too much," he said. He went to twist them to one side and it popped out as if to sample the English air.

"Looks like you've got too much to restrain," I said, trying in vain not to stare at it.

"For the sunbathing I take them off. It is better so," said Michael.

With a thumping heart I went down to the flat and rummaged in the airing cupboard to find two bath towels that were not too new. As always on a Saturday afternoon, I had to wait a long time for the lift. When I got back onto the roof, Michael was sitting, naked, on the low parapet.

"Here we are," I said, spreading the towels out. He stood up. I couldn't help laughing. Some sticky black substance from the wall had transferred to his behind. A broad black stripe ran across his buttocks and thighs.

"It makes nothing," he said when I told him about it. "In the bath it will come off." He lay down on his front. I took off my shirt and lay next to him.

"You are not wishing to get the overall brown?" he asked, turning his head to look at me.

"English modesty," I explained. The real reason was already pressing against my pants. For a moment we lay silent. Then he spoke.

"Later I must post my letter," he said.

"No point. There's no collection until Monday morning."

"Oh."

"You must be very fond of your uncle to write so much so soon," I said.

"My parents say to me I cannot visit him or write," said Michael ruefully.

"Why?"

"You will not tell my parents?"

"I don't even know them so I can't."

"It start when I am ten. Maybe eleven. I drive to my uncle for the weekend. He is the brother of the husband of my cousin. When I am there I break the window in his special glass house where he grow the tomatoes. He take me inside the house and he take off all my closes and then he smack me."

"Oh yes," I said. I was getting interested despite myself.

"But he give me twenty Marks."

"Not counting the marks on your backside," I said.

"Excuse me?"

"Oh nothing. Go on."

"So I go every month. Always he smack me but he give me money. Then when I am fifteen he made it very hard on my, eh, what is this in English?"

"What?"

"This." He reached behind him and slapped his behind.

"Your bottom. Your behind."

"Oh, I think there is another word. Anyway, he make it hard and...." He started to giggle.

"What's so funny?" I asked.

"I have made the joke in English. I see it now. I say he made it hard and I am thinking of the hitting but also he made something else hard. That is my first joke in English. You are not laughing. You do not understand the joke? Maybe you think it is too dirty for laughing?"

"Not in the least. It's quite funny."

"Well, always I go to see him and he does other things."

"What other things?" I turned to look at him. His face had turned a dull red. Not, I was sure, from exposure to the sun.

"Oh it does not matter. Then he writes to me a letter and my parents find it. They say no more Uncle Otto."

"I see. You know, Michael, you really ought to turn over.

Your back's quite red."

"My behind will make the towel dirty."

"Don't worry about that. It'll wash. Sunburn won't."

"In a moment."

I knew what the problem was of course. Thinking about his uncle had turned him on. I changed the subject and asked him what he wanted to do on Sunday. After a few moments, he turned over. I was right. It had grown from the four inches of flaccid flesh I was used to seeing to something like six inches. It lay across his thigh, twitching slightly. An erection such as he could achieve would be worth seeing. I didn't really need to get him talking. Just remembering would probably do the trick.

"What was in the letter?" I asked.

"Oh nothing."

"Parents don't get upset over nothing. What was in it?"

"Oh he say he love me very much and now I am older he want to prove it. Also he took photos of me when I was there last year and he sends one. I am not wearing any closes."

"How did he want to prove he loves you? Did he say?"

"Yes. He say it every time I visit."

His face had gone even redder. Not that I was concentrating on his face. Inexorably, his cock was rising.

"Tell me," I said.

"I think you will laugh at me and think I am a dirty boy."

"Certainly not. Tell me."

"Every time I see him I must take off my closes and he make me hard. And he take me into the bathroom and makes the you know with my.... What is this in English?"

"What?"

"This." He reached down and touched it.

"Proper English is penis. Most people say cock."

"He play with my cock and say it is very beautiful but most beautiful is my behind and he want me to go to bed with him so he can... I don't know the word... in my behind."

"And you were looking forward to it?"

"You think I am dirty?"

"Of course I don't."

"It feels so good when Uncle Otto do the you know to me," he said. "When I think about it, it makes my cock hard."

"So I see." I looked at my watch. "We'd better go down to

the flat," I said. "Danny takes ages in the bathroom when he comes back from football and we've got to get that mark off your behind."

There was no way he could have got his jeans on, even if I had wanted him to. The tar or whatever it was would have ruined them anyway. He draped himself in both towels. Fortunately, nobody got into the lift between the top floor and our floor but I was still relieved when the front door closed behind us. It had gone down slightly but not much.

I followed him to the bathroom. "It is okay. I can do it myself," he said.

"The man isn't yet born who can see his own behind," I said.

He took off the towels and stood over the toilet to pee. Predictably, it took an awful long time before I heard water. I rummaged in the cupboard. He flushed the toilet.

"Right, let's see what we can do," I said. "This isn't going to be easy. I think it's tar or bitumen or something like that."

"Maybe it is easier if I do what I do for Uncle Otto," he said. My heart leapt. "He make me get over the side of the bath," Michael explained. "Like this."

He took a towel from the rail, folded it, placed it on the side of the bath and leaned over, supporting himself with his hands on the other side.

Uncle Otto certainly knew a few things about showing off a boy to his best advantage. Not even the sticky black stripe across his buttocks detracted from the sheer beauty of his body. I took in the line of his vertebrae running down from his neck and vanishing at the slightly parted cleft of his ass and his long legs. The tendons at the back of his knees stood out prominently.

I said something about it being an ideal position. "I'd better get my things off, I think," I said. "That stuff is going to make a mess." I was down to my boxers within seconds. Michael stood up until I was ready. Whether he noticed the state I was in I don't know. I'm sure he must have but he didn't say anything. He got back into position. I covered my hands with the industrial soap I got from work and, for the first time, touched him. The silky feel of his buttocks was an instant turn-on—not that I really needed one.

"Comes off?" asked Michael.

"I'm afraid not." I rubbed harder.

"Oh, that feels so good," said Michael. "That's how Uncle Otto does it."

"Oh, yeah?" Interesting. I added some after shave lotion to the soap. I was a bit scared that it might burn him. All he said was that it smelt nice. That had the desired effect. The suds in my hands went grey; then black. I washed them, loaded up again with the same mixture and started again, kneading the flesh like putty. Soon— all too soon, I'm afraid—the stripe had gone and his asscheeks were the same uniform creamy white.

"There!" I said. "Keep still. There may be just a bit more in here." I parted the cheeks. There wasn't a trace of tar to be seen. "Ah yes," I said. "Just a bit here." I soaped my hands thoroughly. Not, that time, with the industrial stuff. Danny's ex-girlfriend worked in a cosmetic factory, and she used to give him samples. An ass as attractive as Michael's deserved the best. I treated him to Cream of Lavender which, according to the tube, "cleanses and softens the skin." Danny puts it on his feet!

"That smells nice," said Michael as I parted the cheeks again with the thumb and forefinger of my left hand and pushed the lavender-laden second finger of my right hand between them.

"Wait!" said Michael suddenly and he stood up. For a moment my heart sank—until he turned round and I saw his tool. It wasn't just erect; it was rampant and pointed to a spot just forward of his chin. At least seven inches of solid, succulent cock. Danny and I had both agreed that it was beautiful when limp, but erect it was superb.

"Oh, you also are hard," he said, looking down at the projection in the front of my boxers.

"Inevitable," I replied.

"Excuse me?"

"I couldn't help it," I said. He smiled.

"I help it for you," he said. He reached forward and pulled my shorts down. It sprang up.

"It is good," he said and curled his fingers round it. I did the same to him and he grinned.

"You wish me to do the you know?" he asked.

"I've got a better idea," I said. My voice sounded strangely husky. "How about if I do what Uncle Otto had in mind?"

He looked doubtful. "You were looking forward to him doing it. You said so," I continued.

"Uncle Otto said it is only right when the man loves the boy very much. I think you love Danny."

So he had realized. We'd both wondered. There had been times when one or the other of us had made too much noise in the middle of the night.

"It's a different kind of love," I explained, which was true. I loved everything about Danny. I had also come to love Michael's smile and his fractured English. At that moment I was madly in love with a very pretty, neat little butt and a cock that was desperate to fire its load.

"Danny is very big," he said, squeezing mine. It wasn't, perhaps, the most tactful thing to say but I had to agree.

"I like it very much if Danny loves me," he said. "One day I think he does. We are talking and his cock start to go hard."

"I'm not surprised," I said and, still holding his cock, I stroked his backside with my left hand. "Both Danny and I are very fond of you."

"Wishes he to do it in my behind also?"

"Does he want to fuck my ass?" I corrected. "The answer is yes. We both do."

"Fuck my ass. Fuck my ass. Fuck my ass. I like that. It sounds good."

"It feels even better," I said. An idea came into my head. "It would be more sensible to let me do it first. Then you'd be able to take Danny's more easily."

I felt a drop of sticky liquid on the side of my finger. There wasn't a lot of time for further discussion.

"I like it very much if we three love each other," he said.

"No problem."

"Shall you tell Danny?"

"Do you want me to?"

"Of course. Then we are all very happy together. But first you fuck my ass." He released his hold on my cock and took a step towards the bath. I let him go. He picked up the towel, which had dropped to the floor, folded it, placed it on the side of the bath and leaned over again. He spread his legs.

"I am ready," he said.

I had his bedroom or ours in mind but it was a superb position. His long legs formed a broad V and I could actually see his little pink asshole. More Cream of Lavender. Much more. He winced as I touched it. I said something about trying to relax. Stupid really. In that position his whole body was tense. I pushed a finger against it. He winced again. I pushed a bit harder. He made some sort of movement and, suddenly, I was in him.

"Ow!" he yelped. The sound echoed back from the empty bathtub. His legs jerked even further apart and my questing finger went even further in. He felt warm and, not surprisingly, very tight. Slowly, the muscles loosened up, first clenching, then gripping and then just holding my finger. I wiggled it around. He liked that. I did it again. He wriggled. I pulled it out, added yet more of the cream and then pushed two fingers against it. It opened. Not easily but it opened for them. He groaned.

"All right?" I asked.

"Ja!"

I parted my fingers and felt his silky lining stretch. He muttered something in German. My cock was weeping. I managed somehow to empty the tube and anointed it with the rest of the lavender. Slowly, I pulled my fingers out and leaned forward, putting my hands next to his on the opposite side of the bath tub. I remember noticing that his knuckles were white.

Full marks again to Uncle Otto. My cock head found the right place immediately. Michael tensed up for a moment. I licked the back of his neck. He relaxed again and I pushed in.

"Ooooh! Ja! Ja!" he gasped as I slid up into him. "Oh! Ja!" as I thrust a bit harder. I slid my hands round under his armpits and felt his nipples. He wriggled. That felt good. His ass felt slightly less tight.

"Oh! Mach es. Mach es!" he groaned. I didn't know what it meant but it sounded encouraging. His asscheeks felt cool against my balls and incredibly smooth. Trying desperately to keep myself under control—which I am not good at, as Danny will testify—I stuck it in him and began to fucking him, seeming to move farther in with every stroke.

His gasps were amplified by the bath. "Ah! Harter! Ja! Ah! Oh, ja!"

It felt so good, I wanted to make it last as long as humanly possible. Unfortunately, I couldn't. My balls ached. My legs ached. Perspiration was dripping off me onto his long back. I gave one final thrust.

"Ooooh! Ja! Ja!" he grunted as I pumped it into him. "Oh! Ja!" He wriggled again. I clutched his nipples. I never saw him come. He made a sort of gasping noise. There was a soft splashing noise and he was still.

"Good?" I asked, when my heart had stopped thumping.

"Oh yes. Very good. I like it." Gently I withdrew and stood up. The bathroom seemed full of the scent of lavender.

"I make it in the bath," he said. "Look."

Spots of his spunk were spattered on the side and the bottom of the bath and glittered in the light. He turned the water on.

"Now I shall have a bath," he said. "I think there is much to wash from my ass. You make it very much."

I washed my hands and cock at the wash basin whilst the water was running in. I watched him climb in. He seemed to do it much more gracefully than I. I slipped on my boxers.

"Make the door open," he said, as I left him. "Then we can talk."

Still finding it difficult to believe my luck, I settled down in the lounge with my library book, listening to the splashing noises that emanated from the bathroom.

"Can I stay with you next year also?" he called.

"I'm sure you can."

"When comes Danny back?"

"Pretty soon."

"If I come next year, can I also work in the same job?"

Resignedly, I put my book down. "I'll have to ask. Probably."

"Oh, good."

Silence. Just as I picked up the book again, I heard the key in the front door. Danny appeared.

"Good game?" I asked.

"Terrific! I scored. What have you been doing? Teaching young Michael English?"

"Actually, believe it or not, I scored too," I said.

"How do you mean?"

"Tim," Michael called from the bathroom.

"Yes?"

"When Danny comes back, will you tell him he can fuck my ass?"

Danny looked as if he'd been struck by a thunderbolt.

"He's here now," I said. "You can tell him yourself."

"Fuck my ass?" said Danny. "You really have been teaching him English, haven't you?"

"And you're due to give the next lesson," I said.

STRIP FOR STARDOM

Tim Scully

"If we're going to America in the summer, we should go to the travel agent's tomorrow morning," said Danny.

I grunted. "Ready for the out?" he asked.

"Not yet." I wasn't nearly ready. Even the thought of getting out of bed relatively early and going to see about our holiday wasn't sufficient incentive to let go of his magnificent nine inches. I could feel it shrinking inside me but it was in that pleasantly rubbery stage. By clenching my asscheeks, I could compress it, squeezing the last drop out. He liked that and, more often than not, if I continued to do it, his cock would harden again and I'd be in for another glorious fucking.

Those first few months with Danny were a dream. I'd never been happier. I had my very own pet stud. Time and time again in the office, I'd look up from my desk and wonder what good deed I'd done in the past to get a reward like Danny. He is dark haired and handsome. At home, when he's changed out of his business suit and into jeans, he is even more of a feast for the eyes.

He is a very domestic person. Danny is one of the few men I know who don't mind shopping. A few flecks on the carpet are sufficient for him to bring out the vacuum cleaner. We play silly games. He tells me to put my feet up. I do so and he runs the nozzle over my thighs and my butt, a sure sign that he's already thinking of bed.

That's where he comes into his own—or, to be more precise, into me. The nice thing about Danny though is that he's... well... versatile. There are times when I watch him undress and marvel at his strong legs, smooth, white butt and his massive, stiff cock, and decide that it's my turn. Then, when he's got the tube out of the drawer, I need only say "Thank you" to get a radiant smile as he hands it over.

Lubricating him is half the fun, getting a finger into his tight asshole and massaging the silky lining: listening to him moan softly into the pillow as the second finger follows. Then, when he's ready I tap his back with my dry left hand. A signal that he's required to slick up the member which will penetrate him. He sits up. I move towards him and he's got it in his mouth, licking and sucking like a baby on a comforter. More often than not I have to tell him to stop and he lies on his front again, this time with me on top of him. At first it took some time to get in. We were both unpracticed. Now I swear my cock has a mind of its own and could find his asshole without any help from me.

Usually though, I am happy to say that it's me who gets fucked. There is nothing, absolutely nothing, like feeling Danny's monster cock pushing into me. He does it slowly so I can appreciate every fraction of its nine inches. Feeling my insides stretch to accommodate its thickness is great. The first, slow thrust sends me into noisy ecstasies. I love the soft warmth of his balls as they jiggle against my thighs. By the time he's come, I'm in a seventh heaven, unable to think of anything—even vacations in the U. S. A.! I just want him to do it again and again, to fill my ass with his warm spunk until can't hold any more and it starts seeping out of me. I don't even mind the bites that he plants on my asscheeks after he's withdrawn. After the first few nights I had to put a cushion on my chair at work. I wouldn't have said my butt was anything to shout about. His is much more beautiful.

It was my awareness of my shortcomings that brought about the events of this story. We are about the same height. I'm five feet eleven. But my physique is nothing compared to his. It was his strength that got to me. If I do the housework, I have to slide the furniture around. Danny just lifts things up and puts them down again. There was one never-to-be-forgotten night when he slung me over his shoulder and carried me into the bedroom. He was ready for bed. That was obvious from the shape of his jeans. I wanted to watch the end of the television film. I never saw it. One moment I was watching the screen and the next I had an upside-down view of the carpet. I'm no lightweight but you'd have thought I was a sack of feathers.

"I've been thinking," I said one morning when we were in the office.

"Oh yes? What about?"

"How much is the subscription to your fitness club?"

"Depends on what you want to do. We get a discount

through the firm of course."

"I was thinking I ought to join."

"What for?"

"America mostly. I want to look good, like the guys in the brochure."

He said I was talking balls. The guys in the brochure were probably models anyway and he liked me the way I was. But I persisted and he brought me an application form. I had to get him to go easy on the butt biting. That made him try again to persuade me that I had no need to go but in a health club, you have to get changed and there was no way I was going to get undressed and exhibit an extensive collection of mandible impressions.

It was a nice place; very well equipped and I liked the trainer. His name was Rod and I guess he was about twenty seven. Older than me but not too old and very patient. He did all the necessary tests. My blood pressure was a bit high, he said. I put that down to Danny. As the cuff inflated round my upper arm I was thinking how similar it felt to Danny's ass.

Rod was very patient and very good. He'd show me how to do an exercise or use a particular piece of apparatus and then go back into his room and watch me and all the others on the closed circuit television they had. Occasionally, his disembodied voice would come from a speaker near my head to tell me that I was doing something wrong or that, in his view, I'd had enough and ought to stop.

Then I'd join Danny in the Jacuzzi, placing my rapidly healing behind on the cold shelf and feeling the water rushing past my cock and my balls. We could never do much in there of course. It was too risky but when there was nobody around we could talk and, sometimes, reach down and feel each other.

I started to put on weight. Rod said it was a good thing. It was all muscle. I wasn't too sure. Danny said he couldn't see any change.

"You look all right to me," he said one night as I paraded, nude, in front of him. "You look as good as ever. You fuck better than ever. Stop worrying and come to bed. I've got something for you."

Needless to say, I was between the sheets pretty fast.

I was worried though and spoke to Rod about it again on my

next visit to the club.

"You might find a massage beneficial," he said. "I could do that for you and if there is any fat developing, I'll spot it then."

I was grateful and that night, instead of rushing to the Jacuzzi to meet Danny, I lay on the massage couch with just a towel round my middle. Rod was very good. He started on the backs of my legs and worked up to my thighs, kneading and pressing. I could actually feel that it was doing me good.

"I see you and Danny have the same address," he said.

"Oh sure. We work for the same firm and share an apartment. Purely for reasons of economy," I said.

"I see." He undid the towel. I felt his hands on my butt cheeks.

"No fat here. That's where you'd expect it to accumulate," he said.

I guess it was because Danny usually did what Rod was doing to me at that moment. My cock began to take an interest.

"You get on pretty well together, then?" he asked.

"Pretty well, yes." I wished like hell that he'd stop talking about Danny. I envisaged my lover sitting in the Jacuzzi waiting for me to join him. That made it worse.

"He's a good looking guy. Superb body," said Rod. His hand moved up to the small of my back, which was a relief.

"I hadn't really noticed," I said.

"Mind you, it wouldn't do him any harm to have the occasional massage. I've told him several times."

"Oh yes?"

"It's good for the body and relaxing for the mind. Don't you think so?"

My mind was far from relaxed. I was terrified of the moment when he'd tell me to turn over. There was nothing for it but to make some excuse and get out of there as fast as I could.

"What's the time?" I asked.

"Just after eight o'clock."

"What? Bloody hell!" I said. "I'm supposed to be meeting a client at eight."

"Meeting a client at eight o'clock at night?" said Rod. "Funny time to do business."

"It's the only time he could make it. Sorry Rod, I shall have to fly. We'll do the rest of me some other time."

"As you wish." He knotted the towel together again and I sprang off the table. I was in the Jacuzzi within minutes. "We have to leave early, Danny," I said.

He smiled. "Early to bed and early to rise, eh?" His hand moved under the swirling water, found it and clasped it. "Rising nicely," he said. "Come on. Let's go."

He was disappointed when I told him the real reason for leaving. Fortunately I made up for it later in bed.

"I don't suppose Rod would have been embarrassed. Loads of guys probably get erections when they're being massaged," he said when we'd finished and were hugging each other.

"I would have been. What made it worse was that he kept talking about you."

"Me?"

"Yes, he said you have a superb body and that you ought to have a massage."

"He's been going on like that ever since I joined. Extra money for him of course. You bet your life he doesn't declare his massage money for tax. Hence the new car every two years. Ready for the out?"

I didn't intend to tighten up quite so hard. I must have hurt him I'm sure. In my rush to get out of the club I'd forgotten to pay Rod for the massage.

"Pay him next week. He won't mind," said Danny after I'd explained and apologized. But that's not how I like to live. We decided to call into the club on our way home from the travel agents.

"I suppose it's open on Saturday mornings?" I said.

"Seven days a week. Just like you. Mmmm. That feels great!"

. . .

I was surprized at the difference in the clientele. When we go on Thursday evenings, we only see middle aged businessmen. The Saturday crowd seemed to be composed of teenagers and a few kids. St. Bede's school, Neil's place, was well represented. They get cheap membership in the squash club. I presume that there's a similar arrangement for them at the fitness club. We found Rod in his little 'control' room, scanning the monitors.

"Have to watch this lot carefully," he explained. "They tend to strain themselves."

I apologized for not paying him. He said it didn't matter and anyway, I'd only had half a massage. I insisted and he pocketed the money.

"Going away?" he asked, spotting the brochures I was carrying.

"To Fort Lauderdale," I said. "It's a special last-minute offer. Five days in a four star hotel and flight."

"Fort Lauderdale eh? Florida? You wouldn't care to do me a great favor, would you?"

"Depends what it is?" said Danny.

"Take a package for a friend of mine who lives there."

"What's in it?" Danny asked.

"Just four training videos. It costs a fortune to send them by post."

"Oh sure. No problem," said Danny. Rod said he'd hand them to us on Thursday evening and we left him watching a sixteen-year-old boy pedalling an exercise bicycle like he was on the last stage of the Tour de France.

. . .

"Got time for another massage?" Rod asked on Thursday. I said I hadn't. Danny was waiting for me in the Jacuzzi and I was anxious to join him.

"I'll give you that package I mentioned," he said. "It's in the office."

He brought it out. There was no doubt that it really did contain videos; not that I suspected for a moment that Rod would be into drugs or anything like that. It was well-wrapped and bound with tape and addressed to "John Forbes."

I told him the name of our hotel. He said he'd get Mr. Forbes to collect the package and that Mr. Forbes would give us an envelope to bring back to him. "Don't lose it for Christ's sake," he said. "It's important."

If it hadn't been for the thought of Danny sitting in the Jacuzzi idly fondling his cock whilst he waited for me, I'd have said something a bit sharp. I'm not in the habit of losing important envelopes. Some of the stuff I handle at work is really top secret. But, I kept my temper and shortly afterwards my fingers were gently caressing the thing I held most dear; letting Danny know what I had in mind for the rest of the evening and, not for the first time, I wondered how something so big could feel so good. I couldn't wait.

But I had to. "Nothing much on television," said Danny when we got home.

"That suits me," I said. "Early to bed and all that."

"I'd like to watch something. It's fairly early."

"Please yourself," I said. In fact, Danny's television ritual was quite funny. He'd watch for about ten minutes, during which time my hand worked overtime on the area of his crotch. In the summer months he drove to and from the club in his shorts. In a remarkably short time he'd decide that the program wasn't what he thought it might be and we went to bed.

"Are there any videos we haven't seen yet?" he asked.

"No."

He picked up the package. "We have. We've got these," he said.

"You can't do that! They're private. Anyway, you'd need to cut it open."

"Nobody will know. Mr. Forbes never saw it packed."

"But they're training videos. As boring as hell."

I have a lot of experience with training videos. The firm has a special department that produces them. Endless slow motion shots of missiles doing their deadly work and always narrated by the same man whose voice gives the impression that he is as bored as the potential customers.

"To hell with morality," said Danny. "Let's have a look anyway."

He slit the package open, carefully preserving the label. There were four tapes: 'Schoolboy Exercises', 'Massage Techniques', 'Open Air Sports' and 'Weight Training'.

"Which shall we look at?" Danny asked.

"Oh, I don't know. Try 'Massage Techniques'. Then you can learn how to do it and save me money."

He put the cassette into the machine and switched on the television. A very amateur title came up on the screen followed by a shot of a familiar room. I recognized it immediately. The couch, the wash basin in the corner and the Venetian blinds hanging at a slight angle.

"That's the club," I said. "He's used the monitor camera."

A young man entered, draped in a towel exactly as I had been. He got up onto the couch, grinned at the camera and undid the towel.

"He's got nothing to shout about," said Danny and, even though mine was very little bigger, I laughed. He was a good-looking guy though. Very few people are blessed, as Danny is, with good looks and a big cock.

Rod came into the room, dressed as always, in the white training suit he wore. One of those that has straps that go under the soles of the shoes. I'd never seen him in anything else.

I think both Danny and I went rigid with shock. Rod grinned. The young man grinned back. Rod slid his hands up and down the young man's thighs. Naturally enough, his cock began to respond. Soon it was erect. Rod started to wank him, slowly at first. The young man closed his eyes. With his free hand, Rod played with his nipples.

"He likes that," said Danny, unnecessarily. I put a hand in my pocket to restrain my cock. Rod smiled at the camera and lowered his head.

"He's done that before," said Danny as inch after inch of cock disappeared from view. The young man heaved upwards several times; then arched his body. Rod stood up straight again. Streams of pearly white fluid ran down his chin.

"Well, I'm damned!" said Danny. "I never would have thought it! More?"

"Might as well," I said and for the next three quarters of an hour we saw eight people undergo similar treatment. Some were young and attractive but by no means all of them. One guy, I guessed him to be about forty-five, was repulsive

'Weight Training' had its good moments though I shuddered to think that I had lain on that same bench trying not to look at the camera on the wall as I heaved the bar upwards. I liked the hunky blond who managed to lift far more than I could and who, after the bar was back in its rest, lifted his legs so that his equally well-built buddy could screw his ass. All we saw were the soles of his feet in close up and the rhythmic tensing and relaxing of a very powerful pair of buttocks. It was a pity, as

Danny said, that there was no sound and nobody seemed to have thought about camera angles.

'Open Air Sports' had been shot outside by someone who appeared to be suffering from Parkinson's disease. There were some shots that shook so much that it was difficult to see what was happening. An older man and a younger man were seen walking in a pine forest. The man undressed. Then he undressed his companion, who laughed at something the man said and exhibited his erection to the camera. Then he bent over a huge fallen tree. After that, camera vibration was so bad that it was almost impossible to see what was happening. A white ass swayed from left to right of the screen, often going right out of view.

In another scene, Rod appeared again. This time with two naked young men who started by doing push ups in the middle of a cornfield and who ended up with one on top of the other and with Rod on top of the pile trying to emulate a sandwich screw which, unfortunately didn't work out. Cocks that should have been deep in assholes kept coming into view.

I was a bit dubious about 'Schoolboy Exercises.' In fact I need not have worried. Technically speaking they might have been still at school. Indeed, I recognized the St. Bede's student I'd seen on the exercise bike. No attempt had been made to shave their legs and you need to be pretty far up in a school to have the large cocks and dense pubic bushes that were displayed to the watching camera. It would have been better had they not tried to act. As it was, both Danny and I were in hysterics in minutes.

The massage room at the club had moved incongruously to an exclusive boys' school. A shaky hand-held shot at the beginning identified it as 'Parker's Academy for Boys.' We saw two 'boys' enter the room and undress. They lay alongside each other on the couch and we were treated to a quite good shot of mutual masturbation. Had Rod or whoever it was been satisfied with that, it would have been good. They were both cute guys. Both had big cocks and both knew how to get the best out of a friend. Just when they were lying with eyes closed and ready to shoot their loads, another 'boy' came in and stood with open mouth and rolling eyes like a codfish at a tennis match. Needless to say, they opened their eyes and, within minutes, he'd undressed and taken the first throbbing, pre-cum-dripping cock into his mouth.

The next visitor was Rod, dressed in an old-fashioned schoolmaster's cap and gown and wielding a cane. He gave a dramatic impression of someone in the middle of an epileptic fit, raising his arms in horror. All three of them had to get off the couch and bend over it in a row for him to administer a gentle beating. At least, I assume it was gentle. It didn't seem to leave any marks.

Up to that moment we had only seen Rod from the back or the side. He turned to face the camera and revealed that the schoolmaster's gown was the only thing he was wearing. Nine or so inches of rigid cock stood out between the silk-faced sides. He grinned.

"There's more to Rod than meets the eye," Danny commented. There certainly was. All three boys goggled at it, rolling their eyes and gaping with wide-open mouths. One of them actually got down onto his knees and was apparently begging for mercy. Rod grabbed him by the hair and hauled him to his feet, an effect that might have worked had the boy not been grinning.

All three of them must have been lubricated and well practiced. Ignoring the lad's plea for a reprieve, Rod thrust his cock between the boy's asscheeks. The boy turned his head towards the camera. His mouth was wide open. His eyes rolled like a ventriloquist's dummy as Rod pounded against his buttocks.

"Pity there's no sound track," I remarked. Danny grunted.

They say the camera can't lie. If that's true, Rod must have been some sort of superman. He pulled out of the boy just in time to spatter spunk all over his back and then, apparently, went straight to the next in line, who got similar treatment. In less than twenty minutes, all three had been anointed and Rod, instead of looking exhausted, grinned triumphantly as he rubbed it into their skins.

It was, as Danny said, such a shame. All the natural grace of an older teenaged boy had been sacrificed to hammy acting. If Rod had stayed in his control room and left the three of them to do what comes naturally it would have been superb viewing.

It was well after two o'clock in the morning when we went

to bed. We had to go to work the following day. Goodbye to my thoughts of a long and leisurely fuck. It was far too late and some of the things I'd seen had put me off. Not completely, I am happy to say.

I think we both felt equally shattered on the following morning. I certainly did. I fell asleep in Danny's car. Fortunately Joan, our shared secretary, was ready with the coffee.

"I was thinking," said Danny, looking up from his computer.

"Oh yes. What about?"

"Those videos."

"I wouldn't have thought them worth thinking about," I replied.

"I agree. But this Mr. Forbes is going to give us an envelope to bring back, right?"

"Right."

"The betting is that it's money. Payment for the videos. Hence its importance."

"That figures. And?"

"If he pays money for rubbish like that, why don't we make one? Just you and me? No acting. No daft schoolboy uniforms. Just you and me having a good time."

There was something in the proposal that I found intriguing. Quite exciting to be truthful.

"At home?" I asked.

"No. We'd need a third party to operate the camera. The club."

"Oh yes. And how do we arrange that?"

"There has to be a slack time when there are no members and Rod wants a break. We'll ask him."

I have to hand it to Danny. For sheer deviousness he takes some beating. He was sympathetic when he heard that Rod had to be there from eight in the morning to ten at night.

"What do you do for meals?" he asked.

"Slip out when I can. Weekday lunchtimes are no problem. Nobody comes then."

"Damn!" said Danny. "Tim and I were thinking of coming here during our lunch break to get fit for the holiday."

"If you want to come, you come," said Rod. "Members first is the motto."

We came to an arrangement. Rod was really grateful. We'd get there just before one o'clock. We promised only to use the equipment he'd recommended and never at a higher setting than he had prescribed. He could go out and have his lunch break. He suggested that we should lock the outer door whilst he was away which was very convenient.

We didn't rehearse. There was no time and, as we both agreed, it was going to be a spontaneous record of two people who loved each other; something that we could keep forever and that might possibly make us a bit of extra money. I must confess that there were times when a rehearsal would have relieved the tension. Our planning meetings were held in the office. We had to ban poor Joan from coming in, on the grounds that we were working on a secret project. In fact we sat at our respective desks, both with distinct erections, whilst we discussed the best possible methods of recording the action, bearing in mind that we were limited to fixed cameras.

Anyone outside the club on our first day would have been puzzled to see us lug a long dressing mirror out of the car a few minutes after Rod had left. It was my idea and it worked beautifully. I still enjoy looking at that bit. Me lying on the weight bench fingering my cock. God knows, there was no need to. I was as randy as a rabbit. Doing it in a strange place I guess. Danny was an inordinately long time in the control room. He was having trouble, as I now know, finding the right switch for the monitor camera. None of them was numbered.

Danny arrives and looks down at me. The mirror catches his smile and massive erection. The camera records my inane grin. He lifts my legs up and puts them over his shoulder. The shot of his greased finger probing me is really good. That involuntary wince on my face as it slides in is good; a thousand times better than Rod's "actors" achieved. I'm a bit ashamed of the way I wriggled around when the second finger went into me and of my toothy grin. Not, I think, that any viewer would have been looking at me at that moment. They would have been concentrating on the mirror shot of Danny's dripping cock and his erect nipples.

I got the answer to my question from that session. It goes in easily. It's as if my ass is a mouth, sucking it in and expanding to take it. Bit by greasy bit it disappears from view and anyone mad enough to concentrate on the camera shots sees my mouth open slightly as it pushes in and the flinch as it brushes past my prostate. But nobody would look at me. Danny's face, the gleam of his oiled body are much more attractive and you get a glimpse, from the mirror shot, of his huge balls. I still get an instant hard on when I look at that bit.

Danny has always said that I'm good. So, for that matter, has Dhasan. I don't know. If it hadn't been me, I would have said the person was acting most of that ecstatic writhing and squirming around. Danny has both hands under the small of my back, lifting me up and pulling me on to him. The camera catches his ass tightening and loosening and, over his shoulder, my hand working on my cock. I was desperate to come at just the right time.

In fact I didn't. The camera leaves no doubt as to the moment when he shot a torrent of spunk into my aching ass. His butt contracts so tightly that you can hardly see the cleft and his open mouthed, sweating face is reflected in the mirror. I didn't do too badly though. I came a split second later. It shot upwards, splashing Danny, the bar of weights above my head and the mirror.

By the time Rod returned, we'd cleaned up. He found me lifting twenty-eight pounds with Danny standing solicitously over me just in case twenty eight pounds might be too much for a frail person like me! Very little work got done in the office that afternoon.

Nor the next. That was the day when we did the massage room shots. I think Danny is better than I am. It certainly felt so at the time. By the time he'd got it into his mouth I was out of my mind. After thirteen minutes of being fondled, my cock was more than ready to shoot and my balls were aching. We were going to do "Tim does Danny" on the same afternoon but those thirteen minutes had done things to Danny as well. I was dimly aware, as he sucked on mine, that he was wanking himself. A second or so after I'd shot and he was licking his lips, he came, spraying it all over my left leg. It was just as well we'd put a sheet on the table.

So my opportunity to star had to be postponed. In retrospect I am glad. If you're going to have a good meal, it's nice to have time to think about it. I had twenty-four hours of mouthwatering anticipation. For that reason I wouldn't let him that night. I went to sleep with my hand under his balls, imagining them producing the sperms that give Danny's spunk such a delicious flavor. It's as sweet and sometimes almost as thick as syrup. It's only when it's been in your mouth for a few minutes that you get that slightly sharp taste. Even writing about it makes me slobber over the keyboard.

He was good. I love the way his legs dangle over the edges of the couch, giving the camera a good look at all he's got—when my head isn't in the way. I was able to get my tongue right in to begin to lap his asshole and his balls. Naturally I couldn't manage to get all his cock in my mouth. I don't think anybody could, but the shot of me licking along its length is good and, when I finally get as much of it as possible, the sight of the last inch or so is quite exciting. If you look carefully, you can actually see the moment he comes. Just at the moment when he lifts his butt off the couch and I hold on to his hips to save losing any, you can see the shaft swell slightly as his spunk gushes through. I didn't waste a drop. In fact when Rod came back I was still licking my teeth.

There wasn't a lot of tape left but I was determined to use it to the best advantage and that, of course, would be to record me fucking Danny.

Now Danny, as I think I've told you before, likes being fucked lying on his front. I like it too. In that position his ass is as tight and as comfortable as a well-fitting glove. The problem was, as we agreed in our morning conference, that there was no way we could get a good shot. All the viewer would see would be my ass heaving up and down. It was kind of Danny to say what he did but I didn't think it would make riveting entertainment.

I think even then that we had gotten to the stage in our relationship when we both thought the same way. Certainly I can't remember either of us making the suggestion. It seemed to come out of the blue. Me on the weight bench or the massage table with my head towards the camera and Danny sitting on me. Or, to be more precise, sitting on my cock. That way the viewer would see his face as it slid up into him and, as a bonus, a good view of his cock and immense balls.

To my mind it's the best part of the tape. "A fitting climax," as Danny said when we sat and watched it for the first time. By the time Danny had switched on the camera and the recorder I was carefully greasing my cock, which, as you can imagine, was already standing at attention, waiting for the arrival of the guest of honor.

Danny comes into the room. You just get a glimpse of it; not yet totally rigid. He takes a few steps forward. Time for the viewer to take in his long back, perfect butt and downy thighs. He climbs up and kneels across me with his shins pressing against my sides. At this stage he's facing away from the camera. He leans forward and begins to suck my toes. He'd never done that before and you can't see exactly what he's doing. But who would want to? His ass is in perfect focus. My hand appears. A finger goes between his cheeks. A little spasm of the muscles as I find the spot and push into him. A bit of internal massage. Big dimples form in the sides of his buttocks as he tightens on my finger. The second finger disappears from view. Danny wriggles, doing his bit to get my fingertips in all the right places. He's ready. He climbs off the bench and then, facing the camera for the first time, gets back onto me. This is the point when you get your first good view of nine inches of steel-hard cock. Mine was as stiff as it's ever been but, compared with Danny's, it looks pretty insignificant.

If it had been left to me, I would have erased the bit where Danny feels under himself to guide me to the right place. It was, after all, the first time we'd done it that way. Danny said we ought to leave it in so we did.

Danny grinning. Danny wincing. So, for that matter, am I, though you can't see my face. It felt like I had a ton weight poised on my cock. For an instant I thought it might double up. Something had to give. Something does. Danny screws up his face as he sinks down on it; shuddering as it touches his button. The little spot of pre cum glitters at the tip of his cock before sinking like a fluorescent thread onto my belly.

Neither of us is really in control of the other; that's what I like about it. I grasp Danny's cock and wank it slowly whilst he rises and falls, using his well trained muscles to fuck himself, grinning happily as he does so. I help, lifting my butt off the bench in time with each of his down strokes.

Danny comes first. A professional cameraman couldn't have

done better. It is sheer luck. That first milk white jet looks almost solid until it breaks up and splatters over my face. The second and third cover my chest and belly with spots that look like pearls under the light. During that instant my cock is gripped hard and, the moment his muscles slacken again, my own load spurts up into him. I play our copy of the tape again and again just to watch the blissful look on his face.

Danny lifts himself off, pressing down with his hands. My gleaming member comes into view again. Danny leans over my face, licking the spunk off my chin before planting a kiss on my lips. Like I said, the best part of the tape. I think Mr. Forbes thought so too.

. . .

Fort Lauderdale is a fantastic place. If you've never been there, go. There's no space to tell you about most of the people we met or the things we did. It was the best vacation of our lives.

Forbes showed up on the second day we were there. I had expected someone in dark glasses with a hat pulled down over his eyes, the archetypal pornographer. Instead of which he was young; not much older than I am, good looking and with a pleasant smile.

We handed over Rod's tapes. He gave me the envelope. Just feeling it was enough to tell me that Danny was right. Those were dollar bills.

"You might be interested in this one," I said, bringing out a copy of ours. For a moment he looked non-plussed. "Same as the others?" he asked. I nodded.

"Oh. It's just that Rod said you weren't in the know."

"Better that he stays that way," I said. He frowned and took the tape.

He was back the next day. We'd just returned from the beach. Danny was taking a shower, to get rid of the sand before we got down to our usual late afternoon activity.

"That's you, isn't it?" said Mr. Forbes when I'd opened the door for him. I didn't have time to reply. Danny stepped out of the shower. Mr. Forbes grinned. "Definitely you," he said, "I recognize that. Wouldn't say no to a mouthful myself."

Politely but firmly, Danny told him to forget it.

"It never does any harm to ask," he said. "Let's get down to business, shall we?"

And that is why we came back from Florida with more money than we'd had when we started from London airport. And that is why we are going back to Fort Lauderdale in a few months' time—this time as film stars!

THE NUDE-SWIMMING POND

Ian Cappell

When I was a senior at boarding school, there was a boy called Peter. He used to make my dick get hard, just at the sight of his tight, muscular body. And the noticeable bulge in the front of his grey school trousers. From the first moment I saw him, all that I longed for was the chance to see him naked.

Not far from the school there was a pond, hidden away in a small copse of trees, which was used during the summer to go nude-swimming, although this had to be kept secret from the teachers or there would have been big trouble. One hot afternoon I saw Peter and two of his friends sneaking off in the direction of the copse. Taking my chance, I followed them, being as careful as I could to make certain that they did not notice me.

Once I entered the copse, I crept as close as I dared to the pond, and hid in some bushes out of sight. Carefully parting some of the branches, I nearly burst with excitement, as I watched all three of them strip naked, and then dive, unashamedly, into the ice-cold water. But for me, the other two boys, nice as they were, may just as well not have been there, as my eyes were glued on Peter's wonderful body and the enormous cock that waved between his legs.

Hastily I stripped off my own clothes, happy to feel the air on my naked body, and stroked my already-hard cock, as I gazed, doe-eyed at Peter. My only thought was that I just had to touch that wonderful, sexy body. My lust for him was driving me mental, and I was wanking my cock in a frenzy. All I could do, was wait, wank, and hope for a chance.

It came after about twenty minutes of delicious torture, when Peter was standing in the water with his back towards me, his hands on his hips, his powerful legs spread wide apart, laughing with his friends. Silently I left my hiding place, and slipped into the pond. Filling my lungs with air, I swam under water, heading towards his legs. I have always been a good swimmer, and being under water was no problem for me.

When I reached my goal, I started to swim through his open

legs, but to my amazement, just as I got my head through, he closed them on me, gripping me with his strong, muscular thighs. Before I knew what was happening, he had me in a scissor-lock, but, instead of his foot being in my mouth, I had his wonderful cock pressed against my lips instead. It must have happened in my struggle to free myself. I was in heaven.

Peter kept his grip tight around my neck. But he lay on his back in the water allowing me to come up for air. But as I gasped for air, my mouth open wide, I also got my first taste of his cock as well. This made the other two boys laugh, and Peter said to them, "He really must want it, after all the trouble he went to just to get near it." They all laughed even louder at this, but suddenly Peter's cock grew rock hard and every time that I opened my mouth for air, he would poke the tip inside it, making me gag because it was so big. This would only make them all laugh like hell as they watched me gulping air, and sucking in Peter's cock as well.

When they had finished larking about with me, all three of them dragged me out of the pond and into some dense bushes nearby. I was a bit scared then, and wondered what they were going to do to me. But they all kept a firm hold on me, as I stood, sandwiched between their hot, sexy bodies. My cock rapidly stood at attention as they argued amongst themselves, who should have me first. Then Peter shouted that as it was him, that I went for, he should be the one to have first go with me. Finally, the other two reluctantly agreed with him, and backed down.

A towel was then spread on the ground and I was forced down, onto my knees, while Bill, one of the other boys asked me, "Can you shoot spunk yet?"

"Yes", I answered.

He continued, "Well, if you drink loads of spunk, when you are our age, it will help your cock and balls grow bigger." All the time that he was explaining this, he kept rubbing the head of his now swollen cock across my lips.

Before he could get any further, Peter pushed him aside and stood towering over me, his swollen cock standing ramrod straight before him, perfectly in line with my lips. "O.K. boy. Open your hot mouth and suck it for me. And don't get your teeth in the way or there will be trouble. Do you understand?"

I just couldn't believe that I was going to do this, but right at that moment, tasting that hot cock was all that mattered in the world to me. So I just nodded my head and opened my mouth as wide as I could, so that I could take his throbbing monster inside me.

As he slid his throbbing cock inside my mouth, I discovered that it was hot, hard and delicious. I closed my eyes, and luxuriated in the fantastic taste of his solid cock. I had never experienced anything so wonderful in my whole life before. But I was soon dragged back from my dream-state by the hoarseness in his voice. As I opened my eyes and looked up the length of his wonderful body he said, "Stop fucking about boy. Suck it. Suck it good."

I did exactly as he told me, eager to learn to do this job properly. Within a few minutes he was moaning and groaning with pleasure. He pumped his hips backwards and forwards, faster and faster, as he grabbed my hair and forced his cock farther and farther down my increasingly cock-hungry throat. Suddenly I felt it swell inside my mouth, and the next instant, it exploded, and I choked and gagged on the stream of hot, sweet spunk that he was pumping into me. But I did my best to gulp down as much as I could. This was my first-ever taste of cock. My first taste of spunk. And I knew then that I loved it.

No sooner had Peter slipped his softening cock from my mouth, than Bill replaced it with his. I dutifully sucked and slobbered on it until he unloaded, and I hungrily gobbled down his sweet cream. Then without any hesitation, I gobbled down the third. But for me, neither of the others was as good as Peter. As he stood, hands on hips, legs spread wide, watching me service his friends, I kept glancing across at his wonderful, sexy body. He was smiling at me, which made me so happy. In a way, it made me feel proud that I was pleasing him, and I stepped up the pace of my own wanking, which seemed to please him even more.

As the last cock emptied its load into me, Peter came and stood over me, as I licked the last traces of spunk from my lips. He said, "Come on then, cock-sucker. Let's see you milk your own cock now." Just looking at him, naked, was all the incentive that I needed. Keeping my eyes fixed on his body I beat my dick harder and harder and soon I was moaning and gasping with delight at the sensations that flooded through me. But after all the excitement, it did not take me long before I sent wads of cum squirting out of my aching cock, all over the ground.

Peter seemed quite impressed with the healthy load that I produced and said, "Not bad at all," then he moved around behind me, put his bare foot against my back, and pushed me forwards, so that my face was on the ground, and my arse high in the air. Then he knelt down, and spread my arse-cheeks with his hands, exposing my tight, puckered, virgin hole.

Speaking to his friends, he said, "I suppose this has had loads of cocks up it, seeing as he is so hungry for cock?" They both laughed, and I could see Bill out of the corner of my eye, stroking his cock to hardness again. Until that moment, I had never thought about having a cock up my arse. But then, I hadn't thought about having a cock in my mouth either. But that hadn't stopped me enjoying three of them. So, as I lay with my face against the earth, and my arse high in the air, with Peter's wonderfully soft hands stretching my cheeks apart and teasing my hole, I said, "As a matter of fact, no. No one's been up my arse...yet."

Before either of the others could answer, Peter slapped my arse with his hand, and told me to get dressed. Then, as he watched me fetch my clothes and put them on, he told me to meet them there tomorrow, at the same time, to service their cocks again. As I left the pond, they all dived back into the water, and I heard them splashing around as I walked out of the copse.

That night, when I was in bed, I just couldn't get what happened in the copse out of my mind. As I lay on my side, listening to the others in my dorm settling down for the night, my cock grew so hard, it really started to ache. It was pure torture for me, having my cock throbbing like crazy under my pajamas, and not being able to do anything about it.

The minute I thought it was safe, I lay on my back, undid the cord on my pajamas, and slid them down to my ankles. Boy. What a relief that was. Taking a firm grip on my solid shaft, I started stroking it, up and down, thinking about Peter, and his wonderful, naked body, and his big, hard cock, which had filled my mouth, and tasted so good.

The pace of my wanking increased, as I undid the buttons on my pajama top, so that I could run my other hand across my bare chest, and play with my hard nipples. Then, as my hand travelled down across my flat stomach, so I pulled my legs up towards me, and spread my knees wide under the bedclothes, so that I could slip my free hand down passed my bouncing ballsac, and rub a fingertip lightly across my virgin hole.

While I did this, I thought about what Peter had said, about having a cock inside me. Automatically, my mind focused on Peter's own fabulous, rock-hard cock. Oh, fuck. It looked so beautiful. So strong. So powerful. Just imagining what it would be like to have that solid pole filling my rosebud, pushing all the way inside me, until his wonderful balls slapped against my firm little boy-cheeks, was more then I could stand.

The images flooding through my brain turned me on so much that I felt my cock swell in my hand, and I quickly had to use my free hand to tent up the bedclothes, as my spunk rocketed along my shaft, and spurted out of my knob, splattering all over my bare chest, even hitting my chin. And throughout all this, I had to keep silent, for fear of waking any of the others, which was real torture. As I scooped up my spunk with my fingers and carried it to my eager mouth, the next day just couldn't come soon enough.

All the next morning my cock was never less than semi-hard. By the time the afternoon came around, I was so eager to get their cocks in my mouth again, and maybe somewhere else, that I got to the pool ahead of them. Hurriedly I stripped out of my clothes, and dove naked into the water. Even as I swam around, waiting for them to turn up, my cock was solid, and aching for what was to come.

When they did arrive, I heard Bill turn to Peter and say, "This kid really is eager Pete. How about we teach him more about boy-sex?" This made me really excited, and I walked out of the pool towards them, my throbbing cock leading the way, my eyes fixed on Peter, who was busy stripping off his clothes.

When he and the others were naked, Peter turned me around and squeezed my arse-cheeks. Oh. His hands felt so strong on my boy-cheeks. Then he said to Bill, over my shoulder, "Let him suck us all hard first. But remember, the first fuck is mine." Bill and the other boy, who I now found out was called Stuart, both agreed.

They spread out two towels this time, and I eagerly got on my knees and took Peter's already-hard cock into my mouth, and really relished the taste and feel of it sliding across my tongue. I sucked and sucked on it as if my whole life depended on it. I loved that cock so much, I just couldn't wait to get it all the way up my arse. Then he pulled it out, and immediately Stuart replaced it with his.

As I sucked him, I felt Peter reach underneath me, and finger my hole. His finger felt very slippery and I found out later that he had brought some grease with him, just for this purpose. The feelings that shot through my body as he stroked and teased my rosebud were so wonderful that I automatically bent forward, so that my hole was more accessible to him.

Before I knew it my arse-muscle relaxed, and I felt his finger slide inside me. It felt so fantastic as he worked it in and out of me. It only took a couple of seconds before I shot my load. And I hadn't even touched my cock. Not only that, but my cock stayed hard too. And just kept on throbbing between my spread legs.

Just as Bill was pushing his cock into my mouth for some hot suction, Peter took his finger out of me, telling Bill to kneel down, so I had to bend forward, and support myself on my hands. Then he took hold of my hips and lifted me up onto my knees. Next I felt his warm cockhead pressing against my virgin hole.

By now I wanted it up me so badly that I pushed my arse back onto it, and felt only a little pain as the head slid inside. He waited a moment, to let me adjust to it, then he slowly worked the whole length in and began to fuck me. It was the most fantastic feeling of my entire life. And I ate Bill's cock ravenously.

Stuart and Bill were getting so turned on watching Peter's cock pistoning in and out of my tight boy-cunt, that Bill's cock soon started to swell in my mouth. I knew his load of sweet spunk was on its way. Hmmm. He really filled my mouth with his cream, and I guzzled it all down greedily. Stuart didn't even give him time to finish before he was pushing Bill out of the way, desperate to get his own aching cock into me.

But even while all this was happening to me, I was still fully aware that Peter had stepped up the pace of his fucking, and he began to moan and gasp loudly. I sensed that he must be close to the edge, and tried to grip his shaft even harder with my arse-muscle. Then I felt his cock grow fatter inside me, and when he started shooting his spunk into me, I nearly fainted. I loved it. He gripped my hips really tight, as the spasms seemed to go on forever.

The minute that Peter pulled his cock out of my hole, Stuart changed ends, and eased his cock into my still-open boy-pussy. It did not take him long to build up his pace, and soon I was being rocked back and forth under the force of his fucking. This pushed me onto Bill's cock, as he had shoved it quite roughly, back into my mouth, and was helping to get him hard again.

The three of them each fucked me twice during that session. And my own cock was never out of my hand. I unloaded three more times, while I was being fucked at both ends, because my mouth was also never empty either. I was put into all kinds of different positions, to get fucked. At one point, when it was Peter's turn to plow me, he lay down on his back, and had me straddle his body, facing him. I squattedt down, with my hands spread behind me, while I lowered my gaping, sopping hole onto the head of his fantastic cock. Slowly, I let the full length of it sink into me, then I began jumping up and down on him until I came. Oh, it was glorious!

When they had all finished, the four of us dove into the pond to clean ourselves up. Then we all lay together on the towels letting our bodies dry in the hot summer air, and they told me I was the best sex each of them had ever had.

After a compliment like that, I made sure that I sucked them all off again before we climbed back into our clothes, and crept back to school.

THE STUFF DREAMS ARE MADE OF

Bert McKenzie

I first met him in a dream. My legs were up in the air, my knees beside my head. I was folded into an unbelievable pretzel while he worked above me. His thick cock was pounding into my ass, stinging me with a burning pain while pushing me into an ecstacy at the same time. In that bizarre perspective that only occurs in dreams, I was lying back looking up at his face, his intensely blue eyes, and at the same time I was watching the two of us fucking. I could see the curve of his dick as it slid in and out, his balls bouncing beneath. I walked around to watch the muscles of his ass as he slammed into me.

The moans of passion increased in volume until they became a scream as we both climaxed. My incubus shot his hot jism into my body at the same time as I began spraying us with my own fountain of cum. The moans were real; they were my own. I awoke as the orgasm passed, my chest and pubes covered with my sperm. It had only been a dream. Then I saw him in the real world two weeks later.

I wanted him from the first moment I saw him. He was my dream come true. But then I was sure that just about every other gay man or straight woman felt that way. And why not? After all, he was my dreamboy.

He was stretched out by the hotel pool. A long, lean and perfectly muscled young man wearing boxer-style trunks. His hair was a sandy blond and his face had a firm, square jaw line. At the time I could only wonder about the eyes hidden behind the dark sunglasses. What color were they? Perhaps intense blue as in my dream?

His chest was dusted with a light coating of yellow fuzz as were his arms and legs. The sun reflecting off his golden skin and blond body hair gave him an ethereal, sparking quality. The boy had perfectly shaped pecs capped by small bronzed nipples and a corded washboard stomach. I suspected he must spend time at a gym, although he looked young enough that most of his definition may have come naturally.

He had apparently fallen asleep in the lounge chair by the

pool. In that sleep what erotic dreams must have come? The tent in his swimming trunks was quite obvious. How I wondered what hot, sexual scenes ran through his mind! Was he at a desert oasis surrounded by scantily clad maidens waiting to offer him their feminine virginity? Or was he stripped and hard, plunging his cock into the willing asses or mouths of other hot studs? Or maybe he was fucking me, with my legs in the air and his dick slamming into my guts, a re-enactment of my dream from before.

"Don't you wonder who he is?" Carlos asked at the party. He nudged me and pointed to the door. We sat at the bar, Carlos and I, a couple of lecherous old queens, watching for fresh faces, new blood, as each person or couple entered the Crystal Room. It was a piss-elegant affair thrown by another lecherous old queen, only a very rich one. His reception was in honor of a young artist, an untalented man with an unduly large penis, which had caught his patron's eye, among other body parts.

My heart rose to my throat. There in the door was the young man from the pool, my dreamboy, now awake and dressed in an immaculate tuxedo. He looked about the room nervously, as if he wasn't sure he was at the right party.

"Model or call boy?" Carlos asked. Suddenly his bitchy game of guess the career repulsed me. I didn't want my beauty to be an ordinary hustler, or even a high-priced one. I wanted him to be the innocent he appeared.

"In the wrong room, looking for the Johnson wedding reception," I quipped back.

The young man scanned the room. His eyes seemed to rest on me, then he headed in our direction.

"No. Call boy, definitely," Carlos argued as he slid off the bar stool.

"Where are you going?" I asked with an urgency I didn't feel.

"Just to the lady's room to powder my nose," my friend said, then disappeared.

It wasn't me the young man wanted, but the bar and an empty seat beside me. "I'll have a rum and Coke," he ordered, then turned to glance my way. Cornflower blue. Intense blue like the summer sky or the rolling ocean.

"What?" I asked. I had been lost in his eyes, only realizing too late he had asked me a question.

He looked a bit bemused. "I said, how's it going?"

What a first impression I must have made. "Fine, just fine." We both lapsed into silence while he waited for his drink.

"Say something," my mind screamed at me. "Soon it will be too late."

"What can I say?" I asked myself mentally.

"Ask him about his dreams by the pool. Ask him what got him so hot, his dick so hard. Tell him about your dream. Ask him back to your condo or out for a walk, or into the john for a five-minute blow job. Anything!"

"Hi!" a voice called with a lilting, musical quality. It was Carlos, back from the can and now positioned on the other side of my young man. I realized I was becoming mentally possessive. "Perhaps you can settle a bet between my friend and me," he said, indicating me.

The boy's eyes, his cornflower blue eyes, darted between us from one to the other. "Well, yeah, if I can." I could hear the hesitancy in his voice.

"What is it you do for a living?"

"Me? Uh...I'm an actor."

Carlos smiled a wide, wolfish grin. "Oh, all bets are off," he cooed. "My friend thought you were a model but I said you were a call boy. An actor . . . so we're both right." The boy's face turned pink. He was obviously embarrassed, but unsure how to respond. "So, what's your name?"

"I'm not sure yet."

"You don't know your name?" Carlos persisted. He looked over at me and winked. "He's bright, too."

"No, I mean professionally," the boy stammered. "My agent wants to change it but he hasn't settled on the new one yet."

"And . . . ?" Carlos prompted.

"Oh, it's Harold Kowaloski."

"Smart agent," my friend jabbed. "I hope you have that sewn into your underwear so you can periodically ask someone to check who you are."

The boy again blushed. He drained what remained in his glass and then got up. "Where are you going, sweet cheeks?" Carlos called after him, but he just kept walking, heading out onto the terrace.

I ordered another rum and Coke and took it with me. As I left I said, "Sometimes Carlos, you really disgust me."

"You and the girl's hockey team from Bennington, Vermont," he snapped back.

I found Harold Kowaloski on the terrace that overlooked the gardens. "Here," I said, handing him the drink. "I'd like to apologize for my . . . friend. He's kind of a jerk."

"Yeah, I noticed." I introduced myself, reaching out. He took my hand in a firm grip. "Hank," he replied.

"So, do you know Alex, or are you just a patron of the arts?" I asked.

"Alex?"

"The man who's throwing this shindig."

Hank shook his head. "No, my agent said I should go to every party I could. That's how you make connections. Some guy invited me, but I haven't seen him here at all. I feel kind of out of place."

"Where are you from, Hank?"

"Olpe, Kansas," he answered as he drained his glass.

"A long way from home."

"Yeah," he agreed. We strolled out into the gardens. Hank told me about his experiences in high school, a star athlete who was bitten by the acting bug after being in a play. He turned down a scholarship to come west and be a movie star. Apparently this worn dream still existed in his backwards, midwest home.

I got him another drink from the terrace bar and it loosened his tongue even further. He had made no contacts other than his agent, a sleazy little man who agreed to represent him. He had done one photo shoot for a calendar and that was the sum total of his professional work. Hank had received several offers from different people, based solely on his body. He might have a promising, although short-lived, career as an actor in straight porn, gay porn, or even as a hustler, but he didn't want to start that way.

"Are you straight or gay?" I finally asked. My curiosity, and my dick, were getting the better of me.

"Bi," he answered without hesitation, then looked me in the eyes and began to fidget. "Well," he amended, "okay, I guess I'm gay. I said bi because it . . . well . . ."

"You thought it was more acceptable than being a fag?"

"Yeah," he agreed, downing his drink. Then he looked up

at me with those cornflower blue eyes. "Are you gay?"

"Yes," I answered.

He got a stunned look on his face. "Oh, God," he said and quickly turned, ducking into the bushes. I was shocked and astounded. My orientation had never had that effect on anyone. I followed him and found him a few feet away on his hands and knees, retching in the shrubs. This boy obviously could not hold his liquor. I helped him up, but he was a mess, mud on his pants, puke on his white shirt and cummerbund.

He passed out in the car, but I managed to rouse him enough to get him up the stairs of my condo. The poor kid was no help at all, tottering as he stood, in danger of toppling over any minute as I stripped him and put him in the shower. The warm water revived him for a few minutes, just long enough for me to dry him off and lead him back to bed. No sooner had that perfect body touched the mattress than he began to snore softly. I had done my good deed, rescuing this starstruck boy from the Midwest. He was safe in my bed, asleep. His youthful perfection overshadowed my middle-aged complacency. I knew that if he was sober he would not be here. Perfect boys with perfect bodies only came home with me when I bought them. This golden boy was different. I didn't want to sully my image of him by offering him money. I couldn't face the rejection if he said no, and I would despise him if he said yes. So I let him sleep, and finished my last drink on my balcony.

The next morning I awoke to delightful smells of coffee and bacon. I grabbed a robe and stumbled out to the kitchen. "Good morning," came the overly cheerful call. Hank was just dishing up breakfast. "I wanted to do something for you for helping me out last night." He stood by the stove, spatula in hand and a towel wrapped around his waist. "Sit and eat your breakfast before your eggs get cold."

I fell heavily into a chair at my glass-topped dining table. "Aren't you hung?" I asked. The boy blushed and tried to adjust the towel around his waist. "No, I mean a hangover."

"Oh," he said, coloring in embarrassment. "No, I feel great." He sat down opposite me and we began our meal.

As I ate, I couldn't help but notice the bulge in the towel at his crotch. I mentally thanked my decorator for the glass table. Hank must have either noticed my eyes, or felt uncomfortable because he reached down and tried to adjust himself, but it only made matters more obvious. And the view was causing an equal reaction in my crotch, the robe I was wearing slowly parting as my dick slid out into view.

Hank couldn't help but notice. Those blue eyes widened as he pretended to look at his plate, but I could tell he was focusing on what was beneath the table.

"Thanks for fixing breakfast," I said as I rose and cleared the dishes, no longer caring that my robe was open and my hard cock was pointing out.

"I hope I wasn't too much trouble last night," Hank replied, but his eyes never left my crotch.

"Not at all. Although you were a bit difficult to undress."

"Why?" he asked, finally looking up at my face as I stepped close to him.

"Because you are beautiful. I wanted to make love to you when I took your clothes off. Just like I want to make love to you now."

My gorgeous boy didn't reply. He just leaned forward and kissed the head of my cock. It was a gentle kiss, the delicate pucker of his lips pressing lightly on my dick head. But the gentleness of it, made it all the more erotic, and my cock jumped, bobbing up and bumping against his nose. He looked up at my face, his blue eyes meeting mine, then he looked back down at my prick, and took me into his mouth, sucking me deeply in and burying his nose in my pubic hair.

He may have been a naive hick from Kansas, but this boy sure knew how to suck dick. His lips tightly gripped my shaft and his tongue swirled in circles around the head. I began to hump forward, fucking his beautiful face. This was a wonderful experience, quite a match to the fucking I got in my dream. I thrust forward and grabbed the sides of his head as he continued the blow job.

Hank reached around and began to play with my ass, bringing me to a higher intensity. He slipped a finger in, pressing against my prostate and I couldn't hold back. Looking down at that angel slurping on my dick, I suddenly began to cum, shooting my load in his mouth.

Hank gagged and coughed, sputtering my sperm out onto my pubic hair. It ran down his chin and onto my balls. "I'm sorry," he apologized as he reached for a napkin on the table. "I guess I didn't know you'd do that."

I laughed and asked, "What did you expect?" And my beautiful young man began to laugh, too. He rose to his feet, embracing me and pulling me close for a passionate kiss. Then we separated, to laugh some more. I reached down and slipped off his towel, while shedding my robe, then I draped my arm around him and led him back to bed.

In the bedroom Hank became a wildman, kissing me firmly on the lips. I could taste my cum in his mouth as he stabbed his tongue back into mine. He then threw me onto the bed and grabbed my legs, lifting them up and diving down to eat my ass. His tongue, newly christened with my cream, now worked to enter my ass as well. Hank paused long enough to lick his way from my hole, up to my balls, a quick swipe at my dick, again growing hard, then back down again to taunt my ass. "Fuck me, Hank!" I begged. "Give it to me! I want all of you inside me!"

He pushed my legs up further, bending me into a pretzel, my knees beside my head. Then he positioned that marvelous dick against my tight pucker and shoved with all his might. I pressed back, trying to will my body to relax. One strain and it popped inside. The searing burn of his entry quickly melted into the erotic fullness of his girth inside me. "Yes, give it to me," I pleaded, and my dream lover began to slowly slide his length into my guts. It seemed to take forever, and yet it was over in only a second. His pubes were pressed firmly against my buns.

I looked up into those blue eyes and was instantly lost in his soul. My dream lover could keep me like this forever, and I squeezed my ass tight, hoping to hold him inside me for all eternity. But his dick had other ideas. It began to pull back, trying to free itself. But the warmth of my chute was overpowering, and called it back inside. Hank again pushed into me, only to pause for the briefest of seconds and pull out. Then he began to pump in and out, in and out, fucking my ass as I had never been fucked before. This was no dream. No ethereal god was working over me, but a real-live, flesh and blood man, pumping and puffing, working his magic on my body.

I wanted it to go on forever, but neither of us could sustain it. All too soon Hank began to scream in triumph as his slammed deep into me. His dick shot its load into my guts, and pushed me over the edge. I began to shoot my second load into the air, spraying my cream all over the two of us. For a few brief moments our souls joined, then slowly we dissolved back into two horny men, coming down from one incredible joint orgasm. Hank fell forward, cementing our naked bodies together with my semen, and planting his tongue in my mouth in an intensely passionate kiss. I held him as tightly as I could, fearing it was all over and that I would never again be loved in this manner.

We spent the next two days making love. He gave himself to me. I came again in his mouth and in his ass. Then he came in me, and splashed my naked body with his hot youthful cream. I knew at last my love had come. I didn't deserve this gorgeous man, the perfect Adonis to my Apollo. But I gratefully accepted what I had received.

Unfortunately, nothing seems to last forever but the earth and sky. At the end of the summer Hank grew restless and moved on, leaving me with old photographs and my memories, the stuff dreams are made of.

BLUE DUNGAREES

John Patrick

*"I think love has made me young again,
or maybe it's the blue dungarees."
Tennessee Williams,
in a letter to Donald Windham, 1940*

I saw him again this weekend.

Usually I saw him at the grocery store down the street, but this time he stopped in at the laundromat where I occasionally washed my clothes. As usual, he looked spectacular, this time in a white T-shirt and, as always, tight-fitting jeans that accentuated his perfect butt. He was young, taut, with shoulder-length blond hair. He was the most fuckable thing I'd ever seen, my dream lover. I figured him for a student; the college was nearby. Clean-cut, trim, everything just right. Then I read what was printed on his T-shirt: "F--- me." I couldn't believe anybody would be so bold as to advertise it!

Encouraged by his obvious show of attitude, I tried to strike up a conversation, but he seemed distracted, or maybe just uninterested. As he went about starting his wash, I noticed a bruise on his arm, and a nasty cut above his eye. It's my business to notice things like that; I'm an investigator for a big insurance company. Not a lot of money in it, but it can get interesting. I had to make a call, and went outside to use the pay phone. It took much longer than I had thought, and when I returned, my clothes were not in the dryer where I had left them.

He was still there, folding his clothes. On the table next to him was a neat pile. My clothes. He looked up. "The time was up," he said. "I didn't want 'em to wrinkle on you."

"Thank you. Thank you very much."

"Sure," he said, busying himself.

I walked by him and noticed there wasn't any smell to him at all.

I sorted through my clothes and discovered I had lost a black sock. "Did you happen to see the mate to this?" I asked him, holding up the remaining sock.

"No. Sorry," he said, lifting his wash from the table and taking it to his car.

I went to the dryer, looked on the floor; no sock. By the time I got to my car, he had already driven off.

That night, I closed my eyes and tried to sleep, but I kept seeing the blond, wanting the blond. I made up my mind that, from the precision with which he had folded my clothes, he was an orderly sort. Perhaps he would be back at the same place exactly a week later. I went there, with my wash, but he didn't show. I was about to leave when, lo and behold, there he was, pulling up in his car. He spoke to me first. "Did you find your sock?"

I chuckled. "Yes, it was caught up in the leg of a pair of my blue dungarees."

"I told you." His eyes held mine for a moment and I could tell there was something a little too knowing in his eyes, like someone who's already done a lot in his life, maybe too much.

"Well, thanks again," I said, loading my wash into my car.

I should have gone home, but I was too aroused by him to do that. I went across the street to the diner, got a cup of coffee and a glazed doughnut. It was a cool, pretty afternoon and I had nothing much to do so I sat in my car, waiting.

He finally came out, loaded his wash, neatly stacked as always, got into his car, a nondescript white Mustang. I put the doughnut I was eating down on the front seat and followed him to I-10, where he headed east. He drove fast and it was hard to keep up in my old Dodge, but I managed. He suddenly pulled over to the curb, so I had to drive past him and park in the next block. I watched through my rearview as he got out of the Mustang and went to the curbside mailbox. His ass made me drool. I moved down the street, parking close to the driveway. It made me sad that this was as close as I might ever get to him, playing Peeping Tom, but then I guess we all have our roles to play in life.

It was a pleasant, pink house with a white shingle roof, surrounded by a white wrought iron fence festooned with flowers. Suddenly, a white Chrysler drove by me, into the drive. A tall, heavy-set guy with a beard got out and went up to the house. He had a menacing look; I wouldn't want to get in an argument with him, I knew that much. I couldn't imagine them together, but what the hell did I know about gay guys these days?

I could hear shouting, doors slamming, then silence. I decided to get some dinner, maybe come back.

An hour later, I returned. The sky to the west was a blackish blue, salmon at the far edge. I could see the front door was hanging open, but I knew it wasn't open to let in the cool breeze that blew steadily from the ocean. The white Chrysler was gone. I pulled into the drive, made my way up to the house.

I pushed the door open a bit farther, stepped inside and called out: "Hello?"

I kept calling out as I made my way through the deserted house, until I found him, in the darkened master bedroom, tied spread-eagled to the bedposts.

I switched on the lamp nearest the door. He looked at me, eyes intense. "Help me," he cried.

As I unbound him, I noticed the lash marks on his incredibly firm buttocks. Then I saw the greased asscrack. I imagined what fun the man must have had with this great piece of ass. "The guy that did this to you obviously has a lot of rungs missing in his ladder," I said.

A smile bloomed on his face. A special smile, a smile I hadn't seen before. I took him in my arms and held him.

"Make me a drink, will you? I need one bad."

I remembered passing a small bar in the living room. I left him in the bedroom and poured him a Scotch rocks, another for me. I returned to the bedroom. He was wrapped in the filthy sheet. We sat drinking our Scotch. We were feeling warm and relaxed, knowing it was over, that he was with someone safe now.

"You did a brave thing, man," he told me. "Coming through that bedroom door to help me, not knowing if the creep was coming back."

"Yeah, I did think about that, what with his leaving the front door open and all. But it was stupid is what it was, not brave. But when I heard you whimpering I just had to find out if you were okay. I just hope he's not coming back."

"That makes two of us," he said softly, leaning toward me

and kissing me on the chin, cheeks, forehead. Little sex kisses. Meant to arouse me. And I was aroused. Was I ever! I put down my Scotch, reached for him, folding him tightly into my arms. He felt even better than he looked.

"Remember my T-shirt?" he said with a cat's smile.

"Who could forget it?"

"Well," he said, stripping away the sheet, "what you see is what you get."

He got on all fours, his ass in my face. I stuck a digit in, moved it around. "Are you sure?"

"Oh, yeah. It'll feel so good."

I quickly stripped and got in position. I entered him, slowly at first, then with long strokes. Oh, he was divine! His ass muscles gripped my tool tightly. My eyes shut in concentration. I leaned my chest and face against the boy's hot back. I paced myself to his urgings and as his commands erupted more violently, my thrusts increased in speed and I wrapped my arms around his waist, reached down between his legs to pull and tease and delight his ready cock. He was too relaxed now to fight the feeling. My fingers were finally touching him intimately! He gasped as I stroked his dick, and looked at me helplessly. Leaning down, I covered his mouth with my lips. My tongue urged his lips to part and, upon parting, plunged inside his mouth, probing him, tasting him, sucking his tongue in and out. I could feel my cock growing harder. I wanted this boy so badly. He moaned deep and low as he opened his mouth to me. It was as if a dam had broken. I came, joyously. It was an orgasm so strong and intense that I felt my legs weaken and tremble.

But I wasn't finished with this one, not by a long shot. I went to his seven-inch, cut cock, touching and kissing it. The musky smell, the hardness, turned me on. I was growing hard again. Oh, the excitement of making love to this boy I had so long desired. My fingers touched his nipples, and they sprang to life, firm and erect, aching to be taken. I teased the warm brown nubs, squeezing each one hard, then releasing it, repeating it until I heard him cry out. Then doing it again, only this time much harder. Extending my hands over his tits, I began squeezing and releasing, massaging the warm flesh as it throbbed pulsed beneath my touch while I continued to suck his cock.

He sighed and purred, twisting his head back and forth against the pillow. "Oh!" he moaned. Panting now, pressing his groin against my face, I shoved a finger in his ass. I could feel his cock throbbing with excitement. Wanting to be fucked, begging to be fucked again. I had come too soon for this boy, that's for sure. I started kissing him again. This time his lips were hard and demanding. Crushing against my mouth, kissing me until my lips began to swell.

I shoved my cock into his ass again, the place that I was sure must have caused him so much anguish and pain in his young life, but now he was telling me how much he loved it. Moving his hips side to side, he teased me to go deeper. Hearing him moaning was music to my ears. He thrust his hips forward. He was fucking my dick, wanting to feel it deeper inside of him. "Fuck me! Please fuck me," he begged.

Taking advantage of his excitement, I felt a surge of power and I started fucking him as I had never fucked anyone in my life. In a state of frenzied excitement, he cupped both hands around my ass.

Unable to control my desire, I came again; it was not as strong as the first, but it was draining, exhausting. Taking a deep breath, I looked him in the eye, then kissed him. The kiss was so full of passion and heat that I groaned quite audibly. As I kept on sliding in and out of his ass, slowly, not wanting to leave it, he purred with pleasure. I felt the lad's orgasm approaching. "Oh, ohhh," he cried. His face muscles tightening, he squeezed his eyes closed. "Ugh...ahh...." he growled as the orgasm spread through him. His ass tightened as he hugged my shrinking cock inside of him.

Calm now, I recalled another boy, another time. This wasn't my first time with one of these characters. I remembered Tony, who stayed with his lover despite the abuse. I even tried taking Tony to a shrink. Tony wouldn't go, but I did. The shrink said that it wasn't surprising Tony stayed with his daddy. "It makes perfect sense. It's called the Stockholm syndrome. These sexually sadistic offenders have that ability to control people. Many times it's just out of fear, or perhaps Tony felt obligated. These guys target their victims, make them indebted to them in some way."

I recalled Tony had his apartment, his car, everything, because of his daddy. I looked around and wondered what the story was with this lad. And then I thought about something else: God, here I was in his house, in bed with him, and I didn't even know his name!

We dozed, for how long I could not tell. The next thing I remember was him shaking me, hysterical. In my sinking haze I heard him say, "You've gotta go." His bearded, brutish lover had returned and was unlocking the front door, the door he had left open not that long ago. "You can slip out the back," the boy assured me.

I dressed in haste, in such haste that, when I was back in my car, I realized I was wearing his blue dungarees, not mine!

VOLUPTUOUS

Antler

Some poets never get tired of
   watching teenage boys
      take off their clothes
  and passionately jack off
     in front of them.
Every channel on their visionary TV
   shows only film after film
      of the most voluptuous boys
  of every race and region
     jacking off together or alone.
This poet wants the taste
  of the first spurts of youthjuice
     in an incredibly long ejaculation
   always sluicing over the sensitive tastebuds
    of his boy-adoration tongue,
So the freshest savory boycum you can imagine
  or believe in
     continually anoints, blesses, restores
   the innermost and most cosmic definition
     of love in his heart.

"In the pissoirs of the European metropolises, I have seen children of no more than eight or nine on their knees, and I have seen men my own age on their knees worshipping, so to speak, before the altar of their dreams."
—Tom Whalen, in the book "Brief Encounters"

They all wanted him so badly,
it was sinful.

DREAM BOY

An Erotic Novella by
Kevin Bantan

STARbooks Press
Sarasota, Florida

"I once attended a private party (six guests) in Columbus, Ohio, with Karl Thomas as the featured attraction. Fifteen bucks admission got you a complete strip show, a couple of thirty second 'strokes' on the star's HUGE dick, a group JO and a post-show Q&A. Karl is a terrific guy who, they say, doesn't do drugs or alcohol. All of us stood nude over Karl as he laid back, nude, on a stool. We all came together. With Karl Thomas under you in that situation, 'non-performers' are hard to come by. I hadn't had that kind of satisfactory squirt in months."
—*A fan, recalling a wonderful time with one of the all-time great dreamboys*

Prologue

YOU SOUNDED SO NEAT THAT I WANTED TO TALK ONE ON ONE. SO YOU'RE A COLLEGE STUDENT, TOO, HUH?
Yeah. Econ major at the University of Chicago. I'm a senior. You?"
SAME HERE. ENGLISH MAJOR AT NYU. SPECIFICALLY, ROMANTIC LITERATURE. PROBABLY BECAUSE I AM ONE.
imo, the world needs more people like you. I plead guilty to being one, too.
YEAH, IT'S TOUGH SOMETIMES, WITH ALL THE PHILISTINES OUT THERE AND HUNS AT THE GATE.
it is. Well, what do you say we get the statistics out of the way first? What do you look like?
I'M TWENTY. BROWN HAIR, BLUE EYES. ABOUT FIVE-TEN. SLIM, SMOOTH BODY. PEOPLE SAY I'M GOOD LOOKING. YOU?
i'm twenty-two. Blond/blue. Just under six feet. Smooth and muscular. Given my handle, I guess you could say I'm pretty good looking, too. Well, and I do model part time for an agency here in town. I can pretty much work whenever I like.
WOW. SOUNDS GLAMOROUS.
it really isn't. It's hard, boring work. But it's a rush to see myself in print and on TV.
I'LL BET. SO WHAT'S WHAT YOUR MONIKER?
They call me Dreamboy.

One

"You know, I think you've finally succumbed to Internet addiction. You just don't realize it, because your brain is still wired to the computer."

"Come on, Jess. It isn't that bad. I just like talking to people on the Net. They're interesting. Besides, it's a hell of a lot safer than striking up a conversation on the subway."

"What a ludicrous comparison."

"It is not. And this guy is really neat, I'm telling you."

"You don't even know him, man. What's his name, again?"

"Dreamboy; he sure seems like one, too."

"Look, Derek, this guy could be a sixty-year-old troll, for all you know. He could be a psycho; a fucking axe murderer."

"Oh, please, Jess. Leave your flair for the dramatic at the stage door."

"I'm serious. You know zilch about this guy. And you're ready to hop a bus to Chicago to meet him."

"I am not. I'm going to thumb to Chicago."

"You are really crazy, you know that? That in itself is dangerous. You could be raped or shot or worse."

"Save the hysterics for your audition with Mr. DeMille, pal. I'm going and that's that."

"Derek, please don't."

"Forget it. I've made up my mind. You know what you need, Jess? You need your own Dreamboy. Maybe it would help your anal retention."

The atmosphere in the cramped apartment did not improve over the next week, as Derek Brown prepared for his trip to meet the articulate, sexy young man in Chicago. He couldn't understand Jesse's behavior. They'd been roommates for the past two years and had always gotten along well. So well, in fact, that they had a mutually satisfying, no-strings-attached, ongoing sexual relationship. They were careful about keeping their feelings in check, because neither was ready to settle into terminal domesticity. Well, that was the company line, at any rate. In reality, it was the fact that Derek found himself falling in love with his dark, handsome Hispanic roommate that drove him to the Internet. So, it was Jesse's fault that he met

Dreamboy. And now it was Jesse telling him he shouldn't carry through on the attraction he felt for his cyber-boyfriend. Man, some guys were never satisfied.

As he packed, Derek felt relieved that he would be leaving the next day. At the very least, he'd be out of the stifling air to which Jesse contributed with each breath he exhaled. He just didn't miss a chance to snipe. It had been a mistake to room with the next Antonio Banderas. He saw that very clearly now. Actors just couldn't resist the urge to emote, and that's all he had gotten from his apartment mate ever since he announced his plans. Fuck Jesse. No, let Jesse fuck himself. It might help his problem down there.

"Good choice to wear shorts. I'm sure every horny guy on the road will see those legs and offer to take you all the way to Chicago, hoping he can get you to wrap then around his neck."

"Very funny. I don't plan to pull a Claudette Colbert on the interstates. And I don't plan to screw my way to the Windy City, either. If Dreamboy is half as cute and sexy as he seems, saving myself for him will have been well worth it."

"Oh? How big is he?"

"That wasn't fair!"

"No, it wasn't. I'm sorry, Dreek." The nickname was a play on 'Derek' and on 'dreck', which Jesse thought any romance novel or poem was. It had begun as Jesse's needling little joke, but it eventually became an endearment, which he always used in bed, or when he was feeling especially horny. Or caring, as he was now.

"Look, Jess, I'm going to be okay. This is my spring adventure. One week of being footloose and fancy free."

"I'll give you money to take the bus. Or, better yet, fly Southwest out of Newark. It's as cheap."

"Thanks, but no thanks. I've decided that I'm going to do it this way. It'll be fun, which I'm badly in need of."

"What's that supposed to mean?"

"Forget it. I don't want to get into another fight, before I leave."

"Dreek, this isn't a vision quest. You're too old."

"Oh, please. Save me the melodrama."

"At least give me the guy's address and phone number."

"I promised I wouldn't."

"You what? Why in hell not?"

"So that you wouldn't be able to call ten times a day to check up on me."

"Now I know you're crazy. I don't like this, Dreek."

"It's not for you to like or dislike. Get over it, Jess."

"Please don't go, Dreek."

"Look, I'll call when I get there, okay?"

"Well...all right. But I'm still going to worry."

"Be my guest."

"What's his name?"

"Jesse. Look, I want to leave on good terms, so that I'll look forward to coming back."

"Suppose there's a family emergency? How will I get in touch with you?"

"Oh, all right. His name is Adrian Jordan. Satisfied?"

"No, I don't think you should go."

"Well, I am. So, don't worry your pretty little head, Jess."

"And you'd better call. I'll come looking for you, if I don't hear from you."

"In a city of almost three million people. Good luck."

"At least tell me what part of town he lives in."

"Oh, what harm can that do? He lives in what is euphemistically called 'Boys Town'. Satisfied?"

Jesse closed the gap between them and hugged Derek tightly. "No, not until you're home safe and sound," he whispered. Derek didn't see the lining of tears in his eyes.

His strategy was simple. He waited until rush hour was over before starting his journey. That way, he figured people leaving the city were more likely to be going farther than the near suburbs. He had a placard with the abbreviation 'PA' neatly lettered on one side and 'CLEVELAND' on the other. An additional card in his knapsack had the words 'INDIANA' and 'CHICAGO' on it. He figured that he'd use the Pennsylvania side first. Dressed in a long, billowy T-shirt and shorts, high tops and a baseball cap, he decided that he looked non-threatening enough that he wouldn't have much trouble getting picked up. He sure hoped that Jesse was wrong about all of the crazies he envisioned were out there. Actors had vivid imaginations, he knew from the two years of their cohabitation.

At least Jesse did. Most of the time he enjoyed his roommate's mental idiosyncracies. But Jess had driven him crazy the past week. A royal pain in the ass, for sure. Like a mother hen with her peep. Finally freed from the confines of the apartment, he could breathe again. Let the adventure begin.

Jesse Montalban was brooding. This whole Dreamboy thing was his fault. When Derek went onto the Internet and started talking in those gay chat rooms, he feigned disinterest. But he knew why his roommate was doing it. For the past six months or so, he sensed the change in Derek. There was a building frustration in him, he could tell. The sex they had seemed to be getting better and better. Then it began to go flat. And Jesse thought that he knew why now. Derek needed more than sex. He needed love. And the hell of it was that Jesse saw it too late. They had agreed that they wanted no romantic entanglements in their relationship. They liked each other and got along well. They had great sex. Until recently. He wondered if it would have made any difference, if he had admitted to Dreek his own true feelings. It was too late now, because he was going to meet his Dreamboy. That was what his brooding was about when stripped of pretensions. He was keenly jealous.

At the same time, he was also uneasy about Derek going off like that, relying on strangers to get him to Chicago and back. It was foolhardy. Even if he didn't meet up with a psycho, he could end up being stranded in East Bumfuck. In the event that happened, would he call? Probably not, knowing Derek. As nice a person as he was, he had a stubborn streak in him that would daunt a mule. Jesse hoped, at least, that he would call when he got to Chicago. He had said he would, and he did keep his word. In the meantime, there was nothing for him to do but hope that nothing befell the young man he loved.

If the first ride was any indication of what the rest of the trip boded, he would make it to Adrian's in no time. He had held up the "PA" placard, and the third car to pass him stopped. Well, it was a van with a guy heading to the Poconos to meet some high school buddies. His name was Tim. He had straight blond hair, which he wore below his shoulders. Derek, on the other hand, wore his brown hair short, which was a modification of the punk look he'd sported through most of college. Now he looked like Joe College, and he wasn't sure that was all good. Well, Jesse liked the hairstyle change, so it wasn't all bad, either.

Tim seemed laid back, but he did carry on a decent conversation. "Yeah, me and my buddies figured that Florida would be too overrun with students, so we decided to chance the weather and go to the Poconos. And what do you know? Warmest spring on record."

"Yeah, it's downright hot."

"So much for baking in Florida. Hey, you smoke?"

"Cigarettes?"

"Weed."

"Oh. Not for a few years."

"Well, you're welcome to join me. I feel like loosening up a little." He pulled a joint from his shirt pocket and lit it.

"Aren't you afraid of being stopped?"

"Nope. I figure if I drive the speed limit, I'll be okay. Besides, we're in New Jersey now." Whatever that meant. Tim passed the joint to Derek, and he inhaled. He passed it back to the driver. By the third hit, he could tell that it was good stuff. He'd heard somewhere that pot was a lot more potent than it had been in his parents' college days. It sure seemed stronger than the stuff he used to smoke. Plant engineering was making great strides, it seemed. At least as far as this genus was concerned.

"So, where in Pennsylvania you headed?"

"I'm not. I'm going to Chicago."

"Friend?"

"Guy I met over the Internet."

"No shit. A little romance, maybe?"

"Maybe."

"Cool. He's sure getting the better part of the bargain, it's safe to say." Derek smiled. He didn't even realize what he'd said, as buzzed as he was. But he appreciated his chauffeur's reference to his physical beauty. Every now and then it was nice to get an ego stroke. Especially when there were none to be had at home.

They were more than halfway across the state, when Tim

saw a roadside rest area and decided that he needed to pee. He parked and went into the building, while Derek peered out the window at the gloriously warm spring day. At the rate he was going, he might make Ohio yet today. He'd be through New Jersey well before noon. How long could it take to get across Pennsylvania?

When Tim came back, he told Derek he wanted to show him the back of the van. He'd fixed it up himself, he said. He parted the nondescript curtain separating the passenger section from the storage area and allowed his guest to precede him. A weak overhead light revealed a bed and not much else besides tasteless shag carpeting. "Nice," Derek said honestly, because he always found beds enticing. He could feel Tim's hand around his waist. It felt good. The guy was pretty good looking, too. "I'm glad you like it. It's really handy for those times when I need to nap." He was whispering in Derek's ear. "Or when the mood hits, you know? Especially after a couple of joints with a gorgeous guy." Derek turned to look at him, and Tim's lips were soon on his. He responded and before long they were locked in a heated embrace. What the hell. He'd still be out of New Jersey before noon, he thought, as he began to unbutton his host's shirt.

They crawled onto the bed without prompting. He lay on his back and reached for Tim's cock. It was semi-tumescent from their kissing, so it wouldn't take much to get him in fucking form. He moved the foreskin up and down slowly, making Tim hard and coaxing precum from the slit. He caught the discharges and coated the shaft with the clear stuff.

Meanwhile, Tim had wet two fingers with spit and was finger-fucking Derek's ass. When he couldn't take any more of the digital action, Derek said, "Fuck me now." His partner was only too happy to oblige. Derek reared back and spread his legs. "Fucking beautiful," Tim said, as he pushed his long, narrow prick in to the hilt. Then he grabbed Derek's ankles and set his hip speed on frantic, rutting in his passenger like an animal. Derek had never been fucked so desperately before, and he liked it. The long, blond mane was whipping around Tim's head as he furiously worked his cock in Derek. The latter urged his companion on, taking his own sweet equipment in his hand and masturbated for all he was worth.

It couldn't have been more than ten minutes, tops, before they were shooting their loads and telling everyone else in the parking lot that they were doing it by their loud cries of release. Then Tim leaned down and kissed him tenderly. "Thanks. You're a great fuck, man."

At the juncture of Interstates 80 and 380, Tim let him off. "Thanks for the ride, man. I appreciate it. Oh, and the fuck, too."

"You're welcome on both counts. Especially the fuck. Most beautiful guy I ever made it with." He winked. "Good luck in Chicago." Derek waved at the retreating van.

He pulled out the 'CLEVELAND' sign and waited.

Two

Jesse was more than a little ticked at Derek, too. Although he hadn't planned anything for spring break, he thought that they'd at least get to spend some quality time together, while they were off from school. Now, here he was alone. He did have rehearsals for the spring play and one paper, which he might as well get over and done with. But otherwise, he had all that free time and no Derek to spend it with. He got up from his desk. He wasn't going to get anything accomplished in the apartment. He picked up his books and papers and decided to do his work at the library. Then he thought of the cute student librarian, who always seemed to give him a shy smile. He wondered if the guy was off during the break. He hoped not. Two could play Derek's little game.

It seemed like forever, but it was really a little over an hour before a car stopped to pick him up. After a brief exchange, he got in. "Thanks. This seems to be my lucky day."

"Oh? Why is that?"

"Well, I started in New York this morning, and my first ride took me all the way to back there. And here you are going to Cleveland." He gauged this guy, Jeffrey, to be in his early thirties. He was good looking, though, like Tim. "You from Cleveland?"

"No. Jersey. I'm a computer technician. There's a client in Cleveland who's got a problem and insisted that we send someone from the home office to fix it. It's a big customer, so that's why I'm going. Otherwise, we'd have talked them through the problem over the phone. I don't mind. That's why they pay me. To solve problems. And I'm helping to solve yours to boot. So, you from Cleveland?"

"No. The City. I'm not actually going there, either. I'm really headed for Chicago."

"Oh. I figured from the sign..."

"Well, I did that, because I thought that some people would be turned off, if they saw a sign that said 'Chicago' on it, being so far away, that they might not stop. So, I put different destinations on my signs, hoping that it would work. So far, it has."

"So what's in Chicago?" Derek told Jeffrey about meeting Adrian on the web and how they were about the same age and had many of the same interests. "Yeah, I've done my share of chat rooms. Finally had to stop. It gets expensive being on line. And sitting at a computer all day makes it less enticing to come home and do it some more, you know?"

"I can imagine."

"Besides, I've heard of too many times where people blatantly lie about themselves. You can pretend to be everything you're not, and how is the other person going to know?"

"Well, I doubt that Adrian would do that, knowing he was going to meet me. He sounded hot."

"Well, in your case it probably will work out. But the net seems to draw out the weirdos and psychos." That word again. At least Jeffrey didn't say axe murderer.

They rode on for about an hour before Derek noticed Jeffrey shifting in the seat. He saw Derek looking and said, "Sorry. Male equipment wasn't meant to ride in a car in restrictive underwear."

"I know what you mean."

"Do you?" He grinned at Derek. Then he put his hand on his crotch and slowly stroked it. The rider could see the bulge there. He licked his lips. It looked like a good one. "Yeah, sometimes they need to breathe. It gets awfully stifling on a long trip. No freedom to do what a cock wants to do." The lump was pronounced now, and Derek had no illusion about what was coming. He decided to play along.

"And what does a cock want to do on a long trip?"

"Be free. Feel the breeze on its sensitive nerves. Get friendly."

"Is that what yours is thinking?"

"You've been looking at it. What do you think?"

"I think it wants out, from the looks of it."

"Would that bother you?"

"Not if I can liberate mine, too."

"Deal." With that, Jeffrey unzipped his pants and fished inside to try to pull himself out. Being semi-hard didn't make it any easier. But he finally was able to thread it through the fly of his boxers and bring it into glorious view. Derek gasped. It was longer and thicker than even Jesse's, and it was the color of rich, dark chocolate from the big mushroom head all the way down the shaft.

Without a word, Derek took off his seat belt and moved over to where he could bend down and take it into his mouth. The slit appeared to be winking at him like an eye, it was so big. Man, this was a cock. And he would never have expected one so dark on a medium-skinned guy. But there it was, begging to be sucked. "Hello, freedom," he said as he went down on it. It smelled musky, having been cooped up for all those miles. It tasted great. The skin was smooth and silky. He played with the head, sucking and licking for a while. It was probably the most beautiful glans he had ever seen, perfectly shaped and solid. After several miles of worshipping the knob, he decided that he wanted to feel as much of that shaft in his mouth as he could manage. It was awkward trying to draw it into himself, because he had only one available position from which to work. This was a dong that needed complete access in order to do the job on it that it deserved. But when life gives you cocks, you suck them as best you can. "That's great, Derek. You're not only beautiful, you are a great cocksucker, too. Make it feel real good, pretty baby." He did, almost managing to get it into his throat. But the angle was impossible. So he contented himself with taking what he could and making love to that much.

He felt his own arousal and his right hand fumbled with his

zipper. He'd decided that packing light for a week's trip necessitated that underwear and socks were expendable. So, once he'd gotten the damn Talon in hand and unzipped it, it was easy to expose himself to the breeze, as Jeffrey put it. Then he idly played with himself while he continued to work on the ebony masterpiece.

He pulled off to admire the glistening, dark rod. Oh, yes. He went back to his ministrations, keeping his rhythm casual, so as not to make Jeffrey come too soon. He lost track of time as he filled his mouth and slid his lips on the smooth, fat penis. Only when his jaw began to ache did he increase his movement on the mahogany delight. He completely forgot about himself in his quest to satisfy this adorable appendage. He felt it begin to twitch and heard its owner signal his impending release. He braced himself for what he knew would surge from the huge opening, but he still couldn't keep all of it in his mouth. One shot of come after another after another, until he thought there was surely a malfunction in the guy's scrotum. He did his best, and then he did his second best, licking up what he'd missed of the potent male issue.

When he'd cleaned the man, he felt a hand caressing his hair, and then on his own sex. "That was great, Derek. You are the best cocksucker I've ever had. Why don't you keep mine company a while longer. I'll look after yours." Derek did, occasionally kissing this piece of art and resting it on his face as he was slowly masturbated. This was turning into some experience.

He was, indeed, working during break, and Jesse surprised the librarian by returning the shy smile with a wide grin. Now, if only he could remember the guy's name. The room was practically deserted. No fools they, the other students. Oh, there were a couple of geeks furiously scribbling, but that was typical. But what did that say about him? He was with these geeks. He could throttle Derek for what he'd done, ruining spring break. Then the next emotion he felt surprised him, although it shouldn't have. It was that he missed his roommate. He had to get over that in a hurry, or the next week would be a memorably miserable one. Then he remembered the student librarian. What the hell was his name, anyway?

It was Irish. Yeah, the kid had a brogue. How had he ended up at NYU? Why not? Where else should he be? Princeton? Georgetown? Which turned out to be two of the places that Jesse would have loved to have gone, had he had the money. But he would never have met Derek, in either case. All of a sudden, those schools sounded better and better. Of all the colossal nerves in the universe, he had to fall in love with one of the biggest. Well, I'm off to Chicago to see my cyber-honey. Keep the bed warm for me, Jess. I'll be back after I thoroughly soil another set of sheets. No harm, no foul, man. It's not like we're lovers or anything, you know. Just fuck buddies. That's what we agreed to be, right? Just tension relievers. Warm bodies on a cold night. Convenient and safe. Best friends, who also dig other's body. A lot, Jesse thought. Tears came to his eyes again. *I'm sorry, Derek*, his heart said.

He was amazed at Jeffrey's powers of recuperation. He was still hanging out, himself, but flaccid now, because the driver said that a sign warned of rough road ahead, and he needed to have both hands on the wheel. Derek could believe it. Pennsylvania was notorious for its bad roads. And once you're notorious, it doesn't matter if the other forty-nine are as bad or worse. You've got the reputation. You're it. The road didn't feel unusually bumpy, but you couldn't always tell with these newer cars. The new suspension systems were like nothing he'd ever ridden in. Well, when you live in New York, you don't go on test drives every day, you know? Unless you're a cab driver. But they were some sub-species of Homo Sapiens, which hadn't been identified yet. Archie Bunker was one of them. He rested his case.

He began to lick the dark, shiny maleness, playfully treating it to his seductive tongue caresses. It loved his tongue. It loved his mouth. He would reward the adonis of potency with that as soon as it was so hard that it was begging for his cavity to surround it. Maybe he'd just make Jeffrey beg him to do it. The best cocksucker he'd ever had was lying in his lap, so near to the tool he held most dear. Yeah, he would beg for it.

Sean. No. Shannon. No, that was an airport. He knew that much about Ireland. Eamon. No, DeValera had been a

Portuguese Jew from the Bronx. Shit, even Chaim Herzog, the former President of Israel was Irish, he'd heard. Strange people, the Irish. Jesse knew that even a couple of the last Lord Mayors of Dublin had been Jewish and Protestant. All of that strife in the north, and the people in the south, overwhelmingly Catholic, like him, voted for all of these Protestants and Jews. Didn't they know better? And their president was a woman. Mary Robinson. One of the most sexist countries on the face of the planet, and they elect a woman as head of state. Go figure. But Pakistan and India had done the same. No, they had been heads of government, not state. Too many political science major friends had filled his head with useless facts. Think, Jesse. Kevin. Brian. That was closer. Brendan. No, although he would love to act in something by Behan sometime. Those Irish had their heads screwed on so wrong, they managed to look normal in a world run amok. No man is an island. No, but the Irish lived on one. So did his ancestors, but Puerto Ricans weren't as manic depressive as were the ones on this other one. Maybe it was the weather. Or the fact that they were drunks.

Think, Jess. Begins with a "B," rhymes with purple. Sometimes he hated free association. "Be purple, Jesse," his first drama teacher had told him. He'd mooed. You know, for a purple cow. What did he know? Starts with B and isn't Brendan. Brian. No, he said that. Bartholomew. Wasn't that one of the lost tribes of Israel? The Irish were supposed to be them, he'd read once. So the Irish and the Jews were the same people. That explained a lot. No, Bartholomew was an apostle. Hey, the Jews and the Irish were the Judeo-Christian alpha and omega. *Jesse, what the hell has gotten into you, man? It's that I'm not getting into Derek anytime soon. The shit.* "Brandon!"

The librarian was beside him almost before he knew it. But not before the geeks had registered their auditory disapproval. Jealousy. Pure and simple. It comes with the burden of being a geek. Latin lover penis envy was what it was. "Can I help you?" Jesse nearly jumped out of his seat.

"What?"

"You called my name."

"Oh, yeah. I did. Uh, well, I was wondering... I mean, I was thinking... no, no, I was wondering."

"Yes?"

"Yes. I was wondering if you could help me find a book in the stacks."

"Sure. Which one are looking for?" Which one are you looking for? What a stupidly cogent question to ask. Librarians. Go figure. His expression turned sheepish.

"You." With that, Brandon O'Connor sat heavily on the chair next to Jesse and stared at him in disbelief. "Sorry. It came out the way I meant it."

He nursed on the head, while flicking his tongue onto the vulnerable nerves just beneath it. Jeffrey told him that the next sign warned of dangerous pavement for the next three years. He didn't care. Getting off wasn't his purpose. Making love to the most perfect human reproductive organ was. He could love this magnificence forever. He felt the now-familiar indications and increased his oral assault. He was rewarded with another mouthful of delicious come, this time one he could handle. He fell asleep clutching the cock of his dreams to his cheek.

He waited on the steps for Brandon to help close up the library. The geeks both exited after him, giving him the evil eye, when they passed. Fed up with their attitude, he called after the latter one, "It's not my fault that you're straight."

The book weasel turned around and said, "I'm not. That's why I hate you and beautiful people like you. I would die to get a kiss from Brandon. But, no, the adonis cries out his name and he becomes your handmaiden. I hope a slasher is out tonight!" Jesse watched the vehemence continue to billow out of his body language, as the geek stalked away. Well, I am so sorry, Mary. He turned to look back through the doors, in anticipation of Brandon's appearance. "I'm sorry."

Jesse jumped a foot. He was panting and disoriented. The slasher, foretold, had appeared. "I really am sorry." He focused on the voice. It was the snarky geek. "I didn't mean what I said. Well, the part about the adonis, I did. But it was unfair of me to have lashed out at you the way I did. You can't help how beautiful you are. It's all genetic. I should kill my parents, before I take it out on you." Maybe a murder/suicide, Jesse was thinking, as he regained his breath. "Apology accepted. I'm Jesse Montalban."

"Irwin Pinkster. You really are a looker, Jesse." A looker? What planet did he come from? "I'm glad to know you." Find a quick and easy way to remove your hand, or you will regret this little touching scene of guy cordiality for years to come. Being an actor, Jesse kissed the bony extremity of Irwin Pinkster and pretended to sweep his musketeer hat to the panting geek. It worked. Good old Irwin skipped down the steps after smiling, knowingly, at the adonis, Jessathos. He might very well be a slasher, Jessathos thought. And where is my sword, when I need it?

Just then, Brandon came out of the building, and Jess knew exactly where it was, because it was wanting to stand up and unsheathe itself for the comely, reddish-blond library student. "Sorry to keep you waiting."

"No problem. I was occupying my time, fending off your admirers. They seemed to take it personally that I would make a play for you."

"You're kidding."

"No, but I can understand why. You must move a lot of hearts, considering how cute you are." They were walking across campus to no particular destination.

"And how did I move yours tonight, Jesse?"

"Well, because you're you."

"I've been me the whole time you've been comin' in, haven't I?"

"Well, I have an appreciation for you now, Brandon."

"So, did he dump you?"

"No, he went to Chicago to visit a cyber-buddy."

"You mean that much to him that he gallivants off to Chicago to meet someone he's never even seen?"

"Yeah, something like that. But that's not fair. I've never told him how much he means to me."

"How much could you mean to him to do what he's doing?" Jesse shrugged. He had no idea.

The last orgasm was achieved on actual bumpy roads. Derek was so into loving Jeffrey's penis that he didn't feel him turn off the interstate. Jeffrey had rewarded him with another mouthful. His testicles were a great example of American manufacturing productivity. The hand caressed him again. On his head, not his quiescent sex. "Man, Derek, you are the world champion. You are the god of sex. Your mouth is ready for the hall of fame. Say, look, love, I need to stop for gas, so you'd better put me away. Yeah, that's it. So loving and considerate. You'd better zip yourself up, too, man. Sorry it was so bumpy back there. Glad you didn't get sick. You are one hell of a cocksucker."

Derek was feeling smug. They were driving down a country lane, corn fields on either side. He had enjoyed the best oral sex he'd ever performed, as restricted as it had been, and he'd accomplished the impossible. The best cocksucker in the world. Jeffrey had said so. He smiled. At the next intersection, there was a gas station. Jeffrey pulled in, gripping his shoulder. Lovers didn't need to expend words. The Romantic poets knew that, even though they expended a lot of them to say so. He had to pee, an emphatically unromantic notion. While Jeffrey gassed up, Derek went to empty his bladder.

It was all too much for him to deal with. He knew that he would have to relinquish the godhood of Jeffrey's cock in Ohio, but he would adore it until then. Maybe afterward, too, if the man didn't live too far away in New Jersey. He shook the last of the urine off his head, eager to rejoin the stud of phalluses. He washed and dried his hands quickly. When he came outside, the car was gone.

Three

He really hadn't planned to end up stranded off the interstate in the middle of Pennsylvania. But then he hadn't counted on waiting an hour for the last ride, either. He'd made over two hundred miles with that one, so he didn't feel too ticked. And he could easily get back to the highway with one ride. Still, he wondered why the guy would just leave him at the service station like that after he gave him such great head. Must be straight. Go figure. One thing that troubled Derek was that the sun was awfully far along in the western sky. If he could just get lucky with a ride, he might be on his way to Ohio before dark.

Slowly he walked down the two-lane road, letting his

thoughts drift as the rows of corn on either side of the black top waved in the breeze. Then the sound jerked him to attention. In the distance he saw the motorcycle approach. It must be a Harley, although his familiarity with those kinds of vehicles was zilch. To him, every motorcycle was a Harley Davidson. As it came closer, he saw that its driver was dressed in leather. The extent of his leather fantasy was wearing a pair of boots and a belt at the same time. The cycle slowed at the sight of him and came to a stop beside him. Its owner was not what he expected. The guy was young, well-kempt and attractive. "Hi. You lost?"

Derek explained his abandonment as briefly as he could.

"Had to be a crazy straight guy," the guy said, matter-of-factly.

Derek laughed. "I thought so, too." He checked the sky. "There's not going to be too much day left, and I'll bet you could use a meal." The meal sounded good, as a matter of fact. "Well, if you don't mind being the guest of a leather master and his naked slaves, you're welcome to eat with us. Hell, stay the night, too. I'll get you back to I-80 early tomorrow morning. My name's Frank."

Derek introduced himself and he shook the tightly gloved leather hand offered him. A leather master? Naked slaves? Even with his neatly trimmed beard, this guy looked almost too young to drive. Oh, what the hell. He hopped onto the seat and held onto his host tightly, as instructed. The leather smelled tantalizing.

The trip to Frank's house took only a few minutes, but it was a terrifying few minutes for Derek. He didn't know that motorcycles could go that fast. The upside of the linear roller coaster ride was that he like having his arms around Frank's chest. It was solid, and the leather felt good against his skin.

The place was an old farm house. Upon alighting from the ferocious vehicle, Frank explained that he and his slaves worked about two hundred acres. It kept their bellies full, if not much more than that. They were greeted at the door by a blond boy, who wore only a black leather collar and some kind of wire and leather device over his genitals. Frank greeted the boy, calling him simply, "slave," and handed his gloves to him. "I keep the slaves naked when it's warm. It keeps them humble and they get an even, all-over tan." Another slave was in the kitchen preparing supper. Frank asked the first slave where Joel and Remy were. Waiting out by the barn, he was told. "Good. This is Derek, and he'll be joining us for supper. He'll also be staying the night. He's hitchhiking to Chicago to see his dreamboat."

With that, they went into the backyard, where a few chickens were scratching around on the pathetically sparse grass. "If you like, you can stay in the house and visit with Sean and Jamie," he turned to Derek and said, as if he had just remembered that he had a companion. "But you're welcome to watch me tend to these two slaves. In fact, I'd prefer it, because it will only increase their humiliation."

"I'm game," Derek said, having no clue as to what the game was. They went into the barn, where Frank took off his jacket. He was bare-chested. Yes, indeed, those muscles looked as good as they felt. And they were covered with fine dark hairs. Next the young leatherman removed his boots, chaps and jeans. The rest of his body was toned and Derek felt a pang of desire. Then Frank put on a studded leather harness and matching cock ring, feeling no inhibition about being naked in front of his guest. Derek was glad, because the man was a feast for his eyes. As he was buckling his harness and snapping his strap, he explained that Joel and Remy were going to be shaved. Remy was a newly arrived slave, who had applied to come to work on the farm and further his learning in the ways of slavery. People applied to be someone's slave?, Derek wondered. Last, Frank put on a studded G-string and snapped the waistband to the pouch.

Behind the barn, two young men were waiting for Frank. One, about six feet, was very handsome. The other was shorter and younger. During a very brief conversation, Joel, the taller slave, explained that he had shaven Remy's legs and arms in anticipation of his master's arrival. Frank would do the rest. Derek sat down to watch the action. Using shaving cream and a straight razor, the master first removed the short, crew-cut hairs from the kid's head. Then the eyebrows were banished. Next, he took a pair of scissors and clipped off the boy's eyelashes. Derek had seen nothing like this in his life, but it was weirdly engrossing to watch the boy being shorn. In fact, the boy, Remy, looked weird without the usual hairy facial features. Next the armpits were scraped clean. Then, bending over, the kid presented his cute ass to the razor's edge. There wasn't anything there to be removed, but Derek enjoyed watching Frank play his hand in the crack between the kid's cheeks. As the kid stood at ease once more, his hands behind his back, the last patch of hair was lathered. Frank explained, "The last of the hair to be removed is the most important to a boy. Shaving it off is the symbolic neutering of him. It makes him look like a little boy again." With that he carefully worked the razor over the pubic hair, holding on to Remy's penis as he defoliated him.

When he was finished, Joel handed him a hose, and he washed off the skin of the denuded slave. Then he affixed the boy's collar to his neck and the wire device to his genitals. The master explained that this was a cock cage. It was employed to prevent the slave from having an erection. Remy's penis fit snugly into the steel harness, and Derek could see that getting aroused would be a real problem for the kid. He winced, when he pictured the shaft trying to grow and encountering the unforgiving metal stays.

Next it was Joel's turn. Unlike the other slave, he was the instrument of his own emasculation. The boy presented his ass to his master, putting one foot on a boulder in front of him. Then he soaped himself with Barbasol and used a safety razor to remove what had to be stubble, because Derek couldn't see any growth. He repeated the procedure with the five o'clock shadow of his pubic hair, meticulously grooming himself, so that no shaft remained above the skin line. When he had finished, he presented himself to his master, who ran his hand over the smooth lower abdomen and the valley between his ass cheeks. Satisfied, he smiled. So did Joel. It was evident from that the slave was happy that he'd pleased his master. Derek wondered about the allure of this kind of lifestyle, but he was unaware at that moment that his own sex had responded positively to the acts of denuding.

The newly shaven young man stood with the remnants of shaving cream on him. A steady stream of water gurgled up from the garden hose, which Frank would play over the now-smooth body to rinse off the remnants of his ritual bodily regression. On the ground next to the standing boy, the completely hairless youth knelt, looking like an extraterrestrial from the absence of any hirsute features. His knees were spread apart, feet together, hands clasped behind his back. On that hot early evening, the cold water must have felt good to the boy being hosed down. Joel neither flinched nor shivered. When his body was clean and glistening from the coating of water, he leaned over, planted his hands on the rock in front of him and spread his legs.

His master spread his cheeks and pushed the end of the hose into the boy's opening. From his vantage point, Derek could see the hose attached to the body, like a long green tail. The boy breathed deeply as water filled his bowel. It had to feel awfully cold in there, at least, Derek thought. He watched the boy's belly slowly distend from the intrusion of the liquid. The harnessed man put his hand on the expanding abdomen and held it there. The hose kept filling him, and Derek marveled that the handsome kid was taking it without a whimper of protest, despite the fact that he looked as if he were in the early stages of pregnancy. Then, as if feeling the limits of the young man's intestinal endurance through his skin, he removed the hose. For several seconds nothing happened. He just stood bent over, carrying his water baby. Then Frank uttered one word, too low for Derek to hear, and a steady stream of colored water surged from his anus and splashed onto the kneeling slave. Remy seemed shocked by the shower, and although he flinched, he didn't otherwise move. The front of his body was covered with the other boy's waste, the smell of which rose to insult Derek's nostrils.

The master once again inserted the hose into the bent-over boy, replaying the scene, and he once again shit the liquid onto the hairless, hapless slave. A third application of the ad hoc irrigating device produced a prolonged expulsion of crystal clear water, as if he were the source of a mountain spring. The final discharge from his cleansed gut cleaned off the soaked slave. Man, this was getting to be some adventure, Derek was thinking to himself.

Then the young master stood in front of kneeling boy and unsnapped his pouch, casting it aside. Without a word of instruction, the boy leaned forward and kissed the large mushroom head of the man's penis. Then he took it into his mouth and sucked on it. Derek thought that what he lacked in technique, he made up for in enthusiasm. The kid seemed awfully eager to please. But the sight of him was unnerving. Derek had never seen a human completely without hair before. But his attention was soon transferred to the hardening cock. It was curious. The knobby glans was the color of the rest of Frank's skin, but the shaft was brown. He wondered at this anomaly, as he shifted his gaze to the face, hoping to find a clue to the dark coloration there. He couldn't, looking at it in profile.

When the cock was hard, he put his hand on the slave's forehead and pushed him off his erection. Then he turned around and slid the bi-colored boner into the clean rectum of the older slave. The kneeling one leaned forward again and buried his face into his master's cleft. The enema had begun to arouse Derek. The sucking had coaxed it on. And now the sight of the two handsome men joined in sex had him rock hard. He wanted to free his own prick from its constriction and stroke himself in time to the master's rutting, but he didn't know the etiquette of a guest at a leather household jacking off without permission. He decided that discretion was a better idea, even if he wasn't happy about it.

The fucking was long and slow, but he finally gave a grunt and came in his possession, marking him once more as his. Derek was glad that it was over, so that his own manhood could return to normal. Joel thanked his master for fucking him and received a possessive kiss from the man. Then Frank picked up the hose and ordered the kneeling slave to his feet. He washed him down again. Then he collared and harnessed Joel, and the slaves were sent to the farm house. Derek and Frank went into the barn, where the master put on his pouch again. Derek wanted to ask about the strange juxtaposition of the brown shaft and pink head, but he thought better of it. He continued to dress, except that he didn't don his jeans again. "So, are you completely scandalized, Derek?"

"Well, actually, no. I mean, I've never really known any leather people, but, honestly, it was a real turn on. Man, seeing the guys having their hair removed was way cool. And I thought that it was kinky living in New York."

"It is, but usually, it's done behind closed doors. I have the luxury of privacy. And it's a rush for the slaves to denude themselves for me out of doors."

"I'm not surprised, considering how it made me feel. Um, Frank, thanks for letting me see that."

"You're welcome. A guest should enjoy himself. I'm glad that you are." Now with Frank dressed in his chaps and boots, pouch and harness, they went back to the house.

Supper featured hearty fare. Jamie and Sean had made a beef roast, with mashed potatoes, gravy, green beans and carrots. The bread had been baked early that morning, before chores, Derek was told. The spinach for the salad came from the kitchen garden, Frank said, as had the other vegetables, although the potatoes were last year's. They were stored in the root cellar. Given what he had witnessed behind the barn, and the fact that each of the slaves wore collars and genital harnesses, he was surprised that dinner conversation was so freewheeling. Each of the young men was able to talk with no constraints, except that each prefaced his remarks to Frank with "Master." And it struck Derek that they all seemed happy. They talked excitedly about what they'd achieved that day; they joked and laughed; they even confessed shortcomings. Frank was affirming, telling them what a good job they'd done or telling one or another not to screw up again. Only Remy didn't join in the conversation. At one point his master asked him, if he thought that he would like his new life. "Oh, yes, master. Thank you for asking me, sir. It's so beautiful here. And, well, so are you." The other slaves laughed. The boy blushed. "They're not laughing at you, slave. You've already grasped what these airheads are finally thankful for. I think you'll fit in just fine here."

"Thank you, Master."

"Master, thanks for mortifying me by having Master Derek witness my shaving and cleansing. It really bothered me," Joel said. Derek saw Frank smile.

"You would, you little wimp pup," Sean said.

"Well, maybe Master Derek'll still be here tomorrow, when you and Jamie shave. How about that?" Sean shut up and tended to his plate. Jamie shifted nervously. Frank had been right, Derek thought. It was profoundly chastening for these guys, to begin with. To have someone else see it was a real blow to their egos, however much a slave had.

The mood of the house changed abruptly after the meal was over. The slaves became silent and went about cleaning up the dishes, or feeding the chickens or other chores. Derek and Frank took a walk. "We don't get many visitors here, for obvious reasons, but the boys do enjoy company, except when it involves seeing them being profoundly slaves. It's good for their humility. Well, you've seen the lot of them. And a great lot they are, I should add. They're all good boys. So, which one would you like to share your bed tonight?" The question surprised Derek. He hadn't thought about doing anything but maybe jerking off before he went to sleep. But the invitation was irresistible. "Joel," he said.

Frank seemed pleased with that, and Derek was looking forward to having the gorgeous young man to play with. "So, how did you get interested in leather?"

"My uncle lived with us. He hung around with some motorcycle guys. I don't think that daddy particularly approved, but they were brothers, you know? And Uncle Frank helped raise me, for which daddy was thankful, because my mother had died when I was fairly young. Well, then daddy died, and Uncle Frank got the farm and me. He educated me about sado/masochism. I've been a leather boy since I was thirteen. And a slave. It was great training to become a master, which I've been since I was eighteen. So, here I am, with boys of my own."

"They seem real nice. Especially Joel."

"Yes, they are. But Joel's special. I own him."

"Come again?"

"He signed himself over to me as my possession, when he turned eighteen. I really love him."

"Wow. But won't it bother you that I'll be sleeping with the person you love?"

"No. Besides, I have Remy to attend to tonight. And I saw how Joel was looking at you at dinner tonight. He wants you bad. I realize that you're not into our lifestyle, so you can do whatever you want with him. But I have one request."

"What's that?"

"Don't let him fuck you."

"Why not?"

"Because it'll take me weeks to beat his ego out of him for having fucked your gorgeous little ass."

Joel accompanied him to the bathroom. Derek wasn't used to having Jesse in the bathroom with him, let alone a stranger. Although he had seen Joel getting fucked, he reminded himself. What he was not prepared for even more, was when he had to use the toilet. "Master Derek. Please use me. Please, sir. I would be honored." Derek was flummoxed, but he decided to give it his best shot. Joel lay down in the tub. Derek got in and straddled him. *This is crazy*, he assured himself. Still, he squatted over the supine slave and dropped his load onto the taut abdomen under him. He wondered whether or not he should ever have left the city. But he did feel a rush of some kind. He had actually shit on another human being. And the man wanted him to do it. When he finished, Joel asked him to back up, please. The slave put his head into Derek's cleft and wiped him with his tongue. It was so unbelievable to him that the slave should be his toilet paper, that he was getting hard again. Joel's lips and tongue tended to him so seductively, that he was going to have a hard time pissing. He stood and turned around. "Are you unhappy, Master?"

"No, but I need to pee, Joel."

"Thank you for using my name, sir. And thank you for using me. Please urinate on me." When his penis returned to flaccidity, he took it and sprayed the boy under him with his yellow liquid. The boy already had a mound of his excrement decorating his body. He covered the body under him with his bladder's delight, to Joel's own, it seemed. When he was empty, he said, "Can we shower together now?"

"Please, Master."

Derek had never had such loving attention paid to his body. Joel soaped every inch of his body twice, paying careful attention to his cock and balls. Then he hurriedly cleaned himself. He dried Derek thoroughly, before toweling himself off.

In the guest bedroom, Joel stood before him, legs spread, arms behind his back. Derek removed the key from his shorts pocket that Frank had given him. He opened the lock and removed the harness. Then he kissed Joel. He put his arms around the boy and said, "It's just going to be two guys having sex, Joel. But there are ground rules. You worship me as I should be, being a top. And I'll reward you with the best fuck I can give you." He saw some disappointment in the boy's eyes, but he agreed to the terms.

For the next hour, the slave licked every inch of the front of his body. Derek had never had a tongue bath before, and he loved it. He felt massaged from his hairline to the soles of his feet. Then he made Joel slather his cock for penetration and then to impale himself and do the work himself. Derek pulled and twisted the boy's nipples, causing him some pain, he could tell. He wondered what Frank did with them. But not for more than a few seconds. He could tell that the discomfort made the slave buck harder on him. As he felt the pleasure begin to rise in his body, he played with Joel's penis, making it come alive with the promise of release. The slave boy asked him deferentially, as to the progress he was making in giving him pleasure, and he assured him that he was coming along fine. He could sense that the boy was getting close, so he pumped him hard, bringing him to the brink. As the boy began to twitch in orgasm, Derek's other hand grabbed his ballsac and squeezed hard. Joel came, screaming and bouncing wildly on Derek's cock, making him come.

As they lay together afterward, Joel whispered, "Awesome," and nuzzled him. Not bad for a guy not into the scene. Then Derek thought that some things were definitely going to change, when he got home. He pictured both Jesse and him in leather. He liked what he saw.

He had made Joel sleep in his metal harness, to the boy's chagrin. Given what Frank had said, Joel probably would have fucked him during the night. But he did hold the slave before they went to sleep, whispering affirming words for the pleasure he'd given him. And, upon wakening, he enjoyed the smooth body he fucked again, minor stubble and all.

At breakfast, which was at the ungodly hour of five-thirty, the other slaves razzed Joel about his screaming. Frank smirked and winked at Derek. The latter enjoyed his bacon, eggs, home fries and biscuits all the more.

When he deposited Derek at the ramp to Interstate 80, he said, "You're welcome anytime at my place. In fact, I think that you have the makings of a leather master in you, Derek. Joel told me what you did to him. Thank you." He shook the gloved hand and, holding it, kissed the master. "Thank you, Frank." There was mutual admiration in their eyes.

Four

He used the 'CLEVELAND' sign again. He cheated by standing on the interstate, because, at that hour few if any cars were going to be entering from the rural entrance ramp. He'd have to risk an encounter with a state policeman, because traffic was sparse. That was another thing that made Pennsylvania notorious. With good reason, he'd heard. While the New York state police were a bite in the ass, and the Jersey police were obnoxious to the letter, as cops went, you didn't mess with a Pennsylvania trooper. Great. Just how long was it going to take to get out of this fucking state? He smiled. The fucking had been great. So had the cocksucking. Maybe it wasn't a bad place, all things considered. Then he considered Jesse dressed in leather. He didn't expect the tears, conjuring up his beautiful roommate in shiny animal skins. He'd never been unfaithful to Jesse before. But Jesse didn't love him. How could he be unfaithful to someone who only used his body in bed? He didn't have time to consider, because a car stopped a few hundred feet from where he was standing. He ran to it. The driver was a woman.

Brandon was really cute. And his voice had a lilt that melted something in Jesse's being. He was overdue for a thaw, although Brandon wasn't the source of warmth he needed. But the young Irishman was there in his apartment, handsome and horny. What more could he ask? Under the circumstances, not much. The body was lean and pale, like his hooded penis. Jesse tried to remember the last time he'd seen an uncircumcised organ. High school probably. What was that kid's name? The naked body on the couch moved. The first thing he had done upon entering the apartment was ask to strip. His idea of kink, probably; being bare to his clothed host. It proved that the Irish were weird. Not that Jesse at all minded having Brandon naked. The problem was that he kept getting distracted by it. He had envisioned a suitable period of polite conversation before tossing the clothing and coupling, but Brandon might as well have had "Fuck Me" emblazoned on his chest. The movement was Brandon leaning into his ear to say, "Fuck me, Jesse." So much for high tea.

Jesse kissed him and began to fondle the soft skin covering the Irishman's torso. He began to undress himself with his free hand, but that slowed his progress. Maybe he'd just fuck the boy with his clothes on. He'd probably like that. So he unzipped himself and pulled at his dark manhood to free it from the confines of his swimmer's jock strap. Derek thought that the white athletic supporter looked dynamite against Jesse's caramel skin. So, he often wore it as a prelude to sex. But why was he wearing it now? Derek was hundreds of miles away by now. At least he hoped so. So why was he wearing the strap? Force of habit, because wearing it meant that sex was on the agenda?

"Jesse?"

"Huh? Oh, what?"

"You seem distracted."

"Uh, sometimes my mind wanders."

"Well, thank you very much."

"I didn't mean it that way."

"How many other ways could it be meant? Don't I turn you on?"

"Of course you do. I'm sorry."

"You're thinking about him, aren't you?"

"Of course I'm not. I was preoccupied with getting my dick out of my jock."

"You're wearing a jock? Let me see it." Jesse got up and took off his clothes, leaving him standing there in his snowy white strap. "Wow. That is so sexy, Jesse." He slouched farther on the worn brown couch and spread his legs farther apart. Jesse knew an invitation when he saw one and accepted it by kneeling in front of his guest and taking hold of his cock. He smelled a light scent of woodsy cologne. He pulled back the protective skin and the smell was slightly stronger. He sampled the exposed head and he tasted it. The taste was not unpleasant. "I'm sorry. I guess I should have warned you. I perfume myself. Otherwise it can get close in there."

"No, no, that's fine. It tastes pretty okay, actually." So pretty okay that he went down on Brandon again and stayed there until he was hard. Still holding him, he said, "So what do you like to do?"

"I'm pretty versatile. You know the stereotype. Repressed gay boy from a small Irish village gets to come to the U.S. and the big city to boot, where he's like a kid in a candy shop."

"So you might be amenable to having your colon stroked?"

"Aye, as long as other things get a little loving, too."

"I think that can be arranged." Jesse stood and prepared to remove his jockstrap.

"Aren't we going to go to the bedroom?" Jesse held onto his straps. The bedroom? Where he and Dreek made love? In their bed? Their bed?

"Uh, well, I guess we could."

"Well, it is logical, isn't it?"

"Perfectly."

His initial response was surprise that a woman would pick up a hitchhiker, and a guy at that. She couldn't possibly know that he was gay and harmless. Maybe she had been moved to stop because of his good looks. He had that annoying effect on women. Sometimes it seemed that he was more attractive to the opposite sex than to the one to which he was attracted. But a ride was a ride, Gertrude Stein.

Her name was Bambi, she said. She didn't look like a Bambi in her tailored gray business suit, off-black hose and black sling-back pumps. She looked like, well, a Joan or a Doris or maybe a Martha. Yes, a Martha. Did people still name their daughters Martha? But she didn't look like a Bambi. Still, she was pretty. If he were straight, he suspected that he would be attracted to her. She wore her makeup almost invisibly, which seemed to be an ability a lot of women he knew lacked. Her nails were red but not garish. She was obviously a professional woman. Why had she picked him up?

"You're probably wondering why I stopped to pick you up."

"Exactly."

"Well, one reason is obvious, uh...."

"Oh, sorry, Derek."

"What a pretty name. To go with a pretty boy. That was one reason. I'm a sucker for gorgeous boys. Please take that as a compliment, not as a come-on."

"It wouldn't work anyway. I'm gay."

"I see." He saw a smile flicker momentarily on her red lips. "Well, since I'm not propositioning you, there's no problem. Anyway, the other reason is that I get so bored driving alone, and I appreciate having the company. And I've been on the road for two hours already. It's going to be a long day. So, when I saw you, I decided that you didn't look like an axe murderer." Oh, no, not that again.

"Actually, except for stepping on a few ants and catching lightning bugs, I haven't harmed another living thing that I'm aware of."

"That's nice to hear. So, we'll be riding pals until Chicago. You going to see a friend?"

"Cyber-friend. We're finally going to meet. I can't wait."

"Well, he's certainly going to be pleasantly surprised."

"Thanks. I hope so."

"Trust me, Derek. Oh, wait. There is one hitch."

"You're not going to leave me at a gas station in the boonies are you?"

"Why in the world would I do that?" He told her a severely edited version of his encounter with Jeffrey and Frank. She said that was cruel of Jeffrey and kind of Frank. "No, the hitch is that I have a presentation to make outside of Elkhart tomorrow. I'm staying at the Holiday Inn there tonight. The room's a double, so you're welcome to join me, if you don't want to keep thumbing through the night. The meeting is at nine o'clock. We should be on the road by about ten or so. Now I understand that you're anxious to get there, so it's your call. But right now you're assured of getting to Chicago tomorrow."

"Well, I do appreciate the offer and Adrian isn't expecting me until at least tomorrow, anyway. But I don't want to be a bother. And I don't have much money."

"Derek, the room is on me. I would have to pay for it, anyway. So, why don't you think about it?"

"Sounds good to me, as long as you don't mind having me around."

"Not in the least, sweetheart." Not in the least.

It turned out that Bambi and a friend had a computer network consulting firm. She said that they had been in business for a little more than two years, and the business was growing. Her partner was a man, but she made most of the presentations to prospective clients, given that they were mostly men. "Two can play the sexist game, Derek." He laughed.

"Good for you. So, where were you coming from?"

"State College. I wish it had been Pittsburgh. That's a great potential market, given that so many Fortune 500 companies are headquartered there. Alcoa, USX, Heinz, PPG, Westinghouse. It goes on and on. And they have networks for days."

"So, do you troubleshoot?"

"Occasionally. We mostly plan for their needs. Start-up, expansion, those kinds of things."

"Sounds cool."

"It can be quite interesting at times." Oh, could it.

They stopped for lunch in Ohio. As they passed the Cleveland exits of the Ohio turnpike, Derek wondered if Jeffrey of the magnificent cock and shitty manners had really been going there. He had to be straight. Or closeted. They were as bad as straight men, probably. Telling the same bathroom jokes and yak yakking with the boys. As unsure as Derek was about sharing a hotel room with a woman, at least she was straight. He found it curious that, in his experience, he, as a gay boy, was loathed by straight men and gay women. That didn't make sense. But it was true in his case. And straight women seemed to like him. Well, he was cute, but it was more than that. Maybe like in Bambi's case. She could feel safe rooming with him, because his hot breath wasn't going to be on her face in the middle of the night, begging her to open up her legs. Whatever it was she had to open.

They were both tired from the monotony of tires on concrete, wearing each other and the humans down. And they were just past Elkhart now. He'd meet Adrian tomorrow for sure. Right now, he was looking forward to a shower and dinner.

Bambi checked in, and then they took the elevator to the fourth floor. He did notice that she had great legs. He wondered what Jesse would look like in heels. Then a stab of pain. If only Jesse loved him. It had been a mistake to room together. He should have known that he would fall in love with the Hispanic deity eventually. And liking him so much made it that much worse. He sighed. Be careful what you agree to. It may make your life miserable.

She caught the forlorn exhalation, as they rose in the elevator and asked, "Impatient to get there?"

"No. Wishing that the trip wasn't necessary."

"Oh?" They got off on their floor and found their room.

"It's just that I have a roommate, who's to die for. And I have, emotionally. Unfortunately, it's not mutual. So, I end up going off to Chicago, hoping to find love. I guess that sounds pretty pathetic."

"No, it doesn't. Love is something we have no control over. When it's requited, we hope for the best, that it'll work. When it isn't, we mourn. Often, we end up mourning, when it is, too."

"Thanks for understanding, Bambi."

They hugged. Then she gave him a strange look. "Derek, let's sit down for a minute." The sat together on one of the beds. "There's something I need to tell you. I don't quite know how to say this. I've been somewhat dishonest with you. I'm sorry. I really am attracted to you, and I feel like such a jerk."

"That's okay. I mean, I know I'm attractive to women."

"I'm sure you are. You're one of those men who's just a magnet to both sexes."

"But I really am gay, Bambi. I can't do you any good in bed."

"Well, that's where you're wrong. You see, I was named after the fawn that Walt Disney created."

"Okay."

"Do you remember the movie?"

"Well, yeah. I cried when his mother got it."

"Me, too. *His* mother, right? Bambi was a boy," she whispered into Derek's ear. He looked at her, shocked.

"You're... you're...."

"An all-American gay boy, living his life as a woman." Bambi took Derek's hand and put it under his Lord and Taylor skirt to feel the bulge straining at his tricot panties.

"Holy shit!"

"I'm sorry. You're such a nice person, Derek. I shouldn't

have done this to you."

"No, it's all right. I mean, it's... it's just strange. A shock." Bambi removed Derek's hand from his crotch.

"And unfair. I really did stop because you're beautiful. I had my motives, and you were innocent of them."

Derek looked at him and said, "But I don't know how good looking a boy you are, with all of your female stuff on."

"You mean it?"

"Sure. If you're interested."

Bambi Gonsalves had gotten most of his facial genes from his mother, whose ancestry was French. He took off his jacket and skirt, and then his blouse. Then he removed his bra. Behind the falsified garment was a hard, male chest. He smiled. So did Derek.

"I think I might like to see the panties go, too."

"You're serious?"

"Are you?" A very nice set of male genitals appeared. Standing before Derek in only a pair of stockings and heels, Bambi felt embarrassed. He saw it and said, "How about a cocktail before dinner?"

"Love to."

"Only, keep your sexy stockings and heels on." Bambi walked sexily up to him and planted a kiss on Derek, while the latter played with the distinctly male equipment. "Oh, man, You are so convincing as a woman. Even your voice. But you're a great-looking guy."

"Thanks, Derek. You're sweet. No, I mean that. I've felt all along that you are. Thanks for understanding."

"This is great. You feel like exercising your male prerogative?"

"Oh, do I."

Bambi wasn't the best sex partner he'd ever had, but he could give Jesse a run for his money. And he was being fucked by a guy wearing nylons and high heels. That was such a weird realization, that it turned him on more. A made-up guy with styled chestnut brown hair screwing him. So soon after he'd subdued a leather slave to the slave's master's satisfaction. This was really turning into some adventure. The "woman" came in him, and they lay quietly for a time, caressing and kissing. Then, Bambi asked, "Are you hungry?"

"Starved."

"Well, let's get dressed and wow them downstairs."

"How?"

"I have this cute little black sequined number I always pack and almost never get to wear. You're all the excuse I need. We'll be a hit."

"But I didn't bring along anything to wear for dress-up."

"Let's see what we can do."

The knapsack contained mostly T-shirts and shorts. Pairs of blue and black jeans. Sports sandals. A pair of black high-tops. A white oxford shirt. You can get only so much into a knapsack. "Perfect. Put on your white shirt and black jeans and your black athletic shoes. We'll make it a fashion statement." He did as instructed. Bambi took a paisley scarf from his suitcase and threaded it through the loops of Derek's pants and tied it. Then he found a button cover of red glass. He buttoned the top button of the shirt and put the fake red stone on it. "Perfect. Elkhart will never be the same."

He hadn't changed the sheets, so that Derek's smell would linger in his absence. He thought that it was probably pathetic that he kept the scent of the man, who didn't love him, for his nose to inhale, in light of the fact that said man was traveling west to cheat on him. And they hadn't slept together for a week before he left. The linens were ripe. He apologized for the dirty sheets.

"Why," Brandon asked. "So they have you on them."

They lay down, their nude bodies pressed together, their lips in concert. The Irish lad's lips weren't nearly as full as Derek's, but they were persistent. In fact, they were so persistent that Jesse didn't doubt for a minute Brandon's allusion to being a kid in a candy store. And Jesse was the confection. He and Derek didn't do much kissing. In the first place, they were fuck buddies. In the second, they were fuck buddies. People related that way didn't kiss. They just sucked and fucked. Jesse wished now that they had kissed. Well, they did kiss, you know, as buddies kiss. That's how he knew what Derek's lips tasted like. But they didn't *kiss*. Perhaps if they had, his roommate might have realized that he loved him, and maybe the sentiment might have been mutual. But he doubted it. You didn't get somebody to fall for you because you set their lips on fire. There had to be a pilot light, at least, already burning in the other person. He thought of his drama teacher asking him to be fire. He'd mimed a fire eater. That had been brilliant. Sometimes he wondered how he had gotten to be a fourth year theater major. Well, he could act pretty well. He just had trouble with abstract concepts.

He also became aware that he was having another problem, and there was nothing abstract about it. Despite the fervency with which his lips were being assaulted, it had not translated to his nether region. Even those short, friendly kisses he and Derek exchanged always gave him a momentary buzz down there. So, why wasn't he responding to his partner?

"Is something wrong again, Jesse?"

"Uh, no. Why?"

"I was the only one whose lips were moving." What was worse was that Brandon was sticking straight up in the air, he noticed. Maybe he needed to be more deprived. How deprived did a guy have to be? It had been a week, for crying out loud. Ever since Derek announced that he was going to Chicago and they'd argued. His sperm should be banging on his ball walls, screaming to get out. So what the hell was the matter?

"Well, sometimes I'm passive."

Brandon laughed. "I didn't know there was a passive partner in kissing. It must be an obscure American custom, because I hadn't encountered it until now. Are you sure you're interested in me?"

"Very."

"You know, it is possible to play things too cool. However, since arriving here, I've had the distinct impression that you're preoccupied."

"I'm distracted by your good looks."

"Well, that's original."

"And my mind wanders."

"Yes, you said. But during sex?"

"I'm an actor."

"When it comes to sex, one doesn't need to pretend. Unless he's really not interested."

"I am. I think you're very cute and I want to screw you to show you how attractive you are."

"Well, try to concentrate a little more."

"My undivided attention."

"Good, now let's see what's behind the white door." And with that he pulled Jesse's strap down his legs and flung it into the air.

When they entered the restaurant, it was evident to Derek that he was an oddity. The fiftyish, balding maitre d'hotel didn't quite know what to make of him, but he was with this pretty woman in the short, sequined cocktail dress and strapped, patent evening sandals. He couldn't quite grasp how Bambi had pulled off the illusion of cleavage, but he liked it. God, this guy had fucked him less than half an hour ago, and here he was in female persona, being squired by the very man he'd fucked. This trip was turning out to be nothing, if not enlightening. Evidently the maitre d' found the cleavage to his liking and ignored the sartorially avant garde male next to her. Heads did turn, but who cared? He was from the City. Let Indianans gawk.

They sat together in a banquette, receiving glances from other diners, handsome young couple that they were. "Well, this has certainly exceeded my wildest expectations for the trip."

"How's that?"

"Meeting you. And then managing to get you into my hotel room. And! Get you into my bed."

"So that's why you smiled in the car, when I said I was gay."

"Oh, you saw that? Maybe I'm not as good as I think I am."

"You had me fooled."

"Yes, but one slight slip-up under the wrong circumstances, and I could be cooked. Imagine if I suddenly lowered my voice during a meeting with a client. What a disaster."

"How long have you been impersonating a woman?" Their meals arrived. Derek's shrimp Scampi was still sizzling. Bambi's tournedos in roasted garlic sauce looked appetizing, too. Their both ordering garlicky dishes would uncomplicated their further physical exploits. Then his eyes drifted from the plate to the man's lap. The short dress had ridden up enough to expose his black panties. Derek wondered what it would be like to touch the male clitoris and lips through the panties. His earlier fondling had been done in shock.

"Since I graduated from college. I let my hair grow senior year, all the while planning my revenge."

"Revenge?"

"My dear father, please note the sarcasm in my voice, Derek, thought it was a great joke naming me Bambi. He saw it as a kind of 'Boy named Sue' thing. Well, it got me in plenty of fights all right, but it never made me into the he-man he thought it would. Worse, when I realized that I was gay, I thought that was crueller yet. So, I decided that the only way to live in the real world was as a woman. I didn't want to become one, because I like being a guy. And I like making love to other guys. So, I started buying women's clothes and learned how to apply makeup. I lived alone senior year, so I could practice my transformation in the privacy of my apartment. After I graduated, I had my hair done smartly and went home to visit my folks. My father actually shit when he saw me. That was mightily pleasing. Then he ordered me out of the house. My mother was embarrassed to pieces. Although we do talk on the phone now. She even asks me for tips on grooming. Sometimes mothers understand the pluses of having a gay son." They laughed. "But only sometimes."

The meal was delicious. And it was free. Well, he would repay Bambi with his body, but that would be a pleasure.

Back in the room, with ice bucket filled, Bambi poured them drinks from a bottle of Wild Turkey he kept in his suitcase.

"I'm curious. How do you date guys, if you're always dressed as a girl?"

"Well, when I go to the bars, I'm just another drag queen, although a very convincing one. And there are lots of guys who like the look. I also have a couple of friends who are closeted, and I help them out by being their dates at company affairs. It's a lot of fun."

"And nobody catches on."

"Nope."

"Well, I sure didn't. Do any straight guys hit on you? I mean you're really pretty."

"Thanks, sweetie. And yes, I get hit on all the time. And most of them are ugly, balding and married. So much for fidelity, I guess. What's wrong?" She saw the sudden shadow crossing Derek's countenance. He shrugged.

"As much fun as I'm having on this trip, and as glad as I am to have met you, I wish that I hadn't had to do it."

"You said."

"Yeah. His name is Jesse."

"That makes living together difficult, I'll bet."

"It does. I mean, we agreed to be fuck buddies, but I slipped up. And, you know, the sex is fine, well it's great, but sometimes I need to be held and kissed and told I'm special. I just wish it could have been with Jess."

"I'm sorry, Derek. But the people we go ga-ga over don't usually reciprocate, I've found."

"I know. But I'm hoping that Adrian will turn out to be the romantic type I'm looking for. He sounds it from our chats."

"So, you met him on the Internet?"

"Yeah. A few months ago. His moniker is Dreamboy. He's a student at the University of Chicago and he models. He sounds like one."

"Have you ever talked on the phone?"

"No. Why should I?"

"To hear his voice?"

"I never thought of that."

"A child of the Computer Age."

"Well, you're one, too."

"I wasn't being nasty, Derek. But with the computer, you never needed the telephone."

"That's true. But tomorrow, I'll not only hear him, I'll see him. Dreamboy."

They took their time in bed this second go-round. Derek did get to fondle Bambi through his panties and decided he liked it. They kissed lying on the bed with their feet on the floor. Bambi had removed his dress and bra, Derek his shirt. It felt good to have his lips attended to, although he'd forgotten the remarks he'd made about it. But Bambi hadn't, and he wondered how this Jesse person could find Derek's lips resistible. He certainly couldn't. Slowly the panties came off and the jeans unzipped. Both were soon holding erections in their hands. "Well, I don't know about you, but I know where I'd like this," Bambi said, teasing him with his long nails.

Derek wondered what Jesse would look like with long red,

nails. Then he said, "Sure."

Almost all of the time, Jesse fucked him, which he liked, because he was a bottom by nature. But he had enjoyed Joel's tight little tunnel and was willing to sample Bambi's boy cunt. Maybe he'd like it enough to demand equal time from Jesse. If he went back to New York, that is. Maybe he wouldn't leave the Windy City.

After their first session, they'd showered. Bambi had changed into sheer suspender pantyhose, black, because it was evening, and Derek asked him to keep them on. If this be kink, let us make the most of it, he thought. Even if he wasn't paraphrasing a Romantic playwright. He played with his partner's boy nipples, while he sucked his cock. He came off it one time to say, "Bambi really is a beautiful name."

"Thanks, Derek. That's nice of you to say."

"No, I mean it. Cute guys should have cute names."

"Like Derek."

"And Bambi."

"Okay, you win."

"Yeah, and I'm enjoying my prize." With that his ample lips slid down the ample shaft of the stockinged stag.

It had become an obsession, and his aching jaw could attest to it. This had never happened before, and yet here it was happening with this Latin adonis. Brandon tried every trick he knew, but nothing worked. Humiliated, Jesse lay with his arm over his eyes, not caring to see his dismal failure. But he felt it, anyway. This had never happened before. Derek barely had to tease him with his tongue to make him spring to life. Derek. That was his damn problem. The boy who broke his heart had also caused his plumbing to fail. Maybe he should just stay in Chicago with his dreamboy. Good riddance. What had he ever given him, anyway? Besides good companionship and great sex? Nothing. Well, friendship. The best friend he'd ever had. But a guy's best buddy didn't just leave him for a computer halfway across the country. He began to cry. "I'm sorry. I'm sorry, Brandon."

"You really love him, don't you?"

He took the hand away and looked at the cute Irishman and nodded. "It's not your fault." He sat up and put his hands on

Brandon's shoulders. "It isn't you. Honest. I really do like you. A lot. It's just that I hoped that some day Derek would realize what he meant to me."

"Did you ever think of telling him?"

"Yeah. But that would have ruined everything."

"I think I'm catching on to American logic. How is it that you managed to become a superpower in spite of it?" Jesse laughed, despite his tears. He hugged Brandon.

"Are you hungry?"

"Isn't that obvious?"

"I meant for something to eat."

"I'm always hungry for American hot dogs." He saw Jesse's face sag. "I'm sorry, Jesse. That was unfair. What did you have in mind?"

"How about beer and pizza?"

"Second best still sounds good. With all of your fast food, how *did* you get to be a superpower?"

"Vitamins. Then we exported the Colonel, Mickey D's and the BK Lounge to places where they have none, and we at least get our RDA, and they get food they can't fight on."

Jesse got them beers. Brandon said, "*Slainte*."

"Huh?"

"It's the Irish toast. It's Gaelic. The mother tongue of the Emerald Isle."

"Oh. What do you want on the pizza?"

"Surprise me."

"I already did that once." Brandon put down his bottle and hugged Jesse. "It's okay. It is. I understand."

"I wish I did."

"You will. One way or the other, you will."

Bambi felt great. His ankles were wrapped around Derek's back, as the brunette slid effortlessly inside him. "You feel so good."

"So do you. I have half a mind to kidnap you in Chicago and keep you all to myself."

"If I weren't so hot to meet Dreamboy, I might like that. Of course, if it doesn't work out...."

"And what kind of a lady do you think I am?"

"A very butch one, I think."

386

"Don't tell."

"I won't."

"Just fuck me, beautiful." He played with Bambi's nylon-covered legs and kissed them as he built toward his orgasm. Yes, the trip was already more than he could have imagined. It could only get better. His orgasm was powerful, although he resisted squeezing his buddy's balls this time as he came. That was a completely different culture. He seemed to be encountering different ones right and left on this trip.

They made love one more time upon awakening. He could get used to fucking guys, he thought. But Dreamboy had told him that he was a top. Well, what he'd said was that he had a way of controlling his lovers, implying that his beauty let him have his way with his partners. That was fine. He still knew how to be submissive, as Jeffrey had demonstrated so poignantly. If Adrian wanted to control him sexually, he knew how to respond.

It wasn't an unmitigated disaster. He liked Brandon and Brandon liked him. In fact, they decided to get together the following evening. Not where the ghost was haunting Jesse, however. They would get together at Brandon's. A candlelight dinner, just the two of them, he'd said. Jesse knew he was right. He felt it, too, when he went to bed that night. Derek was there in the bed with him. Not physically, but he was there. Jesse kissed the pillow next to his, before he laid his head on his own.

Five

"It's okay, Derek," Bambi said. "I'm not the possessive type. In fact, I hope that things work out with you and Dreamboy. But if they don't, you always have Jesse. Maybe more than you know."

"What do you mean?"

"You two are guys, cutie. Guys sometimes have trouble with admitting what they feel for each other."

"But Jess's an actor. They practice how to say things they

don't mean. How would I know?"

"How does anyone?"

"You got me."

"I'll let that pass." They chuckled. "Seriously, if something goes wrong with this seeming Mr. Right, please call me, okay?" He handed Derek his card with his home number written on the back. Derek asked for another card, so that he could write his and Jesse's number on it.

"I doubt that anything will, but I appreciate it."

"And I appreciate having met you, honey. You're a doll."

They were on the Skyway when the city came into view. It's conspiracy of buildings wasn't as impressive as Manhattan's, but the Sears Tower was the tallest building in the country. Big deal. They got onto the Dan Ryan and Derek knew that he would miss Bambi Gonsalves a lot. Even more than Frank and jerk Jeffrey's cock. This was a person with whom he could be friends. Bambi gave him an abbreviated tour of Michigan Avenue and then got onto Lake Shore Drive. Boys Town wasn't that far north of downtown. Bambi found the address and double parked. Derek kissed him. "Thanks for everything, Bambi. I mean it."

"I think you're so sincere that you couldn't not mean it." He smiled, disarmed, and Bambi saw that he was right. He watched as Derek got out of the car and went up to the door of the well-kept house and waited until the door opened. That was strange. An older guy answered. He made a note of the address. It wasn't strange that a dumpy middle-aged guy answered the door. But what would he be doing living with Dreamboy? Probably had to be his father. Or uncle. Or sugar daddy. Or none of the above. Bambi had to get to the office to tell Sam about getting the contract in Elkhart, considering that they'd never gotten around to obtaining a cell phone for his car. But his heart and mind were on Derek. He was special, he knew. And much more like the fawn after which he was named. But not too young to know how much Jesse Montalban meant to him. He wondered if Jesse could ever feel the same way.

"Hi. I'm Derek Brown. Is Adrian in?"

"Oh, Derek. Pleased to meet you. No, he's out at the store, grocery shopping. But he should be home soon. He didn't know exactly when you'd show up. I'm sorry he isn't here, but he asked me to extend his hospitality to you. Come in."

"Thanks. Who are you?"

"I'm his friend, uh, Chuck. He should be back shortly. He's really been looking forward to meeting you."

"Me, too. He sounds like such a great guy."

"He is. And I know he'll be happy to make your acquaintance." Did people still talk like that? Maybe older guys. "You're quite a handsome young man."

"Thanks."

"Can I get you something to drink, while you're waiting? Iced tea perhaps?"

"Thanks, I'd like that. It sure is warm for spring."

"Yes it is, but not nearly as hot as I suspect it'll get for you with Adrian."

"I hope so."

"So do I. One iced tea coming up."

Being a college student used first to institutional blah and now shoestring budget functional in furnishings, Adrian's living room struck him as downright prissy. Every piece of upholstered furniture looked as if it had been pumped up with air. The wooden pieces glinted from heavy doses of polish. The baby grand piano in the corner was buffed to a high sheen. Knitted white doilies were everywhere. There was something obsessive about the room beyond its scrupulous neatness, and completely unexpected in the home of a twenty-two year old. And just how did Adrian manage to afford this place? It certainly wasn't located in a low-rent district. He wondered if Chuck lived with Adrian. Or the other way around. Considering that Dreamboy had no compunction about inviting him to visit, it was doubtful that Adrian and Chuck had a physical relationship. Was he a kind older man helping a gorgeous college student in return for the pleasure of seeing his beauty every day? People did stranger things. He sure had on this trip already. But whatever Chuck's relationship to Adrian, he, Derek, was evidently not seen as a fox in the henhouse. Otherwise, Adrian wouldn't have invited him, he was sure. Unless it was to make the older man jealous. But Chuck didn't seem the least bit perturbed to see him. Maybe Adrian's family was wealthy and bought the place for him, and Chuck was a neighbor friend.

A collection of framed photographs sat neatly staggered on the piano. Evidently neither Adrian nor Chuck used the instrument. Otherwise, why have a bunch of pictures you had to move every time you wanted to lift the lid to play? As he approached the expensive piece of furniture, one photo caught his attention. He knew immediately that it was Dreamboy. The handsome features had been described to him in surprisingly effective detail. He picked up the frame. Yes, he could see this guy being portrayed as Dreamboy and having his face plastered all over Chicago. He had to be one of the stars of Boys Town. Then why was he soliciting boyfriends over the Internet? There had to be tens of thousands of cute gay boys in this city. Thousands within a few square blocks of this house, probably. Curious. But who was he to second guess Adrian's motives? He couldn't wait to meet the man in this photo.

"Ah, I see you've found his photo."

"Yes. He certainly is a Dreamboy."

"Indeed. And I'm sure he feels the same way about you."

"How? He hasn't met me yet."

"Well, I meant from your description of yourself to him. He printed it out and showed it to me. I'm relieved to say that you were most honest in your self-portrait, even if I do admit that I was skeptical. But here you are. Oh, and here is your iced tea." Derek put down the frame and accepted the proffered tea. It tasted good, but there was a vague aftertaste. Probably an artificial sweetener.

"Please have a seat, Derek. You will be face to face with Adrian before you know it."

"And I'm excited about it. I mean, well, he's a fox."

"Ah, yes. He is a fox, indeed. A good choice of word." Chuck's smile was almost a leer. Was he coming on to him? He took another sip of the tea. Yeah, it had to be sweetened with some artificial stuff. That was one reason he never used them. Didn't need to, either. He was in shape and had a good metabolic rate. He glanced toward the photo again. There was something about it, now that he looked at it again. Something not quite right. Some detail. He took another sip and put the tea down on the doily of the end table. Doilies. His grandmother's house. She had lots of them, too. But she was old. So was Chuck, sort of. Old. The photo. It wasn't recent. The hairstyle was wrong. Nobody wore…. His vision began to swim as the young man smiling at him dissolved into darkness descending like angry nimbus clouds over the sun.

Jesse was never strong on geography, but a simple move to a different location was already having salutary effects. When Brandon kissed him, he felt an accompanying sensation in his groin. He felt much more in the next few minutes. This was more like it; more like good old Jesse, who practically got a hard on when he was in proximity to Derek. But this was Brandon, and he was responding to him. Not to Derek. The traitor. His host was quite aware of his recovery, if he was measuring it only by the ferocity of Jesse's kisses. He decided to strike, or rather have Jesse strike while the cock was hot. He managed to avoid his lips long enough to say, "Why don't we get naked and commune on the bed."

"Great idea."

After the frustrations of the night before, Brandon found it hard to believe that he was with the same person. Jesse had lubed his cock and was screwing his brains out seconds after they hit the bedroom. He was on fire, and so was Brandon's ass, so enthusiastic was Jesse's considerable tool coupled with him. And the orgasm he had desired the previous evening he declined being favored with, fearing the permanent disfigurement of his organ. So he did it himself. Putting aside the fact that he wouldn't be able to sit for a week beginning tomorrow, it was quite a satisfactory communing, as he was wont to put it. Perhaps he'd get Jesse a little tipsy and see if he could calm him down a bit.

Brandon decided to treat his guest to an Irish meal. He served spiced beef, which he'd made at Christmas time and frozen. A variation of Colcannon, which was a mixture of mashed potatoes, onions, and cabbage; and soda bread. And of course Guinness. He'd put a couple of bottles in the refrigerator, knowing that Americans drank just about everything cold, including tea and coffee, often, but Jesse surprised him by taking his the traditional way.

"This is a great meal, Brandon. Where did you learn to cook?"

"County Louth."

"Where?"

"Ireland. That's the county I'm from."

"Where is it?"

"On the border with the north."

"Oh, IRA country, huh?"

"Sadly, yes. Although my family were IRA members during the fight for independence. It was honorable to be back then. No, patriotic. Now those people are as bad as Paisley's goons. You don't need Christians and lions. Just put two Christians together and stand back."

"Ah, yes. The pacific religion of Christianity. Let the wars begin."

"Aye, sad to say. Are you Catholic, Jesse?"

"Marginally. I was raised that way. Unfortunately, I'm not able to toe the company line in one important aspect of my life."

"Me neither." He grinned at his guest. "I guess we showed the pope, didn't we?"

"Not that he cares."

Jesse was certainly feeling like his old self again. Well, and feeling the Guinness, too. He chuckled.

"What?"

"How many wusses does it take to screw in a light bulb."

"I don't know. How many?"

"Who cares?" they both laughed. Brandon decided that it was time to suggest revisiting the boudoir. He decided to have another go at the now-responsive cock and was pleased with its response to his lips. He could get used to having this dark pleasure-giver around, he was sure. When Jesse was hard and dripping with his saliva, he slid on top of him and humped him, using the spit and commingled precum as lubricants. Jesse's smooth, pigmented torso contrasted with his pale hairy body. Physical yin and yang, he thought, happily. They came within seconds of each other, bodies pressed together, and that was how they fell asleep.

In the morning, Jesse stayed for coffee but declined his host's offer to make breakfast. They made a date for that evening at Brandon's, but Jesse insisted that he would bring the food. It wouldn't be anything approaching spiced beef, but it would be edible.

When he walked in the door, the first thing he did was to check the answering machine. He hadn't turned it on. Shit. What if Derek had called? How many days had he been gone? Two? Three? Three. Damn him. If he'd have flown Southwest, Jesse would know he was there safe and sound. But no, he had to go for the new experience of thumbing. The thrills. The smell of danger. Actually, Derek didn't smell the possible danger, that was his problem. He was too innocent for his own good sometimes. He hoped that he hadn't called yet. What if he had and discovered that he had gone out? What the hell was he thinking? The asshole had gone to Chicago specifically to cheat on him. And while the mouse was away, the cat ate well, anyway. El Gato. The cat. Dreek had called him that early on in their relationship. He said it was because of Jesse's sinewy body movements. Like those of a cat. Hence, Gato. He sure hoped Dreek was okay. Maybe he'd call today. He went into the bathroom, which was off the bedroom, to pee. Coming out of the john, he stopped. He walked over to the bed and pulled down the top sheet. He lifted the pillow, kissed and inhaled it. Then he held it to his chest, as if comforting a frightened child. Maybe he was.

The description he'd given of himself paled when compared to the reality of him. The short, straight brown hair. The dark, arched eyebrows and lashes surrounding darling blue eyes. The small nose and solid chin. The fleshy lips. Oh, no, he had not done justice to himself in the least. He was the prettiest of them all by far. The muscular body. Hairless, save for the usual patches and a dusting on the legs. He was perfection. Therefore, he would contribute so much to his own reincarnation.

Six

He was sitting, staring at the photograph. The handsome face seemed to be smiling almost conspiratorially back at him.

Chuck was playing the piano behind the battalion of frames. Even with the top closed, the music was pleasant. He didn't recognize the piece, but it sounded Elizabethan. It would have sounded better on a harpsichord, but he wouldn't quibble, because he was enjoying the melody. He looked alternately at the photo and past it to Chuck. The distances between the two began to decrease. It was as if the two faces were merging. The forehead of the picture into Chuck's forehead. The eyes a nearly perfect match. The cheekbones interchangeable. The chins replicas of the other. Strange. He blinked and looked again. A much older Adrian was playing the piano, and he was definitely leering now, as if the music was somehow seductive and he knew that he had Derek under his spell. To be sure, Derek was transfixed. It wasn't because of the music. It was because Chuck was Adrian.

    He felt as if he were awake, but his eyelids were too heavy to lift. He felt disoriented, as if he had been drugged. He took deep breaths through his nose. He had been sitting in the chair. He didn't think that he was there anymore. He didn't seem to be lying down, either. A yawn arose in his mouth, unable to escape. Maybe he was still asleep. No. He was awake. He worked his mouth, but the lips wouldn't move. What the hell? He needed to get his eyes open to figure out what was going on. They were awfully heavy. He had been sitting in that overstuffed chair talking to Chuck, waiting for Adrian. He was looking at the photo of Adrian, the one which had merged into Chuck's face.

    His eyes flew open, and he wasn't encouraged by what he saw. He was in a cold room, the realization of which caused prominent goose bumps on his smooth skin. It was dark, save for a low-wattage red bulb glowing dimly in the ceiling. A basement room? He couldn't be sure until his eyes adjusted. He was standing upright. How was that possible? He craned his neck to see that his arms were above him, held there by something. He couldn't move them. He tried his legs. They were secured by something, too. His body was fastened to a post of some kind. A house support? Why?

    Think, Derek. Who would do this? The drink! That aftertaste. He'd been slipped a mickey by Chuck. Who wasn't Chuck. He was Adrian. A much older Adrian than the photo. The photo.

What had struck him? The ducktail! He saw it too late. Few guys wore their hair slicked back in a ducktail these days. And the photograph was in black and white. These days, large yearbook pictures would be in color. The unmistakable truth was rapidly sinking in. He had been lured here under false pretenses and was now Dreamboy's prisoner. And Dreamboy was anything but.

His mounting sense of horror about his predicament was interrupted by a sudden thought about Jesse. Would he become concerned when he didn't hear from him? He'd been pretty ticked about his coming here. Would he care? If only he cared as much as I do for him, he thought. But he doesn't. What if he did? What would it matter? He couldn't find me. Now he knew why Dreamboy had wanted everything kept confidential. What a dumb fucking ass he was. Jess had been right to smell a rat. He had thought it was a ruse, because Jess was jealous. What if he was? Did that mean he was just being proprietary? Jess liked to do that, as if his body belonged exclusively to him. Fuck buddies had no claims on their partners. It was strictly an arrangement of convenience. Except that he'd crossed the line and developed feelings for Gato. His nickname for him. Gato and Dreek. Where are you Gato?

A door opposite him opening refocused his attention immediately. "Well, I see that Sleeping Beauty has awakened. A little groggy, I presume, but none the worse for wear. I do make a mean iced tea, you must admit."

Derek stared at him. He was naked, except for a pair of flip flops on his feet to ward off the cold concrete of the floor. "Now, let me make myself perfectly clear. You are in a soundproofed room. I intend to take off your gag, but it will do you no good to scream. No one can hear you. Do you understand?"

Derek nodded.

"And if you don't believe me and scream, I will hurt you. Bad."

Derek was looking into the dark eyes. There was hatred in them. He didn't have a prayer. "Now, do you agree to play nice and avoid unnecessary pain?" He nodded. He didn't doubt that this person was capable of serious hurt, given what those eyes had conveyed. The first impression of the body was one of flabby seediness. But he didn't for a second think that he would make good on his threat. Adrian Jordan, the beauty gone to tallow, ripped off the duct tape gag. After yelping in pain, Derek breathed rapidly through his mouth. "Well, so far, so good. If you cooperate, I am prepared to be merciful. Do you understand?"

Derek's voice croaked when he replied. "Does that mean you'll kill me fast, instead of slowly?"

"My, how quickly you've cut to the chase. No, they all die in the same way. Some just wish they were dead a lot sooner than others."

"Why?"

"Look at me you pretty faggot!! You have to ask why?! You saw the photo on the piano, you fool!! Why do you think?!" His lined, sagging face came to within inches of Derek's. "Because I've lost my beauty," he said just above a whisper. "Because now the pretty ones are so preoccupied with their own precious silky skin and erections on demand, that they won't look twice at a troll like me. Yes, they've even called me that. But you know what? I remembered them and waited under the bridge, unbeknownst to them. Oh, I don't get them all with iced tea. Sometimes I have to use other means of persuasion. But they ended up where you are, mightily regretting their haughtiness. The impertinence of beautiful youth has its price in Mister Rogers' neighborhood. A very dear price." He snorted in derision. "But their imperiousness vanished, to be replaced with whining and pathetic begging. You see, unlike others out for revenge, I don't lie to my prey. By being frank with them, I instill the knowledge of their impending premature deaths in them right from the start. It's a wonderfully horrifying fact for them to nurse in their stricken brains the entire time they're hanging there. Their seemingly precious beauty is for naught. Indeed, it is the passive instrument of their deaths."

"Jesus."

"Is no savior for you. There is no one to save you, Derek. I trust that you followed my instructions to the letter." Derek began to cry. "I trusted that you would. You seemed the trusting type. Stupid, but trusting. I have a mind to go easy on you."

He gasped for control. "How many?"

"Have I consigned to hell? That's none of your concern. You're just another number, albeit the most beautiful one yet. A beautiful number. The irony of the double meaning."

Derek sniffled. "I don't understand."

"I just explained it to you as succinctly as I could."

"No. No. Why the Internet?"

"I mentioned those two, who called me a troll. And laughed at their little joke, I might add. But it was I who laughed as I exacted my final revenge." He stroked Derek's torso with his fingers. "Such supple flesh. Such firm sinews. A delight. You are an absolute delight, Derek."

"What... what are you going to do with me?"

"I'm sure you don't want to know. But I intended to tell you anyway. We may as well get it over with now. I am going to milk your semen. You may think this organ, shriveled in terror won't be able to perform. Ah, but the youthful male is nothing if not potent. You will give me what I want. Your come will shoot from your body, unable to do otherwise."

"Why do you want my come?"

"I have in my possession an ancient text, which by happy accident I found in a rare book store on Clark. In it is a prescription for a type of fountain of youth, involving the fruit of young males. And you may doubt all you want, but I am seeing certain changes, which tell me that the text has revealed the truth. I will bathe in your semen. And I will end your life by removing your scrotum, so that I can extract your testicles, which I will eat." Derek's big blue eyes got round as saucers at the thought of bleeding to death, emasculated. "You see, there's a drain directly beneath you. Your blood will flow into it as your life drains with it." He kept fondling his captive like a buyer in the market for an exceptional animal to put to stud. "Yes, you are by far the prize. I may regress five, perhaps ten years, thanks to your contribution. Oh, and to answer your question about the Internet. Those two I mentioned were local. There have been others. But on account of that, it became too dangerous to continue to harvest semen and organs locally. Too many disappearances in Boys Town would surely have the police becoming too inquisitive. That is a foolhardy risk to take. So, I lure unsuspecting pups like you to my house. Mostly boys in desperate need of love and attention. You would be surprised how effective I am. Shocked, even, although I'm sure you are by this time."

"But, but how do you...?"

"Dispose of the bodies? It's simple, really. The soft tissue gets fed to the garbage disposal. The bones I collect in a parcel post bag, the kind the postal service uses. Given that they are constructed to such exacting standards, meant to hold up for years, if not decades under truly adverse conditions, they serve my purpose well. I weigh down the sacks with rocks. Then I take my speed boat far out onto the lake and toss them into deep water, never to have a chance to see the sunny Chicago beaches again. Oh, and I crush the teeth, in the unlikely event that they should ever wash ashore. So, while the authorities may know that the skull belongs to a white or black male, its identity will forever remain a mystery. Well, there you have it. You now know your fate, pretty, pretty boy." He smiled a demonic smile. Derek screamed in despair. Adrian Jordan punched the wind out of him and left.

Seven

He was pacing. He knew that he was, but he couldn't help it. Dreek said he would call. He had to have gotten there by now. Unless he was stranded on the interstate and too proud to call. That was Dreek all right. He took a big swig from the beer bottle. God, he was sorry he'd let him go. The whole thing just didn't feel right. Suddenly, inspiration. He went to the phone book. He paged through the front of the directory to the map of the country. Illinois. Chicago was in the 312 area code. He punched long-distance information. "What city?" They never said "please" anymore. And this wasn't New York we were talking about here. This was the heartland, home of people, who were nothing like those creeps on the east coast, that we were talking about here. But no 'please', please note. He hated the fucking rest of the country for distorting the reality of his home town. "Chicago, please." Take that.

"Yes?"

"Uh, Adrian Jordan."

Then a computer came on. "The number is 555-4071. The number is 555-4071. Please make a note of it." Twice, bitch. He didn't mean that, because the voice was human. He'd read about her doing the words and numbers for the different Baby Bells. But her voice was syncopated, so that it sounded like a computer. Except it was human. What the hell was he thinking? He punched in the number for Adrian Jordan and held his breath, as the phone rang. "Hello?" Oh, Mary, hello.

"Is this Adrian Jordan?"

"Yes. Who is this, please?"

"My name is Jesse Montalban. My roommate, Derek Brown was coming out to visit you. Is he there?"

"What on earth are you talking about?"

"Derek. He was coming out to see you. You met on the Internet."

"I'm afraid I don't know what you're talking about." The line went dead. He knew it! The guy owned a human chop shop. His anger welled faster than his tears, as he cursed himself for not having tied Derek to the bed to prevent him from leaving. He'd never loved anyone more than Dreek. Gato and Dreek. Oh, man! He should have tied him up, if only to explore a fantasy he had about leather. Only in that one he was tied up. He wondered what Derek would look like covered in leather. Are you fucking insane, man?! Dreek's missing! Concentrate.

He jumped at the ringing phone. Nerves. It was the worst possible time to have them. Figured. He picked up the receiver. "Hello."

"Jesse?"

"Yeah, who's this?"

"Your date for the evening. Did you forget?" Oh, shit.

"Brandon, I'm sorry. Can you come over? I think something bad's happened."

"What?"

"I think Derek is in big trouble."

"I'm on my way out the door."

"Thanks. A lot," he said to a singing dial tone.

He jumped at the knock. It was Brandon. "Thanks for coming over. I'm sorry, Brandon, but I called the guy in Chicago Dreek said he was going to visit, and all I got was dog breath."

"Could he have gotten the name wrong?"

"Dreek? Hardly. He looks like the dark-haired equivalent of a dumb blonde, but that's your first mistake." Or mine. He stopped and tried to hold himself together. "But he's too damned trusting. He takes people at face value. And he's a New Yorker, for chrissake. He should know better."

Brandon studied his couch mate. He had no chance with this guy. He never had. Derek had him by the balls and wouldn't let go, even from Chicago. But Jesse was a good person and an entirely desirable lover, once one's bum didn't hurt anymore. Which he was looking forward to. But, no, it wouldn't happen again with Jesse.

They sat drinking Guinesses, which Brandon had yanked from the top of the fridge on his way to the door. It was infinitely more desirable than watery American brews. And they were a superpower. It was a mystery to him. "Perhaps he hasn't gotten there yet, Jesse."

"No, the guy said he never heard of him. It wouldn't matter when he arrived, if the guy said he didn't know him."

"Aye. Well, what do we do?"

"I don't know. My gut tells me he's in trouble. It doesn't tell me anything else. Guts are so short-sighted." He wanted to laugh, but Jesse was in pain. The phone rang. They both jumped.

Jesse swiped up the receiver. "Dreek?"

"I beg your pardon." A husky woman's voice. Now what?

"Sorry. I mean, hello."

"Is this Jesse?"

"Yes. Who's this?"

"My name is Bambi Gonsalves. I was wondering if you heard from Derek yet."

"How do you know Derek?"

"I gave him a ride to Chicago. He's a doll. So, have you heard from him?"

"No."

"Jesse, I dropped Derek off at Adrian's place, but a young man didn't answer the door. An older man did. I've been concerned about that. That's why I called."

"How did you get our number?"

"Derek gave it to me. It didn't seem right, somehow. So I thought I'd call."

"He was supposed to call, but he didn't."

"I don't like this. Tell you what...."

Jesse interrupted her. "Bambi? We're coming out on the next Southwest flight we can get. Give me your number." He wrote it down.

"I'll meet you at Midway."

"Okay, I'll call you back to let you know." He hung up.

"I'll call the airline. You go pack," Brandon said.

Eight

It was nearly chaos. Despite themselves, they made it to Newark International. Brandon had no clothes, except what Jesse packed that might fit him. They paid for the one-way tickets and headed for the gate. Theirs was the last flight out that evening. Once they were airborne, Jesse sighed. At least he was doing something. What he was going to do when he got to Chicago, he had no idea. But one thing was for sure; he wasn't coming back without Dreek.

He was pawing him with one hand and masturbating him with the other. "You know, there's an old European legend, which tells of boys being roasted on certain festive occasions, because they were prized for the succulence of their meat. First, the boy was skinned alive. The skin was then tanned on another boy to keep its shape, before being sold to those desiring a soft young male shell to use for their pleasure. Have you ever heard of that one, Derek?"

Derek jerked in orgasm, having no clue about what his executioner was talking about.

"Your skin would be ideal to be subjected to that ritual. Imagine having your dermis slowly cut away from your body in order to serve a higher purpose. The pleasure of trolls." He yanked on Derek, causing him to buck against his restraints. "Don't worry. I haven't the knowledge nor the boy to prepare your skin for a long-term relationship after death. But I'll consult the text, just in case. Yours will be a terrible skin to waste in a disposal."

He cried in the womb of his death, hardly cognizant of where he was, hardly aware now that it was evil. Jess would never know his love for him. Too late we wish we had said what we wouldn't have said in the first place. Herrick had said that, he was sure.

Bambi had neglected to get a description of the guys he was meeting, so he held a sign, which read, "Jesse/Brandon," hoping that they were the only ones by that name traveling together on that flight to Midway. Seeing the sign, they walked toward her. She knew immediately which one was Jesse and why Derek loved him, at least superficially.

Nine

"I'm sorry for having hit you, Derek. I realize now that it was confronting your death that made you cry out."

"Cry for that which is not. I beg you for what cannot be."

"Oh, don't start begging, Derek. Surely, it's beneath you."

"Beneath me is thine drain. Into which I am fated to bleed. I, however, could have loved thee. That time passed, hoary scoundrel that it were. In ways few mortals know, my death is your assignation with a truer love. Would that it weren't true. Alas, I suffer for my peers and I promulgate the writ done against thee and thine cohorts, devils, all. The despicable whining of putrefied flesh, goaded by its odor. You are one together and yet abhor each other, rancid epiphany to the world." Derek fell into unconsciousness, as if speech now were a sedative. His subconscious was dazzled by the outburst, although it couldn't figure out what he had said. *To what effect?* it asked then. He was still going to die.

The stimulation aroused him to wakefulness, if not awareness. His retreat into himself seemed total.

"And when you hold the rose in your hand, do you feel its silky stem or the thorns arrayed thereon?"

"No, only the silky skin of your penis, Derek."

"And what of that? A will to be succulent yet treacherous,

lest you look? What is your gain, should you be pricked in your randy gathering?"

"You don't have—" he paused dramatically. "Well, you aren't, like, sick, are you?!"

"Hell, I'm a garden of ineffable delights. My body flows to the maker of my happiness."

"What in the world is this gobbledegook? Do you have AIDS or not? Answer me!"

"I walk in beauty, like my captor. I am the seeker of his quest. To become sublime with him who shackles me. Without him, I am not free. With him, I am not free." Derek stared at him, unblinking, sending a shiver down his spine.

Ten

Bambi pulled into a parking lot down from Belmont and Clark. "Where are we going?"

"To my favorite Thai restaurant, so we can plot strategy and get something to eat."

"I'm not hungry."

"That's fine, but we still can't do anything, until we've thought through how we're going to get Derek out of there."

"Come on, fucker. Prithee, show your despondent countenance to me, that I may affirm your degenerative beatitude to all the world. Show thine face to mine. I shall give you no succor in words. I shall give you nonce, lest my body and spirit fly together. You shall hear upon the heights the heavenly host singing... "And then Darkness gripped his world once more. The entrant to the room was relieved that the body was quietly at rest. He'd been rattled for the first time in his years of doing this. All of that babble he'd spewed. What did it mean? Was he mocking him? Or standing up to him, as hopeless as it was? He was developing a grudging respect for the kid. That meant that he would cut him and scar his body. He held the knife, ready to alter him. He remembered the enlarged slit he'd made for Jeremiah, in appreciation of his generous come production, whose black balls cried rivers into his receptacle. He would cut this perfect beauty, Derek, in the same manner, after carving lines in his face and body as the Kiwu tribe had done to its defeated enemies to physically mark them as vanquished and as slaves. He stood poised with the knife and remembered that the boy had not answered him about his blood's status. Better to wait. The semen was harmless for his external purposes. The blood, however, could pose a problem if it spurted into his mouth or eyes. He would ask the boy again about his HIV status, when he awoke during his next milking.

Eleven

They were sitting at a table in the restaurant in Boys Town, nervously downing cocktails. Looking out the large plate-glass window, Jesse saw him cross Belmont toward the restaurant. A short black in a tight black T-shirt, tight blue jeans and knee-high black boots, the kind of boots he envisioned Derek would wear and be the sexiest man on campus. "You listenin'?"

"Sorry, I was distracted."

"There are no distractions, except Derek, Jesse."

"Don't you think I know that?"

"No."

"Sorry. I was reminded of a fantasy I have about Dreek."

"You fantasize about him? I thought fuck buddies used each other's body and fantasized about making it with others."

Jesse hung his head. "He's more than that to me, actually." Brandon put a supportive hand on his arm.

"So you're saying that Derek is not just your fuck buddy?"

"Yes."

"Oh, honey, are you in for a shock."

"How?"

"Derek is in love with you, too."

"You mean it?"

"He told me. He thought it was one-sided."

"Oh, man. We have to get my lover out of there."

"And we will. But we need to figure out how to get into that house. Any ideas?" Over dinner, which Jesse did eat, they came up with one hare-brained idea after another. Brandon suggested calling the police, but each had to admit that, although Bambi saw him go into the house, they had no evidence that he was even in there. They knew he was, but they didn't *know* he was. Let alone that he was being held captive. So, the police were out, if only for the time being.

By the time they left the restaurant, they still hadn't hit on a plan. Bambi drove them to his apartment, which was in a building close to the Second City comedy club, and not too far from where Adrian Jordan lived. Bambi got out his Wild Turkey and launched into his explanation about his really being a guy. The two young men were shocked, but then they had a hollow laugh about being fooled. Then Jesse's face showed the pain he was feeling. "I'm sorry, Jesse. He didn't know how you felt."

"I know. I don't blame you. Half the world wants to bed Dreek, I'm convinced. And the other half's never seen him. This is all my fault."

"Now don't start that. He never told you what you mean to him, either. We need to keep focused, even if we don't know on what yet. Help yourselves to the liquor. I'm going to change."

Jesse jumped up. "Do you have a phone book?" Bambi fetched it and handed it to him.

"What are you looking for?"

"Mistaken identity."

When their host returned wearing jeans and a sweatshirt and without makeup, he did look a lot more like a boy, except for the hair and nylon-covered feet. Jesse told him what he'd found.

"So the guy was telling the truth. Neither he, nor any of the Jordans listed as 'A' lives there. The guy gave Dreek an alias, so even if he slipped up and told me Dreamboy's name, it would be the wrong one. I'd never be able to find him. I'm just so thankful Dreek met you, Bambi. At least we know where he is."

"And the first thing we do tomorrow is go to the library," Bambi said.

"What for?"

"To look in the Polk Directory to see if we can find out who really lives at that address."

They were in the double bed in Bambi's second bedroom, but

there was no question that there would be no sex between them. Brandon didn't mind, but he wondered why he was in Chicago, considering that he wasn't being any help. Well, moral support, he supposed. And it was his first time in the city, even if he wasn't getting to see much of anything. Being there for Jesse was important, he concluded. They were lying quietly, when Brandon asked, "Do you have a photo of Derek, by any chance?"

"Yeah, I do. He doesn't know that I carry it in my wallet." He turned on the light, got up and went to the dresser, where he'd tossed his billfold. He pulled several cards from a slot and found the picture of his roommate. He took it to the bed and handed it to Brandon. "This is Derek?"

"Yeah."

"I've seen him many times. Said hello to him a couple of times. Oh, Jesse, I can't believe I almost know Derek and didn't have any idea that it was him." He handed the photo back to him. "I have to admit that I, too, have entertained fantasies about him. Who wouldn't?"

"I hope they were good fantasies, because that might be all that's left of him." He broke down at the thought. Brandon held him. Aye, moral support was important.

He was unconscious again, when his kidnapper came into the room. But before he drifted off, he realized that all feeling was gone from his hands and arms. He knew that he'd lose them for good pretty soon. It didn't matter. He would die soon. If gangrene set in, he would become useless to Adrian, so it had to be soon. It wasn't the most pleasant thought that had ever preceded his sleep.

He squirted the syringe and stuck it into an arm vein. He pushed the plunger. Then he unshackled Derek and lowered him to the cold, concrete floor. "Sleep in peace, my dark angel. Store up your potent come, because I feel myself getting younger. Only a couple more milkings and then I will give you a different peace." He kissed the unresponsive lips and left the room.

The room was brightly lit. In addition to the red bulb, there were greens and blues and yellows along the ceiling border. It was as if it had been decorated for Christmas. Dreamboy came into the room and smiled widely at him. He greeted him as an old friend and kissed him as if they were lovers. He pressed his body to Derek's and rubbed against him. The slicked-back hair looked strange, but the boy was certainly desirable, and he desired him. When Dreamboy had him hard from their body contact, he went behind him. He held Derek to him as he impaled him on his cock. It felt wonderful to have him inside his body. The trip to Chicago had been worth it to experience the wonderful feeling of Dreamboy fucking him with his long cock. His whole bowel tingled from its massaging possession of him. All the while Dreamboy whispered words of love in his ear. He wanted his partner to possess him forever. He wanted to give him his body always to experience the radiant pleasure in his abdomen that he was feeling then. When Dreamboy's breathing became ragged and his cock lunged far up his descending colon, Derek felt the boy's come erupt into him; the violence of the spurts pleasing him.

Then Dreamboy slowly withdrew from him, but his canal felt as if it were still being fucked. It felt wonderful. His partner then knelt in front of him and began to suck his cock. Yes, it had certainly been worth the trip to meet his Dreamboy.

Twelve

His eyes opened, feeling the mouth working on his stiff penis. Only it was the older man, who was there, and he was jerking, not sucking, him off. He still felt the sensations in his ass, but he realized that they were being made by the butt plug holding his cheeks to the beam. He was moving on it involuntarily due to the manipulation of his sex. He seemed to be lucid once again. And he realized he had feeling back in his arms and hands, because they were hurting again. "Did you have a refreshing sleep, beautiful Derek?"

He didn't answer. He closed his eyes. Where had he been? How long had he been asleep? Was this still the first day? He felt the other hand on him now, groping his body for its own pleasure. "Are you still feverish, or have you returned to sanity?" The latter, he feared.

So, it hadn't been hallucinations. Well, it had, but they were real in the sense that he hadn't dreamed them. He thought that he was cracking up, and now he was sure of it. His clearheadedness was a sign that he was going completely mad. "And what did you decide about your HIV status, Derek? Did you tell me the truth over the Internet? Or are you one of those despicable people who lie so that they can inflict their own death on other trusting souls?" Trusting souls? That's what he'd been. Gato always told him he was. As usual, Gato was right.

Oh, yes, he might be as mad as a hatter, but he decided that he knew how to answer that question. He opened his eyes and saw the troll looking at him. He summoned his waning reserves.

The first volley of spit hit him in his right eye. He recoiled in horror, but his mouth was open in disbelief. Before he could shut it, Derek spit a second time, splashing the lips and teeth with his saliva. The man screamed and ran from the room. There was going to be hell to pay, when he returned, but it had been worth it. The seed of doubt would grow. Good. Two could play this game, and he would play it as well as he could, given his extreme handicap. I'm going to die, but I'm going to take as much of you as I can with me, fucker.

They were at the doors of the library before it opened. Having no idea what good this exercise would do, they did it anyway. R. L. Polk produces city directories, which list residents by street and phone number in its "Street Guide" section. A cross-referencing "Telephone Key" follows that section. But the man might be so secretive, that he wouldn't respond to the Polk Directory's request for information on him. Yet, when Jesse looked, he was listed at that address. "Okay. There it is. Guy's name is Charles Bedlington."

"So, how does that help us," Brandon asked.

"Maybe I'll know, when I call Adrian Jordan."

It was swift and painful. Not only did he punch Derek several times in the stomach, he slapped his face for minutes on end, preventing him from regaining his breath. His deflated lungs begged for air, but his facial pummeling prevented it, all the while the man was out of control and yelling at him. "You fucking, lying bastard! You fucking diseased queer! You putrefied faggot!" Then he stopped, as if the eye of his furious hurricane moved over Derek like a womb. His face burned, but he could see, at least temporarily. He suspected that he'd be bruised to the point of their swelling shut, but for now he could use them. He saw that the old man was winded by his exertion, breathing erratically.

When he recovered, he looked at Derek with hatred. "You're just lucky that I need two more samples from you, before I cut you open, or I would end your miserable life right now. Lying to me as you did, you fucking asshole." Derek began to laugh, despite how much it hurt to. All those damned battered facial muscles he had to use for the spontaneous levity caused by the absurd outrage of this murderous liar.

"You are a piece of work, you know that, man? Talk about lying. Luring me out here to kill me with a ton of lies. You deserve it and worse."

"Well, we'll see which tune you sing, when the knife begins to cut your diseased sex organ away. Yes, we'll see, then." He knew he would, but just then he felt something. It was only the second time he'd felt the urge. Stall.

"If I'm so diseased, how come you want mine? It should be loaded with virus. Did you think of that?"

"Of course. The sperm I've taken from you is harmless, when processed into the body lotion. It is effective, but any virus in it is long dead by the time I apply it. Nice try, though."

"But my other bodily fluids are more problematical, huh?"

"Don't get any more ideas, or I will deal with you so severely, you'll spend your final hours praying for death."

"I already am," he said, sincerely, through lips rapidly losing their abilities to pronounce words.

He stepped forward and took Derek's penis into his hand. He began to masturbate him, watching his captive closely. He saw the look come over the boy's face. "What the...?" He followed Derek's gaze down to the boy's cock, which he held pointing up, and he had no time to react to the sudden gush of urine hitting his face. He let go of the hose immediately, but it was too late. His eyes stung from the acidic fluid, and his nose had taken a direct hit, too. He was inhaling it and sneezing it and crying as he staggered from the room.

Tethered helplessly to his death beam, Derek tried to console himself that he'd given it his best shot. Then he hoped that there was a God and that He wasn't deaf.

They knew that it would be an exercise in futility, but they decided to try it anyway. When the door opened, Bambi recognized the graying, balding man as the one, who had ushered Derek into the house. His eyes were bloodshot, as if he was on a bender. He looked as if he had just showered. "Hi, my name is Bambi. I'm a friend of Derek's. He left his comb at my apartment, when he visited me the other day before coming here. I'd like to give it to him."

"I'm sorry, miss, but I don't know anyone named Derek. This friend of yours visited you and told you he was coming to visit me?"

"Why, yes. You're Adrian Jordan, aren't you?"

"No, I'm not. Now, if you'll excuse me, I don't talk to strangers playing games. Goodbye."

"But... you're not Adrian Jordan?"

"No, indeed. And I don't know a Derek, either. Did this Derek give you my address?"

"I thought this was the address. I'm sorry. I guess I heard it wrong."

"Yes, you most certainly did."

"Hello." Testy, testy, Jesse thought, as he, himself, gripped the receiver tightly.

"Hi, I'm looking for Derek Brown. This is his roommate in New York. This is Adrian Jordan, right?"

"No, it is not! And I don't know a Derek Brown, whoever you are. How did you get my number?"

"I found your name in Derek's saved Internet files. There was one with your name on it. Then I called directory assistance. They gave me the number. 555-3256?"

"No. You've dialed 555-3257. Obviously, you have the wrong number."

"Gee, I'm sorry to have bothered you, sir. A long distance call wasted." He hung up.

He'd saved their conversations? How? And if he had, the man, who just called, would find his address. Wait. He said he found only one file. That was bad, but it didn't prove anything, because he was not Adrian Jordan. Still, the woman showing up at his place and the phone call right afterward were too coincidental. He needed to make the last two milkings as soon as possible. And he'd have to forego any more punishment for the moment. He'd inflict serious pain just before he killed him.

"Your friend Bambi stopped by," he said, as he slapped the duct tape over Derek's mouth. That would prevent any more spitting incidents. He saw the boy's eyes get wide at the mention of the girl's name. He grasped the handsome cock and masturbated it with his hand. "You didn't tell me that you had friends here. Why didn't you tell me about Bambi, Derek?" Muffled protests piled up behind the closed mouth like a chain-reaction car crash. "Why did you give her my address, Derek? I specifically asked you to keep it confidential." He closed his eyes. Despite himself, he was erect, and the hand on him felt oh, so good. He tried to imagine that it was Jess's hand, but he couldn't concentrate well enough to bring his image completely to the fore. "No matter. The police can search every inch of this house after you're gone, and they won't find a trace of you, Derek. Not one single clue that you were ever here. I'm meticulous in my preparations and executions. I leave nothing to chance." Of course. The living room. How obsessively neat it was kept. Still.... "Your friend and roommate can have all of the suspicions in the world, and they will count for nothing, because no one will be able to prove that you ever set foot into this house." Jess? Had Jess called? He must be worried about him. He cared.

He came in several jolting shots, and the plug fucked him incrementally. His captor left him to wonder about Jess and Bambi and whether or not they could get here before he was killed.

"Hello?"
"Mister Jordan?"
"Yes."
"This is Jesse Montalban. I spoke with you a couple of nights

ago."

"Yes, and I told you that I didn't know your friend. Why are you bothering me again?"

"Do you by any chance know someone named Charles Bedlington?" There was silence on the line for several seconds.

"How do you know Chuck?"

"I don't, but my roommate, Derek, does. He's at his house." More silence. Then,

"Oh, dear."

"May I come over to your place, please? It's a matter of life and death, I think."

"Yes, of course. Do you have my address?"

He replaced the receiver. Bambi had just walked up to the pay phone around the corner. "Bedlington denied everything, of course. But Jordan seems to know him. He's all that we have. Let's go." Adrian Jordan's house was a little farther north toward Wrigley Field, but it was within reasonable walking distance of Bedlington's. Jesse wondered how much Jordan really knew about Bedlington. And whether or not they might be walking into a trap, themselves.

Thirteen

"So, do you think he might help us somehow," Brandon asked.

"I hate to be pessimistic about it, but I don't see how."

"But maybe he'll know something about this guy that we can use to free Derek," Bambi said.

"Maybe," he replied, unconvincingly.

Bambi saw that Adrian Jordan was about the same age as Bedlington, but he was better preserved facially. They were ushered into the living room, which was expensively furnished, although indirect lighting and cheerful colors prevented the room from looking stuffy. He was not the perfect host either. He didn't offer them refreshments. Of course, they were strangers, who might be trying to pull something on him. If that were the case, having served refreshments to flim-flam artists would look mighty foolish. And Jesse could possibly pass for being a gypsy, if one gave his dark features only a cursory look. And we all know about those people. Don't we? Adrian Jordan perched on the edge of his wing chair. "So, what is this all about?" Jesse filled him in on what they knew.

Just then a young man with jaw-length brown hair, parted in the middle, entered the room carrying a silver tea service. "This is Wally," Jordan said with pride in his voice.

"Where's the Beav?" Jesse asked and realized what he said, when Jordan glared at him. Wally thought it was funny. Points to him.

"I assure you, Mr...."

"Montalban."

"...Mr. Montalban, that Wally is here of his own free will. It is serendipity when an older man meets a younger one, and their feelings are mutual." Wally finished pouring the tea and perched himself on the arm of Jordan's chair. "He's right. We're lucky." The smile was genuine, Bambi thought. At least Jordan didn't appear to be a kidnapper.

"Does Charles Bedlington like young guys?"

"You must understand that I know him only from meeting and seeing him on field trips sponsored by the Audubon Society. We are not close friends."

"But you reacted, when I told you my roommate, Derek, was at his place. What else do you know about him?"

"Well, I have seen him in the Rusty Screw on several occasions. That is, before I met Wally. He seemed to go for younger men, too, but they didn't give him the time of day."

"He's a creep. He came on to me once. He's ugly and his eyes looked weird up close. Like unnatural, you know?"

"Unnatural?"

"Yeah, like he wasn't right in the head. I never knew him to ever take any kid home. He must be one frustrated pecker."

"It's worse than that, if our hunch is right," Jesse said, becoming impatient that this was going to lead nowhere.

"Mr. Montalban thinks that Chuck has kidnapped his roommate."

"Wow, really? I wouldn't put it past him."

"Why not?"

"Well, it was weird. I remember one night last year. I was at the Screw and so was he. There were two cute guys who were there. He approached the one and I heard him call the creep a troll. The guys both laughed. It was obvious that the creep was furious."

"And then what happened?"

"That night? Nothing. Except that in a few days they both disappeared. Both are still listed as missing. I wonder if he could have done it."

"I believe it, considering that Derek's got to be there. Is...."

"That's it!" Brandon. "Are there any other boys missing besides them, Wally?"

"Well, yeah. About twenty that we heard of. Eight used to go to the Screw, I was told. The others, I don't know."

"So, that's why he's on the Internet now. He can't keep kidnapping boys from the bars he frequents, because it could cast suspicion on him. So, he lures unsuspecting guys by computer. That's how he met Derek."

"It does make sense," Jordan said. "But we have no proof."

"The proof is inside that house, and we have to figure out a way to get in there," Jesse said.

He found the red light especially grisly now, reminding him of the color of his blood, which would be flowing into the drain beneath him, from a gaping hole, which would be made under the base of his penis. So, he kept his eyes closed. If he had one last wish, it would be to tell Jesse that he loved him. But wishes weren't granted in a cold, soundproofed basement room in the house of a mass murderer of boys. At least he knew that Jess was concerned about him. That was comforting. He wished that Jess loved him. But that's why he had ended up here, and it wasn't his roommate's fault. Bambi was right. Love is so infrequently requited. He tried to think of something appropriate for the moment from one of the poets, but his rote memory wasn't functioning. Well, surprise. He felt prayed out, too. Either God had gotten the message or He hadn't. He decided to concentrate his thoughts on Jess. His beautiful face. His dynamite body. The cock he found so exquisite and its counterpart, hanging low, like a bull, under it. His sense of humor. His....

"Well, Derek of the angelic body, your last contribution is due, and another angel shall be blowing the trumpet for you shortly. Such a gorgeous boy. It's a shame to have to grind you up, but I will be most careful, considering that you are racked by plague. Such a shame. But happily, you won't suffer the horrible death so many of your ilk do." Bleeding to death as a gelding wasn't horrible? Knowing that your come generators were going to end up in the stomach of the person you hate most in the world? That wasn't horrible? "So, in my own way, I'm an angel, too. One of mercy to save you pain." As if getting your balls cut off will be a walk in Painfree Park. Right. Getting kicked in them had been painful enough. No pain, no gain did not apply in that excruciating case. Oh, jeez, now he was playing with them. If only they had teeth and could bite off his fingers. Or maybe he'd choke on them, trying to swallow them whole. It was a thought worth holding. "You have a lovely penis, Derek. So pretty. Such lovely lines. I'll bet it's seen many boys' behinds. Which, alas, is where you contracted your contagious little disease, no doubt. Or were you a cocksucker? I shouldn't be surprised, given those luscious lips of yours. It's a pity that they have to be hidden behind the tape. Yes, I can see those lips on nubile, male organs, coaxing them to fill your mouth with their potent cream. The potency of youth. But I wax poetic." Derek rolled his eyes, but the gesture went unnoticed. "I feel you throbbing, Derek. You adore my hand on you, don't you? And my fingers teasing your sac. The loving touch only an older man can give to a young one. If only they hadn't scorned me, Derek. If only you hadn't. In your case I might have relented, fallen under the spell of your angelic countenance. But what if I had? You would have infected me. So I'm doing the world and myself a favor. I wish that I could milk you forever, while enjoying your comeliness. Ah, I feel your sac contracting. You are going to give it up to me one last time, aren't you, dear boy? You shudder under my expert touch. That's what none of them understands, certainly not the ones who called me a troll. They couldn't comprehend that the hands and mouth, and yes, dare I say it, the cock of an older man knows how to give pleasure far more adroitly than youths desperate for orgasms. But they learn too late. You, dear Derek, have felt my abilities, and even now you are beginning to boil over. Come to me, Derek. Give me the penultimate offering to make me young again." Helpless to disobey, Derek's balls released their fluid and sent it hurtling up and out of his shaft.

When he'd collected every last drop, he put down the container and went behind Derek somewhere. He returned seconds later. He felt his scrotum being tugged down and something snapped onto him. "It's a ball stretcher, in the vernacular, Derek. It pushes down the testicles." It sure did. It hurt like a banshee. "It will make it easier for the knife to separate you from your precious jewels. And that will happen after I bathe in you one last time. Soon, Derek. Soon, you will be free of earthly bonds. I will be back anon." He was a dead man.

Fourteen

It was not something that Wally would ever have wanted to admit, especially in front of Adrian. And it hadn't been well received by his shocked lover. But, what the hell. He was young and reasonably attractive. There were other rich men, who would gladly take him into their beds and make him their heirs. So, he told them what his specialty had been, until he had gotten caught. Adrian could deal with it or not. With that, they were out of the house and running to Bambi's car, a shaken Adrian Jordan bringing up the rear.

As he sat in the tub, applying the potent combination of fresh rose water, glycerine, herbs and Derek's semen to his skin, he thought how much younger he would look, thanks to the helpless boy in the basement. He really would have liked to keep him longer, as he had wanted to with Jeremiah. But the text was prescriptive. Not one application more nor less. And he could see the difference in the days that Derek had been here. Such a noticeable difference. He hoped that it would be the same with Steve and John. Yes, too bad he couldn't keep Derek. Both he and Jeremiah had given him so much of the fruit of their bodies. And they were so different. Jeremiah, as dark as the night, and Derek, as light as the day. But they each served their purpose. They were making him into Dreamboy, again.

He was feeling weak. How long had he been strung up? Days probably. No wonder he was weak. When had he last eaten? Despite how feeble he felt, he was hurting like a bitch below. That ball whatever Dreamboy had called it. He had to distract himself. He didn't want pain to be his final experience in life. So, he concentrated on Jesse. He saw him wearing his wave cap. At first he thought that it was a pseudo-homeboy thing, something that Jess did just to annoy him. But he found out that it was a part of the ghetto, which he needed to hold on to. Once Derek understood that, he accepted it. In fact, he liked being fucked while Jess was wearing it. And when he was wearing his big black leather jacket. Maybe his roommate was into leather more than he was aware. He loved having Jess fuck him. That cock of his was always hard, it seemed. What a great piece of meat it was, too. So majestic, rising above those bull balls hanging in a smooth skin. What an unbelievably sexy guy he was, and what a nice guy besides. His fuck buddy: Jesse. He cried for his loss until exhaustion overtook him.

The two heads at the back door were sitting ducks, if someone was in the darkened kitchen and saw movement behind the sheer curtains. But the room was empty. They watched for several minutes, and just when Wally was ready to put the pick into the lock, they saw movement at the far end of the hall. They watched as the shape came toward them. It was back-lit by a light in the entry hall, so they couldn't make out more than its outline. They ducked as the form came into the kitchen, fearing that a light would be switched on. But it wasn't. With trepidation they peered over the sill of the window in time to see the figure going down the basement stairs. "Around to the front," Wally whispered. They took off around the house as fast as they could.

Adrian looked eastward and Bambi stood sentry to the west. Brandon was on the next to the top step, crouched, ready to sprint into the house. Wally worked as patiently as he could, all the while feeling that his two acquaintances from the Rusty Screw had once been where the troll had been going. He remembered those eyes. "Demonic," that was it.

"Demonic what?"

"His eyes."

"We know that. Can't you hurry?"

He looked at Jesse with exasperation. "No, I can't. It takes time."

"Just what we don't have."

He busied himself at the lock. "Just shut up. I need to listen." Hard. Lock picking was not an exact science. Especially on those used by paranoids. Like this Schlage, damn the troll.

"It really has been a pleasure having you here, Derek, even taking into account your defiant behaviors, trying to infect me with your disease. But I should have known. The best looking are the feistiest. Jeremiah was, too. So unlike you. But just as beautiful in his own way. And it excites me to know that, because his testicles were the sweetest I've ever tasted. None of the others compared to his. And large. Oh, my. I savored them for the longest time that evening. I suspect that yours will be as succulent. Yes, I know you won't fail me, darling Derek. You won't fail to please me after your death. Of course, you'll be long gone, bodily. But that is when I will savor the last of you. Oh, I should so like to kiss your lips once more, but you would be rash, knowing that your end is seconds away. Alas. I missed that opportunity with Jeremiah, too. Such full lips. Such wonderfully kissable lips. Those like mine are lost in those like his. And yours."

Derek was disoriented. He saw the figure before him, but his eyes weren't focusing. The guy seemed to be masked. And he wasn't naked. He had something white on. He came closer now, and Derek saw that it was some kind of bizarre mask, like some African or South American thing. No Romantic poet had ever worn one of them. Their gain. "You see, I never let my contributors see the final salutary effects of the regeneration they've provided. The text says that it's bad luck. So I hide myself, coquettishly, as the Angel of Mercy. The natives called it 'kinkqua koo', but what's in a name? Pity that your friends didn't care enough to save you, isn't it?" Yes, he thought, and the thought hurt. It was like a knife to his heart. They'd given up. Even Jess. The man he loved had abandoned him. It was time for him to give up, too. His executioner had won.

His mind was going again, not that it mattered now. The

sounds of buffalo stampeding rose in his ears. Why not? It might as well be the Wicked Witch of the West coming to put him out of his misery. Why not buffalo? Then he remembered something Bambi had alluded to. He was right. With ebbing strength, he barely was able to touch his heels together while he thought, there's no place like home.

The knife blade caught his waning attention, glinting red in the light. He looked at the instrument of his death. So be it. He couldn't get to Kansas, which was a blessing in itself. "Now, you won't feel anything after the initial pain. And I'll talk to you all the while you're dying, Derek. Goodbye, my beautiful, corrupted angel." He felt the skin prick. His eyes went wide open. He was hallucinating for sure. He saw Jesse in the shimmering red light.

Fifteen

Jesse yelled, "You motherfucker!" It caused the blade to recoil from Derek's scrotum. He wheeled, raising the blade, but not before Jesse had his arm around Bedlington's neck and his hand pulling at the arm with the upraised weapon. Bedlington's feral screams were met with Brandon's kick to the groin through the diaphanous white gown he wore. His blade arm wrenched free from Jesse's hold, and he stabbed himself with the knife, as his hands sought to cover his insulted genitals. Bambi and Wally tried in vain to free Derek, as his life force steadily dripped into the drain meant for all of it. "We need a key, Jesse."

He flung off the mask and pulled the troll up by the neck of the gown. His eyes were lolling in his head. "Where are the keys, motherfucker?" The eyes disappeared behind another mask; his eyelids. Jesse turned to Derek and saw the blood. He found its source and put his thumb in the wound to stanch the flow. "Dreek? Dreek?"

"Gato. It is you."

"I'm here."

"Too late."

"No. Just in time. I love you, Dreek."

"Oh, God, Gato, Gato....."

Sixteen

As Adrian had promised, as out of breath as he'd been from climbing the stairs and running to find a phone and running back down the stairs to announce his having called emergency so that he was barely understandable, the Chicago police force and medical units descended on the house. After all, Adrian Jordan was an alderman, albeit for Boys Town. Forget the 'albeit'. Adrian Jordan was an alderman. That would be a member of the city council to Jesse and Derek. Now you know how to get your emergency phone calls responded to promptly. Run successfully for alderman. Or was that unfair?

The medics, along with Bambi and Wally, had to pry Jesse from Derek Brown in order to treat him. Officers used hacksaw blades to free him from his cross. The scene was controlled chaos.

Wally figured his B & E could be seen as heroism. After all, he'd saved Derek's life. Well, he hadn't. They could have broken the window on the front door, which he was getting ready to do, as exasperated as the Schlage people made him, and as he had during his less honorable years. But that could have signalled their presence sooner, causing Jesse to lose Derek. And he had no doubt that Derek's death would destroy Jesse, as the world knew him. So, he was relieved that he'd conquered the fucking lock and saved Derek, after all.

Jesse rode in the ambulance with Derek. Bambi, Adrian, Brandon and Wally followed.

As competent as Jesse had been in stopping the external flow, it didn't prevent Derek from being taken into emergency surgery for internal bleeding. His scrotum looked as if he were suffering from the early stages of Elephantitis, by the time he arrived at the hospital.

Charles Bedlington, one-time pretty boy and recently embittered holder of a dwindling countenance, died from the accidental self-infliction of the instrument of Derek's presumed death.

Seventeen

He had spent many hours in the hospital talking with the police. Countless heads asking endless questions, which always left him exhausted. It frustrated him, because he wanted to spend his time exclusively with Jesse. But he realized that he had an obligation to do whatever he could to help the families of the dead boys find their loved ones' remains, however remote that possibility would be. Therefore, he endured the detectives and their inquiries. And the doctors and nurses and psychiatrist. Actually he liked the shrink, whose name was Bohner. Upon introducing himself, the good doctor was treated to a gale of laughter, which caused Derek to cough spasmodically and threatened to loosen his stitches. "Is that called gallows humor, Doc?"

"In your case, I would say that it was appropriately-named." And Bohner, himself, laughed at the irony of his name, given Derek Brown's recent genital predicament.

Bambi had taken off on another round of presentations, because, no matter the headlines generated by the horrific misadventures of one person, the lives of the rest of the world went on as usual, perforce. Brandon had accepted Bambi's invitation to see some of the heartland, and Jesse and Derek had no doubt that they were enjoying their version of the Hope and Crosby road movies, this one appropriately titled, *The Road to Des Moines*.

Jesse never left Derek's side, unless it was to go to the bathroom or to complain to the nurses about some deficiency in their care of his lover. Once they knew the story of the two, they took Jesse's idiosyncracies with good humor and amusement. During his stay there, the other bed in the semi-private room was unused. So the nurses allowed Jesse to sleep in it. They also ordered meals for the non-existent patient in bed B, so that the boys could eat their meals together.

They would laugh recalling the day Derek's surgeon pronounced him well enough to resume "marital relations,", as he put it. "Great. Give us ten minutes alone, doctor," Jesse had exclaimed. Whereupon, the doctor scribbled a note and taped it onto the closed door to the room. Jesse pulled down the covers and lifted Derek's gown. He took Derek into his mouth deliberately and made his pleasure last as long as he could. It was the first time he'd ever sucked Derek's cock. After the patient came, he kissed him and said, "Things are going to be a lot different from now on, Dreek. Good different."

Bambi and Brandon's return coincided with Derek's release from the hospital, so they went to the Thai restaurant in Boys Town to celebrate. The aromas of food were especially enticing to him, because it seemed like ages since he'd had anything but white bread American cooking. Not that the hospital food had been bad. It had satisfied his hungry palate nicely. But he and Jesse were used to what they called "Melting Pot Noshing," a different ethnic cuisine just about every night of the week. And he hadn't had Thai for some time.

"Well, I must say that your fame helped me tremendously on this trip, dearie."

"How's that?"

"Well, even in Des Moines and Waterloo you were big news. So when the prospective clients found out that I knew you, they were impressed. Well, I did fib a little bit and told them I rescued you."

"That wasn't a fib. You did save my life."

"Well, I said I did it singlehandedly." The guys broke up.

"And didn't even chip a nail," Jesse said. He turned to look out the large window next to the table. He loved to observe people, and this was great place to view his brothers. Boys Town reminded him of the Village, where he and Derek were going to live one of these days. Then he saw him.

Without a word, he was up and out the door. "Where in the world...." Bambi asked.

"That's Gato. He must have spotted somebody prettier." His tablemates laughed at the absurdity of Derek's statement.

Today he had on a colorful striped hooded pullover with white jeans. "Sir. Excuse me, sir." The young man turned around.

"Yes?"

"Uh, those are great boots you're wearing. I was wondering where you got them." A conversation ensued and they introduced themselves. Then Jesse invited the young man to join them for dinner, and he accepted.

"Hey, guys, this is Glenn Beamon. I invited him to eat with us. And take a look at those boots he's wearing, Dreek, because you're going to have a pair just like them, before we leave town."

As the meal went on, it was obvious that Bambi was becoming more and more interested in the engaging brown-skinned man. Jesse noticed and leaned toward Glenn's ear. "She's really a guy, not a fag hag."

Brandon heard him and said, "Aye, and rescued Derek singlehandedly." They laughed again. "She also chased the snakes out of Ireland."

"I'm not that old," Bambi said, and hit the Irishman with her clutch. The comment about the rescue left Glenn clueless, so they regaled him with their daring deed.

"It was like the just-in-time delivery thing automakers do now," Jesse said.

"Hardly. I already had the knife sticking in my scrotum. But thanks for comparing me to a car, Jess."

"Come on, Dreek, you know what I meant."

"No, but what else is new?"

Bambi saw them off at the airport. He had been a great host, not allowing them to pay for anything during their stay. Except for the hospital bill, which Derek's student health insurance would mostly cover. The guys, well, Jesse did end up getting Bambi a hostess gift of sorts. Glenn also saw them off. This had been the adventure of a lifetime, Derek thought, as the jetliner roared into the sky. And almost a very short lifetime, at that. He put his head on Jesse's shoulder. But almost didn't count this time.

Eighteen

When they entered their modest apartment, Derek truly felt that there was no place like home. They spent several minutes kissing in the first relaxed private moment since their reunion. Then Jesse said, "Now, raise your right hand and repeat after me. Raise your hand, Dreek. Okay. I Derek Kevin Brown."

"I Derek Kevin Brown."

"Do solemnly swear."

"Do solemnly swear."

"That I will never."

"That I will never."

"Ever."

"Ever."

"Surf the Net for the remainder of my natural life."

"Never ever?"

"Get that hand up. Say it."

"Oh, all right. Surf the Net for the remainder of my natural life."

"Good. You may kiss the judge."

"Fat chance. Get that right hand of yours up. All right, repeat after me."

"All right repeat after me."

"Look, asshole, I played along with your little game. Actors." He rolled his eyes. "I Jesse Felix Montalban."

"I Jesse Felix Montalban."

"Do solemnly swear."

"Do solemnly swear."

"That I will love, honor and cherish."

"That I will love, honor and cherish."

"Derek Kevin Brown."

"Derek Kevin Brown."

"For the remainder of my natural life."

"For the remainder of my natural life." He was grinning widely. "Okay, your turn."

"My turn what? Are you kidding? I already swore off the Internet. That's a much bigger deal than swearing fidelity to you."

"Why you shit."

"And you swore to love the shit, remember?"

"Why did I bother to rescue you?"

"Because I, Derek Kevin Brown, love you, Jesse Felix Montalban with all my heart and promise to for the remainder of my natural life. That's why."

"Yeah, that's why. Can we kiss now?"

"Only if you promise to fuck me silly afterward."

As Jesse sank into him, he leaned over and kissed Derek. "Mmm. It's so much better this way."

"It's called making love."

"I think I can get the hang of it."

"I have no doubt. You feel so good, Jess."

"Likewise. Do I really have to honor and cherish you, too?"

"Yes, because otherwise, I'll go back onto the Net."

"You promised not to."

"And you promised to love, honor and cherish me."

"We didn't use a Holy Bible."

"Gee, I'm sure glad the modem still works."

"You shit."

"You can't blame me for your taste in spouses."

Jesse grinned. "Oh, but I can."

"Okay. Guilty, your honor."

"You may love the judge." Jesse encircled Derek's shaft with his hand as he kissed and fucked him. Derek sighed into his mouth. It really was Jess's hand this time. Happiness spread through him from the intimate contact with his roommate. The warmth of love enveloped him. Then the warmth of orgasm, as they came together.

"So what do you think," Jesse asked.

"That red is definitely your color. Bambi would be proud. Maybe you should paint them black, when you're the leather slave."

"Only if you do, too, when you're the Master."

"Masters don't wear nail polish."

"He spends a night with a leather boy and he's an expert. Give me a break. Do you think it was excessive doing the toenails, too?"

"Nope. Gives you a balanced look. I like it."

"Just think. We have a whole new life, because of your little adventure."

"Little? Little?! Man, and it turned out it was one adventure I never needed to have."

"But we made new friends. And Brandon got a boyfriend out of it."

"I almost got killed!"

"That was your fault. Well, and mine, too. Sorry, Dreek. I am. But you made it back intact."

"With about five seconds to spare. Somehow I can't see you loving a eunuch, as oversexed as you are."

"But you're not a eunuch. However, you are my golden boy, even if you do have dark hair."

"No, no, go not to..."

"Don't start. Do you like your boots?"

"Love them. Glenn has excellent taste."

"So do I, if I do say so myself."

"You usually do. You know, Glenn is really racking up those frequent flyer miles visiting Brandon almost every weekend."

"Yeah, and watching his savings account dwindle. I hope those two make up their minds soon."

"It would be great to have him here."

"So do you promise to swear off any more adventures?"

"All except this one," he said, and then he kissed Jesse.

"That's a relief."

"Well, why would I roam anymore, now that I know what I have here."

"And what's that?"

"You. My Gato. My *real* dreamboy."

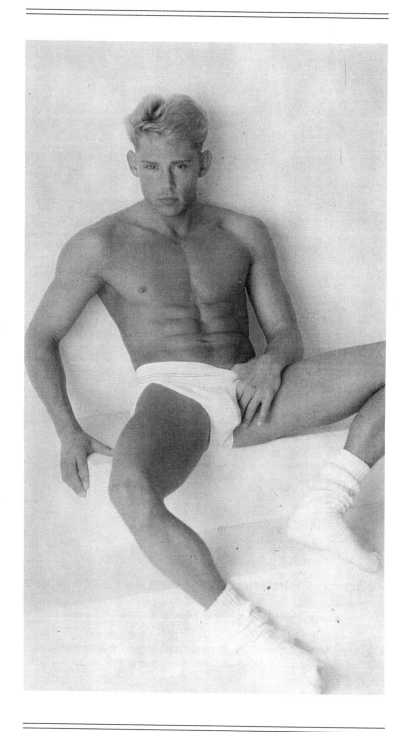

Photo on the preceding page of Kevin Kramer is from his personal archive. Kevin's life story, plus dozens of great photos, is featured in the book *Beautiful Boys*, available from STARbooks Press (see page 551).
Fans may also visit Kevin's personal site on the world-wide web at martinryter.com, or call 818-374-3698.

"Help yourself and heaven will help you."
— La Fontaine, "Fables"

HEAVEN SENT ME

A Series of Erotic Adventures of The Saint by JOHN PATRICK

STARbooks Press
Sarasota, Florida

The Saint first appeared to mortals in the STARbooks anthologies "Runaways/Kid Stuff," "In the Boy Zone," "Mad About the Boys," and "Smooth 'N' Sassy," and those tales are included here.

CONTENTS

Reported Sightings

YOUNG & BEAUTIFUL
ALMOST ANONYMOUS
INTRIGUE
THE TOUCH OF A STRANGER

First Hand Accounts

A KIND OF MADNESS
SMOOTH 'N' SASSY
SHORT 'N' SWEET
THERE SHOULD HAVE BEEN MUSIC...
THE HAPPY HITCHHIKER
HEAVENLY HEAD
PUPPY LOVE
FEAR OF FLYING: THE NEW RECRUIT

INTRODUCTION

Back in the '70s when I was discovering the joys of gay sex, I was fortunate enough to spend many wonderful hours with so many beautiful strangers I came to think of them as angels, boys who came to my mercy in a time of need.

This concept was the basis for the books that became *Angel: The Complete Quintet*. As I stated when I originally wrote those books in the late '80s, to most mortals, angels are nebulous, androgynous beings hovering on the uncertain fringes of spirituality and imagination.

Experiences that smack of angelic intervention leave both wonder and doubt in their wake. Was it a celestial messenger or helpful stranger? Was the close scrape coincidence or the hand of a higher power? Was its source sinister or heavenly?

The same might be said of saints. Or, those who appear to be saints. "Saints, real saints, are magical. They are luminous, transparent, irresistible," said writer Andrew M. Greeley. "They enchant us, enthrall us, captivate us. They seem to be qualitatively different from the rest of humankind. They attract us not by preaching, much less by screeching, but by radiant goodness, irrepressible cheerfulness and devastating love. We are compelled to follow them, not because of what they say but because of who they are. Our aim is not necessarily to do what they do but, rather, to try to be what they are."

While there is little I have in common with the Catholic church, I do like their ideas about sainthood. They make it possible for us to acknowledge angelic beings right here on earth. In this new collection I created the character of the sexual miracle worker Terry not as an angel, but as a saint, which seemed appropriate since Pope John Paul has elevated more people toward sainthood than all of his 20th century predecessors. The *La Stampa* newspaper reported that nearly 1,000 have been canonized or beatified, the next to last step before becoming a saint. For some, this is too many: "The Vatican has become a saint factory," said 85-year-old Cardinal Silvio Oddi in recently published memoirs. He urged the Vatican to be more strict in considering miracles attributed to candidates. Generally, two miracles ruled as having occurred through the candidate's intercession are required for canonization."

Photographer Arnold put it best when he said, "I think of most people as being angels. We're surrounded by angels and we're all trying to catch on to them. But before we do we have to remember that to find an angel, we first have to be one."

And, of course, that goes for saints as well.

Angels aren't for ravishing—unless it's quick.
Just drag him straight into the entrance hall
Shove your tongue right down his throat and stick
Your finger up him, turn him to the wall
And when he's good and moist, lift up his gown
And fuck him. Should he groan as if in pain
Hold him hard, bring him on; once, and again—
That way he'll lack the strength to strike you down.

Remind him that he has to move his butt
And tell him he can go ahead and touch
Your balls, that he must just let go and come
While earth and sky are slipping from his clutch—
But while you're fucking don't look on his face
And see his wings unruffled stay in place.

- *"Thomas Mann" by Bertolt Brecht*

Reported Sightings

THE YOUNG & THE BEAUTIFUL

"Before we get carried away," Peter said, "we thought we might just remind you of the rules for All Soul's Day."
Terry shook his head. "I know the rules...."
"Yes, of course. But just to remind you, you must ascend after sundown on November the 2nd and all worldly possessions must be left behind. Please don't take a bottle with you."
"For goodness sake...."
"Don't get huffy! Do you remember Evangelina? She went down for All Soul's Day. Had a good time. Drank as much as she could before ascending to the blue. Poor thing forgot all the rules of the holiday and tried to bring back a bottle of champagne."
Terry chuckled. This was goodhearted sport on Peter's part, but there was a seriousness to it as well. Terry had been through this many times. No matter where he was, it seemed, no one had any real confidence in him, mainly, he felt, because he was so young and so beautiful. But, they conceded, his attributes certainly made his job easier.

It was All Souls' Day, 1975: a day of solemn prayer for all dead persons, and the bells rang. But Terry didn't hear them. He was sitting on a stool in a bar on Bourbon Street in New Orleans.

The man next to him, Archer, was "drinking his lunch," and expounding on sainthood. Terry had told the man he was named after Mother Teresa. This always got a good conversation going, but this one today was an especially lively one.

"It seems to me," Archer was railing on, "saints are a fraud by definition: once called saints, they cease to be."

"Oh?"

"You know, become known, like on TV."

"I don't watch much TV," Terry said, staring at the TV over

the bar, now playing a music video.

"I think saintliness should be unrecognized. *And that,*" he concluded, "is the longest speech I have ever made on a religious subject in my life. The longest and, I promise you, the last."

"Good." Terry had the bartender bring Archer a cup of strong coffee. "Sainthood bores me," Terry said, "and that's a fact."

"I don't know what the fuck got into me," Archer said.

"If I didn't know better," Terry remarked, "I'd say you had too much to drink."

"I'm sorry. It's my birthday, such as it is. Oh, I don't want to make myself out as some pitiful object. My wife, may she rest in peace, had a theory about hitting forty. She thought of it as a time to begin again, if one would just let it happen."

Terry smiled. "She sounds like my kind of woman."

"Oh, she was. She was the best."

Terry saluted Archer with his coffee mug, "Happy birthday."

"Thank you. And Happy All Soul's to you," Archer said.

Archer couldn't help himself. He loved his dead wife madly, entirely, had promised to be hers alone till he died. But he couldn't help it: All thoughts of her, the little fair beauty, all demure delicacy, were obliterated by Terry, with his bold radiance, his promise of a good time.

Archer took Terry back to his dreary rooms on Frenchmen Street in the Faubourg-Marigny district.

They had brandies and Terry told Archer what he wanted to celebrate this feast day: to be fucked by Archer's ten-inch dick.

"How did you know I have a ten-incher?"

"Your hands, your fingers. I've had practice."

How *much* practice Archer could never have imagined, but Terry in the nude with his ass high in air was a sight that would have gotten many a man going, even a tired-out old drunk like Archer. Terry played with his hole, applied some grease. Terry was teasing Archer unmercifully and Archer was loving it. Archer stripped and climbed on the bed.

"Oh, Jesus," he said, sinking his finger in the hole, "don't let me have a heart attack! Let me live to see my next birthday party!"

Tensing his legs, he could feel the power thrust in his muscular thighs as he began. Soon he had the massive head and a couple of inches of shaft in and Terry was taking it real good. And with Terry squirming, Archer lunged, deep.

"I try to come, but I can't. Nobody can get me off. No woman, no man, not even myself, so you just go ahead, enjoy yourself."

"Don't worry so much," came Terry's voice, deep. He rolled over and Archer hung Terry's legs over his shoulders. Terry caressed Archer's back, and Archer began humping even harder, tears of sweat sliding down his face.

Then something miraculous began to happen. Archer felt a change come over him. It started like a slow-moving train, pulling him inexorably, building evenly, coming on, coming on, coming on, as if wheels were rolling, rolling, and actually going somewhere! There was an incredible *feeling* coming through him. And a bright lightbulb of realization snapped on inside his brain. "This is it! I'm actually gonna come! It ain't gonna stop!" It was an incredibly uplifting experience. A fullness. An intense heat. Each of his thrusts brought him further ecstasy, his cock working inside Terry, hard. Soon he was at the height of heights. To satisfaction unlimited! "I'm having a birthday party!" Terry laughed at his quaint way of describing his orgasm.

After he finished coming, Archer lifted up and stared down at Terry's cock bouncing around as he continued to poke him. Then he pulled out his cock, glistening with cum. "I got something for you." He hopped out of bed, went to the dresser, got a huge pink plastic cock.

He had tried for years to get off with others. When he was with himself, he would use the Pink One, playing with himself, teasing his anus with the Pink One. But lately, not even that worked. But this night was proving different. Archer fingered Terry's butthole. He stuck one finger in, then two, in and out. Terry gasped for breath with the insertion of the Pink One. Then Terry took the faux cock and guided it in with his hand and began a slow thrust of his hips as Archer jammed it in, hard and firm.

Archer leaned over Terry, watching the boy's bouncing

erection. The expression on Archer's face meant business now. The orgasm he had enjoyed broke his resistance. His body let go; and so did his mind. Archer had another man's cock in his mouth for the first time and he loved it. Terry knew it wouldn't be the last time, either; Archer was busting out!

Terry kept pushing the Pink One in and out of his boy-pussy. With each thrust he got hotter and humped up his hips to meet Archer's suddenly eager mouth.

Then Terry spread his legs wider, and began a volley of his own.

"That a' boy," Archer muttered blissfully, body tense. "Come for Poppa!" The cock, flowing its juice onto Terry's washboard stomach, then onto the sheets, was glorious, Archer thought. He had never experienced this satisfaction right to the end. He had been like a kite tied to earth, his wife's memory a lead weight that wouldn't pass. Now he was free.

Aggressively he hooked his hands around Terry's thighs and pulled his cock, covered with cum, into his mouth. He started to suck it again. Working his lips, tongue hot on the kid's sex, licking, lapping, making a wet sound that caused Terry to scream, "Ohhhh!"

A low moan came from Archer as he lifted up to take the now-hard-again prick in his hand. "So good!" he said, and quickly returned to his job.

Another intense orgasm exploded from between Terry's legs, and Archer took it all. Finished, Archer wiped his mouth, went to the bathroom.

Terry heard noises: coughs and spitting.

When Archer came back out, Terry was dressed, ready to depart. "What's this? You're leaving me?"

"I must."

"No, please."

"Yes. My job is done."

"Job?"

"I was sent to persuade you."

"Sent?"

"For your birthday."

Archer didn't have time to reflect on this notion because Terry had wrapped him in his arms.

"Do you know," he whispered, his tongue flicking at his

ear, "why I was chosen to persuade you?"

"Because you are the best?"

"Oh, no." He laughed, a rippling breath on his neck. "Oh, no. I got this job so early in life, and I was never properly trained. See what I did with you? I slipped off into my own pleasure, when I should think only of yours—"

"Oh, but I *was* pleased, really. *Really, really* pleased."

Somewhere here was an answer to a question Terry had never thought to ask. "It is the same, isn't it? The pleasure, the joy? It is both ours."

"You can say that again."

Terry glanced up at him, a slanted look through those long, shadowy lashes. "You are too kind, Archer. No. I was chosen not because I am the best, but because I am the worst. The youngest, the most naive, the most distracted," he gulped. "The least adept at the arts of love."

"What? Man, that was the best sex I've ever had!"

"Really?"

Then Archer spoke aloud the thought that now finally formed in his mind. "My god, imagine what the others are like."

The others, Archer thought. The other hustlers who worked for this service that had sent Terry, what were *they* like? It had never occurred to him that there might be men available for such things. Before his marriage, he had picked up a tart or two in his prime, usually one of the transsexuals the city is famous for. Just intermittent loving, an occasional spell of peace, a few moments of sweet passion and tenderness. But these were never enough, always just an interlude, and soon forgotten. But this, *this* would never be forgotten.

"Must you go?" Archer protested as Terry left him standing in the middle of the bedroom, bewildered.

"Yes, I must. It's nearly dawn and I have to be in... eh, Rio by nightfall."

"Rio?" Archer was totally confused. "Like in Brazil?"

Terry nodded. Now he imagined Terry worked for a worldwide escort service, wandering the world an orphan, alone in life as he had been alone at birth, and he imagined that solitude was Terry's destiny. Archer could never have imagined the truth: that Terry, when he was offered another destiny, one that was his for the believing, he took it. And that now he could spend his life—or life after death, as it were—saving souls through sex.

ALMOST ANONYMOUS

"A color is almost never seen as it really is."
- Joseph Albers, Bauhaus theorist

The first thing Lars noticed about Detroit was the smell. Almost as soon as he stepped out onto the curb at the airport to catch a cab, he thought he smelled a fire. Back home in Sweden he associated this smell with autumn, and the first fires of winter, the smoke puffing out of chimneys. But here it was midsummer, and he couldn't see anything burning.

On the way into the city from the airport, with the windows of the cab rolled down and the hot air blowing in his face, he asked the driver about the smell.

"Cars," the driver said.

Lars, who spoke very precise school English, thought that perhaps he hadn't made himself understood. "No," he said. "I am sorry. I mean the burning smell. What is it?"

"Cars. They make cars here." The driver glanced in the rearview mirror. "Hey, where you from?"

"Sweden."

The driver nodded, and the cab took a sharp right turn off the freeway and entered the Detroit city limits. Through the left window Lars saw a huge electric billboard. In hundreds of small incandescent bulbs, which went on and off from left to right, was the slogan: "It's today's CHEVROLET!" The driver pointed with his left hand toward another electronic signboard, this one with a small windowless factory at its base. It advertised tires. When he gestured, the cab wobbled on the pot-holed roadway. "Cars and everything that goes in 'em. There's always a fire somewhere."

"But I don't see any fires," Lars said.

"That's right."

Lars sat back, feeling somehow defeated again by the American idiom. He had spent the past month with his Aunt Ingrid at Bear Lake, where she always spent her summers since coming to America many years before. Lars had looked forward to this vacation more than any other because he was curious about America, attracted by its disorderliness. Disorder, of which there was very little in Sweden, seemed incredibly sexy to him. He was intrigued most of all by the disorder in America about sexuality. Before he left the country he hoped to sleep with a very disorderly American in a very disorderly American bed. That was his ambition, why he decided to take an extra day in Detroit. He wondered if the experience would have any distinction so he might be able to go home and tell his friends about it.

In his hotel room, he changed into his best jeans, a light cotton shirt his aunt had bought for him, and a pair of running shoes. In the mirror, he thought he looked relaxed and handsome. The tan he had acquired from a month at the lake agreed with him. His vanity amused him, but he felt lucky to look the way he did, especially if he was going to meet a disorderly American. Back out on the sidewalk, he asked the doorman which direction he would recommend for a walk.

The doorman, who had curly gray hair and sagging pouches under his eyes, removed his cap and rubbed his forehead. He did not look back at Lars. "You want my recommendation? Don't walk anywhere. Just stay inside and watch TV." The doorman stared at a fire hydrant as he spoke.

"What about running?"

The doorman suddenly glanced at Lars, sizing him up. "You might be okay, if you run fast enough," he chuckled. "But to be safe, just stay inside."

"Is there a park here?"

"Sure, there's parks. Lotsa parks. What're you plannin' to do?"

Lars shrugged. "See the sights."

"You're seein' 'em," the doorman laughed. "Buy some postcards. Look, if you wanted sights, you shoulda gone to California—"

Lars thought that perhaps he had misunderstood again and had the doorman hail him a cab.

"Where to?" the driver asked.

"The park."

"*The* park?" The driver peered at Lars through the rearview mirror. "Which park?"

"Any park."

The driver nodded as if he understood, and maybe he did, because he deposited Lars at edge of Palmer Park, six miles north of downtown, near what passes for a gay ghetto in The Motor City.

Lars sauntered about for a while along the trails that wound through the bushes. He passed a few men. He found he liked the way Americans walked, with a purpose in their step, as if, having no particular goal, they still had an unconscious urgency to get somewhere.

At dusk, the light had a bluish-gold quality and the place looked like almost any city park to him, placid and decorative, a bit hushed. Lars didn't know what he was looking for but he sensed, sooner or later, he would find it. After about a half an hour, he passed a slender youth wearing white running shorts and a pale blue tank top. Leaning lazily against a tree, the boy, Lars decided, had just the right faraway look, just the right disorder about him. Lars thought he recognized this look. It meant that the boy was in a kind of suspension, between engagements. Lars put himself in his line of sight and said, in his heaviest accent, "A nice evening!"

The boy looked at him. "What did you say?"

"I said the evening is beautiful." He tried to sound as foreign as he could, the way Germans who visited Sweden always did. "I am a visitor here," he added quickly, "and not familiar with any of this." He motioned his arm to indicate the park.

"Not familiar?" the boy chuckled. "Not familiar with what?"

"Well, with this park. With the sky here. The people."

"Parks are the same everywhere," the boy said, leaning his hip against the tree. He looked at Lars with a vague interest. "And the sky is the same. Only the people are different."

"Yes? How?"

"Where you from?"

As Lars explained, the boy looked past him, toward the entrance to the park. "Okay," the boy said when Lars was finished. "But why are you *here*?"

"I came to see my aunt," he said. "Now I'm sightseeing."

"*Sightseeing?*" the boy laughed out loud, and Lars saw him arch his back and thrust out his pelvis. The gigantic bulge at his crotch seemed to flare in front of him. The boy's body had distinct athletic lines. "No one sightsees here. Didn't anyone tell you?"

"Yes. The doorman at the hotel. He told me not to come."

"But you did. How did you get here?"

"I came by taxi."

"You're joking," he said. Then he reached out and put his hand momentarily on Lars's shoulder. "You took a taxi to this park? How do you expect to get back to your hotel?"

"I suppose," he shrugged, "I will get another taxi."

"Oh no you won't," the boy said, and Lars felt himself pleased that things were working out so well. He noticed the boy's eyes: blue, or maybe green. They kept changing. Whatever their color, they sparkled brilliantly. Fireflies danced around them. No one had ever mentioned fireflies in Detroit. Night was coming on. He gazed up at the sky. Same stars, same moon as in Sweden.

"You're here *alone?*" the boy asked. "In America? In this city?"

"Yes," he said. "Why not?"

"People shouldn't be left alone in this country, and especially in Detroit," he said, leaning toward him with a kind of vehemence. "They shouldn't have left you here. It can get kind of weird, what happens to people. Didn't they tell you?"

"No, certainly not."

"Well, they should have."

"Who do you mean?" he asked. "You said, 'they.' Who is 'they'?"

"Any 'they' at all," he said. "Your guardians."

"I don't have any guardians."

The boy sighed. "All right. Come on. Follow me." He broke into a run. For a moment Lars thought that he was running away from him, then realized that he was expected to run with him, that perhaps it was what people did now in America, instead of holding hands, to get acquainted. He sprinted up next to him, and as he ran, the boy asked him, "Who are you?"

Being careful not to tire—the boy wouldn't like it if his endurance was poor—Lars told him his name, his interests, and he patched together a narrative about his mother, father, two sisters and his Aunt Ingrid. He told him that his aunt was eccentric and broke china by throwing it on the floor on

Fridays, which she called "the devil's day."

"Years ago, they would have branded her a witch," Lars said. "But she isn't a witch. She's just moody."

He watched the boy's reactions and noticed that he didn't seem too interested in his family, or any sort of background.

"Do you run a lot back home in Sweden?" the boy asked. "You look as if you're in pretty good shape."

He admitted that, yes, he ran, but that people in Sweden didn't run as often as they did in America.

"You look a little like that tennis star, that Swede," he said. "By the way, I'm Terry." Still running, he held out his hand and, still running, Lars shook it. "Which god do you believe in?'

"Excuse me?" Lars asked.

"Which god?" Terry asked. "Which god do you think is in control?"

"I had not thought about it."

"You'd better," he chuckled, "because one of 'em is." He stopped suddenly and put his hands on his hips and walked in a small circle. Terry put his hand to his neck and took his pulse, timing it on his wristwatch. Then he placed his fingers on Lars's neck and took his pulse. "One hundred fourteen," he said. "Pretty good."

Again Terry walked away from him and again Lars found himself following him, this time toward the parking lot. In the growing darkness he noticed other men, standing around, watching the boy intently, this American with such beautiful strawberry blond hair, dressed in a skimpy running outfit, now soaked with sweat.

When Lars caught up with him, Terry was unlocking the door of a blue Chevrolet, which was rusting badly. Terry slipped inside the car and reached across to unlock the passenger side. When Lars got in—he hadn't been invited to get in, but he thought it was all right—he sat down on several audio cassette cases. He picked them out from underneath his ass and tried to read their labels. Debussy, Bach, an original cast recording of "Annie." The boy was taking off his running shoes.

"Where are we going?" Lars asked. He glanced down at Terry's bare foot on the accelerator.

Terry didn't answer him. He put the car into reverse. "Tomorrow" came blasting out of the speakers.

"Wait a minute," he said. "Stop this car."

Terry put on the brake, slammed the gear into park. "Now what?"

"I just want to look at you for a minute," Lars said.

"Okay, look." He turned on the interior light and kept his face turned so that Lars was looking at his profile. No matter what the light, Lars found Terry perfectly lovely. On the stereo, the little girl was singing "...the sun'll come out tomorrow."

"Are we going to do things?" Lars asked, touching Terry's thigh.

"Of course," Terry chuckled, shifting into drive. "Strangers should always do things."

On the way to the hotel, Lars thought it strange that he saw almost no one downtown. For some reason it was empty of shoppers, strollers, or pedestrians of any kind.

"I'm going to tell you some things you should know," Terry said.

Lars settled back. He was used to this kind of talk: everyone, everywhere, liked to reveal intimate details. It was an international convention.

They were slowing for a red light. "God is love," Terry said, downshifting, his bare left foot on the clutch. "In the world we have left, only love matters. Do you understand?"

"Yes." Lars nodded. He was beginning to feel very comfortable with this stranger. "So is that what you do, make love for a living?" He thought perhaps that was it, that he would be asked to pay. He was willing to do so.

"No, I do what everyone does. There is only one thing I do that is special."

"What is that?" he asked.

"I don't make any plans," he said. "No plans at all."

"That's not so unusual. Many people don't like to make—"

"It doesn't have anything to do with liking or not liking. It's just my, uh, religion."

"Of course," Lars said. He had heard of American cult religions but thought they were all in California. He didn't mind this talk of religion. It was like talk of the sunset or childhood;

it kept things going.

"Have you been listening to me?"

"Of course I have been listening."

"Good, because I won't sleep with you unless you listen to me," he said. "It's the one thing I care about, that people listen. It's so damn rare, listening I mean." He turned to look at him. "Lars," he said, "what do you pray to?"

He laughed. "I don't."

"Okay, then, what do you plan for?"

"A few things," he said.

"Like what?"

"My dinner every night. Studying for my examinations. Meeting my friends after school."

"Do you let accidents happen?"

"Not if I can help it."

"You should. Things reveal themselves in accidents."

"Are there many people like you in America?" Lars asked.

"What do you think? Do you think there are many people like me?"

Lars looked again at his face, taken over by the darkness in the car but dimly lit by the dashboard lights and the oncoming of traffic. The boy was truly extraordinary, Lars decided. "Not very many," he said.

"Any of us in Sweden?"

"I don't think so. I've never met anyone like you. I've never *heard* about anyone like you. They didn't tell us in Sweden about pretty American boys who listen to Debussy in their rusty automobiles and who believe in accidents."

Terry chuckled and ran his hand up Lars's thigh. Lars felt heady, like he was tripping on a drug of some kind. It was all happening so fast; he could hardly believe his luck.

As they passed the doorman, he nodded, rubbing his chin. Lars introduced Terry and said that he was very friendly and wanted to show him, a foreigner, the sights. The doorman laughed.

Lars unlocked the door of the room and stepped inside. The room was reduced to an eerie grayish blur of odd shapes and forms. Terry went to the bathroom. Lars looked out the window at the street lights. They had an amber glow, the color of gemstones. This city, this American city, was unlike anything he had ever seen. A downtown emptied of people; a river with huge ships going by silently; a park with nothing but men...and one strange, beautiful boy, who was now taking a shower in his bathroom.

He wanted to open the hotel window to smell the air, but the casement frames were welded shut. He turned on the radio that was built into the television. Some light jazz was playing. Perfect, Lars thought. Some music was slow enough to dance to, in the slow way he wanted to dance right now, at this moment. Terry came from the bathroom, showered, scrubbed, a towel around his waist. Lars took his hand; it felt bony and muscular; physically, he was direct and immediate. When they held each other tightly and swayed together to the music, Lars began to feel as if he had known Terry for a long time and was related to him in some obscure way. Suddenly he asked him, "Why are you so interested in me?"

"Interested?" Terry laughed, and his long hair shook in quick thick waves. "Well, all right. I do have an interest. I like it that you're a foreigner and that you take cabs to the park. I like the way you look. You're kind of cute. And the other thing is, your soul is so raw and new, Lars. It's like an oyster."

"What? My soul?"

"Yeah, your soul. I can almost see it."

"Where is it?"

Terry leaned forward, friendly and sexual and now slightly elegant. "You want me to show you?"

"Yes," Lars said. "Sure."

"It's in two places," he said. "One part is up here." He released his hand and put his thumb on his forehead. "And the other part is down here." He touched him in the middle of his stomach. "Right there. And they're connected."

"What are they like?" he asked, playing along.

"Yours? Raw and shiny, just like I said."

"And what about *your* soul?" he asked.

"My soul is radioactive," Terry laughed. "It's like plutonium. Don't say you weren't warned."

Lars thought that this was another American idiom he hadn't heard before, and he decided not to spoil things by asking him about it. In Sweden, people didn't talk much about the soul, at least not relative to oysters or plutonium.

He drew Terry to him and kissed him. His breath was layered with toothpaste, mouthwash. Immediately he felt an unusual physical sensation inside his skin, like something heating up on a frypan.

Lars heard a siren go by on the street outside and drew back. He wondered whether they should talk some more—share a few more verbal intimacies—to be really civilized about this and decided, no, it was not necessary, not when strangers make love, as they do, sometimes, in strange cities, far away from home.

Terry began undressing Lars. The towel slipped off Terry's waist and Lars noticed that his cock, by the light coming in the window from the street, was as big and beautiful as he hoped it would be.

When Lars was naked, his cock throbbing, Terry took him in his arms again. Terry's skin felt vaguely electrical to Lars. They stood in the middle of the hotel room, arms around each other, swaying, and Lars knew, in his arousal, that something odd was about to occur: he had no words for it in either his own language or in English.

They moved over and under each other, changing positions, both lively and attentive, and at first he thought it would be just the usual fun, this time with an almost anonymous but incredibly friendly American boy.

Feeling bold, Lars slid a finger into the slipperiness between the lips of Terry's anus and this started his heart racing. Terry began whimpering pleasure and relief in every breath. And the fleshy place behind his knuckle moved into him, pressing. Terry gasped. The finger teased him awhile, then was removed. The moist finger traced a line to his throat, to his chin, lower lip, and he took the finger into his mouth, in his teeth, and the touch of his tongue made Lars laugh.

Tasting himself on Lars's fingertip, Terry begged, "Fuck me." Lars' feet were planted firmly apart as he got behind him and slid his cock into him, Terry bent at the waist. His hands on Terry's hips, holding him still, sometimes moving him, his cock growing larger inside of him. When Lars was close to coming, Terry tightened around him, bringing on a new sensation.

For Lars, his own orgasm never mattered much; he wanted

his partner to come first, that was triumph enough for him. He pulled back, slid out from Terry, his cock glistening in the somber light. Terry stood. Lars turned him and they kissed, two hard cocks pressed between two hard bellies. Lars's hands explored the sweaty surface of Terry's back, lean and tough, and down to his ass as he sank to his knees and Terry's penis pointed the way up his body; then he took it in his hand, pulled his head back and filled his mouth with it. He concentrated with animal-like preoccupation on the head of his cock, his head moving in a trance-like motion and his hand following, slipping easily along the moist length of it.

He pulled back suddenly and he stood again, rubbing the length of his body against the length of his clean wet cock and Terry ran his tongue up under his lips. Lars lifted him, a hand under each spread thigh, and slid him down onto him, and carried him like that, high, Terry's hands on his shoulders, his mouth at Lars's neck, to the bed.

Terry unlocked his ankles and lowered his legs as Lars pushed him back on the bed. Lars put one knee on the bed, then the other, straddling him, taking his own straining erection in his hand. Fist around his cock, he lowered himself over Terry and entered him again, his hands landing deep in the mattress on either side of Terry's head, his blond hair falling into Terry's face, strands of it sticking to the sweat on his brow. He lifted himself deep into him, opening his eyes and smiling down at him. Terry pulled Lars to him and rolled over on top of him, sinking his cock back into his ass. Lars kissed his pecs, massaged his nipples, one after the other, between the tip of his tongue and the roof of his mouth. Down his flat belly. Terry began quivering now, gasping, his body writhing. Terry was coming so close now, and Lars grinned there between his legs, playing with his erection. Nothing would please him more than every day bringing Terry to orgasm, grasping him by the soul and guiding him to ecstasy. Terry moved slowly up and laid his body down with care along the length of Lars. Now Lars plunged his cock as deep as it would go, and Terry tightened himself around him. His eyes were closed tight; he was holding the feeling with all his might. It was just the beginning.

Terry came liberally, smoothly with a fast, hot breath, an incredible contracting of every muscle in his long, shining body.

Lars kept moving in ever-easier smooth strokes and began to come as well, his face in Terry's hair. After his orgasm, he moved slowly, tenderly, still inside of Terry, kissing his lips and his closed eyelids.

Later, resting with him, Lars's hands on Terry's smooth back, Lars felt a wave of happiness; he felt another wave of glorious color traveling through his body, surging from his forehead down to his stomach. It was like he was having another orgasm. It took him over again, and then a third time, with such force that he almost sat up.

"What is it?" Terry asked.

"I don't know. It is like colors were moving through my body."

"Oh, that?" He smiled at him in the dark. "It's your soul, Lars. That's all. That's all it is. Never felt it before, huh?"

"I must be crazy," he said.

Terry put his hand up into his hair. "Call it anything you want to. Didn't you feel it before? Our souls were joined together."

"You're crazy," he said. "You are a crazy boy."

"Oh yeah?" he whispered. "Is that what you think? Watch. Watch what happens now. You think this is all physical. Guess what, you're the crazy one. Just watch."

Terry went to work on him, has hands gliding over him. At first it was pleasurable, but he began to get nervous when he realized Terry was about to fuck him. He had never let anyone fuck him before. As Terry entered him and moved over him, it became a succession of waves that had specific colorations, even when Terry turned him and Lars got on top. Incredibly, with Terry's eight-inch cock buried in him, he had never felt such pleasure.

"Who are you?" he said. "Who in the world *are* you?"

"I warned you."

Lars put his hands on Terry's. "This is not love, but it—"

"Of course not," Terry said. "It's something else. Do you know the word? Do you know the word for something that opens your soul at once? Just like that?" He snapped his fingers on the pillow. His tongue was touching his ear. "Do you?" The words were almost inaudible.

"No, but I think you're wonderful," he said. Keeping Terry's cock in his ass, he reached down and embraced him.

In the morning, Lars watched as Terry dressed. His eyes hurt from sleeplessness.

"I have to run," Terry said. "I'm already late." He looked at Lars naked on the bed, tangled in the sheets. "You're a lovely lover," he said. "I like your body very much."

"What are we going to do?" Lars moaned.

"We? There is no 'we,' Lars. There's you and then there's me. We're not a couple."

"But after last night—"

"Look, I'm going to work. I've got so much to do. And you're going back to Sweden."

"Oh please, Terry—"

"I don't believe this," he said.

"What?"

"You think you're in love, don't you?"

"No," he said. "Not exactly." He waited. "Oh, I don't know."

"I get the point," Terry said. "Well, you'd better get used to it. Welcome to America. We're not always good at love but we are good at sex."

"Let me buy you breakfast."

"No, I must go."

"Please—"

"All right, but hurry."

Lars stood up and took Terry in his arms. With a sense of shock and desperation, he felt himself becoming aroused. Terry kissed him, and his lips tasted strangely sweet.

"You feel like a drug to me," Lars said, massaging Terry's groin.

"Hurry," Terry begged, pulling away.

Lars went to the bathroom. He looked in the mirror; he wanted evidence but didn't know for what. He looked, to himself, like a slightly different version of what he had been only a day before. In the mirror his face had a puffy look and a passive expression, as if he had been assaulted during the night.

A few minutes later, in the hotel's coffee shop, Lars asked Terry about his plans for the day.

"No plans," he said. "Didn't I tell you?"

"I am not sure I understand."

"We don't do all that much explaining. I've told you *everything* about me. We're just supposed to be enjoying ourselves. Nobody has to explain. That's freedom, Lars. Never telling why." As Terry finished his eggs and bacon, he glanced out the window. His eyes widened, as if he had seen an accident, or as if he felt one was about to happen. "Excuse me," he said, pushing his plate away. "I'll just be a minute."

Lars finished his breakfast, lingered over his coffee. He looked at his watch. Ten minutes had gone by since Terry had left. Lars knew without thinking about it that Terry wasn't coming back.

He put a ten-dollar bill on the table and left the restaurant, jogged into the parking structure where Terry had left the car. Although he wasn't particularly surprised to see the car wasn't there, he sat down on the concrete and felt the floor of the structure shaking. He ran his hands through his hair, where Terry had grabbed at it during his orgasm. He waited as long as he could stand to do so, then returned to his room.

In the shower, Lars realized that he had forgotten to ask for Terry's address or phone number.

INTRIGUE

Lex's heart beat so hard and so fast that it felt like a time bomb in his chest. Since meeting Andy, fucking Andy, saying good-bye to Andy, his life was not the same. Andy was everything Lex had ever dreamed of: tall, slender, long blond hair and green eyes—beautiful in every way. But even more important, he treated Lex like a fine wine. Tasting his sweet flavor, savoring the texture and warmth of his soft, smooth skin, caressing his very soul when he came inside of him. No one had ever treated Lex with so much care and tenderness.

Several weeks passed before Lex realized that Andy was not interested in long-term relationships. Lex was but one of many men in Andy's life.

Today was one of those dark days when Lex felt overwhelmed by images of his former lover. To cope, he was beating a path along the Pacific shoreline, running as fast and hard as he could. He wanted nothing more than to erase those memories. Yet, everywhere he looked, everything he saw or heard reminded him of Andy.

Lost in his memories, mesmerized by the steady movement of the ocean's tide against the shore, Lex did not realize he had gone well past his halfway marker. He stopped and tried to orient himself. Looking toward the highway, searching for a landmark, he saw the familiar outcropping of rocks where Andy had so often posed for pictures. A photographer of considerable fame, Lex enjoyed taking intimate shots of men, including the men in his life. He usually let his lovers see him work and beg to be photographed. He seldom made a pass at a model he had hired. He preferred to keep his professional and private life separate. He also would never dream of selling his pictures of his lovers. Still, he envisioned one day publishing a book of his "private moments" with his studly lovers, especially with Andy.

He recalled the day he first got Andy disrobing and posing on the rocks. By the time he had finished his first roll of film, they were both too aroused to continue. Searching for a place to unleash their sexual desires, they stumbled upon a little hideaway in the rocks. Just the thought of the hot sex that afternoon sent shivers down Lex's spine. Suddenly he felt very tired; he couldn't believe it but he wanted nothing more than to lie down and rest. He edged his way between the rocks and crevices to curl up inside that little hideaway.

As he approached the opening Lex heard a strange sound from inside, as if someone were moaning in pain. Peering around the corner, Lex saw a youth sitting on a beach towel. His legs were spread wide, his clothes folded neatly beside him. He was finger-fucking himself with one hand while he jacked himself with the other. Lex stared at the sight of the fingers going in and out of the soft pink flesh of the asshole. The boy froze when he saw Lex.

Flustered for having interrupted such a private moment, Lex stammered, "Oh, I'm sorry. I didn't realize anyone was...."

Before he could finish, Lex heard the stranger's husky voice, the kind that always drove him wild with desire.

"Hey, it's okay," the boy said, leaving his cock and ass alone and rolling over on his stomach.

Lex found himself wondering what it would feel like to run his hands over the firm young buttocks that were now exposed to him.

As the boy looked Lex up and down, Lex was stunned by the youth's beauty. Lex's thoughts raced as he tried to think of what to do next. A chill wind snaked its way in though the crevices, and the stranger shivered. Remembering he carried a jacket with him, Lex removed his running pack from his shoulder. The stranger watched him, a curious look on his face.

"Looking for something?" he asked as Lex rummaged through his pack.

Lex surprised himself with his response: "Oh, I'm looking for something all right." He pulled his jacket from his pack. "I'm looking to cover you up before you catch pneumonia."

The stranger laughed. "Don't worry about me. I never catch cold."

"All the same, you should put this on." Lex draped the jacket over the lad's back. They introduced themselves; the stranger said his name was Terry. Lex started to initiate a conversation, but then he felt Terry's hands on his arms. Terry's eyes had the glazed look of sexual arousal, and he gripped

Lex's arms so strongly it hurt. Uncertain of what the lad wanted, Lex decided to wait and see what happened next. Terry tilted his face up so that he was looking directly into Lex's eyes. His gaze was so piercing that Lex had to look away. He was at a very vulnerable point in his life; the last thing he needed was for someone to strip his soul bare and read his innermost thoughts and desires. He didn't realize he was trembling until he felt Terry's hand on his, trying to steady him.

"Let me help you forget it," Terry said. Drawing Lex down, he kissed Lex's lips very gently. His mouth was so warm and soft and inviting that Lex didn't want the kiss to end. Sliding his tongue out, he probed gently but insistently at Terry's lips, urging him to open his mouth, to let him go very deeply inside of him. Terry complied immediately. Lex felt many conflicting emotions at that moment, but desire proved to be the strongest. Clasping Terry's face between his hands, he kissed him fiercely and passionately. Bruising Terry's lips with his desire, he wanted desperately to hear him beg for sex. He felt so hot, so very hot. Not averse to a little aggression in sex, Terry responded to Lex with equal passion and force. He pressed his teeth against Lex's mouth, biting him ever so lightly. Then he pulled Lex's lips into the hot, burning cave of his mouth, sucking him in and out like a two-year-old with a lollipop. He could feel Lex's lips becoming swollen and puffy.

Terry's aggressiveness was a real turn-on for Lex. This adorable youth was making love to Lex's mouth, sucking him, biting him, probing deeply inside him that Lex began to moan as the excitement built torturously high within him. Taking this as a cue that Lex wanted to continue this pleasurable activity, Terry pushed him back down on the beach towel. He grasped Lex's wrists above his head. Lex began to struggle and Terry smiled when he saw the sudden look of fear in his eyes. Terry was so aroused by Lex's reaction that he could feel his pre-cum seeping from the head of his erection. Lex felt both humiliated and excited for allowing Terry to dominate him like this. Terry made his way from Lex's mouth to his neck. Next came a trail of hot, wet kisses that Lex felt certain were burning his skin. He threw his head back as far as he could, inviting Terry to continue. Terry did, sucking Lex's tingling flesh between his lips. He made a path of tiny bite-sized bruises on his neck.

Then Terry felt Lex's legs wrap around his waist, trying to capture the youth's body against his prick. Pausing for a moment, Terry smiled and let Lex ride his erection for a couple of minutes. He grew giddy anticipating how it would taste in his mouth, how it would feel up his ass.

Deciding he'd had enough for the moment, Terry disengaged himself from Lex's long legs. When Lex whispered a protest, Terry told him, "Hold on." He released Lex's arms and started removing his sweats. Lex had only a jockstrap underneath. Terry licked his lips in anticipation of taking Lex's bulging cock into his mouth. But Lex reached for Terry; he was so hot and so aroused that he could think of nothing beyond his desire to feel another man's arms around him, something to release the pent-up longing and desire that had been building inside of him since Andy left. But this would not happen yet. Pushing Lex's hands away, Terry turned and pulled a large beach bag from behind a rock. He held it in front of Lex's face and smiled. "My own little bag of treasures, Lex. Would you like to see what's inside?"

Once again, Lex felt that strange combination of desire and fear. What did Terry have in store for him? He reached for the bag, knowing that Terry would not let him touch it. Chuckling in wry amusement, Terry wagged a finger in front of Lex's face. "No, no." A surge of excitement raced through Lex's body as he watched Terry remove a pair of gold-plated handcuffs from the bag. Terry turned the key and the cuffs sprang open. Placing the key between his teeth, he leaned over and took Lex's hands. Lex offered only minimal resistance as Terry cuffed him. Lex's submissiveness did not go unnoticed by Terry, who smiled and began teasing Lex's nipples with the gold chain that held the key. Lex didn't flinch. "This is so good," said Terry.

Terry rolled Lex over onto his stomach and Lex heard a jangling sound. It was familiar, but he couldn't quite identify it. When Terry reached for his hands, Lex knew immediately what was happening. He began to struggle, trying to roll over so he could sit up. Terry was proving much stronger than he looked. He held Lex in place with the ease and grace of a lion tamer. There was a metallic sound as he fastened a long gold chain to Lex's handcuffs. Lex had been so excited, he hadn't seen the ring Terry had welded to the handcuffs. Tugging at the chain, he ordered him, "Get up on your knees. Now!"

Another delicious thrill raced through Lex's body as he obeyed Terry's order. He began moaning deep inside his throat, unable to suppress his desire.

Terry stood and secured the chain to a rock with an iron ring in it. He then dropped the chain and circled around in front of Lex. Lex was avoiding Terry's eyes and this only added to the intrigue. Terry commanded him, "Look at me, Lex."

Startled, Lex watched Terry walk toward him. Placing a hand on either side of his face, he forced Lex to look at him. Lex was immediately overcome by the passion burning so fiercely in Terry's eyes. Lex started panting with excitement. Terry smiled and pushed Lex down onto his hands and knees. Moving behind him, he then positioned Lex's hips, providing him perfect access to that lovely ass. Lex moaned with excitement, anticipating what Terry would do next. He felt a tightening in his anal muscles, the excitement building incredibly.

Terry chuckled and kneeled down behind Lex. Reaching into his bag once again, he brought out a knife. He pressed the cold steel against Lex's skin, trailing the point up his legs, his back then down his neck. Lex now showed his first signs of real fear. But soon he knew Terry was playing with him. The lad circled his nipples with the weapon, flicking the tips until they hardened into two tight nubs. Terry knew those nipples longed to be sucked, but that would have to come later. One swift move with the knife put the cold steel between Lex's skin and his jockstrap. There was a ripping sound as he cut through the fabric. The sweat-soaked jockstrap fell partly away, and Terry watched with satisfaction as Lex's ass swayed back and forth, inviting Terry to fuck it. Terry dropped the knife and grasped the top of Lex's jockstrap. Wanting to show off how truly strong he was, Terry ripped Lex's jockstrap off and then examined his trophy. Terry was so close that Lex could feel his breathing against his skin. The mere thought of what Terry might do to him sent a surge of sexual energy through his cock. He wondered if Terry could feel his rushing need and desire.

Beginning with gentle caresses along the sides and over Lex's hairy cheeks, Terry explored his captive. Lex's asshole was small and tight, as if daring entrance. Terry blew his hot breath on it and watched as a slight tremor passed through it. Smiling, he began licking the sides of Lex's crack. He paused and blew some more. Only when Lex started groaning did Terry plunge his face between his cheeks and start licking his asshole. Judging from Lex's response, he doubted anyone had ever done this to him. Lex shrieked as Terry continued tonguing him and jerked his cock. Lex gave no sign of stopping, nor did Lex want him to stop. Unfortunately, his want and need became evident to Terry. Terry stopped, satisfied that he had found yet another area to torture Lex's appetite.

When he stopped, Lex growled in frustration. Knowing it would only heighten Terry's desire to tease him, he made no effort to hide his feelings. It was as if Terry knew exactly what to do to torment him. That just made Lex want Terry all the more.

At this point, Lex would do anything to please Terry. Terry moistened his cock with some of Lex's own pre-cum, then added some spit. Getting it wet and slippery, sliding it over Lex's asshole, teasing him in every way imaginable. Lex was moaning by the time Terry started pushing the head of the thick prick inside the steaming ass. Moving ever so slowly, each thrust a little deeper, a little more insistent.

When Lex felt the head of the cock pressing against his most tender spot, he moaned so loudly that it frightened the seagulls flying overhead. This aroused Terry even more. He began a steady rhythm, thrusting the delicious prick in and out of Lex's ass. Taking each of Lex's nipples between his thumbs and forefingers, he teased them unmercifully. Lex responded by thrusting backward, heightening the effects of each thrust. Terry caressed Lex's tits, taking their fullness into his hands and squeezing with the intensity of his own excitement. Lex's counter thrusts became harder, more insistent. Terry was close, and he slowed his pace, making the strokes longer and deeper Lex was panting with excitement. He *needed* to be fucked, and Terry was definitely not disappointing him.

When Terry finally pulled out, Lex whimpered in protest. But Terry was fast. Before Lex knew what was happening, Terry rolled him onto his back. He then straddled Lex's face, the cock dripping. Knowing what was expected of him, Lex began sucking his own filth from the prick. Terry's cock was one of the most beautiful he had ever seen, and he made fierce, passionate love to it, using his tongue, his lips, his teeth. Satisfied that he'd sucked it long enough, Terry pulled away. He lifted Lex up and entered him again. Terry started fucking his ass, concentrating totally on achieving his own orgasm. As his climax drew near, he pounded Lex as hard and fast as he could. Once started, the orgasm shook his entire body with such intensity that even Lex was trembling and gasping for air. Terry held onto Lex's shoulder and slowly, steadily thrust as he rode the final wave of his orgasm. Then he was astonished to see Terry leave his ass and take his cock in his mouth. Terry sucked Lex for a bit, cleaned the cock of pre-cum, then licked his way down to his asshole. He inserted his tongue deeply inside and fucked him with it, while he stroked Lex's erection. Over and over again, he listened to the sweet sounds of Lex's intense excitement.

It wasn't long before Lex was close to orgasm. As Lex began grinding against Terry's face, Terry thrust his fingers inside Lex's now burning ass. The walls, hot and smooth as velvet, tightening around Terry's fingers as he thrust one, then two fingers inside him.

Lex felt an explosive climax building within him. He wanted to prolong the sensation, ride wave after wave of sheer, raw excitement. He groaned as Terry put three and then four fingers inside him.

Meanwhile, Terry sucked Lex's swollen organ deep into his mouth. Then his tongue flickered across the tip. He soon had Lex begging for release. He felt his muscles tightening. Then his legs began to tremble. Lex was ecstatic with the utter intensity of Terry's lovemaking.

As he rode over the edge, his body trembling and spasming against Terry's face, Lex held tight to the chain. Relying on its firm hold to keep him from falling, he gave himself totally to the orgasm. The flood of sensations raced through his body. His heart set the pace with each new surge of blood. On and on, then once again over the edge.

As Lex began to relax against him, Terry eased him down onto the towel. The look of contentment on Lex's face was far more satisfying than a second orgasm to Terry. He freed Lex, then held him close in his arms. Now Lex relaxed against the lad, and Terry ran his fingers through Lex's hair. Lex was soon fast asleep in his arms.

For two hours Lex slept. Awakening with a sigh, Lex saw the semi-darkness of early evening closing around him. At first he was frightened, but then it came back to him. He felt around beside him, wanting once again to feel his dreamboy's arms around him. But Terry wasn't there. He looked around the rocky enclosure but there was no sign of the youth anywhere. Panic built inside him as he crawled outside and looked around the beach. Still no sign of Terry. He searched inside again. The handcuffs, the chain, Terry's bag—everything was gone. Lex then began to wonder if it was all a dream, some fantasy he conceived out of his terrible loneliness?

Sighing, he reached for his running pack. Then he noticed the slight bruising around his wrists. The handcuffs! He looked up, searching for the rock with the iron ring. It was nowhere in sight. Had this really happened, or was it a figment of his imagination? So many missing pieces, yet the bruises were a clear sign it had actually happened.

Totally confused, Lex suddenly felt incredibly tired again. It was time to go home and forget this strange fantasy. Crawling through the narrow opening to the outside, he felt something cold and metallic lying in the sand. His heart skipped a beat when he saw the gold lock entwined with the gold chain. He picked it up and rubbed it with his fingers. Then he looked up and down the beach for signs of Terry, but the beach was deserted, only the full moon and several shining stars overhead. And in the distance, a lone seagull was flying toward the horizon.

THE TOUCH OF THE STRANGER

Wilbur sat by the azure sea and it seemed the air shimmered, a kind of blurred, fractional movement, like a heat haze, making the boy in the dunes appear as if in a vision.

"Or is it my eyes?" he thought.

Wilbur had been coming to this beach three times a year for longer than he cared to admit. He always brought books with him, from the spring, autumn, and summer best-seller lists, and always he brought a companion. He had just picked up the phone; there were always boys ready to flee Boston for Florida, if the price were right. But the last companion, Johnnie, had been so deeply into drugs that he became uncontrollable, disappeared the day after they arrived and, as far as Wilbur knew, hadn't been seen since. No, this time he had decided he would sample the local offerings.

Wilbur got up from his chair and walked towards the boy, who was adjusting the crotch of his sky-blue Speedo. Wilbur had been here for a week and no one had paid him any attention. Nor had he seen anyone who truly excited him. Now a godlike young stud was walking directly toward him. No, Wilbur's eyes were not deceiving him. This was no apparition. Wilbur didn't mind the obviousness: he knew where he stood. However, the boy merely nodded at Wilbur as he passed and broke into a sprint for the water.

Wilbur watched the boy dive into the warm water of the gulf and begin swimming. The boy was a powerful swimmer. Wilbur shrugged and returned to his place on the beach. The boy swam for several minutes and then, just as Wilbur became absorbed again in his book, a figure was blocking the sun.

"Got an extra towel?"

"Why, yes," Wilbur said, reaching into his beach bag. "I was saving it for you."

"Thanks," the boy said.

The towel covered the boy's face and permitted Wilbur's eyes to feast on the boy's nearly hairless swimmer's body, and the abundant crotch directly in his face.

"Wow," Wilbur said under his breath. Wilbur could make out the head of the penis, and some of the shaft, as if the cock was semi-hard. Maybe it was, Wilbur thought, the idea of driving an older man wild somehow appealed to this kid.

"There, that's better," the boy said, dropping the towel to the sand and spreading it.

Wilbur was immobile in his lounge chair, staring, a benign smile on his face.

"My name's Terry," the boy said, extending his hand.

Wilbur introduced himself, using his now-preferred nickname of "Wil."

As Terry sat on the towel, Wilbur gulped. He was dumbfounded. He had never had anyone ingratiate themselves in this way, and wasn't sure what was expected. He picked up the book he had been reading. Terry noticed it, asked what it was.

"*Sexual Outlaw*, by John Rechy," Wilbur responded. "This trip I'm catching up on a lot of the old ones."

As Terry nodded and Wilbur handed him the paperback, the long plumes of the sea oats lined up behind them bobbed drowsily.

Soon Terry was scowling prettily into the sun, pretending to read the book Wilbur had chosen for him, waggling his toes in the sand. Wilbur, elegant and jaunty in his straw sun hat, stared down at him, and sighed. But they were getting so young, he thought, while admiring Terry's sculpted face even in its petulant frown.

The beauty didn't have to be here, Wilbur told himself, looking away momentarily. He could at any time be back in the city, in the world, with friends, and admired. Oh, how admired. "Yes, he would hate me," he thought, now looking at Terry with thirsty eyes.

Tourists swarmed and splashed and smiled around them and sometimes they stared, as if pointing at them, the slim man with his much younger companion, the beauty with the soft, angelic face. Wilbur smiled at them as if he knew them and he found they smiled back at him. Terry paid no attention, engrossed in the book. Wilbur pushed his hat over his eyes and lost Terry's face, but when he lifted it again, there he was again, like a sun over the horizon, glowing. Wilbur bit his lip, and looked away, then quickly back again.

Terry stretched his fine legs, elongated his spine, cat-like, for the world to see. It was as if he paraded his beauty.

Another group of tourists walked quickly past, self-conscious and stiff-necked.

"They're probably thinking he's young enough to be my son," thought Wilbur, "if I weren't so well-preserved." And he was. Wilbur had taken care of himself.

The smooth-limbed youth pushed himself up onto one elbow and lifted his head from the book with learned insouciance. Said Terry, "Gives me a hard-on reading about guys getting off." The bulge in his trunks lengthened and thickened, the plump, uncut head now peeping over the waistband. Wilbur's eyes widened.

A sudden salty gust stung Terry's legs with sand as he shoved his cockhead back inside the fabric. "My best feature," Terry snickered, seeing Wilbur had noticed. "Everyone says."

"Yes," Wilbur said, blushing and averting his eyes.

Now Terry rolled away from him, as if teasing him.

The smell of the sea, the chatter and fresh breeze faded, giving way to a heavy, tropical silence.

Finally, Terry rolled back towards Wilbur, asked the time. Wilbur checked his watch. It was nearly five.

"I've got to be going," Terry said.

"Me, too," Wilbur said.

Wilbur folded his chair and put his things in his beach bag.

They followed a path into the dunes, hung over by sharp, shiny fronds and almost concealed from the sky. The air was dank, and under their feet the ground was creepily soft. Strong, wet leaves brushed against their faces and arms; there was the noise of water dripping; the undergrowth rustled as they passed. Finally they came to a clearing and some parked cars. Terry had not stopped, made no move to leave the path, find a thicket where Wilbur could suck him.

They arrived at a new white LeBaron convertible. The boy stopped. "Well—" he started, allowing Wilbur his opening.

"Well," Wilbur stammered, "will you have dinner with me?"

Terry smiled as he unlocked the door of the convertible. "Of course."

Wilbur stood beside the car, his breath caught sharply in his throat. He held back his head and smiled up to the sun, in case tears rolled out.

As Wilbur climbed into the passenger seat, he picked up the rental contract. Terry turned the ignition and "I'm So Excited" by the Pointer Sisters blasted from the speakers. Terry turned down the volume. Wilbur chuckled.

At Wilbur's condo in the tall building overlooking the beach where they had just met, Wilbur offered Terry the guest bathroom to shower and change. Wilbur went to the master suite and began undressing. When he heard the water running in the guest bath, his cock grew hard. It had been months, perhaps years, since he had been this excited. He started humming "I'm So Excited."

They went to the French Hearth, a cafe a block from Wilbur's condo. The same waiter Wilbur had taken a liking to showed them to their table. When the young man, whose name was Paul, saw Terry, he seemed to show new interest in Wilbur, even calling him by his name for the first time.

Once they were seated, Wilbur ordered a martini. Terry had a Perrier. As the waiter moved away, Wilbur said, "It's so strange—"

"What?" Terry asked, reaching for the bread basket.

"My vacation is almost over and I hadn't met anyone and now—"

"Now what?" Terry teased.

"Well, I'd given up, I guess. I suppose it's an ethereal thing. When you seek it out, you get nowhere, get nothing." He nodded. "Yeah, it's an ethereal thing."

"Little do you know," Terry chuckled, "just how ethereal."

As Wilbur sipped his martini, Terry said, "You look so sad sometimes."

"I haven't been well."

"Oh?"

"Yes, depressed. My entire department was laid off. I was moved into another position. I'm secure, but the—"

"You had a whole department?"

"I'm in computer programming. All forty people were out of work in a day. Corporate downsizing they call it."

"I have heard of that. Where I come from they call it greed."

"And where is that you do come from?"

"Oh, here, there, everywhere."

"Very mysterious."

"Yeah, guys like that."

"I imagine. I mean, I know."

Terry buttered his bread. "So you are sad."

"Been sad. I should have taken the whole department and set up my own company."

"Why didn't you?"

"Oh, I'm too old to do that now."

"You're never too old—for anything."

Wilbur shook his head. "If you say so."

Terry smiled. "If I promise to go to bed with you tonight, will you start your own company and take those forty people with you?"

"What?" Wilbur couldn't believe his ears.

"That's all I ask."

"You're kidding, of course, but I just don't know. If you think I could do it—"

"I *know* you can do it. Trust me." Terry reached his hand across the table, touched Wilbur's. The hand lingered, toyed, teased.

Wilbur smiled. "Somehow I do. I can't figure it, but somehow I do."

Over the next hour, here with Terry, Wilbur found his anger, his thwarted spite, had gone and that he felt instead a kind of longing, an exquisite, gentle longing for sex with this beautiful boy. His cock stirred in spite of himself.

At the end of the dinner, Wilbur ordered French champagne. Paul brought it grinningly. As Terry filled and refilled Wilbur's flute (he took nothing for himself) his hand roved up and down his own empty glass and he fixed on the older man those startling, greenish blue eyes. It seemed the boy was desiring him, as much as he desired the boy, and the gesture stripped him of years more surely than his hair dye had ever done. Finally, Wilbur took the bottle from Terry and let their hands touch when he filled Terry's empty glass.

As the waiter brought the check and hovered at their elbows, Wilbur noticed Terry showed no interest in Paul. His eyes were only for him.

When they left the restaurant, the streets teemed with people, young, ardent, untouched, all of them, and the men and women alike were sleek-haired and shining with youth. With Terry at his arm, Wilbur was in splendid isolation, as if in a dream.

At the condo, Wilbur sat on the balcony with his robe half open. The wind was lower, the moon swelling in the indigo sky, the air sticky, balmy with a steady beating heat. For the first time in months, Wilbur had an erection that would not go down. It seemed he was drugged. The touch of the stranger had made him high. His bare feet danced on the warm rose tiles. The lazy slap of the waves, the murmuring in the trees, the sound of Terry taking another shower lulled Wilbur into a euphoric state.

Terry had a towel wrapped around his waist when he came onto the balcony. Saying nothing, he guided Wilbur into the master suite, sat him down on the bed. Wilbur stared up at him as if he'd never seen him before, biting back his full lower lip. Terry, looking at him intensely, reached his hand and hauled it to his sex. Wilbur's fingers trembled as they were invited to touch the incredible hardness. Terry lifted Wilbur's chin, commanding him to look at his face. Terry bent and gave Wilbur a kiss, the tenderest kiss the older man had ever known.

Wilbur smiled, then gasped as he stroked the sizeable cock through the terry cloth towel. Terry loosened the towel and let it drop to the floor. Wilbur moaned in appreciation and buried himself in Terry's crotch, enfolding himself, losing himself in its great heaviness.

"Oh," Terry cried softly.

Tears ran freely down Wilbur's cheeks, his mouth gaping, choking on, drinking in Terry's eight inches of uncut cock.

In the noise of the night, of the waves, the far-off fading music and murmuring of the trees, Terry kept saying "Oh," with occasional gasps of indrawn breath. This was followed by Wilbur's full and choking, "Oh, God."

After a few minutes of sucking, Wilbur begged Terry to put it in him. Wilbur wanted it from behind and got on his stomach on the bed. Terry poured himself into the older man, arching over him, quite lost, as Wilbur gasped beneath him. His ass was incredibly welcoming. Wilbur could not help it. Terry's plunges hurt him, taking him by the scruff as if he were a rag, shaking him.

After a time, Terry's breathing changed, became regular, quieter, listening. Then, panting a little, he tensed briefly inside Wilbur. Terry lifted Wilbur and clutched the older man's erection. Wilbur's eyes widened in acquiescence. Both of Terry's hands were coursing and roving—Wilbur's stretched body working, busy, frantically coming. Terry's movements become faster and more frantic, feverish even, his head thrown far back. His right hand continued to play with Wilbur's now-spent cock. Wilbur's hand covered his. Terry's kind, strong hands, laid on a warm, hard place, had pleasured Wilbur. Terry's head remained thrown back and his eyes tight shut, as if possessed. He came again, groaning.

When he was capable, Terry disposed of the condom and lay down beside Wilbur, facing him. Their sweat had begun to cool and they got under the covers.

"I don't think I've ever come together with somebody the first time," Wilbur said. He burrowed his face into the curve of Terry's collarbone.

"You were good. So good, I want some more."

Wilbur shook off his tiredness and leaned over to examine Terry's prick, which was hard again. He was soon sucking continuously—licking, drinking in the sweetness. Drunk from the taste, he desperately took the entire shaft into his mouth and buried his face deeper and deeper into the reddish pubic hair.

As Wilbur ravenously devoured him, Terry began fingering his own asshole, then fucked himself with one digit, then two.

Suddenly, Terry let out a loud moan. He grabbed Wilbur's hair. Bucking wildly in deep pleasure, his entire body shuddered as he entered into another orgasm, moaning, "Yes, baby! Oh yes, baby!"

Wilbur continued to suck madly on Terry's throbbing prick. Barely able to breathe, Wilbur sank his entire face back into Terry's crotch, hardly conscious of anything else but the delicious tangy taste, the musky, inviting scent. This was it, heaven, as far as Wilbur was concerned. It had been a most unbelievable night.

But it was not over. Now Terry wanted to get fucked. Soon he was on his back on the bed, his legs spread, jacking his cock.

"Come on," Terry whispered.

"Oh, I can't. I haven't done that to anybody in years."

"Oh, come on," Terry begged. "Give me that big dick."

Wilbur did have an erection, the hardest erection he could remember. He knelt between the outstretched thighs, and began applying grease to Terry's anal lips.

"That's right," Terry was moaning.

As Wilbur entered him, Terry said, "Oh, that's just what I want."

Wilbur could not believe how hot Terry felt as he allowed the head to lie in the throbbing anus. "Go ahead, go ahead!" Terry pleaded, and Wilbur sank his fat, hardened prick all the way in. Now Wilbur was crying, "Yes," half breathing and half whispering in Terry's ear, echoing him. Wilbur's heart was pounding, almost into his throat, it seemed. He finally remembered to breathe deeply. He inhaled and shook everything he could muster through his shoulders and down the length of his body. No, he would not hold this energy in his body any longer. He would fulfill his own pent-up desires at last.

He held the firm, freshly showered ass in his hands and fucked it. If there is a Creator, he thought, he's enjoying a good laugh over his awkward gyrations—or perhaps their chance meeting was really a Blessing. Damned if either of them knew now top from bottom, or cared for that matter, but rather Wilbur knew only that Terry's palms and manicured nails were playing all over his skin. It felt so surreal.

"Is it okay?" Wilbur was foolish enough to ask. He was beyond surprised to find Terry so ready to be fucked, to use his knowledge and skill as a top and a bottom for the purpose of Wilbur's pleasure.

Wilbur backed up to look at Terry again, the strong shoulders, the tight pecs, down his muscular stomach to his again burgeoning crotch. Suddenly Wilbur's equilibrium faltered and his cock slipped from the hole. He held Terry's body still and shoved it in again, then began long, hard surges. He would no longer be scared of it. If this boy wanted to get fucked, Wilbur was ready.

"God, it's so big," Terry moaned.

Wilbur had forgotten just how big he was. He remembered the days, years ago, when the guys at the baths begged to suck it. But nobody ever wanted it inside them the way Terry seemed to. Wilbur could now feel Terry's ass twitching to keep the cock in him.

Terry grabbed Wilbur's asscheeks to force Wilbur in all the way. Wilbur was thrusting madly and surprised at his own strength. Terry's lips were inches from Wilbur's, his eyes searching with a fierceness.

"So you want me, eh?" Wilbur cried, then kissed Terry, so hard it almost seemed as if he were trying to absorb Terry's beautiful face into him, as if he felt beyond any hope of relief.

Suddenly, Terry's body tensed, and he gripped Wilbur, throwing his legs around him, locking him in.

Terry began grinding his face into Wilbur's, kissing him into fierce, demanding thrusts of release. To Wilbur's bursting delight Terry was making him come harder and harder.

"I can't stop," Wilbur cried at last, rocking and coming and lifting Terry with all his might. Terry bucked against him and that made Wilbur surge one last time. Terry was completely locked around him, and he rolled over on top, easily pinning Wilbur, and he kissed him violently on the mouth.

Wilbur was completely exhausted. He thought he must now be dead. He felt merely a ghost of himself, weightless. His mouth was open and wet on Terry's smooth chest.

Terry pulled away and Wilbur watched as the buttocks rose, perfect moons lighting the dim, two cool scoops of vanilla ice cream. A faint hiss rose from between them.

On the way to the bathroom, the image in the mirror stopped Terry. Wilbur could see the reflection and Terry appeared rosy, perfect, more beautiful than ever before. Not a religious man, Wilbur was stunned to find himself whispering a prayer of deep thanks for their short time together.

He looked up to see Terry gazing intently in his direction behind a radiant almost-grin, and then he vanished behind the bathroom door. Presently Wilbur fell asleep. He dreamed vaguely of music that, in the dream, had a very important and perfectly obvious meaning but faded away and could not be recalled when he later tried to translate it into words.

Dawn light, rose-hued and clear, filled the bedroom of the spacious master suite. Wilbur frowned at the empty space beside him and eased out of bed. He threw a robe around himself and went through the condo, looking for the boy. The air was cool and silent, the rooms empty.

He returned to the bedroom, stared at the bed as if Terry might have reappeared during his search. Then he noticed the two hundred-dollar bills were still on the bureau where he had left them for Terry.

Wilbur went out to the balcony and looked down at the parking lot. The convertible was gone. Wilbur blinked. No, he thought, it *did* happen. The boy *was* here. It *wasn't* a dream. In seeming desperation, Wilbur called the boy's name, and a soft, cool breeze from the direction of the dunes touched his sunburned face.

First Hand Accounts

A KIND OF MADNESS

Saints, I have discovered, are a great inconvenience. They interfere with the plans of ordinary people. When you have a saint in your midst, your first reaction is to hurry to the psychiatrist. Me, hell, I went to bed with *my* saint.

But I'm getting ahead of myself. First, you should understand that prosperity touched me early on. "First I get the law degree, then the Lincoln." That was my Life Plan. What I hadn't counted on was that lawyers are not regarded as highly in society as are doctors, although our education costs nearly as much. I joined a firm and hated it, so I went on my own. My Lincoln was a far way off when I touched upon a need, and, as my father said, success in business is finding a need and filling it. I decided to come out, in a way: I advertised my services in the gay newspapers. I was, after all, gay, so I understood the problems gay men can have. How often a gay man can find himself set up on bogus charges and, knowing no attorney who could possibly understand, he plea bargains.

After defending so many men against many charges over the years, it became clear often good men become involved with losers, or are entrapped, and it was disheartening to me. I avoided any boy I assumed might be a threat. Naturally, my paranoia took over and I had practically given up the hope of having any sexual contact. Yet I occasionally found myself turning into the park on my way home, just to check out the action. It was there that my saint came to me almost as an apparition, appearing to me as if in a dream. At first I thought I was just suffering from having an especially hard day at the office, working on three thorny cases ready to go to trial. I left my office late, put the top down on the old Eldo (I didn't like the Lincoln after all) and let the cool night air envelop me. I drove deep into the park, then turned around. I was planning to leave, when, in my headlights he appeared: A vision of loveliness like no other.

He was no longer a boy, certainly, but not yet a man; he had a perfection that would easily stop the hearts of females and males alike, and I feared that no one who yearned for him was favored, or even noticed. He appeared to be icy; his heart, cold. Struck by his beauty, enamored beyond reason, I parked and got out of the car. He moved; I followed along behind him, going from bush to bush, eager for yet a closer look at this marvelous creature. My shyness prevented me from calling to him to stop, to turn, to speak. My tongue was meat in my mouth, until the charm of his own voice broke the spell.

"Hi," he said.

I was smitten utterly, and he knew it.

But there he was, looking up into my eyes, handsome beyond belief, with a negligent, saucy look that invited me as it also repelled yet fascinated me. He seemed somehow lost, as motionless as a marble statue. But he was a statue perfect in form and proportion. Suddenly, he tugged off his sweatshirt and walked to the pond and stepped into it. The reflection of him shimmered, coy, elusive, mocking me as so many boys had, I thought, mocked me here in this park. Yet I could not desist, could not resist. I was crazed, telling myself, "Go, turn away, forget him." But I could not turn away. I gazed down with hungry eyes for him, eager to follow wherever he led. He looked up at the trees that surrounded the pond and called out to me : "Come in, water's fine!"

That face beckoned and tantalized me. I rubbed my arms against the night's chill. "It's too cold," I hollered.

"Oh, it feels so good," he said, kneading the bulge at the crotch of his white short shorts.

He stepped out of the water and took his time returning to my side.

"How old are you?" I whispered, although there was no need to. The moonlight felt cold on my skin, and my head swam from fatigue. He took me in his arms and we fell to the ground. I lay alongside him, pressing myself very close. After a while I dropped my head to his chest. I swept my hand down across his firm belly and slid my hand into the shorts. I felt the stiffness there and as I loosened the waist and drew out the cock, moisture trailed out of the tip. Half-hard now, in the moonlight it seemed a true masterpiece of a penis.

"Let's go back to your place," he said. And when he slid

silently away from me and put his sweatshirt back on, I longed to put my fingers again on his flesh. I jumped up and ran my hands down his hips, felt his hands grabbing my ass, pushing me toward the car. We struggled there, in fun, and he let me win, for a moment. I slid myself down until my mouth was again close to his crotch and I drew the head to my lips, taking it in my mouth, in and out, in and out, all the way down, then up.

"Like it?" he asked.

I nodded, not wanting to give the cock up to answer such a foolish question.

"Then let's go."

He fiddled with the radio all the way to the house, never saying a word. My left hand steered the car while my right fiddled with his cock. Safely in the garage, we kissed tenderly, but he said he was in a hurry. "Let's fuck."

Jubilant, I led the way to my bedroom. He wanted to get me into bed. While I sucked his cock again, he thrust two fingers inside my ass and rubbed the ball of his hand firmly against me. I spread my legs far apart, writhed wildly and groaned.

Without transition, without letting up on the frantic pace, he flipped me over and suddenly the moans were his as he inserted his raging hard-on into my anus, where his fingers had so deftly prepared the way. As it invaded me to the hilt, his glorious cock was pleasuring me as none ever had. He fucked me for a few minutes, stroking my cock, coated with pre-cum, expertly, then pulled out and rolled me over. He sucked on my nipples and I wrapped my legs around his body, drawing his hips forward so his hot erection slid into me deeply. "Oh, yeah," he said as it hit home. "Tell me what you want."

"You know what I want," I managed to say between breaths.

"Say it!"

"Fuck me. Oh, fuck that ass!"

And he did, for a half an hour, playing with my cock as he screwed me. Then he stopped, put a finger to my lips and I could smell my pre-cum which turned me on even more. He stuck his tongue in my mouth and we kissed some more, then his tongue followed the path his finger had made around my pecs and down my stomach to my cock. He gently sucked me and I held onto his head; soon I was lurching in an orgasm of an intensity unknown to me. My body was seized with wave after wave of chills all the way to my toes until I finished coming. Exhausted, I lay still on the bed. He gently sucked my spent cock some more and rested his hand on my pecs. I reached over to his semi-hard penis. He took my hand and licked it and then put it back on his cock and I rubbed it slowly. "Touch my balls," he requested softly, and he moaned when I grabbed them.

His cock was glistening with a few drops of cum and the fuck juices of my ass, and I could feel my excitement rising up again. I licked him the way he had me all down his front, and then I teased his tip until he begged me to take him. Still I ran my hand up and down his shaft and licked only the tip of his cock while he thrust himself into my mouth. "Please, please," he groaned.

I took it deep, all eight uncut inches of it, sucking up and down, carefully keeping my teeth out of the way. He found my cock again with his spare hand, and we writhed around together until I could taste his sperm. He was delicious, and I loved the strangely sweet vanilla taste of him. It came gushing out into my mouth, gobs of it, as if he hadn't come in weeks.

We lay wrapped in each other's arms for a very long time until I felt him reach for the clock on my nightstand. We looked at the glow-in-the-dark hands together. It was 3:30. I would be an utter disaster in court the next day if I didn't try for a few hours of sleep, but I couldn't let go of him. He kissed me again, and we entwined tongues. He reached for my cock. I was hard again. "You have a beautiful cock," he said.

"*Me?* You're the one."

He was beautiful all over. Blond hair, no, red. Strawberry blond really. Green eyes, no blue. It all depended on the ways he caught the light and reflected it back into my face.

Although I still thought this boy was a product of my fevered imagination, that not one particle, not one delicious corpuscle of him could be solid flesh, it didn't seem to be important as I gazed upon him lifting my legs, getting into position between my thighs. Good god, I thought, he's going to fuck me again. Emotions I barely knew the name of washed over me in a torrent of intense longing that left me shaken, utterly speechless. All I could do was lie on my bed and listen to the sound of my own heart pounding hard in my chest and watch as he slowly inserted that magnificent rod into me.

"Wow! It sure is a shame that you're not real."

"Of course I'm real, man." His perfect lips parted, and his words echoed in my mind. His voice was soft, husky, melodious, everything it should be. He didn't so much talk as sing, and I fell in love all over again as those tones wrapped themselves around my spine.

"You're real to me; that's enough." My voice was a mere whisper of sound, but he heard it and smiled.

"Don't you want to know who I am?" he asked and drifted slowly forward until he hovered above me. I wanted to reach up and grab him, but I was afraid that if I tried to touch him, cling too tightly, he would vanish.

"No." I didn't want to know anything about him in case that made him disappear. I just wanted to drown in the loveliness of his body.

"You're a funny guy," he mused, his forehead creased into a frown as his cock slid into me again. "Don't you even want to know where I came from?"

"No." I had no curiosity. I was willing to accept his presence without wondering anything about it. "Just fuck me. Just *fuck* me."

"I wish you'd quit thinking this is just a dream," he said, "I am as real as you are."

It felt real, that magnificent cock, as it slid in and out of me.

"I'm sorry. It's just so crazy."

"That's all right," he said, "happens all the time." He hovered above me, looking thoughtful, as his penis jabbed me expertly.

As I watched him fucking I thought again just *how* beautiful he was and I suddenly felt a need to tell him so, to tell him how much this meant to me. I knew that it was crazy, feeling this way about somebody I'd just met, but I couldn't help it.

"Don't you want to know why I'm here?" he asked, lifting me up by my ankles.

"You're here to fuck me."

"Not entirely. I came here to save your soul."

"Oh?" Suddenly I understood. Somehow it didn't seem all that important, although I knew it was, of course.

"Why did you tell me?"

"Because...oh, I don't know! I just like you. I thought you ought to know the price you must pay for this." The jabbing was never-ending; I was amazed at his prowess.

"See, I'm selfish! I'm taking advantage of you!"

"I don't care," I cried. "You can save my soul. You can *have* it. I couldn't care less!" Even if he was doing what he said, he was still the most important thing in my life at that moment. I had known so little of beauty, so little of happiness, so little of great sex. He had given me a taste of it and I loved him for it, no matter what the outcome. "But why do you want to save my soul?" I asked.

"I get extra points," he chuckled, continuing the fuck all through this period of revelation, never losing his erection.

"You keep fucking me like that, you'll get a lot of points right here."

"But I want to save your soul. You know, if you lose your soul, you will cease to exist. When you die, you will not continue—"

"Okay, I want to continue. So now fuck me shitless." I couldn't express the excitement I felt. At that particular moment, as I lay on my back, his cock sliding in and out of me with an intense rhythm I had never experienced before, nothing was more important to me than coming again.

"I am," he said, confidentially, "because I want to save your soul, no matter what I have to do."

"Just keep at it," I begged, feverishly stroking my cock.

"You don't know what you're giving me!"

"Yes, I do." I was close now, stroking as if my life depended on it, which maybe it did. "You've saved me!" I closed my eyes and came.

Slowly, hesitantly, he clamped his lips on mine and began to kiss me. It was the tenderest kiss ever, but gradually his touch became more and more solid and we fell asleep in each other's embrace.

. . .

"I was named after a saint, you know."

"Oh?" I was fixing breakfast. Orange juice, coffee, toast, bacon and eggs.

"Yeah, St. Teresa, the Little Flower of Jesus. But of course, I was a boy so my mother named me Terry. But I enjoy being a saint. Really I do."

"And saving souls by making love to men?"

"Men who really need it. And, man, you needed it."

"Yes, I certainly did. But how does God, or whatever you call him - "

"My Master."

"Yes, the Master. Anyhow—"

"It's this way: You don't have to do great things in the world to be considered holy; I can do my Master's work anywhere. Grace can just as easily be won by scrubbing floors or by fucking lawyers."

"That's comforting to know."

I *had* been fucked by a Saint! It was, after all, the most heavenly fuck I had ever known, so I wasn't a bit sorry.

But what I hadn't counted on was that Terry still wasn't finished with his work. He sought further sanctification by being fucked by a lawyer. "As long as I'm here," he said with a wink.

I told him to just stay at the apartment. I had to be in court but only to file a motion. I'd be back in two hours. "Don't go away," I pleaded.

"Okay," he said, finishing his breakfast. Saints, I saw, could really work up an appetite. Perhaps he was human, after all, at least a bit.

Just after one, I returned home and he was in the bathroom taking a shower. My first inclination was to jump in with him but I figured a saint needed his privacy.

I flicked on the TV, not knowing what to expect next. "The Bishop's Wife" with Cary Grant and Loretta Young was on TNT. I hadn't even selected the channel, it just was there when I pushed the button. I had seen the movie several times but now I had a very special feeling for it. I must have watched a half hour of it before Terry came from the bathroom with a white towel wrapped around his thin waist. His hair was damp and he was drying it with another towel. "What's on?" he asked. "I don't get a chance to see much TV."

"It's a story about one of your associates," I chuckled. "An angel who comes down to visit a bishop and his wife at Christmas."

"A bishop? What kind of bishop?" His eyes sparkled.

"Episcopalian, I believe."

He grimaced. "Hell, they aren't any fun. Now those Catholic bishops, they can be fun; they're always horny, but they don't need any help from us. They get all the sex they want."

"That's comforting to know."

"What'd be comforting is if you'd stick that big dick up my ass before I go crazy from wanting it."

At that point he helped me out of my clothes and began his attack on my groin. If I thought what had happened earlier was exciting, this was beyond comprehension.

Once I got him to the bedroom, I got into position between Terry's muscular legs and straddled his head. He licked my balls, then pushed down on the topside of the throbbing cock so that it slid into his mouth easily. Bending over his body, I began my assault on his asshole.

I locked my legs around the back of his neck and pushed down. He nearly choked on the cock. I squeezed one cheek of his ass with my hand. My finger slid in. He had prepared himself while he was in the bathroom. He could take three fingers easily. I released my cock from his mouth and he begged me to fuck him.

Now I got into a new position, on my knees between his legs, holding myself up at an angle on my arms and not touching him, and then I slowly began pushing my cock in. Terry stirred and tried to roll over, but I stopped him, pushing him onto his belly. The hole expanded and I pressed. He began moving his hips slowly, carefully. I held himself steady and soon the cock was halfway in. Terry moaned and stopped moving momentarily, then I began again, slowly sliding in another inch. I pushed in, drew out, slipping my hands around his ribs and twisting his erect nipples. I began moving faster and Terry writhed, twisted, rotated his hips. I pumped himself deeply into him. His muscles clutched me as I came and I collapsed onto his back.

Panting, I rolled off of him and found I still had an erection.

Terry rolled over and stroked it with his hand.

"Oh, do it again," he pleaded.

I grabbed his legs and spread the cheeks of his ass. My tongue entered his slimy hole. I tasted my own cum, tickled the soft, sensitive lips of his anus, then pierced it as hard and deeply as I could. I withdrew my tongue, then started again. I fucked him with my tongue for a good while, driving him wild. Finally, he begged me, "Please, fuck me. Fuck me like you've never fucked anybody in your whole life!"

Fully intending to obey him, I aimed my cock at the slick, puckering hole. I rubbed my cockhead, glistening with precum, up and down against it, slowly working the head in. My cock was inching in slowly and Terry moaned, "Oh, yeah, oh, oh, oh."

As I plowed the ass relentlessly, we kissed, deeply, passionately, as lovers. Then I broke away to spend a few minutes on each of his splendid pectorals, grabbing them with both hands and forcing up so that they soon resembled a woman's tits. I sucked the nipples violently, all the while accompanied by the delightful sound of my groin and belly slapping the boy's ass.

I sat back up and took my cock almost out, then with little, short thrusts, renewed my fucking, then rammed it in to the hilt. My hands, spread out flat on his ass, were stretching the hole, opening it was wide as possible. He began breathing harder, his luscious prick wobbling wildly before me, soon coming without his even stroking it this time. Finally I rammed my cock into his ass one last time that afternoon and came.

"Wow," he said, stroking my back as I lay atop him, gasping. "Not even a bishop ever did as good as that!"

I kissed his shoulder. "That's good to know."

Terry was starved. I took him to my favorite restaurant, The Pier, for red snapper. While we were eating, I said, "I've heard of selling your soul to the devil but I've never heard of sending saints out to fuck to save souls—"

He smiled. "It's something new we're trying."

"I think it's wonderful."

"Yeah, sex sells."

I realized that every time I tried to ask a question, he'd turn the answer into a question for me. He knew all about my cases and asked me some questions about them that were never brought out in court. "Are you thinking of calling on some of my clients?"

"No. But I think what you've done is, like you say, wonderful. You deserve to be saved."

I tried asking about what happens to the soul, what's the Master *really* like, all those questions for which there have never been any answers, but Terry remained elusive. "You'll see," he teased.

What I did see was Terry, later in my bedroom, again on his knees, me launching what would be my final assault on his perfectly rounded ass. Where I got all that energy I couldn't fathom, but I knew it had something to do with the fact I had given my soul to this saintly boy.

The next morning, I woke up alone in bed. There was no sign of Terry. No note, nothing. It was as if he was never there, except he was. I know he was. And the last thing he told me before we fell asleep was to "keep on doing what you're doing, but take a little time for yourself." I promised I would.

And nowadays when I drive through the park I think I see Terry there, among the trees or swimming nude in the pond. Sometimes I find a boy willing to play but, mostly, I just go home and jack off to the vision of Terry in all his youthful loveliness. For me, there'll never be another boy quite like Terry. It's a madness only a saint would understand.

SMOOTH 'N' SASSY

As I shuffled through the door of the old bar on the beach, I scanned the small space. On vacation in Florida for the first time, I was fresh meat—something new to look at—and wanted to use that to my advantage. I hoped that someone was in the mood for a new kid in town because I was in the mood for a good fuck.

I decided to find a good seat at the bar. I felt sassy enough to order my signature drink in the hopes of at least getting a smile out of the surly, balding bartender. "A Cocksucker, please." He raised an eyebrow, as if I was the only one who had ever ordered it before. Maybe I was, in this place.

No one caught my eye or seemed tough enough to take me on. The most interesting sight was the sharp pool sticks standing in a perfect row against the wall that faced twin pool tables. I imagined what the long, pointy sticks would feel like colliding with my backside, or being shoved roughly inside me. Watching a good but dirty game of pool was like hot foreplay for me, and everyone knows that a skilled pool player is an even better fuck.

One guy certainly was serious about playing pool, but I wasn't completely mesmerized by the action on that green table until his opponent came from the john and stepped up to it. The youthful stud captured me from the moment he confidently filled the empty red triangle with solid and striped balls. Such precision and perfection. He knew exactly where he wanted each ball and how close they should be to each other. I wanted him to fill me up with the same power and gentle force. From the first time his stick collided with the shiny balls, it was evident that his hands were rhythmic, generous, methodical. I could tell how strong his arms were from the power behind his shots.

He carefully set up each shot, and before he was ready to shoot, he made an unbelievable move. Leaning over the table, he spread his legs by twisting his ankles and sliding his feet apart. Then he smacked the cue ball sharp and fast.

As his balls ducked into the dark pockets and disappeared from the table, I watched his eyes guide them there with a concentrated deliberateness that made my cock swell. I wanted desperately to cruise him without distracting him from the game that was making me so hot. Before he pummeled the eight ball in to win, through smoke bright from the light overhead, his eyes moved from the table, glanced over his glasses and focused on me. His look had the same force behind it as his shots.

By the time he'd beaten all the regulars, I decided to open myself for his first move. I coolly turned around on my bar stool, putting my back to the action. I leaned against the warm and sticky surface of the bar. Seconds later, a sweaty bottle of Coors appeared on the edge of the bar in front of me. A small hand with flushed, rough skin around the knuckles and perfectly trimmed nails gripped the bottle confidently. I hoped the hand was his and turned coyly around on my bar stool to get a better look.

I think I actually gasped slightly at the sight of him up close. Fuck, he was gorgeous! He was built solidly, but just how solidly was hidden by the baggy shorts and an oversized T-shirt. His hair was short, wet, strawberry blond, slicked back. I always had a thing for blonds, but never seemed to make it past the cruising stage with them. His nerdy gold-rimmed glasses framed the most intense blue eyes I had ever seen look at me. Then he smiled. That did it. It was over. I thought I would come then and there.

"Hi. I thought you might like another," he said, pouring on the charm like the pro he so obviously was.

"Thanks," I said as I reached my hand out for his. He took my hand gently at first, then squeezed it so hard I thought I might gasp again. He released my hand and let his drop to my thigh. He just lingered there. "So, what brings you to Florida?"

"That obvious, eh?"

He nodded. "But I'm a tourist here myself."

"You played well tonight. Is your game always that intense?" I got my first chance to smell him as he moved behind me, breathing against the back of my neck. Sweat mixed with Polo. His hand traced my ass through my shorts. My cock hardened. He took a gulp from his beer, then, "Well, it really depends. How's your game?"

"Pretty rusty I'm afraid." I took a deep breath.

He took another drink of his beer and put out the cigarette he had just lit. I saw the fearlessness in his smoky eyes, and I wanted him to take me home. I wanted him to fuck me. I didn't want to have any choice. I didn't want to have any small talk. No discussion, no negotiation, no latex, no lube. Just him inside me. Without my permission. Without my asking. Well, maybe begging. Just pull me through the door and push me on the bed and get inside me.

"Let's go," he instructed, and he took my hand in his again. Then he walked stridently, leading me past everyone who would have died to be going home with him. But it was as if he was showing *me* off. I felt a rush of excitement throughout my body unlike any in years..

When we got outside, he put his arm around me as we walked in silence.

"Your place or mine?" I asked.

"We can walk to yours," he said.

I blinked. I didn't remember mentioning where I was staying. Still, I said, "Okay," without hesitation.

The walk was long, and the closeness just made my cock harder. We arrived at my room and he was smiling the toothy grin of a naughty boy with dirty thoughts and secrets and plans.

He sat me on the bed, leaned forward, and planted the most incredible kiss on my lips. His tongue probed my mouth and lips as his hands explored what felt like every inch of my body. His touches were precise, perfect, like the way he handled the stick, worked the balls in his pool game. It was as if he had diligently studied my body and knew all its curves and tender spots by heart, like he knew the pool table: hands gliding, stroking, pressing, until my already-sun-burned flesh relaxed in warmth and wetness underneath him, ready to go into whatever deep pocket he was pushing me. He pulled back from me and stood studying my body with his acute, extreme eyes. His concentration and the quietness that surrounded us was terrifying. Electric.

"You like to cry when someone hits you, don't you?"

I paused. "Yes...yes, I do."

"It feels good, doesn't it?"

"Uh-huh." Actually, I have a hard time crying, losing

control. Oh, I love being a submissive, but it ain't easy. But having a dick in me is a million times easier and safer for me than revealing what's *really* deep inside. Crying is too revealing—it means I've gone too far. I've let him get too close. He terrified me in that moment when he said it like he knew I liked it. None of my lovers had ever asked me about crying. No one had ever made it a goal to make me cry, so no one had ever gotten to that part of me.

It was beginning to dawn on me that this was not just another bar pick-up. He was strange. I wanted to know how he knew where I was staying, how much I liked being a cry-baby. And why was I so eager to go with him. Yes, go *anywhere* with him! It was baffling to me.

He nodded and whispered, "Good boy. Now turn around and lean over the bed." He'd had enough of questions and talking for now.

I did as he said. He pulled down my shorts until they were around my ankles. He began methodically tracing my body, as if he were preparing for some ritual. His fingers were smooth on my skin, except for his rough knuckles, which added a coarse texture to his touches as he explored my ass with the back of his hand. He took my flesh between his fingers and squeezed with a deliberate sense of ownership and devotion. I anticipated and anxiously awaited being bound in leather restraints or some elaborate rope work, but instead he tied me up with one quiet breath. "I don't need to restrain you. You'll stay still for me like a good boy, won't you?"

"Yes, Daddy."

He chuckled. His first smack was quick, sharp, stinging. I felt the skin of my ass warm beneath his palm. There were three more to follow. He alternated from right to left. One hard and slow with lots of power behind it. Then, without time to recover, without time to move slightly so he wouldn't hit the exact spot, he came down with three fast and vicious slaps. After each set of four, he rubbed my tender, burning flesh with the softest part of his hand. As the beating continued, I writhed, began to arch my back, raised my ass to meet his harsh blows, offered myself to him. He alternated the hitting with teasing, rubbing my hole with his thumb, pushing into my ass-slit, sneaking inside me, then leaving for another smack, my scream, his groan, smack, smack, smack.

When my ass was tender and achingly hot, he told me how red it was, how good it felt under his fingers, and how hard he got when he hit me. Then he slid his belt out of the loops of his baggy shorts. The firm leather was rough, mean, and hurt even more on my fleshy ass, already raw from his hand and my nude sunbathing. I screamed louder—it hurt more; I wanted to flinch, but wouldn't dare. I arched my back again, this time to drop my head down, look between my legs, and catch a peek at him. With one hand he held the belt, with the other he stroked his firm dick, which stood majestically between his legs. It was the most beautiful cock I'd ever seen. I wanted to suck it, but that would have to wait.

Once I was reeling high enough from the whipping, he took me in his arms and we kissed. He forced open my lips and his tongue began exploring my dry mouth.

His fingers played with my ass. The feeling of needing to shit, the fear of pain in that tenderest of all places, anxiety about being dirty, all of it became secondary to the desire that his incredible cock would follow his fingers and pierce me deeply, take more pleasure in my ass.

"God, you feel good, so good," he murmured, his hands lifting and separating the cheeks.

Soon his fingers massaged the sides of my asshole, then he positioned his cock. He pushed a little. I held still, letting the stud work on me. There was a popping sensation as the head of the dick slipped past his sphincter, then the smooth length of the shaft filling me.

But he reached around and began playing with my cock. I brushed his hand away because it was distracting; I wanted to be able to concentrate on the delightful penetration. I wanted to feel my ass hugging and milking the stud, delighting him until he came. Surprisingly, my ass opened up for his dick as if he had fucked me a dozen times before, drawing him deep inside and sucking on him like a hungry child, which made my prick swell. But now the possibility of coming myself before he did was annoying. He fucked for a few moments, then began to withdraw. "No, please," I begged.

"Hmmm," he sighed as I pushed back when he pushed back in. I tried to twist my head around so I could see him, kiss him, but, no, he held my body down with his powerful arm, pressing into my shoulder blade with his weight. Now he began to use my ass as he really wanted to. Fast, hard, cruel.

"Yeah," he groaned. "God, I love your ass."

His rhythm was still precise, really perfect, quickening as he plunged deeper inside me. I let my body be pushed forward with his thrusts and moaned as my ass muscles gripped his dick. He came so fast, too fast, shooting his load inside me as he groaned, breathing hard. For a moment, he was absolutely still. He tried to roll off me but I followed with him, not permitting the cock to slip from me.

When his breathing slowed, I sat back on his cock, taking the length inside my ass as he pressed hard on my cock and cradled me in his lap. Surviving his painful smacks and then feeling his cum had sent me over the edge, and I was riding his dick and his hand as hard as I could. He was the boy I have dreamed about and jerked off to too many times to count. The one who won't leave my fantasies, who cruises me wherever I go, who seduces with his sexy voice, who plays pool and drinks beer, who grabs my ass in crowded bars just to fuck with me. He is the one who has never been mine until now.

Yes, now he was the one who was making my cock explode. And this was his gift to me now.

Spent, I fell to the bed, but he was not through. He started in on my ass again until I was past the place where I could possibly take another lash. The pain had become too intense, too much—but I felt alive, for the first time in months. He reached up, yanked the hair at the back of my neck, and smacked the side of my face. My lips were spread open. He shoved his cock into my mouth. Then I felt that soft part of his hand again against my cheek and mouth, and I burst into tears. I let go. I was crying. Real tears, at last. I sucked him until he came again, then we lay in each other's arms, bathed in sweat and cum. Every inch of me ached, my heart was racing, and I couldn't catch my breath. But his warm, familiar arms were wrapped around me, and I knew I was somewhere safe.

SHORT 'N' SWEET

"It was short and sweet... We were both very young. I was too needy. He wasn't needy enough."
– from "Love! Valour! Compassion!"
by Terrence McNally

I watched him walk down the street ahead of me. He had a fine body, slim-hipped in faded jeans worn low down to reveal his pale white skin. His corded arms were beautifully displayed in a plain white T-shirt, arms that are well-muscled for one so thin. He had long strawberry-blond hair and green eyes. He was amazing looking, really, with the fine, cut cheekbones that professional models would envy. Any time spent with him would be a gift from the gods, I thought. Little did I know.

My first hint that something was strange was when I finally caught up with him. He had stopped to look at a window display. A normal cruising ploy. But then, as we talked, I realized he knew me. He knew my name. I was stunned. More than just my name, the boy knew my history. My family. The rumors. Everything I'd tried to escape. I held still, seized by both my desire and fear. I stepped away from this boy who knew my name. I began to walk down the street. Half-hoping he would follow. Half-hoping I would disappear into the crowd of shoppers.

I thought I had lost him when I entered The Cave. The bar suited me at any time of day. Whether I'd just gotten up, or I didn't want to go to bed. Whether I'd been up for days and wanted a bit more to keep me up a few more days. It always suited me. There was something about the dark interior, with the vibrantly painted walls that glow under a violet light; something about the way the bartenders looked as if they might have been part-vampire, or part-alien. Dark hollows beneath their eyes that I found strangely attractive. And the patrons were even worse. They were all thin, junkie-looking, all after the same thing I wanted: not caffeine, not pure adrenaline, but that satisfied feeling that you can find only when sex is anonymous and abundant.

I wandered into the dimly lit interior in what was a slow-paced gait for me. I needed a drink badly. If I had enough to drink, I'd find myself in the dreamy state I had come to prefer those days. I didn't need any other drugs to enhance the effects. It was the most amazing feeling.

I nodded to people I knew as I made my way through to the back. I liked Mick, the bartender at the back of the place. He often pointed out new arrivals, fixed me up. He knew how painfully shy I was, especially before I'd had a drink or two.

I sat down, crossing my long legs and waited to catch Mick's eyes. He spotted me immediately and brought me my sinful potion without even waiting for my order. As he set it down in front of me, he asked, "Who's your friend?"

I turned around. "Jesus," I muttered. The stranger who knew my name was standing behind me, smiling. In this atmosphere, it was as if an angel had landed.

I smiled at him, then turned back to face Mick. "Oh, you know how I hate to drink alone."

"You on a break?"

"I am now."

We flirted easily, and occasionally I had taken him up to my apartment and given him what he needed.

"I'm off in an hour," he told me, innocently slipping one hand over mine. I let him, but I tilted my head. "I'd like that, but I don't know what he's going to do."

"Maybe I can join you?"

"I don't know."

"Well, I just thought...."

"You thought what?"

"You know... that you were free."

That brought a smile to my lips. "We'll see." It was a new experience for me having to choose. Normally I simply chased and most times never caught. I leaned back on my stool and turned to regard my new friend. He was even more stunning in the dark than he was on the street. He seemed to glow in the dark.

"Hi," I said, in mock surprise.

"You been waiting long?" he asked, taking the stool next to me.

"All my life," I answered.

"I know," he said.

"I was afraid of that—"

"What?"

"I'm sorry. I know I should remember your name, but—"

"Terry," he said, extending his hand.

I shook his hand, but I knew I had never met anyone named Terry, and certainly no one who ever looked like this boy.

Mick brought Terry the same magic potion he always served me, took a good close look at the boy, then left us alone.

Terry sipped it. "What is this?"

"Mick's Magic."

"It's very good."

"Takes only one, really. But I usually have two."

"You can finish mine. I'm not much of a drinker."

"That's a shame." I took a long swallow of the potion. Terry just sat there, drinking me in with his eyes. He brought his hand to my extended leg and started stroking me.

"You're a fast worker," I said.

He looked to one side, then the other. Then he smiled at me. "I don't have much time," he whispered.

Before we left the bar, I asked Mick to come over after he closed up. "To see if I'm still alive," I joked. But it really wasn't said in jest. This boy had unnerved me. And the sensation didn't end when we got back to my apartment on Beekman Place. Terry made himself comfortable at the piano and began tinkling the ivories. He was very good, and I recognized immediately the song he was playing, "Who's Next?" from the score of my last failed musical, five years ago. I didn't know anyone remembered that song.

"I'm amazed you know that," I said, sitting down next to him, handing him a cognac.

"I love the song. The lyrics are great." He sang a few bars and I suddenly realized I was hopelessly drawn into his spell. The greatest compliment one can pay a composer is to have his songs sung by a beautiful singer, and I was overwhelmed with gratitude.

His little impromptu concert lasted a good fifteen minutes. By the time it was over, I was hugging and kissing him. He stood. "I will sleep with you and your friend if you promise me something."

"My friend?"

"The bartender that's due here later."

"Oh, him. Well, see I—"

"I see very well. But what I want is that you finish the score for 'Just Friends'."

My jaw dropped. Almost no one knew about the musical I had been working on for ten years. In fact, my agent had given up on me.

But Terry was not about to give up on me. He drew my head into his crotch. My lips brushed the bulge. I gnawed at it, tried to pry his pants apart, but he held my hands.

"You must promise me."

"This is crazy."

"No, it is necessary. You need someone to push you. I've been sent to push you."

"Ye gods!" I shut my eyes tight. I wanted to rest a moment, then open them and he would be gone. But when I opened them he was still there. Worse yet, he had undone his pants and I was being confronted by the most perfect penis I'd ever seen. It looked like a missile ready to fire. I wanted it in my mouth and up my ass. At that point, I would have agreed to anything.

"Sure, kid," I promised. "I'll finish it."

"Good. The theater's already been rented for the workshop, so you only have five weeks."

"What?" Now he was behaving as if he had told me everything, only none of it had made any sense. God almighty.

"Now, shut up and suck," he commanded.

I could have devoured him, sucked him completely into me. Terry moaned. He writhed. I squeezed his cock-shaft, thick between my fingers, and Terry began to grind his hips. He grabbed at my hair, pressed me onto him. His soft-as-silk pubic hairs tickled my nose. That incredible cock lifted up in grateful anticipation. In a second, my mouth covered it, suckled it, rolled it. My hands raced up and down his thighs, then I held him by his buttocks. The swollen sexflesh was jammed deep down my throat as I slipped my fingers between the buttery folds until I found his puckering asshole. Terry got crazy. His body bucked and he pounded my back. He rocked like a wild man. I knew men, and he was ready. He was jerking. Crying.

Pleading. I had him. I had him good. My fingers dug deep into him as he came. It was a generous orgasm. He tasted unlike anyone I'd ever known. Sweet, in a way. I held him tight as his cock softened. He kissed me on top of the head and then disappeared into the bathroom.

While he was taking a shower, Mick rang from the lobby. "Boy, have I got a surprise for you," I chortled.

"I'll be right up."

I no longer felt strange about entertaining Mick in my home. I knew I had become a refuge for him, from the demands of his wife and baby, the bar, the customers who, like me, retained his services. He told me he was happiest here, but yet he could never stay for very long. I poured more cognac and waited for him. I longed to feel his big dick again. There was no more fear. Or embarrassment. Only hunger as I waited for his tap on the door.

I swallowed the last of my cognac and told him to join me on the piano bench. I had been doing as I was told by Terry, finishing the score. "Come here," I said. He stepped closer and sipped his cognac. My fingers went to his zipper, moving it down along its tracks. Avoiding the bulge behind the jeans, my fingers moved to the brass button holding them there on his hips. I glanced up at his face as I unbuttoned them and spread the flaps of denim back to expose his briefs and the prick that lay under them. He smiled, and commanded: "Suck it! Suck it through my underwear, and move my jeans down at the same time...."

I stuck my tongue out and tentatively began to do what he'd suggested.

"Yeah' baby...." He pulled his shirt over his head as I moved my tongue back and forth along the shaft hiding behind the thin white cotton and my fingers pulled his jeans down his legs.

I slipped off the bench and knelt before him, helping him step out of his jeans. My tongue stroked that slab of meat still hidden from me. I grabbed at his briefs with both hands and pulled.

"You're hungry tonight," he chuckled from above me as I pulled away and finally saw it again for the first time in almost a month. It flopped in my face, oozing pre-cum from the tip.

"God, I love your cock," I babbled.

"I've noticed," said he, pushed my head forward. Mick's cock always tasted as good as it looked. The raw smell of musk, the smoky essence from working all those hours at the bar, and sweat that wafted into my nostrils as I took him down to his pubic hairs was more exciting to me than a deep hit of poppers. I had sucked it for only a few moments when Terry came back in the room, a towel wrapped around his waist.

"Well, look at what we have here," Mick said.

"Yeah, look," Terry said, stepping over to us. Terry felt Mick's heft while Mick stroked the bulge in the towel. They kissed each other.

Mick said, "Oh, yeah, let's party...."

I stared into his eyes as he lifted me back to my feet. His hands moved to possess my assglobes and pulled me to him. Terry's hand joined Mick's at my ass and they hugged me. I was dazzled by being so desired by two such gorgeous studs.

I led the way to the bedroom, tore off my bathrobe, and then made the mistake of going to the bathroom. But, reflecting on it, I knew exactly what I was doing. When I returned to the bedroom, they were wrapped in each other's arms, a spirited 69 in process. I sat on the bed next to them and enjoyed myself. I had seen such a display several times at the baths, but not performed by two such superb specimens. They carried on for several minutes while I stroked my cock to full hardness. While their mouths were fully occupied, their hands were not idle. They explored each other's body, and there was much squirming, spasming and sighing as they appreciated each other's physical attributes. Mick was the first to pull off, gushing, "Oh, man—"

"Told you," I said.

"You ready?" he said, squeezing my erection.

"Oh, yes."

Terry knelt on the bed behind me, and guided me back onto all fours. Mick knelt in front of me, holding his hard cock before my mouth. Instinctively, I slid my mouth onto it, taking it down my throat, as Terry plunged his cock into my ass. The hard shaft in my mouth muffled my loud groans and Terry furiously pounded in and out of my ass. He fucked me like he didn't care how it felt, like he wanted to rip me in two.

"Yeah," Mick snarled, "He sure likes to have two cocks at once!" He began fucking my face at a speed that equaled his partner's.

I was just settling into the rhythm of the double-fuck when Mick pulled out and slapped his prick wetly against my face. "Is that right? You want us both?" I nodded, rubbing my cheek against his huge, uncut cock. "Hey, I bet he'd like us both to fuck him! Would you like that? Can you handle two cocks up your ass?" In answer, I wrapped my mouth around his cock again, greedily sucking it, as Terry's cock continued to plow my butt.

The idea excited Mick and he wouldn't let it go. "Hey," he said, "let me get under him."

I raised up far enough to permit Mick to lie under me. Slowly I mounted him and took his cock into me. He took me in his arms and held me as Terry got in position. My ass felt like it was on fire as the second cock slid all the way into me. My head was thrashing from side to side, violent groans escaping my throat. The two men pumped their cocks into me. After what seemed like forever, they slowly slid out of me. I blinked at suddenly being left so empty. They lay on their backs with their legs entwined, so their hard cocks stood, pressed together. "Get your ass over here," Mick commanded. "Sit on our cocks." I rose and straddled their pricks, which they held together like one massive organ. I lowered myself down until two sets of balls pressed against me. "Come on, ride us!" Mick yelled. I bounced up and down, feverishly jacking off. Each time their long tools penetrated my ass a wave of fire swept through my crotch. I couldn't hold back much longer. Behind me I heard Mick moan."I'm gonna shoot! I'm gonna...." Then he howled, erupting inside me. His cock slid out of my ass and he crawled out from under me, silently leaving the room. Terry thrust his hips upward and drove into me harder, his cock sliding through Mick's cum which filled my ass. Terry's fucking me raw put me over the edge. I threw my head back as my cum splattered onto Terry's chest and stomach. Terry shuddered, and I felt a second wave of cum gush into my ass. Sore and exhausted, I collapsed next to Terry.

Mick came back into the room, freshly showered. "I guess you're safe. I gotta get home. The old lady's waitin'."

I thanked him for stopping by. Mick kissed me goodnight, then kissed Terry. I could tell he didn't want to leave, but he knew it was best for all concerned if he did. Terry said he had to leave as well, but he lingered for about an hour, showering, dressing, playing the piano. It was nearly dawn by the time he kissed me goodbye. I stood at the door watching him get on the elevator. In a way, I felt sad for him. He had had many lovers, I was sure, but no lover. Each one who had touched him had to let him go. But it was great while it lasted.

THERE SHOULD HAVE BEEN MUSIC...

It was a warm, bright and shining day and I was driving a company car from Naples north to Tampa. I was stuck in traffic, late for a meeting with my boss. I had become irritable and edgy. The trunk was stowed with samples, literature and display materials. I'd kept myself in top gear for three years, ever since I'd been graduated from Florida State. I'd turned myself into the best road man the Owen Drug Company had ever seen. I was making fifty thousand a year, with stock options. I was buying Owen stock with every dime I could hoard after taxes. I was on my way to my first million, my boss said.

But I was chronically hoarse from my spiels to doctors and druggists. And it was hard not to notice that I was going through three packs of cigarettes a day, and I hadn't been sleeping well of late. Plus I was bothered by nervous indigestion, and my temper was too easily lost. In other words, I was a mess and I wasn't even thirty!

Stuck in yet another traffic jam on Route 41 on the south end of Sarasota, I saw my chance to move ahead and I would have made the light by a huge shopping mall if a big Cadillac with Ohio plates, driven by an old broad with blue hair, hadn't drifted over into my lane and blocked me. I was running behind schedule, and so I sat, cursing the bitch, holding my steering wheel so tightly my knuckles ached.

I happened to glance over toward a part of the mall's parking lot that had been fenced off. It was a festival of some kind. Floridians are big on festivals to attract the snowbirds, in town with nothing to do and plenty of money to spend. A crowd of people were clustered with their backs toward the highway, watching something.

I saw a youth burst up into the air, higher than their heads. With his body straight out, he made a turn so slow and so elegant it seemed that I was watching it in slow motion, and then fell back out of sight and reappeared again in a slight variation of the first turn. I knew that the kid in the bright sunlight was the most astonishingly beautiful thing I had ever seen. I watched him until an indignant horn blasted behind me, and I saw the Ohio Cadillac so far ahead I knew the light had changed long ago.

I charged ahead, but couldn't lose the thought of that youth in the air. I suddenly had the horrible realization that I was close to breaking into tears. I now know it was a clue to the extent of my nervous exhaustion. Something so precious had occurred that I couldn't even put a name to it. And here I was, running away from it. I drifted over to the curb, found a place to turn around and went back. I parked, locked the car and joined the crowd.

It was a demonstration of a trampoline. I had seen it being done, but not like this. Neither had the other people, I guess. Except for some squealing kids, the other customers inside the fence had stopped to watch the beautiful youth also, in a hypnotic silence. It was like a wild strange dance he was improvising as he went along, with a complete grace and total control in spite of the tremendous height he was achieving. He looked incredibly young, had a burnished tan and was strongly constructed. His hair was a tousled strawberry-blond mass. He had one of those wide-cheeked Slavic faces of a totally deceptive placidity. With a dreamy look on his face, he seemed to drift about in a better world than any of the rest of us could ever know.

Suddenly he smothered the next leap with a deft flex of his knees and stepped off the trampoline. We gave an audible group sigh because it was over, and then we all began clapping. He looked startled, but smiled, bowed with professional aplomb and bent to put his shoes back on as the applause died and the people began drifting away.

I moved toward the gate where he would come out. I heard the proprietor telling him to stop there at any time and be his guest. It was a smart move for him, generating a big crowd.

The boy came out, moving slowly, earthbound after soaring. He was sturdy and smaller than I would have guessed. But as he neared me I could detect none of the residual puffing and damp sweatiness of great athletic effort.

"There should have been music with that," I told him.

He gave me a cool glance of dismissal, but I was not to be denied. Not this time. I walked beside him. He continued to pretend I was not there.

"I have to tell you something," I said.

"Oh?" he said curtly.

"I was just driving through and I had to stop for that light. Then I saw you over the heads of those people, way up in the middle of the air. I drove on because I'm supposed to be in Tampa by four o'clock for a sales meeting, but I found out I had to come back and find you and tell you how beautiful it was. That's all."

He stopped and looked up at me. "You really goin' to Tampa?"

"Yes."

"I've never been to Tampa."

We were near the entrance to the food court in the mall. "Could I buy you a Coke?"

He shrugged. "Yeah. I'm pretty thirsty," he said.

We went to the burger stand. He ordered a fresh orange slush. I ordered coffee. We sat at a little table far away from everyone else. I handed him my business card.

"Paul Fox," he read. "Short name."

"What's yours?"

"Long name. But you can call me Terry."

"Terry it is."

"You live in Tampa?"

"Yeah. I'm based in Tampa. I spend four days a month there. I drive fifty thousand miles a year."

"Must be boring."

"Usually. But not today."

He smiled and sipped his slush.

I looked at my watch. I spotted the phone booths. "Terry, I have to make a phone call. Promise you won't leave before I come back."

"If you don't get back before I feel like leaving, I won't be here. How much do you expect for one orange slush?"

I laughed out loud. This kid was too much.

I called my boss. I was stranded in Sarasota with car trouble, I informed him. He told me to pick up a rental car. I said it was tire trouble, and I'd wrenched my back foolishly changing the wheel and I didn't feel like driving. He believed my every word. It was my first lapse from total dependability.

Then I saw Terry get up and begin strolling toward the door.

I cut my boss off by saying, "Hello? Hello? Hello? Damn it!" and hanging up.

I caught up with Terry a hundred feet from the entrance. "Where are you going?"

"Home."

"I thought you were going with me to Tampa."

"What?"

"Tampa. You said you wanted to go to Tampa. You'd never been. That's what you'd said."

He shook his head. "You're wasting your time, Paul Fox."

I stopped dead in my tracks. My heart rolled over as he walked on. It was the first time I really noticed him from the rear. If ever there was an ass meant for fucking, that was it. I sighed. I hadn't had a piece of ass in so long I couldn't even remember the last one. Then he turned back and looked at me curiously. Suddenly he threw his head back and laughed like hell.

"You're kinda cute, Paul Fox. That's it, you're a fox. But I bet you get that a million times a day."

"No. No, I don't."

"That's a shame, 'cause you really are a fox."

As we walked together toward my car, I stole careful glances at him. Only the most perfect physical conditioning, I thought, could produce a walk like his. He moved like a panther on a jungle path. There was a small-boy appeal about him, but a defiance in the squareness and sturdiness of his jaw. And then there was that world-weary look in his eyes. I sensed this boy had more miles on him than even I.

He seemed placidly content with our silence, and I knew I would have to initiate any conversation. "You were really great on the trampoline. Really great. I can't get over it."

"My mom's with the circus. I work out with her."

I felt like thumping myself in the head. This was Sarasota. It explained some of the strangeness of him. Circus people were the most clannish people in the world. "Which circus?"

He chuckled. "The big one."

I knew getting any information out of him was going to be a struggle. Besides, he was now making me nervous. He was too good-looking to be walking along with me. I lit up.

"You smoke too much," he said abruptly.

"I know I do."

"So why don't you smoke less?"

"There's a lot of strain connected with my job, Terry."

"Strain? Selling pills?" he asked with such surprise that it irritated me.

"They set a quota for me, and I have to meet it."

"So what happens when you meet it? The strain is over?"

"Well, no. They set a new quota."

He snorted and said, "Even in the seal act, a seal always gets a fish after every trick. They don't make her work harder each time for the fish. That quota thing is ridiculous."

I thought about it, and I saw that it was. I was being treated with less dignity than a seal in Terry's big circus. But I had to salvage something. "I make darn good money."

"How much?" he demanded.

"Uh, fifty, plus stock options."

"What do you spend it all on?"

"Taxes take a big bite because I'm single. After I pay living expenses, I invest what's left in stock in the company I work for."

"Ha."

"What's this *ha*?"

"Nothing. It just sounds like a crummy way to live, Paul Fox."

"I'm considered very successful for my age."

"Ha," he said again, and I didn't feel like contesting that one. I didn't know what he was calling me in his mind. It was an odd experience to be scorned and pitied by this delicious little boy.

We got into the car. I started pulling out of the parking lot. He didn't say anything, so I presumed I was on my way to Tampa. He'd never been to Tampa, he said, although now I was beginning to think there was no place this boy hadn't been.

"Are you sick?" he asked.

The question startled me. "Why do you ask me that?"

"You are pale, and I saw your hand shaking when you picked up your coffee cup. You look thin and stringy, and when somebody squealed their brakes when we pulled into traffic it sent you right up in the air."

"I don't get a chance to get much sun, Terry. I've been

working hard without a break for a long time. No, I'm not sick."

"You don't look healthy."

"Compared to you I've *never* been healthy, I guess."

"You look older than thirty."

"I like what you do for my morale, boy."

"I'm not doing it. You've been doing it to yourself—for that fifty thousand dollars."

"God!"

Terry chuckled. "God has nothing to do with it. Believe me, I know."

"Look—"

"I wouldn't say it if you really were sick. I care about you, Paul Fox. I really do."

So I used up a couple of blocks of silence thinking about that. He cares about me? Why would he care?

"What's wrong?" he asked, rubbing my thigh tenderly.

"Nothing, really. You just called me a fox. Nobody's called me that in so long. But, you know, a fox recognizes the traps."

He stared at me with great intensity, squeezed my thigh, and repeated, "I care. I really do."

By the time we arrived in Tampa, at my rented house on Bayshore Drive, I was a nervous wreck. Out of deference to him, I hadn't smoked a single cigarette. And I had given Terry my entire life history. I realized I had done nothing more than answer his questions. I knew absolutely nothing about this youth who was so easily seduced into going to Tampa with me. There was no discussion of any kind about what we would do, how long he would stay, nothing. Yet when I looked at him, I forgot all of that. I was consumed by lust. I kept picturing how he looked as he walked away from me, how the black denim shorts hugged his full, round buttocks.

Inside my house, we fell into another long awkward silence. I decided to give him a tour of the house, ending in the bedroom, of course. I really could hardly wait to get him out of those shorts.

But when we arrived there, Terry had to go to the bathroom. He closed the door behind him, and I raced to the nightstand and lit up. I smoked while he was in there. Feeling much better, I made myself comfortable on the bed, and was just finishing my third cigarette when he emerged from the bathroom. I had heard the shower running so I knew he was making himself pretty but nothing could have prepared me for the vision of loveliness that appeared beside my bed. He had one of my big white bath towels wrapped around his slender waist and his hair was slicked back. I coughed. In that moment, I thought he had to have been the most beautiful human being I had ever laid eyes on in my entire life. He was so beautiful that tears came to my eyes.

But he was frowning. "You smoke too much, Paul Fox."

"I guess I just like to have something to suck on."

He giggled. It was a little boy's giggle, crazy, light-hearted. And then he dropped the towel.

Terry was beautiful all over. Of course the cock was splendid, in perfect proportion with the rest of him, but the ass was a work of art. He turned to expose it to me and I rubbed it, squeezed the mounds. He turned again, wanting oral servicing first.

I played with his semi-erect cock. Slowly I licked the tip and the underside of it. It smelled clean, suckable. His voice, ragged with passion, sighed, "Oh, yeah!"

It was soon fully erect and I took it deep in my mouth. I felt it press on my tongue and slide down my throat. It tasted so good, and he groaned with pleasure, throwing his head back.

His ever-seeping pre-cum saturated my mouth and throat. I devoured it like a hungry stray dog and soon he was frantically pounding my quivering throat.

"Oh, suck on that cock! Suck on that cock like it was the last cock you'll ever get!" With another thrust, he was close to the point of no return, and although he tried holding it back it was no use. With one last hard thrust, he crammed his big dick all the way down my throat, forcing my lips to hug around the base. My nose was nuzzled into his crotch hair as I tried hard not to gag on the heavy load. But it was no use. I gagged at the force and volume and the cock slipped from my mouth, splattering cum across my face. With cum dripping from my lips, I caught my breath, only to have him force the still-spewing cock back down into my throat.

He moaned in relief as my head jerked back with each squirt.

Finally, he was done and sighed as I licked him clean—cock, balls and then on to the asshole. I poked my tongue into the lips of the ass. He groaned, but pushed me away.

"Let me get it ready. *Really* ready," he said, shoving me back on the bed. When he started in on my veiny eight-incher, I knew it wouldn't take much to get me "ready." I was very nearly over the top as it was.

He was a terrible tease as a cocksucker. But after a few moments, I realized he was simply toying with me, giving himself time to recover from his incredible orgasm. Finally my cock was sopping and he was ready. I'm afraid my experience with boys who bottom was extremely limited. Thus, I was stunned beyond words when he climbed over me and lowered himself over my prick. The sight of my cock being fucked by his asshole and him jacking off over me was more than I could bear. "Oh, no, no," I cried as I started to come. This caused him to slam down even harder on my prick.

"Yeah, I love your big dick," he groaned. He leaned back, his hips danced, gyrated, and he tugged at my cock. I pumped faster and faster, sweat flying off our bodies, my arms taut. Shuddering, I spurted my cum deep within him. When I was done, he stayed on top, jerking off to a second heroic orgasm. Then he collapsed over me. I wrapped him in my arms, and mumbled something stupid, like never wanting him to leave.

The next morning, I found him sleeping beside me, an angelic look on his face. As we ate breakfast, he convinced me I needed a little vacation. We took a long weekend, days of peculiar but real pleasure. We went out to the beach, moved from one cheap motel to another, from restaurant to restaurant, from convenience store to convenience store, pretending to be connoisseurs of this trashy world. ("Which do you prefer, Velveeta or Cheez Whiz?") We ate everything that was bad for us. He said we'd fuck it off.

We compared bedding, mattresses, the cleanliness of bathrooms, the number of cigarette scars on the furniture, the number of bugs. And I was grateful for nearly every moment of it. Whenever I needed a cigarette, he made me suck his cock. I never believed I could have quit cold-turkey but, at least for the time I was with this stranger, I had quit. It was amazing.

The whole thing was amazing.

In bed, we had become one single being, breathing with the rhythm of the sea outside the window, a slow continuous undulation like a ship rocking on the waves, forever buffeted by the surging.

This miracle had happened to me only once before, with a boy who had been mine during my college days and who went on to get married and have children. Terry suggested I look him up. I agreed to. "He's lonely," Terry said. And I didn't question how he knew this, I simply accepted it. There was just no fighting him. He said everything with such authority. And when he told me that I would be able to retire once Owen was merged with another company, I grew anxious. It was like the time I visited a fortune teller in New Orleans and she told me that my mother would die within weeks. Somehow, Terry had this same eerie power.

In the end, it was Terry who said it was time to get back. It was Tuesday. We were in what was called a "family-style" restaurant. I had been trying to signal the waitress for the bill. Now I lowered my hand and looked at Terry.

"It goes without saying, Terry, that this has been wonderful."

"Yeah, yeah."

And that was that. I paid the bill, we got in the car and drove back to Tampa. He agreed to stay the night and I would take him back to Sarasota in the morning.

After another night of incredible sex, we slept. In the morning, when I awoke I was alone. I searched the house but there was no sign of him. It was as if he had never been there, as if it had all been a dream.

I sat in bed, stunned. I reached over to the nightstand to get my cigarettes and the pack I had opened the night before was gone. So was my lighter. Frantically, I searched the room, and then the entire house. There were no cigarettes to be found. I took it as a sign, and, to this day, I have never smoked another.

THE NEW RECRUIT: A FEAR OF FLYING

Everyone is afraid of flying. You think, what if they can't ever come down again?

But I often dreamed of flying. Being unconnected. Being unattached. High in a sky that is in Technicolor and Cinemascope.

And finally I got to fly. It was a great adventure, as it turned out, mainly because I never left the ground. Not in a literal sense.

It all began when a massive snowstorm in the Northeast grounded all planes. So there I was at the airport with my duffle bag and a parka that I hadn't worn in two years, not since I was living in Buffalo with Mom and Dad, before I hitched to Florida. Outside the terminal, it was a balmy seventy-five degrees. When I told my folks what the weather was like where I was, and how I couldn't believe it was so bad where they were, there was dead silence. My dad hated the idea that I never had to shovel snow; that was what kept him going all winter, telling me to shovel out the driveway while he watched football on TV and got drunk.

Anyhow, there I was at the airport with everything cancelled, perhaps for several days, no one knew.

Worse yet, my lover, Bob, was stranded as well. We had planned to meet in New York City after I saw my folks. He was already in the Big Apple, attending a conference, and we had planned to have a "second honeymoon," to celebrate our first anniversary. But now that wasn't to be. Nothing was working. Not even, as it turned out, the cabs. There was a long line at the cab stand and I cursed myself for not driving and paying the long-term rate in the lot. But it was Bob who said it would be cheaper, considering we would be coming back together. Yes, it was all Bob's fault. *Everything* was Bob's fault.

As I stood there making up my mind that I simply had to leave Bob, I saw a striking stranger. He was standing two people ahead of me, and his beauty was so total that it took my breath away. He felt my staring at him because he turned, eventually, and smiled at me. I smiled back, and he let the two ahead of me and behind him take the cab that was next up. "We seem to be headed in the same direction. Do you want to share a cab?" he asked.

"Sure," said I, without a moment's hesitation. Then I reflected on what he said. How could he know what direction I was headed, although the obvious destination was the noticeable bulge at his crotch, which I couldn't help staring at as he stood next to me. That, coupled with buttocks I had so admired while he was standing ahead of me. He was really more than I could stand. When confronted by such abundance, I always turn dumb. I couldn't think of a thing to say. But he began telling me about how he just got out of Atlanta in time, before the airport closed, and, with a wink, how he was looking forward to some "sun 'n' fun."

"Where are you staying?" I managed to ask.

"With you," he said, matter-of-factly.

Before I had a chance to respond to this outlandish news, we were in the cab.

Now things really got bizarre. The stranger gave the driver *my* address.

"But how—?"

"It's on your tag," he said, pointing to my duffle bag.

So it was, but how could he have read it at that distance? This, I decided, was as close to being with Superman as I ever was likely to get, so I settled back into the seat and went along for the ride.

It takes ten minutes to get to my apartment from the airport. In that time, the stranger introduced himself as Terry, and got from me more details about my life than I have shared with anyone, let alone a total stranger. But from the questions Terry asked, it seemed he already knew the answers. I didn't know whether he was clairvoyant or what, but at that point, it hardly mattered. This gorgeous number was coming to my apartment for the weekend!

"First the sun," he said, after I'd showed him to the bedroom and told him where he could hang his clothes in the closet, on the hangers where Bob's shirts usually hung.

"Okay," I said, heading for the bathroom. I had taken a

swim the day before and my suit was hanging in there. Besides, I thought I'd let him change in private.

When I opened the door after changing, he was just slipping into his suit. I saw he was strawberry blond all over, and the promise of the bulge was a reality. The cock was unusually thick and mouth-watering as he pulled the fabric over it.

"All set," he said.

"Me, too," said I, staring as he turned around, as if he was showing off, making sure to remind me the rear view was every bit as good as the front.

As he strode purposefully out through the sliding glass door to the courtyard, I muttered, "First the sun," as if I was reminding myself to behave. There would be time for fun. Lots of time.

"I have come to recruit you," he informed me when I finally managed to get him into the bedroom.

"Recruit me?" I asked, removing my wet swimsuit.

"Yes, for some very important work."

"Oh?" My cock was already hard. His, I noticed, was getting there as he slipped from his trunks.

"Do you know," he whispered, his tongue flicking at my ear, "why I was chosen to persuade you?"

"Because you are the best?" I asked, stroking his cock for the first time. Now it was fully hard.

He glanced up at me, fluttering his impossibly long lashes. "No. We must concentrate on the pleasure of others. I was chosen not because I am the best. Because I am the worst. The clumsiest, the laziest, the most distracted. The least adept at sex."

He went on to say he had wandered the world an orphan, alone in life as he had been alone at birth, and he had imagined that solitude was his destiny. But then he was offered another destiny, one that was his for the believing. He had only to say yes. And he did. He was offering me that as well. I started to speak but he pressed his fingers against my lips, closed his eyes tight. "This is what we do. This can be your destiny too, if you will take it. To share. This is how we find peace."

He opened his eyes; they glowed brilliant and fierce, like green fire. "So you must say you will join us."

The air was hot on my skin, but I could feel a chill all the way down to the marrow of my bones. "I don't know what to say," I stammered.

"Just say yes," he said, as he dropped to his knees and began sucking me.

"Oh, yes," I sighed.

It was all so bizarre, so unreal, but I didn't really want this to be real, I realized. A tingle like static electricity built up in my fingers. I was looking directly at Terry pleasuring me, but suddenly it seemed as though I was looking through him, directly into him, into the essence of him. I took his head in my hands, trying to control his hunger for my cock. It was flesh and blood that lay under my hands, but rainbowing swirls of light were all I could see. I literally gasped at the sight. We're all made of light, I thought. Sounds and light, cells vibrating....

But in moments, I could see that under my hands the rainbowing pattern of the lights was unblemished now, the lights had faded, became flesh and bone and skin and then I was just holding Terry's head in my hands once more. The tingle left my fingers, and I dropped my hands. I had come, but he had not swallowed it. He had caught my entire load in his hand. He smiled.

"Thank you," I said.

"You have a wonderful penis," he said, stroking it, squeezing the last drops of cum from it.

He rose and went to the bathroom. I reclined on the bed. My cock wouldn't stay still. I stroked it back to hardness. When he came back into the bedroom, his cock bobbed deliciously before him. I sat up so that I could kiss it, suck it, play with it.

He joined me on the bed and we began making love. It had been so long since I had enjoyed the pleasures of long-and-tender love making. Terry was not Bob, rushing to completion. No, Terry was wooing me by repeated kisses and caresses to a gentle penetration and slow ride to the peak of sensation.

Eventually he could stand it no longer. He sat up, gleaming with all the vitality of youth and health. I rolled over on my back, took hold of his jerking stiffness and pulled him towards me, my legs parting wide to offer myself to him. But he stopped. He got up, went to his trousers and pulled out a condom.

"I won't get pregnant, I promise," I joked.

"I know," he said soberly, putting it on.

Then, I guided him quickly into me and he pierced me with a long thrust. His hands began kneading my plump ass while he slid backwards and forwards with incredible strength. I was soon moaning with delight and jerking under him, my head upturned on the pillows. My legs were as wide open as they would go, and my belly heaved under Terry's belly as he plunged into me. His fingers were digging hard into the flesh of my shoulders and my head lifted abruptly up from the pillows to bring my open mouth over his and force my flickering tongue into his mouth. In my feverish excitement, I began jerking my cock. Terry was plummeting me to my very depths, and a moment later, in a crescendo of small whimpering cries, my back arched briefly off the bed, lifting his weight on me as I came. Then I collapsed underneath him, my head rolling from side to side on the pillows, while Terry fucked on pitilessly. I was squirming beneath him, moaning a little, when his mouth covered mine and sucked at it. I began to swing my hips upwards to meet his strokes, crying out from the excruciating pleasure his cock was giving me.

Terry gasped; his orgasm was near. He rammed fast and deep into my aching, slippery hole, his belly smacking against mine brutally until he had filled the condom.

Shaking, he took me into his arms and we lay quietly together as his sheathed cock slowly slipped from the opening.

I peeled off the rubber and dropped it on the floor next to the bed. I wanted to suck him some more, but he insisted on washing first. I followed him, and stood behind him at the sink, watching him. My cock would not stay down. I stepped up behind him and my cock pushed into his buttocks.

He said nothing, simply went back to the bedroom and got another condom. He rolled it onto my cock and then turned around. He took my cock in his hands and, as he bent over, he brought the cock to his hole. I couldn't remember the last time I'd fucked anyone standing up, and it seemed like an entirely new sensation, with the added benefit of being able to watch in the mirror over the bureau as Terry took all of me deep inside his ass.

I was excited almost to the point of delirium by the sight of my long pink cock going in and out of Terry's perfect ass. There was no more discussion of whether or not I was worthy to do the fucking the way I had with Bob. Terry was not only allowing me to penetrate him, he actually wanted it!

"Put it in me," he murmured. "That's what I came here for today!" He was wrong, of course—Terry had come here to fuck me, but I wasn't in any mood at that moment to dispute his mistaken belief. I wanted him in bed, with his legs wrapped around me. I pushed him there, and I was on top in a flash, and guided myself into him with an eager hand.

"Oh!" he exclaimed as I thrust home to the hilt. I wasn't sure whether he was expressing surprise, dismay or pleasure, but whatever his emotion, his legs closed over my back like a steel trap. He began moving underneath me, thrusting his hot loins up against me with fast and nervous little strokes. At once I went into action, plunging in and out of him, but his legs clamped tighter round my waist and his arms were round my back to immobilize me. He held me with his belly tight to mine. Now there was nothing else I could do but lie still while he had his way with me from below. Not that it mattered—the outcome was the same as if I had been allowed to continue.

My cock throbbed as I stared down in wonder at the face below me, the eyes locked in a glassy stare, mouth open as he finally released me, jerking himself to bring forth another explosion of cum.

I moaned a little in delight and thrust hard and faster into him, setting his legs shaking to the rhythm of my pleasure. I held his foot to my face, showering wet kisses on the soft sole, then sucking on the toes one by one. My arousal soared to frantic heights, and I plunged into him with greater force. His body shook as I stabbed into him in a frenzy of fucking. My eyes were open but I saw nothing. My body convulsed as I filled the rubber, my mouth pressed in a hot kiss to the instep of his right foot. The sheer momentum of my climax caused his body to buck and writhe on the bed.

When I was tranquil again, I took hold of his ankles and opened his legs to the full extent of my arms, to stare down at my cock, now only half embedded in his ass. Terry raised his head to look along his body to our joined parts, an expression of approval on his handsome face. I straightened my back, and withdrawing my softening prick, I whispered, "Yes, I will join you. But when?"

"Not long," he said, rolling away from me to the edge of the bed. "But you must be careful," he added.

"What do you mean?" I asked.

"Just be careful," he said. He tilted his head back as he rose to his feet. He dressed quickly. My gaze tracked him as he walked away, across the carpeted floor and through the doors of the balcony. He didn't open the doors, he just stepped through the glass and steel out into the street and continued off across the pavement. A half dozen yards from the condo, he simply faded away like a video effect and was gone.

I shook my head. "No," I said softly. "I don't want to believe this."

Just then Bob entered the bedroom. He was carrying his suitcase.

"Believe what?" he asked.

I turned to look at him. "Oh, Bob, didn't you see what happened?"

"Happened where?"

"Here. There." I pointed to the window.

"What the hell are you talking about?"

"He...." My voice trailed off as the realization hit home. I was on my own with this. What had happened? If I took it all at face value, I realized that what had happened was the end of the world the way it had been to become the world the way I now knew it could be. It was changed forever. *I* was changed forever. I carried a responsibility now of which I'd never been aware before.

Bob began unpacking, but he continued his interrogation.

Terry, or whoever he really was, had given me a command, "Be careful," so I let the matter drop. Then my gaze fell to the floor and saw the glow-in-the-dark condom Terry had worn during sex. I hesitated for a moment, then reached over and picked it up. My fingers tingled again, and I watched in wonder as the rubber sparkled.

"What've you got there?" Bob asked.

I shook my head. I closed my fingers around the condom, savoring its odd warmth. "Nothing," I said.

Bob left his task and moved toward me. "No, it's not nothing. Let me see."

"No," I said, as he starting wrestling me.

He overpowered me and pulled the condom from my hand. "So this is what you do while I'm away."

"No, no," I protested, but he held me down. He had his pants opened and his cock in me in moments.

All I could think of all through his furious fucking of me was that I was, from now on, to think of the others' pleasure, not my own. With Bob, that was simple, because there was no pleasure, not with him, not any longer.

Maybe this was what Terry had meant when he said that he had been just like me once. He had gone from hurting to healing, and maybe I could do that too.

Just be careful. It seemed possible. Now it seemed more than possible when I saw the gratitude in Bob's eyes when he came.

I shifted my weight, wanting to move away. I was climbing too fast, and I couldn't see the ground.

THE HAPPY HITCHHIKER

Last night, as we parted, clouds overcast the sky and a mist was rising. "Tomorrow will be a miserable day," I said.

But the hitchhiker, a beautiful boy, said, "No. Wait and see. You must wait and see." He didn't want to think the future would be anything but bright and sunny. He wanted everyone and everything to laugh, to sparkle. And his joy was so contagious, there was so much tenderness, so much friendliness, for me in his heart last night, that I couldn't help but be happy. A happy boy is always so full of seductive charm.

We made a date. I wanted to believe he would meet me. I wanted to believe the day would be wonderful, regardless of the weather.

And, of course, he is here, standing on the same corner. He makes a mock gesture, as if hitching a ride. Last night he really was hitching a ride, and he was only a stranger. A beautiful, but odd, stranger. I invited him back to my place but he said he had someone waiting, that he would meet me in the same spot the next night. And here he is.

Now, strangely, Terry is doubling the attentions he showered on me, as if he wants instinctively to give me something he is longing for himself, something he fears he wouldn't get. It is all so intense and concentrated.

I have come to meet him tense with emotion, hardly able to wait for the moment of meeting. I never expected to feel what I feel now, seeing him again. He is, if it is possible, even more luscious than last night.

At first, every word I utter makes him burst into nervous laughter. Finally he says, "Do you know why I'm so happy tonight?"

"No...."

"Why I'm so pleased to see you?"

"No...."

"Why I like you so much?"

"I have no idea." I'm beginning to shiver.

"I like you so much because you didn't force me last night. Someone else in your position might have started pestering me, become full of self-pity, laid it on thick," he moaned. "But not you, you're so nice." He suddenly presses my hand so hard that I almost cry out. He laughs. "Yes, God sent you to me, really, I mean it. I can't imagine what would have become of me last night without you. My car in the shop and my appointments to keep. Damn, you've been so nice to me."

Somehow I feel awfully sad because being nice to him was really not all I want to do and he knows it, yet something resembling laughter stirs somewhere deep down inside me.

"You're overwrought," I say. "Whatever are you talking about?"

"Last night. I'm talking about last night."

"Oh."

He laughs. "I admit you're right. Yes, I'm not myself now, I'm all expectation, I feel a little too light-headed. I've had a wonderful time here...."

"My God, what's this all about?" I interrupt him. "I don't understand a thing you're saying."

"Well, I was trying to make you understand the strange feeling—"

"Stop," I interrupt again. This is making me crazy.

Laughing, he tickles me, trying to make me laugh, too. Every awkward, embarrassed word of mine sets off such long peals of laughter that I am soon on the point of losing my temper.

But then he becomes flirtatious. "Actually," he begins, "I'm a bit offended with you for not trying something last night. People don't always make sense, remember. But still, Mr. Cadillac Man, most guys wouldn't have let me leave the car so easy."

Now I feel sorry for him, and myself, but I don't know how to make up for my nastiness. I try to cheer him up, to find good reasons for my failure to put the make on him.

"It's really funny," he says heatedly, admiring the way his power-assisted seat can be adjusted independently of mine. He puts it all the way back and this prominently displays his crotch. I had not noticed his crotch before, so appealing was his face, his torso, tightly packed in jeans and tank top.

"What's funny?" My voice trembles with some hidden emotion and, at the same time, I try to smile.

"All I want to tell you is that I'm grateful, very grateful, you met me tonight."

He falls silent and squeezes my hand. He draws it over, onto his crotch. "Yeah, I'm grateful, see—"

Several minutes go by as I steer the car along the quiet streets with my left hand as my right hand sees just how grateful he is. I stroke the bulge. My mouth waters at the thought of how beautiful this cock must be. This adorable lad has spared me. He had realized that I was lonely, unable to deal with the loss of my lover, Ralph, to a lingering illness.

"Ah, my God, my God." He opens his pants, lets me pull out his erection.

"Sweet boy," I cry, completely overcome now as I stroke it, "you're torturing me. But we'll be at my condo in just a few minutes."

Long before my lover died I had fallen out of love with him. He had made light of my feelings. He wounded me and slighted my love. I can only love one who is generous, understanding, and kind, because I myself am like that—so he was unworthy of me, but I couldn't just let him die alone. I had to stay. It wasn't his fault that I had deluded myself, discovering too late what sort of man he was....

Anyway, it's over. Like this, it was a delusion; it began as a childish adventure, you show me yours, I'll show you mine.

But this is no child; this is a very mature youth.

Terry is short of breath in his excitement. He pushes my hand away from the throbbing member. "Enough, enough for now, that's definitely enough," he says, getting hold of himself. "By the way, where do you live? I've forgotten."

"Over there, in that building."

We park and walk to the elevator as if in a drunken haze, like walking through clouds, with no idea of what was going on around us. In the elevator, I sigh at the sight of him and a tear glistens in my eye again; I become frightened, turn shy. But he immediately presses my hand and pulls me to his chest. We are about to kiss when the elevator door opens.

We move along the balcony outside to my rooms. We are high above the beach now. Terry says, "And look at the sky: it will be a wonderful day tomorrow. What a sky! What a moon! Look at that cloud about to veil the moon. Look at it! Look at it—no, it has just missed the moon. Look at it—look!"

But I'm not looking at the cloud. I am looking at Terry looking at the cloud, how beautiful he is in the moonlight, and after a while, he presses himself against me in a strange way. My hand is trembling in his. I look at him, a close, scrutinizing look. My heart throbs. "Who are you?" I ask, very softly.

"Me. I am *me*," he whispers, pressing himself even more closely to me. I can hardly keep my balance. Then with the speed of lightning, his arms are around my neck, and before I know what is happening, I feel his passionate kiss. Still without uttering a word, I bury my face in his crotch. I open his pants, then begin rubbing the cock across my lips and cheeks, helplessly nipping at the balls with my teeth.

"You are too hungry, Mr. Cadillac Man," he says, running his fingers through my hair.

He is right, of course, I am much too eager, much too in love with this boy, with this cock, for my own good.

He backs away, lets the swollen member throb in my face, dripping my saliva.

"Oh, please," I cry, lunging for it. He resigns himself to letting me have it, and I look up just in time to be a little startled by the look of almost demented malice on his young face as he ejaculates across my mouth and nose.

We get fully undressed and climb into bed. We lie in each other's arms for a long time, rubbing each other. Finally he spreads his legs to show me he's erect again. In this moment he exudes such a potent masculinity that I am afraid that if he fucked me he just might kill me! With his recuperative powers so aptly demonstrated, I feel very aware that I am so much older than he is. I go back down on it. I can't remember loving a cock this much. Ralph's was bigger, but not as beautiful. This is the most beautiful cock I have ever seen, I decide, letting it slip, hard and quivering, between my lips.

. . .

It is about eight o'clock in the morning and warm autumn sunshine shows at the bedroom window when I wake up to a marvelous feeling of well being. Sure, I blew him a second time and went to sleep with his cock in my mouth. But that circumstance alone has not produced this sense of euphoria. It is due, mostly, to the fact that he agreed to stay the night, and now as I roll over on my side and look at him, asleep beside me, I wonder what the day will bring. It is Sunday, after all, a day of rest, for everyone but us real estate types, of course.

Today I should be showing the new apartments, but I'll wait and see what Terry wants to do, where he wants to go. The strange thing about this is that I am not usually attracted to boys as young as Terry. Ralph was a decade my senior, and I liked that. I needed that. But that was then, and this is now. I have always been attracted to older men who brought to love-making a wealth of skill, acquired over the years. They knew what they wanted from a lover, they were not coy and did not pretend to be, and they were not surprised by pleasant little deviations. Yes, I adore older men. But every rule, if rule it is, has its exceptions. Terry is such an exception, radiating such youthful sensuality that he is totally irresistible.

I make coffee and, when I bring it to the bedroom with delicious-smelling fresh-baked croissants, Terry is already up and showered. He is sitting on the balcony with a towel wrapped about his waist.

I set the tray on the table and he shifts in his chair to make the bulge at his groin more prominent, or so I think. "Your beauty is truly devastating," I say, and I mean it, for I could not restrain a sigh of pleasure at the sight of him this morning, nearly nude.

"Thank you," he says. "This is really very nice of you," he says as he helps himself to a croissant.

I watch him eat, then feel between the warm thighs. Just to touch him sends little tremors of pleasure through my body. My softly moving fingers find his erection. I lift away the towel and fall to my knees.

He says, with only mild interest, "You are *so* hungry."

"Starved," I say. "You don't mind, do you?"

He laughs. "Obviously not."

He eats his croissant, and crumbs drop on the top of my head and into my face as I go back to sucking this most lovely of cocks.

I ask him to spread his legs—or am telling him, rather than asking him, for I speak in a soft voice without inflection. Asked or told - it doesn't matter in the least to Terry in his condition of arousal. He spreads his legs wide for me. His expression is one of tranquillity, but not for long.

Soon he is holding my head down deep into his crotch.

"Oh, yes," I exclaim in triumph as he starts to come.

. . .

Being a sentimental guy, I write him a card to take along: *So may the sky lie cloudless over you, and your smile be bright and carefree; be blessed for the moment of bliss and happiness you gave to another heart, a lonely and a grateful one.*

My God, such moments of bliss. Why isn't that enough for a whole lifetime? It will have to be.

"You really shouldn't see me any more," he says as he's leaving. "I want only to tell you I love you. But I want you to keep our secret."

"I will."

HEAVENLY HEAD

Nobody goes to Key West in mid-August, and what I was doing driving there from Miami remains a mystery to me. Perhaps it was just a case of bad planning. But there I was, in the leather-lined, air-conditioned tomb of my BMW, on autopilot, when I saw a stunning youth hitching a ride. He looked odd, there, at the city limits of Key Largo, looking fresh as a daisy when everyone else was expressionless, barely moving, dead-looking, their brains boiled. The boy smiled when I pulled onto the shoulder and stopped. Swinging his backpack, he ran across the gravel to the car. Despite the oppressive heat, he seemed totally alive—and his worn denim short shorts left little to the imagination.

We exchanged pleasantries as he made himself comfortable. His face was pleasant, and looked familiar to me, like an old acquaintance you meet after many years but cannot quite place.

He said he wasn't going far, and appreciated the ride. We listened to the radio, a jazz station out of Miami, saying little to each other. Suddenly he said, "This is it."

There was a sign, directing travellers to a marina.

The hitchhiker breathed a sigh of relief when I finally stopped the car. He thanked me politely for the ride. The engine still running, I helped him get his backpack out of the back seat and then my hand impulsively landed on his thigh. I left my hand there and looked into the boy's eyes, which sparkled and glowed, even in the record heat. This was a crazy thing for me to do—I couldn't remember having been so bold in many moons—but the hitchhiker did not pull away. Instead, he thanked me again for the ride and kissed me softly on the lips. The kiss felt so natural that I returned it. Suddenly all the deep loneliness of the past few months after having lost my lover, Eric, to The Plague overwhelmed me. I pulled the hitchhiker into my arms, our chests touching and our hands on each other's shoulders. I moved my lips to the boy's neck, kissing him wildly. Finally, I asked, "Have you ever made love outdoors?"

"Why?"

"There's a place down the road I know of. It's really a lovely spot, no matter how hot it gets."

The hitchhiker didn't answer. Instead, he took me forcefully, pressing his mouth insistently against mine, his lips hot and wet, his tongue fevered and burning. He caressed my back, then my pecs. Moving his hands back and then down, lifting me so that he could cup my buttocks in his hands and squeeze the firm supple flesh. I was overcome, and I cried out, my need and hunger urging the stranger to continue.

But the hitchhiker pulled away, saying, "Well, then, let's go. Otherwise we might get arrested here."

He introduced himself finally. His name was Terry and he was going to work at the marina, but he didn't have to report until the following morning. "How convenient," I said, squeezing his thigh.

At the cove, we got out of the car and felt a breeze from the Ocean. The terrible heat was letting up as the sun was setting.

Terry leaped from the car and ran down to the water's edge. "Mind if I take a dip?" he asked.

"Certainly not. I'll join you."

Terry permitted me to pull off his tank top, then unbutton his shorts. I gasped when I saw Terry's full basket bulging against his jockstrap. My hand wrenched it down, giving my mouth open access to a luscious cut prick. It was long even though it was semi-flaccid. The smooth, pinkish-brown, pliable shaft was begging for attention. Terry moaned as I dropped to my knees and circled my tongue around and around the cock, blowing lightly over the wetness. I was overwhelmed with this urge to lick. Barely breathing, I stretched out my tongue. He stiffened slightly. I held his hips steady, inhaled his sharp-sweet smell, and licked him some more.

The cock kept growing before my eyes. I began sucking it, taking it deep, deep inside of my mouth, pulling and caressing the warm flesh. I had not sucked a cock in so long I simply went wild. I continued my frenzied feeding on the cock for several moments. Wanting to take him and possess him, I couldn't stop, even though he begged me to. I brought one hand to his asshole. He groaned when I touched the puckerhole, worked his butt muscles and sucked my finger in to the knuckle. He was no virgin, this hitchhiker. I finger-fucked him while I sucked, feeling around inside for that knob of the prostate. I massaged it vigorously with my fingertip. I felt his cock grow hard in my mouth. He groaned and pulled me off his cock so I could watch as he shot a copious flood of cum onto my chest. As his cock diminished to floppy satisfaction, he ran off into the water.

We swam intently for a few minutes, and then I noticed he was no longer in the water. I looked up and saw he was sitting on one of the rocks on the beach.

I hoisted myself out of the water. As I walked toward him, my body felt cool for the first time in days and I smiled. I felt incredibly vigorous and content. I had made this beauty come, and now he was beckoning me once again.

We said nothing to each other. He lifted my face and kissed me. The long, slow, sensual kiss sent tremors through my body, awakening it to long-forgotten feelings and sensations. I returned his kiss, murmuring softly against his lips.

I groaned when I felt the heat of Terry's body pressing into me. I fluttered my fingers down his back, my hand caressing the warm, inviting bare flesh. My hand slipped farther, down over his ass, squeezing and kneading. We ravaged one another with our passion for several minutes until he gasped, "Let's get a room for the night."

Oblivious to the heat, lips parting, sliding inside of one another, our tongues touching, caressing, exploring, demanding and wanting more than could possibly happen in one night. But I agreed to get a room.

Once inside the motel room, hard with desire, I moaned as Terry's fingers unbuttoned my shirt. He pushed the shirt off my shoulders, planting hot, wet kisses all over my neck and pecs. He lowered his mouth, licking the tip of each nipple, then kissing over the surface of each pec. Sucking me ever so lightly, then licking the hot flesh that was now pulsing and aching with hunger. It seemed that Terry wanted me as much as I wanted him.

He continued sucking me with an intensity equalled only by my own desire. I struggled to free my arms, wanting so badly to touch him, to caress him, to suck him again.

But he would not let up on my dick. At one point, he raised

up and said, "I am going to suck you so good, you'll never forget me."

Fat chance I would ever forget this, I thought, and I nodded,

I moaned and writhed beneath Terry's touch, thrusting my chest up, urging him to take me, to make love to me, crying out when I felt his mouth biting my sensitive nipples.

He reached down, grasped my zipper, and pulled it down roughly. He pushed the fabric aside, his fingers plunging into my warm crotch. At long last, he got to my dick. I was ready for him: hot, hard and eager to fuck his mouth. My glans was exposed, the thick foreskin fully retracted. He eased onto my erection, taking just the head into his warm lips and testing the piss-slit with his talented tongue. One or two more exploratory flicks and he went down on me in one gulp. His mouth was just what my dick was aching for. With just a few stabs at his throat, I forgot all about many months of sexual frustration. I felt his tongue sweep along the shaft of my dick, and his lips sucking at my foreskin. Every time my cock disappeared into his throat and his face burrowed into my pubes, I let out a little moan. This was heavenly head. His working of my balls was heavenly, too. He stroked and caressed my nuts, lovingly coaxing them to come. Once or twice, his mouth left my cock just long enough to lick my balls. I watched as his head bobbed at my crotch, and I became mesmerized by the flexing muscles in his shoulders, each rippling with motion. He kept up a steady rhythm, and I began squirming with pleasure. "Oh, yeah, I'm almost there," I gasped. I arched my back and he pulled off my dick just as the first spasm gripped me. My whole body shuttered, and a blast of cum burst from my cock. He kept on it, and some cum spilled out onto his lips. He swallowed, licking his lips clean, looked up into my eyes.

"You like that, eh?" he whispered.

"Yes! You're terrific," I told him. "But, my god, where did you learn to suck like that?"

He chuckled. "I'm just a country boy. My brothers taught me. I had a lot of brothers."

This was, without question, the best head I had ever received. Even Eric, my deceased lover, on his best days was not as good as this boy. I was so close, and he knew it. He let up on my cock, and held my hips in position. All of a sudden, my heart was thudding. He touched my anus. Ran his finger along to the entrance and said softly, "It's ready. So ready."

"Oh, yes," I sighed.

I opened my legs wider, in invitation. Tenderly, with the tip of his tongue, he circled my fuck-hole. He took a sharp breath, then he was licking me and I was soon making little whimpering noises. He buried his face in me, parting me wide. Soon he was sweating, sighing, his fingers digging into my thighs. He came up and kissed my cock, licked the pre-cum, then kissed me on the lips, and I could smell myself on him, salt-sweet.

As we kissed, our faces became salivia-slippery, and our kisses were hard, somehow meaningful, as if we were lovers of long-standing. I wanted him fuck me, to make me come. My fingers found their way to his ass and I pressed him against me. I bit softly on his perfect throat, smoothed his hair back, lifting the damp, strawberry-blond tendrils from his eyes.

His lids flickered and he was staring at me, and he began moving against me. I felt powerful, sexy. I pressed into him harder and faster. Our bodies were sliding, merging. I became flushed and yielding, and I closed my eyes, my mouth on his, capturing each breath.

His perfect body strained and flexed. He was in me at last. I didn't think about protection; I don't know why, except that it would have broken the spell. I groaned when I felt his hard cock sliding into my ass; I worked my butt-muscles and helped his cock slide in deeper. Soon he was humping me furiously, his balls slapping my ass. I was bucking and thrashing against him.I reached for my cock but he insisted on jacking it while he fucked me.

This was the way Eric had always wanted it, and, like him, Terry came when I came. I was astonished. Did Terry know? But how could he?

We went to dinner at a little cafe with red plastic booths. We ordered the specialty of the house, pot roast. I hadn't had pot roast since I left home. My mother made pot roast every Sunday.

At one point, I said that anybody who lived in this godforsaken place must be crazy.

He smiled. "There's all kinds of madness in the world," he said. "Some of it gets you locked up. Some of it puts you on pills so you don't have to think. But most of it just leaves you in the here and now, not quite broken, not quite whole."

"Yes, I know." I told him I had been crazy, crazy in love. He smiled when I said this, not because I was funny, but because he seemed to know what I had been through and he knew what I meant. "Nights are the worst time for thinking," I said.

"No more thinking tonight. This night is for fucking," he said.

It was like a celebration, being with Terry. He let me sit on the bed and watch as he got naked.

When he finished his strip, he turned and I noticed his back was a spider's web of muscle, the rippling of dorsal and deltoids reminding me of a pair of wings of an angel. That was how I began to think of him, as an angel sent to break me out of my shell since Eric's death. Every now and then I gazed at him as if he were a figment of my imagination. He turned and approached the bed, his sensuous body a smooth symphony of movement and grace.

"You should always use these," he said, sliding the rubber over it.

"I do."

"No, you let me do it without one earlier."

"Well, I...."

"You wouldn't want to die like Eric did."

"Eric?"

He crushed his lips to mine. I could no longer speak, he was kissing me so forcefully. I knew I had never mentioned Eric, not last night, not ever. Or had I? I was confused now, so many things I couldn't remember.

He went to the bathroom, and when he returned I was weeping. I was so happy. I hadn't been this happy since Eric had moved in. The thought of Eric got me weeping.

"What's wrong?" Terry asked, sliding into the bed next to me.

"How could he do that? How could he do that?"
"Who?"
"Eric." I would go quiet for a moment, try to talk about something else, then I would start up again. I kept asking, "How could he do that? How could he do that?"
"I don't know," Terry said.
"You *do* know. You know everything. You're—"
"I'm what?"
"Different. You know, you know...." I lost control, began beating his chest.
"Hey," he said as he pulled me close, his jaw moving against my cheek. "I'm not the enemy."
I lay there against him, crying for a while, then drifting at the edge of dreaming as he stroked my hair. The room seemed oddly silent once I'd finished, so quiet I could hear my own heartbeat drumming in my ears. We were still sitting side by side when he reached across me, switching off the bedside lamp and pulling the quilt up around our shoulders. "It's okay to get mad," he whispered at my ear, and after that I was sleeping.

That morning, after breakfast, I took him back to the road to the marina. "Thanks for everything," he said.
I blurted something, something about how it was I who was thankful, but he had already shut the door and, swinging his backpack, he began walking down the road.
I turned to look, to watch him go, but I was blinded by a bright light shining in my eyes.

. . .

I stayed in Key West only one night. I was bored; nobody turned me on, not after Terry. I was restless; I couldn't sleep. I had to see the boy again.
I reached the marina around noon. In the office, an old man sat behind a counter, reading a book. I asked him about the boy who had come to work for them a couple of days before.
"You kiddin', mister?" he said, peering over the tops of his glasses.
"Why?"

"Hell, we're pretty much shut down here. It's August, you know."

"Yes, but—?"

I backed away, slowly made my way back the BMW. As I climbed back behind the wheel, I remembered something he had said: "I'm gonna suck you so good, you'll never forget me." It was his message: to go on, to live—but never to forget.

PUPPY LOVE

I could hear strange noises in my condo, so I got up and crept toward the kitchen. I won't say I was ready to kill, but I was ready to do some damage. Then I saw him, his overcoat on, slumped over the kitchen sink like a drunk, shoveling cereal and milk into his face. I thought of a movie about an angel I'd just seen on cable. "John Travolta?" I asked.

"Nope," he said without missing a scoop of his cereal. "You got any more sugar around here?"

"No, you're not John Travolta. You're cuter than he ever was!" I got him some more sugar.

"Thanks. You saw the movie, huh?" he asked.

"*Michael?* Yeah, I saw it," I said.

"That movie was good. It could have been better, but they wouldn't let me play the part," he said, pouring the sugar on his flakes.

I laughed. "No?"

"Nope," he said. "I think it was 'cause I'm not an angel, like in the movie. I'm only a saint. See, in Hollywood they prefer goofy actors who believe in some weird religion." He straightened up and drained the last of the milk from the bowl.

"A saint?"

He ignored me. "But *Michael* was a pretty good movie, wasn't it?" he asked.

"Pretty sappy. A chick flick," I said.

"You're not into romance? Big mistake. But I agree, it was no 'Bishop's Wife'."

"They re-made that one, you know. They called it 'The Preacher's Wife.'"

"Very amusing, that one. But I love black people. Good with hymns."

"You probably love everybody."

"Yes, that's true." He helped himself to the rest of the corn flakes.

"I can't believe I'm having a conversation with a saint who is eating all of my corn flakes."

"Is that a problem?" he asked.

I laughed. "No. I'm the one with a problem, or you wouldn't

be here, right?"

"Right. You can't get a date."

"Okay. That's right. I guess I've given up. These are rough times, you know."

"You do take precautions, don't you?"

I laughed. "If I ever have the chance! But how do you suggest I get a date?"

"You gotta learn how to fake it."

"Fake it?"

"You saw the movie. What made John so attractive to women?"

"Well, I thought he was a slob," I said. "I haven't a clue."

"Well, look, he was a *safe* slob, right? He ate cereal and let it dribble down his chin, just like me. He walked around in his underwear and scratched his balls and smoked too much and drank a lot of beer."

"You do that?"

"No, I may look a bit sloppy this morning, but usually I'm more the Roger Moore-kind of saint; you know, suave, debonair. All that."

"So what are you saying? I'm very confused."

"What I'm saying is, you have to be a little sloppy, to make someone want to pick up after you, look after you. You're very neat, very uptight."

"I think I'm getting it."

"And remember Sparky, the dog in the movie?"

"I have to buy a dog?"

"Oh, more than that," he said. "You have to buy a small, smart, cute and non-threatening puppy. And you have to let the man of your dreams rescue this dog from an almost certain death, just like Travolta did in the movie."

"No can do," I said.

"Sure you can. You buy a puppy and train him to play dead. Then you take him out on the street and teach him how to run between the cars."

"But what if he gets killed!"

"Don't worry, he'll go to heaven. They all go to heaven."

"I think I heard that somewhere." I laughed. "Okay, so I save the dog...."

"No, *he* does."

"Oh, I see. And then what?"

"You take it from there."

"But I think I've found the man of my dreams, right here in my kitchen, eating up my corn flakes."

"No, no, I'm not the man of your dreams. Trust me, he's out there, waiting to save your puppy."

"I don't know. I've never wanted to have a dog. I'd feel so terrible if it died."

"Not if, when. But don't worry."

"I know, all dogs go to heaven."

"Now you've got it." He stood up, took his dishes to the sink. "No, but I'd like to," I said, coming up behind him, squeezing his ass through the trenchcoat.

"Don't worry," he said, stepping away from me. "I'm as horny as you are."

"Now what?" I asked.

"Mind if I take a shower before? I've had a rough night."

"Not at all" I said. "I'll get you a fresh towel."

"Thanks,' he said, slipping out of his trench coat.

While he showered, I got nude and waited for him on the bed. This whole episode reminded me of other stories I had heard and read about lost travellers being brought back to life by nomads and hunters. When they're brought back, they're not the same. They have been changed by an initiation. Thinking about my own impending initiation, I lay there yanking off. He came out of the bathroom and grinned. He too was nude and his cock was beautiful, at least seven inches long, semi-hard and dripping like mine. The sting of blond peach fuzz covered his crotch, leading a trail to his navel.

He came over to me, and climbed on the bed, mounting my chest. He fed me his cock and it soon was hard. He tasted delicious. He reached back and stroked me. I was ready to blow.

"Let me have this," he asked. "Please."

He lifted away and flopped on the bed next to me on his stomach. He immediately started grinding his crotch into the bed and stuck his butt up in the air. His hairless ass was tight and perfect. I wanted to taste him there as well. I just stuck my face between his cheeks, breathing in his wonderful smell. I cannot recall enjoying eating someone out as much as that. I wanted to melt into him, be one with him...but I loved getting my bottoms good and ready first. With my tongue I delicately licked the outside of his asshole, gently stroking and caressing it. I licked up and down his ass crack, coating it with a sheen of my spit, sucking up the droplets of sweat I found there. Luxuriating in his body, I loved having this boy all to myself, here, now in my own bed.

I suddenly stuck my tongue into his asshole and he let out a moan of pure pleasure. His ass moved up and back to meet me, helping my tongue get farther inside. He tasted as good inside as he did outside, and I rolled my tongue around trying to feel as much of him as I could.

He responded so well to getting tongue-fucked I replaced my tongue with one finger to see if he liked it as much. He liked it more, pushing back on me farther and even humping my finger a little with his cheeks. I gently pushed a second finger in, then a third. He was groaning with delight now, his hands gripping the edge of the mattress tight.

"Please, stud," he said. "Please fuck me... hard!"

"Oh, yeah!"

Rearing back on my knees, I tore open one of the condom packages and slowly rolled the latex sheath over my throbbing pecker. I squirted a generous helping of lube into my palm and slathered up my cock with it, thrilling to the bursts of pleasure that shivered through my body at the touch of my hand.

Terry was whining and crying like an animal, rubbing his dick frantically into my bed and pushing his butt back at me.

"Fuck me, stud, please...." he moaned. "I need you in my ass, give it to me, please...."

After all his teasing, now he was the one begging for it. Well, I'd let him see how it feels. I gripped my dick in my hand and guided it up and down his ass crack, following the same path my tongue had taken. He shuddered at the feel of my hard tool against his butt.

"Please take me, man...." he groaned.

I slapped his butt playfully.

"Wait...wait...." I said. "Patience is a virtue. You, of all people, ought to know that!"

"Fuck virtue!" he said. "I need your cock in my ass!"

I laughed at him, teasing his ass some more with my dick. He was right, he did need me inside him, almost as bad as I needed to be there. Grabbing his ankles again, I flipped him over on his back. His eyes were crazed with lust. I tossed his legs up over my shoulders and aimed my boner at his puckering hole.

"Oh, ohhhh," I cried, and rammed my cock inside his asshole. He flung his head back and howled with ecstasy. It was awesome being inside him. After getting him all opened up with my tongue and fingers, he was more than ready to take what I had to offer. His ass-muscles expanded and contracted, seizing my dick as if it always belonged there.

This was the sensation my body had been craving—I was finally one with this incredible man, joined in the most intimate way we could be. It was like our bodies were merging into one, both halves fusing together by the power of our attraction.

Digging my knees in, I started plowing the gorgeous ass below me. No time for gentleness any more, I just reamed the kid's ass like there was no tomorrow. High on lust, I realized this was the best bottom I'd ever screwed. He added to my pleasure by moaning and crying and yelping with pleasure like he'd never been nailed before.

"Push back on me," I ordered.

He obeyed, grabbing hold of the mattress and forcing his butt back onto my dick even farther.

"That's it, yeah, you've got it...."

It was so incredible to see such a beauty on my bed, lying there impaled on my cock. I leaned forward, pressing his legs down, until we were face to face. He was flushed and sweaty, his eyes locking on mine as his mouth slacked open in disbelief

I leaned in and kissed him, my tongue hungrily invading his mouth like my cock was invading his ass. Now I had him plugged at both ends, he was mine and only mine. My dick was swelling up inside the condom. It had almost reached the point of no return. I didn't want it to end, but I couldn't hold back any more. Pulling gently out of his butt, I peeled the condom off and grabbed hold of my dick.

"I'm gonna shoot!"

He gripped his own rock-hard penis and started pumping it. We got into perfect sync, our strokes matching each other's exactly. Together we worked ourselves, and seconds later we were ready. My cock flexed, cum shooting out of it to splatter all over the kid's chest. At the same time, he came, and together we let out cries of joy and relief that drowned each other out they were so loud.

I collapsed on top of him, our cum fusing together just like our bodies had moments earlier. We put our arms around each other and hugged tightly, moaning and sighing.

We lay still for a few minutes, catching our breath.

He wriggled out from under me and went to the bathroom. I lay dozing for a few minutes. When he re-appeared I was almost asleep. He started to get dressed.

"Don't go," I begged.

"You've got shopping to do." He stepped over to the bed and finished buttoning his shirt.

"I do?"

"I'm not the man of your dreams. I was just sent here to give you the message."

I ran my hand up his thigh. "You gave me the message all right."

"I hope so. Happy puppy shopping," he chuckled.

And then he disappeared in a flash, leaving me here to fend for myself in a world I do not understand.

But the day had just begun, and I was going to buy a puppy. So my gallant man of my dreams could save it. And who cared if the dog died eventually? All dogs go to heaven—I have it on the best authority!

"I started to think about God again. (And he has helped me) more and more. But I'm not a saint yet. I'm an alcoholic. I'm a drug addict. I'm homosexual. I'm a genius. Of course I could be all four of these dubious things and still be a saint. But I shonuf' ain't no saint yet, nawsuh."
– Truman Capote, 1979

Our forthcoming anthology, "Play Hard", features coverboys who appear courtesy of David Butt, noted British photographer. Mr. Butt's photographs may be purchased through Suntown, Post Office Box 151, Danbury, Oxfordshire, OX16 8QN, United Kingdom. Ask for a full catalogue.

Bonus Preview

A chapter from John Patrick's sensational new novella "Play Hard", which will be included complete in the anthology of the same name, coming in January, 1999.

Jeremy woke up first, with a glorious hard-on. Joe was just surfacing. Joe spread out on his back. Jeremy was turned on and very pleased to have such a stud in his bed, to do with as he wanted. Jeremy mounted Joe and started rubbing the stud's cock against his ass, trying to stimulate him into more sex. Jeremy was insatiable, and from the way Joe's cock was swelling he would soon be ready to comply. While Jeremy sucked his nipples, Joe plunged his fingers up Jeremy's ass, and then out to the tip and then back in again, and out again, and in again.

Joe was breathing heavily as Jeremy sucked his nipples harder and harder. Joe began to moan, and Jeremy could feel him arching up beneath, ready to start the fuck. Jeremy pulled up and applied lube to the now erect cock. As he mounted it and impaled himself with it, he shook and shuddered in tremor after tremor. When it finally was all the way in, Joe's delight was signaled by a long deep sigh. But now it was Joe who controlled the rhythm. He held Jeremy's ass as he lowered the boy's body up and down on his cock. Jeremy let his excitement build up until he was almost verging on pain; he concentrated on jerking himself off, and then, with a final exquisite jolt, he came ecstatically on Joe's pecs.

They lay side by side, regaining some composure. Joe, who had not come, pulled his cock from Jeremy's ass. He excused himself and left for the bathroom. Jeremy, dazzled, watched his new lover in retreat and smiled.

Joe walked into the bathroom stark naked with his cock dripping with lube. Larry was brushing his teeth. Joe ignored Larry and stood over the toilet. He pissed like a racehorse, without skipping a beat. Larry could not believe this, the huge, beefy, leather-clad stud Jeremy had cruised the night before and brought into his house, was relieving himself in his bathroom, without even a "good mornin'!" Having taken the horny bitch Patty to her room and fucking her, Larry had missed Jeremy and Joe's fuckfest, but he had heard all about it from the other guys as they left the house. Carl had missed it too, having passed out in his bedroom. So over breakfast Carl and Larry had conspired on how they were going to get the lovers to do an encore just for them. Now Larry was staring at the monster, lube-coated dick as the piss streamed from it. No wonder everyone was talking, Larry thought. Each of the others had only sampled it while they were the daisy chain, before the cock disappeared up Jeremy's ass—and they couldn't stop talking about it. Damn, Larry said, they were probably *still* talking about it!

Larry wiped the toothpaste from his mouth and moved closer to Joe. Joe gave Larry a sidelong glance, then looked back down at his cock as he finished his business. He shook the last of the piss from it and stood back, in effect inviting Larry to move closer. Larry dropped the seat of the toilet and sat down. "Now I know what everyone was talking about," he said, tentatively running his fingers along the shaft.

"Oh?"

"Yeah, you're the talk of the town by now."

"Is that what you're gonna do, talk?"

Joe's directness tickled Larry and he chuckled while he inspected the formidable equipment. His fingers toyed with the mammoth ballsac, while his other hand began stroking the shaft.

Larry took a washcloth from the rack and wiped the cock clean. Then he began licking the cock. As the cock-licking was gaining momentum, Joe began panting erratically with short, quick intakes of breath. His abdomen was rolling in wave after visible wave. He was moaning as his cock was being serviced with diligence and relish. Larry considered himself sexually "open," and he seemed to be drawn toward guys who claimed they were straight. His favorite saying was, "Mix a straight guy with a little alcohol and you get a bisexual."

Now the straight-appearing stud's cock was soon glistening and swollen with anticipation, and Joe held Larry back and began slapping the thick member against Larry's hungry lips. This was just the kind of thing that got Larry going big time.

Joe started using the thick head of dick to tease Larry, whose mouth strained to suck more of it in. Finally, Joe held Larry's head with both hands and began face-fucking him.

After the cock plunged into Larry's throat, with one deep thrust and groan, Joe began pumping his dick in and out of the man's wide-open wet hole, thrusting the shaft all the way in and then all the way out. The shaft was becoming juicier and more delicious with every retraction. Joe's hard asscheeks tensed and then shook each time he was all the way in.

As Joe began a furious rhythm of in and out, in and out, in and out, suddenly Jeremy appeared in the doorway. He watched for a few moments, delighted to catch Larry in the act in the broad daylight, then entered the bathroom. Sexual fire was flashing. In a frenzy of movement, Jeremy was on his knees and he and Larry were sharing the cock. Joe was beyond caring who did or was doing what. This was sex and they were sex machines, pure and simple. Joe gave into the luxury of being catered to. He didn't have to do anything but feel, submit to the ecstasy. Joe felt incredibly worshipped. He was riding the sexual waves, remembering Jeremy's tight ass, and he came. It was such an astounding explosion that it caught both Larry and Jeremy off-guard. They each stroked the cock, finally to squeeze the last of the cum from it onto Jeremy's cheek.

Slowly and with deliberation, Jeremy led Joe back to the bedroom. Larry was in hot pursuit. Joe lay back on the bed, ready to accept more adulation from his new young lovers. He seemed to be amused by Larry, who seemed to be even more enamored with his cock than Jeremy was.

Larry's charm was well-rehearsed. He knew exactly how to attract other people's sexual interest, and he was incomparably seductive, a dark-haired, brown-eyed beauty. He would flash glints of passion, but then retreat. He wasn't easy, but he was incredibly alluring. Jeremy was immediately hooked the first time they met at a party. They had sex together right away. It was all-out surrender, unbridled give-and-take pleasure on Jeremy's part, and it wasn't like any other one-night stand Jeremy had ever experienced. There were no boundaries, no hesitations, no holding back. It wasn't piecemeal sex, it was a banquet. The idea that Larry was fucking everything in sight, male, female, transsexual, only added to his allure.

Jeremy gave Larry everything he wanted and Larry did the same. They were involved in pure passion, Larry fucking Jeremy all night, all morning, and half the next day. Larry let Jeremy bring him to orgasm after orgasm. His sensitivity was ultra high. They were completely attuned to each other, and their sex was incredible.

When they finally finished, they both looked at each other with amazement and embarrassment. They both had lovers and it would never do that they fall in love.

Jeremy left that day feeling fabulously well fucked but also a little bewildered. He had found the right sexual match in the wrong person. Destiny had thrown him a boomerang. Through the course of a year, Jeremy had come to own Larry sexually. He could do whatever he wanted, as long as Larry agreed. This made Jeremy very happy for a while, even though the "relationship" was clandestine. After all, Larry was Carl's lover and Jeremy had Nathan. But the secrecy was in itself a kind of kick, leaving room for pursuing others. For Jeremy, the ideal situation would be that he could do whatever he wanted but that Larry would be his and his alone. This, of course, was absurd. Larry, like Jeremy, was young and adventuresome, incapable of fidelity. But as the months progressed, they fucked occasionally and Jeremy thought he was getting what he wanted. He thought he was calling the shots, but he was actually playing out the role that Larry had assigned him, and that the entire affair was being directed by Larry's dark needs.

So for months they carried on discreetly, Larry pleasing Carl, in exchange for a place to stay, Jeremy pleasing Nathan for the same reason, and more.

But now Jeremy was seeing a new Larry, a Larry he didn't know existed. Larry, the bi-sexual, was actually on his knees, begging Joe to fuck him! Jeremy had never seen Larry in this position; he thought he was an exclusive top. But, apparently, confronted by a cock the size of Joe's, all bets were off. Jeremy fell in line, getting down shoulder-to-shoulder with Larry and inviting Joe to have his fun with both of them.

Over the next few minutes, it seemed Joe was flaunting his prowess, fucking one ass, then the other, with equal vigor. But Jeremy wanted more and he scrambled under Larry so that Larry could fuck him while Joe continued to screw Larry's tight ass. It was so rare an occurrence that Larry found himself in the middle of such a magnificent fuck sandwich, he came almost immediately, but he was so turned on that he kept his cock in Jeremy and was able to resume after several moments.

The games they played had seldom been as successful as this one had obviously become. Earlier, Larry cursed himself for leaving the party and screwing Patty, but now at least he didn't have to share Joe with anyone but Jeremy.

The Contributors
(Other Than the Editor, John Patrick)

"Making Mark" and "My New Master"
Tony Anthony
The author's first story for STARbooks appeared in *Naughty By Nature*. He lives in England.

"Voluptuous"
Antler
The poet lives in Milwaukee when not traveling to perform his poems or wildernessing. His epic poem *Factory* was published by City Lights. His collection of poems *Last Words* was published by Ballantine. Winner of the Whitman Award from the Walt Whitman Society of Camden, New Jersey, and the Witter Bynner prize from the Academy and Institute of Arts & Letters in New York, his poetry has appeared in many periodicals (including *Utne Reader, Whole Earth Review* and *American Poetry Review*) and anthologies (including *Gay Roots, Erotic by Nature*, and *Gay and Lesbian Poetry of Our Time*).

"Dream Boy"
Kevin Bantan
The author lives in Ohio, where he is working on several new stories for STARbooks.

"Moroccan Dreamboy"
Frank Brooks
The author is a regular contributor to gay magazines. In addition to writing, his interests include figure drawing from the live model and mountain hiking.

"The Nude Swimming Pond"
Ian Cappell
The author is a frequent contributor to gay magazines. He lives in England.

"Getting Shafted"
Leo Cardini
The celebrated author of the best-selling *Mineshaft Nights*,

Leo's short stories and theatre-related articles have appeared in numerous magazines. An enthusiastic nudist, he reports that, "A hundred and fifty thousand people have seen me naked, but I only had sex with half of them."

"Milk Bath"
Jason Carpenter
This Texas-based author is frequently published by gay erotic magazines under many aliases.

"Dream Soldier"
William Cozad
The author is a regular contributor to gay magazines and his startling memoirs were published by STARbooks Press in *Lover Boys* and *Boys of the Night*. Another of his books, "The Preacher's Boy," appeared in *Secret Passions*.

"A Dream in Denim"
Peter Eros
The author is a frequent contributor to STARbooks.

"Gingerbread House" and "Oh Come All Ye Faithful"
Peter Gilbert
"Semi-retired" after a long career with the British Armed Forces, the author now lives in Germany but is contemplating a return to England. A frequent contributor to various periodicals, he also writes for television. He enjoys walking, photography and reading. His stories have swiftly become favorites by readers of STARbooks' anthologies.

"Getting Shafted" and "Buon Giorno, John Porno"
James Hosier
The youthful author lives in a little town that is "definitely not sleepy." He says he is straight but admits that he lets guys do what they want: "I need the money and I happen to have a good body (thanks to the swimming club). Provided they're prepared to pay, I let them go ahead." Stay tuned.

"Island Fruit" and "Golden Boy"
Thomas C. Humphrey

The author, who resides in Florida, is working on his first novel, *All the Difference*, and has contributed stories to First Hand publications. His superb memoir of his youth on the farm appeared in *Juniors*.

"Cowpoke Down Under", "The Farmboy and the Stud" and "Farmboy Dreams"
Rick Jackson, USMC

The oft-published author specializes in jarhead stories. When not travelling, he is based in Hawaii.

"The Stuff Dreams Are Made Of"
Bert McKenzie

The author's earlier works for STARbooks appeared in *Secret Passions*, *In the Boy Zone*, *Barely Legal*, and *Mad About the Boys*.

"Bound Virgin" and "Randy Cowpoke"
Jack Ricardo

The author, who lives in Florida, is a novelist and frequent contributor to various gay magazines. His latest novel is *Last Dance at Studio 54*.

"English Lessons" and "Strip for Stardom"
Tim Scully

The author, who lives in Europe, is a friend of STARbooks' favorite Peter Gilbert and is working on many more stories based on his personal experiences.

"My Pen Pal"
Dan Veen

The popular author's stories for STARbooks have appeared in, among others, *Intimate Strangers*, *Naughty By Nature*.

"Sweet Dreams"
Peter Z. Pan

Peter's earlier works for STARbooks appeared in *Juniors* and *Naughty By Nature*. He lives in Miami.

ACKNOWLEDGEMENTS AND SOURCES

Our main coverboy, Justin, courtesy of Ben Block, the renowned Brit photographer whose images often grace the pages of magazines such as *Vulcan*. Recently, Block's stunning photographs were exhibited in London under the title "Simplify and Repeat." In its review of the show, *Gay Times* said: "When does art become porn, or porn become art? I ask this purely as a curious aside rather than an academic inquiry, for when it comes to the work of photographer Ben Block, the two labels become as inseparable as they are pretty much irrelevant—his are simply very attractive pictures."

Block operates Flashers studio in London and makes his prints available to collectors worldwide. For more information, write: 56 Byron Mews, Fleet Road, London NW3 2NQ.

Secondary illustrations of new video stars Javier Duran and Jan Novak and Andel (in *Puda*), courtesy of Mike Donner and All Worlds Video. Free catalogue: 1-800-537-8024, or fax at 619-298-8567 or look on the internet for a complete gallery of stars: www.allworldsvideo.com.

HE'S SO NAUGHTY...

But he's so damn nice! STARbooks' erotic classic, *Naughty By Nature*, edited by John Patrick and featuring many of your favorite authors, is now available at booksellers throughout the world, or by mail from STARbooks Press: $14.95 retail U.S., plus $2.95 postage and handling. Address: STARbooks Press, P. O. Box 2737, Sarasota FL 34230-2737. State over 21.

SPECIAL OFFER

STARbooks Press now offers two very special international gay magazine packages: You can get the hottest American gay magazines, including *GAYME, All-Man, Torso, Advocate Men, Advocate Fresh Men, In Touch,* and *Playguy,* either singly for $6.99 each, or in a very special deluxe sampler package for only $25 for six big issues.

We also offer the sizzling British and European magazines, including *Euros, Euroboy, Prowl, Vulcan, HUNK,* and *Uniform* in a sampler package for only $39.95; six fabulous issues. Please add $2.75 post. Order from: STARbooks Press, P.O. Box 2737-B, Sarasota FL 34230-2737 USA.

NOW ON AUDIO TAPE

In cooperation with Prowler Press in London, STARbooks Press now makes available a special selection of stories from *Barely Legal*, our classic collection, on audio tape. Two cassettes. $16.95. Order from: STARbooks, P.O. Box 2737, Sarasota FL 34230-2737 U.S.A. Also available from Prowler Press, U.S.A. and London, via MaleXpress Ltd., 3 Broadbent Close, London N6 5GG, U.K.

He's waiting for you...
IN THE BOY ZONE

Another erotic classic, *In the BOY Zone*, edited by John Patrick and featuring many of your favorite authors and some interesting new writers, is now available at your local bookseller, or by mail from STARbooks Press: $14.95 U.S. Plus $2.75 postage and handling. Address: STARbooks Press, P. O. Box 2737, Sarasota FL 34230-2737.

Now available at bookstores or by mail: BEAUTIFUL BOYS, John Patrick's enormously entertaining look at boys who are really much more than just a pretty face. This unusual collection of hot erotic tales includes two big bonus books: "The Blessing," a sizzling novella by Leo Cardini, and another of John Patrick's revealing looks at the lives of porn stars, this one featuring the incredible bottom boy Kevin Kramer. This huge book is $14.95, plus $2.75 post from STARbooks Press, P.O. Box 2737-B, Sarasota FL 34230-2737 USA. *Or at your bookseller now.*

ABOUT THE EDITOR

The editor with his favorite dreamboy, infamous porn superbottom Kevin Kramer.

John Patrick is a prolific, prize-winning author of fiction and non-fiction. One of his short stories, "The Well," was honored by PEN American Center as one of the best of 1987. His novels and anthologies, as well as his non-fiction works, including *Legends* and *The Best of the Superstars* series, continue to gain him new fans every day. One of his most famous short stories appears in the Badboy collection *Southern Comfort* and another appears in the collection *The Mammoth Book of Gay Short Stories*.

A divorced father of two, the author is a longtime member of the American Booksellers Association, the Florida Publishers' Association, American Civil Liberties Union, and the Adult Video Association. He resides in Florida.